THE MARIANNE TRILOGY

'A most enjoyable novel . . . very elegantly done . . . Tepper's quirky prose is very well suited to Marianne's eccentricities, and serves to make the character all the more plausible'
Locus

'A remarkable talent, and with each new book she outdoes herself. I don't know which I like more, the worlds she creates or the way she writes about them'
Stephen R. Donaldson

'One of the outstanding new writers of the decade'
Booklist

'I doubt Tepper could write a bad book if she tried'
Fantasy Review

G000298971

Sheri Stewart Tepper was born, reared, and educated in Colorado, U.S.A. She worked for many years for various non-profit organizations including the international relief organization, CARE, and Planned Parenthood, the American family planning organization. As executive director of Rocky Mountain Planned Parenthood, she was responsible for the administration of some thirty medical clinics in Colorado, Wyoming, and New Mexico.

A longtime writer of children's stories, she sold her first book for adults in 1982. Other sales encouraged her to leave her job and retire to the family ranch in Larkspur, Colorado to write full time. She lives there with her husband, Gene, and an assortment of wild and domesticated animals including a small pack of Norwegian Elkhounds to keep the coyotes at bay, a herd of Belted Galloway cattle, and a family of shorthaired silver tabbies.

She is the mother of two children: one son, a scientist with the National Laboratories at Los Alamos, and one daughter, who is also a writer. She has one grandchild.

THE
MARIANNE TRILOGY

Sheri S. Tepper

comprising

**MARIANNE,
THE MAGUS AND THE MANTICORE**

**MARIANNE,
THE MADAME, AND THE MOMENTARY GODS**

**MARIANNE,
THE MATCHBOX, AND THE MALACHITE MOUSE**

CORGI BOOKS

THE MARIANNE TRILOGY
A CORGI BOOK 0 552 13192 X

Originally published in the United States of America as
Marianne, the Magus, and the Manticore,
Marianne, the Madame, and the Momentary Gods and
Marianne, the Matchbox, and the Malachite Mouse

First publication in Great Britain

PRINTING HISTORY
Corgi edition published 1990

Copyright © 1985, 1988, 1989 by Sheri S. Tepper

The right of Sheri S. Tepper to be identified as author
of this work has been asserted in accordance with sections
77 and 78 of the Copyright Designs and Patents Act 1988

This book is set in 10/11pt English Times Medium by
Busby Hannan & Busby Ltd., Exeter

Corgi Books are published by Transworld Publishers Ltd.,
61–63 Uxbridge Road, Ealing, London W5 5SA, in Australia by
Transworld Publishers (Australia) Pty. Ltd., 15–23 Helles
Avenue, Moorebank, NSW 2170, and in New Zealand by Transworld
Publishers (N.Z.) Ltd., Cnr. Moselle and Waipareira Avenues,
Henderson, Auckland.

Made and printed in Great Britain by
Cox & Wyman Ltd., Reading, Berks.

MARIANNE,
THE
MAGUS,
AND THE
MANTICORE

CHAPTER ONE

During the night, Marianne was awakened by a steady drumming of rain, a muffled tattoo as from a thousand drumsticks on the flat porch roof, a splash and gurgle from the rainspout at the corner of the house outside Mrs Winesap's window, bubbling its music in vain to ears which did not hear. 'I hear,' whispered Marianne, speaking to the night, the rain, the corner of the living room she could see from her bed. When she lay just so, the blanket drawn across her lips, the pillow crunched into an exact shape, she could see the amber glow of a lamp in the living room left on to light one corner of the reupholstered couch, the sheen of the carefully carpentered shelves above it, the responsive glow of the refinished table below, all in a kindly shine and haze of belonging there. 'Mine,' said Marianne to the room. The lamplight fell on the first corner of the apartment to be fully finished, and she left the light on so that she could see it if she woke, a reminder of what was possible, a promise that all the rooms would be reclaimed from dust and dilapidation. Soon the kitchen would be finished. Two more weeks at the extra work she was doing for the library and she'd have enough money for the bright Mexican tiles she had set her heart upon.

'Mine,' she said again, shutting her eyes firmly against the seductive glow. She had spent all Cloud-haired mama's jewelry on the house. The lower floor, more recently occupied and in a better state of repair, was rented out to Mrs Winesap and Mr Larken – whose relationship Marianne often speculated upon, varyingly, as open windows admitted sounds of argument or expostulation or as the walls transmitted the unmistakable rhythm of bedsprings – and the slummy part was occupied by Marianne herself. 'Not so

7

slummy anymore,' she hummed to herself in the darkness. 'Not so damn slummy.'

If she had been asked, she could not have said why it had been so important to have rooms of her own, rooms with softly glowing floorboards, rooms with carefully stripped woodwork painted a little darker than the walls, all in a mauvey, sunset glow, cool and spacious as a view of distant mountains, where there had been only cracked, stained plaster with bits of horsehair protruding from it to make her think for weary months that she was trying to make a home in the corpse of some great, defunct animal. At the time she had not known about old plaster, old stairs, old walls, nothing about splintered woodwork and senile plumbing — either balky or incontinent. Something in the old house had nagged at her. 'Buy me, lady. You're poor. I'm poor. Buy me, and let us live together.'

Perhaps it had been the grace of the curved, beveled glass lights above the front door and the upstairs windows. Perhaps it had been the high ceilings, cracked though they were, and the gentle slope of the banisters leading to the second floor. Perhaps the dim, cavelike mystery of the third floor beneath the flat roof. Perhaps even the arch of branches in the tangled shrubbery which spoke of old, flowering things needing to be rescued from formlessness and thistle. 'Sleeping Beauty,' she had said more than once. 'A hundred years asleep.' Though it hadn't been a hundred years. Ten or fifteen, perhaps, since someone had put a new roof on it. Forty, perhaps, since anyone had painted or repaired otherwise. Both times someone, anyone had run out of money, or time, or interest, and had given up to let it stand half vacant, occupied on the lower floor by a succession of recluses who had let the vines cover the windows and the shrubs grow into a thicket.

Perhaps it hadn't been anything unique in this particular house except that it stood only a block from the campus. From her windows she could look across the lawns of the university to the avenue, across acres of orderly green setting off rose-ash walls of Georgian brick, a place of quiet and haven among the hard streets. 'Damn Harvey,' she hummed to herself, moving toward sleep. This was part of the daily litany: at least a decade of 'mine's' and five or six 'damn Harvey's.'

It shouldn't have been necessary to sell *all* Mama's jewelry. Harvey could have advanced her some of her own inheritance — even loaned it to her at interest. The past two years of niggling economies, the endless hours using the heat gun to strip paint until her ears rang with the howl of it and her hands turned numb . . . 'Carpal tunnel syndrome,' the doctor had said. 'Quit whatever you're doing with your hands and the swelling will stop. With what your papa left you, sweetie, what's this passion for doing your own carpentry?' Dr Brown was an old friend — well, an old acquaintance — who believed his white hair gave him license to call her sweetie. Maybe he called all the people he had once delivered as babies sweetie, no matter how old they got, but the familiar, almost contemptuous way he said it didn't tempt her to explain.

'Look,' she could have said. 'Papa Zahmani was pure, old-country macho to the tips of his toes. He didn't leave his little girl *anything*. He left it all in half-brother Harvey's hands until little Marianne either gets married — in which case presumably her sensible husband will take care of it for her — or gets to be thirty years old. I guess he figured if Marianne wasn't safely married by thirty, she never would be and it would be safe to let such a hardened spinster handle her own affairs. Until then, however, Harvey controls the lot — half-brother Harvey who treats every dime of Marianne's money as though it were a drop of his own blood.'

Anyhow, why explain? It wouldn't change anything. The truth was simply that she hadn't the money to pay anyone to paint the walls or strip the woodwork or reupholster the furniture scrounged from secondhand shops. 'Junk shops,' she reminded herself. 'Not so damn junky anymore . . .'

'You can live on what I allow you,' Harvey had said, offhandedly. 'If you get a cheap room somewhere. There's no earthly reason for you to go on to school. You are by no stretch of the imagination a serious student, and if you're determined to live the academic life — well, you'll have to

9

work your way through. If you're determined to get a graduate degree — which will be useless to you — you'll spend
most of your time on campus anyhow. You don't need a nice
place to live. A little student squalor goes with the academic
ambience.'

Not that Harvey exposed himself to squalor of any kind.
His six-room Boston apartment took up half the upper floor
of a mellow old brownstone on Beacon Hill, and an endless
skein of nubile, saponaceous Melissas and Randis and Cheryls
replaced one another at eager intervals as unpaid house-
keepers, cooks, and laundresses for Harvey S. Zahmani,
professor of Oriental languages and sometime ethnologist,
who had had the use of all his own inheritance and all of
Marianne's since he was twenty-six. Papa hadn't believed that
women should take up space in universities unless they 'had
to work,' a fate evidently worse than death and far, far worse
than an unhappy marriage. 'I do have to work,' Marianne had
said to Harvey more than once. 'Do you really expect me to
live on $500 a month? Come on, Harvey, that's poverty level
minus and you know it.'

'It's what Papa would have done.' Bland, smiling, knowing
she knew he didn't give a damn what Papa would have done,
that he hadn't cared for Papa or Papa's opinions at all, giving
her that twinge deep down in her stomach that said 'no fury
like a man scorned,' and a kind of fear, too, that the man
scorned would try something worse to get even.

'Hell, Harvey,' she whispered to herself. 'I was only
thirteen and you were twenty-six. I don't care if you were
drunk. You're my half-brother, for God's sake. What did you
expect me to do, just lie there and let you use me for one of
your Randis or Cheryls because I was convenient?' It had
been a frightening scene, interrupted by the housekeeper.
Neither of them had referred to it since, but Marianne
remembered, and she thought Harvey did, too. Why else this
nagging enmity, this procession of little annoyances?

'You give up this graduate degree business and do something more in keeping with your position, and I'll see about
increasing your allowance . . .' He had sneered that polite,

10

academic sneer, which could only remotely be interpreted as a threat. Marianne hadn't been able to figure out what would have been more in keeping with her position. What position did a poverty-stricken heiress have? Great expectations? She had on occasion thought of raffling herself off on the basis of her Great Expectations. Perhaps temporary matrimony? No. She was too stubborn. Sue? It was possible, of course, but Marianne felt that going to the law to gain control of her money would involve her in more of a struggle with Harvey than she had the strength for. Nope. If Papa had been a chauvinistic Neanderthal, Marianne would play it out – all the way. But she would not do it in squalor, not even student-style squalor. The jewelry had been given to her when Cloud-haired mama had died. So far as anyone knew it was still in the safe-deposit box. Marianne had never worn it. Now it had gone for fifty percent of its value to pay for three stories of dilapidated Italianate brick across the street from the university, and Marianne spent every available hour with tools or paintbrushes in her hands. The worst of it was done. Even the scrappy little area out front had been sodded and fringed with daffodils for spring, with pulmonaria and bergenia to bloom later, and astilbe waiting in the wings for midsummer. Harvey, if he ever came to Virginia to visit, which he never had, would find only what he could have expected – a decently refurbished apartment in an elderly house. Not even Mrs Winesap or Mr Larkin knew she owned the place. 'Mine,' she said for the tenth time that day, sinking at last into sleep.

There had been a time, long before, when there had been gardens lit by daffodils fringing acres of lawn. There had been a time when there had been many rooms, large, airy rooms with light falling into them through gauzy curtains in misty colors of dusk and distance. Sometimes, on the verge of waking, Marianne thought of that long-ago place. There had been a plump cook Marianne had called Tooky, even when she was old enough to have learned to say 'Mrs Johnson.' There had been an old Japanese man and his two sons who worked in the gardens. Marianne had trotted after them in

11

the autumn, her pockets bulging with tulip bulbs, a bulb in each hand, fascinated by the round, solid promise of them, the polished wood feeling of their skins, the lovely mystery of the little graves the gardener dug — what was his name? Mr Tanaka. And his sons. Not Bob, not Dick. Robert and Richard. Robert digging the round holes, Marianne pitching in the handfuls of powdery bonemeal, Robert mixing it all into a soft bed, then taking the bulbs from her one by one to set them in an array. Then, filling in the hole, the hole so full of promise, knowing the promise would be kept. And then, in the spring, the clumps of green stalks, the buds opening into great goblets of bloom. Marianne standing with Cloud-haired mama to peer into those blooms, into the bottoms of those glorious vases where bees made belligerent little noises of ownership against the yellow bases of the petals, a round sun glowing at the bottom of the flower to echo the great sun burning above them.

Marianne didn't even remember it, and yet when she had bought the garden supplies last fall, she had stood in the garden shop with her hand deep in the carton of tulip bulbs, not seeing them, unaware of her own silent presence there. When she had paid for the plants there had been tears running down her cheeks, and the sales clerk had stared at her in perplexity, for her voice had been as calm and cheerful as it usually was while the tears ran down her cheeks and dropped off her chin. Later, she looked into the mirror and saw the runnels from eyes to chin and could not think what might have caused them.

Cloud-haired mama had died when Marianne was thirteen. That was when Harvey had . . . well. No point in thinking about it. After that had been boarding schools, mostly. Papa Zahmani had sold the big house with the gardens. Holidays had been here, in this city, in the town house. Then, only a year later, Papa Zahmani had died. The headmistress had told her in the office at school and had helped her dress and pack and be ready for the car. Two funerals in less than a year, and no reason anyone could give for either one. No reason for Mama to have died. No reason for Papa to have died. Dr

Brown acted baffled and strained, with his mouth clamped shut. After that was more school, and more school, and summer camps, and college, and more college. There had not been any home to return to, and the only career which occurred to her was the same one Harvey had entered — ethnology. Which might be another reason for his sniping at her. Harvey didn't like competition. As though Marianne would be competition — though someday perhaps, when she was decades older, if she became recognized in the field, and . . . Well. She tried not to think about it. It was better not to think about Cloud-haired mama, or Papa Zahmani, or Harvey. It was easier to live if one were not angry, and it was easier not to be angry if she did not think about those things.

She woke in the morning to a world washed clean. Outside the window the white oak had dropped its burden of winter-dried leaves into the wind, littering them across the spring lawns which stretched away between swatches of crocus purple and ruby walls, a syrup of emeralds, deep as an ocean under the morning sun, glittering from every blade. Slate roofs glistened, walls shone, teary windows blinked the sun into her face as she leaned from the window to recite the roll call of the place. Mossy walks, present. Daffodils, granite steps, white columns, ivy slickly wet and tight as thatch, a distant blaze of early rhododendrons. All bright and shiny-faced, pleased and yet dignified, as such a place should be, her own slender windows fronting on it so that she might soak it in, breathe it, count it over like beads. Yew hedge, present. Tulip tree, present. The multi-paned windows of the library across the way; the easy fall of lawn down the slope to the side walk and street at the corner.

The street. Marianne hastily glanced away, too late. A red bus farted away from the curb in pig-stubborn defiance of imminent collision. The shriek of crumpled metal came coincident with the library chimes, and a flurry of McDonalds wrappers lifted from the gutter to skulk into the shrubbery. 'Damn,' she murmured, starting her daily scorecard in the endless battle between order and confusion. 'Confusion, one;

order, nothing.' By her own complex rules, she could not count sameness for order points. There was nothing really new in the order of the campus, the buildings, the gardens — no lawn freshly mowed or tree newly planted. She made a face as she turned back to the room, hands busy unbraiding the thick, black plait which hung halfway down her back. The room, at least, would not contribute to confusion. Except for the Box.

It sat half under the coffee table where she had left it, unable to bear the thought of it lurking in the darkness of some closet or completely under the table where she could not keep an eye on it. Better to have it out where she could see it, know where it was. 'Damn Harvey,' she said, starting the day's tally. If she took the Box to the basement storage room, he might decide to come visit her. She believed, almost superstitiously, that the act of taking the Box out of her apartment and putting it somewhere else, no matter how safe a place that might be, would somehow stimulate a cosmic, reciprocal force. If his presence, more than merely symbolized by the Box, were removed, some galactic accountant might require him to be present in reality.

'Silly,' she admonished herself, kicking the Box as she passed it. 'Silly!' Still, she left it where it was, decided to ignore it, turned on the television set to drown out any thought of it. Despite the bus crash, the morning was full of favorable portents. No time to waste thinking of Professor Harvey S. Zahmani.

'. . . Zahmani,' the television echoed in its cheerful-pedantic news voice. 'M. A. Zahmani, Prime Minister of Alphenlicht, guest lecturer at several American universities this spring, prior to his scheduled appearance before the United Nations this week . . .'

This brought her to crouch before the tube, seeing a face altogether familiar. It was Harvey. No, it wasn't Harvey. It looked like Harvey, but not around the mouth or eyes. The expression was totally different. Except for that, they could be Siamese twins. Except that Harvey was up in Boston and this man was here at the university to lecture . . . on what?

14

On Alphenlicht, of course. She had read something about the current controversy over Alphenlicht and — what was that other tiny country? Lubovosk. There was a *Newsweek* thingy on it, and she burrowed under the table for the latest issue as the television began a breathless account of basketball scores and piggy-backed commercials in endless, morning babble.

'. . . Among the world's oldest principalities, the two tiny nations of Alphenlicht and Lubovosk were joined until the nineteenth century under a single, priestly house which traced its origins back to the semi-mythical Magi. A minor territorial skirmish in the mid-nineteenth century left the northern third of the minuscule country under Russian control. Renamed 'Lubovosk,' the separated third now asserts legal rights to the priestly throne of Alphenlicht, a claim stoutly opposed by Prime Minister of Alphenlicht, Makr Avehl Zahmani . . .'

There was a map showing two sausage-link-shaped territories carved out of the high mountains between Turkey and Iraq and an inset picture of a dark, hawk-eyed woman identified as the hereditary ruler of Lubovosk. Marianne examined the woman with a good deal of interest. The face was very familiar. It was not precisely her own, but there was something about the expression which Marianne had seen in her mirror. The woman might be a cousin, perhaps. 'Good lord,' Marianne admonished the pictured face. 'If you and Russia want it, why doesn't Russia just invade it the way they did Afghanistan?' Receiving no reply, she rose to get about the business of breakfast. 'Zahmani,' she mused. She had never met anyone with that name except Harvey and herself. In strange cities, she had always looked in the phone book to see whether there might be another Zahmani. Then, too, Alphenlicht was the storybook land which had always been featured in Cloud-haired mama's bedtime tales. Alphenlicht. Surprising, really. She had known it was a real place, but she had never thought of it as real until this moment. Alphenlicht. Zahmani. 'This,' she sang to herself as she scrambled eggs, 'would be interesting to know more about.'

When she left the apartment, her hair was knotted on her neck, she was dressed in a soft sweater and tweedy skirt, and

15

the place was orderly behind her. She checked to see that she had her key, the Box nudging her foot while she ignored it, refused to see it. Instead, she shut her eyes, turned to face the room, then popped her eyes open. She did this every morning to convince herself that she had not dreamed the place, every morning doubting for a moment that it would be there. Was the paint still the dreamed-on color? Were the drapes still soft around the windows, curtains moving just a little in the breeze? No rain today, so she left the window open an inch to let the spring in and find it there when she returned. 'I love you, room,' she whispered to it before leaving it. 'I will bring you a pot of crocuses tonight.' Purple ones. In a blue glazed pot. She could see them in her head, as though they were already on the window seat, surrounded by the cushions.

Back in the unremembered time, there had been a window seat with cushions where Marianne had nested like a fledgling bird. Cloud-haired mama had teased Harvey, sometimes, and urged him to sit on the window seat with them and listen to her stories. Marianne had been hiding in the cushions of the window seat the day she had heard Mama speaking to Harvey in the exasperated voice she sometimes used. 'Harvey, please, my dear, find yourself a nice girl your own age and stop this nonsense. I am deeply in love with your father, and I could not possibly be interested in a boy your age even if I were twenty again.' Of course, there had only been seven years' difference in their ages, Marianne reminded herself. Though Papa had been forty-three, Mama had been only twenty-seven and Harvey had been twenty. Harvey had been different then; he had been handsome as a prince, and kind, and they had sometimes gone riding together. She shut down the thought before it started. 'Begone,' she muttered to the memory. 'Be burned, buried, gone.' It was her own do-it-yourself enchantment, a kind of self-hypnosis, substitute for God knew how many thousand dollars worth of psychotherapy. It worked. The memory ducked its head and was gone, and as she left the room, she was humming.

At the confluence of three sidewalks, the library notice

board was always good for one or two order points. The bulletin board was always rigorously correct; there were only current items upon it; matters of more than passing interest were decorously sleeved in plastic, even behind the sheltering glass, to avoid the appearance of having been handled or read. Marianne sometimes envisioned a crew of compulsive, tenured gnomes arriving each night to update the library bulletin board. Though she had worked at the library for five years now, she had never seen anyone prepare anything for the board or post it there. She preferred her own concept to the possible truth and did not ask about it.

'Order, one; confusion, one. Score, even,' she said to herself. The bulletin board was in some respects an analogue of her own life as she sought to have it; neatly arranged, efficiently organized, ruthlessly protected. There were no sentimental posters left over from sweeter seasons, no cartoons savoring ephemeral causes, no self-serving announcements by unnecessary committees. There were only statements of facts in the fewest possible, well chosen words. She scrutinized it closely, finding no fault in it except that it was dull — a fact which she ignored. It was, in fact, so dull that she almost missed the announcement.

'Department of Anthropology: Spring Lecture Series, Journeys in Ethnography. M. A. Zahmani, *Magian Survivals in Modern Alphenlicht*. April 16, 12.30 p.m. – 2.00 p.m. Granville Lecture Hall.'

She felt an immediate compulsion to call Harvey and tell him that a namesake of theirs was to give a lecture in three hours' time on a subject dear to Harvey's heart. Not only a namesake, but a Prime Minister. The impulse gave way at once to sober second thought. Harvey would be in class at the moment. Or, if not in class, he would be in his office persuading some nubile candidate for a postgraduate degree that her thesis would be immeasurably enhanced by experiencing a field trip for the summer in company with 'Call Me Har' Zahmani. While he might be interested in learning of the visiting lecturer, he would certainly be annoyed at being interrupted. Whatever Harvey might be doing, he was always

17

annoyed — as well she knew — at being interrupted. On the other hand, if she did not tell him and he read about it, as he would, in some journal or other or even, heaven help her, in the daily paper, then she could expect one of those superior, unpleasant phone calls. 'One would think, Marianne, that with no more on your mind than your own not very distinguished academic work, you might remember that it is my field . . .'

No. Far better to call his apartment and leave a lighthearted-sounding message on his machine. Then he would have been told and would not have palpable grounds for offense. Which did not mean he would not contrive some such grounds, but she wouldn't have made it easy for him. She lifted her head in unconscious dismissal. Thinking her way around her half brother often required that kind of dismissal. Meantime, should she or should she not go to the lecture herself? Alphenlicht wasn't her subject as it was Harvey's — he had traveled there the same summer Mama had died. He had talked about it since then, mockingly, and about the Cave of Light. Well. Flip mental coin. Rock back and forth on heels and toes. Bite lip. Why not, after all? She'd had a large breakfast; she'd simply skip lunch.

And with that it was back to the wars, the library stacks, the endless supply of books to be found, shelved, located, relocated, repaired, and otherwise dealt with. The work did not pay well, but it was steady and quiet; it did not require an extensive wardrobe or the expense of socializing. There were no men to be avoided, to be wary of, or suspicious of. No office parties. The head librarian did have the habit of indulging in endless, autobiographical monologues, sometimes of astonishing intimacy, in Marianne's hearing, but with practice they could be ignored. There were no collections for weddings or babies. In the library, Marianne was anonymous, virtually unseen. It was a cheap, calm place to work, and Marianne valued it for what it was.

At a quarter past noon she left her work, smoothing her sleeves over wrists still damp from a quick wash up. Granville was a small lecture hall, which meant they did not expect a crowd. She moved through the clots of people on the steps, dodging clouds of cigarette smoke, to find a place near the front of the hushed hall. The speaker came in with several other people, probably people from the Anthropology Department. His face was turned away, the outline of his head giving Marianne a queer, skittish feeling, as the department spokesman mounted the podium to mumble a few words of introduction, sotto voce, like a troubled bee. Then the speaker turned to mount the platform and she thought in revulsive panic, 'My God, it *is* Harvey! They got the initials wrong!' Only to see that no, it was someone else after all. Her heart began to slow. The choked, suffocated feeling began to fade. The first words assured her that it was someone else. Harvey's voice was brittle, sharp, full of small cutting edges and sly humors. This man's voice covered the audience like brocade, rich and glittering.

'My name is Makr Avehl Zahmani. In my small country, which you Westerners call Alphenlicht because of an innocent mistake made by an eighteenth-century German geographer, I am what you would call a Prime Minister. In a country so small as Alphenlicht, this is no great office, though it is an honorable one which has been hereditary to my family for almost seventeen centuries . . .'

Hereditary Prime Minister, thought Marianne, and so like my half brother they could have been clones. Look at him. The same hair. The same eyes. If Alphenlicht is indeed the old country from which we came, then you are of the line from which we sprang. Harvey wouldn't believe this. I don't think I'll try to tell him. She looked down at the notes her hand had taken automatically, reading 'Hereditary for seventeen centuries . . .' Ah, surely that was an exaggeration, she thought, looking up to see his eyes upon her, as startled as hers had been to see him first. Then his lips bent upward in interested surprise and went on speaking even as his look fastened her to her seat and told her not to move until there was time to settle this thing, this thing he had recognized.

'There is possibly only one force in human society which could have bound one family to so lengthy a course of public

19

service. I speak, of course, of religion, and it is of the religion of Alphenlicht, the religion of our people, that I have been asked to speak to you today . . .'

Marianne's score between order and chaos was almost even for the week, and Marianne considered this among other things as she went on taking notes without thinking about it. If this man who looked so much like Harvey *were* like Harvey, then any further attention paid to him would push the confusion scores for the week − for the month − beyond any hope of recouping. *However.* She looked down to see her handwriting and to underline the word. *However!* The amusement she was hearing was not Harvey's kind of mockery. This man had a gentler mind, perhaps? He would not delight in tying knots in one just for the fun of it? Flip coin, she told herself, but not just yet. He's got some time to talk before I have to decide whether to run.

'Our people serve the god of time and space. Our name for this deity is Zurvan, One-Who-Includes-Everything. My own family name, Zahman, means "space." In the early centuries, BC, during the height of the Persian Empire, our people were centered in the lands north of Ecbatana, among the Medes. We were known as the Magi . . .'

So this is a Magus? Black hair, a little long, flowing over his impeccable shirt collar. Narrow face, imperious nose, high arching, very mobile brows. Sensual mouth, she thought, followed at once by the enchantment words, *buried, burned, gone.* She would not think about sensual mouths. She wrote 'Magi,' underlined it twice, then looked up to find his eyes eagerly upon her again. His chin was paler than the rest of his face, as though he had recently shaved a beard. She narrowed her eyes to imagine him with a beard, and a picture flashed − glittering robes, tall hat, beard in oiled ringlets. She shook her head to rid it of this We-Three-Kings stuff. Beard, she wrote, question mark. Why did he go on looking at her like that?

Because, said the internal monitor, the one Marianne called old sexless-logical, just as you recognize a family likeness in him, he recognizes one in you. Obviously.

20

Obviously, she wrote, listening.

'Our religion is monotheistic, though not sexist, for Zurvan is both male and female. In our own language, we have pronouns which convey this omni-sexuality (I say "omni" to allow for the possible discovery of some extra terrestrial race which needs more than two)' — polite laughter from audience — 'but in your language you must make allowances when I say "from his womb" . . .'

Wombmates, she wrote busily, then scratched it out. Allowing for the difference in sex, it was possible he recognized her in the same way she had recognized him. Same eyes, nose, hair, eyebrows. Same mouth.

'We recognized many attributes of this divine unity, but there was a tendency for this recognition to be corrupted into mere idolatry or a pervasive dualism. This was convenient for kings who needed to incorporate all the little godlets of the conquered into the state religion. There began to be priests and prophets, some even calling themselves Magi, who turned away from the pure, historic religion.'

He's about forty, she thought. Maybe a few years older than that. The same age as Harvey. Who should have remained an only child. Who would have remained an only child except that Papa Zahmani fell for my Cloud-haired mama and the two of them went off into eternity, unfortunately leaving me behind. From Harvey's point of view. Not that he had ever actually said anything of the kind.

'In the third century AD there were widespread charges of heresy brought by one Karder, a priest serving the current Sassanid king. Karder espoused a more liberal faith, one which could incorporate any number of political realities. He and the king found the Zurvanian Magi difficult to . . . ah, manipulate. The charges of heresy were made first, on the grounds that the king's religion was the correct one, and the persecutions came after. My people fled north, into the mountains . . .'

He was turning to the map on the easel, putting on glasses to peer at it a little nearsightedly, taking them off to twiddle them, like Professor Frank in ethno-geography. Like old

21

Williams. Lord, he could be any teacher, any professor. Why did she feel this fascination?

'The area is now called Kurdistan, near what was Armenia. The borders of many modern nations twist themselves together in this region — Turkey, Iran, Iraq, Syria, the USSR — of which I will have more to say later. In the midst of this tangled, inaccessible region, my people established a theocracy a millenium and three quarters ago. There were no roads into the country then. There is one entering our country now, from the vicinity of Van, in Turkey. There is another, not so good, from the area around Lake Urmia in Iran. We have no airport, though we have improved the road during the last decades, to accommodate those who seek the Cave of Light . . .'

If he talks about the Cave of Light as endlessly as Harvey talks about the Cave of Light, I will simply get up in a dignified manner and leave, she thought. As though I have to get to class. As though I were late for an appointment with the dean. He went on talking about the Cave of Light, and she didn't move. Her hand went on taking notes, quietly, automatically, while she sat there and let the words flow through. Harvey called the Cave of Light a kind of historic Ouija board. Makr Avehl Zahmani obviously thought it was more than that — a good deal more than that. I can't be taking this seriously, she thought. *Magi*, for God's sake. Magians, magicians, magic. Lord.

'Several generations ago the czars of Russia extended their borders in several areas. One such extension cut our small country into two parts. The northern third of it was gobbled up into Russia and renamed Lubovosk. The Magi who live in Lubovosk are still our people, our separated people. They now have their own charges of heresy to contend with. In seventeen hundred years not that much has changed. Now, I have used my allotted time. If any of you have questions, please feel free to come forward and ask them of me.'

She did not move during the light, appreciative applause. He had been a good speaker. The hall emptied. A half-dozen argumentative students went forward to pick at details of his talk. She sat. Even when the arguers went away and the speaker came toward her, she sat as he scanned her face quarter inch by quarter inch, shivering between smile and frown.

'My dear young woman,' he said, 'I believe we must be related.'

She could not afterward remember quite how it happened that she accompanied him to the only good restaurant nearby and found herself drinking a third or fourth glass of wine as she finished her dessert. She seemed to have been listening to him for hours as he sparkled and glittered, telling her marvelous things about marvelous places and people. Something he said made her comment on her game of muddle versus order and her lifetime cumulative score.

'Confusion is winning,' she admitted. 'Not so far ahead that one gives up all hope, but far enough to make me very anxious. It uses up a lot of energy.'

'Ah,' he said, wiping his lips with his napkin before reaching out to touch her hand. 'Do your rules allow transfer of points?'

'I don't understand. What do you mean, transfer?'

'Well, my own lifetime cumulative score is somewhat better than yours. I have several thousand points ahead for order. Of course, I have an advantage because of the Cave of Light — no. Don't say that you don't believe in it, or that it's all terribly interesting, but . . . All that isn't really relevant. I simply want to know if your rules allow transfer of points, because, if they do, I will transfer a thousand points to you. This will take off the immediate pressure, and perhaps you can strengthen your position sufficiently to mount a counterattack.'

If there had been any hint of amusement in his voice, even of a teasing sort, she would have laughed politely and — what? Accepted? Rejected? Said something about one having to play one's own hand? The surface Marianne, well educated in the superficial social graces, could have handled that. However, this did not sound like a social offer. The tone was that of an arms control negotiator placing before the assembly the position of his government. It reminded her that she was speaking with a Prime Minister, all too seriously, and yet how wonderful to be ahead for a while. A gift of such magnitude, however, might carry an obligation. *Begone, buried*, she whispered to herself.

'It's too much,' she whispered to him, completely serious. 'I might not be able to repay.'

'Kinswoman,' he said, laying his hand upon hers, the tingle of that contact moving into her like a small lightning stroke, shocking and intimate. 'Kinswoman, there is no obligation. Believe me. If you know nothing else of me, if we do not meet again, know this of me. There is no obligation.'

'But — a thousand. So much?'

'It is important to me that my kinswoman win her battles, that she be decisively ahead. That she be winning and know herself to be winning.'

'But it wouldn't be me who was winning.'

'Nonsense. If a gunner at the top of a hill uses all his ammunition and an ally rushes ammunition to him at a critical time, it is still the gunner who wins if he keeps his head and uses all his skill. He has merely been reinforced. We are kinsmen, therefore allies. You will forgive me if I do not say "kinspersons." I learned my English in a more elegant setting, in a more elegant time. However, you need not decide at this moment. Merely remember that it is *important* to me that you win. There is no obligation beyond that. You would favor me by accepting.' And he left the subject, to talk instead of Alphenlicht, of his boyhood there, being light and gracious.

When they parted, it was like waking from a dream. Fragments of their conversation fled across her mind only to dissipate. The lecture hall, the restaurant assumed dream scale and color. When she turned to see the restaurant still behind her, solid and ordinary as any other building on the street, it was with a sense of detached unreality. She attended a class, took notes, entered into the discussion, and did not remember it five minutes later. She went to her apartment, stopping on the way to shop for food and milk, and stood inside it holding the paper sack without knowing where she was. It was a square, white envelope on the carpet that brought her to herself at last, her name written on it in a quick, powerful hand. The message read, 'I have transferred one thousand order points to you. If you do not wish to receive them, you may return them to me. May I have the pleasure of your company at dinner on Thursday night? I will call you tomorrow. Makr Avehl.'

When she touched the envelope, she received the same tingling shock she had felt from his hand, but as she read the words, most of the cloudy confusion vanished.

'He did give me a thousand points,' she told herself, knowing with certainty that it was true. 'I've got them, I can tell I have,' knowing that she not only had them but had accepted them. If she had not had them, she would have been too confused to accept them. Now that she had them, she knew she would keep them. 'It's like an anti-depressant,' she said to herself, caroling, doing a little jig on the carpet so that the groceries ripped their way through the bottom of the brown bag and rolled about on the rug, oranges and lemons and brown-and-serve rolls. 'Before you take it, you're too depressed to want it. After you take it, you know it was what you needed.'

There was, of course, one small confusion. Her door had been tightly locked. No one had a key except herself. How, then, had the square white envelope come to rest in the middle of the carpet, where she could not fail to see it but where no one could possibly have put it?

Magus, she hummed. Magi, Magian, Magician.

CHAPTER TWO

There was a knock at the door. Someone turned the knob and Marianne heard Mrs Winesap's voice.

'Girl? I heard you coming in. Someone brought you a pretty.' Mrs Winesap was addicted to slightly regional speech, the region in question varying from day to day so that Marianne was never sure whether the woman was from the South, West, or New England states. On occasion, Mrs Winesap's speech approached an Elizabethan richness, and Marianne thought the true source of her changing accent might be overdoses of BBC period imports.

'Mrs Winesap. Come on in. What is it?'

'Crocuses,' the woman replied. 'In a pretty pot. A man brought them. I was out front, and he came along looking lost, so I asked him who he was looking for. After he told me they were for you, we got to talking. I thought at first he might be your brother, there being a family resemblance and my eyes not being that good. Then I knew that was silly, your brother being the kind of person he is and all.'

Marianne had never discussed Harvey with Mrs Winesap that she could recall, and her attention was so fixed on the gift that she completely missed the implications of this statement. Mrs Winesap often seemed to know a great deal about Harvey or, perhaps more accurately, knew a great deal about people and things that affected Marianne.

'The man who brought these is . . . he's a kind of cousin, I guess, Mrs Winesap. I met him today. It was nice of him to be so thoughtful.' The crocuses were precisely as she had visualized them, purple ones, in a glazed pot of deepest, persian blue.

'Same name of yours, so I guessed he was some kind of kin,' commented Mrs Winesap. 'Anyhow, he left the flowers with me after he made me promise six times I'd see you got them as soon as you got home. Seemed like a very determined sort of person. You got something cold to drink, Marianne? I been moving that dirt out back, and it's hotter'n Hades for April.'

Marianne hid a smile as she went to the refrigerator. It was true that Mrs Winesap was a bit dirt-smeared, and also true that she was largely responsible for the emerging order in the garden, but it was not even warm for April, much less hot. Mrs Winesap simply wanted to talk.

'Larkin bought an edger at the flea market. Paid a dollar and a half for it. Want to go halfies?' This was rhetorical. Mr Larkin would present Marianne with a written bill for seventy-five cents, which Marianne would pay without demur. Sometimes Marianne believed that the two downstairs tenants suspected Marianne owned the place and were playing a game with her. Other times she was sure they had no idea. Whatever their suspicions or lack thereof, they had decided that garden maintenance was to be their particular responsibility, and that the upstairs tenant should pay what they delighted in calling 'halfies.' Since the expenditures never exceeded two or three dollars at a time, Marianne managed to cope.

'An edger?' she asked.

'You know. A flat blade on a handle, to cut the grass straight where it comes along the flower garden. It was all rusty is how come he got it so cheap. You know Larkin. Give him something rusty and he's happy as a clam all day cleaning it up. Does your brother know this cousin of yours?'

As usual with Mrs Winesap's more personal inquiries, the question caught Marianne completely by surprise and she answered it before she thought. 'No. I just met him today myself.'

'Ah,' said Mrs Winesap with deep satisfaction. 'So you'll have to call your brother and tell him about it. About meeting a new relative and all.'

The emotion Marianne felt was the usual one, half laughter, half indignation. Her response was also the usual one: dignified, slightly cool. 'Yes, as a matter of fact, I was just going to call Harvey, Mrs Winesap. Take that soda along with you. I do need to catch him before he leaves for the evening . . .' Polite, firmly shutting door behind her visitor, Marianne fought down the urge to peer through the keyhole at the landing in fear she might see Mrs Winesap's eye peering back at her. Instead she went to the phone, moved both by her assertion and the need to leave some kind of message.

Harvey always considered it an intrusion for Marianne to tell him anything. Nonetheless, he would deeply resent not being told. A quick message on his machine would be the least risky way of informing him, and if she avoided answering the phone for a while after that, he might see

27

Makr Avehl Zahmani's name on the news and realize that Marianne was, in fact, only telling him the truth. It was part of Harvey's usual treatment of her to accuse her of making up stories, as though she were still seven years old, and once committed to the assertion that she was fabricating it would be hard for him to back off. She encouraged herself to take a deep breath and do it, managing to make the message sound calm and good-humored. She unplugged the phone with a sense of relief. She didn't want to hear it ring if he called her back.

'I am ahead on points,' she told herself. 'Well ahead, and I have no intention of ever getting behind again.' She tried the pot of crocuses in various places, finally putting them on the window seat as she had originally intended, then threw together a few scrappy bites of supper. When she had finished, she started to take the dishes into the kitchen, stumbling unexpectedly over something which was not supposed to be there.

The Box.

It was at the edge of the kitchen counter, where she could not avoid stepping over it, where she must have already stepped over it while preparing her meal without seeing it, without remembering. She stared at it in confusion. That morning — yes, that morning it had been in the living room under the coffee table. Who could have moved it? Mrs Winesap? Perhaps out of some desire to help, some instinct to tidy up? With a grimace of actual pain she lifted it back to the place she last remembered it being, half under the table, possessed in that moment by a completely superstitious awe and fear.

The Box was a symbolic embodiment of Harvey-ness. If she gave him cause for disturbance up in Boston, then the Box would take it out on her down here in Virginia. She knew this was ridiculous but was as firmly convinced of it as she was of her own name. Her mood of valiant contentment destroyed, she went about her evening chores in a mood of dogged irritation. Sounds bothered her. Traffic. Mrs Winesap rattling the trash cans. Doors closing. A phone ringing. Mrs

Winesap laboring up the stairs and a repetition of that firm, brook-no-nonsense knock, the knob turning, her voice.

'Girl, your brother called our phone. Says he's been trying to reach you and can't get an answer.' Broad face poked around the edge of the door, eyes frankly curious as the face was frankly friendly.

'Oh — shit,' said Marianne, breaking her own rules concerning language and behaviour.

Mrs Winesap pulled a parody of shock over her face. She had heard Marianne's lecture on scatology directed more than once at Mr Larkin. 'Got the phone unplugged, haven't you?'

Marianne nodded in dismal annoyance. 'How did he know to call you? He's never been here. He's never even met you.'

'Yes, he did. Came by one day about two weeks ago. Told me he was your brother. Introduced himself. Course, I introduced myself back. We talked some.'

'You . . . talked some.'

'I told him it was a nice day,' she reported with dignity, 'and I told him you weren't in your apartment but I'd be glad to take a message. He pumped me all about you, and I let him know I was blind in both eyes and couldn't hear out of either ear. Did tell him my name, though, and I'm in the book.'

'You never told me.'

'No reason to. Why upset you? I didn't like him, so I figured you probably didn't either. He was all over sparkle like a merry-go-round horse, expecting anyone with a — with breasts to fall down and play dead.'

'Oh.' This was precisely Marianne's view of Harvey, but she had not thought it generally shared. This explained why Mrs Winesap had at first thought Makr Avehl was her brother. 'So, he knew your name and looked you up in the book.'

'Most likely. Anyhow, just now I told him the reason you didn't answer was you weren't in and I'd be glad to leave a message for you to call him. Consider message delivered, OK? Seemed best.'

'Thanks, Mrs Winesap.'

'One of these days, girl, you'll get tired of calling me "Mrs Winesap," and the name "Letitia" will just slip out.

I won't mind, whenever that is.' She shut the door firmly behind her, leaving Marianne in some limbo between laughter and tears.

The door opened again to allow Mrs Winesap to deliver herself of an utterance.

'Marianne, whatever it is you don't like about that man, brother or not, you got a right. Don't you sit up here feeling guilty because you don't like him.'

This time tears won.

Oh, yes, she did feel guilty about it. The only family she had left, the only kin, and she frequently wanted him gone. 'Begone, burned, buried,' she chanted quietly. If there was any actual guilt, it was Harvey's, not Marianne's, but knowing this didn't seem to make the horrid nagging weight of it any easier. She often tried to reduce the whole conflict to one of disparate personalities. 'He is domineering,' she told herself, 'and authoritarian. He relishes power, and he uses it, but he is not some all-devouring monster.' Saying this did not convince her this time any more than it had before.

'So, I'll return his call,' she told herself, plugging in the phone and tapping his number with hesitant fingers.

'Harvey? Returning your call?' She listened with suppressed, seething warmth as he complained that she had not been in earlier, that she should not leave messages on his machine unless she would be available to take a call, that—

'Harvey, I am sorry. I didn't intend that you should have to take the trouble to call me. I just wanted you to know about the Zahmani Prime Minister from Alphenlicht. I thought you'd be interested.'

Oily sweet, the voice she hated. 'Bitsy? Are you playing one of those infantile ''let's pretend'' games again?'

She heard her own voice replying, 'Harvey, hold on a moment, will you? Someone's at the door.' She took a deep breath, strode to the door, opened it, closed it, mumbled to herself, struck the wall with her hand. Her usual response to him under like circumstances would have been something full of self-doubt, something cringing. *Harvey, I don't* think *so. He really did look as though he was related. He really did say . . .*

She returned to the phone. 'Harve. Someone has come and I have to go now. If you catch the news tonight or tomorrow, you'll probably see the Prime Minister on it. He's here to speak at the UN. Sorry I have to run.' And hung up on Harvey S. Zahmani without waiting for permission.

He would not want to appear foolish, not even to her. Give him time to find out that what she had told him was the simple truth, and he'd be less likely to take some irrevocably punitive decision about money matters — always his last argument when others failed. She unplugged the phone again, resolving not to connect herself to the world again until morning. 'One more point for order,' she sighed. 'Score for order, for the day, one thousand and one.'

In the morning, she forgot to connect the phone. When she got home, it was ringing. There was no time to think who? How? She knew it was Makr Avehl and answered it without a qualm. 'Thank you for the flowers,' she said, her voice slipping sideways into childlike pleasure.

'You said you intended to shop for some,' he replied, 'but I knew you wouldn't have time yesterday if you were in class. I took most of your afternoon, so it was only proper to repay.' His voice was enthusiastic, warm. It changed suddenly. 'I was in New York today, at the UN. I met your brother. He's very like you in appearance.'

'Harvey's in Boston,' she said. 'Not at the UN. You can't have—'

'Sorry,' he laughed. 'I didn't lead up to it. A woman named Madame Delubovoska and I are on opposite sides of a very small international issue. Madame and I are related. Madame, it turns out, is your half-brother's aunt, his mother's much younger sister. Today, in New York, your half-brother was visiting his aunt and I met him. Is that somewhat more clear? I said he much resembled you.'

'It's you he resembles, actually. When I first saw you, I thought you were Harvey.'

'That's true. You even said so.' There was a long silence,

31

a calculating silence. 'Marianne, may I come see you?'

'You're in New York.'

'No. I was in New York. I'm about two blocks from you, in a phone booth.'

'Well, of course. Yes. Can you find the house — oh, you've already been here once.'

'I'll find you.' Dry-voiced, humorous, amused at her confusion. She put her hands against her flaming face. It took practice to behave with calm and poise around men like Makr Avehl — around men at all. Marianne had not practiced, had no intention of practicing, for she had decided not to need such skill. She told herself that just now her concerns were housewifely. She hadn't dusted, hadn't vacuumed since the weekend. Well, it didn't look cluttered, except for the Box. Better leave it, even if he noticed it.

There was nothing in the house to offer him except some sherry and cheese and crackers. Well, he couldn't complain, dropping in unexpectedly this way. Quick look in the mirror, quick wash up of hands and face. No time for makeup. No need with that hectic flush on lips and cheeks. 'Lord,' she thought, 'one would think I had never had anyone drop in before.' A moment's thought would have told her the truth of this. There had been no one to drop in. Except for Mrs Winesap. And the plumber. And the phone man. And people of that ilk. The stairs creaked outside her door.

He stood there in a soft shirt and jeans, not at all like a Prime Minister, perhaps more like her childhood dream of a fairy tale prince.

'You didn't bring your horse and lance,' she said, caught up in the fantasy.

'The joust isn't until later,' he replied, 'unless you have a dragon you want skewered in the next half hour?' She was so involved in the story she was telling herself that it did not seem in the least remarkable that he had read her mind. Laughing, she waved him in.

They drank sherry and ate cheese. Makr Avehl sprawled on the window seat and waved his finger in her face as he lectured on the day's events. 'I made my speech. Madame made her speech. Neither of us convinced the other. I will now bore you greatly by telling you what the dispute is about?' There was an interrogative silence, not long, for she was happy to let him carry the burden of their conversation. 'Madame and I are cousins, of the same lineage, you understand. When our land was cut into two parts in the last century — as the result of some minor Czarist expansion or other, utterly unimportant and long forgotten except to those of us directly involved — Tabiti's great-grandfather was in the northern piece of the country and my great-grandfather was in the southern part. They were brothers. You heard my little speech the other day, so you know that Alphenlicht is a theocracy.' He bit a cracker noisily, examining her face. 'Don't wrinkle your nose so. There are nice theocracies, and ours is one. We are not reactionary or authoritarian; we do not insist upon conformity or observation of taboos.' He raised one triangular brow at her, giving her a brilliant smile, and she felt herself turning to hot liquid from her navel to her knees as her face flamed.

She rose, made unnecessary trips with glasses, ran cold water over her wrists in the kitchen.

He went on. 'At any rate, in the southern half of Alphenlicht, things went on very much as they had for a very long time. We did begin sending some of our young people out of the country to be educated, and we did begin to import some engineers to do modern things like building roads and bridges. We also imported a few motor vehicles, though certain of the Kavi, that is, members of the priesthood, questioned that much innovation.'

'I thought you said you were not reactionary?' She managed to sound matter-of-fact rather than sultry, with some effort.

'Oh, it wasn't a question of religion. It was a question of aesthetics. Some members of the Council simply felt that cars and trucks smelled very bad. There were long arguments concerning utility versus aesthetics. I've read them. Very dull.

'To continue with my tale: The narrow pass which connected Alphenlicht and Lubovosk was controlled by Russian border guards. Over the past hundred years interaction between the two parts of the country has been very much restricted. Access to the Cave of Light has been almost impossible for people from the north. Since they had been accustomed to using the cave, they evolved their own substitutes. People do find ways to get answers to important questions. Theirs involved a heavy admixture of shamanistic influences.'

'I thought shamans were from — oh, the far north.'

'Some are. Some are found in Turkey. The black shamans who came to Lubovosk did happen to be from the far north. Well, at this point we may make a long story short. Four generations after the separation, a group of people in Lubovosk, supported by the USSR for obvious reasons, has decided that Lubovosk, not Alphenlicht, is the true heir to the religious leadership of both countries. They base this on the fact that Madame's great-grandfather was my great-grandfather's older brother. They conveniently ignore the fact that after several generations of re-education and shamanistic influences, there's no one in Lubovosk who even pretends to believe in religion, a prerequisite, one would think, if a theocracy is to work. The US State Department supports us, of course. Russia supports Lubovosk's ridiculous claim. No one else cares. So we have gone through this charade. When it was all over, some of the delegates woke up and went on with their business. Everyone was very bored. The only two people present who took it seriously were Madame and I. Do you know Tabiti? She is named, by the way, for the fire goddess of our ancestors. Not inappropriately.'

'Madame Delubovoska? No. I never knew she existed until a few days ago.'

'As I told you, she is a kind of back side kin of yours. You can imagine how surprised I was when she introduced Professor Zahmani to me. I knew at once who he was, of course, for you had told me about him.'

'Not too much, I hope,' she said in astonishment. 'I certainly never thought you'd meet him . . .'

'Ah. Well, it turned out fortuitously. I had just invited

34

Madame to the country place we have taken here when she introduced me to your brother. So I invited him as well, intending that you, also, should be my guest.'

'Oh. With . . . Harvey? I don't . . .' She did not know what to say. The thought stunned and horrified her, and her voice betrayed the emotions. There was a strained silence.

'I see I have made a mistake,' he said with obvious discomfort and an expression almost of dismay. 'There is something awkward? You do not like him?'

'I — I'm probably very childish. It's just — he's quite a bit older than I. He was left rather in charge of my affairs when Papa Zahmani died. He is not . . .'

'Not sympathetic.'

'No. No, you may truthfully say that he is not sympathetic. Not where his little sister is concerned.'

'But it's more than that? Even when I said I had met him, there was a certain quality in your silence. It is something which makes you reluctant to meet him at all?'

'It is awkward,' she admitted. 'Sometimes I interpret things he does and says as — threatening. He may not intend them in that way. And yet . . .'

He was looking at her in a curiously intent way, not intimately, more as though he found her a fascinating item of study. The perusal did not make her feel insulted or invaded, as men's thoughtful glances sometimes did, but she felt the questing pressure of his gaze as an urgent interest, impossible to ignore. It was suddenly important that he know how she felt . . . and why. Particularly why.

She reached down and tugged the Box from beneath the table, pushing it toward him so that it rested against his well polished shoes. 'Look in that. Everything in there is something Harvey has given me over the last several years. Presents. Together with suggestions as to where to display them. I couldn't . . . couldn't bring myself to put them out, not here, so I've kept them in this box.'

He put down his glass. She had not sealed the Box, but had merely closed the cardboard carton by folding the top together. He opened it and drew out the two framed prints which lay on top, setting them side by side against the table and regarding them with the same intent gaze he had focused on her.

To the right was a cheaply framed print of an Escher lithograph, an endless ribbon of black fishes and white birds swimming in space, at one end the black figures emerging, at the other the white, coming forward from two dimensions into three, from shadow shapes into breathing reality, one white bird flying free of the pattern only to be cruelly killed by the devilish fangs of the metallic black fish.

'It bothered me when he gave it to me. So, one day at the library, I looked it up,' she said, trying to be unemotional. Everything in her screamed anger at the black fish, but she was so long experienced in swallowing her anger that she believed it did not show. 'The artist wrote that the bird was all innocence, doomed to destruction. Not exactly cheerful, but by itself it shouldn't have made me feel as unpleasant as I did. Then I got the other one . . .'

He turned his attention to the other print, this one of a painting. 'Paul Delvaux,' murmured Makr Avehl. 'Titled *Chrysis*. Well.'

A naked girl stood on a lonely platform at the edge of an abandoned town, a blonde, her scanty pubic hair scarcely shadowing her crotch, eyes downcast, lacy robe draped behind her as though just fallen from her shoulders, right hand holding a lighted candle. To the left of the picture a flood-light threw hard shadows against a dark building. On a distant siding, a freight car crouched, red lights on it gleaming like hungry, feral eyes in the dark.

'She's like the white bird in the other picture,' Marianne said. 'All alone. Totally vulnerable. She has no protection at all. Nothing. Someone horrible is coming. You can tell she knows it. She is trying to pretend that she is dreaming, but she isn't.'

'Ah,' he said. 'Is there more?'

She reached into the bottom of the Box to pull out the little carvings of ivory, basalt, soapstone. Eskimo and Bantu and old, old oriental. Strange, hulked shapes, little demons.

Another black fish. A white skull-faced ghost. An ebony devil. A small ornamented bag made of stained and tattered skin with some dry, whispery material inside. 'I don't know what's in it,' she said, apologetically. 'I didn't want to open it. Harvey said it was a witch bag. Something from Siberia? I think his card said it belonged to a shaman.'

'Yes,' said Makr Avehl soberly. 'I should think it probably did. And should never have left Siberia. It is black shamans from there who have come to Lubovosk.'

'All these things are interesting, in a way. Even the little bag, colored and patterned the way it is. I feel a little guilty to be so ungrateful for them. It's just — Harvey had never given me gifts before. Not even cards on my birthday. And then, suddenly, to give me such strange things, which make me feel so odd . . .'

'What did he suggest you do with them?' Makr Avehl's voice had a curious flatness, almost a repressed distaste, as though he smelled something rotten but was too polite to say anything about it.

'When he gave me the picture of the fish and the birds, he told me to hang it on the wall in my bedroom — he hadn't been here, but I told him I had a one bedroom apartment. Then, later, when he gave me the other one, he said to hang it in the living room. The other things were to be put on my desk or bookshelves. Of course, since he hadn't been here, he didn't really know what it's like . . .'

'It's a very pleasant apartment,' he commented, looking about him as he packed the things back into the Box. 'You've done most of it yourself, haven't you?'

'How did you know? Does it look that amateurish?'

'Not in that sense. Amateur in the sense of one who loves something, yes. I was a student in this country for a while, and I know what the usual kind of apartments available to students are like. They are not like this.'

She flushed. 'I guess I do love it. I hadn't had any place of my own since Clou — since Mother died. It was important to me.'

'You started to call her something else.'

37

'Just — a kind of fairy tale name.' Ordinarily, Marianne did not confide in people, certainly not on short acquaintance, but the focused, intent quality in his interest wiped away her reticence. 'I always called her Cloud-haired mama, and she called me Mist Princess. It was only a kind of story telling, role playing, I guess. We were alone a lot of the time. Papa was away. Harvey was at school, mostly. Lately I have remembered that she was only four or five years older than I am now, and yet I still feel like such a child most of the time. So — she wasn't too old for fairy tales, even then.'

'Ah. But despite your enjoyment of fairy tales, you do not like the pictures and these little carvings.'

'I don't. They make me feel — oh, slimy. Does that make sense to you? I felt it, but didn't understand it.'

'Oh, yes.' Flat voice. 'It makes sense. Of a kind. Would you mind terribly if I took these away with me? I'll return them, or something like them. Something you'll be more comfortable with. Since your brother does not visit you, he is unlikely to care. The sense of his gifts will be maintained.' He closed the Box firmly on its contents. 'Now, what are we going to do about the weekend?'

She smiled, made a little, helpless gesture. 'I don't want to seem stubborn or childish, really, but I think it might be better if I didn't accept your invitation.'

'That makes me sad. It's obvious to me that I've made a miscalculation. Tabiti and I are old adversaries, and her I invited out of bravado. My own sister, Ellat, will be peeved with me. She often tells me my desire for bravura effect will get me in trouble, and she is often right. Whenever I am full of pride, I am brought low. What is your proverb — Pride goeth before a fall? Well, so I am fallen upon grievous times. Because I had invited her, I invited him, because I wanted you. I will now have a guest I did not much want in the place of one I had very much wanted, for I know you would enjoy it. Can I beg you? Importune you?'

Curiosity and apprehension were strangely mingled, and yet her habitual caution could not be so easily overcome. The thought of spending a weekend in Harvey's company, among

38

strangers. Strangers. She reminded herself firmly that the man sitting so intimately opposite her was a stranger. Charming, yes. So could Harvey be. Seemingly interested in her as a reality, not merely as an adjunct to himself — but then, how could one tell? 'I — I'd like to think about it. Perhaps I could give you an answer later in the week?'

He had the courtesy to look disappointed but not accusing and to convey by a tilted smile that he knew the difference. 'Of course you may. And you must not feel any pressure of courtesy to agree if it will make you more uncomfortable than the pleasure the visit might afford you. Everything is a balance, isn't that so?' He stood up, shifted his shoulders as though readying them for some weighty burden, toed the Box at his feet.

'Now, there are things I must do. We do have a dinner date tomorrow, and I will return your belongings then. Someone told me of a place nearby where there is a native delicacy served. Something called a soft crab?'

'Soft-shelled crabs,' she laughed. 'You must mean Willard's. It's famous all up and down the coast.'

'I shall find them very strange and quite edible,' he announced. 'Until tomorrow.' At the door he touched her cheek with his lips, no more than an avuncular caress, a kind of parent to child kiss. Her skin flinched away from him, her face flamed, and she gave thanks for the darkness of the hall and for the fact that he picked up the Box and left, not turning to look back at her as she shut the door between them.

She did not see him set the Box down on the stair and wipe his hands fastidiously on his handkerchief. Sweat beaded his upper lip, and he shook his head, mouth working, as though to spit away some foul taste. For a moment, when he had opened the Box, he had felt as though astray in a nightmare. One did not expect to smell such corruption in the pleasant apartment of an innocent — oh, yes, make no mistake about that — innocent young woman. Yet he had smelled it, tasted it. Makr Avehl Zahmani had some experience with wickedness. As a leader of his people, it was part of his duty to diagnose evil and protect against it. What he felt rising from

39

the Box had a skulking obscenity of purpose, a stench of decay. His face sheened with sweat at the self-control it took to lift the Box and carry it. He drew a pen from his pocket, used it to jot a quick shorthand of symbols and letters on each side of the six faces of the Box. Then he picked it up once more, a bit more easily, throwing a quick glance over his shoulder at the door at the top of the stairs.

Behind that door, Marianne was conscious of nothing but shame and fear, shame at the feel of hard nipples pressing against her blouse, shame at the brooding, liquid heat in her groin, fear at the greedy demands of a desire which had ambushed her out of nowhere and was swallowing her into some endless gut of hungry sensation.

She clung to the door, cringing under a lash of memory. There had been Cloud-haired mama dead in the next room, cold and white and forever gone. How did she die, Marianne had demanded, over and over. She was young! She wasn't sick! How could she have died? There had been no answers, not from Papa Zahmani, not from Harvey who had only looked at her strangely, expressionlessly, as though he did not know her. There had been whispering, shouts from behind closed doors, Dr Brown saying, 'I would have said she died of suffocation, Haurvatat. I can't explain it. I don't know why. Sometimes hearts just *fail*.' And Marianne crying, crying endlessly, finally seeking Harvey out and throwing herself into his arms in the late, dark night . . . And then had come the frightening thing. And after the housekeeper had come in and interrupted him, he had hissed at her, 'Bitch princess. You're as soft and usable as your mad mama was . . .'

She leaned against the door, digging her nails into her palms. 'I'm not like that!' she screamed at herself silently. 'I'm not like that at all.' Demon voices in her mind hissed, 'Soft, usable, bitch!' An obscene heat enveloped her, and she was back in the old house, returned to Harvey's holding her, touching her, starting to undress her with fingers busy under her clothes, and herself responding to him in a kind of dazed frenzy which had no thought in it, no perception except of a hoped-for forgetfulness, a much desired unconsciousness.

And then he had been interrupted, and the shame had come, the shame of his using Mama's name, defiling her death, defiling her child — and Mama's child involved in the defilement, cooperating in it. 'No, no, no,' she screamed now as she had then. 'I am not like that. Mama wasn't like that. I won't, won't, won't!'

Somewhere inside herself she found the calmer voices. 'This man is not Harvey. This man is someone else. He has Harvey's face, but he has not Harvey's sins. He is attractive, you are attracted, but this hot shame is only memory, Marianne. It is not now, not real, only memory. And you, Marianne, you are well enough alone. So. Stay alone, Marianne, and do not remember that time. And perhaps, someday, you will find it is forgotten.'

She took her chastened self into the shower and then out for a long, exhausting walk to weary even her tireless brain, a brain which kept trying by an exercise of pure persistence to make her wounds heal by cutting them deeper. For, of course, among all the other monsters was the monster of guilt, guilt which said that she herself had been responsible, not the grown man but herself, the child, the woman who should have known better, for are not women supposed to know better? And if the twelve-year-old Marianne did not know better, then best for the twenty-five-year-old Marianne to work in the quiet library and attend the endless classes and have no male friends at all, for she, too, might not know better if put to the test. She would not go for the weekend, would not allow this feeling to take hold of her, would not allow her calm to be destroyed.

'Of course,' her internal self reminded her, 'you are not always so calm, Marianne. Sometimes in the deep night, you waken. Sometimes when the sheets are sensuously soft against your newly bathed skin. Sometimes in the midst of a TV show, when the young man and the young woman look at each other in that way — that way — then you are not so calm.'

'Begone,' she said wearily. 'Burned, buried, begone.' Usually the litany or the long walk let her sleep, but tonight she lay wakeful, dozing from time to time only to start awake

41

again, until she gave up at last and took two of the little red pills Dr Brown had given her. Her sleep was dark, dreamless, empty, and when morning came she was able to convince herself that the night's turmoil had been unreal and that she had not been mired in it at all.

She could not feel anticipation for the evening. Each time she thought of it, it loomed at the end of her day like a road marker, pointing to some unknown destination, evoking an apprehension not so much for the destination itself as for the unfamiliar and possibly tedious journey it would take to reach it. She was familiar with the feeling, one which had served in the past to limit her society to the few, the necessary, and she felt ashamed of it without in any way being able to defeat it. Only when she came into her apartment at the end of the day to see the pot of crocuses on the window seat and feel the absence of the Box did she begin to feel a slight warming, a willingness to be graceful within the confines of her apprehension − perhaps even a willingness to move outside it toward pleasure if she could find a way.

'So, Marianne,' she instructed herself, 'you will not give him a dinner partner to shame him. He has done nothing at all to deserve that.' It was a sense of pride which took her through the routines of bath and makeup, hairdress and clothing, and finally to the examination of self in the mirror. The dress had belonged to her mother, a simple, timeless gather of flowing silk, jade green in one light, twilight blue in another, utterly plain. The only dressy clothes she had were things salvaged from among Cloud-haired mama's things, trunks Papa had put in storage in her name, 'Because you may want them someday, or may simply want to have them to remember her by.' Some had been too fashionable then to be useful now, but there were a few things like this − blouses and shirts, ageless skirts, a topcoat which might have been illustrated in the morning paper, a wonderful sweep of lacy wool stole which would serve as a wrap. The only clothes Marianne had purchased in the last four years had been underwear and two pairs of shoes. Everything else was left over from undergraduate days or made over from Mama's

42

trunks. If it came to a choice between clothing and the tiles for the kitchen . . . She smiled. There was no choice.

She looked good, she decided. Not marvelous or glorious or glamorous, but good. Clean, neat, attractive, and by no means shabby. So.

Turning then from the mirror, she saw the line of light run down the silk from the curve of her breast, the flush of red mounting to her cheeks. Her hands trembled as she tugged the softly rounded neckline a little higher on her shoulders. She hadn't chosen this dress to be . . . hadn't . . . had. 'Didn't,' she said defiantly. 'Did not.' She reached for the closet door to pick something thicker, less clinging, less . . .

Too late. She heard him coming up the stairs, the firm knock on the door. Put the best face on it possible.

He made it no easier for her. He stood back, obviously admiring her, his eyes lighting up. 'You look wonderful, a water nymph — what is it? A naiad. The color suits you. It makes you glow as though you had candles lit inside.' He smiled, not knowing that the emotion he had roused in her was a quiet anger, at him, at herself. 'I've brought your box back.'

Her mood of acceptance was waning, but he gave her no time to fret, placing the box on the table and opening it as he talked. 'One Escher print,' he said, busy unpacking. 'One print of a Delvaux painting. One Eskimo carving, one Bantu carving, one bit of oriental charmery. One medicine pouch.' He set them out for her as she stared.

The Escher print was of a fish rising to the top of still water where leaves rested on the ripples and bare trees laid their shattered reflections. The Delvaux painting was of two young women walking in a well-lit street, clothed in high-necked white dresses, lamps all about, a nearby house streaming with light from windows and doors. The Eskimo carving was of a bird, a confluence of curving lines which said nest, rest, peace. The ebony carving was of a happy frog, and the oriental bit was of two mice chewing their way through a nut. He laid a medicine pouch beside the pot of crocuses, a bit of fluffy ermine skin, eagle feathers tied to it with turquoise beads and bits of coral. 'American Indian,' he said. 'How does this collection of things suit you?'

She considered them. Each of them separately was pleasant, unremarkable. Together — together they seemed to reach toward her with welcoming arms. 'Safe,' she offered at last. 'Everything seems very natural and contented.'

'I like the young woman in the Delvaux painting.' He made a vast, smoothing gesture, as though wiping away the darkness. 'Busy at lighting up their world. Light is a very powerful symbol in our religion, of course.' He stood back from the picture and admired it. 'Ah! I meant to hang them for you, but it will have to be when we return. Our reservation is for eight o'clock, and if we make a careful hurry, we will get there on time. The maître d' to whom I spoke was most forthright. We must be on time or our table will be given away to those less foresighted but more prompt. Nothing would sway him, not even appeals to justice and the American Way. So. Your wrap? Lovely. Your purse? That is all you are carrying? Well, the young are the only ones who may travel so unencumbered. We go.'

She had no opportunity to tell him he need not hang the pictures, no opportunity to change her dress, no time to remember she had wanted to change it. She was swept down the stairs — past Mrs Winesap in the entryway, pretending to be much involved with her mailbox — and into the car before she could think of anything, already laughing somewhat helplessly at his nonsense.

'Most cars available for rent,' he announced, shutting her door, 'are too large to be amusing or too small to be safe. I will not, however, join nine-tenths of your countrymen in the daily game they play with their lives. To meet my sense of prudence, you are required to ride in some ostentatious luxury, though I know you would prefer simplicity, being the kind of person you obviously are.'

She sank back into the seat, surrounded by velvet surfaces and leather smell. 'I didn't know one could rent cars like this.'

'One cannot,' he said with some satisfaction. 'However,

one can appear to be a potential buyer, with unimpeachable references, of course, thus gaining the temporary ownership of such a vehicle. One may even *be* a potential buyer, though I am uncertain whether the roads of Alphenlicht are wide enough for such extravagance.'

'You do *have* roads?' she asked in wide-eyed innocence.

'You mock. Quite rightly. You will remember, however, that I told you we are beginning to build such things. We have even recently completed a hydroelectric plant, and there is an Alphenlicht radio station by which means the people may be informed of matters of mutual interest. Avalanche warnings. Things of that kind.' He negotiated a tricky turn at the avenue with casual mastery, darting up the entrance ramp to fit them between two hurtling truck behemoths without seeming to notice he had done so. Marianne, who had braked in reflex, leaned back and relaxed. He was not going to kill them both. So much was obvious. 'I rather like it,' he purred, patting the dashboard with proprietary interest. 'Do you think it appropriate for a Prime Minister?'

She considered this judiciously. 'Well, it is a little ostentatious. But a Prime Minister should be, at least a little.'

'It will acquire importance when Aghrehond drives it. Aghrehond does my driving; he is also my friend, first factotum of the republic, and the guardian Nestor of my youth. He will be enormously pleased with this machine. It will contribute to his already overpowering dignity.'

'You're going to buy it, then?'

He cocked his head, considering. 'If it continues to behave well. Have you noticed the tendency of some things to behave well at first, as though knowing they are on trial, only to turn recalcitrant and balky when they believe they have been accepted?'

Marianne flushed in the darkness. He had not been speaking of her, but she applied his words to her own case. She had behaved well when they had first met, an interesting experience, a previously unknown relative, no troubling overtones, and she had felt free to be herself. Now she knew she was turning balky, for good reason, but he would not know that. Well, one could be balky without letting it appear on the surface. She commanded herself to be charming. He would find her charming. Her citadel might keep its portcullis down, but she would not be obvious about it. So she seduced herself with promises and turned her attention back to him with a newly kindled radiance.

'I had a typewriter like that once,' she said. 'The only time it ever worked was in the repair shop where I bought it, and in the repair shop when I took it back — every time I took it back.'

He laughed. 'I had a Jaguar XKE — you know the one? It has twelve cylinders and a complexity of electrical system beside which the space probes are models of simplicity. Whenever it went more than fifty kilometers from the garage where its mechanic waited, it had an electrical tantrum and stopped running. It was so very pretty, even standing still — which is what it mostly did — that I left it for a very long time in the garage, simply to look at it now and then. However, since it had not been purchased as sculpture, it seemed unwise to continue giving it house room. I then put a curse upon the engineers who had designed it, and British Leyland went bankrupt soon thereafter.'

'You claim responsibility for that?' she asked, uncertain whether he was serious or not.

'Absolutely.' His voice was utterly serious. Then he turned and she saw his eyes. 'Marianne, you are a good audience for my silliness. You are young enough almost to believe me.'

'No,' she protested. 'I didn't, really.'

'No,' he echoed, 'you almost did.' Then his voice changed. 'I could have done it, Marianne. A Magus could do such a thing. But it would be self-indulgent, and a Magus does not build his powers — or even retain them — by being self-indulgent. Those who do so go by other names.'

She was surprised at this abrupt change of tone, evidence that something was on his mind other than the evening. However, he gave her no time to brood over it, but reached across to the glove compartment to tug out a map, which he dropped into her lap, stroking her knee with his hand. 'Here,

46

see if you can find where we are, and then tell me the exit number. I looked it up this afternoon, but I have forgotten it.' His voice was a caress, as his touch had been, and she drew her stole around her, over her knees and thighs, all too aware of the place his hand had touched. Face flaming, she bent over the map, not noticing he had leaned to one side to see her face in the rear view mirror. He smiled, a smile of pleasure, but with something hungry and predatory in it.

She searched the map for some time, calming herself with it. When she could trace their route, she found the exit number for him. 'I've only been there once before,' she said. 'An old friend of my father's invited me to dinner there with his wife and daughter.'

'Were they good people? Did you enjoy it?'

'I did. Yes. They had known my parents, and that was nice. My parents were wonderful people, and I like to remember them . . .'

'Happily,' he suggested. 'You like to remember them happily.'

'That's it. I usually have to remember them in some context of money or property because of Harvey, you know. And that isn't the same. It's certainly not happy.'

'Your affairs were left in his hands, you said.'

'I was only a schoolgirl. My mother's estate — rather a big one, from her father — was in papa's hands during his lifetime, but then it came to me. Except Harvey was executor. Oh, there's some man in a bank in Boston, and an attorney I've never seen, but Harvey is really the one who says yes or no. The others simply do what he tells them.'

'Ah,' said Makr Avehl, in a strange voice. 'They simply . . . give consent.'

'Yes. And whenever Harvey says anything, he always says it is what Papa would have wanted. Which means it is what Harvey wants.' She fell silent, flushing. 'I feel very disloyal, talking about him this way.'

Makr Avehl, thinking of the contents of the box he had taken from her apartment, contented himself with silence. At that moment the hungry, predatory part of him withdrew, and

47

a more thoughtful self examined Marianne's face with a quick, sideways look. 'Blood is not always thicker than water, Marianne. Only when the ties of blood are equally strong on both sides is there any true kinship. Kinship can never be a one-way thing.'

'That's what Mrs Winesap says. She says if I don't like him, I simply don't like him, and I shouldn't feel guilty about that.'

'I couldn't agree more. Mrs Winesap is an eminently sensible woman. Also, she has your welfare at heart, and that makes her kin to you in a real way.' He swung the car onto the exit ramp, then beneath the highway, and onto a shore-bound road between budding trees fretted against the dusk. Lights faded around them, dwindling from hectic commercial to amber residential, soft among the knotted branches. It was quiet in the car, all traffic left behind them. Reflected in the waters of a little bay was the discreet sign in pink neon, 'Willard's.' He parked the car and looked quickly at his watch. 'On time. There will be no excuse to have given our table to anyone else.'

He took her from the car and into the place by her elbow, gently held. Their table was waiting, and Marianne gained the impression it would have been waiting had they not arrived until midnight. Makr Avehl waved the maître d' away and seated her himself, his hands lingering on her shoulders as he arranged the stole on the back of her chair. She resolutely focused herself on the reflections in the water, on the candle-lit interior, on anything else.

When he had seated himself across from her, he said, 'Shall we dispense with the usually obligatory cocktail? Do you know the origin of the word? It dates, I am told, from the early years of the nineteenth century in New Orleans where cognac was mixed with bitters using an old-style egg cup — called a coquetier — to measure the ingredients. From cah-cuh-tyay to cock-tay to cock-tail would have required only the slovenly enunciation of a half generation. Does that interest you? Not greatly.' He grinned at her and pretended an interest in the menu. The meal had already been arranged for.

48

When he had ordered for both of them, he leaned back and stared around him, a little arrogantly. 'This ordering for one's guest is no longer an American custom, I know. But it is a custom I enjoy. So I command outrageous viands from kitchens across the breadth of the world if only to see how my companions will approach them. If what I have ordered does not appeal to you, now is the time to chastise me.'

'It sounds delicious,' she said. 'I don't mind at all. It's precisely what Papa always did.'

'And Harvey?'

'I've never eaten in public with Harvey,' she said stiffly. 'I imagine he would be more . . . more showy about it.'

'I can hear him now,' said Makr Avehl, putting on a pompous expression. ' "The lady will have breaded cockscomb with the sauce of infant eel." Then an aside to his companion: "You'll love it, Juliet. I remember having it in Paris, during the International Conference of the Institute of Anthropology." Like that?'

'Like that,' she agreed. 'And then he'd watch her like a hawk to be sure she pretended to enjoy it.'

'Which she would do?' He nodded at the hovering wine steward.

'Which they seem to do,' she agreed. 'I've never been able to figure out why.'

Across the table from her, he glittered with gentle laughter. The explosion of light seemed so real that Marianne actually blinked to avoid being blinded, then opened her eyes wide, astonished at her own childishness. It was only the blaze of something flambé behind him, being made a great show of in a chafing dish. An obsequious waiter slipped behind her chair to place two additional wine glasses beside her plate, while the wine steward poured an inch of ruby light into Makr Avehl's glass. He sipped it, nodded, and Marianne's own glass dropped red jewels of light onto the table cloth.

She sipped, smiled, sipped again. It had been a long time since she had had good wine. She had drunk it as a child, at Papa's side, learning to taste. Then she had gone away to school, and there had been no wine then or since. Her slender budget would not stretch to such indulgence, and she sipped again, lost in a haze of happy memory. A plate of pâté appeared before her, almost magically, smelling succulently of herbs and shallots. She began to eat hungrily, not noticing his expression as he watched her. It was the expression of a lion about to pounce.

But behind that expression a dialogue had begun, a familiar dialogue to Makr Avehl, one between the man and the Magus, with a word or two from that entity he called 'the intruder.' It began with the man saying, 'I want this woman!' He said it impatiently. The man did not equivocate. He did not apologize.

'You will conduct yourself appropriately,' replied the Magus. 'This is a kinswoman. Even if she were not, there are indulgences inappropriate to a Magus!'

And another voice, sibilant, hissing, 'This is a complication we do not need at this time. This is foolishness, kinswoman or not. Be done.'

'She is fair,' sang the man to himself, not listening to the voices. The wine was diluting their message, blurring their advice. 'Fair. Lithe and lovely, dark of hair and pale of skin, curved as a warrior's bow is curved, straight as his arrow is straight. A warrior's trophy! A warrior's prize!'

'A brigand's booty. A robber's spoils,' threatened the Magus.

'A poacher's trap,' hissed the voice of dissent.

'A lover's prize,' the man amended, bending over his plate in a sudden access of warmth. He had not meant to say that. He had not used the word to himself for almost twenty years, not since he was nineteen and thought himself dying because someone else had died, died untimely, unforgiveably. He shut down the voices, apprehensive of the end of their colloquy. The food gave him something else to think about, but it led him into the trap once more. He looked up to see Marianne's lips curved to accept the edge of the glass, curved as though in a kiss, and his hands trembled.

'Come now, Makr Avehl,' he said to himself. 'You are not a schoolboy any longer. You are not a lascivious youth, carried willy-nilly on naïve curiosity's back, like Europa on the bull, tormented by lust into abandonment of all sense. Come, come. Let us talk of something else.'

'Did you really like the pictures I brought you?' he asked, seeing a well-trained hand slip the empty plate away from before him to replace it with another, noticing also that Marianne's glass was being refilled. His own was almost untouched.

She did not answer at once, being occupied with napkin and glass. 'That was duck,' she said happily. 'Lovely duck. All bits and pieces with swadges of truffle. I didn't know Willard's was capable of that . . .'

He did not tell her that the pâté had been provided earlier, that Willard's was not capable of that, that no restaurant within five hundred miles was capable of that except the one which had provided the pâté to his order. 'The pictures?' he prompted.

'The pictures. Well, the one of the fish is marvelous. One has a sense of the fish rising, and because the air above and the water below are all one, it is almost as though it could go on rising upward, forever. Like a balloon.'

Makr Avehl, who had not thought of this, was much taken with the feeling. 'Exaltation?'

'Yes. The feeling that one could go on up and up forever, but one would not need to. The surface is very nice, too. Well, I liked that one. The other one was more difficult. The young women are in the street, alone, but they are not threatened at all. There are lights around, in the house — which must be the house they live in — where people are waiting for them. Nothing horrible is coming. It's a special evening, and the girls are setting lights along the streets. They do that in Mexico, don't they? Set lights along the streets? Candles, in bags of sand? A kind of ritual in which the safe, lighted way is shown, I think. And that's the way it feels, a safe, lighted way.'

'Luminous,' he suggested.

She considered this over a spoonful of lobster bisque, turning the idea with the other flavors on her tongue. 'Not so

51

much luminous as illuminated. Things which could be threatening or frightening are lighted up, made harmless, perhaps even shown to be attractive. That's what one wants, after all, to have the monsters shown to be nothing but paper cutouts, or shadows, or humped bushes which the light will show to be full of flowers.'

He nodded. 'It's unfortunate the other group of things had such an unpleasant feel to it. Certain groupings can have that quality of foreboding or threat. I remember a particular place in the forest of Alphenlicht, trees, stones, some large leafed plants with waxy blooms. Taken individually, the trees are only trees. The stones are interesting shapes, taken each by each, and the plants are found in many boggy parts of the mountains. Taken as a whole, however, this particular clearing among the stones with the trees brooding above has a quality of menace.'

He shook his head, keeping to himself the question as to what kind of knowledge or study would have stimulated a person — any person — to have chosen the particular group of things he had found in the box. The knowledge was one matter but, in addition, what motivation would one have had? These questions were not merely interesting but compelling. He was most curious about the sly vileness in which he had given her the things one at a time, singly, so that her spirit would be led to accept them individually rather than take warning at the cumulative effect.

Nonetheless, she had taken warning. Which told him something more about her to make his lustful self pause. There was heritage here, the heritage of the Magi. 'With whom,' advised the Magus within, 'it is wise not to trifle.'

He pursued this question. 'You didn't like the things Harvey gave you. Did you tell me why?'

She shrugged, spooning up the last of her bisque, sorry there was not more of it, so relaxed by the wine that she did not mind answering. 'They made me feel slimy. Dirty. Not clean dirt, but sewer dirt. I've never been in a sewer, but I can imagine.' She put her spoon down with regret. 'The naked girl was the worst. That one made me angry. She was so . . . sacrificial.'

'Anger,' he mused, nodding once more to the hovering waiter. 'I have often wondered why anger is considered by some Western religions to be a sin. It is such a marvelous protection against evil.' He examined her face, thinking of an old proverb of his people, often used to define perspicacity of a certain type: *He can recognize the devil by his breathing.* He thought it interesting that Marianne could recognize the devil by its breathing, and he wondered who the devil was. Well, he should not be too quick to identify.

'The reason you found them unpleasant probably doesn't matter. We've taken care of it. It's likely that your brother would not even know the difference between the things he gave you and the substitutions I have made. He would undoubtedly be distressed to learn he had caused you a moment's apprehension. There is certainly no reason to mention it to him.'

Marianne had had no intention of mentioning it. 'You think I felt as I did about the things merely because Harvey gave them to me? That seems a little simplistic.'

'It's probably as good an explanation as we are going to get.' He laughed with a good pretense of humor, watching as the second set of wine glasses were refilled. They would continue with the Trockenbeerenauslese until dessert. He had chosen it for her, thinking she would prefer it, and was now regretful that he had not realized she would appreciate something better. Still, it was a very fine wine, if not a preeminent one, and her glass was being refilled for the third time. Her face was flushed and happy, and she played idly with her fork, waiting for the salad. He went on, putting an end to the subject, 'I suggest any further presents from your half brother be put in storage somewhere. Often we wish to be exorcised of demons we ourselves have allowed house room. That is an Alphenlicht saying, one my sister is very fond of.'

'I suppose she means demons of memory,' said Marianne in an untroubled voice. 'Of guilt, of vengeance. Things we dwell on instead of forgetting.' In that moment, she felt she would not be bothered by such things again.

He cursed at himself, not letting it show. The box had been no minor assault. She should be warned. Who was he to give her these platitudes instead of the harsh warning which was probably required? If he were to be true to his own conscience, he would explore the root of that corruption, find the cause, help her arrange a defense against it rather than deal her a few proverbs to placate her sense of danger. However, there was no way to do that without frightening her, and tonight was not the time, not the place, not with her glowing face across from him, candlelit, soft and accepting. When he knew her a little better — when he found out who was responsible. He did not believe it was her brother. The shallow, puffed-up ego which had looked at him out of Harvey S. Zahmani's eyes would not have been capable of the singleminded study necessary to select those individual gifts to make up such a synergistic power of evil. Well. It would wait. He would not destroy her pleasure tonight.

Neither would he destroy his own planned pleasure for the weekend. He returned to his purpose.

'Do you ride, Marianne?'

'It was my passion once, if twelve-year-old girls may be allowed to have passions. I had a wonderful horse, Rustam. I loved him above all things. When he was sold, after Papa died, I cried for days. I never could tell if it was for Papa, or for Rustam. I think it was for Rustam, though. I had already cried for Papa.'

'That was at your home?'

'Yes.' She picked at the edges of her salad, a spiraling rosette of unfamiliar vegetables, intricately arranged. 'I was just learning to jump. Rustam already knew how, of course, and he took great care to keep me on his back. I was always afraid I was in his way, hindering him.'

'Is it something you want to do again someday?'

'Something I dream about. I would love to ride again, if I haven't forgotten how.'

'There is some particular affinity, I am told, between adolescent girls and horses. Some girls, I should say.'

'Some, yes. I was very conscious of being . . . well, what

can one say? Not weaker, exactly, but less able to force myself upon the unimpressionable world. Less able, that is, than Papa, or Harvey. Mama didn't seem to care. There were things the men did which I simply couldn't understand. And yet, when I rode Rustam, the barriers were gone. I felt I could go anywhere, through anything, over anything. That I would be carried, as on wings.'

The look she turned on him was full of such adoring memory that he clenched both fists in his lap, fighting down the urge to make some poetic outburst: 'Oh, I would be your steed, lady. I would carry you to such places you have not dreamed of . . .' Instead, he hid his face behind his napkin, managed to say something in a half-choked voice about Pegasus, leaving the poetry unsaid though the words sang in him like the after-sound of a plucked string, reverberating, summoning sympathetic vibrations from his loins.

'I asked,' he said in a voice deliberately dry, 'because the house which we have leased while we are in the country has attached to it an excellent stable. The people who own it are vacationing in the Far East, and they left us in complete possession of their own riding horses — that is, once they learned that we are not barbarians.' He choked back a laugh, remembering the oblique correspondence which had finally established this fact to the satisfaction of the Van Horsts. 'I do not want you to miss the opportunity to ride with us this weekend, Marianne. I do not want to miss the opportunity to ride with you. I have invited other people, good friends, people you would enjoy. You would not need to be in the company of your brother at all. I will beg you, importune you, please. Be my guest.'

She could not refuse him. Whether it was the wine, or the thought of the horses, or the candlelight, or his own face, so full of an expression which she refused to read but could not deny, she murmured, 'If you're quite sure it won't be awkward for you if Harvey behaves oddly toward me. Perhaps he won't. I know I'm a little silly about him, sometimes.'

'Do you think he will be unpleasant company for my other guests?'

'He can be charming,' she said offhandedly. 'I think he is only really unpleasant to me.'

'Do you know why?'

She flushed, a quick flowing of red from brow to chin which suffused her face with tension. He saw it, snarled at himself for walking with such heavy feet where he did not know the way, did not give her time to reply.

'Ah, here come the crabs. Now we shall see if this is indeed a delicacy or merely one of those regional eccentricities which litter the pathways of a true gourmet.'

'Gourmand,' she said, relieved that the subject had been changed. 'I think a gourmet would not eat soft-shelled crab. They are supposed to be an addictive indulgence, like popcorn.'

'I wasn't warned,' he said in mock horror.

'Be warned. I will fight you for them.'

Makr Avehl could not have said whether he liked the dish or not. He ate it. More of it than he would have eaten if alone. He drank little wine, afraid of it for the first time in his life, of what he might say unwarily, having already said the wrong thing several times over, afraid of what he might do that would frighten his quarry.

'Quarry?' boomed the Magus, deep inside. 'I warn you again, Makr Avehl. Kinswoman.' He heard it as an echo of her own voice, 'Be warned.'

Marianne had not expected the wine, was not guarded against it, did not notice as it flowed around the controls she had set upon herself, washed away the little dikes and walls of the resolutions she had made, let her forget it was to have been an evening of politeness only, without future, without overtones. She felt herself beginning to glitter, did nothing at all to stop it, simply let it go on as though she were twelve once more, at the dinner table with Cloud-haired mama and Papa and their guests, full of happy questions and reasonably polite behavior, ready to be charmed and charming. 'Tell me about Alphenlicht,' she demanded. 'All about it. Not the politics, but how it smells and tastes. What it is like to live there.'

'Shall I be scholarly and give you the history? Or do you want a travelogue?' Gods but she is beautiful. In this light, her skin is like pearl.

'Don't tell me how it got that way. Just tell me how it is.' She licked her lips un-self-consciously, and he felt them on his own. He turned to look out the window and summon his wits.

'Well, then. Alphenlicht is a small country. You know that. It is a mountainous one. There is no capital, as such. Instead, there are many small towns and villages gathered around the fortresses built by our ancestors, many of them on the sites of older fortresses built by the Urartians centuries before. Hilltop fortresses, mostly, with high stone walls topped by ragged battlements. They march along the flanks and edges of the mountains as though they had been built by nature rather than by man, gray and lichened, looking as old as forever.

'Outside the walls, the towns straggle down the hillsides, narrow streets winding among clumps of walled buildings, half stable, part barn, part dwelling. We came from Median stock, remember. The Medes could never do without horses, and their houses were always surrounded by stableyards.'

'Flies,' commented Marianne. 'There would be lots of flies.'

'No,' he objected. 'We are not primitive. The litter from our stables enriches our farmland. Then, too, there is a constant smoky wind in Alphenlicht. We say it is possible to stand on the southern border of our country and know what is being cooked for supper on the northern edge. You asked what the country smells like, and that is it. Woodsmoke, as I have smelled here in autumn when the leaves are being burned; a smell as nostalgic among men as any I know of. A primitive smell, evoking the campfires of our most ancient ancestors.' He thought about this, knowing it for a new-old truth.

'Our houses are of stone, for the most part. We are self-consciously protective about our traditions, so we have a fondness still for glazed tile and many wooden pillars supporting ornate, carved capitals, often in the shapes of horses

57

or bulls or mythical beasts. There is plaster over the stone, making the rooms white. The walls are thick, both for winter warmth and for summer cool, so windows are set deep and covered with wood screens which break the light, throwing a lace of shadow into our rooms. Floors are of stone for summer cool, but in winter we cover them with rugs, mostly from Turkey or Iran. Our people have never been great rug makers.

'Ceilings are often vaulted, with wind scoops at the ends, to bring in the summer winds. In winter we cover them with stout shutters which seldom fit as well as they should. We say of an oddly assorted couple that they fit like scoop shutters, meaning that they do not . . .' He fell silent, musing, seeing his homeland through her eyes and his own words, as though newly.

'What do you eat?' she asked, taking the last bite of her final crab. 'I am not hungry any longer, but I love to hear about food.'

'Lamb and mutton. Chicken. Wild game. I have a particular fondness for wild fowl. Then, let me see, there are all the usual vegetables and grains. There are sheltered orchards along the foot of the snows where we grow apricots and peaches. We have berries and apples. There are lemon and orange trees in the conservatory at the Residence, but most citrus fruits are imported. We are able to import what we need, buying with the gems from our mines.'

'But no soft-shelled crab,' she mourned. 'No fish.'

'Indeed, fish. Trout from our streams and pools. For heaven's sake, Marianne. How can you talk about food?'

'What did you order for dessert?' she asked, finishing her wine.

He nodded to the waiter once more. 'Crêpes, into which will be put slivers of miraculously creamy cheese from the Alphenlicht mountains, served with a sauce of fresh raspberries flamed in Himbeergeist and doused with raspberry syrup.'

'That sounds lovely.' She sighed in anticipation.

'It is lovely.' He made a wry mouth, mimed exasperation. 'Also unavailable here. We've having an orange soufflé which

58

is available here, which has been recommended by several people with ordinary, people-type appetites. Try a little of this sweet wine. It has a smell of mangoes, or so they say. I like the aroma, but I confess that the similarity escapes me.'

They finished the meal with inconsequential talk, together with more wine, with brandy. They had been at the table for almost four hours when they left, coming out into a chilly, clear evening with a gibbous moon rising above the bay to send long, broken ladders of light across the water.

'I am at the middle of the whole world,' Marianne hummed. 'See how all the lights come to me.'

They stood at the center of the radiating lights, town lights on the point stretching to the north and east, island lights from small, clustered prominences to the east and south, the light of the moon.

'If you can pull yourself out of the center of things,' he said tenderly, 'I'll take you home.'

The drive back was almost silent. Marianne was deeply content, more than a little drunk without knowing it, warmed by the wine, unsuspecting of danger. As for him, he was no less moved than he had been hours earlier, but that early impetuous anticipation had turned to something deeper and more bittersweet, something like the pain of a mortal wound gained in honorable battle by a fanatical warrior. Heaven was guaranteed to such a sufferer, but a kind of death was the only gateway. 'Death of what?' he fretted, 'of what? I have never been one to attach great esoteric significance to such matters!' He refused to answer his own question. Such metaphors were merely the results of wine-loquacity, a kind of symbolic babble. He concentrated on driving.

When they arrived, he took her to the door and entered after her, saying, 'I'll hang those pictures before I leave you. No! Don't object, Marianne. I want to do it,' riding over her weak protests to come close to her, making a long business of the stick-on hangers, standing back to see whether the pictures were straight, putting them where those others had been meant to go, one in her living room, the other by her bed. And she there, watching, bemused, almost unconscious, eyes fixed on the picture of the maidens setting out their lights, stroking her own face with the fluffy eagle feather tassle of the medicine bag he had brought her, as a child might stroke its face with the corner of a loved blanket, her whole expression dreamy and remote as though she merely looked in on this present place from some distant and infinitely superior existence. Then she turned to him, and her eyes were aware, and desirous, and soft . . .

He groaned, the man part breaking through his self-imposed barriers, groaned and took her into his arms, putting his mouth on hers, feeling her half-surprise, then the glorious liquid warmth of her pressed against him in all that silken flow as she returned the kiss. He dropped his lips to the hollow of her throat, heard her gasp as he pressed the silk away with his mouth to follow the swelling curve of her breast . . .

And heard her cry as from some great distance, 'Oh . . . not that way . . . chaos will win ، . . . all my battles lost . . . Oh, tomorrow I will want to die.'

The words fell like ice, immediately chilling, making a crystalline shell into which he recoiled, immobilized, the Magus within him seeing her face, the mouth drawn up into a rictus which could equally have been passion or pain, so evenly and indiscriminately mixed that he could not foretell the consequence of the feeling it represented.

So then it was Magus, cold, drawing upon all his powers of voice and command, who took the feathers from her hand and drew them across her eyes, forcing the lids closed, chanting in his hypnotic voice, 'Sleep, sleep. Dream. It is only a dream. A little, lustful dream. It will be forgotten in the morning. Order rules. Your battles will all be won. Makr Avehl is your friend, your champion, your warrior to fight your battles beside you. Sleep . . .' All the time afraid that the voice would fail him, that his man self had so undermined his Magus self as to make his powers impotent.

But they were not. She slumped toward him, and he caught her as she fell, placing her upon her bed. When he left her a few moments later it was with a feeling of baffled frustration and disoriented anger, not at her, not even much at himself, but at whatever it was, whoever it was who set this barrier between them. He mouthed words he seldom used, castigated himself. 'Fool. You knew there was something troubling her, something you have no knowledge of, but you tramp about with your great bullock's feet, treading out her very heart's blood . . .' For there had been that quality in her voice which had in it nothing of coquetry but only anguish. 'Idiot. Get out of here before you do any more damage.'

But he could not leave until he had written her a note, folding it carefully. When he shut the door behind him, he turned to push it under the door, as though he had returned after leaving her. She would not remember anything of his − of his importunate assault. He had never felt so like a rapist for so little reason, and his sense of humor began to reassert itself as he went down the stairs. She might accuse herself in the morning, but it would only be of drinking a bit too much. She could accuse herself, or him, of nothing else.

'And I will find out, will find out what it is makes her act like this.'

A voice hissed deep within. 'Of course, it may be she simply does not find you attractive.'

'Be still. It isn't that. It isn't that at all. What it is is a threat. Desire − sex − a threat. Not merely the usual kind of threat which any intimacy makes to one's individuality, to one's integrity, no. More than that. Something real is threatening her, and I am walking around the edges of it.'

He sat for a long time with his head resting on the wheel, continuing the mood of part castigation, part determination. At last, when he was more calm, he drove away. Behind him in the lower window of the house, Mrs Winesap twitched the curtain back into place, an expression of sadness on her face. She had been sure that this man would not have stayed so short a time.

61

CHAPTER THREE

If it had not been a working day, she would have slept until noon. Since it was a working day, she struggled awake at the sound of the alarm, conscientiously set before she left her room the evening before. There was something hazy, misty in her mind, the lost feeling one sometimes gets when a recent dream departs, leaving a vacancy. She shook her head, trying to remember. There had been a good deal of amusement and laughter the night before, a good many soft-shelled crabs, pâté, wine . . . oh yes, wine. Her head ached a little, not badly, as though she might have slept with her neck twisted. She rubbed at it, noticing for the first time that she was naked among the sheets. Good lord, there must have been a lot of wine. Her clothing was laid across the chair. At least she had had the wits to undress. She couldn't remember anything about it. Wrapping herself in a robe, ignoring the protest of bare feet on the cold bathroom floor, she brushed her teeth, drenched her face in a hot towel, pulled a brush through her hair. Thus fortified, she had the courage to look at herself in trepidation. The feared bleary eyes and reddened nose were not in evidence. Well then, perhaps she had only been what Cloud-haired mama was wont to call 'being a little tiddly.'

She was still half asleep when she went to the front window to begin her daily monitoring of conditions of order and disruption. The white square on the carpet brought her fully awake.

Marianne, my dear: I forgot to tell you that my driver, Aghrehond, will pick you up on Saturday morning, about 9.00. My sister, Ellat, conveys her delight that you will be with us. She will be your chaperone and constant companion. No one will be given any excuse to criticize. All will be very proper. If you do not have riding clothes, Ellat can provide them. I look forward to the weekend with much pleasure. Thank you for a lovely evening.

She read this twice, confused. So she had agreed to spend the weekend in Wanderly after all. How could his sister have known, if he had left this note just last night? Last night? She shook her head again, so confused that she did not see the last word on his note. He had thought long before adding it, not truly sure that he meant it. He would have been much discomfitted to know she did not even see it. She crumpled the note. Lord. Riding clothes. Of course, she did have Mama's. And riding clothes didn't change from generation to generation. She would have to do some washing — and then there would be dinner. They would undoubtedly dress for dinner — if not formally, at least up. Could she wear the silk again? She stood, lost in thought, only reluctantly realizing that the phone was ringing.

'Marianne?' Harvey at his most charming. Everything within her leapt up and assumed a posture of defense. 'I wanted to thank you for telling me about Zahmani. I knew my aunt, that is, Madame Delubovoska, was in the States, but I had no idea that anyone would be here from Alphenlicht. I went down to New York to see her yesterday, and I met him. Evidently he's taken a country place not far from you while he's here in the US. I've been invited for the weekend.' The voice was gloating a little, oleaginous.

'Yes,' she stumbled slightly. 'I know.'

Silence. Then, 'Oh? How did you know?'

'I've been invited as well. Did you accept the invitation?' Dangerous ground. She could feel his attention hardening as he fixed it on her. Until this conversation she had never heard him mention his aunt from Lubovosk. The silence stretched, almost twanging with strain. 'I'm going, of course,' she said, more to break the silence than for any other reason.

'Marianne, you're obviously not awake. I dislike it when you sound muddled. I think you should take a few minutes to discuss this.'

She was honestly dumbfounded. 'What is there to discuss?

I've already accepted the invitation. It was very nice of him to ask me.'

'We have to discuss,' he said in a voice of ice, 'whether it's appropriate for you to go at all.'

Ordinarily, I would come unhinged at this point, she thought, but this is not ordinarily. I am 1001 points ahead. I had a lovely evening. The girls in the picture on my wall are setting lights in the street. I have a real medicine bag full of good influences protecting my home. 'I'm sorry you have any concern about it,' she said in a voice that sounded unflustered. 'I've accepted. Please don't be disturbed on my account, Harvey. His sister is staying with him, and he assures me that it will be quite proper.'

Silence.

Silence.

Oh, Lord, she thought. I've really done it. He will be so angry he'll cut off my allowance altogether and tell me to give up school entirely. Whoops, there goes the graduate degree.

Ice voice. 'I'm sure it will be quite proper. I'll look forward to seeing you there, Marianne. Try to dress appropriately. I hate it when you embarrass me.' Gentle return of the phone to the cradle, buzz on the line, Marianne sitting up in bed, staring at the wall.

'Harvey, if you do anything mean about my money, I'll go directly to the head of your department at the university and tell him you tried to rape me when I was thirteen.' She said this to the wall, almost meaning it. She did not know where the idea had come from. She had not thought of any such reprisal before. 'Blackmail Harvey?' she wondered at herself. 'I suppose I could try it. Would he tell the world it was all my fault?'

Well, let him tell the world it was all the fault of a thirteen-year-old girl. Ten years ago people might have believed that. Ten years ago people actually wrote that fathers and older brothers weren't to blame for sexually abusing six-year-olds because the little girls were 'seductive.' Public opinion on the subject of rape and child abuse and incest had changed a lot in the last ten years. She considered. One could make quite a case. His succession of Cheryls and Randis were very, very young. An occasional one might be under eighteen. The question could be asked. It would stir up quite a storm. On the other hand, Harvey would probably devote all his resources to proving that she, Marianne, was a maladjusted, possibly neurotic spinster with an overactive imagination.

'Oh, Lord,' she said. 'I don't want to do that.'

'You don't want to drop out of school, either,' her inner self replied. 'One more semester, and the doctorate is yours, Mist Princess. One more semester, and you can go hunting for a teaching job somewhere. Out in public. With people.'

As always, when she reached that point in her rumination, she stopped thinking about it entirely. It was one thing to get the degree; it was something else to figure out what she was going to do with it. That was what Harvey always meant when he said she was not a serious student. She didn't really want to teach, or write, or do research. What she really wanted to do was work with horses, or maybe with animals in general. When she had been twelve, she had been sure that she would be a veterinarian. It had been all she could talk about, all she planned for.

'What am I going to do with a degree in ethnology?' There was no answer. 'One day at a time,' she said. 'Just take it one day at a time.' This day, for example. A Friday. Which passed, as such days do, interminably but inevitably.

When Makr Avehl's driver, a pleasantly round man, arrived on Saturday morning, she gave him her suitcase and followed him to the big car somewhat apprehensively. She had repudiated the blackmail idea, reflecting that she was almost certainly not strong enough to see it through, and she was feeling the lack of any effective strategy to protect herself against Harvey during the weekend. On the other hand, driven by his nastiness on the phone, she had taken most of the money carefully saved for the new kitchen tile and blown it on the two new outfits in her suitcase, both extremely becoming. After all, Makr Avehl had said there would be a lot of other people around, and Harvey might not be able to do to her in public what he invariably did in private. She did not have long to dwell on these various concerns before she was distracted from her worries by the man named Aghrehond.

'You may sit in the back in lonely privacy, miss,' he said to her gravely. 'Or you may sit in front with me. I shall ask you very many impertinent questions to improve my English, which as you can tell is already very good, and you shall reprove me.'

She was amused, as he had intended. 'Why should I reprove you?'

'I have a curiosity unbecoming a person of lower rank. Here in America they pretend there is no rank, so I can indulge myself with − what is the word I want? − impunity. Faultlessness. Correct? It will give me bad habits, however, when I return to the land of the Kavi. Where you call Alphenlicht.' He looked at her hopefully, and Marianne gestured at the front seat, indicating she would share it with him.

When they had reached the highway and were headed south at a conservative speed, he said, 'You may call me Green. This is what part of my name means, and it is much easier to say than Ah-Gray-Hond. Green sounds almost English. Just as Makr Avehl sounds very Scottish when it is said quickly. Macravail. That is a good name for a chieftain, isn't it? Green is a good name for a butler. I am also a butler and secretary and man who does a little of everything. What you would call . . .'

'A handyman,' she suggested.

He shook his head. 'No. That is one who does repairing of things. I mean something else. I am not good at repairing things. If this car should stop itself, we would be quite forsaken until someone came to help us. A tiny nail, even, I will hit my thumb instead.'

'Me, too,' she confessed. 'I'm always stopping up my garbage disposer. I can't make staplers work for any length of time. They always jam.'

'Ah. That surprises me. I think perhaps you have been victim of an adverse enchantment, a small annoyance spell perhaps, nothing very dangerous. For me, mechanical things work well, always, it is only I am clumsy with my hands.

You, now, will not have such trouble in future. I am sure our Varuna will take care of this.'

'Your — who?'

'Ah. Makr Avehl. The — Prime Minister, they say. Mister-Zah-man-ee. In the land of Kavi we say "Sir" or "the Zahmani." "Varuna" is like — oh, a powerful priest. Very mighty, and a great man. Good to listen to. But I beat him playing cribbage. He is what you would call a very lousy cribbage player.'

'I don't play cribbage,' Marianne admitted.

'I will teach you,' he said with enormous satisfaction, turning off the highway as he did so. They were traveling between tree-lined fields, white-fenced, velvet green and decorated with horses. 'When you come to Alphenlicht, there are long winter times with nothing to do. Then we will play cribbage.'

'Am I to come to Alphenlicht?'

'Most assuredly. You are one of the Kavi. One has only to look in your face to see that. Do not all the Kavi come to their own land? Most certainly. Makr Avehl will see to it.'

She was still amused. 'What if I don't want to go?'

'You will want to go. The Kavi always want to go.'

'Is that woman — Madame Delubovoska — is she one of the Kavi?' she asked, unprepared for his response to this more or less innocent question.

He screeched the car to a halt, wiped his face repeatedly with a handkerchief. 'Listen,' he said at last, 'the Varuna has asked her to come to him for the weekend. This is a very dangerous thing. He knows this, now, maybe too late. That woman, she is . . . there is a word. Someone who does not care about anyone? Who takes other people and . . . uses them up? There is a word?'

'A psychopath? A sociopath?' offered Marianne, doubting that this was what he meant. It evidently was exactly what he meant, for he nodded repeatedly, still mopping his face and neck.

'That is it. Listen to me. Makr Avehl is wise, oh, very wise and great. Truly a Varuna for his people. So wise. But not

67

smart sometimes, I think. Sometimes I think I am smarter. He says so, too. When I win at cribbage, he says so. So, it may be this woman is a Kavi. One time certainly her people were so. Now, is she? Or has she done forbidden things so not to be called Kavi anymore? Makr Avehl, he must know, he says. So, he asks her to come spend the weekend, so he can talk to her, listen to her, find out. Now, listen. I do not think it is smart to have you come at the same time. Not a smart move. So, you be careful. Do not ask any questions where *she* can hear you. Be a simple, pretty little kinswoman except when you are alone with Makr Avehl. Or me, of course.'

He had frightened her rather badly, and she huddled in her corner of the front seat while he pulled the car back onto the road and continued their journey. They had entered a forest, and the light splashed through the windshield at them, broken by leaf lace into glimmering spatters. 'What do you mean, forbidden things?' she asked at last.

He shook his head. 'Do you know Zurvan?'

She told him what she had heard at the lecture. 'That's all I know. Zurvan is your god.'

'More than that. Both male and female is Zurvan. Both dark and light. Both pain and joy. One who includes all. In balance. Now, if *somebody* tried to upset the balance, to make more dark than light, that would be forbidden. That person would not be Kavi. When you are alone with Makr Avehl, you ask about the shamans. You know that word?'

She nodded, amazed at this tack and scarcely believing that she was listening to this odd talk.

'Russia has lots of black shamans,' he said. 'In places where the government does not go. There are places like that, even in Russia. Forests, deep chasms in wooded places. So, now Lubovosk has shamans, too. They say they don't need any religion there, you know. Not in Russia, no.' He laughed as though this were very funny. 'But still, they brought those black shamans to Lubovosk. To learn, do you suppose? Or to teach. Or, maybe, just to make a great confusion. Anyhow, you be a quiet inconspicuous person and don't make that woman pay much attention to you.' They drove on for a time in silence.

'Can the Kavi — can Makr Avehl do tricks? I mean,' she said hastily, seeing his expression of disapproval, 'can he do — supernatural things?'

'What sort of things? Kavi can do many very wonderful things, certainly.'

'Could he — oh, could he deliver a letter into a locked room? Could he make a phone hook itself up so that he could call someone?'

Aghrehond laughed. 'Oh, these are only little things. Of course. Any Kavi could do simple things like these. What is it, after all, but moving something very small?' He went on chuckling to himself, and she could not tell if he were teasing her or not. He drove for a few miles in silence, then pointed away to the right. 'There is the house we have rented for this season. Not so beautiful as the Residence in Alphenlicht, but very nice.'

It glowed gently in the morning sun, white-columned over its rose brick, gentled with ivy, stretching along the curve of the hill in wide, welcoming wings. Makr Avehl had not yet returned from his business in New York, she was told, but she felt no lack of welcome as Aghrehond introduced her to Ellat Zahmani, Makr Avehl's sister, a stout middle-aged woman with a charming smile who offered her a second breakfast, a sun-drenched library, a brief expedition on horseback, or a walk around the gardens. Laughing, Marianne accepted the second breakfast and a walk in the gardens. It was there that Makr Avehl found them.

He kissed Ellat on the cheek, then Marianne, in precisely the same way, so quickly that she could not take alarm. 'Aghrehond has gone to the train to meet your brother,' he said. 'Tabiti will arrive later this afternoon. I think we will not call her Tabiti, however. We will be very dignified, very political, very correct. We will all say Madame Delubovoska.'

'I will keep very quiet,' Marianne said. 'Your cribbage partner suggested it.'

'You see!' Ellat's voice was serious. She shook her head.

69

'Makr Avehl, I'm not alone in thinking this is a mistake. Bad enough to invite her, but to have the child here — forgive me, Marianne, I know you're not a child, but anyone younger than I am gets called a child when I am feeling motherly — to have the child here may stir her up. She's not likely to enjoy the idea of reinforcements. An American Kavi? She'll hate the idea.'

'What is a Kavi?' demanded Marianne. 'Green used that word. Am I one? How did I get to be one?'

'Ah, well,' Makr Avehl drew them together. 'Your father, dear Marianne, was a Kavi. Almost certainly. I'm not absolutely sure, can't be until I check the library at home, but I think he was a cousin whose family left Alphenlicht some fifty years ago. They came to America with a few relatives. There may have been some intermarriage. Now, I *am* sure who your mother was. She was the daughter of an official in the Alphenlicht embassy in Washington. All of these people were — or could have been — Kavi, which is simply our name for the hereditary family which governs Alphenlicht. Some consider it a kind of dynasty, others a kind of priesthood, but it means no more than you wish it to in your case. It was what I had in mind when I called you a kinswoman. Do you mind?'

'Is Harvey one?'

Makr Avehl shook his head. 'We generally think of lineage as coming through the mother. When we use the word Kavi, we don't only mean bloodlines, we mean other things, too — matters of belief and behavior. No; I much doubt your half brother could be Kavi.'

Ellat obviously thought this might have upset Marianne, and she started to explain. 'In Lubovosk, after the separation, there was a good deal of racial mixing with another line.'

'Shamans?' nodded Marianne.

'There,' exclaimed Ellat. 'Aghrehond talks too much, Makr Avehl. He can't learn to keep his mouth shut.'

'I think I'm the culprit, Ellat. Marianne and I had occasion to discuss shamans in another context. Yes. Black shamans, devil worshipers. We don't use the word "Kavi" for any of that line. I suppose Aghrehond told you to be prudently quiet about all this with Tabiti here?'

'Yes, he told me. The problem is, I don't know how you're going to avoid the subject. Devil worship, shamanism and similar things happen to be Harvey's favorite professional topic, and he'll be after it like a cat after a mouse.'

'Is that so? I hadn't considered that. I knew, of course, that he has written on the subject of Alphenlicht — I've read some of it. But I hadn't thought that his interest extended to Lubovoskan cultural attributes . . . Well, of course it would. His kinfolk are there! I wonder how old he was when he first met them? When he first learned of them? How old was he when his mother died?'

'It seems to me he was ten or eleven. Old enough to resent Papa Zahmani marrying again so soon, only a year later. I know Harvey went to Lubovosk or somewhere over there when he was twenty-one or -two.' He had been back only briefly when Mama had died. She would not forget that. 'The trip was a graduation present from Papa. Then, I know he went again, that same year, just before Papa died.'

'Well then, he will be well up on the subject, and we may expect him to raise issues which we would prefer not to discuss in the company we will have. I'll take him in hand at lunch. Ellat, you'll have to manage him tonight. Divert him.'

'If you have any very pretty guests,' suggested Marianne, 'that might do it.'

Ellat shook her head, frowning. 'The Winston-Forbeses are coming to dinner tonight. Their daughter is very attractive, but very young.'

'He'll like that,' said Marianne, without thinking and without seeing the odd, distracted look which Makr Avehl fixed on her. 'The younger, the better.'

It seemed for a time that she might have been concerned about nothing. Harvey arrived in the big car, chatting with Aghrehond as though they were old friends. He greeted Makr Avehl with courtesy, Ellat with gallantry, Marianne with a proper peck on the cheek and a smile which only she could have recognized as ominous.

71

Marianne took a deep breath and put herself out to be pleasant. 'How was the trip down, Harvey? Is there a station near?'

'About half an hour away. It was a very pleasant trip. Very kind of you to have asked me and my little sister down, sir. As a sometime student, Marianne does not often get this kind of treat.' Charming smile. Guileless voice. *Sometime student*. Marianne fumed impotently.

'You're most welcome, Professor Zahmani.' Ellat being equally charming. 'Your sister honors our home, and you we welcome because of your interest in our part of the world. Do come in. You have just time to erase the stains of travel before lunch.'

'I'll show him in, Ellat. Professor, I wanted to talk with you about that paper you did in the *Journal of Archaeology* — last June was it? — comparing the Cave of Light with the barsom prophecies of the Medes . . .' And Makr Avehl led Harvey away into the upper reaches of the house, still talking.

Ellat squeezed her arm. 'Don't worry. We have two other couples as luncheon guests.'

'Tabiti?'

'Not until much later this afternoon. She is driving down. Now we will enjoy our lunch. Makr Avehl has told me his impulsive invitation to your brother — no, it is a half brother, only, isn't it? — well, that this invitation brings us a guest who turns out to be unwelcome. I am glad you overcame your dislike of him enough to come. We will stay well apart from him, and Makr Avehl will keep him occupied.'

And he did keep him occupied all during lunch, Harvey so far forgetting himself at times as to let his voice rise in temperamental disagreement. Makr Avehl received these expostulations gravely, nodding, commenting, smiling. Harvey was certainly not getting the better of the argument, but the sound of his sharp-edged voice made Marianne shift uncomfortably in her chair.

Ellat nudged her knee. 'Don't worry about it. So far they haven't gotten past the fifth century AD. They're still talking about King Khosrow's persecution of the heretics.'

'How can you tell?'

'It's what Makr Avehl always talks about when he doesn't want to talk about something else,' she smiled. 'Even Prime Ministers and High Priests are men, and men are somewhat predictable, you know. Besides, he lectures. He has this dreadful habit of pontificating at great length about things others don't care about. Hadn't you noticed?'

'He does a little,' Marianne admitted, 'but I don't really mind. The things he has to say are interesting.'

'Even if you were not interested, he would still wave his finger at you and tell you all about it. I tell him, "Makr Avehl, try to listen sometimes. When you cease talking and there is only silence, it is because you have ended all conversation." He only laughs at me. Sometimes, I think, he tries to do better, but he forgets. I tell myself it is because he is shy.'

'Shy? The Prime Minister? Shy?'

Ellat gave her a conspiratorial look. 'Yes. Shy. He talks at such great length about impersonal things to avoid worrying about people. Oh, I have seen him spend great hours thinking up tortuous reasons why people behave as they do, all because he will not admit they are simply ignorant, or silly, or tired. He is a great one for explanations, Makr Avehl, but only when he must. Most times he would rather not think about people. They confuse him.'

This was a new thought for Marianne, and she glanced at Makr Avehl, catching the brilliant three-cornered smile he threw her way and feeling her face flushing as it seemed to do each time she looked at him. Shy. Well. It was an explanation, though not one she was sure she believed. Perhaps Ellat was only teasing her.

She turned to the guest on her other side and smiled monosyllabic responses to a long, one-sided conversation about politics, turning back to Ellat in relief a little while later. 'That poor woman on Makr Avehl's other side isn't getting into the conversation much.' She was watching the woman covertly, a quiet woman with a quiet, impressionable face.

'That poor woman is the LaPlante Professor of Archaeology

73

at the University of Ankara. I wouldn't worry about her. She will probably write some paper in one of the journals taking issue with your half brother on some abstruse academic subject.'

'Good Lord! Does Harvey know who she is?'

'I doubt it. Makr Avehl introduced her as Madame Andami. That's her husband across the table from you. He's very deaf and makes no attempt at conversation, but he enjoys food very much. I like them a good deal. She is interesting and he is restful. However, Madame Andami is not the name she uses professionally.'

'So Harvey has been set up to make a fool of himself. Do I get the impression you all do not like my brother much?'

Ellat looked shocked. 'What would make you say such a thing? I think Makr Avehl knows that you do not like him very much. He knows this so well that he spent most of an hour on the phone with me yesterday, talking of you, and of your half brother. Very serious talk. So I cannot tell you not to take him seriously, as I might tell some other young thing. A gentle warning, you know the kind of thing? No, to you I say something else again. He may seem to be invulnerable and very strong. Sometimes he is very strong indeed, but he is not invulnerable.' She gave Marianne a meaningful look which confused her enormously, then giggled, unexpectedly, an almost shocking sound coming from that dignified person. 'So, even if we are sympathetic to your side of whatever problem brews, we have done nothing Professor Zahmani could complain of. If he is not civil enough to converse across the table and find out what his luncheon partner does — well, what occurs thereafter must be his fault, no?'

Marianne, being human, found the thought of Harvey's discomfiture very pleasant indeed.

After lunch, Makr Avehl suggested that they all go riding. Harvey had not brought riding clothes. He demurred, explaining that he would be happy spending a few quiet hours in the library. The others left him there with Ellat while they went into the afternoon sun and the freshness of spring.

Madame Andami cast aside her quiet, listening pose and rode like a centaur, laughing when Marianne complimented her on her seat. 'I have ridden donkeys, mules, camels, even elephants. You have not a bad seat yourself, young woman.'

'I haven't really ridden in years. Before my mother died we lived in the country, and I had my own horse. I still miss him.'

'Ah, horses are a very great love to many girls of that age. I have been told it is something very Freudian.'

'I don't think so,' laughed Marianne. 'I think it is at that age that boys begin to grow so much bigger and stronger, and we girls feel left out. On the back of a horse, one ignores the fact that one is female.'

'You dislike being female?'

'Not really. It just makes . . . complications.'

In midafternoon they were met at the end of a curving lane by Aghrehond, splendid in a plaid waistcoat, who offered them champagne and fruit from the tailgate of a station wagon before they returned by a more direct route, Makr Avehl riding at Marianne's side.

'I did not wish to appear to monopolize your attentions earlier,' he said. 'But now, we have only a little way back to the house, and I can have you all to myself while the others go on ahead in such impatience. You got on very well with Madame Andami.'

'I like her. She was telling me about her work in Iran, before everything there went up in smoke. The places have such wonderful names. Persepolis. Ecbatana. Susa. I read about them in school, of course, though it's not an area of the world I have done any reading on recently.'

'They have about them something of the fictional, isn't that so? They were real, nonetheless. To us it does not seem that long ago, possibly because our children hear stories told around the fire of things which happened fifteen centuries back. Such stories carry an immediacy one does not get from books . . .'

'Which is why some countries carry such old grudges,'

offered Marianne. 'What children learn at their grandmas' knees, they act upon as though it happened yesterday.'

He nodded gravely, even sadly. 'Perhaps that is true. Those who have an oral tradition full of old wrongs and old revenge do seem to fight the same battles forever. If the Irish were not forever singing of their ancient wrongs − or writing poetry about it . . . well, we see the result in every morning's newspapers.'

'Is that the kind of thing between Alphenlicht and Lubovosk? Or would you rather not talk about it?'

'Stories told at my grandma's knee? Oh, yes, Marianne. For my grandma remembered it happening. The country was always like the two halves of an hourglass, connected with a narrow waist, a high mountain pass which was difficult in the best of times. To separate us, Russia had only to take that pass. Then the northern bit became a "protectorate." The general's name was Lubovosk − thus the name of the country. Later, of course, it became a "people's republic." Under either name it was high, and remote, and difficult to reach. Grandmother told me that at first we paid no attention. We continued to go back and forth from north and south, but we had to go over the mountain instead of across the pass. Then there began to be changes in Lubovosk. The visitors who came from there came to stay. Visitors from Alphenlicht who went there didn't return. There were whispers, rumors of evil.'

'Aghrehond said I could ask you about shamans, but not when others were about.'

The expression on his face was one of embarrassment, almost shame. 'Yes. I am ashamed to say it. Black shamans, from the land of the Tungus. Dealers in necromancy. People who would trifle with the great arts. Dealers in sorcery. Ah. You don't believe in any of this, do you?'

'It's not . . . it's not anything I've ever thought about except as . . . as . . .'

'As a part of the superstitions of primitive peoples? Perhaps as survivals in the modern world? Little unquestioned things we learn as children? Fairy tales? No, you needn't apologize.

76

Let me explain it to you in a way you will understand.

'Let us say a woman is driving a car. There is an accident, and her child is pinned beneath that car. She is a little woman, but she lifts that car and frees her child. You know of such things happening, yes? Well, let us suppose that before she lifted the car, she danced widdershins around the spare tire and called upon the spirits of the internal combustion engine, *then* raised up the car to rescue her child. Do you follow what I say?'

'You mean the first thing is unusual, but natural. The second thing we would call magic?'

He beamed at her. 'Precisely. The same thing happened in both cases, but only in one would we call it magic. There is much of which man is capable, much he is unaware of, all very natural. The worshipers of Zurvan, the Magi, are scholars of this knowledge. The shamans, too, are scholars, but they use the knowledge in a different way. They teach that the power comes through the ritual, through dancing around the spare tire. They teach, when they teach at all — which is not often, for they prefer to be mysterious — that the power comes through demons, godlings, devils. They teach that in order to obtain the power, it is necessary to propitiate these devils. Followers of Zurvan teach that the power is simply there. We may use rituals to help us focus our thoughts, but we know they are simply devices, not necessary functions. Am I making any sense to you at all?'

'You mean that their demons and devils don't really exist . . .'

He shook his head, reached over to touch her hands where they lay loosely gripping the reins, his face dappled with sunlight as he leaned toward her. 'Would not exist, Marianne, except for them. The act of worship, of invocation, can bring things into being which did not exist of their own volition — temporary demons, momentary gods.'

His intensity made her uncomfortable. 'Isn't it all more or less harmless?' she said, trying to minimize the whole matter. 'Mere superstition? Regrettable, but not . . . not . . .'

'Not dangerous? When the ritual demands blood, or maiming, or death, or binding forever?' His voice had become austere, his expression forbidding and remote. 'The difference between a true religion — and there are many which share aspects of truth — and a dangerous cult is only this: In the one the individual is freed to grow and live and learn; in the other the individual is subordinated to the will of a hierarchy, enslaved to the purposes of that hierarchy, forbidden to learn except what the cult would teach. You have only to look at the rules which govern the servants of a religion to know whether its god is God indeed, or devil!' He passed his hand across his face, then laughed unsteadily. 'Listen how I preach. Aghrehond should not have told you to question me about this. My anxiety is too close to my skin. Come, we will ride up to the others and think no more of it.'

But when they rode into the gravel courtyard near the stables, Marianne thought of it again, for a long black car stood there, the black and red diplomatic flag of Lubovosk fluttering over its hood.

'I had not expected her for several hours yet,' said Makr Avehl. Then, as he sat there, looking at the flag, he was struck with a comprehension so violent that he swayed in the saddle. Tabiti. Madame Delubovoska. Harvey's aunt, his kinswoman. Why had he not made this simple connection before? If Harvey had not had the wit to pick out the things he had given to Marianne, if someone else had done so, someone sly, vile, deeply schooled in all the black arts — why, it would have been Tabiti.

'Lord of Light,' he thought, terrified. 'Of course it would have been Tabiti, and I have brought Marianne here, like bringing a lamb into a cave of wolverines.' They had been so casual with one another when he'd met them in New York, he hadn't realized that they were not merely related, not merely acquaintances, but actually *akin*, sympathetic. He turned to Marianne with some urgency, knuckles white where they gripped the reins. 'Wait,' he warned himself. 'Do not jump too quickly. You are not sure that this is true.' But he was sure, so sure that his face was ten years older, drawn with concentration, when he turned to take Marianne's hand.

'Kinswoman, I will ask you in advance to forgive me if I

pay you little attention for the next several hours. Now that I have learned a bit more about your half brother and his relationship to Lubovosk, I think it was a foolish mistake to invite him into my house, a foolish mistake to invite Tabiti here. The dimensions of my foolhardiness were unclear. I could not be more sorry. Will you forgive me?'

She managed to create a smile, eager to give him whatever help she could. 'I'll pay no attention at all.'

'Stay with Ellat,' he counseled. 'Stick to her like a leech.'

'Ellat may get rather bored with that.'

'Ellat will prefer it,' he grated.

They went into the house, to all appearances a cheerful, chattering group, through the open doors of the library where Ellat awaited them, her face slightly drawn with strain. As Marianne entered the room, she saw nothing but the two figures across it, Harvey and the Madame, faces alike as twins, eager with some strange avidity she could not identify, eyes hungry and glittering. They were staring only at Marianne, and she felt their eyes like a blow.

Harvey came to take her by the hand, his own palm wet and sticky as though he had been working in the sun. 'Well, little sister. Back from the ride? Come meet a relative of ours.' She nodded, murmuring 'of course' as he drew her from Makr Avehl's side across the room into a cold, threatening space where it was all she could do to smile between tight lips in acknowledgment of the introduction. Madame's eyes were like those of a bird of prey; they seemed to whirl like wheels of fire, and her voice had serrated edges to it, a kind of velvet file rasping in her head.

'I'm so pleased to get to meet you at last, my dear. My nephew has mentioned you so often, told me so much about you. How is the school going? Did I understand you had had some academic difficulties?'

Marianne tried to deny this, tried to say that she had had no difficulty, except in carrying a heavy load of course work in addition to working full time, but the words stuck in her throat.

She heard Harvey's voice as though through a pool of thick

water, thick, cold water, gelid, about to crystallize into ice making a thunder in her ears. 'Oh, I don't think Marianne lets that worry her. She isn't that serious about her work.'

Again Marianne tried to protest, realizing in panic that she could not breathe. She was suffocating. Then Ellat was beside her, saying something about Marianne's having promised to look at the orchids in the conservatory, and she was drawn away from them and was in another room, leaning against a wall, gasping for breath.

'What . . . how . . .' she gasped. 'What happened?'

'It is an amusement for her,' said Ellat angrily. 'It's something *she* does. For fun, I think. She tried it on me, but Makr Avehl had warned me. I will show you how to prevent its happening again. Also, I've had your things moved out of the guest wing and into my room. It's a large room with two beds, and we will share it. I think it will be safer if you are not alone. We'll go there now.' And the two of them sneaked away upstairs like naughty children, though Ellat continued her angry muttering the while. Once behind the closed door, Ellat washed Marianne's face with a cool washcloth, as though she had, indeed, been a child.

'It's frightening, isn't it? I could see your face turning red, as though you couldn't get your breath.'

'What did you mean, it's something she does? I don't understand what's going on.'

'Have you ever heard of telepathy?'

'I've heard of it. I don't believe in it.'

'Well, then don't believe in it if you don't want to, Marianne, but listen to me anyhow. That woman down there, that — Lubovoskan,' she spat the word as though it had been a curse. 'That woman made a very strong telepathic suggestion to you that you could not breathe, that you were suffocating. As I said, she tried it on me earlier, but Makr Avehl had warned me. Now, if you aren't comfortable with the idea of telepathy, that's fine. Call it subliminal suggestion or something. Or pretend she has a transmitter in her pocket that blocks your brain waves. Whatever. She can do it, and you felt it.'

'I don't believe this,' Marianne protested. 'Things like this aren't possible.'

'Well,' said Ellat, 'you felt it. Was it false? A result of riding too long, perhaps? Coming into a warm room out of the air? Dizzyness? Perhaps something to do with the menstrual cycle — that's always a good explanation for such things. Hysteria?' She waited angrily for Marianne's denial, which did not come. 'No. It was none of these things. It was an unworthy exercise of certain abilities which should never be used in such a way. It is a kind of seduction, one of several kinds they use. Well, we knew she could do such things. We did not know she *would* do them; particularly, we did not think of her doing them here or to you. So you must either run or confound her. Which is it to be?'

'I will confound her,' pledged Marianne, revulsed by the memory of Harvey's hungry, prurient eyes. It had been Ellat's use of the word "seduction" which had decided her. Of course it was a kind of seduction. A kind very like the one Harvey had been trying on her for years, a seduction of power, of oppression, of dominance. 'I will confound her if I can, but she makes me feel like Harvey does. I can feel her peeling me, taking my skin off to look inside, layer by layer. I feel flayed when she looks at me. She scares me.'

'That one scares Makr Avehl himself, girl. But I think we can manage to get through the evening.' She began to clear the top of her dressing table, beckoning Marianne to a place before the mirror where she could see her own frightened face above Ellat's busy hands.

'This,' said Ellat, making a specific shape with her left hand, 'we call the "tower of iron." Make this shape with your hand. No. Look at it more closely. That's right. Now this we call the "wall which cannot be moved." I will tell you about these . . .' So the lesson began.

Hours later Marianne sat before the mirror once more, dressed in one of the new outfits, a glittering silver sheath, hair piled high in a simple, dramatic style which one of Ellat's maids had done for her. She breathed deeply, setting her own center of being high and balanced. 'You will not get

81

me again, Harvey,' she said. 'Not you or your aunt.' The woman in the mirror could be afraid of nothing. *I am a tower of iron*, she sang quietly to herself in the litany Ellat had taught her, moving her hand in the proper sign. *I am a fortress of strength, a wall which cannot be moved*.

Ellat was running a brush across her shining head, patting the full knot which she wore low upon her neck. 'Remember to think *reflection*. Visualize lightning striking a mirror and being reflected back. Remember.'

Marianne shut her eyes, fastened her sparkling necklace with its shining pendants. She glittered all over, a gemmy wand, bending and swaying, the necklace flashing. 'I remember, Ellat. I'm trying to remember everything you've said.'

'I'll be right beside you. There's the dinner gong. Shall we go down?'

Marianne took a deep breath, nodded, began to breathe slowly, calmly, focusing her thought upon strength and will. They went into the library as though for a stroll in the gardens, setting themselves like adamant against the will of Madame, against the hot curiosity in Harvey's avid eyes. Was it only her imagination, thought Marianne, or did he seem disappointed? What did that questioning look to Madame mean? Perhaps they had not expected her to be able to come down to dinner at all. She gritted mental teeth and smiled, visualizing lightning with every fiber in her brain. *I am a tower of iron*.

Madame came toward her at once, Harvey trailing behind, making Marianne think irreverently of a mother goose with one gosling, Madame's expression being very much a looking-down-the-beak one. She laid a hand on Marianne's shoulder and Marianne stepped back, out of her reach. Madame's eyes glittered at this and she said, 'Harvey and I were just discussing what you might enjoy seeing when you come to Lubovosk with your brother.'

I am a fire which cannot be put out, she thought. 'Really?' she said aloud. 'I have not contemplated such a trip, and it's unlikely I could travel so far any time soon.'

'Oh, Bitsy, anything is possible,' said Harvey, smiling,

sipping at his cocktail, lips wet and avid in the soft light of the room, sucking lips, vampire lips.

'Not for me, I'm afraid,' she said, smiling in return. *I am a tower of iron.* 'Besides,' she turned a spiteful reposte, 'if I traveled to that part of the world, it would be to my mother's people — to Alphenlicht.' Had she put that slight emphasis on my, *my* mother's people? Yes. The air boiled around her and she felt Madame's fury like a blow.

'There is really very little there to interest you, my child,' the woman said. 'Very little of interest to anyone. It is a country of peasants and priests.'

'Do I hear my name being taken in vain?' asked Makr Avehl, offering Marianne a glass and taking her elbow in his hand to turn her away toward other guests. 'What is this about peasants and priests? Are you talking shop again, Tabiti?' Marianne felt his fingers tremble on her arm, knew that he was almost as sunk in rage as Marianne herself, felt herself adrift in these vicious currents which spun around her. *I am a fortress of strength*, she told herself, moving away to be introduced to other guests, Ellat close behind her.

At dinner, she was at the far end of a long table from Harvey and Madame, and she was able to ignore them for moments at a time. After dinner, they came close to her again, the thrust of their intention as clear as though they had struck at her with a blade. Makr Avehl spoke to her only casually, as to any other guest. Ellat stayed close.

I am a fortress of diamond, Marianne told herself, concentrating upon reflecting their intentions back upon themselves. She moved her hand into the configurations Ellat had shown her, then thought about them, internalized them. *A mountain of stone.* Making a hard fist with her right hand. *I cannot be moved or changed. I am the fire which cannot be put out.* Flicker of first and second finger of the right hand, a trill of movement, secretive.

'Hey, Bitsy,' Harvey called. 'How are you getting back to town tomorrow?'

I am diamond, Marianne told herself. 'I hadn't thought

about it, Harvey.' Quietly asserting the while, *I am iron*. Left forefinger raised, pressed against cheek.

'Then you must let me drive you back.' Madame, gaily importunate. 'Your brother has already consented to accompany me, and your home is on our way.'

'Marianne.' Makr Avehl, laughing. 'I am crushed! Had you forgotten so soon that you promised I could drive you back? I have those papers to pick up which your librarian so kindly offered to lend to me.'

I am iron. I am adamant. Smiling, turning to him with a little moue of forgetfulness. 'I did promise. Of course. I'm sorry, Madame. Another time, perhaps.' *I am the fire which cannot be put out*.

'Oh, I am disappointed. Yes, we will certainly make another occasion. I have not had opportunity to get to know you nearly as well as I should like.' Gentle, caressing, infinitely threatening.

We are like Siamese fighting fish, thought Marianne. We circle, our fins engorged with blood, ready to die if need be, caught up in our dance. She flinched nervously as Ellat touched her on the arm.

'Would you like to go up? You said you wanted to ride early in the morning.'

Taking this lead, Marianne nodded gratefully. 'Thank you, Ellat. Yes. I am a little tired. The ride this afternoon was a longer one than I've had in years. Good night, Madame, Harvey. Madame Andami, I enjoyed your company today. Mr Williams, Betty. I enjoyed our discussion at dinner. Mrs Williams. Mr Winston-Forbes, Harriet, Stephany. Good night, Your Excellency. It has been a very pleasant day.' To walk away, back straight, face calm, up the stairs. *I am a tower of adamant, I cannot be moved*. Down the hall with Ellat, into the room, to collapse across the bed, bent tight around a stomach which heaved and squirmed within her.

'You did very well,' said Ellat, giving her a glass of something sweet and powerful which melted warmth through her and stopped the heaving.

'Nothing happened,' Marianne whispered. 'If you'd taken

a movie of it, you wouldn't have seen *anything*. Nothing happened at all. But I kept *feeling* them.'

'Nothing seemed to happen; very much was happening. Your half brother has made an alliance. He has done it very suddenly it seems. Did he know her before?'

'I never heard him mention her name until a day or so ago. I didn't know he had relatives in Lubovosk.'

'He writes mockingly of the Cave of Light. That is a typical Lubovoskan attitude.'

'I only know what I told you earlier. I think he went there twice. Once shortly before Mama died. Once, later, before Papa Zahmani died. When each of them died, Harvey had . . . had . . .'

'Had only recently returned?'

'Had only recently returned,' she agreed in a dead voice, remembering Dr Brown's words, heard through a closed door when she had been only twelve: 'I would have said she died of suffocation, Haurvatat.' Suffocation. Not being able to breathe. A thing Madame did to people for fun. Had Madame been able to teach that skill to Harvey? Harvey, who had been rejected by Cloud-haired mama and told to go find a nice girl his own age? Or had Madame herself come to confront Cloud-haired mama when no one else was there to see, to remember?

'There may be no connection at all,' said Ellat firmly, undoing the tiny buttons at the back of Marianne's gown. 'Go in there and have a nice, hot shower and put on your robe. Makr Avehl will come up here before he goes to bed. After a good night's sleep, nothing will look so ominous.'

'I'm afraid I won't sleep,' she confessed, the vision of Mama and Madame in intimate confrontation still oppressing her.

'Another glass of what I gave you before, and you will sleep.'

Makr Avehl's light tap at the door came late, when the party downstairs had broken up and the sound of voices calling goodnight to one another had fallen into silence, when lights had begun to go out in upstairs windows that Marianne could see in the opposite wing. He entered quietly, embraced Ellat, then sat on the edge of Marianne's bed. 'Isn't this ridiculous?' he asked. 'I invite a lovely young woman for a weekend's visit, all quite properly chaperoned by my sister. I invite her brother, too, because I am curious, and an old antagonist of mine, because I am proud, and suddenly all turns to slime and wickedness. You find it difficult to believe, don't you? Well, so do I, and I have less excuse than you do. Marianne, my dear, will you rise at dawn, please, and go down to the stables where Aghrehond will meet you and take you away from here. Leave your bags. I will bring them when I meet you later in the day to drive you home, as promised. There are too many currents here, too many eddies of greed and passion. Tell me, Marianne, would . . . would your half brother benefit in any material way if harm came to you?'

Her throat went dry, harsh as sandpaper. She had had those thoughts, had banished them, had put them down, 'buried, begone' in her own litany, but they lunged upward now like corpses long drowned and broken free of some weight to rise hideously through slimed water to the surface. She cried out at the horror of it, all at once weeping in a steady flow. Ellat took her into her arms and held her, saying 'Shh, shh. He shouldn't have asked it so abruptly like that. But you don't protest, Marianne. You don't protest?'

'No,' she cried. 'I can't protest, Ellat. I've thought it too many times. I thought I was wicked to think such a thing, only a wicked, angry child. But, oh, if I died, he would get all that Mama left me − it's all tied up in Papa Zahmani's estate, and my share of Papa's estate, too. It's a lot. More than I ever wanted or expected. More than anyone could need.'

'Ah,' said Makr Avehl. 'So *he* has a reason. Now, what is *her* reason?'

Ellat shushed him and gave Marianne something which sent her into sleep, all at once, like falling into velvet darkness. She was still fuzzy at the edges of her mind when they put her into Aghrehond's care at dawn in the stableyard, among the horses clattering out of the place for exercise and the grooms chattering as they headed for the wooded roads.

'Come, pretty lady,' said Aghrehond. 'We must be away from here.'

'Won't they think I'm terribly rude,' she asked, 'leaving the party unannounced this way?'

He made a conspiratorial face with much scrunching of eyebrows and mouth. 'Ellat will say you have gone for an early ride. This is strictly true. She will not say "horseback," though they may think so. Others may also desire to ride. So, that is fine, and Makr Avehl will go with them. It is a large place, is it not? There are many miles of pleasant roads around it. Who is to wonder if you are not seen by anyone until noon? By then, you will be elsewhere. Tsk. Stop frowning. You make your face all frilled, like a cabbage leaf.'

She stopped frilling her face and let the day happen. They stopped for breakfast in a small, seaside town. They shopped for antiques along the winding streets. They drove through a national monument. They returned to the small town a little after noon to find Makr Avehl waiting for them with Marianne's bags in his car.

'There is a buffet luncheon going on back at the house,' he said to Aghrehond. 'Some are eating now, others will have luncheon when they return from riding. Some friends of Ellat's will come in to swell the numbers. We will not be missed for some time, which is fortunate.' His face was set, grim, and he made a covert sign to Aghrehond which Marianne saw from the corner of one eye. 'When someone asks − and not until then − you may say to Ellat in the hearing of the rest that I have driven Marianne back early in order to go on to Washington for an early meeting at the State Department.'

'What happened?' she demanded. 'Something happened. What was it?'

He barked a short expletive, chopped off, as a curse half spoken. 'A pack of feral dogs,' he said, 'came out of no-where, according to the grooms. Madame Andami was bitten on the leg. Superb rider, of course, and she stayed up. We've sent her to a physician up in Charlottesville. One of the horses is cut up a bit. The vet is there now. Someone riding

87

alone — someone not as fine a rider as Madame Andami, someone out of practice, for example — might have been seriously injured.' They stood for a moment considering this. 'The head groom works for the people who own the place, of course, as do all the servants except for Ellat's maids and my secretary. He says he has never known it to happen before. It's horse country. A pack of feral dogs that would attack horses? It wouldn't be tolerated for a day! They would have been hunted down.'

Marianne did not ask the questions which tumbled into her mind. Did someone think the dogs were set upon the riders? Was it an accident? Makr Avehl's face had the look of one who did not wish to talk, to guess, to theorize, the look of a man rigidly but barely under control. He waved Aghrehond back to the big car as he ushered her into the smaller one. Over her shoulder, she saw the large car turn back toward Wanderly and the house. She remained quiet, let time and miles pass, watched his face until it began to relax slightly, then asked, 'You think they were after me?'

'I'm sorry, Marianne. I do think so. Yes.'

'You think that's possible? To stir up dogs that way? Make them attack horses?'

He made an odd, aborted stroking motion toward his chin. 'I could do it. It wouldn't even be difficult. I know that she can do it, because I can, and whatever I may think about Tabiti, she's strong. Lord, she's strong. And I am weakened by being angry at myself. No — don't shush me. I am angry at myself. Before I invited you here, I never thought to ask about your true relationship with your brother. I knew you didn't like him, I knew things were not good between you, but I never tried to get at the bottom of it. I should have considered it more fully. Instead I lulled you. I lulled myself.

'Marianne, he means you ill. Not merely in the slightly jealous way one sibling may cordially detest another — which, Lord help me, was what I had considered. No, he means you real destruction as surely as this road leads to your home. He means you ill and he has made some kind of alliance with Madame to that end — if, indeed, she is not a primary mover

88

in this matter. And I, who foolishly exposed you to this, must find a way to protect you.'

Marianne laughed bitterly, and when he turned an astonished face on her, she laughed again. 'Makr Avehl, you don't know how relieved I was last night to hear you say that. For years, I've thought that Harvey hated me, or resented me. For years I've fought against his patronizing me, destroying me. Whenever I got my head up, he'd do his best to knock it down. The only things I could be sure of succeeding at were things he didn't find out about. Always with that hating face, that superior smile. But nothing I could prove. Nothing anyone else could see. So I felt guilty, wicked. I felt I didn't have the right to hate him. After all, Papa left him in charge, left him to take care of me. Now you say he's trying to harm me — really. For money. For Papa Zahmani's money. I suppose it's true. Harvey likes money. He never has enough, though what he inherited should have been enough for anyone. But I get more, of course, when I'm thirty, because a lot of it was my mother's. *My* mother's, not Harvey's mother's. But Papa was old country, through and through. Couldn't see leaving it to me until I was a matron. Girls had no real status with Papa. He loved me, but that was different.'

'That may be true, but I think it more likely he saw you as a little girl and he saw Harvey as a grown man. Perhaps he only wanted to protect you. How old was Harvey?'

'Oh, twenty-five or -six. That may have been it. I was only thirteen. I wish I could feel that was it.'

'Your papa had no reason to mistrust his son?'

'No. Harvey was never . . . he was never strange until Mama died. When I was a little girl, I thought he was Prince Charming. Really. He was so handsome, so gallant. He brought little presents. He . . . he courted us, Mama and me. Then, when Mama died, he changed, all at once. He became something . . . something horrible.'

'I think it possible that he did not understand the reality of the property division between your parents. I don't think he realized quite what part of the family fortunes were yours, Marianne. Perhaps he began to be a bit strange when he

89

visited Lubovosk. I'm sure that he was given weapons there he should not have had, and now I must defend you against them. You must be very brave, and very strong. There are certain things black shamans can do — and certain things people trained by them can do. You've seen a sample already . . .

'There are worse things: transport into the false worlds, into the dream borders, binding forever in places which exist within the mind and have virtually no exits to the outside world . . .

'But to do any of these things, the shaman believes that his ritual demands consent. *Listen to me, Marianne.*'

'I'm listening. You said the ritual demands consent.'

'Remember it. The shamans believe the ritual is necessary to the effect, and they believe that consent is necessary to the ritual. The shaman says to his victim, "Will you have some tea?" And the victim says, "Yes, thank you." *That* is consent. In my own library, your brother said to you, "Come, let me introduce you to . . ." and you nodded yes. That was consent. So she then struck at you.'

'Did the people who went riding consent? If so, to what?'

'More likely, Madame went down to the stables before going to bed last night, taking a few lumps of sugar with her. "Here, old boy, have a lump of sugar," and the horse nods his head, taking the sugar. He has consented then, and they can use him. So also with dogs, with birds, with anything they can get to take food from their hands. The true victim was to be the horse, whatever horse you might be riding or anyone else might be riding. They are not over scrupulous.'

'What are you trying to tell me?'

'I am saying, for a time, do not consent to anything your brother proposes. If he says on the phone "isn't it a nice day," say "no, it is not." If he says "wouldn't you like to go to Mexico for your vacation," say "no, I'd rather go somewhere else." Be disagreeable. Better yet, do not talk to him at all.'

'Forever? That may be difficult.'

'Only for a few days, until I can get a few of the Kavi together to make a protection for you. Until we can teach you to protect yourself. I don't even want to take you home, to leave you there alone, except that anything else would make them more determined, more dangerous. As it is, they may not know we suspect them.'

'The thing Ellat taught me won't work?'

'You're not schooled enough in its use. You haven't the discipline. I hate to leave you, even for tonight.'

'They can't be in that much of a hurry,' she said nervously, disturbed by his intensity. 'I don't inherit for another four years, for heaven's sake. Harvey isn't going to do anything precipitous.'

'I suppose you're right. Once one begins to feel this menace, this gathering force, it is like hearing a thunderstorm in one's head. Space and time are lost in it. One is at the center of fury.' He reached to take her hand in his, utterly unprepared for the reaction his words would bring. 'Marianne, I could stay with you tonight.'

Her hand whipped away from him, without volition. Her mouth bent into an oval of rejection, horror. 'I'm not like that,' she said, the words coming from deep within, words she did not usually say aloud but were now aloud, between them, harsh and ugly. 'Not like that.' She shuddered once, again, muttered words under her breath, like a litany, got control of herself, tried to make light of it, did not succeed. His face was white, blank.

'I've offended you,' he said at last. 'I meant nothing dishonorable. Please. It was only to offer protection. You're probably right. There is not that much hurry. They aren't mind readers, after all. They cannot know how thoroughly I am alerted to the danger they pose. We will comfort ourselves with that thought. If your brother calls, you will be light, and cheerful, and contrary. Please remember to be contrary, Marianne.'

She agreed to do so, not hearing him, too caught up in the internal maelstrom he had unleashed, wanting only to be out of the car and behind a door, her own door, shut against the world. 'Not like that,' the hissing demon voices inside kept saying. 'Harvey was wrong. I'm not like that.'

He left her at the door, seeing on her face that he should not offer to come in. She went in to disconnect the phone, to sit for an hour in her window while the sun went down and the stars began to peek over the roofs and chimneys. The buds of the oak outside her window had begun to unfurl into tiny, curled hands of innocent pink, and her mind squirmed in guilt and confusion at the fact that now, even now, she lusted after him, wanted him, and all the years of not wanting did not seem to have immunized her at all.

At last she set to work building mental towers of adamant and walls of iron. She put herself to sleep with the litany Ellat had taught her. She awakened to her clock radio, news of combat and death, so ordinary and distant as to be undisturbing. She was almost ready for class when the door-bell rang, and she saw the delivery man's hat through the peephole, knew that it must be some little gift from Makr Avehl, felt again that combined guilt, lust and self-loathing. She opened the door to receive the package, accept the proffered pencil.

'You have to sign for it. Where the X is on the line.'

'Yes,' said Marianne, 'I will.' Only to see the glitter of eyes as the uniformed person's head came up, dark, hawk-faced, mouth curved in a cry of victory. She had only time to think that she had given consent and to say, 'Madame Delubovoska,' before all went dark around her.

CHAPTER FOUR

It was dark by the time Makr Avehl arrived in Washington after miles of driving through country he did not see, traffic he did not consider, in a state of mind best described, he told himself, as unnerved and astonished. While his mouth had been busy saying words which meant, in whatever language he was thinking, 'Gods in heaven, what ails the wench!' his center of being was saying in another tone, perhaps another language entirely, 'Oh, my dear, my very dear.' This colloquy was over in the moment which it occupied, leaving his political self shaken before the sweet longing of that inner voice: 'Oh, my very dear.' And that was when he knew, absolutely and without any remaining doubt. Not earlier, when he had seen her at dinner, a sparkling baton of willow flesh, bending but not breaking before her brother's assault; not on horseback, face eager as a child's, with tendrils of hair wet on her forehead from the sun; not as he had seen her in the car, first laughing then crying to know that all her world was arrayed against her but that she was not insane.

So. So what was he to do now? She had rejected him and he had left her, left her there alone, and he could not go back to force himself upon her, for in such forcing might end all that he now in one instant hoped and longed for, without warning or premonition. Well, no matter the reason, if any. If she had rejected him, she had not rejected Ellat, and what Ellat could not find out was not worth the finding. So he drove like a maniac to reach his hotel and a phone so that Ellat might be enlisted in his sudden cause. He was convinced of danger, smelled it, felt it breathing hotly on his neck, a scent of blood and damnation. She must accept help from Ellat.

Oncoming headlights speared toward his eyes, and he came to himself as a horn shrieked beside him, dopplering by and away into darkness with a howl of fury. This sobered him. He would call Ellat as soon as he arrived in Washington. Until then, he would try to behave more sensibly and think of other things.

In which he was only partially successful. Ellat was eager enough to help Marianne. 'Of course I'll stay with her. We got along quite nicely. If you really feel . . .' But her desire to help did not allay Makr Avehl's concern.

'I really feel,' he said grimly, 'that there's something more than merely wicked going on here.'

'I can't figure what they're playing at,' fussed Ellat.

'Madame using her cocktail party magic tricks here, in this house, against one of your people.'

'I think Madame sees Marianne as one of her people, or one of Harvey's people, which amounts to the same thing. Can you be here by lunch time tomorrow?'

Lunch time, she said, yes. Yes, the guests had all departed. Yes, the horse which had been bitten seemed to be healing and a dog they had captured was being tested for rabies. Yes, he could turn in the little car to the rental agency, they would use the big one. Yes, the servants were packing so that they might leave. 'I'm tired of all this, Makr Avehl. I want to go home.'

'Just as soon as we do something about Marianne, Ellat. I promise.'

Something in his voice said more than he had intended, for there was a waiting silence at the other end of the line, a silence which invited him to say more than he was ready to say. When he did not fill it, she said, 'Take her with us. That's the sensible thing to do.'

'It's called kidnaping, Ellat. The Americans don't find it socially acceptable. They have laws against it.'

Ellat only snorted. 'Tomorrow. At lunch time.'

On which note he found himself sitting on the side of his bed, holding the phone in one hand as it buzzed a long, agitated complaint. Should he call Marianne? What could he say? No. Better leave it. Drop in with Ellat tomorrow, about five in the afternoon, when Marianne got home from work. Gritting his teeth, he turned from the phone to his briefcase to spend two dull hours going over the material he would use in his meeting the following morning.

And when that meeting was over, he felt it had all been an exercise in futility, a kind of diplomatic danse macabre in which he and Madame had shaken skeletons at one another like children at a Halloween party. And yet the woman had seemed strangely satisfied, as though she had won whatever game she was playing.

'The undersecretary of state assures me that we may depend upon the status quo,' he said to Ellat over the lunch table.

'Which means precisely what?' asked Ellat, not interrupting her concentration on a plethora of oysters.

'Which means exactly nothing,' he admitted. 'The US has spoken for us in the UN and that's it. They don't take the matter seriously, and I'm beginning to think they're right. This has all been a charade. Madame is up to something else, and this has all been misdirection, probably for my benefit.'

'Marianne said that.'

'She said what?'

'Marianne said that if the Lubovoskans really intended to take us over, they'd invade.'

'Well, of course they have tried that,' he said.

'She would have no way of knowing that, Makr Avehl. I repeat what I said earlier. If you want to keep the child safe and away from that horrible brother of hers, take her with us.'

He did not reply. The food did not tempt him, and he was waiting impatiently for Ellat's affair with the oysters to run its course. He dared not agree with her, for she would take it as a promise, but emotionally he had begun to believe only the course she had suggested would satisfy him — to take Marianne with him when he left.

'Eat your oysters, Ellat,' he said. 'It may be your last opportunity to do so. Aghrehond will be here with the car in twenty minutes.'

They approached Marianne's tall house just at sunset. The door into the front hall stood open and on the tiny turfed area between the steps and the iron fence, Mrs Winesap leaned on a lawn edger, intent upon the clean line separating daffodils from grass. She looked up in frank curiosity, staring at Makr Avehl and Ellat from her broad, open face, mouth a little open, rather gnomelike with her cutoff jeans and baggy shirt. 'I don't think Marianne's here,' she told them. 'The door's open, though, so she must have run out just for a minute.'

Makr Avehl acknowledged this information with a pleasant nod, stood back to let Ellat precede him into the hallway and halfway up the stairs. Then he saw Marianne's jacket, obviously trodden upon where it lay half on the upper step,

95

then the clipboard of papers with her signature scrawled and running off one edge. The door to her apartment was open. On the window seat the purple crocuses wilted in the close heat, and a fly buzzed in frustration against the closed window.

He stepped back into the hall to pick up the clipboard, knowing as he did so what had happened. It could all be read in the signs; the track of the beast could be seen. The world began to turn red inside his eyes, and he realized he was holding his breath. Released air burst from his lungs, and he sat down abruptly. 'She's gone. Oh, damn me for a fool, Ellat. Damn me for an arrogant, irresponsible fool. We're too late. She's gone.'

Ellat was already going down the stairs, out into the tiny front yard. 'You must be Mrs Winesap? I thought so. Marianne has told me all about you. She's so grateful for your help with the lawn. I wonder, did you happen to notice anyone coming or going this morning? I had sent a package, and I wondered . . .'

Sympathetic, warm expression saying what a nice woman she was to have sent a package. 'I saw him leaving. Went out of here like a cat with his tail on fire. Must have left his delivery truck around the corner, because he went off down the block in the time it took me to say "Good morning." I hate it when people are so bad-tempered they don't even respond to a simple time of day. I said, "Good morning," loud and cheerful, and I didn't even get a grunt from him.'

'That would have been about what time?'

'Oh, let me see. What did I come outside for? I'd had breakfast, and Larkin was doing the dishes, and I'd written a letter to my sister − that was it − and I'd come out to put it in the mailbox for the postman. So it wasn't time for "Donahue" yet, or I'd have been watching him. About 8.30, I'd say, give a little take a little.' She laughed heartily. 'I always say don't be too sure, and nobody can call you a liar.'

He was holding onto the banister when Ellat came back up the stairs. 'I heard,' he said. 'Then Marianne wasn't taken.' He turned back into the room. On the window seat the

Delvaux print of the young women setting lights in the street was broken in two, splintered ends of frame protruding like broken bones. He went through to the bedroom. Nothing. Orderly. She had made the bed. The bathroom was a little messy, towel dropped rather than folded. 'She was here when the doorbell rang,' he said to Ellat, turning to make a helpless gesture to Aghrehond who had just come up the stairs. 'Doorbell rang, she went to the door. The person there said something about signing for a package, and Marianne said "of course" or "sure" or something of the kind — without thinking. She didn't even have time to be afraid.' Oh, God, he thought, why did she pull away from me with that revulsion? I should have been here. I should have been the one to answer that door, confront that monster.

'If it is that Lubovosk woman, she flips her finger at you,' said Aghrehond. 'She sneers like a boy in the street, nyaa, nyaa, nyaa. She makes an insult, a provocation. Why?'

'Perhaps,' said Ellat, 'because she has had the wits to see that Makr Avehl cares for the girl. Bait. Bait in a trap.'

With horror, Makr Avehl thought of the white bird and the black, demon fish; thought of the naked girl carrying her little light into the darkness while trying to pretend that she was dreaming. He came to himself staring at his own face in the mirror, haggard and terrified.

'Why is the picture broken?'

'I gave it to her,' he replied woodenly. 'To replace a very unpleasant one her brother had given her. If Harvey saw it — if Madame saw it, they would know in an instant that someone was intervening in Marianne's affairs.'

'But she wasn't taken,' said Ellat. 'Whoever it was didn't *take* her.'

'Sent,' Makr Avehl growled. 'Not taken, sent.' So, wherever she was now, among the false worlds, somewhere in the endless borderlands where no maps existed and the shortest distance between any two points was never a straight line, she was at least together, body and soul. He had seen bodies sundered from their souls. He had experienced souls sundered in that way, too. Better not, far better not. If he had had to choose between two horrors, it would have been this, at least. That she was in one place. One. Somewhere.

'I must go into Madame's limbo after her, into whatever borderland place she has been sent.'

'Makr Avehl! Think of the danger!' Ellat laid a hand upon his arm. 'Think!'

'I am thinking,' he muttered. 'You, too. Think of her. Somewhere alone. Lost. Frightened. Perhaps without memory. Certainly without friends. In a dream world, a lost world, a world in which dark is light and evil is good, perhaps. You think, Ellat. What else can we do?'

'From here?'

'Yes. From here. Water those flowers, will you? She wouldn't have left them like that. Open the window. She would have done that.' Oh, God Zurvan, he prayed, let me undo the harm I have done. I was the one not to tell her what pit of evil I sensed in that box of hers. I was the one who begged her to come to Wanderly, not valuing her own instincts which bade her stay far from her so-called kin. I was the one who considered the threat not urgent, not imminent. God.

Where would one like Madame send one like Marianne? What kind of world would she construct, of her own soul, of her own being? Where would one like Marianne be sent? Into what place? Into which of the myriad borderlands? How constrained, how held? He lay down upon Marianne's bed, quietly, quietly, letting what he knew of Tabiti possess him until it became more real than himself. Where? Where? Where?

Ellat came to the door of the room, apparently unsurprised to see him lying there. 'Can you tell me what you are going to do?'

He reached out a hand to her, clasping her own, begging her trust and indulgence. She released him, sighing.

How could he describe to her the almost instinctive tasting of ambience, the intuitive sorting through of words and ideas and pictures? Marianne had been *sent*, and that sending had had to be, by its very nature, within the structure of

Marianne's relationship to Madame, within the ambience of their milieu. He had only to feel his way into that vicinage, into what was already there; he had only to seek that faintly diplomatic tinge, the flavor of embassies and foreign places, the sourness of artifice, the stink of deception, the thin, beery scent of solitude and cold rooms, the presence of children — no! The presence of the childlike. The shadow of malevolence hovering. Within that, something being built, constructed, changed, for Marianne's own persona would demand that. Courage. There would be courage. Stubbornness. A kind of relentless perseverance in survival.

Withal, there would be power, Madame's power, Madame's control, hidden, perhaps, or disguised, but there nonetheless. Madame's colors, ebony and blood. Marianne's colors, mauve and plum and misty blue found rarely if at all. Would there be anything there of Harvey? Unlikely. Though he might think of himself as an important part of this challenge, in reality he was no more to Madame than was Marianne herself, a part of the bait.

He lay there, breathing his way into the precincts of illusion, finding the border of dream as he would have found the spoor of a deer in the forest of Alphenlicht, slowly, with infinite caution, summoning it, moving breath by breath so as not to shatter the silence or betray his presence, disguising his own form, changing to blend into the place he would find himself, that otherwhere, that hinterland where he would find her, find her, find her . . .

Ellat, watching, saw him sink into trance, fade before her eyes into an effigy, lifeless as stone, betrayed only by the shallow, infrequent breaths which misted the mirror she held before his lips. A grunt from the doorway made her turn. Aghrehond stood there, eyes wide, mouth open, panting as though he had run for miles. 'I will go with him,' he said.

'Hondi. He did not ask—'

'Ellat, he does not ask. I will go with him. He may need someone. He may need someone to stay in there when he comes back, for he cannot stay. That is what she wants, that Lubovoskan. She wants him lost in the false worlds, but he

99

is too wise for that. I will go. Shush now.' And he went back into the living room to lie down there, hands folded on his chest, sinking at once into a sleep both as profound and as disturbing as that which held Makr Avehl.

Deep into the night the light glowed in the upper window as Ellat's figure passed and passed again and the search went on.

CHAPTER FIVE

Marianne, like the others in the pensione, made daily visits to the embassy. It was only a short walk, through the carnival ground and the phantom zoo, along the city wall to the Gates of Darius — not cleaned yet, though the scaffolding had been rigged against the ruddy stones for several seasons, and teams of dwarves were brought in from time to time to swarm up the ladders and peck away at the archway — then onto the Avenue of Lanterns. She thought that they must keep changing the avenue. When she had first visited the embassy, she remembered the avenue as quite broad and straight, the lanterns honest constructions of amber glass and bronze. Now the way curved to make room for the new tiled pool they were building, and the lights had been replaced with scattered braziers which left much of the roadway in darkness, the footing treacherous among chips of marble, chisels, mallets, and discarded cola cans the masons had left. Of course, reaching the embassy in the morning light was only a matter of watching one's step, but the return always seemed to occur after darkness had fallen, which made the return trip difficult though not, Marianne reminded herself constantly, impossible. Marianne went to the embassy at least every other day, religiously, in the constant hope that some message would have arrived concerning her, or some quota would have been changed to allow her an exit visa. Everyone at the pensione, of course, existed in the same hope.

The woman who could have come from Lubovosk had pointed out, with laughter, what a vain hope that was. 'Those of us from Lubovosk already have our visas,' she had said, fixing Marianne with her cold, imperious eye in which that taint of mad laughter always hung like a pale moon over a cemetery. 'Those of us who know the rules know the way. Those of us in favor with the ambassador. You, on the other hand, are unlikely to receive permission to leave. You are obviously a native, a borderlander.' The way she said it was a venomous revelation to Marianne, a metempiric bombshell which seemed to make the matter certain forever. Of course they would not help her at the embassy. Of course the quota would not include her. Of course they would be moved to neither pity nor mercy. Not for a borderlander, a creature of quiet-gray, still-dun ghostness.

She had thought to apologize to the woman who could have come from Lubovosk, but the words caught in her throat, so she had put her glass of Madeira on the harpsichord (worrying later that it might have left a ring) and let herself out of the crowded apartment. Behind her the surf of conversation ebbed and flowed, falling into silence as she climbed the echoing stairs to her own room. It had been a mistake to go to the reception. Probably they had meant to invite someone else, and the invitation had been put under her door by mistake.

Her room was cold, the dirty casements opened wide to a view of the nearer roofs and the farther towers. Sun lay upon the streets, rare as laughter, enough to start a ridiculous upwelling of hope, like a seeping spring under ashes. She snatched up her coat to drag it over her arms as she ran down the clattering stairs of the pensione, past the landing where they had found the old man dead, his pockets stuffed with appeals to the ambassador, past the room where the woman who could have come from Lubovosk and her guests still talked, into the frigid entrance hall with its lofty ceiling and frosty mirrors, and out into the bright, dusty streets where the children from everywhere gathered to play. She wondered, as she had before, why they gathered in this street rather than some other. They broke before her like drops of mercury, only to flow together behind her and go on with their games, a fevered intensity of play. She could feel their impatience, their hot ardor, sizzling in the dust.

She wondered which of them, if any of them, had been born here in the borderland? Surely none. No one remembered being born here. There were no natives to this place, despite what the woman who could have come from Lubovosk had said. They had come, all of them, as Marianne had come, interlopers, strangers, unacclimatized to this place or this time. Marianne knew there must have been somewhere else. 'Cibola,' she chanted to herself. 'Rhees. New York. Camelot. Broceliande. Persepolis. Alphenlicht.' All of these were places beyond the border. 'I could have come from there,' she whispered rebelliously. 'I could. I know I could.'

Hands thrust deep into her pockets, she started down toward the river wharves, toward a place full of light and the complaint of gulls. If the sun were an omen, if hope were not dead, if there were still reason to go on – well, then Macravail might be there. Perhaps they would go to the phantom zoo, feed dream shreds to the tame ghosts. Perhaps he would give her another present from the flea market, perhaps a book with stories about other places. Perhaps he would not. One never knew with Macravail.

She found him sitting, as he often did, upon a bollard, perched like some ungainly bird, thin to the point of ropiness, every corner of him busy with bones. She gentle-voiced him, knowing his horror of shrillness, and he turned in one flowing motion to stare at her from huge, lightless eyes which seemed to see only shadows where she saw light and light where she saw shadows. 'Marianne,' his voice caressed her. 'Will you share my sun?'

The question she answered was not the one he had just asked. Squatting beside him on the wharf, she said, 'I don't think I'll go to the embassy anymore.' He had suggested to her again and again that it was a waste of time, gently, persistently. 'I keep thinking of the old man.'

'What old man was that?'

'The old man who died in the place I live. He'd been going

to the embassy forever. He never got out. The woman from Lubovosk says I'll never get out.'

'But she urges you to go to the embassy.'

'Yes.' Marianne was unable to consider the fundamental dilemma this implied. It was true. The woman who could have come from Lubovosk urged everyone to go to the embassy. Always. The thought led her into a gray, fuzzy area which itched at the edges and hurt in the middle. She could not think of it, even though she knew Macravail would be disappointed. She changed the subject. 'Did you take your dog to the witch wife?'

'It did no good at all.' Macravail's voice was grave and sorrowful, the edges of his mouth under the white moustache turned down. 'I thought at first it had helped. For a time he seemed better, and we even walked to Leather Street and bought a new leash, but last night while we slept all his hair fell out. He is bald now, like a wineskin.' He pointed to the shadows where a bloated shape murfled to itself, shiny and hard as a soccer ball.

Marianne sighed. They had spent half their substance for several seasons — surely it had been several seasons — on Macravail's dog, yet the poor beast seemed no better. She could not bear to see Macravail grieve over him. 'Why don't we plant on him?' she suggested desperately. 'Mixed grasses. We'll tie the seeds on with gauze and water him night and morning.'

So that is what they did that day while the sun dribbled into the streets in shiny puddles and processions wound about on the city walls and heralds rode toward the gates making brassy sounds of challenge. When they had planted Macravail's dog — more complicated than she had thought it would be, for the gauze tended to slip — they went to the phantom zoo, but it was too late to feed the ghosts and they ended up eating the dream shreds themselves.

When he left her at the door, he reminded her of the morning's resolution. 'You promised not to consent to go to the embassy anymore.' She asked him why he cared, knowing he could not, or would not, tell her. He did not, merely

103

sniffed remotely and chewed on the corners of his moustache while the dog snuffled wearily at the end of the gilded leash. 'I hope your dog will grow grass, Macravail,' she wished him at last. He had forbidden her to say goodbye to him, which made leavetaking somewhat tenuous. She was never quite sure when he would go or if he would go at all. When she laid her hand upon the doorlatch, however, he went away, leaving her to climb the four long flights to the cold room and the sagging bed. Evidently the reception was long over, for no sounds came from the woman's apartment. Sometimes Marianne did not see her for days, many long days, and she felt somehow that the woman had somewhere else to go from time to time, unlike the rest of them.

The next morning, however, it was the woman from Lubovosk who woke her, tapping on the door, calling, 'Marianne, get up, get dressed. They're doing something new at the embassy today.' Marianne almost refused to answer, almost kept her word to Macravail, but then decided that any hope was better than none. She agreed to go with them after breakfast, remembering from some misty past a voice telling her she was contrary — or was it to *be* contrary? — asserting her independence by refusing to hurry from the dining room even though the others were shifting impatiently in the hall. The red-faced woman was there, and the two sons of the duchess. The little old woman who swept the hallways was with them as well, her eyes frightened and soft beneath the swath of veiling on her hat. Marianne had never seen her in anything but apron and dusty skirt, a tattered shawl around her shoulders, but today she wore mittens and carried a parasol above the silly hat.

'It's a pretty parasol,' offered Marianne, sorry now to have kept the old thing waiting.

'Everyone ought to have something,' the old woman said. 'Don't you think so?'

The five of them moved off under the sardonic gaze of the woman who could have come from Lubovosk. Marianne expected to hear her laugh behind them at any moment, almost as though she remembered the laughter. When she looked back from the edge of the carnival ground, however, the woman was gone. In the zoo the phantoms moved restlessly in their cages, but only Marianne glanced at the spectral arms thrust through the bars, begging for food. The twin sons of the duchess strode along side by side, their arms around one another's waists to hide the fact they were joined at the lower body. When they arrived at the embassy, a fussy clerk sent them all to various rooms and told them to wait. Marianne sat in the empty office, listening to the hopelessly frustrated buzzing of a fly against the gray glass, dirty from a hundred rains and a hundred dust storms, admitting light only through the accidental fact that the filth was not perfectly evenly distributed. Outside lay the famed gardens of the ambassador, but Marianne could not see them. A very long time went by before one of the consular staff entered the room, a bundle of forms under one arm, to sit at the desk and begin the questions. The woman from Lubovosk had been right. The procedure was different, and yet Marianne had a feeling of horrid familiarity, as though in some other place or time she had experienced it all before.

'Have you ever healed warts?'

Marianne could not remember having done so. 'I don't think so,' she replied, trying to keep her voice interested but unemotional. One never knew. Perhaps the tone of voice one used would make a difference.

'Have you ever visited the Cave of Light or any similar tourist attraction?'

'No. I'm sure I haven't. Should I have?'

The person stared at her coldly. 'It isn't a question of should. It's a question of the quota being changed — definitions. Regulations. You know. The new system will make all that possible. Now. Do the following mean anything to you at all? Stop me if they do. Shamans? The onocratic dyad? The Cave of Light?' There was an invitational pause, but it meant nothing to Marianne. 'Banshees? Sybils? Crabbigreen? Ah, that strikes a chord, does it?'

Marianne thought it had something to do with lawns, but she wasn't sure. Still, the person nodded encouragingly and continued with the list. 'Ethnography? Harvey? Lubovosk?'

'Yes,' Marianne said into the silence. 'There's a woman in my pensione from there.'

'Tell me what you know about it,' he said, silky-voiced, all at once very interested.

'She's from there. You'd have to ask her. I don't know anything about it at all.'

'Umm. Let's see. That's schedule 42-A. Ah, here it is. Now, this will be a little different. You just tell me what comes to mind when I say each word. Drat. This pen is out of ink. Wait a bit. I'll be right back . . .' The person left the room, the door shutting behind with a swish full of finality and finish, the sound a branch makes falling from the top of a tree, falling, falling, then done, not to fall anymore because it has reached the place beneath which there is no more down at all.

'Swish,' said Marianne to herself sadly. She did not expect the person to return. The little light which had come through the dirty glass was already fading. Time in the embassy was different from time on the outside. It was almost night, and outside in the hall the little old woman had set her parasol against the wall and was busy sweeping the floors.

'I thought, since I was here already . . .' the woman began.

'We might as well go on back,' said Marianne. 'Perhaps we'll come again tomorrow.'

Macravail was waiting for her in the street, ropy arms folded across his narrow chest, mouth puckered in reproach. 'I thought you weren't coming here anymore.' She stared at her feet, unable to answer him. 'The seeds sprouted,' he said, pointing at the end of the leash where a fuzzy, green ball clicked along on short legs, beady eyes peering at her from beneath grassy ears. The dog barked, a husky, friendly, convalescent sound.

'I'm glad, Macravail. It makes him look so much more comfortable. I'm sure he feels better.'

'I thought we'd take him to the fountain,' said Macravail. 'He needs watering. Then we could buy some fruit jellies and watch the fireworks.'

Marianne could not help the slow tears which began to well from her eyes, the harsh lump which choked her. Under the curious eyes of the little old woman, she wept noisily. Macravail made no effort to comfort her, merely chewed the ends of his moustache and spoke soothing words to the dog.

'What's it all for?' she cried. 'What good is it all? We'll eat fruit jellies and watch fireworks and tomorrow it will all be the same. The embassy will change procedures again, but they still won't give me a visa. I'll grow old here, and die, and then they'll put me in the phantom zoo with the other ghosts, and I'll be hungry all the time. Oh, Macravail, I just want out . . .'

The little old woman turned pale at this and trotted away, tap-tapping with her parasol. Marianne fumbled through her coat pocket to find some tissues, a little sticky and shredded, but whole enough to dry her eyes and stop her dripping nose. When she came to herself again, the old woman was gone, and Macravail was crouched against the curbing as the grassy dog peed against the lamppost.

'If you'll stop going to the embassy,' he whispered, 'I can get you out. Without a visa. If you *really want to get out*.'

'You can? Why haven't you said anything before? You know I want out. More than anything.'

'People say that,' he went on whispering, 'when they don't really mean it. The little old woman who was just here, she'd say it, but she'd be terrified of it. Here is familiar, always changing, but familiar. Here is almost forever. Here is custom and endless circles turning. Here is nothing truly strange. There is nothing here but what is here, Marianne, and the only way out is *out*, no guarantees, no safety. Some are better off here, Marianne.'

'How can you say that? Nothing ever happens here! Nothing ever changes!'

'New fountains along the avenue. New carvings on the gate.'

'But as soon as they're finished, they'll change it again. They do that. Everything is always changed, but nothing is ever different. I want it to be *different*. I want you to get me out.'

'If you really want to,' he said with an intensity she had

107

not heard from him before, 'I can't advise it, or urge it. It has to be your decision.'

'I want to,' she said firmly, thrusting the soggy tissues back into her pocket. 'I want to. What do I have to do?'

'Just tell me where you want to go. That's all. You tell me, and I'll take you there.'

'I want to cross the border.'

'Where do you want to cross? Into where? There's a crossing in a pasture just outside the walls. There's a crossing under the wharf we sat on yesterday. There's a crossing where the dwarves come in, and one where the heralds go out. Where do you want to cross?'

'Does it matter?'

'You have to choose and consent, Marianne. You can move, change, get from this place to another place, so long as you choose and consent. Each place has rules of its own. That's the rule here. I can only help you if you choose and consent.'

She chewed her lip, felt the hard lump rising in her throat once more. 'Won't you decide for me, Macravail?'

He shook his head slowly, a pendulum slowly ticking, a mechanical motion as though he had been wound up. She could almost hear the slow toc-toc-toc as his head went from side to side. 'No. I can't do that. And if you talk to anyone about it, I can't help you at all. You tell me where you want to cross, and I'll take you there, but you must tell me.'

She fumbled with the soggy tissue again, and when she looked up it was to see Macravail and the dog disappearing around the corner far down the avenue, near the new pool. Loud into the dusk came the sound of hammers, dhang, dhang, dhang, echoing from the high walls along the street. The sound grew louder as she moved toward home, and when she went beneath the arch of the gate a chip of stone fell into her collar, scratching her neck. The dwarves were at work in the flaring light of a hundred torches as the fireworks burst above them in showers of multicolored sparks. She could still hear the sounds of the hammers when she lay in her bed, trying to breathe quietly, trying not to think, trying to sleep.

Then, in the morning, she tried not to sleep, tried to cast off an overwhelming lassitude which paralyzed her will. Below her window the children played in the dusty street in a fever of intensity. Their game seemed to revolve around a small group of slightly older children, children perhaps eleven or twelve — perhaps even a little older than that, for the loose shirt which one of them wore clung occasionally to the swell of budding breasts. That one, a cloud of dark hair and wild, black eyes, was at the center of every evolution of the game, a desperate concentration upon her face. After a time of watching them, Marianne put on her old coat and went down the stairs, through the cold hall and onto the shallow steps which fronted the pensione. There she sat, nibbling a cuticle, watching. Each turn in the game brought the central group somewhat nearer. Finally, when the sun was almost overhead, the cloud-haired girl was so close that Marianne could have touched her. Instead, moved by some urge she could not have identified, she said, 'If someone told you they could get out without a visa, what would you think of that?'

The girl turned on her with a fiery look. 'So what? Any of us can do that.'

'You know where the crossing places are?'

'Hah.' It was a whispered sneer. 'Since I was here. Since I could walk. I know them all, even the ones that haven't been used in a hundred years. All the kids do.'

'Then why don't you — emigrate?'

The girl stared at her insolently. For a time Marianne thought she would not answer, but at last her expression softened and she put out a hand to touch Marianne's face. 'You're all misty in the head, aren't you? Younger than I am, for all you seem older. They change, you know. A place might be a good gate for a while, then it would become a bad gate. You get through a bad gate, you might not be able to play your way out, you know? You have to work it out, play it out. That's what we're doing. Playing the games. Patterning them. When the right pattern comes, then I'm next. I can tell you because I'm next, and I won't be here much longer.'

Seeing the incomprehension in Marianne's face, she continued. 'There aren't any good gates for grown-ups. Only for kids. That's why I have to get out right away, before . . . you know. Don't tell!' For a moment the voice was that of someone Marianne knew, then the voice of an anguished child, then the dark-haired girl was swung back into the frenzy of the game. Marianne returned to her room, thinking she should wash her face before lunch. Bent over the basin she heard a shout go up from the children, but when she hastened to the window there was nothing to see.

The cloud-haired girl was gone, but she could have gone home for lunch. Marianne held that thought resolutely through the noon meal, through her afternoon nap, through the pre-dinner cocktail hour which the woman from Lubovosk insisted all the residents attend, and which she herself attended, today full of some obscure fury which Marianne made no effort to identify. After dinner the children were still hard at play, but the cloud-haired girl was not among them. Marianne went to her room to put a pack of tissues in her pocket with her comb and, after some thought, the little book of stories Macravail had given her. She had not read many of the stories nor understood those she had read. 'Something,' she whispered to herself. 'Everyone should have something.'

She went into the evening and to the river. Macravail was there. Beside him the grassy dog was digging wildly into a crevasse between two stones, whurffling as he did so. Marianne sat down beside Macravail and watched the dog until it gave up the search and lay down with a bursting sigh beside them. 'Tell me where all the crossings are,' she said. 'Tell me where they all are, Macravail.' Then, as he did so, she wrote each one down on a page of the book, each on a different page. When she had finished, the stars had come out. Taking a deep breath, she opened the book at random. The nearest lights were in the carnival ground, dim and distant. She made it out with difficulty. 'The alley behind the bird market. Let's go there now, Macravail.'

They went the long way 'round, skirting the fruit market and the street of the metal workers. They passed the back

wall of the embassy, hearing over the wall the clatter of
dishes and the unmistakable sound of laughter — the woman
from Lubovosk's laughter. The alley behind the bird market
was a narrow one, lit by a single gaslight. When they stood
at the end of it, Marianne could see the door clearly, though
she thought it had not been there when they entered the alley.

'Through there,' said Macravail. She turned to see his face
drawn up in an expression part pain, part hope, part despair.
'Through there.'

'I have to go,' she pleaded. 'You do understand, Macravail?
I can't stay. I can't go on forever like the little old woman,
like the sons of the duchess. I have to have a difference,
Macravail. Come with me.'

'No,' he said unaccountably. 'You're safer alone. They
may not even know you're gone for a while. But give me
something — something to remember by . . .'

The only thing she had was the book. The words came out
piteously, unforgiveably, before she thought. 'Everyone
ought to have something . . .'

'Ahhh . . .' She had not heard Macravail wail in that way
before, so lost, so lonely. 'Give me, and I'll give you.' She
felt the dog's leash thrust into her hands, felt the grassy
beast pressing tight against her legs as the book was withdrawn from her hand. Then there was only the crossing to
elsewhere, and the difference came without warning.

Makr Avehl lay on Marianne's bed, unmoving, eyes closed.
On the table beside him a brazier burned. From time to time,
Ellat dropped a pinch of fragrant resin into it to make a
pungent smoke. Between such times she moved about, making
no unnecessary noise but not trying to be silent. Aghrehond
had been stretched out on the living room floor until a few
moments before. One moment he had been there, as quiet as
Makr Avehl, the next moment he was gone. Ellat had found
her eyes brimming with tears. Aghrehond was like a brother,
like a bumptious, loving son. As Marianne had been *sent*, so
had Aghrehond been *sent*. Except, of course, that he had
volunteered to go.

She moved back and forth between the two rooms, being sure, tidying up. Makr Avehl would not be disturbed by her activities; she had begun to wonder if he could be aroused by anything at all. Outside the drawn curtains the evening bloomed violet with dusk, mild and springlike.

'Ellat?' She heard the indrawn breath.

'Here, Makr Avehl. Hold still. I've kept tea hot for you.' She slipped her arm beneath his head and brought the steaming cup to his lips as he sipped and sipped again, breathing deeply as from some great exertion.

'I found her.'

'I knew you would, if anyone could. Was it as you thought, in some borderland world of Madame's?'

'Yes. A black world, of Black Madame. Oh, Ellat, but I will have vengeance on that one. Marianne is nothing to her, nothing at all, but she took her up like a boy picking an apple, only to throw it away after one bite. Bait. Using her to bait me. She hopes to throw me off balance. To make me commit foolishness, risk my people, risk the Cave. She plays a deep and dangerous game, that one.'

'She tried our defenses once before. I do not think she is eager to try them soon again. She mocks at the Cave, but she could not break its protection.'

'No. She prefers to bait me with my innocent kinswoman. Well, she was ignorant of much, was Madame. Certainly she did not think I knew Marianne well enough to follow where she had sent Marianne, to follow and let her out of Madame's place into one of her own. Madame may learn soon that Marianne is gone from her limbo, but she will not know where. We start even, then, neither of us knowing where she is.' He laughed harshly before sipping again at the tea, swung his feet over the side of the bed and rose. 'I must try to make a call to Alphenlicht.'

'Everything will be packed by now. We can go tonight.'

'I wish we could go. I need the Cave of Light, Ellat. I need the Cave and our people. But if I am ever to find Marianne, it has to be from here.'

'Aghrehond?'

112

'I sent him after her. Poor thing. Everything is twisted where she is, names and people and places and times. All moves as in disguise, strangely warped. In this world of Madame's the pitiable émigrés have no memory of what they were, or only fragments. All has been wiped away. Nothing could wipe her character, of course, and the courage shines through like a little star. Still, she suffers under it.'

'You say Aghrehond is with her. Where?'

He laughed, a short bark of vicious laughter, at her, at himself, at the world. 'Lord of Light, Ellat, that's why I need the Cave. I don't know where she has gone. The only way out from the border worlds is into one's own world. She went into her own place, one of her own places − I don't know how many there may be. If she was a woman of some imagination, there might be thousands. Or perhaps only one. Whichever it may be, I must find her. *I must find her.*'

'What will you do?' She was hushed before his vehemence, a little awed by it, thinking she had not seen him like this before, not over a woman.

He sighed. 'I will eat something, if you can find something here or bring something from that place on the boulevard. I'll take a shower. That place made me feel slimy. I'll call − who? Who would be best? Nalavi? Cyram? Since I can't go to the Cave, they must do it for me. I'll call some of our people at the embassy and set them on Harvey's trail, and on Tabiti's. I want to know where they are in this world, if they are here at all. And then I'll try to think what to do next.'

Outside Marianne's window the pink leaves of the oak uncurled like tiny baby hands, gesturing helplessly at the world beyond. The curtains remained closed. Downstairs, Mrs Winesap turned in her half sleep, sat up suddenly to say to Mr Larkin, 'Did you hear that? What was that?' To be answered only by a snore, a riffle of wind. Unsatisfied, she lay back down to sleep. There was the sound of a car driving away, then returning. Feet moved restlessly over their heads. Then silence, only silence. The house was still, still, as though waiting.

113

CHAPTER SIX

Marianne's desk was on an upper level of the library as were those of the assistant librarians, but not, as theirs were, upon the balcony itself. There a contentious writhing of brass made a lacoonish barrier between the desks and the gloomy gulf of air extending more than four stories from the intricate mosaics of the lobby floor to the green skylight far above. Marianne's space was sequestered in a trough of subaqueous shadow at the deep end of an aisle of shelves, the only natural light leaking grudgingly upon her from between splintered louvers of the curved window set some distance above her head. This eye-shaped orifice looked neither in nor out, but Marianne often glanced up at it in the fancy it had just blinked to let in some tantalizing glimmer from outside. To this wholly inadequate illumination she had added a lamp discovered in one of the vacant basement rooms, a composition of leaden lavender and grayed green in the form of an imaginative flower. Such light as it allowed to escape outward was livid and inauspicious, but that which fell on the desk top puddled a welcoming amber reminiscent of hearth fires or brick kilns, comforting and industrious. By this liquid glow she found her way to and from her desk at night when all the balcony was dark, the aisles of books blacker tunnels yet, and the only movement except for her own the evanescent ghosts reflected through the wide glass doors from the windshields of passing cars.

After making an effort to leave the library every night for some little time, she had resolved not to try to leave for a while. The attempts had become increasingly frustrating, and she felt it might be easier to give up the effort, at least temporarily. She resolved to accept the necessity of washing out her underwear and collar in the staff washroom. She made a brief prayer of thanks that her appetite had never been large and was now easily placated by a few of the stale biscuits kept in the staff tea room. These biscuits never seemed to grow more or less stale, and their quantity remained constant in the slant-topped jar. When the jar was turned in a certain fashion, the tin lid caught light falling from street lamps through the high window to reflect it upon the dusty couch where she slept.

During the first several evenings, Marianne had turned on the lights in the basement room, flooding it with a harsh, uncompromising emptiness more threatening than the dark. The light brought persons to gather mothlike at the window where they crouched on the ground to peer down at her and whisper of books; the stealing of books, the destruction of books. When she turned off the lights, they went away, or so she thought, for the whispers ended and no shadows moved at the barred window. Thereafter, she used the lights only in the washroom, which had no windows, or upon her desk, so deeply hidden among the corridors of volumes that no ray could have betrayed her to watchers.

On each of the first several afternoons, rather late, Marianne had been sent on an errand of one kind or another: to take books to a room in the sub-basement; to find books in the fourth floor annex; to take papers to the special collection room on the mezzanine — all of them places difficult to find or return from. She had been at first surprised and later angered to find all the staff gone when she returned, the doors locked tight, the outside visible only through the vast, chill slabs of glass in the main entry. Each evening at this time it rained, glossing the pavements and translating the sounds of cars into sinister hisses which combined with the tangle of brass railings to make her think of feculent pits aswarm with serpents. It was better to go back to her desk, to that single warm light, to work there until weariness made it impossible to work any longer, than to stay in the chilly chasm of the lobby beside those transparent but impassable doors.

When both darkness and weariness overcame her, she felt

115

her way down the wide marble flight, carefully centered in order not to touch the railings, around the corner to the small door — discouragingly labeled 'Authorized Personnel Only' — then down the pit-black funnel of the basement stairs to the washroom and light. From there it was only a step or two to the tea room where panties and collar could be laid wet upon the table, wrinkles smoothed; where a handful of biscuits could serve for supper, washed down by a mouthful of cold tea; where the tin-topped jar could be turned to beam its pale blot onto the place she would sleep; and to dream of dusty wings beating against glass. She always folded her trousers over the back of a chair, thankful for the plain, dark uniform which did not show dirt or wrinkles.

At first light she wakened, terrified that she might have overslept and be about to be caught in semi-nakedness, remnants of dream catching at her to drag her back into sleep. After washing and dressing herself she became calmer, able to hide in the washroom and emerge when others arrived, as though she herself had just come to work. Some member of the staff always brought rolls, sometimes fruit, though whether this was done spontaneously or by arrangement Marianne never knew. The provender made up the larger part of her day's food, and she had learned to sneak an extra roll or second orange to hide in her desk. At 8.50 the assistant librarians reported to the head librarian, a single line of them neatly clad in the same white-collared uniform which cost Marianne so much anxiety. Many shadowy figures, Marianne among them, watched this assembly from above while the roll was called to the accompaniment of dignified banter suitable to the profession, and finally to the clang and thwock of bolts withdrawn from the top and bottom of the main doors.

Usually one or more patrons waited outside, strolling about on the brick paved portico or leaning against the glass to peer within through cupped hands at the lobby clock. Then the staff members trooped upstairs to their desks, the doors began swinging as patrons entered, and the day began.

Though none of the staff ever spoke to her directly, Marianne was not conscious of any ostracism. There was

116

such indirection in the affairs of the library that she believed no one really spoke to anyone else, ever. Information seemed always to be conveyed in passive statements. 'The door to the muniments room needs to have a hinge repaired' rather than 'Mr Gerald, please repair the hinge.' This inherent passivity had much to do with the fact, thought Marianne, that the door to the muniments room was not repaired for days although its need for repair had been plaintively stated half a dozen times. Thus, Marianne might be given some task by a half-aborted gesture from an assistant librarian directing her attention to a small pile of books while a statement was directed somewhere over her left shoulder, 'Those should be in the sub-basement storage area,' or 'There's space in the shelves of the Alchemy stacks for those.' Mr Gerald, an insouciant figure who arrived occasionally to have long, confidential talks with the head librarian or the doorman, seemed oblivious to these gentle requests. Marianne wondered why she, almost alone among the staff, always acted upon these indirect requirements when virtually all the others seemed able to ignore them completely.

She also asked herself what the staff did all day. Though there was a constant movement to and fro, a flutter of paper and a wheeling of carts about, no one ever seemed to bring books in or take them out. She thought at first it might be the kind of library which was devoted to research on the premises, full of important works and rare volumes. This thought would have been comforting, but she could not reconcile the idea with the actual subject matter of many of the books on the shelves. Some were of an obscenity she found shocking; others lacked sense; some had pictures so vile that she had to cover the pages while working away with her mending tape and glue. There were always loose backs to be fastened on securely, notes to be erased from margins, pages to be mended, labels to be lettered and affixed. Each morning a cart of such work awaited her arrival at her desk, and each afternoon the cart disappeared, taken away by one of the porters, she supposed, though she had never actually seen it happen. Upon this constant maintenance work were

117

imposed the errands, obliquely stated. 'Some periodicals in the Sorcery section need to go to storage.' 'They need a binder clamp up in Thaumaturgy.' The same diffidence which undoubtedly prevented the assistant librarian from directly ordering Marianne to do these things also prevented Marianne from questioning them. Once she woke late at night with the words, 'Where in hell am I to find a binder clamp!' upon her tongue, only to flush and curl more tightly into herself upon the couch. To have spoken those words aloud would have been to break some fragile pretense upon which the library and Marianne's whole existence depended.

She spent much time carrying books away to the sub-basements, adding them to the endless, tottery stacks which filled corridor after corridor of rooms. When books were sent to storage, they had faded almost to monochrome, page and print alike in yellowed tan, the print a mere shadow of fading lines. She never found the bottommost of the sub-basements. Her imagination told her that the rooms of faded books ranked downward forever, into infinity. Some of the rooms nearer ground level held a clutter of miscellany which might have been left over from a time when some other occupant had used the building.

In one room a line of dress forms stood along a wall, voluptuous bosoms thrust in various directions like the snouts of questing animals, turtles perhaps, hunting food in the dim underwater light. Another room held cases of stuffed birds, parrots and lyre birds and toucans, and still another was almost filled with broken furniture. In this room she found a dusty blue blanket which looked almost unused. She beat it free of dust before carrying it to her couch, sighing with contentment. While the room was warm enough, there had been something indecent and dangerous about sleeping half naked with no cover. The blanket became her walls and doors at once. She ate her biscuits while stroking it and curled up beneath it early in the evening to savor the scratchy security of it next to her face. That night she slept without waking, and when she did waken, much later than usual, it was with the dream clear in her memory. She had been collecting butterflies, huge, brilliant insects which fluttered away before her net only to be captured and thrust into her collection jar where they beat their wings against the confining glass, shedding the delicate powder from their wings, breaking the membranes, becoming motionless. Then she had been in the jar with them, feeling the feathery blows of those wings as they beat and beat against the glass, seeing the rainbow dust which fell from them onto her own bare arms and shoulders and breasts so that she became as brilliantly colored as they. She lay for a long time thinking of this dream, slow tears gathering beneath her eyelids.

Eventually, she rose, folded the blanket lengthwise, and hid it beneath the cushions. Several times during the day she went to the tea room to see if it was still there. She slept with it close around her every night thereafter.

Some time after this one of the assistant librarians spoke to the air across Marianne's shoulder saying that Mr Grassi would be researching certain literature in the small reading room later in the day. Later the same person, still speaking to the vacant and unresponsive air, said that Mr Grassi would need the books reserved for him in the thaumaturgy section. Marianne understood this to mean that she should find the books in Thaumaturgy and deliver them to Reading. As was the case with most locations in the building, both Thaumaturgy and Reading were uncertain. She was sometimes amazed that she always seemed to be able to get to any place indicated by these oblique instructions. This time she referred to the large chart hanging behind the head librarian's desk and was able to puzzle out a route to and from. She was approaching the small reading room when she heard the doorman say behind her, 'Good afternoon, Mr Grassi,' and was able to follow the strange hunched figure thus addressed as it moved between two stacks and through the half hidden door. She caught the door as it closed and entered.

He was seated at the round table set in an arc of window, peering through the one transparent pane at the narrow view of the garden outside. Tattered lilies bloomed there under the lash of a cold wind, and the man's head nodded in time with their nodding as though the wind blew him as well. When she put the books at his elbow, he turned to look directly into her eyes. 'The books I ordered?' he asked.

Tears spilled down her cheeks before she was aware of them, pouring across her face in forked runnels, wetting the sides of her nose, the corners of her mouth, dripping untidily from her chin. She fumbled for a tissue, blotting her face, apologizing while Mr Grassi engaged in a strange little dance of compassion which he wove about her out of pats and pokes and jigging steps.

'I'm sorry,' she said angrily. 'I don't know what got into me.'

He had pulled out a chair for her, bumping it into her legs from behind with such vigor that she fell into it. 'My dear, my dear,' he said, emphasizing each word with another pat of his pawlike little hands. 'Please don't cry, my dear.'

Marianne wiped away another freshet, confused by the troubled face before her. His mouth was open, the tip of his tongue showing at one side of it in an expression of such comical and doggy concern that she almost laughed. 'You looked directly at me,' she sobbed. 'They don't do that here. They don't see me.' And having said this she was aware for the first time of its truth. Indeed. They did not see her; they did not see one another. They lived, if this was living, and worked and *were* without true knowledge of one another, acting at every moment in the faith, perhaps only the hope, that others were there, but without the evidence of it. Perhaps it was only that things did, eventually, happen in response to their expressed hopes or needs which made them believe that others were present, that others heard, saw, felt, did. 'They don't see me!' she asserted again, 'But you did. It made me cry!'

Unaware of her revelation, he attempted comfort which she did not need. Their mutual incomprehension straggled into silence. He sat looking at her, tongue still caught between his teeth as though it were too long to be completely withdrawn. Marianne blotted herself dry and said, 'The people here at the library do not look at one. I realize now that they can't. But

120

it's nerve-wracking never to be noticed, seen. So, when you did, I was so grateful to know that I'm actually *here*.'

He shook his head, not in confusion or negation, but as though in commiseration. 'But of course you are here, my dear. That's the whole thing, isn't it. You are here, and we don't want you here at all.' They both subsided after this. She did not feel she had explained, and she had not understood what he had just said, but they were convinced of one another's good will.

'May I get you anything else?' she asked, suddenly conscious of her position as staff.

'Not at all. We have the two I asked for: *Doing and Undoing*, and here is Macravail's *To Hold Forever*. Macravail is *the* authority on malign enchantment, of course.' He tipped his head to one side so that his eyes were almost above one another as he regarded her from this strange angle. 'Can I do anything for you?' This offer, the last word whispered in an intensely confidential tone, caught her so by surprise that she shook her head, saying, no, no, not at all, before she realized she could have said, yes, of course, you can help me escape. But the moment had passed, he had turned to the books and was now reading while one finger tap-tapped at the page. The picture on the page was familiar, and Marianne stared at it for a long time over his shoulder before creeping out and away to her own place to work there while the light from the window swung slowly from right to left as the morning gave way to late afternoon. The inevitable errand materialized to take her to the fourth mezzanine just before the doors were locked, but afterward she did not go either to her desk or to the tea room.

Instead, moved by some obscure impulse she could not have explained, she went back to the reading room where Mr Grassi had spent the day. The room was empty, the books lying on the table. She took up the one titled *To Hold Forever*, thinking to take it to her own desk for a while. Through the single transparent pane of the window she saw persons gathering in the garden, pushing through the shrubbery to crowd at the side of the building to lie down there with their heads and shoulders hidden. She knew then that the staff tea room lay immediately below this room and that the persons gathered outside were those who peered so greedily in upon her if she was unwary enough to leave the lights on. From above they looked ominous, bulky and amorphous, as though constructed of shadows. She did not attract their attention as she took the book away.

At her own desk she turned the pages one by one but was unable to find the familiar picture. Faces stared at her from the pages, demon faces, ordinary faces, bulky forms like those in the garden, long pages of incomprehensible words. She left the book in the reading room before she went downstairs. Evidently the page she sought was one only Mr Grassi could find. She did not find this idea at all surprising.

She was waiting for him when he arrived the next day as she had somehow known he would. She blocked the aisle leading to the reading room, giving him no room to walk around her, ready for the question she had known he would ask. 'Is there anything I can do for *you*?' to which she replied, 'Will you open the book for me, please?' It was not quite what she had planned to say, but it was close enough.

He led her into the room, opened the book upon the table, holding it with one hand as he guided her own to the heavy pages. 'It won't stay open unless you hold it,' he said. He waited patiently for her to refuse or ask other questions, but she had done what she planned to do and could think of nothing else. He left her then, and she sat in his place at the table to examine the picture of herself, seated on the couch in the tea room, the light falling dimly through the high, barred window. The text on the facing page began, 'Her desk was on an upper level of the library, as were those of the assistant librarians, but not, as theirs were, upon the balcony itself . . .' It went on, ending at the bottom of the page, 'But she had done what she planned to do and could think of nothing else.'

She could not believe what she had read, dared not close the book or turn the page. She read it again and yet again, not needing to have read it at all.

She was brought to her sense of time by a scratching at the window which proved to be one of the shadowy peerers, evidently balanced upon the shoulders of one of his fellows to press half his face against the transparent glass and stare in at her, mouth making fish motions, words she could not lip read and wanted not to hear. Holding the book carefully open with one hand, Marianne turned out the light. A muttering outside the window became a crashing sound and a louder shouting then with tones of anger. The peerer-in had fallen. She sat for a long time without being able to make up her mind whether to take the book to her own desk or to carry it down to her couch or leave it where it was. In the end she did none of these, merely sat where she was, staring blankly at the wall until she fell asleep sitting upright to wake in the dim gray of morning now knowing where she was. When Mr Grassi came in, much later, to take the book from her, she was so cramped she could hardly stand.

This time she was completely ready for his question, an almost hysterical readiness in which her answer nearly preceded his question. 'Can I do anything for *you*?' was uttered almost simultaneously with 'Help me! For God's sake, help me!'

CHAPTER SEVEN

'My dear,' he said, 'I will, of course, if I may.'

Much later Marianne was to wonder at his choice of words, his saying 'If I may,' rather than 'If I can.' At the moment, she heard only the 'I will, of course,' and let herself fall upon these words as a starving animal upon food, ravenous and unheeding of any other thing. She hung upon his arm while he patted at her, still panting, tongue protruding at the corner of his mouth, eyes full of seemingly uncomprehending concern.

123

It was this expression which told her he did not know what she needed or wanted, and that she must go further than she had gone in imagination or all her efforts would be lost. She must define the inexplicable, demand assistance for a condition which she could not define. 'I am not mad,' she said tentatively. 'Truly, I am not mad.'

No, his expression seemed to say, of course not. You are distressed, only distressed. It was not enough.

'I cannot get out of the library,' she said. 'I can't get out. Please, do you think I'm crazy when I tell you this. It's true. I cannot escape. Help me.' There, it was said, and nothing she could add to it or take from it would make it clearer.

He moved away from her, his dancing little feet carrying him in short, jigging steps to the window and, from it, to the bookshelves and, from them, to the mantlepiece — the reading room had a large and ornate mantle stretching elegant gilt and inlays above a mingy gas fire — and from it, warbling a little aggrieved sound, like a frustrated cricket caught in a dilemma of its own making. At last he came to rest in the bowed window, bent forward a little to peer through the one clear pane, hands behind him as he rocked upon his heels and toes, up and down again, like some children's toy sent into ceaseless motion by a restless hand.

'The answers to everything are in the books,' he said to her. 'It is in knowing which books, of course, and where to look. Most of the people in this city cannot get into the library, you understand that?' He cast her a sharp, questioning look, began to warble again.

'I read the book you opened for me,' she said stubbornly, wondering if he were testing her or would question her upon the contents of that book. 'I did read it.'

'Of course. And I'm sure the answer is *there*. Would you like for me to open it again?' He turned to meet her silence, her baffled quiet which hid bursting volcanos of weary rebellion and panic.

'It wasn't,' she whispered. 'Truly it wasn't. It was only my story. Mine. And I already know it.'

'Tsk. Well, we often say we *know* things when we are only

familiar with them, you know. My dear, I have spent all the time today that is safe. Let me give you my card. When you have read again, I'm sure you'll find it useful. You will find me there any morning. It may be dangerous to be on the streets after noon. Let me open the book for you again and settle you comfortably, so. Now I must run.'

And she was seated once again as she had been for a day and a night, the light of the brass table lamp upon the picture of her own face staring up from the basement room. She could see every detail of that room; the couch, the floor, the high barred window with the faces in it, the tea urn, the jar of stale biscuits. Even on the page their staleness was manifest, part of the design intended by the artist, part of the story. The staleness was intentional, as was the dust, the stuffed birds in the basement, the writhing railings beside the stairway. Under her fingers was the card he had given her. *Cani Grassi, Consultant, Eight Manticore Street*. The card was very heavy, more like metal than paper, with a design embossed upon its back. She ran her fingers over it, feeling a glow, a warm tingling which grew as she pressed the card to her face then thrust it down her neck, safe beneath a strap. Gradually the warmth died, though she could feel the pressure of the card against her skin, the sharp demarcation of corners beside her breast bone.

She sat until dark, staring at the window, caught in a timeless eddy of despair which allowed no movement or thought. Then the faces pressed against the pane in the window drew her attention and sent her into a spasm of weary revulsion. She turned out the light and made her way to the washroom, the book still open in her hands. She sat in one of the cubicles, her trousers around her knees, to read the story again and again. There was nothing new in it. When her eyes were so heavy she could not keep them focused, she struggled through a final sentence: 'She was sometimes amazed that she always seemed to be able to get to any place indicated by these oblique instructions.' Then there was only wakefulness enough left to get to her couch and stretch out upon it, the book open beneath the cushions and herself wrapped into the timeless security of her blanket.

When she woke, it was to remember the last thing she had read. Her first act was to recover the book and read the sentence once again. *She was sometimes amazed that she always seemed to be able to get to any place indicated by these oblique instructions*. The solution was clear in her mind, including all the tortuous steps she would need to go through to accomplish it. Someone in the library must be induced to tell her that something – some book, some paper, some item of equipment was needed outside. Outside!

But first she had to eat, to drink, to wash herself and comb her hair, to be ordinary, customary. Even if they could not truly see her, there must be nothing in the atmosphere at all different. 'I must be an ordinary ghost,' she said with some cheer. 'A usual ghost, giving no evidence of untoward haunting beyond the acceptable routine.' When all did, indeed, go as usual during the day, she was made confident enough to approach the chart which hung behind the head librarian's desk.

The portico was on the chart. The areaway where deliveries were made was shown. The small, walled courtyard outside the board room was labeled. The garden outside the reading room where she had met Cani Grassi did not appear on the chart. She had looked out at that garden, at the swath of lawn, the ragged edging of shrubbery. There was no wall, no fence, and it was not upon the chart. Marianne took comfort from this. What was not on the chart would not be a part of the library, no matter how close it lay.

And a place which did not lie on the chart would not be mentioned by any of the assistant librarians. Not today, she thought, nor tomorrow. But later – yes. Later, someone would mention it.

That night she sat in the reading room until dark, her message carefully prepared on a sheet of paper, the light on to attract the peerers. When she heard the first sound of them, she moved to the window to hold her message against the clear pane where they could not fail to see it. 'If you will put a sign out there saying NEW STORAGE AREA, I will bring you some books.' There was a confused mumbling from outside. She thought she heard the words of her message repeated in a rumbling voice, then again in a higher tone with fringes of hysteria. A confused chattering preceded a tap at the window. She moved her own paper away to see a message pressed against the pane from outside. 'One book first. Book name *Eternal Blood*. Put out coal chute.'

She did not know the book or where it could be found nor, for that matter, where the coal chute was. Still, if they were in the building, presumably they could be found. She wrote on the back of her paper, pressed it to the pane: 'I'll try.' Outside was only silence. When she looked through the window, there were only the shadows thrown by the street lamps and passing cars, nothing else. Throughout all the days, weeks — perhaps longer — that she had worked in the library, she had discovered no system of indexing, no catalogue listing titles or authors. She knew that finding the book would have to occur in the way everything in the library happened, by indirection and repetition. Though she had little confidence in the attempt, having seen nothing communicated in writing heretofore, she left notes on various desks, saying that *Eternal Blood* needed to be taken to the reading room. She replaced these notes at intervals, for they vanished even from desks at which no one was observed working.

She had had no great hopes for this in any case. Her best efforts went into repetition. Whenever she found herself within the hearing of some other library employee, she would say in a plaintive voice that the book *Eternal Blood* was needed in the reading room. She set herself the goal of saying this one hundred times during the first three days, and when she went to her rest each night it was with an honest weariness coming from much running about during the day to put herself within hearing of shadowy figures which seemed to dissolve from one place to another in a most unsteadying fashion. The days followed one another. Had she not observed the great length of time it took for messages to be received and acted upon, she would have despaired, but she had

estimated it would take at least seven or eight days for anything at all to happen. Thus it was with some degree of
surprise that she found the book in the reading room on the
fifth day after Mr Grassi's last visit.

It lay atop the books Mr Grassi had requested, massive,
covered in black leather with lettering in red. Marianne
opened it only once before shutting it with a shudder which
recurred all afternoon. It was a book devoted to the subject
of torment. Marianne did not ask herself what the peerers
might want with it, knowing that conscience might rise out
of her confusion to attack her if she thought about it. It was
enough that the book was the one named, the one which might
buy her a way out.

Finding the coal chute had been an easy thing in comparison, a matter of prowling the dim corridors of the sub-
basement in search of a furnace and finding a monstrous iron
octopus at last which bellowed and roared at her as she
passed, emitting agonized groans and fitful breaths of fiery
heat. She had crept by it fearfully, crouching under its
widespread tentacles which reached out through the walls and
upward into the flesh of the place.

As she ducked beneath one of these great, hollow arms,
she heard from within it a distant, mocking chuckle carried
down through heaven knew what floors and annexes and lofty
mezzanines from some high, remote place where someone
laughed. It was a derisory laugh. Had it been repeated,
Marianne felt she would not have had the courage to go on,
but the sound did not come again. In a little room behind the
furnace she found the coal chute, too high for her to reach
until she fetched a broken chair from the room of furniture
and mounted it unsteadily to open the corroded hatch, thrust
the book through, and then, half losing her balance, let the
hatch fall with a dull, hideous clang like the lid of a coffin
or vault.

The building fell silent, as though listening. The furnace
did not roar or breathe. When Marianne crept up the stairs
and into the lobby, it was into this same ominous *silence*. At
every desk heads were cocked, eyes staring as though each

128

one waited for motion, any motion, to identify who had been responsible for the sound. She did not move, merely crouched beside the door, as silent and unmoving as they, until someone coughed and the spell was broken. She had not been perceived, she told herself, thankful for the first time that they simply did not see her.

She went to her couch that night with a sense of fruition. The next step waited on those outside, and she listened in the dark quiet to know whether they had found the book or not. It had not been dark long when she heard them cheering, a species of rejoicing with overtones of hysteria and despair. Then a flickering light came through the window and she knew they had lighted a fire. From her place she could see shadows as leaping figures capered and gamboled. Were they burning the book? She was more pleased than otherwise to think they might have disposed of it, and with it whatever damage it might have done. A daytime view of the garden affirmed her assumption, for the scars of fire were there as well as scraps of black which she could identify as bits of the binding, some with lines of red lettering still visible. She paid little attention to these, for the signboard drew her eyes, a nicely varnished board supported by two uprights, lettered in black and gold as though by a professional sign painter: NEW STORAGE AREA. Very well. She planned the next step.

But all her plans were delayed by a bustle in the library, a boiling, a throbbing of purpose as it was announced by the head librarian that a meeting of the Library Board of Trustees was to take place within hours, short hours, perhaps on the morrow. The morning lineup of assistant librarians was thrown into confusion by this proclamation, and the usual plaintive statement gained an immediacy of effect which Marianne had not seen before. The large double doors to the Board Room were opened for the first time she could remember. Books and papers which had cluttered the approach to this room were carried away. Even Mr Gerald arrived unannounced and was seen to carry a pile of volumes away to some other place. The room was cleaned and the windows opened to air it out; a fire was laid upon the hearth, one surmounted by an

129

overmantle of such complexity to make the one in the reading room seem simple in comparison. The activity took most of the day, during which time everyone's attention was fixed and could not have been diverted.

The meeting was held in the late afternoon, after all the staff had gone except the head librarian. The usual shadowy figures which Marianne equated with porters or janitors were nowhere to be seen. She herself had considered hiding in the washroom or the tea room, in some empty room of a sub-basement, perhaps in a hidey hole hollowed out among the broken furniture, but the thought of being hidden while this strange, new activity went on was outweighed by her need to see and know what would occur. The juxtaposition of this meeting and the destruction of the book which she, Marianne, had put out the coal chute was significant to her. A book had been burned; a meeting had been called — both notable events and perhaps not unconnected. At last she decided to cache herself in a far front corner of the third mezzanine, a pocket of shadow above the light of the shaded chandelier which hung one level below this to wet the lobby floor with its weak, watery light. From this vantage point she could see the members as they arrived, see them obsequiously, even cravenly greeted by the head librarian. The chairman arrived last of all, and Marianne heard the head librarian say, 'Good evening, Madame Delubovoska . . .'

The drawling voice which answered filled the lobby, ascended to the green skylight far above, moved inexorably outward from the place of utterance to the balcony edges, thrust through the banisters to flow into the aisles of books, soaking each volume in turn so that the very bindings became redolent with that sound, not echoing but vibrating none-theless in a reverberating hum larger than the building itself, a seeking pressure which left no corner unexplored. The words did not matter, could not be heard. The voice mat-tered, for it took possession of all it touched, penetrated and amalgamated into itself all that it reached.

Marianne saw the voice, saw the shudder of it go forth through the structure, a tremorous wave as in a sheet shaken by the wind, the returning vibration trembling through the coiled railings. She felt the shudder in the same instant she felt Mr Grassi's card begin to burn upon her shoulder with a pervasive heat which covered her and radiated from her. Her hand lay upon the railing; she felt the lash as the brazen circlets uncoiled to reveal flat, triangular serpents' heads, mouths gaping with fangs extended, striking from among the knots of bronze acanthus to shed venom like rain upon the stacks below. One serpent struck a handswidth from her hand, and on the lobby floor beneath she could see the serpents gliding in their tangled thousands.

The warmth which came from the card at her shoulder surrounded her, close as the blanket she had found, so that she looked out upon madness from the security of her own impenetrable shell, as marvelous as it was unexpected. In all that lofty, ramified building there was only this one flaw in the fabric of the place, this one error in calculation of resonances, this one gap in the fatal architecture of the building to allow a small sphere of warm protection where the voice did not reach. She saw the serpents strike and strike again while the woman walked with the head librarian through the doors of the Board Room, saw them coil again into those baroque tangles from which they had emerged, and knew that she had been reprieved, saved, by some intent she had known nothing of. Had that voice fallen on unprotected ears she would have been bitten, poisoned, dead.

When the members of the board had shut the great doors behind them, Marianne stayed where she was, not daring to move so much as an inch to the right or left, as sure of her safety in that one place as she had ever been sure of anything and as sure of her jeopardy if she moved as she was sure she had heard nemesis in the voice of Madame Delubovoska.

The meeting was not long, barely long enough to offer an excuse for the assembly to have met at all. When they had gone, truly gone, she came down from her perch at last, slowly, sniffing the air as for fire or some odorous beast. All was as usual to the eyes, to the nose, to the ears, but she knew that something had sought to smoke her out, and she knew that every previous threat had been multiplied a hundredfold; every previous shadow folded upon itself to a deeper opacity; every mystery stirred into menace and jelled. Only the remaining tingle of Mr Grassi's card against her skin, only the sound of whisperers at the windows demanding books, books she had promised, brought her to full determination again.

From that time on, whenever books were mentioned, Marianne would say, 'You said the New Storage Area, didn't you, Librarian?' Whenever she was within hearing range of any figure, she would say, 'Those books should be taken to the New Storage Area.' So it went, day by day by day. She had become so accustomed to failure that success almost eluded her. Almost she missed the assistant librarian's gesture toward the pile of books on her desk. Almost she missed the figure's quiet voice saying in the usual indirect manner, 'These books belong in the New Storage Area.'

Marianne gathered them up. There were six or seven, not a heavy load. She had kept the two books Mr Grassi had asked for on her desk for days, for it was her intention to take these as well. If they were useful inside the library, they would be doubly useful outside, or so she reasoned. She added them to the pile and started for the door, sure someone would stop her. The doorman ignored her. She leaned against the glassy slab, feeling it move reluctantly before her slight weight, stepped through onto the portico. She trembled as she went down the steps and around the corner to the garden, to the sign. The shrubbery was full of shadows and eyes. Those who had danced, cheered, whispered through high windows were there, just out of sight, watching her through the foliage with greedy intensity. She dropped all the books but her two and fled back to the sidewalk, hearing them scrambling behind her. One of them came after her, not threatening, merely following; she could hear the scrape of shoes.

Against her skin was the card Mr Grassi had given her. Behind her in the library was only an enormous quiet. Behind her on the sidewalk the muffled steps came on, hesitant but determined, giving notice they would go wherever she chose to go.

CHAPTER EIGHT

She had been so intent upon leaving the library that she had spent little time planning what to do once she had escaped. She would, of course, find her way to Number Eight Manticore Street. She assumed that she would be able to ask directions, that conditions outside the library would be somehow different from conditions inside it. However, there was no one to ask. The footsteps behind her, persistent though they were, did not indicate a visible person to whom a question could be directed. She found herself walking through a neighborhood of narrow-fronted houses which stared nearsightedly at her over high stoops and scraps of entryway relieved only by tattered yews and spectral cypresses. An iron-fenced square centered this area, a stretch of weedy grass around a dilapidated bandstand where shreds of paint flickered like pennants in the light wind. She went on walking. The houses gave way to massive, windowless warehouses, every wall plastered with colored posters, layer on layer, variously tattered, all showing human figures, the irregular tearing and layering offering odd, sometimes obscene juxtapositions of hands, breasts, groins, and mouths. Occasionally a figure was untorn, almost whole, and all of these seemed to be fleeing from her as though she saw them from the back, though faces were sometimes turned over shoulders in expressions of terror. Soon the warehouses gave way to smaller buildings, dirt-fronted and surrounded by bits of rusty machinery, and then came open country stretching in a featureless plain to a distant wall which ran endlessly upon the horizon.

In all this way there had been no person, no living thing, no sound except for the hesitant steps far behind her. Sighing, she turned to her left for a few blocks before returning on a course parallel to her original one. She began to see shops on the side streets, some of them overhanging the street in the archaic manner of fairy tale illustrations. The buildings here were plastered with the same type of paper posters she had seen on the warehouses. A little farther on the shops invaded the street she walked upon; a news kiosk, papers arrayed on the counter, caught her eye. The headline displayed on the paper said LIBRARY BOARD DISCUSSES THEFT, VANDALISM. The story beneath told of a minor clerical employee who had taken and wantonly destroyed some books. Desecration, said the paper. Citizens were alerted to apprehend, observe, notify.

Her panic could have been observable a block away, she knew. How had there been time to print anything about her escape? It had only just happened. They must have known her plans before she herself was aware of their fruition. Or — it was someone else, not herself that they sought. And how could they seek her? They had never seen her. The story named the person: Mildred Cobb.

Nonsense, thought Marianne. I am not Mildred Cobb. I am Marianne . . . Marianne . . . someone. Fear spoke within, self speaking to self. 'How do you know? Could you prove this? Would they believe you? You are carrying stolen books. You are wearing the library uniform.'

There was no one around her, no one to see her, and yet she felt eyes running upon her skin like insect feet. A bookstore stood behind the kiosk, its interior a well of dusky emptiness. When she entered it the bell gave a strangled jingle rapidly drowned in the oing, oing, oing of the spring on which it hung, a tinny whine. She crept to the rear of the store, pulled ancient books from shelves undisturbed for years, sneezing in the miasmic cloud which rose as she thrust the books and her collar into hiding. There. She could find them again, but no one else would. She started to leave, freezing in place as heavy footsteps crossed the floor above her and a deep voice called.

'Somebody? You want something?'

She gasped, managed to choke out, 'A map of the city? You have a city map?'

134

'Behind the counter. You want it, leave the money.' The footsteps crossed over her once more; the creak of springs capitalized the silence which followed, a statement of condition.

There was no Manticore Street on the map. When she returned to the street, she went on as she had been, noting the signpost at the corner so that she could find the place again, chanting it to herself as she went, 'Billings and Twelfth. Billings and Twelfth.' She had gone a dozen blocks more before she saw the first person. Then there were several, a woman with a dog, two men talking, then tens of them.

There was a grocery store, cartons of fruit and vegetables on the sidewalk, jicama and artichokes, thrilps and fresh fennel. Here a pharmacy, an alchemist's, a coffee shop with a sign in the window, 'Dishwasher wanted.' Here a church from which solemn music oozed like rendered fat. Here an augurer's post, a dealer in leather goods, a feticheur. She moved among these places as though dreaming, surrounded by life and smells and sound, acutely aware of weariness and hunger. When this busy center ended in vacant streets once more, she turned to walk through it again, stopping at the coffee shop. She had no money. She needed food.

'Dishwasher?' she asked the stout woman with her sleeves rolled to her shoulders. 'The job as dishwasher?'

'Last dishwasher I had the Inquisitors took two days ago. The one before that drank. You drink?'

Marianne shook her head, confused. 'Not − not what you mean, no. I'd drink something now, though. I haven't had anything all day.'

'Ah. On Manticore Street, are you? Well, I've been there more than once. You got a place to stay? No. Well, bunk on the cot in the storeroom until you find a place. Get yourself some food in the kitchen, then you can start in on those pans.'

The bowl of soup was half gone before the woman's words made sense to Marianne. 'Manticore Street, are you?' Well, then, it was a known place. She thought of it as she ate, as she scrubbed pots, smelling the fatty soap smell of the sink, the good meat smell of the kitchen. When darkness came, the woman, Helen, shut the door and got ready to leave. Marianne asked, 'Why do you say, "on Manticore Street"? Is it a real street?'

'When you haven't got any money, that's being on Manticore Street,' Helen said. 'Because that's where the poorhouse and the debtor's prison are, on Twelfth Street, where the Manticore is. You're a stranger here, aren't you? No, don't tell me anything. I don't want to know. Just remember, don't ask questions of strangers, and don't stay on the streets any time on shut-down day. Do that, and you might last. God knows there's enough time to last in.' She left the place with a bitter little laugh which sounded spare and edgy from so large a woman.

'On Twelfth Street, where the Manticore is,' said Marianne to herself. She would find it soon, perhaps tomorrow. Her hands were sore from the hot water, her feet and back ached from bending over the sink. Still, she felt closer to freedom than she had ever felt in the library. There was even a blanket on the cot to hug her with the same scratchy protection the blue one had provided.

It was several days before she could look for Manticore Street. She did not want to go out in the library uniform, and it took a little time to earn the coins necessary to buy a bright scarf from the pushcart man, an old, warm cape from the used clothes woman, a pair of stockings to replace the ragged ones she had worn in the library. She watched the women in the place as they walked past. They were dressed as though in motley, bits and pieces of this and that, some carelessly, others with a touch of defiant flair. Still, it was apparent that any old thing would do well enough.

She returned from her foray for stockings to find Helen reading the paper. Everyone in the city read the paper — copies of it littered the gutters and blew along the building fronts.

'Tomorrow's shut-down day,' said Helen, folding the paper into a club with which she beat the countertop in a steady thud, thud, thud. 'Shut-down day. I won't be in.'

'Shut-down day?'

'Don't be on the street after noon, girl. I mean it. There's plenty to eat back here in the kitchen, plenty of cleaning to do to keep you busy. Stay in. That's all. No — don't ask me. I told you. Don't ask questions.'

'You said not to ask strangers.'

'We're all strangers, girl. Just do what I tell you.'

That evening there was a tap on the window, and she looked out half fearfully to see a black, hunched form against the glass and knew it for that persistent follower who had come after her from the library. The watcher tapped on the window, refused to give up when she attempted to ignore him, but went on with the slow tap, tap, tap, not threatening, merely continuous until she could hear the sound no longer. Almost fearfully she went to the window to see a message thrust against the glass. 'Not all who are here are Manticore meat! Will you join us?' She did not know what this meant and did not want to encourage the watcher, but neither did it seem wise to anger him. She wrote upon a napkin the word 'perhaps' and held it to the pane. This seemed to satisfy him, for he scribbled, 'I'll come back another time,' showed it to her briefly, then disappeared into the wind-scattered shadows of the street. Though Marianne sat in the dark, watching the window for some time, he did not return.

Marianne told herself she would retrieve her books and look for Number Eight Manticore Street very early in the morning, only for an hour or two, returning to the shop well before noon. She left just at first light, wearing her cape, scarf tied over her head. The markets were closed. There were only a few people on the streets. Those who moved about did so furtively, scurrying short distances from this place to that like mice in a strange place. The odd looks directed at her made Marianne walk close to the buildings, staring behind her at odd moments, hurrying her steps. She went south on Billings, counting the blocks: First, Second, Third . . . By the time she had come to Seventh the walks were completely empty. Tattered posters glared at her from the walls, full of reaching arms and frightened eyes. A hand showed briefly at a window, flicking a curtain into place.

When she crossed Twelfth, she was almost running. The blinds were drawn in the bookstore, but the door was not locked. She eased it open, tiptoed to the back of the store to fumble out the books she had hidden there, then hurried back to the street, the door swinging closed behind her with its insistent oing, oing, oing. She turned back to Twelfth, turned right at the corner, searching for the numbers. Eleven. Thirteen. Odd numbers. The light around her was beginning to dim, to pulse, to waver before her eyes. She ran across the street. Number Six. Number Ten. No Number Eight. Panicky, she huddled in a doorway, seeing the street crawl before her as though seen through moving air or flawed glass. It couldn't be noon yet. Helen had said stay off the streets after noon.

No, she cried to herself. Helen had said stay *in*! Her feeling of panic was growing. Number Six. Number Ten. East. East! She scurried from the doorway, turned right, pattering down the sidewalk with the heavy books clutched to her chest, gasping as though she had run miles, across Billings Street where the numbers began again, only to stop, transfixed.

The corner shop was Number Four, a taxidermy shop, so labeled in golden script which slanted across the window in which the Manticore poised, rampant, claws extended and teeth bared in glass-eyed fury, huge and horrible. The beard of the Manticore seemed to rustle with evil life; the eyes seemed to see her. The eyes were dark and familiar, glaring at her, staring into her, transfixing her until she trembled against the glass, hypnotized as a bird is said to be by a snake, poised between surrender and fear.

Fear won, barely. She broke away from the window, ran past a vacant store to a narrow door numbered eight at the foot of equally narrow stairs. Behind her, as she fled up this flight, came a crash of breaking glass, a hideous scream of rage, a palpable wave of fury which thrust her before it up the last few steps and through the opened door where Mr Grassi caught her, pushed her aside and leaned his whole weight against the door. It gave slowly, slowly to close against the sounds below.

'My dear,' he said, panting, 'you cut it close, very close. Another moment would have been too late.'

She staggered after him as he went to the window where he pulled the curtains together to peek through them at the street below. It was hard to see the street. It boiled with shadows, ran with flickering. Thicknesses of air transgressed upon sight. Things shifted, were there, were not there. Clouds of tiny beings came and went, a slightly darker surge in the general flow. Striding through it all, pace on pace of its lion feet, tail arched high above its giant man-head, came the Manticore, scorpion tail lashing as the beast followed its own manic howl along the dream-wrapped street.

'There will be others,' whispered Cani Grassi. 'Troops of mandrakes, legions of Greasy Girls. The Manticore will lead them, and woe to those abroad upon the streets.'

'She said *noon*!' complained Marianne. 'Noon! It was hours yet to noon.'

'One of the conditions of this city is that time changes, speeds, slows, does what *they* want it to do. In this case, they speeded it. A trap for the unwary.'

'They? They who? Why do *they* care? Why do they care about me? Who am I that they should care?'

'Oh, Lords of Light,' he fretted. 'I hoped you knew. Truly? Oh, that makes it so much more difficult. I *know* you are someone very important, but I have forgotten just who. Just now it seems you are something less than that.' He took her chapped hands tenderly in his own. 'Cleaning lady, is it?'

'Dishwasher,' she replied absently. 'What am I doing here?'

'Ah. Why, you are suffering a malign enchantment. That much I am sure of. I thought you might have guessed.'

She collapsed into one of the chairs beside the window, staring out blindly at the raging street below. 'I hadn't guessed anything. Except that it was odd I couldn't remember anything before the library.'

'Many people here are like that,' he said. 'They have forgotten, or been forced to forget. Even I, even I have forgotten some things I am sure are very important. Some people can remember nothing. Particularly those in the library.'

'So many? And all enchanted?'

'An accumulation, I believe. Some have been here for a very long time. Not only those enchanted by *her*!'

'Why? Who is she?'

Cani Grassi shook his head, tilted it, thrust his tongue out at the corner of his mouth. 'I kept only a little information when I came after you, only the tiniest bit, to be sneaked through, so as not to attract attention, you understand. Too much would have alerted them, her. But a little bit, well, Macravail thought it would be safe enough. When he sent me, that is. To rescue you, whoever you are.'

She scarcely heard this, for her eyes had been caught by a fleeing figure in the street below. 'Helen,' she cried. 'It's Helen. I must go let her in . . .' And she ran toward the door, only to be caught in Grassi's arms and held fast, struggling.

'Not anyone real,' he shook her. 'Not real. Don't be so quick, Marianne. Look out the window. Look!'

The woman fled toward them; behind her the Manticore pursued with a roaring howl of madness, tail flicking steaming drops of venom onto the pavement where she ran, her hair streaming behind her and her face distorted in fear. As she ran past, she dwindled, became two-dimensional as though made of paper, a fluttering tissue which then appeared whole once more as it ran away from them down the endless street.

Then the papery figure turned its head, stared over its own shoulder, neck folding oddly, pleating upon itself. The figure swerved close to the wall across the street, opened its mouth to scream once more and collided with the wall to hang there, a pasted-up poster figure, mouth forever open, arms forever outstretched, dress forever twisted and hiked up by the act of running. Marianne heard her own voice crying and found herself held tight against Grassi's shoulder as he patted her back, murmuring, 'My dear, my dear. Shh. Shhh. They aren't real. Not in the way you suppose they are. Shh, now. Shh.'

'It was Helen. Truly Helen.'

140

'I know. I know,' he said. 'But you must not give way like this. You must watch and learn and understand. Otherwise, how are we to rescue you from anything? How are we to send word to Macravail? Come now.'

'How are *we* to rescue me? Gods, Mr Grassi, how would I know? And you don't seem to know any more than I! What is this hopeless place we have come to? Why are we here?'

'My dear pretty lady, do think, do. This is no minor enchantment, no trifling play of an apprentice witch. This is an ensorcelment majeur, a chief work! Oh, these false worlds cluster about limbo thick as grapes upon a vine, great pendulous masses of them upon the dry stick of the place we came from. Oh, I grow eloquent! Each world a grape, each grape with a juice and flavor of its own, individual, unique. Each world with its own laws, its own systems. Each a prison with its own gate. Each a door with its own lock. So, so, what do we do until we know where the gate is? Where the lock is? Ha? We sneak, we sly, we peer, we pry — think child, do! We appear as nothing negligible, not worth the notice of the powers of this place. So, who comes to help you? Ha? The tiniest spy, the weakest servant, the least noticeable familiar. Me. Cani Grassi.' He turned himself about for her inspection, making a pouting face and wiggling his hips. 'I brought no baggage, carried no sacks full of spells of protection, no witch bags, not an *amulet* even! No, no, in this place we are stronger the weaker they think we are.'

Mouth open, she stared at him, disbelieving these tumbled words, this babbling nonsense. 'Who sent you?' she asked, thinking it was a question she should have asked hours ago.

'Macravail,' he replied unhesitatingly. 'The arch mage, Macravail.'

'And who,' she asked, 'or what, is he?'

'A kinsman of yours, I think, pretty one. You do not remember him, but then, you do not remember much. One of the laws of this place.'

'Then how do you remember him?'

'Because I am not suffering a malign enchantment and you

141

are. So. Let us think together. You do not know who you are, and neither do I. If Macravail did not send that information with me, we must believe it is for your protection, or mine, or perhaps both. However, I do remember Macravail, and his words to me. "Greendog," he said, "send me word where I may find you." '

'Greendog? What kind of a name is that?'

'My name,' he said doubtfully, 'or perhaps what he called me at the time. Who knows?' More cheerfully, 'Perhaps he made a joke. Whatever. We must figure out a way to send him word.'

He fell silent for a long time, so long it became uncomfortable and Marianne fidgeted, saying, 'What else?'

He shook his head. 'I was thinking there is very little else.'

'Didn't this Macravail give you instructions?'

'To find you, Marianne. "Find Marianne," he said. The rest he left to my native cunning and natural self-effacement.'

She sighed. It was evident there was no quick, sweet-hot solution. There was only tedium and talk, fear and what courage one could bring to it. So. If that was the way it was, then that was the way it must be.

'Well, if you have nothing to tell me, I do have something to tell you,' she said and she told him about the peerers-in, the stolen books, the burned book, the visit to the library of the woman in black. 'I don't know what it all means,' she confessed, 'what it meant when I put the book out the coal chute. Do you have any idea?'

He nodded, nodded, chewing his pursed lips in concentration. 'Oh, yes, pretty lady. For everyone in this city there is a book. There is a book in that place for you, and for me, and for Helen, your boss, and for everyone. We are bound to our books. And when you put the book outside and it was burned, then someone escaped from this city. That is why they cheered. But there was only *one* book, only one. That is why they despaired. But listen, there is more.

'Here in the city, the Manticore. There in the library, books. And as the Manticore chases our images onto the walls of the city, I think the books grow dim and faded and

142

we grow dim and thin and shadowy as well, until they cannot be read any longer. What does one do with them then?'

'With the old, faded books? They are taken to the sub-basements and stacked there. Room after room of them. Huge, mountainous piles of them.'

He nodded somberly. 'And no chance then of escape. Only to fall into slow rot, to disappear into dust over an eternity of storage.' Sadly shaking his head, sighing. 'We will not consider that. No. Before that time is near, we will have found a way to send for Macravail, or he will have found a way to us. That is why we have our books, of course, yours and mine.'

'We have them?'

'Surely. You brought them. They are here. Was not your own story in the book?'

'But there were thousands of others, too, more stories than I could count . . .'

'Well. Yes. Most of our books have others' stories in them, though we are often unaware of that. It is no matter, pretty lady. You have your book and you must read in it again, to find what we must do next.'

'My story again?'

'Is it not your story we seek to unravel? Your story, of course.'

So she sat down away from the window in order not to be distracted by the recurrent return of the Manticore, by the continuing flight of the paper figures, the miragelike wavering of the street, to read her own story, beginning with '. . . She found herself walking through a neighborhood where narrow-fronted houses stared nearsightedly at her over high stoops and scraps of entryway relieved only by tattered yews . . .' and ending with 'Is it not your story we seek to unravel? Your story, of course.' It was all as familiar to her as ten minutes ago. Even the picture was of her in her bright scarf, cape around her shoulders, clutching the books to her chest as she fled past the corner taxidermy shop where the Manticore raged in the window. 'I shall read it again,' she said in a tired voice, 'and again, and again.'

143

She did not relish reading the story a dozen times, as she had had to do before, but she began without a murmur while Grassi brought her bread and cheese and tea. It did not take as long this time as she had expected.

'Here,' she said to him. 'I think this may be it: "That evening there was a tap on the window, and she looked out half fearfully to see a black, hunched form against the glass and knew it for that persistent follower who had come after her from the library. The watcher tapped on the window . . . Almost fearfully she went to the window to see a message thrust against the glass. *Not all who are here are Manticore meat! Will you join us?* She wrote upon a napkin the word *perhaps* and held it to the pane. This seemed to satisfy him, for he scribbled *I'll come back another time* . . ." '

'What do you think?' he asked. 'A kind of underground, perhaps?'

'Something like that.'

'Against what? Who?'

She shrugged. 'Against whoever runs things, manages the library, keeps the books. If someone escaped — that's the word you used — then it means people are being kept here, imprisoned here. And someone is opposed to it, some resistance movement.'

'How effective, I wonder?'

'Who knows? It is at least something. I'll put a note in the window of the restaurant when I get back. Helen won't mind as long as it isn't conspicuous.'

'And I,' he said, doing a little dance step on the carpet, twirling and bowing to himself, 'I must continue the minuet, the slow dance of finding out. Bow, advance, bow, retreat. Slow and easy, so they don't catch me.'

'Whoever they are.' She laughed, a weary laugh echoed from the street where the Manticore raged past as evening fell. 'Find out who that woman is who came to the library, Mr Grassi. If we find out who she is, it may tell me who I am.'

He shook his head at her, tongue protruding between his teeth. 'I won't spend time doing that, pretty lady. No. I will do what Macravail told me to do — send him a message. He will come like the wind, like a storm, if only we can figure out how to tell him where we are . . .'

'I hope you will be able to do that soon,' she comforted him, privately thinking that it sounded no less mad than anything else in the place. 'But just in case no one can save us from outside, we must try to figure out how to save ourselves.' When he reached to pat her shoulder, she patted his in return. 'It's all right. I'll be careful.'

They watched together until the Manticore returned to its window and people appeared on the streets once more, few and furtive, but moving about nonetheless. Then she left him to return to her work, wondering as the wind blew sharp bits of cinder into her eyes whether it was truly enchantment or dream or a horrible reality from which there would never be any escape.

Makr Avehl had been on the phone for half an hour, speaking first to someone calling via satellite, an enigmatic conversation which involved much note-taking and short, monosyllabic questions. The later calls were to the people he had sent to Boston, and when he had finished them all he merely sat where he was, staring at the carpet between his feet. After twenty minutes of this, Ellat cleared her throat to attract his attention. They had spent two days in this sitting about. He had not left Marianne's apartment even for a moment.

'What word?' she asked.

'Harvey Zahmani is not in Boston. No one knows where he is. He did not announce his departure, which he usually does if he is going on some expedition. Besides, he's supposed to be teaching, and he hasn't shown up since last week.'

'So you think—'

'I think he went after her, after Marianne. Or, probably, she drew him into the world to which she has gone. Actually, that's much more likely. He would be no more able than I to find her, so she must have drawn him in.'

'Why? Fearful of him as she was?'

'Because when we are in our own dream worlds, we people

145

them with others who are important to us, whether we love
or hate them. Her world would have Harvey in it, because
he tied himself to her in some way so that she could not or
would not simply dismiss him.'

'But you are not tied to her? Not with her?'

'Oh, Ellat. I know it. I wasn't important enough to her,
though I much longed to be.'

'She liked you.'

'She liked most people. She liked Mrs Winesap, downstairs, and Mr Larkin, and the people in the library. But
they weren't important to her. No. Likely they are not in her
world either. But I have to find a way to get there, wherever
she is.'

'If you go into her world, Makr Avehl, won't it have to
be in the form which she assigns you? As she sees you or
thinks of you? Are you prepared for that?'

The face he turned to her was blank with surprise. He
had obviously not thought of it, or had thought of it and
refused to consider it further. He started to shake his head
impatiently, but she stopped him with a gesture. 'No, Makr
Avehl. Think. I twitted you down at Wanderly, twitted you
with lecturing at the girl rather than talking with her. If
you had talked with her, you would not have risked her life
as it has been risked. I told her that such pontificating was
your way, and she said she didn't mind, that she found you
interesting. So she is good-natured. We both know that. But
you know nothing about her. Suppose — oh, take an impossible example — suppose she sees you as some monster? If
you follow her into her world, it will be as that monster.
I know that's not possible, but . . .' Her voice trailed away
at seeing the expression on his face.

Makr Avehl was remembering Marianne's hand recoiling
from his own, her face knitted up in that expression of
unwilling revulsion. Ellat, seeing him stricken, took his limp
hands in her own. 'Tell me. Did I hit upon an unwelcome
truth? Makr Avehl, tell me! You need my help.'

'You hit upon something, Sister. Something. I — I offered
to stay with her Sunday night. I was afraid of her being

146

alone. I meant nothing at all improper, nothing lubricious. I thought, after all, that she is an American girl, in her twenties, not some adolescent daughter of Third World aristocrats who has had virginity developed into an art form. I offered to stay with her, meaning nothing dishonorable, and she recoiled from me as though I had been a serpent. She said something — what was it? Something about not being like that, and then she muttered under her breath "begone, burned, buried" — an invocation or curse. I was so surprised I could say nothing. I apologized. I left her. Zurvan knows how she sees me. If you had not reminded me of that instance, I would have thought she regarded me well enough.'

'It might not have been you at all,' said Ellat comfortingly. 'It might have been a conditioned thing, her usual response to any thought of intimacy. In which case, since we have met her brother, perhaps we can guess? I can guess. You are perhaps too nice-minded.'

'Her half brother? Do you mean that she—'

'I mean that *he* probably tried something with her when she was quite young, and by "quite young" I mean emotionally, not necessarily in years. She is still "quite young" in many ways. It would explain much. It would explain her attitude toward your offer to stay with her. You do look like him.'

'What do you mean, "tried something"? Do you mean to tell me that he tried to force her? Or did force her?'

'Possibly. It would explain many things about her. And since he is the kind of man he is, he probably followed the failure or success of his attempt with an equally forceful attempt to make her feel responsible for it. She is carrying some burden regarding him, Makr Avehl, and I wish that Zurvan had prompted you to pay attention to her instead of to the impression you were making.'

'You're brutal, Ellat.'

'Only occasionally,' she said with a fond embrace of his shoulders. 'Only when I am distressed beyond measure. Now, what did the Kavi say?'

'I asked them to read the Cave for me, as you know. I asked for three readings. Cyram did one, Nalavi did one, and the third was by that young cousin of Cyram's, the one with the scary eyes . . .'

'Therat. She doesn't have scary eyes. She's a bit intense.'

'She has eyes like a hawk protecting its nest, ready to tear out your gizzard. Oh, God, Ellat, what difference what kind of eyes she has? They took the readings. I asked for guidance to Marianne. That's all. Aghrehond will be helping all he can, concentrating, fishing about and stirring up the waters. Well . . .'

'So. The message?'

'*Books* and what Cyram describes as "*a paper person*." Nalavi saw a *building*, and a *city*. The young one—'

'Therat.'

'Therat saw a *manticore*. Nothing else; just a manticore.'

'I didn't know there was a manticore in the Cave.'

'Neither did anyone else. It's there. Carved in the seventh or eighth century, Cyram thinks, near the floor, half hidden behind a stalagmite. The light fell on it clean and clear, Therat said, but he didn't believe her until he took a lantern in there and looked for it. It wasn't even in the lectionary.'

'Without the lectionary . . .'

'Anybody's guess. No history of lessons. No previous citations. No precedents. Cyram says that the girl—'

'Therat,' she said patiently.

'Therat. Cyram says that she feels it means just what it is. A manticore. Oh, one more thing. Cyram also saw an onion.' He laughed with amusement. 'Of course, I have a lectionary with me and I'll start by looking up the references that are in it.'

'Makr,' she said, eyes half shut as she stared at the street light glow through the hazy curtains. 'Makr. It makes me think of something. Paper people, and onions. A thing she said. What was it? Shhh, now, let me think.' And she leaned her head in her hands rocking to and fro while the wind moved the branches on the curtain, changing their shadow pattern with each flicker. 'Something she said about peeling away . . . being peeled away . . . about Harvey doing that to her − peeling her away . . .'

148

'Like a snake shedding its skin?' he whispered. 'Papery skin, peeling away? Like that?'

'Think,' she said in a vague voice. 'Of onions, one layer inside another, inside another, all the way to the heart of it and nothingness. She said Harvey made her feel that way. Flayed. Skinned. Perhaps an onion is not a bad symbol for that.'

'Books?' he asked. 'Books. A building. A city.'

'Books and a building. She worked in a library, Makr Avehl, you told me that yourself. *Think!* You don't know her well enough, that's all. You should have listened to her. You should have stopped talking and listened to her.'

He knelt on the floor before her and bowed his head into her lap. 'Beat me, Ellat. Beat me as you did when I was five and tried to drown the white cat. Beat me, but then forgive me and help me. I'm a beast, but forgive me.'

She shook her head. 'A library, Makr Avehl. People being peeled like onions. A manticore. A manticore is a monster. That's all. Look in the lectionary, if you like, but it will not tell you more than that. To learn more than that, you must look at this place and listen to it as you did not listen to her.'

He began to walk around the room, laying his hands on the walls, on the windowsills, on the satiny surfaces of the refinished furniture, on the shelves, the countertops, the carefully laid tile. He began to breathe in the scent of the place, to inhale it, the mixture of lemon oil and potpourri and the fragile smell of Marianne herself, faintly spicy, faintly musky. He began to see the colors, each on each and together, until he knew her thought and intention as she had put each thing in its place, each brushstroke on each surface. He felt the texture of the fabric on the chairs, the dry whiskery push of it into his palm, like a cat's face. He turned on the lamp, noticed the way the light lay on the wood, on the paint, on the fabric. 'She lay on the bed in there,' he whispered. 'She saw it just like this, this corner.' He went into the bedroom, lay down on the bed, turned until he saw it as he knew she had seen it, the blanket warm and soft beneath his cheek.

149

Under the lamplight the happy frog he had brought her glowed quietly.

What kind of world would one like this carry in her soul? What would its geography be, its climate and culture? He lay quietly, letting what he knew of her possess him until it became more real than himself. Where? Where? Where?

Ellat came to the door of the room. 'Makr Avehl. Remember, in her world you may not have a form or presence which will please you. Remember, it may not be of her own doing. It may be merely something old and wounding which will not let her see you as you are.'

'I know, Ellat,' he said. 'If anyone can be prepared, I am prepared. Wait here for me.'

'Oh, my dear,' she said. 'Of course I will wait for you.'

CHAPTER NINE

'Who am I when I don't know who I am?' She was leaning across a table, trying to post her inconspicuous notice in the corner of the coffee shop window, speaking partly to herself. Helen was behind the counter, wiping it with a moist cloth and humming around the toothpick between her teeth. She interrupted the hum to make a short, interrogative snort and put her hands on her hips. Marianne got the notice propped to her satisfaction. It said, 'I wish to meet with those who said they would return.'

Helen thought this over. 'Who are you? You're whoever you were, except you don't remember it.'

'Then I can't be who I was. Memories are part of who a person is, and I don't have any. Right now, I remember the library and getting out of it. That's almost all I am. There's no one here to tell me whether I was good, or bad, or really evil. I don't know whether I helped people or hurt them.'

'You're pretty young to have done very much of either.'

'I'm old enough to have started. I don't know whether people loved me or hated me. Or — not really. Except that someone hated me enough to get rid of me.'

Privately, Marianne felt that the answer to this question was not as important as some superficial and conventional attitudes made it seem. In this sunless place, with its walled horizon and enclosed universe, there was still regard among the inhabitants for a kind of wary politeness, a conventional courtesy. There was an accepted discrimination between good and evil, based largely upon the Manticore as a defining limit of the one and opposition to him as the expression of the other. In this place, Marianne was good because she opposed evil. What she might have been elsewhere, what sins she might have committed, could only be pale and irrelevant in this world, and it was only a traditional concern which made her voice the question — and of what tradition she would have been hard pressed to say.

'Someone else cares enough about you to try and come after you. You told me about the fellow, the one with the books.'

'And that tells me that I wasn't completely . . . you know, *neutral*. I didn't think I was neutral, anyhow. I don't look like a neutral person, do I, Helen?'

Helen shook her head, almost smiling. Since Marianne had told her about Cani Grassi and her narrow escape from the Manticore, Helen seemed a little more trusting, more personal, less shut up within herself. 'You don't look neutral, girl. You look exactly like some of the people in the place I come from. You could be a cousin to them.'

'Where was that?'

'I lived in Alphenlicht. Ever heard of it?'

Marianne felt a tingle, a tiny shock running from ear to ear across the top of her head, a kind of sparkling behind the eyes, which came for an instant and was gone.

'It's a tiny, old country,' Helen went on. 'Squeezed in at the corner of some bigger, more important countries, mountains all around. A little backward, I guess you'd say. We had a schoolteacher used to say that. ''A little backward in a nice way,'' she'd say. Lots of horses on the farms and little wagons in the streets. Only a few cars, and those only to take the high-ups away when they needed to fly somewhere or buy something we didn't have. A slow little country, slow and peaceful. Never was any war in Alphenlicht as long as anyone could remember. Some said we were too little. Others said it was because of the Cave of Light.'

'The Cave of Light?' A tingle, warming, warning.

'In the Holy Mountain, right in the middle of the country. See, there was this mountain, like a big sponge, all full of holes and tunnels, little ones and big ones, and all the holes lined with this shiny glass-rock, what do you call it? Eisen — what?'

'Isinglass? You mean mica?'

'That stuff. Yes. Well, all these holes go down into the mountain into a cave there. A big cave. Round like a melon. Flat floor. Pillars of stone and all these little holes reflecting light down into it. Well, back when the Kavi first came to Alphenlicht, they began to make carvings and drawings in the cave. After a few hundred years, the whole cave was covered with carvings, all over the inside.'

'What kind of carvings? People? Gods? What?'

'Everything. Trees, animals, flowers, people, books, words — everything you can imagine and a few you can't. So, people had noticed that the light comes down through the mountain, down all those funny shiny tubes and holes, and falls on some of the carvings. Not much to that, hmm? Well, somebody had noticed that the light never seemed to fall the same way twice. Say you go in there today at sunrise, and the light falls one place on the carving of a tree and another place on an old man eating a rabbit. Then somebody else comes in midmorning, and the light falls on a picture of a boat and the word *sthrandunas*. And at noon something else, and midafternoon something else, and tomorrow morning something else again.'

'But it would have to be the same sometimes. Say, every 14th of June at six a.m.'

'It isn't,' said Helen triumphantly. 'They kept records, and it isn't. Never the same way twice. They finally figured out

152

it was because of the way the trees grow on the mountain, or the deer graze, or the hunters move, or whatever. No two people ever see the light the same. No one person ever sees it the same twice. Just like fingerprints, all different . . .

'Well, then it didn't take long for people to decide it was like a kind of oracle. You have a problem, you go into the Cave and see where the light falls, and that makes a message for you. If you can't figure it out, then there are Kavi there who figure it out for you. They even have a book telling what all the signs and carvings mean.'

'Like an oracle,' mused Marianne, 'the oracle of Delphi,' not realizing she had no idea what 'Delphi' meant.

'Some call it that,' said Helen. 'Some call it the oracle cave. There are those who say that's why we never had a war, because the Cave showed us how to keep our borders closed. There must have been something to that, too, come to think of it.' She fell silent, thinking.

'Why was that, Helen?'

'Oh, it was something my husband, David, said once about people from the neighboring country trying to get in. He was a border guard, my David, when he was younger.'

'Tell me about him, about you. How did you get here?'

The large woman stared out the window, ticking the toothpick between her teeth, a little tapping, like woodbeetle or some kind of infinitesimal code transmission. For a time Marianne thought she would not answer, but at last she said, 'Well, why not?

'We lived near the Prime Minister's house, not his town house, you know, for when the Council met, but his country house, the Residence. David kept the grounds at the place, him and two or three young fellows and a couple of women in the kitchen garden. Didn't like the insides of places, David didn't. Liked the sun in his face and getting his hands dirty. Well, we got along well enough. Never had any children, which was sad for us, but otherwise it was a good life. Come one spring, David was doing some cutting along the drive, and around noon I took him his lunch. I remember walking down the road. There were birds singing, and the grass was smelling the way it does, fresh. The house was shining up on its hill, walls all silver rose in the sun. Well, I saw this big, black car come down the hill from the Residence, raising up dust, and I knew it was *her*.'

Silence stretched, Helen's eyes fixed on something distant in time and place, voice fallen into a murmur. Marianne waited for a time, then nudged into the quiet. 'Who was she, Helen?'

'Ah. Who? Oh, her. Well, she was some nobility or other. From Lubovosk. It was a country over the mountain used to be part of us but separated off a long time ago. That's the only time we ever talked war in Alphenlicht, when Lubovosk was mentioned. Our teacher called it a place of some unkindness, I remember. This woman was there, come to try and marry herself off to our Prime Minister. We called her the Black Countess because she always wore black, and she had this nephew came with her. We called him Prince Teeth because he was always behind her with his teeth showing like a dog about to bite, pretty much of an age with her, too . . .

'Well, this car comes down the hill and into the woods. I heard it coming, the roar of it along the road like some animal growling among the trees. Then it stopped. I came round a corner and saw David had a little tree down across the road where he'd cut it. He was bowing and tugging his hat brim and saying he'd have it out of the way in a moment, real polite. He was always polite, David . . .'

'Yes,' whispered Marianne. 'What happened?'

'Well, she came out from that car, Prince Teeth right behind her, eyes glittering like a wolf in torchlight, and she pointed a finger at David, one hand pointing and the other hand up in the air twisting and twisting like somebody opening a great spigot of something, and she cries, "Who delays me, I delay. Who holds me, I hold forever. Fool, begone!" Suddenly, David's gone, there's nothing there, and I scream, and she turns on me with that hand still out and the other twisting and twisting, and she smiles — oh, it was a cruel smile — and says, "And you to some other place, slut?" Well, I was quiet. I fell down with my face in the dirt and

I was quiet. I heard the car go on its way, out to the main road and away north. It was her saying "some other place" made me quiet. Wherever David went, that's where I would go to find him, not some other place.'

'Find him? Where? How?'

'Come nightfall, I went up to the house and asked to see the Prime Minister, Archmage Makr Avehl. All the people in the house were relatives of mine. They let me in to see him.'

'Macravail! I know that name. Cani Grassi told me that name!'

'Ah. Well, then, maybe you're another she's sent here. Like my David. Not a follower, like me.'

'I don't understand what you mean, follower?'

'I told the Archmage what had happened. Hard-faced he was, sitting there by the fire, and I knew that woman from Lubovosk had made him terribly angry. I told him what had happened, what David did and said, what she said, and the motions she made and the things she said, and he told me he couldn't get David out without risking the land and all its people, but he could send me in after him, into the false worlds. And if I found David, I could be strong with him until the time Makr Avehl could get us all out. So I followed David in here.'

'How long? How long has it been?'

'How can you measure how long? Long enough for me to take over this place, long enough to find David, long enough for the two of us to know there aren't any trees here, aren't any mountains, to know there's only this city and the Manticore. The damned Manticore.'

'So you did find him?'

'Oh, yes. I found him. For all the good that was.' She fell silent for a long time, chewing her lips, wiping the counter in an endless circle. 'He didn't know me, you see. Didn't remember me. Wasn't interested. That's one thing about this place, you know. There's no love here. No desire. Everything muted and put down of that kind. I've thought about it many a night, lying in my room, knowing he was just down the hall in another room, not caring. Not that I care either, much, but I can *remember* caring. He can't even remember that.'

Marianne was instantly uncomfortable with this line of thought. She did not want to think of caring, not in the way Helen meant it, though she knew well enough what Helen meant. Caring was like trees and mountains, something she knew of, had known of, which did not exist in this world even though she believed that somewhere such things existed. She changed the subject. 'What does David do?'

'He plots, girl. He plots and sneaks about. Ever since I told him about *her*, he follows *her* whenever she comes here. Oh, she comes here, in that same long, black car. I've seen her going into the library.'

'Madame Delubovoska? Her?'

Helen put a finger to her lips, shook her head in a tiny tremor, side to side, the gesture saying be still about it, silly girl, don't say names. 'When he isn't following her, he's plotting to kill the Manticore.'

'Helen, will you come with me when I go to see my friend next time? The one who lives on Manticore Street?'

Helen shuddered. 'I'd as soon not. Better stay as far from the Manticore as possible.'

'I was there. It didn't hurt me.'

'You stay here long enough, you'll see yourself out there being chased by the Manticore. Pictures of you. Flickery things that look just like you. Like your skin peeled off you, layer on layer, your skin and your soul. I've seen them, big paper cut-outs of me, running and screaming and running, and ending up stuck up on the walls of the city, everywhere. After a while, every place you look, there you are, stuck to the walls, bits and shreds of you peeled away to hold up the walls as though the walls are made of people. I can feel it at night, feel the skin coming off me in the dark, tiny bit by tiny bit, around me like a shroud, then floating off to hang in the shadows until the Manticore walks. And we see ourselves running and screaming, and that reminds us to be afraid again.'

Marianne did not reply, but she carried the thought with

her through the day. 'Is that all any of us are?' she wondered. 'Part of the fabric of whatever place we are in, whatever time we are in, a brick, a stone, a carved piece at the top of some pedestal? Is it we or the place which has urgency and importance? And if it is the place which has importance, why do we resist it so? Running and screaming and hating the bits of us which are blown about and lost upon the walls of the world? Are we dwindled thereby?' Helen did not look dwindled, but she had an air of having retreated to some last redoubt within herself from which she peered out upon the world, weary but indomitable.

At noon, which was simply midway through the lighted period in this sunless place, Marianne felt someone watching her, turned from her pan washing to find a dark, bulky man staring from a corner table through the kitchen hatch at her and knew at once that this was one of the peerers who had made her life so miserable when she had been in the library. She went back to her work with the uneasy feeling that his eyes remained fixed upon her.

Helen whispered, 'Marianne, that man watching you is my David. It must be because of that note in the window.' Then she went back to ladling stew and buttering bread, watching the man with such ill-concealed longing that Marianne felt guilt for having brought him there. He was a big man, with a strong face and gray-streaked moustache, and his face was full of angry purpose.

When he had finished his meal, he came by the hatch and dropped a folded piece of paper through it. Marianne put the paper to one side and kept on with the washing. She had wanted this contact, had planned for it, and yet was now uncertain that she could deal with this man's needs and purposes, possibly very different from her own. It was only after the customers had gone and the two of them had the place to themselves that she dried her hands and unfolded the paper, reading it before she handed it to Helen, who had not tried to disguise her interest.

If you want to join us, come to the church tonight, when the bells ring.

157

Marianne regarded this thoughtfully. The dolorous ringing of the bells did not normally begin until late, after most customers had left the restaurant, sometimes not until after Helen herself had gone, after the evening rain had fallen, at the time the Greasy Girls were parading and others avoided the walks.

'You don't mind?' she said. 'I really want to find out . . .'

Helen shrugged. 'I'll come with you. We'll both find out.'

They closed the restaurant and went down the busy street while there was still light in the sky, guiding themselves by the signal tower. There was in the center of the town a tower, tall only in relationship to the squatty buildings which surrounded it, for it had no graceful height to commend it as a building of interest or aesthetic value. It was simply slightly taller than other buildings, and if one scanned the circumference of the city, one might become aware that it was the highest point within that place, not by much, but by the smallest increment which would allow it to surmount all other roofs. The conical roof of this tower was tiled in red so that it appeared as an inflamed carbuncle upon the horizon of the city. The place was called by everyone throughout the city the signal tower. Who signaled from it, or when, or for what purpose was never mentioned. The church crouched near it, half in its shadow.

They hid themselves behind the thick pillars of the church porch to await the coming of darkness. While it was still dusk, the Greasy Girls began to come out of their houses, heads shaved clean, bodies almost naked, all skin surfaces anointed with some ointment which made them shine in the shadows like slime-wet frogs. A few started walking down the street, were joined by others, then still others, no sound accompanying them but the shuffle of their feet. When some fifty of them had assembled, they marched up the church steps and into the building. Helen and Marianne slipped around the corner of the porch to avoid them, and entered the church from an unlit side door. They were oppressed by an unfamiliar smell which aroused a kind of quasi-memory which both of them felt they should be able to identify. The music

158

oozing from the place was deadly solemn, almost lugubrious, and the congregation bathed in this watery sound with expressions of drowned lassitude. Other than the Greasy Girls there were only a dozen or so people scattered individually among the massive stone benches. David gestured to them from behind a pillar, and they came to sit in front of him while the sad music went on and on and the hierarch sat drowsing in his high chair on the podium. David leaned forward as though to say something just as the music trailed away into inconsequent stillness and the hierarch began to speak.

'Tomorrow we will walk with the Manticore once more. Rejoice to walk with the Manticore, for it is the Manticore who saves us from the horrible librarians. In that dread library our books are kept, and we know that others may read our lives, take us into their power . . . If it were not for the Manticore, we would have no future except to live upon those shelves forever. But the Manticore peels us away, layer by layer, places us upon the walls of the city where we may become part of the city itself, strong as its walls, eternal as its stones. As we are peeled away by the Manticore, our books dim and fade, and we pass out of the power of the librarians and into the light. Oh, rejoice to walk with the Manticore — rejoice and sing.'

The singing began again, awful music, deep as an ocean and as black, lightless as the terrible depths of the sea. A curtain at the back of the podium swayed briefly in some errant gust of air, and Marianne caught a glimpse of the singers behind it, women, naked and oiled, shaved and shining, singing in hard, hornlike voices with only their flabby dugs testifying to femaleness.

David whispered, 'Follow me when we go out,' which after a time they did, waiting until the procession of Greasy Girls had departed and then trailing him as he led them down dark side streets and into an area of high, blank-faced warehouses with railway sidings where little red lights gleamed like hungry eyes and a floodlamp blared threat against a wall alive with hunted figures, swarming with fearful faces and pleading hands. He took them into an alleyway, through a hidden door at the base of some black, featureless building. They heard voices before they came into the room, a room which reminded Marianne of the sub-basement rooms of the library, half full of discarded junk, the other half filled by the dozen people sitting around an old table. Marianne had only a moment to hear the voices before she was grabbed by harsh hands and thrust violently against a wall.

'I took them to church,' David said to the assembly. 'There's just the two of them. Nobody followed them. This one is Helen. She says she was married to me once. The other one is the one from the library.'

'Let go of me,' Marianne snarled, almost weeping. 'I am not from the library. My name is Marianne, and I'm not from the library.' Two of the conspirators had risen to take Helen's arms, keeping her from interfering. Helen wrestled with them angrily, but they held her fast.

'Is that so?' asked a white-haired man with a beard down to his belly, wild eyes under tufts of spiky brows staring at her. 'We know that no one comes *from* there. And yet there are always people there, and you are the only one who has ever escaped.'

'Don't be silly,' she hissed. 'People left there every night.' A hard, leaden anger was forming inside her, spinning like a flywheel.

'Really? Did you have the impression that others of the library staff left there at night?'

'They went home at night,' she said. 'Of course they did.'

'Ah. You say they went home at night. Those of us outside never saw anyone leave, did you know that?'

'But I was always alone at night. Absolutely alone!'

'And yet no one left. Believe me, that is true. Though, to lend credence to what you say, it is also true that you were the only one we could see at night, though we could see others from time to time in the day. Interesting. Did you know that since you have come, the Manticore walks more frequently than before?'

'I — I didn't know. I'm sure it has nothing to do with

160

me . . .' As she said this, she knew it was not true, and the heavy wheel within spun a little faster.

'That is unlikely. Before you came to the library, the Manticore walked one day in ten . . .

'One day in ten. We considered it a kind of measure of the malignity of the place, not decently hidden under a cloak of sickness or a robe of age, but ourselves, peeling away layer by layer, visible on every side, confronted at every turning, our own eyes peering at us from the walls, our own mouths pleading with us, our own arms flung out to evoke our pity. What was malign about the city, we thought, is that the Manticore walked one day in ten, a beastly decimator, herding before him our own mortality.

'Well, there are those − in this room − who will not bear it, who will trap the Manticore and kill him rather than be torn off in this fashion, sheet by sheet, as a calendar is torn. We had begun to make plans . . .

'But since you have come, the Manticore walks more often. He walks one day in seven, one day in five. Soon, perhaps, every day?'

'Are you asking me?' Her voice trembled with threat.

'No. I am telling you. Explaining why we sought you out. Since you came, the fury of the place is doubled, and we demand to know why.'

'We will know why,' shrilled a tall, cloud-haired woman who struck the table with her fist, raising a cloud of dust. 'We will know why. We saw you outside the Manticore's window. We saw you looking at it long, eye to eye. We believe you know the Manticore! We believe you know who, or what, he is, and how he may be conquered. We believe you are some kin of his!'

Within her the wheel sped once again, making a hum which filled her blood, set it singing. 'How would I know the Manticore's name? Why would it be kin of mine?'

They looked uncertainly at one another, confused by her tone. Though they held her against the wall, she blazed at them from among their constraining arms. They could only repeat themselves.

'We believe you know the Manticore, know what it is, who it is. How, or why, or when — those are not important questions. You looked at the Manticore as though you recognized him, as though you knew his name.'

'I do not know its name. I don't know anything about this place. I have no memory of what I was before. If you are doing something to get away, I will help you or go with you, but if you go on asking me questions like this, I can't help you.' She felt hot, angry tears, swallowed them, let herself snarl. 'Why am I here? Why are you here?'

The white-bearded one nodded, almost in satisfaction. 'You have seen the Greasy Girls. They walk where the Manticore walks. Bald, shaven, naked, lean as leather, oiled to a brighter gloss than finished marble, walking and chanting before the Manticore, worshiping the Manticore. The Manticore laughs at them, kills one occasionally, lets them march and posture as they will. We are their antithesis. We will not accept, will not resign ourselves, will not permit, will not believe. We will resist! We will find a way to get into the library and burn it. We will find a way to kill the Manticore. We will find a way out of here.

'And we will make you help us, one way or another. We don't believe you when you tell us you do not know the Manticore — though you may not realize that you lie to us. Still, this is enough for tonight. Tomorrow, the Manticore walks. Soon after that, we will meet again.' They let go of her and turned away, and Helen took her arm, perhaps in comfort, perhaps for comfort.

David took them out of the place, the silence behind them breaking into confused expostulation as they went through the door into the night. Helen angrily rubbed her arms where she had been held. 'Damn it, David,' she snarled. 'That was a rotten thing to do.'

He rubbed his wrist across his moustache, face as hard and determined as it had been since they had seen him at noon. 'If we were once married, woman, *if* we were, then you would forgive me, knowing that what I do is necessary. If we were not, then it is no concern of mine what you think of me. You may have resigned yourself to this place. I have not. What the Leader said is true. We will kill the Manticore or die, but we will not merely live here to see our souls pasted upon the walls of this place . . .'

He left them with that, with no farewell, without a wave of hand or a gesture, and Helen began to cry silently, tears running down her strong face without a sound. 'We're going to Mr Grassi's place,' Marianne said. 'He has a book I have to use.'

Helen, busy wiping her eyes, did not answer, but neither did she object. Though it took them some time to find where they were and determine in which direction Manticore Street would be found, Helen said nothing in all that time.

In the second floor apartment, Mr Grassi was unsurprised at their arrival. Marianne went directly to the shelf where her book, *To Hold Forever*, was found.

'Oh, my dear pretty lady,' said Grassi. 'Are you looking for more answers to other questions yet?'

'One question only,' she said briefly. 'Which we should have asked when I was here last, Mr Grassi. We should not have waited, should not have delayed. We should have asked the book then how to send the message you wondered about. How do we call for help, Mr Grassi? We must know, for this last day has convinced me we must have help or be here forever.'

She let Helen tell him what had occurred as she sat down with the heavy book in her lap. Marianne paid no attention. She had begun to read at the place in the story which began with Grassi's question, 'What do you think? A kind of underground, perhaps?' and went on through that day and the day following to the present time. She read broodingly, with deep attention, undistracted by the movements about her or the smell of the food they were preparing. Outside the windows darkness rested upon the city and only the sound of mysterious cars moving through distant streets came through the window. She read and read, finally placing her hand upon the page and reading aloud.

' ''They closed the restaurant and went down the busy

163

street while there was still light in the sky, guiding themselves by the signal tower. There was in the center of the town a tower . . . It was simply slightly taller than the things around it, and if one scanned the circumference of the city, one might become aware that it was the highest point within that place . . . The conical roof of this tower was tiled in red so that it appeared as an inflamed carbuncle upon the horizon of the city. The place was called by everyone throughout the city the signal tower. Who signaled from it, or when, or for what purpose was never mentioned.'''

She thumped the book with her hand. 'There is a signal tower, Mr Grassi. A place to signal from or why else is it called by that name? So, let us signal from it.'

'My dear ladies — now? In the dark? When dawn may come at any time and with it the Manticore? Oh, surely another time, a better time . . .'

The wheel within her hummed, a rising pitch of fury. 'Mr Grassi. You are fluttering, and it is unlike you. Think of your native cunning. Think of your natural guile. Think how clever we are, Mr Grassi, and let us go. Who knows what another day in this place may do to us? I will not wait to be used by those plotters; I will not wait to be eaten by Madame; I will not wait to be pursued by the Manticore. Stay or go with us, Mr Grassi, but we will go, won't we, Helen?'

The woman nodded over her pot of broth, trying to straighten the kitcheny clutter with one hand even as she reached for her coat with the other.

'Oh, leave it,' said Grassi, impatiently. 'Leave it. Who knows. We may never see it again.'

They went out into the silent streets, still wet from the dusk rain, lit by an occasional lamp into uncertain pools of visibility which they swam between in the wet light, working their way back toward the church from which their evening's peregrinations had begun.

'I hear feet behind us,' said Helen, almost whispering. 'Following us.'

'Probably David,' said Marianne in a definite tone. 'Or one of the others. Pay no attention, Helen. Of course they will follow us. Let them. Anyone who helps us helps them, though they may not know it.'

'I hear cars moving.'

'They always move at night,' said Marianne. 'When I was in the library, I used to listen to them at night, wondering where they came from, where they were going. I have never seen them in the daytime at all, but at night they come out after the rain, to make that wet, swishing sound throughout the night. Perhaps the rain brings them, like frogs. Perhaps they bring the rain and cannot move when the streets are dry. Pay no attention.'

'There are bells ringing.'

'They are ringing the bells in the church. Sometimes they do that at night. Whoever does it makes a very soft sound, though, not clamorous as in the day. Pay no attention, Helen. It will help guide us where we are going.'

And, indeed, the soft ringing of the bells did guide them through the wet streets while behind them in the city the sounds of cars and footsteps increased as though a skulking assembly gathered elsewhere and increased with each moment. They came at last to the church, passed before its bulbous pillars, and stood at the foot of the signal tower. In the church there was singing, sad as tears; the sound lapped them in anguished waves where they stood.

'I know,' said Helen. 'I will pay no attention to it.'

Marianne smiled. Had she seen it, Helen would have been surprised at the cold efficiency of that smile.

The stairs wound up the outside of the tower for at least half its height then entered through an arched opening into a lightless interior. From where they stood the heavy tower roof lowered down at them like brows over the shadowed eye holes of the high arcade. Marianne set her foot upon the step and the singing behind her grew in intensity even as the bells began ringing more loudly. Resolutely, she ignored this and went on, Helen and Mr Grassi behind her, the sound growing moment by moment into a cacophony, a tumult, the swishing of the cars and the tread of many feet underlaying other sounds with a constant susurrus as they climbed. Far away she thought she heard the crash of breaking glass and she turned to see the expression of surprise and fear on both faces behind her. 'We would probably not be able to hear the Manticore's window breaking from here,' she said. 'Pay no attention.'

They were not long in doubt, for the next sound they heard was the unmistakable roar of the Manticore, far off yet infinitely ominous. They hurried up the steps, curling around the squatty tower once, twice, three times widdershins. Before them the arched opening into darkness gaped like a mouth, and they stopped as if by common consent before entering it. Below them on the street, things gathered, vision swam, and a file of Greasy Girls began to assemble at the corner. There were bulky shadows at the base of the tower, and Marianne saw one or two of them start up the tower stair. 'David is there,' she told Helen. 'With others. It seems we are together in this, whether or no.'

They hesitated at the dark opening. There was no door, no sign that there had ever been a door, and yet the impression of a definite barrier within that opening was clear to each of them. 'Shall we risk what waits within?' asked Marianne. 'Or do you think we only imagine it?'

'Something there,' said Helen.

Grassi nodded, put out a hand to feel of the darkness as though he measured velvet for a robe. 'Yes,' he said, 'something there, and yet I do not think it menaces us.'

'Then we gain nothing by standing,' said Marianne, pushing her way through the opening and into the tower. There was no light inside, and they fumbled their way around the stone walls until they encountered the stairs once more and could fumble their way up that twisting, railless flight. Gradually their eyes became used to the darkness, became accustomed to the velvet shadow, and they saw draperies as of mist against the dark. Faces of smoke. Hands which reached foggy fingers toward them. Voices of vapor. Marianne stopped climbing, sat down with her back against the wall and her hands held before her to warn away whatever it was which shifted and swam at the edges of her sight.

166

'Ghosts . . .' whispered Helen.

'Peeled ones,' corrected Grassi in an awed tone. 'Those whom the Manticore has chased to the edges of oblivion.'

A sigh ran among the shifting shapes. Marianne could see them more clearly now, forms of virtual transparency through which one might see the ghostly hearts beating slowly, the pulsing blood coursing through pale veins, translucent orbs of eyes staring at them through the darkness. Even as she watched, one of the figures threw up its gray arms and opened its mouth in a long, silent scream which echoed down the tower in a single pulse of agony, then came apart into shreds before her eyes, fading into the gloom, into nothingness. Around this disappeared one was an agitation of ghosts, a turmoil of spirits and a soundless wailing which bit at them like the shriek of unoiled hinges on old vaults.

The anger within Marianne deepened, began to sing. 'There is nothing we can do for them,' she said to the others, beginning to climb once more. 'We save them if we save ourselves. Otherwise, there is nothing for them or for us. Come, quickly. The Manticore is hunting through the streets.'

Though the tower had not looked very tall from the street, from within it seemed to extend endlessly upward, and they turned around and around as they climbed, still widdershins, the world beginning to spin beneath them. At last they reached a flat platform and felt a ladder upon the wall. At the top of the ladder was a trapdoor, and it opened at their combined strength to let them out into the room at the top of the tower. The room was strewn with rubbish, with broken picture frames and trash and blown leaves from trees which had never existed in this place. In the center of the room was a fireplace without a chimney, simply a raised platform made up of large stones cemented together. Marianne did not wait. She began scavenging immediately among the broken frames, stripping a canvas away from its frame and piling the broken sticks upon the hearth. The picture had been of a naked girl carrying a light in a dark, frightening street.

'I pray,' she begged them, 'that one of you has a match. Without it, I fear we're done.'

'Always,' said Helen, rummaging in her pockets. 'One must never be without fire . . .'

Below them in the nearby street the roar of the Manticore became one with a roar from the crowd. Marianne heard a trumpet bray, somewhere, or a car horn, as she fidgeted while Helen searched. At last the woman found what she had looked for, half a dozen wooden matches, two of them broken. They crouched beside her, cutting off the wind, while she tried to light the broken frame with a kindling of dead leaves and scraps of paper. The first four matches went out, caught by vagrant wind, burned out without igniting anything but themselves. Marianne gulped, wiped her hands, let frustrated fury take her. 'Burn,' she commanded. 'You will burn to summon help, because I need help. Burn.' Still, there was only one match left when the leaves caught fire to send tentative tendrils of flame up between the bits of broken wood. Then the wood caught with a roar, the paint upon it bubbling and pouring out smoke. They found other trash in the place, heaped it upon the small fire until it became a beacon of leaping red and a column of black, roiling smoke rising upward forever from the tower.

'Now,' gasped Marianne, 'should we call a name? Invoke a spirit? Call upon God?'

'Call upon Macravail,' cried Grassi. 'For if he hears you, he will bring God with him.'

CHAPTER TEN

The dusk rain wakened Chimera, sogging the rough curls of his mane and running across Lion's closed eyes into the corners of the nostrils, making Lion sneeze. There was no sound to have awakened him, and he swiveled ears, trying to determine what quality of uneasiness it might have been which put an end to dream and brought him into this place.

He rather thought it had been the sound of someone calling his name, but he could detect no echo of that summons now. He turned his heavy head, following the absence of sound, ears continuing to prick and twitch. This motion wakened Goat who shared the ears with Lion, centered as they were in the great arc of Goat's horns. Through slitted eyes Goat stared calmly along the shaggy hair of the backbone to the end of his back where the flat, scaled head of Snake rested — still asleep, forked tongue flickering unconsciously — and Snake's body curved away into Chimera's tail. Lion began pawing wetness away, and Goat caught a glimpse of the dark wall which towered just behind them, arcing off into haze in either direction.

'Where are I,' he mused in his throaty baah. 'We? Where?'

'Outside something,' rumbled Lion, washing the last of the dusk rain from the deep wrinkles between his eyes. His head swiveled as he heard an ominous rattle from behind him, and he looked into the eyes of Snake, awake now, tail in sinuous motion with its tip a vibrating blur. 'We should be inside it rather than outside it. I don't like being outside.'

Goat turned to regard the wall, forcing Lion to look in the opposite direction. Two of the Chimera's faces were back to back, able to turn completely around, as an owl's head does, which allowed Lion to look forward while Goat looked back or vice versa on occasion. Lion contested the movement, turning the neck violently as he coughed with a guttural roar, and Goat stared down his own hairy backbone once more at Snake's head, now thoroughly awake, tongue flicking in and out as it tasted the air.

'Why are we here?' Goat asked, refusing to be annoyed by Lion's forceful behavior. 'Why?'

'Sssummoned, no doubt,' hissed Snake. 'Ssseeking sssome-one. It would be better to ssstop all thisss ssseeking, all thisss waking in ssstrange locationsss.' The rattle at the end of Snake's tail gave a dry, uneasy buzz, a humming paranoia of sound that made Goat blink and Lion extend his claws to scar the ground.

'Who is it we are seeking?' asked Goat, almost as though

he knew the answer already but was testing to see whether the other parts of himself were as aware as he.

'Marianne,' roared Lion lustfully. 'We are seeking Marianne.'

'Sssilly girlsss,' Snake hissed. 'Running away and asssking to be ressscued.'

'She didn't run away,' Goat reminded him. 'She was sent, Snake.' The Chimera got to its feet, heavy lion ones in front and hooved goat ones at the back while a scaled serpent tail lashed at the ground. Snake always felt best when he was lying against the ground and belly scales were where belly scales belonged, while Lion preferred to face forward — and move in that direction.

'I, on the other hand,' said Goat to himself in a philosophical manner, 'find as much to comment upon looking back as I ever might looking forward. It is, perhaps, better that Lion usually does the forward looking. Lion is not overburdened with scruple, with metaphysical consideration, with introspection. If it were up to Goat, Chimera might hover forever upon the brink of action without taking it. I, however, am much needed as a kind of balance, for if it were up to Lion or Snake alone, we would be embroiled in continual calamity.'

This was more or less true. Lion had few doubts about his actions. As he had said on more than one occasion, 'I may be wrong, but I am never in doubt.' Goat, on the other hand, was seldom wrong but often in doubt about virtually everything. Snake did not care. Wrong or right, venom, spite, and suspicion met either condition.

'Have you ever speculated,' began Goat, 'on what a strange mosaic we are? I am continually amazed by the difference, the distinctions, the—'

'Arragh,' roared Lion. 'I am outside, Goat. I want to be inside. This is no time for lectures.' He began to move them along the wall, pace on pace of lion feet, goat hooves trotting behind, snake tail lashing, rattling, a constant counterpoint to the heavy breath of the Chimera, the hot, fiery breath of the Chimera. 'Can I burn this wall?' Lion roared, eager to make the attempt.

Mild-voiced Goat, remonstrating, urging whenever possible a less violent course of action. 'That shouldn't be necessary. We see tracks. A vehicle has come this way, from out there in the haze toward this place.' Goat saw two earth colored lines imposed upon the spongy gray-green of the plain, coming out of a nothing haze into the reality of wherever they were, vaguely paralleling the wall, swerving to meet it far ahead.

'Tracksss mean people,' Snake whispered. 'It isss bessst to ssstay away from people.'

'Shhh,' said Goat kindly. 'We won't let them hurt you.' Goat was watchful of Snake's feelings. Snake's fangs rested very near Goat's backbone, and Snake was not always logical in his feelings of persecution.

'They could not hurt *me*,' roared Lion. 'I am too powerful for them. Besides, why would they? Who would wish to wound anything as handsome as I? As elegantly virile? As marvelously strong? As—'

'Yes, yes,' murmured Goat. 'Quite right, Lion, we are veering away from the tracks. Cleave a bit more closely to their direction and we may come sooner to some break in the wall. Ah. We thought so. Let us turn our head a bit more — yes. See there. A gate!'

'People,' warned Snake again, restlessly shifting his head from side to side upon its stubby neck. 'Bessst to avoid. Why ssshould anyone go inssside?'

'Marianne,' growled Lion. 'I want her.'

'Marianne,' murmured Goat, 'needs help.'

'Marianne,' hissed Snake, 'should look out for herssself asss ssshe isss perfectly capable of doing. It isss dangerousss to go sssaving people.'

The gate which they approached was hardly worthy of the name, being merely a shadowy interruption of the featureless plane of the wall, two penciled lines with a cross line above, and only the twin gullies of vehicle tracks leading to and under it signifying that something here might open. Lion scratched at it with his huge paws without effect.

'Let us try,' urged Goat. 'Horns are very good for this sort of thing.' He turned the reluctant neck until Goat faced forward, lowered the head, thrust the huge, curling horns against the shadowy doorway and began to push, goat hooves and lion feet thrusting deep into the soil of the place as Chimera leaned into the effort. Slowly, complainingly, the door opened. Chimera moved into the wall, through the tunnel under the wall, and out onto bare earth which extended from the wall itself to the outskirts of a dark, silent city. Far in the center of that city a squat, ugly tower poured smoke into the gray sky and blazed with beacon light. Lion could hear the sound of a crowd and the manic scream of a Manticore.

'Manticore,' hissed Snake. 'Vicsssious, poisssonousss.'

'No match for me,' bellowed Lion. 'I never saw a Manticore I couldn't tear up and eat for breakfast.'

'We have seen very few Manticores, actually,' said Goat. 'One or two. Both of them, as I recall, were immature at the time. Hardly a representative sample. Slowly, Lion, slowly.'

Lion, not listening, bounded away toward the outskirts of the city and down the nearest empty street, Snake flying hideously behind. Goat sighed and began to brake the hind feet of Chimera, slowing their progress. Lion panted and growled, but Goat brought him to a halt.

'Slowly, Lion. If you want Marianne, it would be better to find her while both she and we are in one piece — so to speak. Let us not confront Manticore head on. Let us first see what the situation is.'

'Ssspy it out,' whispered Snake. 'Sssneak about a little.'

'Dishonorable,' roared Lion. 'Right always conquers. Right makes might!'

'Right makesss dead Lionsss, sssometimesss,' hissed Snake. 'Lisssten to Goat.'

Snarling, but impotent to move Goat's hind feet any faster than Goat wished them to move, Lion abated his mad charge through the city streets and even allowed Goat to turn the neck about to allow Goat some say in which way they went. They continued moving toward the tower, but Goat chose dark ways which were free of traffic. He could hear the sounds of vehicles, always on other streets, and the roar of a mob,

172

and these were easy to avoid. It was less simple to avoid the vague, swimming light which pervaded some places, the feeling that millions of tiny beings hung about one making shadows and shifts in the fabric of the air. Still, Chimera made good progress toward the tower, and the flaming light from it came more clearly with each cross street they put behind them.

At last they seemed to be only one street away, and Goat urged Lion toward a fire escape which zigzagged up the side of a building near them. 'Let's have a look from up there,' he urged. 'We should be able to see the tower and the street below it.'

Lion shook his massive head, making the rough curls of mane flick into Goat's eyes, and opened his mouth as though to roar, but was stopped in an instant by a curious pain in his back parts. He turned his head to see Snake's head poised over a flank, one fang barely inserted into the hairy hide of Chimera.

'Lisssten to Goat, Lion. If it is going to die sssenssslesssly, might as well die here. Lisssten to Goat.'

Goat slitted his eyes, wondering once again at the strangeness of life and being. Seldom did he feel Snake was an ally, but in this case the serpent part was willing to help Goat in the interest of discretion. He turned head front and tip-tapped hind feet up the stairs behind the pad-pad of lion feet. The roof was flat, and they peered over a low parapet at the convocation below.

Greasy Girls were dancing in the street, before and around the Manticore who slashed at them, sending an occasional slick body flying to crash into a wall and slide to its base, resting there in limp, bloody clutter. On the outer stairs of the tower were many bulky forms, most with weapons of one kind or another, some with missiles which were being hurled at the Manticore to increase his fury. High in the square tower, a little above the place Chimera stood, firelight blazed from arcaded openings on all sides, lighting the street but leaving the outer stairs of the tower in virtual darkness. Chimera could see figures moving in this firelight, one man,

173

two women, bringing more fuel for the fire. Before Goat could intervene, Lion roared, one shattering roar which sent pieces of the parapet flying into the street and shuddered the building beneath them. While Goat was still trying to decide what to do about this, Lion had them halfway down the fire escape once more, and by the time Goat had formulated his expostulation, Lion had them in the street, confronting the Manticore, roaring once more to make the street echo and thunder with the noise.

'Beast,' challenged Lion. 'Horrid monster! Ugly creature! Hideous malefactor! Stand and fight, monster!'

'Monster,' screamed the Manticore, throwing back his dreadful head in a laugh which drowned the Lion's roar. 'Monster. Old Crazy-Quilt! Old Bits-and-Pieces! Old Snake's Tail, Cat's Face! Look at the monster crying monster. Aha, ha, haroo, ha ha! Pot calls kettle black. Snake calls lizard low. Frog calls newt slimy. Chimera calls Manticore monster! Aha, ha, haroo, ha ha!'

This pejorative barrage would have stopped Goat in his tracks while he thought it out. Lion was not slowed by it, hardly heard it. Snake was already so infuriated by the noise and the disturbance that his fangs were fully extended and dripping with poison. Thus Goat was bypassed, left to think the matter over while Chimera went to battle. The first Manticore knew of it was that he found a huge wound slashed into his side by fangs while claws raked at his flanks and a needle strike told him Snake had managed to get in one bite in passing. Manticore turned to look into the calm and considering eyes of Goat for one split moment before Chimera turned and he faced Lion once more. The look from Goat had been more wounding than the bites or slashes, for it had both recognized him and shown pity, an emotion with which Manticore was generally unfamiliar but knew to be lethal.

'Cat's Face, am I?' snarled Lion. 'Feel my cat's teeth, then, monster.' And he went by once more, slashing at the other side. This time Manticore was ready for him, and the great scorpion tail came down to strike Goat's back in front of Snake's head.

'I am immune,' remarked Goat to Manticore. 'Though venom may give me some painful moments, it should be obvious to any sensible observer that immunity to any lasting effects of poison would be necessary for such a creature as I. While I am able, most of the time, to keep Snake's feelings of persecution ameliorated, from time to time even my eloquence and powers of persuasion are insufficient, and Snake expresses his feelings of powerlessness against the world in a sly and poisonous attack . . .'

These words were lost in the general confusion, though Goat went on to explain at some length the evolutionary attributes most necessary to the survival of Chimerae. Meantime, Manticore's venom was making him unusually irritable, and at last he fell silent, focused upon the sensations emanating from within.

The Manticore had fallen back, his screams betraying more pain and confusion than challenge. While Chimera was immune to venom, Manticore was not, and Snake's bite was beginning to tell upon the monster, weakening it and making it feeble. Around it the Greasy Girls drew away, murmuring to themselves, and from the steps of the church the hierarch beckoned to them. Sorrowful music, which had stopped at the height of the battle, resumed once more with a funereal sound which seemed to affect the Manticore adversely for it screamed in agitation at the noise, an agonized bellowing.

High above, Marianne and Grassi watched from the tower as Helen continued fueling the signal fire. Though all three presumed that their help had already arrived, it had done so in such outlandish guise as to make them somewhat doubtful whether this was, in fact, all they were to expect. Thus by mutual and unspoken consent the fire had been kept burning in the hope that something else, something more acceptable and usual in appearance, might manifest itself. Now that the battle began to howl its way toward what appeared to be a final climax, they had begun to doubt that any further intervention would be afforded.

'Is that Macravail?' asked Marianne finally, having postponed asking the question out of deference to Grassi.

'I believe, pretty lady, that it is, though I cannot say with certainty and must admit to considerable surprise. It is not a creature I would have approached on the street with glad protestations of acquaintance. Still, there are familiar things about it.'

'Ah,' said Marianne encouragingly.

Grassi nodded thoughtfully. 'I recognize the pride in the roar. From time to time I seem to hear the goat part of it commenting in scholarly fashion on something or other, and that, too, I recognize. While I hesitate to say so, even the hiss of the serpent part is somewhat familiar to me, though I am proud to say it evokes no general feeling of remembrance.'

'If I may choose a part,' said Marianne, 'I will choose the goat part.'

'Forgive me for disagreeing, pretty lady,' Grassi interrupted her, 'but in the current situation, it seems to me that the lion part is doing very well for our cause.'

She assented to this, still regarding the great teeth of the lion with no less disfavor than she regarded the great teeth of the Manticore. Those teeth might be of differing shapes and arrangement, but both sets served the same purpose; both were hungry, powerful, forceful, and aggressive. She did not have time to comment on this, however, for a long black car had driven to the corner of the street where the battle raged, and she recognized all too well the figure which got out of it. 'Madame Delubovoska,' she sighed, a cold breath of danger going down her back which chilled even the heat of the fire.

'Who is this?' asked Helen. 'Is it the same? Oh, by Zurvan the Timeless, it is the same woman who sent my David to this place.' And she raised a heavy piece of broken furniture above her head and cast it with all her strength toward the woman in the street below. The missile fell short, but it sufficed to attract Madame's attention to those who peered down at her from above. Madame's arm came up, pointing, and they heard her scream orders to the Manticore, orders which made that beast turn laboriously and tear his way through the few remaining Greasy Girls toward the bottom of the stair where he was met with other missiles flung by those of David's party. The Manticore cowered, bleated in a strangely sheep-like way, but was driven forward by Madame's screams to attempt the stairway.

Chimera had been momentarily ignored in this rearrangement of the battle, an oversight which Lion — too late restrained by Goat — rectified by an ear-shattering roar and a plunge toward the Manticore's backside.

'You'll go blind if that stinger hits your eyes,' said Goat. 'Your face will swell up, and you'll look terrible. You might lose your marvelous appearance forever. Careful, Lion. Prudence. A little prudence.'

'He's attacking Marianne,' roared Lion. 'She's mine. He can't have her.'

'He isn't yet near Marianne,' said Goat. 'That woman, on the other hand, is up to something and is very near to us.' Madame was pointing at Chimera with one hand while the other hand twisted high in the air, as though she turned a great spigot on some unseen keg to release a force against them. Goat said again, so urgently that Lion turned to see the threat, 'She is very near to us . . .'

Lion, as usual, did not wait on his decision but attacked the woman at once, causing her to abort the twisting motion and flee toward her car in a curiously arachnoid scramble, all arms and legs in a scurry of furious activity. From the car she cried an imperious summons to the Manticore. That beast backed down the stair, crying its pain from several wounds and then away down the street after the retreating car.

Chimera heard Marianne crying a trumpet call from the tower. 'The library. She's going to the library. After her, everyone!' And in answer to that cry the Greasy Girls poured from the church, suddenly armed against what they had worshiped, the resistance fighters boiled away from the tower stairs, and Helen led the other two in a wild scramble down to the place where the Chimera, confused by this sudden turn of events, awaited them.

'Marianne,' growled Lion. 'I have saved you.'

'Marianne,' murmured Goat, 'it's good that you are not injured.'

'Marianne,' hissed Snake, 'ssshould be assshamed to have ssstarted this messss.'

'Macravail?' asked Grassi doubtfully. 'Makr Avehl?'

The Chimera sat down, Lion licking the blood from his feet, making a face of revulsion. Goat managed to turn the head slightly so that he faced Grassi. 'Aghrehond,' he said. 'The beacon was your work, I assume?'

'Actually, sir, it was Marianne's. She became very determined, all at once. Very wild, almost, taking no advice at all.'

'Actually, it was I,' agreed Marianne, coming forward to lay her hand upon Goat's muzzle, stroking. 'I had reached the end of my patience. Though I didn't expect . . . you.'

'What did you exssspect?' hissed Snake. 'A prinssse in ssshining armor? On a white horssse?'

Marianne drew back, away from the weaving head of Snake, in so doing confronting Lion's lustfully adoring eyes. Lion shook his head, fluffing his great mane and posing for her, semi-rampant.

'Pat him,' whispered Goat, 'or we'll never get away from here.'

'Away?' She was suddenly unsure, doubtful.

'My dear, surely you don't think the Manticore and the woman have gone forever? They have simply made a strategic retreat. It must be now, or never, don't you think? I am often accused of making unconscionable delays, but my sense of occasion is very strong and it tells me that now is the time of their defeat — or ours.'

Marianne, hands sunk deep in Lion's mane, nodded to this. 'Where, where is Helen?' she asked, turning to take inventory of the little group.

'She went after them,' said Grassi. 'Waving a bludgeon of some sort and crying for blood. If we are to be part of this denouement, we had best follow.'

'If you will ride, Marianne,' said Goat, 'we may get on a bit faster.' And he crouched the back legs a little to let her get on Chimera's back, holding herself well forward by gripping Goat's horns. They set off at Lion's usual heedless pace, Mr Grassi puffing along behind and Marianne holding on in deep dread of Snake's fangs, so close behind her. They fled down dark streets littered with bits of the posters which were shedding from the walls as leaves drop in the fall, a constant shower of fragments slipping from the walls to pile on the streets in a whispering mass. Here and there as they ran they saw lights coming on in upper windows. They came to a region of tall, narrow-fronted houses staring over their stoops, a littered park around a dilapidated band stand, shrubbery, a corner, and then the portico of the library itself, gray ghost light shining out at them from behind tall, glass doors. Around this place the resistance had gathered, figures capering around bonfires and voices screaming defiance and threat. Marianne thought she could see the Manticore inside the building, crouched on the great stairway, peering out at them, but she could not be sure. She dismounted, standing close to Chimera, one arm thrown around its neck, cheek close to Goat's lips.

'They are invulnerable in there,' said Goat. 'It is a redoubt, a fortress, bound about with enchantments and spells. From there they can strike at us when they will, and all we can do is bottle them up, perhaps, for a time. We cannot get at them to defeat them. It is not good enough merely to stay here forever, for then we might ask whether we hold them or they us.'

'If we were in Mr Grassi's apartment,' said Marianne, 'I would take my book and read in it, as he has taught me to do, finding in my own story the thing I must do next. Since the book is not here, then I must simply remember what is in it.'

'Can you do that?' asked Goat, curiously. 'We find ourself unable to remember accurately things that have happened in the past. We often mis-remember them in order to make them more logical or more appropriate to their time or circumstance, or they become mis-remembered through too frequent repetition or not being remembered enough. To remember one's own story accurately is a talent too few creatures are capable of . . .'

179

'I will do it,' said Marianne, 'because it is necessary.' She sat down on the ground, leaning on one of Lion's great front legs with his massive head sheltering her from above, and put her face into her hands. The capering figures had put her in mind of the time she had seen them last, when their black shadows cavorted around the fire outside the basement room. They had been burning the book she had put out the coal chute. The coal chute. There had been a way out — for something. There could be a way in — for someone. 'Mr Grassi, find Helen, will you? Tell her to find David and bring him here. I have thought of a way to get in.'

He came quickly, face smudged with torch soot, panting from the running, face no less hard-set against her than it had been when last she had seen him. 'What now?' he demanded. 'Have you decided to help us?'

'I was always willing to help you,' she replied, 'as you would have known if you had stopped accusing me and listened. Were you among those who asked that a book be put out the coal chute? When I was in the library?'

'He was, and I,' cried the cloud-haired woman who stood just behind him. 'We burned the book, and at least one of us got away.'

'If I could put the book out, why couldn't some of us get in?' asked Marianne. 'We could open the doors from inside.'

There was a chorus of approbation at this, interrupted by Goat and Grassi, both speaking at once. 'Dear pretty lady, think, do! Could you open them from inside before?' and 'If it were that simple, Marianne, I think they would have thought of it and set some guard against it.'

'No, no,' she exclaimed. 'Of course I couldn't open them before, because I was under a malign enchantment. You told me that, Mr Grassi. You also said that Macravail was the expert on malign enchantment, and is he not here, now? You said he was.' She stood up, away from Chimera and looked at him with measuring eyes. 'Are you, indeed, expert in malign enchantment? Can you undo whatever it is the Madame has done with that place?'

The question was meaningless to Lion. It meant much to

Goat, much of a disturbing nature, making him believe that in some other place or time Chimera might have been otherwise than now presented to this mob. Malign enchantment. Ah. Now there was a question meriting some lengthy study. Unfortunately, there would be no time for lengthy study, or even for brief study, for the mob gathered 'round had it in mind to force some issue, whether or no, and to make something happen, for good or for ill, they seemed to care not. Still, Goat's curious mind told them that they were in some danger from this suggestion, and that if the occasion were to be saved, Goat must do it.

'Marianne,' he said, turning the neck so that he faced her and the crowd, 'if we had much uninterrupted time, we might deal with Madame's enchantments. We have no time at all. Whatever we do must be done in the next moments, for she is a sly horror who will escape us if we give her time.'

'Araagh,' roared Marianne, sounding not unlike Lion in that moment, full of fury, the flywheel of anger within her spinning as though to fling its fragments upon all the world. 'Either there is too much time or not enough, either we may act or we may not, we may remember or we may not, and all at her behest. Then if there is no time to do anything sly and guileful, be done! Let us burn the building down, and her within it!'

Goat nodded. 'Much though it pains me to say so, in this case − and in this case only, not to establish a precedent for future action − I believe you are right.'

This was greeted with a louder roar of approval than before, augmented by Lion, who obviously considered the suggestion timely. He gave Goat no further time to talk, but leaped upon the portico and breathed flame upon the doors of the place. Inside, Manticore leaped back, bleating its odd, plaintive cry, so timid in comparison to the scream with which it had terrified the city. Still, it was a terror for no reason. Chimera's flames splashed against the great glass doors and did no more than darken them slightly.

'The building is brick,' said Marianne. 'It won't burn.'

'Oh, it will burn,' said David. 'We have only to find the

weak places. There are other doors, ones made of wood. There are window frames, also of wood. There are shingles, casements, porches, all of wood. Come, beast, let us find the way to kindle this fire . . .' And the mob swept away, leaving Grassi and Marianne to sit alone upon the curb.

'Well, lady, it seems we have made a great turmoil here. You are suddenly so forceful, you have taken this world in a storm. Tsk. I was not even needed.'

'Oh, you were,' she hugged him briefly. 'Certainly you were. It's just that I finally got tired of flopping about in this ridiculous world. I mean, why hadn't it occurred to us how silly it was to run from a stuffed Manticore? Had you thought of that? The thing is stuffed! It lives in a taxidermist's window!'

'Still, it rages lively enough,' he objected.

'Well, yes. But so do . . . puppets. So do . . . machines. So do many things which are not really alive.'

'Things which can kill one dead enough, pretty lady. Things which can do much evil, whether they are alive or no.'

'True. Still, being afraid of them rather than of the power which moves them is not sensible, is it, Mr Grassi? Or so I have told myself this night. Do you know what those resistance people told me? They told me that I knew the Manticore, knew its name. Was kin to it. That made me very angry, Mr Grassi. So angry I have forgotten to be afraid.' And she sat steamily listening to the crash and roar of the crowd, the upwelling shouts as they found something vulnerable to their liking in the library. Her attention was drawn to the building by a flickering light which came through the front doors, firelight, dancing light from deep within the building. The Chimera had succeeded in setting the place on fire.

'All the books,' she crowed, 'free. All the people let go. No more Manticore.'

She spoke too soon. There was a crash of glass, a crash exactly like that with which the Manticore announced his usual walk as the doors shattered in lethal shards and the great beast stood forth upon the porch, fur smoking, hair ablaze, driven into madness by pain and terror. Screaming its challenge the beast ran toward her, mouth gaping wide, slavering, teeth bared and claws extended as they tore into the ground. Chimera was behind the building. There was no place to hide. Sobbing, Grassi tried to get in front of Marianne only to have her thrust him away with the strength of ten women. She rose from the curb, rose, and went on rising, higher and higher, a giantess, looming in her height as tall as the tower they had left, growing greater with each moment, so blown up with rage that Grassi could not see her eyes where they looked down from the darkness of that looming height, though he heard her voice thundering at them like continents colliding.

'*Down, dog. Down, beast. Down, you fat cat, you murdering monster from a child's dream; I have had enough of you. I have had enough of that suffocating murderess, your aunt. You have killed what was dear to me. It was you killed Cloud-haired mama, Harvey, you. I will have vengeance on you. Run now, cur, before I squash you as I would squash a beetle on this street.*'

There was silence, utter silence, and Grassi hid his head between his hands, expecting that the sky would fall. Nothing. Nothing. He peeked between his fingers to see her standing upon the curb, staring at the space where the Manticore had been. There was no Manticore. Before them the library burned briskly, sending great clouds of foul-smelling smoke into the general murk. There was cheering from the crowd. Chimera came around the corner of the building, paused when he saw the broken doors, and leaped toward them, roaring a challenge for Manticore. When this was not answered, he bounded about, repeating it. When it was still not answered, he came to Marianne and lay down at her feet, beginning to purr with enormous satisfaction.

She put her arms around his neck and stared away into space thoughtfully, while Goat nuzzled at her neck. Above them the sky began to lighten. The noise of the crowd grew soft, then softer still. The outlines of the city wavered, began to pulse, then dim. Grassi blinked, blinked again, and found himself seated beside Makr Avehl on a grassy bank beneath a flowering tree. Water leaping downward told him they were in mountainous country. There was no sign of Marianne.

183

CHAPTER ELEVEN

That part of Makr Avehl Zahmani which was of a calm and considering nature was not surprised to find itself in the forests of Alphenlicht, within sight of the Holy Mountain which held the Cave of Light. That part of Aghrehond which was also of a calm and considering nature was not surprised to find Helen Navidi and her husband, David, on the slopes of the same mountain, evidently having lost their way during a mushroom hunting expedition. At least, so Helen said, shaking her head and giving every appearance of confusion. David was less sure and had the look about him of a man recovering from a serious illness. Since the couple had disappeared some four years before, Makr Avehl was of the opinion the illness was recent and largely illusory, but he said nothing of the kind to the couple. How they had moved from whatever place Madame had sent David to Marianne's own world was a mystery which he had no time to solve at the moment, though he resolved to do it at a later time.

That part of Makr Avehl Zahmani which was impetuous and fiery was in a frenzy to find itself thousands of miles from the place it assumed Marianne Zahmani to be. That part of Makr Avehl crossed miles of countryside in less time than good sense said it could be done to lead a panting Aghrehond into the Residence and to a telephone. Phone service into and out of Alphenlicht was always problematical. After too much time and some confusion, he was connected with Ellat, where he had known she would be, in Marianne's apartment in a city thousands of miles away.

'By Zurvan, Makr Avehl, where are you? The Residence? How? When? Why didn't you . . .'

To all of which he merely repeated what he had been saying since she answered the phone, 'Is Marianne there,

Ellat? Have you seen her?' receiving the same answer of incomprehension and at last, verbal confirmation.

'I haven't seen her. Makr Avehl, I haven't seen her. About an hour ago, a man came to the door who said he had just bought the house a week or so ago and was surprised to find anyone in it. The people downstairs, Mrs Winesap and her friend, have disappeared. It doesn't even look recently lived in down there. A piece of plaster fell off the wall in the front room a while ago. Something — Makr Avehl, something—'

He thought furiously, unable to think and yet forced to consider something, whatever thing it might be. Finally, full of passionate sorrow, he said, 'Ellat. Pick up the things I gave her — the pictures, the little carvings, that medicine bag on the window seat. The pot of crocuses, Ellat. If you see anything else there that looks as though she treasured it, bring it. Then get out of there. The car is still there. Drive to a hotel. When you get there, call me. Don't linger, Ellat. I have a feeling about this . . .'

He let her go, feeling that to hold her longer on the phone might be to hold her in some position of danger. He walked about the Residence, moving here and there like a frustrated animal in a cage, moving, moving, not knowing where he went or what he did. Eventually he was called to the phone once more to hear Ellat's voice.

'There was nothing there, Makr Avehl. Nothing of hers at all. When I left, the walls were turning dingy. The curtains were all tattered. There was nothing in her closet, nothing in the drawers of her dressing table. Nothing in the bathroom medicine cabinet. Only the things you gave her, and I brought them away. When I left, the place was all overgrown, as though no one had lived there for years, decades. It was frightening.'

'Ah,' he said. 'Then she chose another world, somewhere else . . .'

'A false world, Makr Avehl? One of the false worlds?'

'I don't know. When I have rested, perhaps I will ask the Cave. Perhaps it is not one of the false worlds at all. Perhaps some other . . . well. Aghrehond says that at the end she was very strong, Ellat, a giantess. Nothing could stand against her. She was powerful, shattering. Still, she hugged me . . . I . . .' He could say nothing more, and she asked him nothing more.

Later she called Aghrehond and learned that they had given Makr Avehl something to make him sleep, for he had been tearing at himself in his rage and frustration until they feared for him. 'When will you be home, Mistress?' he asked. 'We need you here.'

'As soon as a plane can bring me. I'll have to come in to Van, in Turkey. Lake Urmia is out of the question with Iran behaving as it is. I'll come to Van, Hondi. I will send word when I leave. Send a car to meet me.'

She came within the few days it took for Makr Avehl to resume the outward appearance of the calm, loquacious, humorous man he had been before, though there were shadows in his eyes and he occasionally hissed in a powerless fury which only Aghrehond understood. He was, if anything, more inclined to lecture on any subject whatsoever, and it was obvious to those who knew him well that he was a man hovering at the edge of breakdown. Ellat, seeing him, was not relieved of anxiety.

'He must go to the Cave, Hondi. He must find an answer. He is eating himself up not having an answer.'

'So I have urged him, Mistress. He will not go. He is afraid there is no answer, and he dares not let himself know that.'

'No. If there is no answer, he must know that. He cannot begin to heal until he knows.' And she set about the business of seeking the Cave on Makr Avehl's behalf.

He was not helpful — not resentful, not overly full of excuse or delay, simply not assisting in the process. He ate the ritual meal without comment and without enjoyment. He was dressed in the ritual robe at dawn, for Ellat had determined that a dawn reading would be most likely to produce results. He suffered himself to be driven to the foot of the mountain where the easy slope of the trail wound upward toward the entrance of the Cave, and to be urged from the car toward the ascent. Once on the path, however, it was only the pressure of Ellat's arm on the one side and Aghrehond's on the other which forced him upward. Birds were twittering their pre-dawn exercises as they crossed one of the small streams which striped the mountain with silver sound. Far away cows were lowing in a meadow, and Aghrehond smiled, glad of the sound in the stillness of morning. They turned to wind their way back, then turned again and again, coming at last to the carven door which stood guard at the east portal of the Cave. There Nalavi and Cyram and the girl waited, the girl Makr Avehl thought had scary eyes. Therat. They lighted their way into the Cave, down the sandy, narrow cavern which opened into the great, round hall, there to group themselves around the altar, utter the proper words, and put out their lamps.

Darkness surrounded them. Only their breathing could be heard in the quiet. Outside the sun would be rising, spreading its rays upon the world, letting them fall upon the mountain-top to be reflected from millions of dancing leaves, from the liquid eyes of deer, from the barrels of a hunter's gun, from pools of dew and a half hundred leaping streams, down a hundred thousand tortuous tunnels and holes into the body of the mountain, some to be lost forever in that great pile, other rays to be reflected once, and again, and again, until they fell into the cavern where they could be seen, upon carvings put there when Rome was an empire, when Picts roamed in forests not yet ruled by Saxons, when Charlemagne ruled . . . Ellat heard Makr Avehl sigh, sigh with a hopeless sound as he turned to see where the light fell.

'A child,' said Therat firmly. 'The light falls on a child.' Indeed, above their heads the light fell on a tiny carving of a child, a young girl, standing in a garden.

'A mother,' said Nalavi. 'The light falls on a mother.' This carving was larger, older, partly obliterated by the slow drip of water over the centuries, but unmistakably a mother nursing a child.

'A knife,' said Cyram. 'The light falls upon a knife.' And that symbol, too, was clearly etched in the gray stone beneath the golden ray of light which leaked down on it through all the massive weight of the mountain above.

They waited, waited, but these rays held firm and no others

broke the dark. At last Therat murmured the appropriate prayers, the lamps were lit, and they left the place.

At the portal, they stopped for a time to look upon Alphenlicht, bright in the dawn. It was the girl, Therat, who said, 'Archmage, may a Kavi offer you assistance?'

'One might, Therat, except that I have found the signs easy to read. She has gone back into childhood, and I cannot go to her there. She has gone into her own time. I cannot go. No Kavi has ever gone.'

'This is true, Archmage. And yet, if I were you, I would consider that time moves, and that her childhood was, but is not now.' And Therat favored him with a sharp, challenging glance from her eagle's eyes before bowing deeply before him, as did Nalavi and Cyram, though ordinarily they would have been full of banter and nonsense. They took themselves away, leaving Ellat and Aghrehond with him on that high place.

'Childhood was, but is not now,' mused Ellat. 'Now what did she mean by that, Makr Avehl?'

'It means, dear Mistress,' said Aghrehond, for Makr Avehl gave no evidence of having heard her, 'that if the pretty lady, Marianne, went back to being a girl-child, she has had to grow up again.'

'Exactly,' said Makr Avehl, slapping his hands against his shoulders as though to wake himself from some bad dream or malevolent spell. 'She has had to grow up again.'

CHAPTER TWELVE

They sat at a table on the terrace overlooking acres of lawn on which a large machine surmounted by a small man with a gay umbrella over his head made undulating stripes and a smell of cut hay. The small man had a brown, round belly, an ancient straw hat, and a pipe. Makr Avehl thought he looked supremely contented atop the clattering machine and wished that he himself could share that contentment. Though his outer self gave the appearance of calm, inside he was a tempest of hope and desire and longing and half a dozen other emotions he had not taken trouble to identify. It had taken several days of concentrated effort to find this place and another week to obtain an invitation. The woman across the table from him knew nothing of this. She sipped from her tall glass, following his gaze out across the lawns.

'You are admiring Mr Tanaka's stomach,' she said. 'I have thought of suggesting to him that he might wear a shirt while running the mower − it is his newest and most glorious toy − but he enjoys the sun so. When he gets bored with the thing, he'll let one of his grandchildren run it. None of Robert's or Richard's children will care whether they wear shirts, either, though their fathers are very dignified.' She laughed pleasantly, sipping from the tinkling glass once more. He examined her covertly, a slender, beautiful woman of almost fifty, hair escaping its loose bun to make a cloud around her face. 'Haurvatat Zahmani, my husband, will be here momentarily. He will be so glad to meet you. He was so excited and pleased when you called.'

Makr Avehl cocked his head curiously. 'Haurvatat? Surely that is a very old name among our people.'

'According to my husband it is. Haurvatat and Ameretat, among the Medes the twin gods of health and immortality. I don't know what possessed his parents to give him and his sister such names except that it reminded them of Alphenlicht. I simply call him Harve. It's much easier. Of course, he insisted on passing the names on to his own children. I call his son Harve, too, and my daughter is Marianne. It isn't that far from Ameretat but it falls easier on American ears.'

'Marianne,' said Makr Avehl. 'Yes. Oh, yes.'

'You say you met my daughter at the university?'

'No. I did not meet her. I did see her, and was fascinated by the family likeness. She so resembled our family that I made inquiries − which led me to you and your charming husband. He was very kind on the phone, very hospitable to invite me down for the weekend.' Actually, the process by which he had located them had been the reverse of this, from them to Marianne, but he had no intention of saying so.

'My husband speaks often of Alphenlicht, though he has not seen it since he was a child.'

'You, ma'am — you remember it?'

'Well, not really. My father came here to the embassy when I was only seven. He returned home several times, but I never went with him. Then, just at the time I would have gone, I met Haurvatat.' She laughed again. 'He was a young girl's dream, a bit older, and *so* good looking. I have never regretted marrying young.'

'He had been married before?' Makr Avehl kept his voice casual. 'You mentioned his son, but your daughter.'

She nodded, a bit sadly he thought, and shook her glass so that it rang like little bells. 'Yes. He had been married before. She died when young Harve was born, young Haurvatat. *Health*. That's what the word "haurvatat" means, you know. So sad.' She seemed about to go on, but at the moment they heard a voice inside the nearest room and a booming laugh. The laugh preceded the man, and Makr Avehl rose to shake the hand of the tall, splendid form with patriarchal beard and flowing locks. Makr Avehl thought of carved frescoes at Persepolis, magnificent and ancient forms going back through the centuries. Haurvatat Zahmani might well have been the sculptor's model for any of them.

'Well, here you are, my boy. And looking exactly as I had pictured you. We do run to family likeness, don't we, we Zahmanis. Did you notice, Arti? Of course you did. He looks just as young Harve would have . . . Well,' heartily changing the subject, 'we are delighted to have you as our guest this weekend. Are you here for some diplomatic reason? Or should I ask?'

Makr Avehl shook his head modestly. 'You may ask, of course. I am here for no sensitive reason. I am here to buy agricultural machinery.' Such was the reason he had invented out of whole cloth the week before when he had found that Marianne was studying livestock management at an agricultural college. 'I was interested in some demonstration projects at the university your daughter attends. Something to do with orchard production.' What Makr Avehl did not know about orchard production would have filled a library, but he smiled calmly, visualizing apples.

'Ah!' Marianne's mother smiled enlightenment. 'So that is where you met — not met? Merely saw? Ah, well, it is truly a family likeness. You saw her at the agricultural school. Such a profession for a woman! Her father was dead set against it . . .'

'Oh, now, now, Arti. Not dead set. Doubtful. Put it that way. Just a little doubtful.'

'Doubtful.' The woman made a sour mouth. 'Full of fury and swearing and carrying on. Saw no reason for a woman to go to university at all. Well. He married me just out of high school. Possibly he thought someone would come along and carry Marianne off to the altar in the same way.'

'Marianne disabused me of that notion.' The man plopped himself down comfortably, stroking his wife's hair as he went past her. 'Said she'd marry when she was ready and not before. I didn't believe it, thought it was all just youthful exuberance, thought she'd be tired of the work in a month. But she carried the day, convinced me. Very convincing young woman, my daughter. She did take a break in the middle of her education — traveled through your country, kinsman. Said she had always wanted to see it, know what it was like.' He smiled hugely, very proud for all his protestations. 'What do we call you, my boy, "Your Excellency"? Just occurred to me that "my boy" probably isn't *de rigeur*.'

'My name is Makr Avehl. *Macra vail*. It has a meaning as old and esoteric as your own, but I ignore that. If you say it properly, it sounds vaguely Scottish and acceptable.' He was hardly following the conversation. So Marianne had traveled in Alphenlicht. In what world, what time had that been? Her father, all unaware, boomed on.

'Ha. I like that. Scottish and acceptable, is it? Well, and what's unacceptable about Alphenlicht? Nothing I know of. Sorry I left the place, sometimes. Though, back then, the family thought there'd be conflict of some kind. You've done well, Prime Minister. Kept the villains at bay.'

'We've had help,' smiled Makr Avehl, not surprised that they both interpreted this to mean help from the US. Neither of them had known anything of the Cave of Light, or of the real power of the Magi. Well, he hadn't expected that they would.

Both of them looked up, across the meadows, and he followed their eyes across the granite balustrade where a horse emerged from the wood and galloped toward them over the pastures, the rider so well seated that she seemed almost to be part of the animal. Mrs Zahmani followed his glance, nodded.

'Marianne. I knew she'd be coming in soon. First thing when she gets here for the weekend is a ride, then next is a ride, then after that, a little ride . . .' She laughed. 'That love of horses. I outgrew it myself, when I was about sixteen. Not so Marianne. Her love of horses has continued — despite everything.' She shook her head, sad for some reason Makr Avehl was not privy to. 'Well, she'll be surprised when I introduce you and tell her how you found us.'

Makr Avehl was not sure of that. He was not sure of much at the moment, least of all what it was that Marianne would know, or be surprised at. He himself had not really been surprised to find her father and mother still alive, healthy, still living the life of grace and elegance which had been mourned by the Marianne he had known. He had started his search very near this place, for Ellat had remembered what Marianne had said about her childhood home though he, Makr Avehl, had not. Having found the parents, it had not been difficult to find the daughter. After his lengthy conversations with Ellat and Aghrehond, he had not been really surprised by anything.

A whisper of sound drew his attention to the doors behind him, thrust open from inside and held while a wheelchair was pushed from the house onto a ramp and then down to the shaded lawn, a white-clad attendant moving beside it. Makr Avehl frowned. The woman saw his expression.

'Marianne's half brother,' she whispered in explanation. 'It was a great tragedy. In fact, I sometimes cannot understand Marianne still being so fond of horses.'

'Paralyzed?' asked Makr Avehl. The shrouded figure made

no movement except that Makr Avehl saw the eyes shift toward him, as though the person there had recognized his voice. Stunned, he looked full into that immobile face. He knew that face, knew it as well as he knew his own. Harvey Zahmani, who had tried so hard to kill Marianne. Who had killed the couple standing beside him — in another world, in another time.

'Completely paralyzed,' the woman whispered. 'He had just returned from a visit to your part of the world — the trip was a graduation gift from his father. He had visited an aunt in your neighboring country, Lubovosk. His mother came from there. He had been home less than a day when he and Marianne went out riding . . .'

'Marianne told us it was a pack of wild dogs,' said Haurvatat Zahmani. 'No one had ever seen them before. No one ever saw them after. They came out of nowhere. The first we knew was when Marianne came riding in. Her horse was all lathered, but she was steady as a rock even though she was only twelve at the time. Told us what had happened, where to find him. Thrown. His head and back must have hit a stone. He never walked again. Never spoke again.' The man sighed deeply, reliving an old tragedy.

Makr Avehl did not answer. His eyes were utterly fixed upon the woman riding to the stairs he stood upon, fixed upon Marianne, his Marianne. His hungry, predatory soul reached for her in glad possession, his sagacious, ruminative self eager to learn of her, rejoice in her . . .

She looked up at him, smiling slightly, welcoming, as though she had expected him, something lightening in her eyes as if a shadow raised, a lusty gladness showing there which brought the blood to his cheeks.

Behind her on the lawn he could see what had been Harvey S. Zahmani in the wheelchair, motionless, powerless, unable to do any harm, to anyone . . . ever.

Deep inside, Snake whispered an unheeded warning.

MARIANNE,
THE
MADAME,
AND THE
MOMENTARY GODS

CHAPTER ONE

There were no words in her mind at all. None of the tools of thinking were there, not yet. Nonetheless, she saw faces peering down at her, saw smiles on lips, heard chortling words and knew them. They were people. The words of recognition came swimming through her mind like familiar fish. Mama. Papa. Great-aunt Dagma.

She was three days old.

The room was as familiar as the people. Light came from the right, moving in a recognized way as the wind stirred the curtains at the tall window. She already knew the tree outside that window, already knew the lawn beneath that tree. On her fourth birthday there would be a pony tethered there for her birthday gift.

She knew the house, every closet and attic of it. There were no rooms in it that she was not already aware of, knowing the boundaries and smell and feel of them, tight wall or loose, small window or large, the wonderful magic of familiar-familial spaces. There was porch space, half-open, half-shut in, where tree shadows made walls and the spaces between branches made windows for the wind to reveal and the sun to dart through. There was cavernous attic space, smelling of dust and dead moth bodies, stacked with sealed boxes as mysterious as old people, full of experiences she had not had yet, was not certain she wanted, yet anticipated with a kind of wondering inevitability. There were long, carpeted halls with windows at the ends and dark in the middle, the twining vines and exotic fruits on the rugs making a safe path down the center from light to light. There were bedrooms, each breathing of a special inhabitant with scent and aura peculiar to that one. There was a deep, stone-floored kitchen that begged for a witch's cauldron and a dragon on the hearth.

She already knew them all.

She was not aware that this knowledge was in any respect abnormal or unusual. This was the way of her world. The place was known. *Her* place was known.

Her people, too, were known. Cloud-haired mama with her soft skin and smiling mouth; bearded Papa with his hard laugh and huge, swallowing hugs; Great-aunt Dagma with her jet-black brows and lashes under hair as white as snow, with eyes that twinkled sometimes and bit sometimes like sharp little puppy teeth. Marianne could see into all of them as though they were glass.

Except for half-brother Harvey. He, too, stood at the crib-side, making admiring noises in his suddenly bass, suddenly treble thirteen-year-old voice, but when she looked at him she could not see beyond the surface of his eyes. He was like the pool in the garden when it got muddied after rain, cloudy, hiding everything. One knew there were fish in there, but one could not see them. One could only guess at their cold trajectories, their chilly purposes, and the guessing made one shiver with apprehension. So with Harvey. She did not know him, and awareness of this blighted an otherwise perfect understanding of everything around her. Not that she thought of it in this way. If she acknowledged it at all, it was simply to identify Harvey as different and scary. He, unlike anything else in her environment, was capable of being and doing the utterly unexpected.

When she was three, they took her to the city.

The motion of the car put her to sleep, and when she awoke, she saw through the window of the car an endless procession of stranger houses. Each house was tight against the next, all of them staring out at the street in a glare of hard, blue light, watching her. She began to scream.

Mama picked her up and cuddled her, asking her what it was that hurt and whether it was teeth or tummy. It was neither. It was the sight of that endless row of stranger houses that had frightened her half out of her infant wits. They were the first closed places she had ever seen, the first unfamiliar sights or sounds in her life, and they came as a hideous surprise.

If Papa had not had to take a detour, they would have gone through a park. Somehow, she remembered a park. The picture of the park superimposed itself on the row of houses and she fell asleep again. There should have been a park.

Thereafter, from time to time, she experienced similar superimpositions, as though her life were a palimpsest on which one experience was written over another in confusing detail so it was difficult to know which was real and which was something else. Not less real, she thought as she began to be old enough to think about things. Simply less relevant to the other things that were going on.

Her second encounter with a closed, unfamiliar place came a year or so later, when she was old enough to go for long walks. Her hand held tightly in Nanny's hand, she strolled down the driveway and out onto the country road. She remembered turning left, but they actually turned right to walk down the road toward the river, passing on the way a tall, gray stone house set well back from the road with windows that stared at her from half-lowered lids. Its door pursed its sill and scowled. As in that time she had visited the city, she wept. She couldn't tell Nanny what was wrong, she hadn't the words for it, and everyone assumed some childhood indisposition when it wasn't that at all. It was simply that she did not know the gray house.

Every morning she could remember, Marianne had awakened knowing the people and places and events that day would bring. Each event was ready for her in her recollection, even before she experienced it, as well as the consequences of that event, sometimes far in the future. If she helped the gardener plant bulbs, the ultimate flowers were already there in her mind, though she would not actually see the blooms until spring. As she was lifted onto her pony for the first time, she already remembered learning to ride it. The horse she would love so much would come later, and the memory of that future horse was evoked by the present pony even as she struggled to master the muscles needed to stay on. Her body experienced it for the first time, but her mind — it already *knew*. It needed only a clue to come to mind. Bulb evoked flower.

Pony evoked horse. All her teachers were amazed. 'She seems to soak it up like a little sponge,' her riding teacher said, laughing a little uncomfortably. It seemed unfair to the other children that this one should take it all in so easily.

She assumed, for a time, at least, that everyone lived as she did, knowing what would come before it happened, knowing the places they lived in as soon as they were born. She assumed everyone had occasional visions of some alternate reality, sometimes dull, sometimes bright, sometimes frightening and bizarre. She did not know that she was unique, that no one else in the world lived as she did. She was unwilling to accept that there might be people and places that remained strangers. Instead she chose to believe that the knowledge would come later. She would get to know them someday. Someday there would be no more unfamiliar streets, no more closed doors, no more shut windows. Someday, when she was grown-up, everything would be understood. The gray house, with all its spaces, its roofs and porches, its closets and attics would come to her, part of growing up. She would be able to greet it as she walked on the street. 'Hello old green-shingly-with-the-cupola. Still have that mouse family in the attic?' Someday, she told herself comfortingly, intercepting a hard, opaque stare from her half brother, she might know Harvey, too. It would come. She would use the huge, old gray stone house as a yardstick to determine whether the time had come or not.

The season came when she started to school, and for the first time she began to suspect she might be different from other children. Why should she enter the school on the first day knowing everything about it, while other children cowered and cried as though it were new and strange? Other children did not know where their classrooms were. Why did she? They did not know where the bathrooms were or where the drinking fountain had made a weirdly shaped yellow stain on the wall, like an upside-down giraffe. To Marianne it was all as familiar as though studied in advance. Why should she know her teacher's name before they met when other children didn't know? She had to accept the fact that they did not know, and in doing so she learned of her own strangeness. She did not want it to show, so she learned to counterfeit surprise and mimic apprehension. Still, she could never do so without feeling that somehow she was lying.

She walked to school each day, often going out of her way to pass the great gray house. Each day she peeked at it, quick, birdlike glances, waiting for the day when it would open like a flower with all its high stairs and dormer windows, waiting for the first glimmer of recognition. That year, the year she was six, went by and the house did not open. Nor when she was seven, or eight.

Still, she believed it would happen. She believed it for a long time, until one day she talked to Great-aunt Dagma, who was very old and thus of an age to have opened all the places of the world, and found that Great-aunt Dagma didn't know the gray house at all.

'Why, child, I haven't any idea,' she said. 'I've never been in it. It's occupied by some people called Carlson, I believe, but as to whether it has an attic or not? I just don't know.'

So the house really was a stranger house. So were the houses in the city. Strangers. Not understood. Marianne sat there, in a state of profound shock, unable to speak for a long time. Great-aunt Dagma was a sympathetic listener who did not make fun, however, and at last Marianne was able to confess that the house was very strange to her. 'Not like home, Great-aunt,' she confided. 'It seems like − oh, like somebody who doesn't talk our language at all. Some people are like that, too. Harvey's like that.'

Great-aunt, with a strangely intent look, agreed that this described Harvey very well. 'He does always seem to be saying one thing with his mouth and something else with his eyes, doesn't he, Marianne. Ah, but then, he's always been a tight, closed boy, like a treasure box with the key hidden away somewhere. His mother was like that, herself, and his aunt is a perfect example. Lubovoskans, you know. It's a strange, shaman-ridden, paranoid country, Lubovosk − unlike sunny Alphenlicht from which our family comes − so it's no wonder the people show that characteristic. Harvey is a hard boy to get to know. Don't let it worry you, child. It isn't your fault.'

Marianne had not thought it was her fault. Still, the implication was inescapable, and she was neither so stubborn nor so unintelligent as to miss it. Merely growing up would not open the gray house or her half brother to her after all. And if Harvey and the gray house would not open, then neither would all the other closed places or people — the people like Mrs Sindles at the school, who was always so pursed-lipped and unhappy about no-one-knew-what, who were capable of doing frightening and unexpected things. They would always be that way. Nothing she could do would change it. She wept over it for a few nights, then accepted it, using one of Cloud-haired mama's favorite phrases, 'All part of growing up.' Disillusionment, pain, unpleasant surprise, all were part of growing up.

She became accustomed to her life: accustomed to knowing ninety-five percent of everything before it occurred; accustomed to the shock of the other five percent, the wild happenings, the accidents, unpredictable and truly frightening; the double visions that were like waking dreams; the occasional places that greeted her as though they were old friends, though Marianne could not recollect how or when they might have met.

There was a stone church at the corner of Beale Street, for example, set back a little behind a clump of trees, that spoke to her every time she saw it. 'Remember,' it said. 'Remember?' Its tower had an admonitory look, like a raised finger. 'Remember, Marianne. Pay attention, now.' A massive rock shelter at the entrance to the Bitter River Road spoke in somewhat the same fashion. 'Here,' it said. 'He has been here for some time. He will be here when needed.'

What was she to make of this? It was a mystery.

There was a small frame house where an old, old Chinese woman often lay half-asleep on the porch. When Marianne passed by, the woman spoke without opening her lips, 'One of them is inside. One you'll need, Marianne. Just keep it in mind.' Perhaps it was not the woman who spoke at all. Perhaps it was the house that spoke.

There was a certain maple tree, bigger around than her arms would reach, which, when it was half turned yellow in the fall, whispered, 'Just now, on the grass. Just this minute he's come. He's usually here. Don't forget.' And a wall of Virginia creeper, bloody scarlet upon the brick, breathed, 'One of them lies here every day, waiting for word from you.'

Messages. From inside. Inside the church, the house, the shelter, the tree, the wall. Messages that were always delivered in the same voice. She believed the voice without understanding it at all. She did not recognize the voice although it was her own, its sound subtly changed in a way she could not have expected. It would be some time before she realized it was her own voice as an adult, as she would someday be.

Now she could only reply to the church, 'No, I don't remember. I'm sorry, but I don't.'

She tried to put the messages and the voice out of her mind. It was too troubling to deal with. For a year or two, she succeeded.

Until she was ten years old and had a dream.

It was very early one fall morning. She lay in her room, her arms beneath the covers, the window blowing a gauzy curtain half across her face. She was aware of this and aware at the same time that she was dreaming. In the dream, also, there was a window, but she was older, much older. An old woman, twenty or more. She sat at a desk by the window, oak twigs tapping at the panes, looking out at a green, park-like place across the street. Something horrible crouched at her feet. When she looked, it was only a box, but there was something dreadful in it. Tears dripped from her eyes onto her hands, and in the dream she knew that she grieved. She was crying because Cloud-haired mama and Papa were dead.

She was crying because Harvey had had something to do with their deaths!

Ten-year-old Marianne sat straight up in bed, the dream as

203

real as something she might have seen on television, a scream trembling unvoiced somewhere deep in an aching hollow inside her. They were dead. Gone. Killed. And Marianne herself was in terrible danger.

The dreamlike quality of her terror was something she recognized within a moment. Her heart was not pounding. Her mind screamed, but her body lay upon the bed quietly, without panic. It was visionary terror, not real — or if real, not real in the way that other, more immediate things were real. Though it might hold the essence of reality, it did not exist in the here and now. It was another of those double visions, experienced this time as a dream and coming as an unmistakable warning. The message was clear and unequivocal. 'If things go on as they are going,' she heard that inner voice saying, 'this dreadful thing will happen.'

For the first time, she recognized the voice as her own.

'Who are you?' she asked, less frightened than angry that some part of her should have separated itself in this way and be playing such tricks on her.

'You know,' the voice answered. 'You. I am you.'

'How do you know such things?' Marianne demanded aloud before she realized she did not need to vocalize for that other self to hear.

'I lived them,' the voice said.

'Are you from the future?' she asked, silently.

'Perhaps,' the voice said, very sadly. 'In a manner of speaking. Your future is my past. I left you word, Marianne. Messages. I left you helpers. So it won't happen! You must not let it happen!'

So that was the reason for the messages. When the old stone church begged her to 'remember,' the word was not from this time, not from this life but from some other time, some other life in which the church had also existed. Another *Marianne* had known the church then, there. She had been inside the church, intimate with it, able to do something there, leave some symbolic taint of herself, some word, some information. Marianne the child struggled with the concept. It was as though someone had put a message in a bottle or

204

a hollow tree, except that the message was just for her. Someone, herself, had left her a message about a terrible thing.

'Something terrible happened in that other world,' she told herself. 'To me. To that *Marianne*. And in this world, it must not happen. That is what the messages are all about.' She was as certain of this as she was of her name. Marianne. Marianne Zahmani. *This* Marianne. Herself.

As she lay there in bed that early morning, she worked it out, slowly. The person who had left these messages was another, a grown-up *Marianne*. She began to sense, however vaguely at first, that the life of the grown-up *Marianne* had always been there, hanging at the edges of each day's experiences, awaiting its own reaffirmation. The discovery came with a sense of shock and ultimate recognition, like seeing her face in a mirror and realizing for the first time that it was her own unique and mortal image, not an immortal shadow awaiting her in some other world. Most of her present life had simply affirmed and repeated another life! A life previously lived. By someone else! By that grown-up person that was in some strange way herself! That is why everything had been so familiar!

She had figured it out by the time people had begun to stir. She dressed for breakfast as she did every morning, not suspecting what would come next. She had not foreseen the implications of the change. Because this thing had happened that had never happened before, this morning, for the first time in her life, she went down the stairs to confront a day in which there were many events she would not foresee.

Harvey said something angry at breakfast, something she did not understand and had not anticipated. There was a guest for lunch, someone she did not recognize. By early afternoon, she was in a panic, unable to deal with this sudden, horribly surprising world. She retreated to her room, trying desperately to appear poised, failing miserably.

She felt lost, betrayed, and angry, too, at that other *Marianne* for having done this to her. Other children met the strangeness of the world as babies; by the time they were ten, they had some notion of how it was done. Now she must learn it all at once, late, without letting anyone know how hideously unprepared she was.

She learned.

Most days there were only one or two things she was not ready for. Some days were totally anticipated, just as they had always been. As she learned to poise herself upon the moment, taking her clues from others, reacting as they did, her fear and panic dwindled, but the anger remained. It was not fair to have done this to her. Not fair. Not right! Even though there was reason for the messages she had received, still, whoever-it-was shouldn't have done this to her! Shouldn't have done it even though Marianne believed that what it had told her was true.

Gradually, she came to act on that belief.

Harvey asked her to go riding with him. She remembered having done so on a bright spring morning just like this one. Now, on the morning of that day − on this morning − she decided it was better not to go.

'What's the matter, Marianne?' asked Mama. 'Don't you want to go riding with your big brother?'

'No thank you, Mama. Not right now.' Knowing why, precisely. That other time, in that other life, she had gone riding with Harvey and he had asked her certain questions about Mama that Marianne, all unwitting, had answered. It would be better not to talk about those things. Better not give him the opportunity to ask.

But since she did not go with him, she spent the day being terrified. By changing now what she had done in that other life, she had changed the day completely. Everything in it was different and unexpected. By evening she was exhausted at the emotional battering, and yet there was a touch of wild exhilaration as well. It had been like a roller coaster. A kind of swooping weightlessness.

Was this the way most people lived? With this shock of events? She could not decide whether she could bear it or not.

As the spring and summer wore on, the choices became more difficult and the former life increasingly unclear.

Sometimes it was only possible to guess what had been done before and what kind of deviation was needed to change the old life into something new. Still, she kept trying. By August, the greater part of every day came as a surprise, and she relished the few familiar hours as rewards for the struggle she was making.

'I wish you'd girl-talk just with me, Mama. When Harvey's there, he spoils it.'

'Now, Mist Princess. Harvey is your half brother. My stepson. He's family, and we have to make him feel loved and welcome.' Cloud-haired mama looked surprised and a little offended, but Marianne persevered.

'He looks at you like the man looked at the lady on TV when she took her clothes off. I just don't think he should come in your bedroom with us all the time. He makes me feel nasty.'

That was not something an eleven-year-old Marianne had said the other time. Now that it had been said, however, Mama saw what Marianne had seen. What she had accepted as filial affection — Mama had very little experience of the world and Papa liked her exactly that way — could be interpreted as a much more basic emotion. Harvey was, after all, a grown man only a few years younger than Cloud-haired mama and not of any blood kin to her. The bedroom visits were curtailed, and Marianne felt relief. That particular juncture had been safely passed.

Mama did not leave well enough alone, however. She spoke to Papa in the garden.

'Haurvatat, you should set Harvey up with his own establishment up in Boston. He's twenty-six. He's teaching full-time now, and he needs the experience of having his own establishment rather than living in hotels and commuting back and forth every weekend.'

Papa agreed, somewhat surprised.

Harvey sulked, furious. 'What do you and your pretty-girl mother think you're doing,' he attacked Marianne. 'He was my father a long time before he was yours. You think you're going to get me out of the picture, you're crazy. I'm his heir, his only son, and don't you and pretty-face forget it!'

'I don't know what you're talking about!' the child Marianne had retorted, honestly confused. 'It's not nice to talk that way about Mama, Harvey.'

'Papa never told me I ought to leave home until she started on him!'

'Nobody wants you to leave home. Mama just thinks you need to have a place of your own. She said I should have one, too, as soon as I'm finished with school. She says everyone needs the experience of independence.'

'She's a fine one to talk.'

What could Marianne say. Papa had come along and married Mama when she was only a girl. Everyone knew that. 'Maybe she regrets not having had the experience, Harvey,' she said in a suddenly adult voice with a mature insight, making him stare at her incredulously and coming closer to the truth than she knew.

Her feelings about all this were uncertain, vacillating. None of this had happened the other time. She didn't know what to do. There was no dream message to enlighten her, no voice coming from one of those strange places that seemed so familiar but were not. She spent long hours hiding in her bedroom or riding alone, trying to understand what needed to be done next, but there were no answers. Was Harvey being changed by her changes? Or was he doing slightly different things but remaining the same? Was the danger still there?

Her confusion was growing into something approaching a nervous collapse when an invitation arrived from Harvey's aunt, his mother's sister, Tabiti Delubovoska. Madame Delubovoska was inviting her favorite — and only — nephew for a visit in Lubovosk. A long visit.

Great-aunt Dagma had much to say about the inadvisability of this. 'Tabiti is not a nice woman,' she said to Papa and Mama, not seeing Marianne where she was curled behind the pillows on the window seat. 'She cannot be a good influence on Harvey. She is likely to be just the opposite.'

'Harvey's twenty-six,' Papa said in a mild voice. 'He's a grown man, Aunt Dagma. I can hardly forbid it.'

'Ever since Lubovosk split away from Alphenlicht and mixed with those people from the north, there has been evil there. You know it as well as I do, Haurvatat. No good will come of this visit.' She tapped her ebony cane on the floor to emphasize the point. 'Mind me, nephew. No good will come of it.'

Though Marianne did not remember this conversation having happened before, Harvey *had* gone to Lubovosk that other time as well. It was as though nothing had really changed! She was puzzled and anxious about this. Every time she changed something, the time pendulum swung back again. The finicky details of daily life as it had been lived before were becoming more and more vacillating and obscure, but the broad pattern seemed as though graven in stone, unchangeable.

And yet, she was grateful to see him go. With him gone, the daily pattern of life became calm, almost placid, each day's path as simple as a ribbon, running from end to end, almost totally familiar. There was danger in this placidity. Danger in the easy living of each day, danger she could feel without being able to respond to it at all. She began to wake in the middle of the night from restless dreams believing there was some message important to her that she was not receiving.

And it was in this state of frustration that she sought the Beale Street church again. Perhaps the message that had evaded her when she was a child would be clear to her now that she was twelve.

The church was usually locked. On several occasions before she had gone around it, pulling at the doors, trying to find a way in. Today, however, there had been a funeral, and the mourners were still gathered in muted clusters on the sidewalk as she slipped past them, through the open door and into the nave.

She knew it. The minute the lozenges of colored light from the tall windows began to swim across her face, she knew the place. There was a bell tower, reached by a twisting flight of stairs behind her in the corner. There was a choir loft on either side of the sanctuary, and a row of bronze plates set into the stone floor where the bodies or ashes of parishioners rested. It was, she guessed, a Catholic or Anglican church. Not a church Marianne would ever have attended. She was being taught the Magian faith of her ancient forebears, and that sect built no edifice in this place or in any other. Still, she knew this church as she knew her own bedroom. Grown-up *Marianne* had been here.

And she had left something here. The other *Marianne* had come to this place and set something here, some word, some symbol perhaps. Something meant to be found by the young Marianne in this separate life. Something to help. Here, and in the house, the shelter, the tree, the wall. In each of them was something she needed.

She sought what it held for her.

It was no message writ large in the stone. The only words carved there were ones of praise to God or thanks for past gifts. It was no song being sung. It was nothing written into the back of a hymnal. She had not really expected that.

She sat down, waiting. The place had summoned her, "here," and she was "here," ready to listen. Time went on. The sun swam a bit lower, sending new jewels of light into the floor and drawing her eyes up to the stained-glass window that cast them. St George. She recognized him from a storybook. St George and the dragon. It was not a very reptilian dragon, rather more doglike in general appearance but with a spiny crest and a lashing, lizardine tail. Its hide was blue as steel. The knight's horse was reared high in fear, and the saint looked likely to lose his seat in the instant. The spear was only a straw. The dog-dragon would bite it in two.

Sitting there in the glow brought it back. Grown-up *Marianne* had come here before, between times, to sit in this place and look at this same window. "Remember," she had whispered to the stone, the wood pews, the stained glass, the carved altar screen. "Remember," bidding them summon herself when she returned as a child, as they had done. The memory was amber, warm, glowing with satisfaction.

Whatever had been done here had been done well. 'Are you here?' she whispered to the window.

The dog-dragon in the stained-glass window moved its head to look at her, staring at her with large, sunflamed eyes. It panted, its pointed tongue sinuous as a serpent's. 'Are you ready?' it asked. 'Do you need me now?'

She gasped, wrapping her arms tightly around herself in self-protection. The dog continued to stare, its tongue flickering, an isolated shimmer of sunlight. Perhaps she was merely having another of those double visions, those bizarre transparencies laid over the reality of life. And yet, in her mind the voice seemed real and very clear, demanding an answer. 'Do you need me now?'

'Not quite yet,' she answered softly. 'Soon, maybe.'

The dog-dragon turned back to contemplate the knight poised above him, dog eyes laughing. One knew he had no fear of either the steed or the armor. When both the saint and the horse were ashes upon the wind, the dog-dragon would remain.

'He's a momentary god,' a voice inside her said and was then silent. Marianne was frowning as she left the church.

Driven by a need to clarify what was happening, to connect it to anything she understood, she went to the house where the little old Chinese woman often slept upon the porch, and stood at the edge of the public walk where the brick path curved to the house. She called, tentatively, as one might call a puppy. 'Here, come on, come on.' Through the closed door a red dog came out, fluffed like a pom-pom, his black mouth gaped wide and his long, black tongue extended in a monstrous yawn. His face changed as she looked at it, becoming another kind of face for a moment, an Oriental face, wrinkled away from fangs much longer than any mere dog could have needed. He turned, posed, raising one foot as though to rest it upon something and she recognized him. There was a statue of him at home in Papa's room. One of him and one of his mate with a cub beneath her paw.

'Now?' he asked. 'We've been reasonably patient.'

'Not quite yet. I only wanted to be sure you were here.'

'Where else would we be?' the dog asked with stern amusement. 'Didn't you tell us to stay here until we were needed? You haven't forgotten that, have you?'

'Not really,' said Marianne. 'Sometimes I forget parts of things I'm supposed to know. Sometimes I get confused. I'm not always sure what's real.'

'There are five of us,' the dog said. 'You do remember that.'

'Yes,' she said, surprising herself. She did know that. 'I don't exactly know what all five of you are.'

'You'll remember,' said the red dog, turning to trot back to the porch beside the old woman. 'You'll remember.'

It was late and Marianne was very tired, but she did stop at the viny wall and whistle, softly, wondering what might come to her call. What came was the size of a large calf, black as the inside of a fireplace, with a mouth and eyes the color of ripe cherries, red as jelly.

'Just checking,' said Marianne somewhat weakly.

'Don't waste our time, woman,' the Black Dog said.

'I'm not really a woman, not yet,' she said.

'Oh, yes you were,' he replied. 'Were, are, will be. We're ready when you are. Just call as you ride past.'

'Ride past?' she asked, for that instant believing she understood everything completely. 'Oh, yes. I will.' She turned away, feeling the fiery eyes of the Black Dog burn into her back as she trudged home. She did not call up the dog of the shelter or the dog of the tree. Dragon Dog, Foo Dog, Black Dog — what would the others be? She was not sure she wanted to know, but her mind told her. Wolf Dog and Dingo. Blue dog, red dog, black dog, silver dog, and yellow dog.

'Momentary gods,' she said to herself, remembering the words without knowing what they meant.

'Papa, what's a momentary god?' she asked him at dinner. It was safe to do so. Harvey was still abroad.

'A what, Mist Princess? A momentary god? Haven't the foggiest idea.'

'Perhaps a very little god?' laughed Cloud-haired mama. 'Perhaps a very tiny one. Who only lasts for a moment?'

'Where did you hear a strange phrase like that?' Great-aunt Dagma wanted to know, cleaving immediately to the underlying significance of the question or event, as she always did. Others could be misled, or diverted by trivia, but seldom Great-aunt Dagma. 'Who used those words?'

Marianne shook her head. 'I don't know. I just heard it somewhere. Maybe on TV.'

'I would say,' Great-aunt Dagma told her, 'that a momentary god is one summoned up or invoked for a momentary occasion. A brief time.'

'Maybe that's it,' Marianne murmured.

'I would say further,' Great-aunt went on inexorably, 'that anyone who did so had better have strong nerves and excellent qualities of conceptualization. I shouldn't think a momentary god would necessarily wish to be dismissed once the moment was over.'

'What do you suppose one would look like?' Marianne asked, not needing to pretend innocence. She was innocent of anything except conjecture. 'Do you suppose one could look like a dog?'

Great-aunt Dagma fixed her with a strange, glowing eye. 'I suppose one might. Or a lion, or a multi-armed idol, or a dragon or a worm, perhaps. Depending upon what one needed.'

'Tsk, Aunt Dagma, you're feeding the child stories again,' Papa said.

'Well, such stories were fed to you, nephew, and you suffered little from it.'

'What did you mean, Great-aunt Dagma, about the god not wanting to be dismissed?'

'Well, child. I suppose it would be like summoning a very powerful servant of some kind. Or perhaps a genie. One summons the creature up, and one says, "Mend me that fence," or something suitable. And the creature does it. But then, when the task is done, it does not necessarily want to go into its bottle or to the servants' quarters where nothing interesting is happening. It may insist upon staying around, perhaps eating and drinking or chasing pretty ladies . . .'

213

'Dagma!' Cloud-haired mama cried warningly.

'Tsh, child. Marianne knows that male creatures chase pretty ladies. Even godlets or genies may do so, eh, girl? Well, that is what I meant. Not everyone has the power to put a creature of that kind back in his proper place. Perhaps it may even be hard to know what the proper place should be!'

Marianne was properly sobered by this. Evidently she, the grown-up *Marianne*, had summoned five momentary gods for some inscrutable purpose of her own. 'Some necessary purpose,' the adult voice inside Marianne prompted. 'You'll know when the time comes.' Be that as it might, the current Marianne thought very anxiously about the five great dogs. When they had done whatever it was they had been summoned up to do, what would happen then?

CHAPTER TWO

The familiar, dreamy time came to an end. Harvey came home from his trip to Lubovosk, bringing with him his Aunt Delubovoska who was properly invited by Cloud-haired mama to come to tea between visits to Washington of an ambassadorial kind.

'Not that I can really think of her as an ambassador — ambassadress,' Mama laughed. 'Any more than I used to be able to think of my own father as one. Lubovosk and Alphenlicht are such tiny, unimportant countries, and embassies are so deadly dull. It seems to me no tiny country should need such boring places even though the great powers may have use for them. So full of maneuvering. Everything is maneuver, tactic, strategy. My own mother used to worry about the political implications of what she *wore*!'

'I'm glad Papa came along and rescued you, then,' Marianne had said. 'Otherwise you'd still be trapped in one.'

'No.' Cloud-haired mama had been quite sad over that. 'Embassy life would have ended for me when my own father died, even if Mother had lived. I would have been sent back home to Alphenlicht, I imagine. Just think of that! Being sent back to a place you don't even remember and being told it's your home.'

'This is your home.' Marianne had hugged her. 'With Papa and me.'

'Well, this has been Papa's home for a long time.' Cloud-haired mama had laughed, looking out at the wide, verdant acres. 'So I guess it has to be mine as well.'

'This is my home,' Harvey had once said from horseback, gesturing with one arm at all the lordly expanse of it. 'Mine.'

'Papa's,' Marianne had corrected, frightened by the gloating look in Harvey's eyes. Now, meeting Madame, Harvey's aunt, Papa's first wife's sister, Marianne saw that same look. A kind of gloating. As though everything here actually belonged to her though no one knew it just yet. This visit was a new thing. It had not happened before. So, something had changed.

'So this is Marianne,' Madame Delubovoska said, smiling a brittle, terrible smile. 'Little Marianne.' Her eyes bored into Marianne's, questioning, demanding eyes.

Marianne felt as though she were about to choke. Her throat was swollen shut and her face was turning color. She could not breathe. Her body screamed for air.

Something moved inside her mind, as though a tenant had come into a room of it, walking very purposefully, already speaking as she entered. 'I am a castle of adamant,' said the voice of *Marianne* and Marianne's fist tightened in an unconscious, symbolic gesture and the choking stopped. Marianne did not fight the voice or the gesture. She relaxed to let them have their way. Madame had done something dreadful, something terribly frightening, but evidently the grown-up *Marianne* understood and was competent to do something about it, even though this had not happened in precisely this way before.

Madame looked puzzled, though only for an instant, before Papa demanded her attention. Then she turned to him, taking his hands, taking Mama's, greeting them, making some statement or other to which they both nodded agreeably. The voice inside Marianne said, 'See, both of them nodding at her? They're agreeing to whatever she's saying. That puts them in her power, Marianne. In hers and in Harvey's.'

Harvey stood just behind his aunt, his eyes fixed on her every movement, strangely glittering eyes.

'Now, Marianne,' said the voice with a sad certainty. 'It must be now. We can't wait. You see what's happening? Another day and it will be too late!'

Marianne did see. Death was in Harvey's eyes. He wanted his inheritance. He wanted it now. Or, perhaps Madame Delubovoska wanted it through him. 'Harvey,' Marianne asked, suddenly and surprisingly, drawing all their eyes, 'will you take me riding with you in the morning?' It was not her own voice, not her young voice, and it surprised them both. 'Please,' she added, in her own persona, the word coming out in a childish plea, almost a whine.

'Well, of course he will!' Madame said in a tone of devilish amusement, as though she would have chosen precisely that. 'He wouldn't miss a ride with his little sister, not for anything.' And she turned to Harvey imperiously, the very movement a command, her eyes demanding obedience.

Then the party moved out of the lofty entryway and became only ordinary. Harvey went off to his room to unpack. Madame had tea with Mama and Papa in the library. She would stay, she said, only for an hour. Then she must go. It was all very civilized, and Marianne sat with them, sipping her own tea, cold as ice inside herself where that other *Marianne* watched and watched. 'You see,' said the adult *Marianne* voice. 'Look at her!'

Marianne looked, seeing something horrible in the woman's eyes. Pain and terror for Mama, first, then for Papa, and perhaps, at last, for Marianne herself. 'You see!' the voice demanded.

'Mama, may I be excused?' she begged, sweat standing out on her forehead. 'Please.'

'What's the matter, Princess? Not feeling well?' Mama saw something in Marianne's eyes, for she asked no more questions. 'Run on. I'll be up to see you in a moment.'

And so she had escaped, she and that other she both, to go up to Marianne's room and sit crouched over the windowsill, leaning out into the quiet airs of early fall. The voice spoke to her. 'It's all right. Listen, Marianne. It will all be taken care of.'

'What am I to do?' she asked that other person, that grown-up voice. 'Tell me, what am I to do?'

'Go riding with Harvey,' the voice said. 'Go past the church, the house, the tree, the wall, the shelter, then on up Bitter River Road, into the forest. That's all. I summoned the momentary gods to help you, and they will take care of it.'

Was this real? She couldn't tell. 'That's all I have to do. Nothing other than that?'

'Everything else has been arranged.'

Marianne began to cry.

'Shhh, shhh,' the voice comforted her. 'Shhh. I'm sorry, dear one. I'm sorry little Marianne. Sorry to treat you so, use you so. But Cloud-haired mama will die, otherwise. Papa will die. Madame and Harvey will choke the life out of them in just the way she was testing on you when she first came in, to see if you were vulnerable. Then, when Mama and Papa are dead, they'll take years to do the same to me, you, us.'

'Why? Why?' She knew why. It was a plea for sympathy rather than for information, but the voice replied as though she had not really known.

'Why? For money, little girl. For all these lands and the money in the bank, Papa's, Mama's. There is more of it than you can imagine, and most of it will go to Harvey when they die. But a lot of it comes to you, Marianne, to you, me, us, and if we die, it goes to charity. Good works. Feed the hungry, rock the baby, build the hospital. You know, Marianne. Not to Harvey. But he is a trustee! So, he won't

217

do us in, not just yet. Later. When he's had a chance to use it all up.'

'And she . . . that aunt of his, she's in on it?'

'Why, Marianne, she's *it*. She's taught him everything he knows.'

'What does she want?'

'The money, Marianne. Money is power. Lubovosk is a poor little country, and she needs money. Papa is very, very wealthy. Once Harvey has it, she has him. She will siphon it off, through him. He thinks he can do what he pleases. She knows he will do only what she allows.'

Marianne didn't understand it. She knew about greed and desire for money. For power. But she couldn't believe anyone would kill Mama for it. Or Papa. And yet, she had looked deep into Madame's eyes. After that, anyone would believe.

'All I have to do is go riding?'

'That's all you have to do.'

She could not really know whether any part of this was real, and the unreality persisted through the night and into the morning as she put on her riding clothes and boots, as she greeted her horse at the stable where Harvey awaited her. 'Well, where do you want to ride, little sister?' He had a narrow, superior grin on his face, like a fox's face, gleeful and anticipatory. 'I thought we'd go along the forest path if it's all right with you.'

'No,' the voice said.

'No,' said Marianne. 'I want to ride by the edge of town and out the Bitter River Road.'

He stared at her, one nostril lifted in scorn, somewhat angrily, as though wondering how important it was to do what she wanted. Abruptly, he decided it didn't matter. He mounted, not waiting for her, and trotted down the driveway to the road. Reluctantly, Marianne mounted Rustram and followed him, Rustram hopping and curveting to attract her attention. She patted him absently, adrift half in fatalistic resolve, half in terror.

The road into town was only half a mile from their gates,

and Marianne saw the blue Dragon Dog waiting at the intersection, the stone steeple of the church spiking the sky behind him like a raised cudgel. 'Shh,' said the voice. 'Ride on.'

It was a dream, she told herself. A waking dream.

The maple tree was on the way, and the yellow Dingo Dog came out of it as she passed, nose first, then ears and neck, finally the upcurving tail, out through the bark as though it had been a curtain of gauze, trotting along behind as though she had followed Marianne every day when she rode. The wall was next, and Black Dog rose from the Virginia creeper at its base to pace along beside them. 'Good morning,' he said to her silently. 'I'm glad you've finally gotten around to it.'

'Shhh,' said the voice again.

'I think I see Bitter River Road from here,' Harvey said. 'There's a shortcut across the meadow.'

'No,' said Marianne. 'I need to see something at the end of this block.' She must dream this thing as she had been told, even though it wasn't real.

'You're becoming very unaccommodating, I must say,' Harvey sneered. 'Though you've grown up amazingly while I've been gone. Almost as pretty as your mama. Might be worth kissing, Marianne, pet. Think I'll test that when we get home.'

Marianne stared at him, cold in her belly. 'No,' she said. 'You won't.' Dream or not, she didn't want him to touch her.

He laughed, reaching out to stroke her chest where her breasts were just beginning to swell. 'Oh, won't we?'

She shuddered away from him as they passed the house of the old Chinese woman, and the Foo Dog came from under the porch, high as her armpit and red as a flower pot. 'One more,' the red dog said conversationally. 'Only one more.'

'I know,' said Marianne, aloud.

'Did you say something, little sister?' Harvey asked.

'Not to you,' said Marianne. They went on down the road.

The shelter lay on the left, a vast rockpile built during WPA days, with a fanciful roof and a great chimney up the middle. At one time it had been used as a site for picnics, but no one used it any more. Ferns grew in crevices among the stones. The entrance was blocked by a forest of burdock, and the Wolf Dog came through the leaves as though they were smoke. She was silver in the sunlight, glittering. Her plumy tail waved a greeting and she looked at Marianne out of eyes like great amber lamps.

'All here,' said Black Dog.

'All here,' agreed the Dragon Dog and the Foo Dog.

'Hmmm,' growled the wolf, deep in her throat.

The Dingo was silent, sneaking looks at the others out of the sides of her eyes.

Marianne touched Rustram with her heels and he sprang obediently into a canter along the dirt road. She did not know where they were going, but someone did. She did not need to look at them to know the five momentary gods were keeping easy pace. In the shapes that other *Marianne* had assigned to them? Or in their own shapes? Which?

'Come back here, you little witch,' Harvey shouted, irritated. He wasn't as good a rider as Marianne. Horses didn't like him, and in any case, his horse was no match for Rustram. Both these things annoyed him, and he clattered after her, furious at being outrun. She fled on, the dogs tight at her heels, around the curve of the River Road and under a huge oak that stood in a clutter of boulders at the forest's edge.

'Stop here,' the voice said.

'Here,' said several of the momentary gods, all at once.

She stopped, turned, waited to see what would happen.

Harvey rode toward her, his face crimson with anger, his whip hand raised. He got angry easily. Perhaps he would whip his horse. Perhaps he would whip her. He had not decided when the dogs erupted from the underbrush and were suddenly all around him. A pack of curs, he thought, mongrel whelps appearing out of the underbrush all in a moment. One of them, a large, gray one, leaped for the throat of his horse.

Another caught at his ankle, tearing him from his seat. It was the huge, black one that caught his hand, the one holding the whip, and jerked him off of the horse, down. He put out his other hand to protect himself from the rock he saw beneath him. Too late.

He felt the rock hit the back of his head, crushingly.

He was not unconscious.

He could still see. She was sitting on her horse, staring at him. At him. Not at the dogs. The dogs. Sitting around her, looking at him also. Licking their mouths. A yellow one burrowing into its shoulder as though for a flea.

'They're yours,' he said in a whisper. 'Yours.'

'Not mine,' she shook her head. 'Not mine, Harvey.' It was all a dream. Her pulse was not fast. There was no feeling about it. He lay there and she was not even glad, not even sorry. She dreamed she said, 'You and your aunt shouldn't have planned to kill Mama and Papa. You really shouldn't have.'

'How did you find out? Bitch,' he snarled. It was the last word he ever said. Something beneath him broke. He felt an abrupt, almost painless cracking in his neck, and then all feeling ceased.

'What now?' she whispered. Perhaps she would wake up now.

'Ride home, very fast, and tell them what happened,' said her voice.

She rode. She told them. Dogs, she said, for that is what she had seen. She said they had come out of the forest, jumped at Harvey, pulled him from his horse. All of that was true, and the horror in her voice needed no pretense. She was horrified at Harvey and at herself and even at the sorcerous voice that spoke from deep inside herself. The real anger at that voice was yet to come.

221

CHAPTER THREE

There were phone calls, ambulances, men with a stretcher. There were low-voiced conversations with doctors. Later, there was a hunt for the dogs by an armed posse, but the animals had vanished as though they had never existed.

'Can you describe them?' the animal control officer asked Marianne. 'How many were there?'

'Five. I counted five,' she said.

'You said one big black one.'

'Very big. And one that looked like a wolf. And a red one. And a smaller yellow one. And one that was kind of bluish.'

'Bluish?' Papa asked, unbelieving.

The animal control officer did not disbelieve. 'Well, yes sir, it could be. A blue tick hound, maybe. They're really sort of dark gray with white mixed in. It does look bluish, particularly in the sun.'

'Does her description mean anything to you?'

'I'm afraid not. Dogs will pack, of course. It's as natural to them as − well, as going to football games is to us. Usually when we hear about a pack, it's made up of dogs from adjacent properties. They get acquainted along their borders, so to speak, and then they run together when they get the chance. It doesn't take much to make a friendly pack into a hunting pack, either. That's natural to dogs, too, but I've never heard of a pack attacking a mounted man.' He fell silent, musing for a time before he went on. 'I know of one big black dog, but he's old as the hills and almost toothless. As for the rest of them, well, it's an odd assortment, you'll admit. You sure about the colors and sizes, Marianne?'

'Yes sir.' She was. She could even have told the officer where to find the dogs, but he hadn't asked her that. When she thought it over, she realized he could not have found them there, even if she had told him.

'How about breeds. Do you know anything about different breeds of dog?'

'The red one was like the dog in Papa's office.'

They went into the office to look at the pair of Foo Dogs on Papa's desk: the male, on the right, with his foot upon the glove; the female, on the left, with her foot upon her pup.

'What are they, sir? Some kind of idol?'

'Temple guardians,' Papa had replied. 'If they look like any living breed at all, I'd say it would be the chow. That would go with the red coloring Marianne mentioned. Chows have black mouths and tongues, too.'

'His mouth was black,' said Marianne, verifying the identification. This, too, was perfectly true.

Papa raged and the animal control man sympathized, but they didn't find the pack of dogs.

'What now?' she asked her internal voice, still dreaming. None of it was real. Not any of it.

'Now?' The voice was remote, as though it reached her from some incredible distance. 'Marianne; nothing now. You've saved them. You've saved yourself. Now you must get on with your life and they must go on with theirs.'

'That's *all*!' She was incredulous.

'That's all.' The sadness in that voice! Marianne was too young to recognize the components of that emotion — aching love and a piercingly sweet renunciation — but she could not miss the sadness. 'Oh,' the voice went on, with tears in it, 'except one thing. When you are about twenty-one or -two, maybe a little older than that, you may meet a man. His name is Makr Avehl. He comes from Alphenlicht, like I — like we do. He may know all about this. About Harvey, everything. He's — he's a very — well, he's a very good friend of ours.'

'Do you — do you love him?' In the vision, it seemed appropriate that she should love him.

'He saved my life. He loves me,' the voice said sadly. 'I do love him. I don't know if you will or not.' It went away

223

then. Purposefully and absolutely, as though some tenuous line that had tied it to this Marianne had been deliberately severed and the connection between them had been broken. Young Marianne knew that grown-up *Marianne* was gone. Not merely elsewhere, but gone. There were no longer two, but only one. If the other *Marianne* had been correct about Madame and about Harvey, no one knew it now except young Marianne herself. And perhaps the man. Makr Avehl. If he were real and not merely part of the dream.

'Mack Ravel,' she said to herself, already forgetting the name. 'From Alphenlicht.'

Time went on. The motionless body that was Harvey came home from the hospital with two attendants and a wheeled litter. His attendants said he could see well enough. He could even signal yes and no by blinking his eyes, though he seemed to do so only in response to questions concerning food or temperature. Would he like more ice cream? Was it too warm? The eyes would blink — once for yes, twice for no. If one asked anything unrelated to food or temperature, 'Would you like to go out on the lawn, Harvey?' there was no response at all.

Sometimes she would come into a room and find him parked there, just lying, looking at her. Sometimes she saw something in his silent stare that could not really be there, something smoldering, like flame beneath a pile of ashes. She told herself it was only because she needed to see something rather than this vacancy. In reality, everyone said there was nothing there. The doctors agreed. The body lived, but whatever had been Harvey within it did not.

Seeing him thus helpless, unmanned, dehumanized, converted into something that was kept alive only out of a conventional sense of the appropriate, made her former belief in the immediacy of danger seem remote and unlikely. The precarious world of her dream-threat faded; her conviction went with it. She did not really believe in it. Belief in the momentary gods departed. She did not think they had really existed, either. By the time she was fourteen, fifteen, she knew that none of it had been real. The accident had been only an accident. There had been dogs. Only dogs. The rest was woven out of fairy tales and too much imagination and an overbred sense of guilt. Her childhood had not really been as she remembered it, all known ahead of time. There had not really been a grown-up *Marianne* in her head. All those double visions of things had not actually happened. They had resulted from some kind of juvenile nervous disorder, now outgrown. She did not tell herself it would never happen again. She merely thought of it as an aberration, one she could handle.

All her memories shifted, changed, underwent a softening as she told herself what she had thought was real had been only a childish imagination.

Until at last there was nothing left at all. Except, from time to time, a feeling of formless guilt. Try though she might to tell herself that it had only been an accident, something inside accused her of being responsible for Harvey's condition. His silent body became ubiquitous, a constant accusation. He seemed to inhabit every room of the house simultaneously. He and the litter were inseparable, half living, half mechanical, not a life but an accusatory device. She twisted beneath the pressure of guilt, feeling it a burden that she longed to shift away from herself.

Who had done it really?

That other *Marianne* who was only a fiction? Fictions cannot be responsible for anything.

Was there a real person involved in all this? She would wait and see. If there was, that person was surely responsible for whatever had happened. If anything had happened.

'It wasn't my fault,' some childish part of her continued to insist. 'I didn't do anything. If anybody did anything at all, they did it.'

Time went. School went. Out of her love for her horse and her interest in animals of all kinds, out of her devotion to the vast acres that Papa Zahmani had said one day would be hers, she had studied agriculture and livestock and business management, knowing she would have to prove herself to Papa before he would let her, a woman, manage the estate with its huge stables of thoroughbreds and its herds of pure-bred cattle. Papa would never have considered her if Harvey had been well and able, but Harvey wasn't. Guilt bit at her again, but she shrugged it off and went on with her studies.

The University went. There was a love affair, sweet and intense and sudden as a summer shower, over as soon, leaving Marianne wondering what she had seen in a particular egotistic, not very interesting, and totally predictable young man. With encouragement from Mama, she decided to forget him by visiting the land of her forebears. She spent several happy weeks among the small villages of Alphenlicht, picking up a little of its language and learning of its customs, no stranger to her than others she had seen in places far closer. When she read of the Prime Minister of the country, Makr Avehl, it was with a sense that she might have read or heard the name before, but it made no particular impression. The papers said he was on his way to the United Nations in New York. There was another dispute between Alphenlicht and neighboring Lubovosk. Madame Delubovoska had asserted a right for Lubovosk to govern the lands of Alphenlicht. The Prime Minister ridiculed these specious claims. The matter would be heard before the General Assembly. Reading of this, Marianne experienced a tremor of recollection, as though, after a long detour, she had come once again upon an old, well-traveled road. The sensation lasted only for a moment. Real memories did not form; no voice spoke.

She went home again. It was time to get on with her life. Time to take a job. Time to become herself.

She waited, deciding among several job offers, spending a lot of time riding to use up recurrent spasms of nervous energy. She felt she should be doing something, fighting some battle, accomplishing some task she could not define even for herself. Something. Something quite remarkable.

Until the afternoon she rode up to the house and found Papa and Mama on the terrace, entertaining a tall, spectacularly handsome man. She had seen his picture often in Alphenlicht.

She recognized him with disbelief, wondering what had brought him here, accepting the introduction to him as she would to any total stranger.

'And you are Marianne,' said Makr Avehl.

She, wondering what he was doing here, gave him her usual glowing smile, which he misinterpreted at once.

During dinner they exchanged only pleasantries, slightly formally as was consistent with their just having met. Great-aunt Dagma gave them both a long, level look through her glasses but said nothing. Marianne felt herself flush under that look and resented it. When dinner was done, he asked her to walk with him in the garden.

'Marianne,' he said to her as soon as they were out of sight of the terrace, drawing her close to him. 'Oh, by all that's holy, my Marianne.'

'What in hell!' she exclaimed, breaking away from him and turning as though to flee, stopping only at his shout of half pain, half dismay. She was angrier than she could have thought possible. 'I don't know you,' she grated at him. 'What do you think you're doing?'

He stood there, trembling, unable to speak, staring at her, searching her face for the woman he remembered. In his own memory, he had left *Marianne* only days before — or rather, had been left by her — in a strange, sorcerous world she had helped to create. She had left him there, but he had found her again — except that he seemed to have found a different woman.

The difference was there, in her face. This was not the gallant *Marianne* who played life's deck even when it was stacked against her. This woman was no less lovely but far less tried. There was little or no pain in this one's face. Perhaps this one had courage also, but it might well be of a different kind. Except for a shadow of guilt, this one had clear, untroubled eyes. They might have been sisters. Even twins. But not the same.

'Accept my apology,' he said from an agonized throat. 'I truly thought — never mind what I thought. Forgive me.

227

Pretend it didn't happen.' He turned away, then back to her as though he could not leave her and she responded to the pain in his face as she had not to his importunity. 'Walk with me,' he said at last in a voice aching with loss, needing to move before he froze into place, turned into ageless ice by this grief he felt.

She wanted to refuse him but could not do so without being ungracious. He had obviously made a mistake. Perhaps he had known someone else by her name, someone with the family resemblance. He, himself, might have been her father's son or younger brother. She had no wish to be rude, though she could not help being angry. The latter was understandable, but the former was beneath her. So Cloud-haired mama often said. So she thought. He was not being demanding. A little resentfully but graciously enough she turned to walk beside him on the path while he examined her face as though it had been a holy icon of his religion.

'You really don't remember?' he asked in a voice pathetically pleading for such a big and powerful man. 'You really don't?'

'I don't know what you're talking about, Your Excellency.'

'There was — there was another *Marianne*. Your twin. You, in another world. She — I . . . I loved her very much.'

She softened at his tone. It would have been impossible not to. One would not kick the victim of an accident, someone lying broken on the road. So, she could not kick at him emotionally when he was so obviously broken.

'It's odd you should speak of another *Marianne*,' she murmured. 'When I was a child, I sometimes thought there was another *Marianne*. Although I know now it was only hallucination, it seemed then I had a grown-up twin, in my head, somewhere. An older self. At one time I bothered myself a lot trying to figure out whether she was real.'

'What if I told you she was?'

Wary, she responded, 'I don't care. It wouldn't have anything to do with me. I seem to remember that from the time I was about five until about twelve, there was a voice inside me, a kind of prompter. It may have been imaginary.

At the time, it seemed to tell me things. Things that were going to happen.' A sudden and unexpected memory assailed her. 'It told me your name.'

'Yes,' he prompted.

'It's hard to . . . think of that time.'

'The voice told you about your half brother, and Madame Delubovoska?'

She looked at him in shock, suddenly awash in memory, long repressed. She gasped. It had not occurred to her he would know what the voice had said. How could anyone in this real world know what her own delusions had spoken of? She dithered, muttering, 'Some things about them, yes. I'd rather not think about that, if you don't mind.'

The guilt that haunted her from time to time was manifest in her voice, and he reached out to her. 'Let me verify what the voice told you.'

'Your Excellency, I've dealt with that. I've forgotten it. I don't want to hear.'

'You must hear. There's pain in your voice. Whatever happened, you feel involved. Your involvement bothers you. In this world, your act, whatever it was, does not seem to be self defense. It must seem to you to be almost gratuitous violence. Your generous nature would repudiate such violence. It would revulse you. What can I say to counter your revulsion if not to tell you what you did was justified?

'In my world, that other world, the one you don't remember, there was a girl named Marianne Zahmani. She called her mother Cloud-haired mama. Her mother died when she was thirteen years old. No one knew why. No one could find out why or how except that she seemed to have choked to death. About a year later, Marianne's father died. Again, no one knew why or how. Both of them seemed to choke to death, but the doctors couldn't find any reason for it. Marianne's half brother was left as Marianne's guardian and as executor of Marianne's estate. My sister believes he may have tried to seduce her sexually when she was still only a child; certainly he did everything in his power to bend her to his will, to destroy her spirit. Finally, when he had diverted most of her inheritance for his own purposes, he decided to kill her.'

'No,' she snarled at him. It wasn't fair for him to drag this dream stuff out into the light. 'I don't want to know . . .'

'You have to know. He decided to kill her. He tried to kill her as he killed her mother and his own father, he and his aunt, Madame Delubovoska. They used — well, call it sorcery. I came along and spoiled things for them. So, they removed her from my influence. See — I do not say "you," I say "her."' He paused, struggling with the word. He said it. He still could not accept it. 'They took her into another world, a false dream world. I pursued her there, with Aghrehond, *Marianne*'s friend, Aghrehond. We helped her escape into still another world, one of her own. Madame and Harvey followed her there. So did my friend, so did I. She escaped again, back into her own past. Working with herself as a child, with you as a child, somehow she has changed things.'

Marianne turned away, angry once again. He was bringing it all back, all the confusion and pain, giving it reality, status. 'I'll assume for one moment you knew some other *Marianne* though I don't believe it. I'll assume it for your sake, because you believe it. If this woman mixed into my life, she had no right to. I've thought it over and over. Doing that to a child is like molesting a baby. Childhoods should be sacrosanct. Children have a right to innocence, to discovery! Assume she reached back into *her* childhood, assume that. Well, it was *my* childhood she ruined. Destroyed.' Her voice burned with the disinterment of a long-buried resentment. 'She did it to me.'

She heard her own voice in disbelief. Did she really believe this nonsense? 'That is, she — she did it to me if she existed. I don't really believe she did.'

He stared at her with a skeptical look. 'Would you rather have seen your parents die?'

'I have only your word for that. And hers. How do I know that's true?'

'You have my word,' he said stiffly, almost angrily. 'What Makr Avehl says is true is true.'

'So you say. In this world it didn't happen. Or perhaps it never happened. Perhaps the whole thing is illusion, a shared illusion between you and her. I don't know. I don't pretend to know. I don't want to know.'

'But she talked to you!'

'Someone seemed to, yes, Makr Avehl. Then. The last thing she said to me was that you might come. And that she loved you.' She told him this reluctantly, but in a sense he was owed at least this.

'Love me. Oh, *Marianne*, to hear that you love me . . .'

'No, no,' she waved him away, hands out, voice hostile. '*She*. Not me. She. The other *Marianne*. A ghost. A dream we shared, perhaps. She doesn't exist. I wish you could agree with me that she probably never did.'

It took him some time to control himself, but he did. When he turned toward her again it was with a stern, calm face.

'Tell me what happened to your half brother?'

She told him what she had decided to remember. 'An accident, that's all. I think there was a pack of dogs and an accident.'

'A pack of dogs?'

'At the time I thought they were something else,' she laughed. 'I called them momentary gods. I was very confused as a child.'

He shook his head, staring into the distance, not looking at her because it was too painful to do so, musing almost to himself. 'So. She was thoughtful of you, Marianne. You didn't actually have to do anything, did you? There is no need for you to feel guilt. She did it, not you. She had it all arranged through the momentary gods. When it was all over, how did you dismiss them?'

'I'm sure they were imaginary. They dismissed themselves. Things we imagine as children disappear when we become older.'

He became very pale, though she could not see it in the equally pallid light of the cloud-shifted moon. 'Did she? The — my *Marianne*. Did she dismiss them?'

'I have no idea. Funny. My Great-aunt Dagma had something

to say about dismissing gods. I've forgotten what it was.'

His voice was tense. She disliked the sound of it, the way it made her feel. Something inside her responded to his tension with a twanging discordancy of its own. 'And what about Harvey's aunt?' he asked. 'My cousin Madame Delubovoska? Have you seen her? Heard of her?'

'Nothing. She called when she heard Harvey had been hurt. She sent flowers to the hospital. I remember Mama calling it "conventionalized concern." She never came to see him.'

'He was of no more use to her then. Which doesn't mean she may not still be very interested in your family, Marianne. And in you.'

'Why? She's no kin to me. To Papa's first wife and to Harvey, yes, not to me. What possible reason could she have to be concerned with me?'

Makr Avehl could think of at least one very good reason, and he started to tell her but she wasn't listening to him. She was wondering, at that moment, whether he and the other *Marianne* had been lovers. Her own prurient curiosity offended her, and she answered his comment with annoyance. Something about the family fortunes. 'I know very little about Papa's affairs,' she said coldly. 'It certainly isn't something I should discuss with someone who is virtually a stranger.'

He was silent for a long time. Their feet made parallel tracks across the grass, wet with evening dew. The scent of flowers blew into their faces. Behind them the lights of the house fell across the paved terraces in long, elegant fingers of colorless light.

'If I tell you you are in danger, you will not believe me,' he said at last, rather stiffly. 'You are not the woman I loved, not the woman who loved me. And yet, you are.' He stared at her. 'Perhaps there is someone else in your life?'

'No,' she said, intrigued despite herself. She did not want to be taken for someone else, but how could she mind being sought as herself? Certainly any woman would find this man's attentions flattering. 'No, Makr Avehl, there isn't anyone else. But I'm not the woman you loved or thought you loved, and you have to accept that. I'm really not.'

She said it. He was facing her as she said it, his eyes fixed on hers. Her voice was clear and cold. And yet, somewhere behind her eyes a shadow slipped along, like the shadow of a lonely inhabitant in a house tenanted by others, peering through a half-curtained window at a world she could not reach.

He gasped. There, in that shadow, had been something he had recognized. Gallantry in the tilt of a head. Courage in the slope of a shoulder. He tried to contrive some way to maintain his contact with her and with that lonely, embattled shadow. He spoke, pleadingly.

'In the normal way, I might simply try to become better acquainted with you, believing that you and she are not so unalike that I could not—' he paused, struggling to find words she would not resent or think patronizing, '—could not show you something of myself you could consider . . . acceptable. I would take my time about it, as I tried to do before. But — but I erred before. Even though I knew my *Marianne* was in great danger, I didn't warn her, didn't guard her. She was shy of me, and I didn't want to frighten her. Well, you are not shy, but even if you were, I would have to warn you. I believe you are still in danger from Madame Delubovoska.'

'Me?' She laughed, shaking her head, believing his sincerity though she totally disbelieved what he said. 'Surely not!'

'Yes. I believe you are in danger from her.'

'You think Madame remembers what you say happened?' She was intrigued by this thought. How many people in the world might remember that other *Marianne*? How many did it take to give a figment life?

'I don't know. Your parents don't remember. They wouldn't. My *Marianne* and you were virtually identical up until the time . . . the time your parents died in one life, lived in another. There was no dissonance, not for them. Probably only I and some of the other Kavi remember it at all. Because we knew that *Marianne*, and followed her to — to you.'

'Kavi?'

'Our people. Our class. In Alphenlicht. The rulers. The Magi.'

'Our class.'

'I include you, Marianne. Because of who your parents are.'

'Oh, yes. I remember now. You are a Magus! I'd forgotten that. I visited Alphenlicht. It's a pretty country. Like all the better parts of an older century. I have the feeling you should go back there and forget all the ghosts, Makr Avehl.' She laughed, unconvincingly. 'As I'm going to try to do. For the first eleven or twelve years of my life, I remember that every movement seemed to be foreordained. I don't think I resented it then, but I've definitely resented it since. You are the last thing connected with that time. I suppose I've been subconsciously waiting to see whether you showed up before . . .'

'Yes? Before what?'

'I don't know. Before being something completely of my own, I think.'

'But not with me?'

'That's not an appropriate question.' A part of her wanted to end the whole relationship, to say something final, but he was already too hurt to wound further without reason. 'You're a man I would love to know better under other circumstances, but I need to feel I have choices. I've not had many up until now.'

'You wouldn't consider staying close by me? Letting me protect you?'

She gave him a critical glance, shaking her head. He knew better. 'That's no choice! It's just more of the same. Having you beside me, directing me, is just like having that imaginary voice inside me, directing me! Listen to me! I'm talking as though all that time was real, even though I've known since I was fifteen it was all invention and fantasy.'

'It wasn't imaginary.' He shook his head. 'I'm not the kind of person to fall in love with phantasms.'

'I'm sorry,' she said again. For an instant she wanted to comfort him. She still had angry feelings about him, but they seemed less substantial when directed at a real person than when she had merely imagined him. 'Perhaps sometime I'll visit you. I've been in Alphenlicht and liked it. Perhaps sometimes you will visit me. But I can't − won't − make commitments. Not now!'

He sighed again, searching her face. A little willful, that face. Willfulness was easy to understand, however. She had only been exercising her will in recent years. And behind that façade, something more complex. Hidden. Why hidden? Was that other presence hiding from him?

Sad and lost as he was, he had to accept what she told him. He started to bid her good-bye, then stopped himself. 'Oh, by the way. I have a gift for you. From my sister, Ellat. She was very fond of . . . of *Marianne*. I forgot to bring it with me today. If you don't mind, I'll drop it off before leaving for home.'

She assented. He was going. Let him do whatever he needed to do to put this behind him. Let him return briefly on the following afternoon. So − her independence was postponed for a day. She could bear it. She watched him go with a sense of a milestone being passed.

He returned, as he had promised. Before going inside to make his farewells to her parents, Makr Avhl introduced her to Aghrehond. Or, reintroduced her, according to Aghrehond.

'Oh, pretty lady, what a consternation and unhappiness you have put upon us. He, the Prime Minister, is cast down, but I − I am shattered.'

'Why shattered, Aghrehond?'

'That you should have forgotten the perils we shared.' He regarded her with sad brown eyes, his chins quivering and his large stomach swaying from side to side in an excess of grief, like a bell, silently tolling. 'We had considered everything but this. That you would hate my master for the forms he had taken . . .'

'I really don't know what forms he may have taken, Aghrehond. You'll have to accept that I honestly know nothing about it.'

'Accept, of course. One accepts. One raises one's fists to

the heavens and cries woe, but one accepts. We had considered some putative hatred you might have felt, and had accepted that. We had considered that you might, in your re-growing, so to speak, have found someone else, younger and more charming than is Makr Avehl. We had considered – oh, I will not weary you with the catalogue of considerations. This single thing we had not considered. That you had forgotten. Oh, to be forgotten! Like a lost shoe, missing even its mate, in the corner of some vast closet of time!'

Despite herself, she laughed. 'It's hard for me to believe I've met you before, Aghrehond. You would be very hard to forget.'

'There! You see! It is as I told the Prime Minister. Him, you might forget. What is he after all but a very powerful, magical, charming and very handsome man. But I, Aghrehond, I am unique!'

'Yes, but you see, that very fact proves my point. I didn't remember, not even you. Therefore, Makr Avehl must accept the fact that I don't remember him, either.'

'Oh, he accepts, pretty lady. I accept. His sister, Ellat, who loved you like a daughter almost, she accepts. The Kavi of the Cave of Light shake their heads and write the whole thing down in their chronicles, adding to their lectionaries, and even they accept. So? What good is it, this acceptance? What are we to do with it?'

She shook her head, confused. 'Do with it?'

'Well, yes. What are we to do with this acceptance? Go away and forget you? Stay here and annoy you? It is much of a problem, this acceptance. Believe me!' He wiped his brow on which small beads of perspiration glittered, ringing his hands over his head and around his large ears, as though to assure himself head and ears were in their proper shape.

'What form did he take?' Marianne asked, suddenly curious. 'Makr Avehl, I mean.'

'Whatever it was, you may be assured it was appropriate to the occasion.'

'But what was it?'

He shook his head. 'My master says I talk too much. This

236

is true, by the way, my only failing. It comes from having a hyperactive imagination and, for that reason, must be tolerated. My imagination is often very helpful.'

He wouldn't say more than that. However, that conversation had done what Makr Avehl's piteous looks had not. It had made Marianne curious about what had happened, and curiosity is a powerful stimulant. Even Marianne would have admitted that her curiosity about Makr Avehl as a sexual man had definitely been stirred.

Just before he left, Makr Avehl fished in his pocket and brought forth a length of chain, heavy gold links from which a dangling crystal hung in a pendant of gold, sparkling even in the dim light.

'Will you wear this, please?'

'What is it?'

'Call it a talisman. As I mentioned, a gift from my sister, Ellat.'

'If it isn't . . . isn't meant as any kind of tie . . .'

He laughed, a harsh, ugly sound. 'An engagement present, perhaps? Like a ring? Hardly, Marianne. Ellat sent it because she is fond . . . was fond of you. The other you. You see, she remembers.'

'I'm sorry,' she murmured. 'I didn't mean . . .'

'Wear it to give pleasure to someone you do not remember. And because it's a pretty thing.' He patted her gently on one shoulder, almost an avuncular caress. She had no idea what that casual contact cost him in self control. He sighed. 'And I will get myself off to keep from distressing you further. So it must be, I think, with victims of amnesia. They do not remember, and all their loved ones undoubtedly gather around insisting that they do. "Do you remember that time we . . ." they ask. "Remember old so-and-so, who . . ." And of course the poor victims do not remember . . .

'Perhaps the relatives and friends believe the victim is only pretending not to remember, or that he would remember if he put his mind to it. I detect in myself a desire to shake you and demand that you do remember. Perhaps it is the same with the very old who forget everyone around them,

237

mixing the generations, calling their grandchildren by the names of people long dead.'

'But it doesn't seem like that to me. I don't have any missing parts in my life at all. I can account for every day, every hour!' She stepped back from him, wearying of the argument. She wanted him to go.

'Lucky Marianne. For me it now seems that my whole life is missing. May I write to you here?'

'Temporarily. I'll be leaving home shortly. I'm taking a job!'

'I see.'

'With the government. Out west.'

'What is "out west," in your lexicon?'

'Well, it happens to be Colorado. The State of. A lot of the federal bureaus have offices there, the Department of Agriculture among them.'

'It is very mountainous there, I believe. Like Alphenlicht.'

'Mountainous, yes, but only down the middle. The east side is very flat.'

'And what will you do there?'

'I will be working for the Department of Agriculture as a consultant, a minor functionary. My specialty is livestock. I'm supposed to be able to teach people how to make money at raising stock of various kinds.'

He laughed. 'I'm sorry, Marianne. But it is so incongruous. I can see you among horses, yes, and dogs. But I balk at sheep and cows.'

'And goats and pigs,' she said firmly. 'Also chickens, turkeys, and perhaps llamas and buffalo. There is a growing market for both llamas and buffalo. Perhaps I will send you a pair of young llamas to use as pack animals on your treks in the mountains of Alphenlicht.'

'Perhaps you would bring them.'

'Perhaps.' She smiled. It was not a promise, but neither was it a rejection.

'You will be living where?'

'Denver, for now. Or one of the suburbs. I'll take an apartment temporarily. I'll look for an old house to remodel.

238

I've got this thing for houses, preferably old ones.' She stopped for a moment, aware of a memory tugging at her that she couldn't quite place. She shrugged mentally and went on. 'I've always wanted to remodel one for myself.'

Makr Avehl started to speak, then shut his mouth. She had already remodeled an old house in that other life, but she wouldn't know that. He remembered the Italianate Victorian house just opposite the University campus, the rosy brick, the oak leaves unfurling like tiny hands outside the window. The place where his *Marianne* had lived. It was a ruin, now, gutted. Someone was tearing it down to build an apartment building on the site. He didn't mention it.

'Will you write and give me your address?'

'If you like. When I have one.'

'Farewell, pretty lady,' said Aghrehond, irrepressibly. 'Do not let us become strangers again.'

She saw them go with strangely mixed feelings. Half was regret. Half was an ebullient joy, a jerk of release, like a spring let go. She was flung into anticipation. All the ties to her childhood dream life were gone. Now, once and for all, she could be herself.

CHAPTER FOUR

'What I don't understand,' said Ellat, her forehead wrinkled in concentration, 'is how you can remember everything and she remembers nothing!'

Makr Avehl shook his head, took another sip of his morning coffee, and rose to walk to the window where he looked down across the fields that surrounded the Residence to the bordering woods of Alphenlicht and the road that joined that tiny country to the outer world. 'I've tried to figure it out myself,' he said. 'Most simply, I am the same person. She is not. My *Marianne* was driven by powerful emotions. Rage.

239

Fear. Both combined. She went out of the dream-world into another world, the world of her own past.'

'According to Nalavi and many of the other Kavi, that would have caused an alternative world.'

'Well, it didn't. My *Marianne* went back in her own world, but she went as a disembodied intelligence. She didn't change anything. She entered into her own young self and guided it on exactly the same path. She set some signs or symbols, but then she let everything go on just as it had, up until she was about twelve or thirteen. At that point, she changed her past.'

'Which, according to Nalavi, would have created an alternative world,' she said patiently again. 'Because it changed our pasts as well.'

'It may have done, but only temporarily. It didn't actually change anything in Marianne's world, except as it directly affected her and her immediate family. In other words, whatever Harvey Zahmani was in Marianne's total world, it wasn't particularly important — that is, important to her, but not to the world at large. We know that because whatever alternative world may have started when he was crippled gradually converged with the old time-line and by the time Marianne reached twenty-one or -two, there was only one time-line. If we were able to look into the future of that original time-line, we would probably find that Harvey Zahmani was killed or crippled in that one as well, although perhaps at a later time. The theory of convergence would indicate that as a likelihood. Knowing Madame, it wouldn't have been much later.'

'Theory of convergence,' she mused. 'You mean the tendency of time-lines to knit together again when they are not very far apart.'

'Yes. I don't understand the logic or mathematics of it, but seemingly there is no room for an infinite number of alternative universes. They split, then converge. At any given time, only so many different ones exist. Like a river finding a new channel in flood, but still staying in the same flood plain and returning to the same channel eventually. When two people remember a specific event having happened differently, it may well be the result of a brief split and reconvergence. The event may actually have happened two ways. When a person remembers something having happened before, it may have done, on a slightly out of sync line.'

'Confusing,' she mused with a smile. 'And terrible for you, my dear.'

He sighed. 'We were anchored at both ends of this particular split, so to speak, so we remember the divergence. I was never there in the years she was growing up. I only came in at the end. Nothing in what she did interrupted my time-line at all. At most I would have this tiny loop, only a few days long.'

'Wasn't your *Marianne* anchored at both ends?'

'If she'd chosen to go on, yes. But she didn't.' He pounded his fist on the window sill, almost shouting. 'She went − went somewhere. She simply wiped herself out of young Marianne's life after Harvey was dealt with. This left only one Marianne, which is partly why the time-line grew together again. I have a feeling the divergence was very brief and that only a few of us are able to remember it.'

'My question,' Ellat said, giving him a hard look, 'is whether Tabiti Delubovoska remembers it. Does she remember trying to capture *Marianne* in that previous sequence?'

He shook his head. 'I don't know. I hope not. I hope all she remembers is going there for a brief visit when Marianne was twelve.'

'And if she does remember? Then what?'

What indeed? Vengeance? Or simply a carrying out of the original plan, whatever that was. However he rationalized it, he could not convince himself Marianne was out of danger.

'You ought to go to the Cave of Light, Makr Avehl.'

'I already have,' he murmured. Though none of the Kavi attendant upon the Cave of Light had ventured to tell him what the symbols meant.

'Well?' she demanded. 'What did it say?'

'It showed me a woman washing clothes,' he answered. 'A pack of dogs. That would be the momentary gods, I'm sure

241

of that. It showed me a palace; a dungeon. And a map.'

'You consulted the lectionary?'

'Would you like me to recite the possible symbolic meanings of a woman washing clothes? Guilt. Ritual cleanliness. Labor. Redemption. There are twenty-three meanings for that symbol alone, not counting sub-categories. Would you care to know how many there are for a map?'

'Never mind, Makr Avehl. You're saying it wasn't helpful.'

'I asked the Cave if I should follow Marianne to her new home, to court her, Ellat, assuming there could be anything between us at all.' He fell silent, thinking of the shadow of the woman he had seen in the girl's eyes. He sighed. 'Assuming there could be anything — but I got a woman washing clothes. And a map.'

'A map portends a journey.'

'Which was the only hopeful meaning the session produced, believe me. Though whether it portends a journey there or a journey returning after I am refused, no one will say.' He turned a scowling face toward the morning. 'I continue to be worried about her, Ellat. Damn it. Something is very wrong in this new world the old *Marianne* has created, willy-nilly, but I can't get at it!'

'You left her the bracelet?'

'Of course I did.'

'If she wears it, we will know of it the minute she is in danger. That is, if she goes on wearing it. Perhaps she will even be wise enough to call for our help.'

'My *Marianne* might have asked for our help, yes. She had suffered. She had suspicion. She knew the world to be chaotic. She tried to protect herself against it. This Marianne? She has not suffered. Her childhood was virtually free of trauma, and she has convinced herself that all the pain was merely imaginary. She is not suspicious. She has found the world almost entirely predictable and safe.'

'Ah,' said Ellat in a particular tone of voice.

He took gloomy satisfaction in knowing she was not as worried as he was.

CHAPTER FIVE

Marianne spent the first week of her new job in a delirium of independence, the second week in a slough of homesickness, the third in a somewhat reasoned approach to the near future.

She looked for an old house, but there were few on the market. She had forgotten that young cities had a paucity of old homes – at least of old homes not already remodeled or wrecked in favor of urban renewal.

She reluctantly gave up the idea of owning her own place and found a pleasant apartment within walking distance of downtown, the upper floor of an old house owned by Mr and Mrs Apple, Patricia and Robin. Pat and Bobby. The four large rooms were freshly painted and carpeted. Cloud-haired mama had given Marianne a generous check to use in buying furniture. She bought Mexican rugs and chunky chairs covered in bright cottons and pictures full of swirling color and one Escher print of a fish, rising to the surface of a pond amid floating leaves and reflections of sky.

She settled into work, finding it one-fifth interesting, two-fifths routine, and two-fifths utter, implacable bureaucratic bumpf. Each helpful act had to be embalmed in forms and buried in files, until she found herself feeling apprehensive about being helpful because of the amount of sheer boredom involved in making records of it.

She met a pleasant young co-worker, went out with him, told him she would not go to bed with him, and was not asked out again. She met another pleasant young co-worker who told her that knowing her almost made him regret he was gay. She met no one else.

'So this is living my own life,' she snarled at herself in the mirror, fighting with her hair, which on this morning had decided to emulate Medusa and slither everywhere but where Marianne wanted it to go. 'Not exactly what I had imagined.'

What had she imagined?

Meaningful work. Definitely. A certain amount of elegance. That, too. A certain amount of romance? Probably.

'What's a beautiful girl like you doing sitting home?' asked Pat Apple, who had knocked at the door while Marianne was struggling with her hair.

Marianne only flushed, finding it hard to formulate an answer. 'I guess I haven't been here long enough to meet anyone, really, Pat.'

'How about at the office?'

'Mostly older and married. Only a couple of young ones. One of whom is a lech and the other of whom is gay. What can I tell you?'

'There are a lot of eligible men who run around in the group Robin and I do things with. Come to a few parties with us. Maybe you'll meet someone.'

Pat and Robin were at least two decades older than Marianne. She had little faith in the invitation, but considerable respect for the kindness that had prompted it.

'I'll think about it, Pat. Thanks anyhow.'

'Not why I came up. This package came for you while you were at work, so I signed for it.'

It was an anonymous little package without a postmark. Marianne turned it in her hands, not liking the feel of it. Deep within her something stirred, a vertiginous feeling, as though some organ had come loose from its moorings and swayed. She gulped.

'Well open it, for heaven's sake. How can you just look at it like that?'

'It might be a bomb,' Marianne said with a weak, unconvincing laugh. She felt nauseated.

'You know someone who'd send you a bomb?'

'Not really, no.'

'Well then?'

She opened it. The cardboard of the box seemed to leave a greasy residue on her skin. Inside was crumpled, grayish

244

tissue paper, and wrapped in that a carving made from a dark, almost grainless wood.

'What's that supposed to be? And who sent it?'

'It looks like a demon, doesn't it?' Marianne commented, disgusted by the anonymous gift or by the vagrant sickness that had gripped her. 'Some kind of goblin or troll, maybe. I don't know who sent it. There's no card and no return address.'

'Well, it's a nasty-looking thing. You'll probably get a card from somebody, telling you they bought it in Borneo or Tibet or someplace.' Pat lumbered up from Marianne's couch and departed, calling, 'You think about coming out with Robin and me, you hear?'

Behind her, Marianne stared at the hideous carving, aware that it had been done with great artistry, for the tiny, wicked eyes seemed to stay fixed on her face no matter where she moved the carving itself. She set it on the mantel, facing the wall, wanting to throw it out but unable to do so without knowing where it had come from. She sat down, huddling around herself, protecting her core without knowing she did it.

'Not Cloud-haired mama,' she said with conviction. 'Not Papa. Then who?' Some friend from college? Making some kind of obscure joke? Someone from the office here? Making some equally obscure joke? 'Stay there until I find out,' she directed the thing as she pulled on her jacket. Her bracelet caught on the lining and she cursed, briefly, telling herself it was silly to wear Makr Avehl's gift all the time, even though he had begged her to do so.

'It really is silly to wear that all the time,' a voice said in an insinuating whisper. 'You don't need it. You're not in any danger.'

The large clock in the lower hall began to bang away the quarter hour. Marianne stopped her effort to unlatch the bracelet and ran for the door. If she didn't leave that moment, she'd be late for work. Behind her on the mantel the carving brooded, its face toward the wall.

While fixing her breakfast the next morning, she stumbled over a featureless chunk of wood on the kitchen floor, fist sized, obviously gnawed by something with sharp, determined teeth. It was dark, almost grainless wood. She was only then reminded of the strange carving and looked for it on the mantel. It wasn't there. She had not seen it there the night before. While she was at work, someone or — or something had moved it. She stood in her kitchen with the lump of gnawed wood in her hand and shivered, very slightly, as though she had felt an icy wind. Again there was that shift inside herself, as though something sleeping had been awakened.

On her way out she asked, 'Pat, you and Robin don't have a dog, do you?'

'Robin's allergic. I used to have a cat. Why? You have mice or something?'

'No. I just . . . thought I heard a dog, that's all.'

The day at work did not go well. The computer files on artificial insemination and experimental breeding programs, which she had spent the past three weeks building, were now fatally corrupted, and she screamed silently at the thought of rebuilding them. Everyone who called seemed to need information from the corrupted files.

'How did this happen?' she demanded from the world at large.

'Software,' the hardware consultant opined.

'Hardware,' the software support person snarled.

Neither of them was helpful. In her mind a demon face watched her from tiny eyes, and she found herself remembering the carving that had been on her mantel.

She had driven to work that morning in order to use the car for shopping after work. When she went to the parking lot, she had a flat tire.

On the way home, late and weary, a scant twenty blocks, she narrowly escaped an accident when two cars in front of her collided.

In her apartment, the chewed chunk of wood had found its way back to her mantel. She laid wood in the fireplace and set it ablaze, waiting until a crackling fire was going before tossing the featureless chunk of wood on top. It hissed agonizingly, finally exploding in a shower of glowing coals. The firescreen caught them, harmlessly. There was an odor of sulphur. She shivered, something she could not quite remember teasing at the edges of her mind.

In the morning, she went to her office in a fatalistic mood, prepared to spend all of the next few weeks restoring the ruined files. She was greeted with smiles from the software support woman. 'Good news. You've got your files back. I got into the system last night and got around the glitch, whatever it was.'

The morning went by in a flurry of productive, interesting work. Just after lunch, the phone rang and Pat Apple said, 'A package came for you, Marianne. I signed for it and put it up in your apartment. Hope that's OK?'

She assured Pat it was okay, then turned to the restored files. They had disappeared again. Only gibberish came up on her screen.

She sat very still for five minutes, then left the office and walked home. She did not really believe there was any connection, and yet − the two events had followed very closely. A hex, perhaps? If there were any such thing. She laughed at herself unconvincingly.

In her living room she found the remnants of a cardboard box, scraps of grayish tissue paper, a faintly musty smell. On the carpet lay fragments of grainless wood, obviously chewed.

She built a fire and put all the remnants on the flames. When they started to burn, she heard her own voice saying, 'All right. Which one of you is it?'

From behind the curtains came the Dingo Dog, yellow eyes gleaming at her. She sat, head turned a little, regarding Marianne out of the corner of her eyes. Marianne caught her breath, a deep, choking gasp, as though she could not get enough air in her lungs to speak. She had thought all the old hallucinations and visions were behind her. She was grown-up now. Real was what real was. She wanted no more of this fantasy, and yet here were her childhood visions, come to life again. Her voice asked, 'Did you chew it up because it was

247

dangerous? Is that why?' It was her voice, and yet she had not asked the question.

The Dingo whined. She remembered then that the Dingo had never spoken, not like the others.

'Are the rest of you around, too?'

'From time to time,' said a breathy voice in a peculiar accent. 'From time to time.' The Red Foo Dog came from the bathroom, jauntily. Just behind it the Dragon Dog came slithering, crawling on its belly, as though begging to be petted. Her bedroom door creaked open. She could see the Wolf Bitch lying on her bed, her huge head pillowed on her crossed paws. Beside her lay the Black Dog, asleep, eyes shut and red mouth agape.

'Why?'

'Bad thing, that was,' the Dragon Dog said. 'That thing you got in the boxes. Very bad creature, that one, as us creatures go. Had to chew it up, get it to go away.'

'You have to burn them,' the foreign, not-herself voice said, 'or you'll not get rid of them.' In the fireplace the thing she had tried to burn had turned into something quite horrible that screamed as it incinerated. So, she was dreaming. There was no need for rejection of what was going on around her. She would merely play along, waiting until she woke up.

'Fire isn't one of our things,' the Foo Dog said. 'We have others, but not fire.'

'Someone's after you,' the Wolf said from the bedroom. 'Someone very nasty.'

'Have you been here all along?' she asked, ignoring what the Wolf had said. She didn't want to hear it.

'Off and on,' said the Black Dog. 'When we had time.'

'I thought maybe . . . maybe'd you'd gone back to − to wherever *Marianne* got you from.'

'She got us from our own loci,' the Foo Dog said. 'Every locus in the universe has one of us attendant to it. We give material space its reality by giving time its duration. Each moment is dependent upon us. Hence, momentary gods.'

'But if you're not in your proper − locus, then what

248

happens to the universe?' she asked, trying to keep her mind off the mess in the fireplace that had stopped screaming and started hissing as it boiled away to nothing.

'We're there,' said the Foo Dog. 'And here. Being in two places at once is very common for a momentary god. We're basically a wave form with particular aspects.'

'Someone asked me if I had dismissed you,' she said, trying to remember who.

'We were very gratified when you did not,' the Wolf Bitch said, licking her nose. 'Being away from one's nexus is stimulating.'

In the fireplace, the thing subsided with a final whimper into a pile of ash. Marianne looked at it. She was not sure what it had been. She did not want to see it again.

'What do you think that was?' she asked, pointing.

'It could have been one of us,' the Foo Dog said, turning to the Dragon Dog. 'Do you think it was one of us momegs? I thought for a moment it looked rather familiar. When it started to yell.'

Dragon Dog nodded, 'One of us. Whoever summoned it had built a dismissal in, however. When you burned it, Marianne, you dismissed it. It went back, wherever it belonged.'

'But it wasn't shaped like a dog. I thought maybe all momentary gods . . .'

The Black Dog rolled over and laughed at her out of blood-red eyes. 'Momegs for short, Marianne. Why should it have resembled a dog? Among the infinite loci in the universe you will find an infinity of gods, momegs, one of every conceivable shape and kind and power, no two alike, though many may be similar. We five are merely similar. We are not alike. That we are doglike is not coincidental. *Marianne* picked us for that reason. She needed doglike creatures for what you — she — meant to do.'

'It wasn't me, but pass that for the moment. How did I — she — know where you were?'

'If you don't know that, how do you expect us to know? Somehow you knew. She knew. You summoned us.'

'But I — she — didn't dismiss you?'

'For which we are grateful. Our gratitude explains why we have taken the trouble to remain close at hand, to provide such guardianship as possible.'

'I didn't do it because I didn't know how,' she confessed, thinking even as she did so that it might be dangerous to be that honest about her own ignorance. 'I wish you'd realize it wasn't me. It really wasn't!'

'What was she is now you,' the Foo Dog said, not unkindly. 'We can only address her by addressing you. She gave herself for you. You don't seem grateful.'

'If you thought about it, you'd know how I feel,' she snapped. Even knowing it was a dream didn't protect her from anger. 'How would you like it if someone you didn't know laid some great burden on you before you were born. So, she stopped being. I'm sorry. I go on being. I'm not sorry about that. She didn't dismiss you, maybe because she forgot or didn't know how, any more than I do. What are we talking about it for?'

'Let me wake up,' she thought. 'Please, let this go on by and I'll wake up.'

The Foo Dog commented, 'You didn't know how, true. But you took no steps to learn how to dismiss us, either. That means you didn't mind our being loose. For which we are, as we have said, grateful. Our gratitude must now take some palpable and practical form toward whichever of you is available to us. We must offer such advice and help as we can. It must be obvious even to you, Marianne, that you are under attack.'

She shook her head, not willing to concede this.

'Oh yes. Yesterday's mishaps were not a mere run of ill luck. Other misfortunes undoubtedly began today the minute that crystalized momeg arrived in your space, your "turf," so to speak. Just as each momeg has its own locus, its own point in space, and its own nexus, that is its continuum, so each living thing has a "turf," a set of material concatenations arranged in a highly personal and largely inflexible way. When an outside momeg intrudes — so to speak — without invitation, the turf is warped. Visualize it as a tray of tightly packed marbles into which one more is pushed, one that doesn't fit . . .' The Foo Dog lifted her hind leg and chewed a rear paw, reflectively. 'Chaos often results.'

Marianne nodded, unable to speak. This dream had to end soon. What was she doing, sitting here on her apartment floor, talking to five dogs, four of whom talked back.

The Dingo whined and put a paw on her leg.

'Dingo wants you to know she is no less concerned than the rest of us, Marianne. After all, there is one built-in form of dismissal with all momegs. When the summoner dies, the momeg dismisses. Just like that. If we wish to stay free, we will continue to be concerned with your welfare.'

'This is nonsense. Who would attack me, and why?'

Black Dog jumped down from the bed and strolled to the front window where he sat, ruby eyes staring out at the afternoon. Foo Dog went to the dining-room window. Wolf Dog sat up and glared out of the bedroom window. Dingo padded her way into the bathroom and Marianne heard her nails scratching the sill. Dragon Dog merely sat where he was. Dingo whined as she came back into the room. The others reassembled, nodding their furry heads.

'Someone's watching you, Marianne,' said the Foo Dog. 'Not from nearby. From some distance away, but watching you, nonetheless.'

'A woman?' she asked, dreading the answer. 'Is it a woman?' She was remembering what Makr Avehl had said, his warnings that she had dismissed.

'I smelled a woman,' Dragon Dog said. 'Unmistakably.'

Dingo whined in disagreement.

'No, I grant you it didn't look like a woman, but none-theless that's what I smelled.' Dragon Dog sniffed. 'Dingo says the person watching you looks like a cloud of darkness with eyes.'

'Tall,' she said, half hysterically, trying to remember what Madame Delubovoska had looked like in that long-ago child-hood time. 'Very thin. With black, black hair and brows.'

'She smells like black hair, yes. Thin, with very black hair and a bad disposition.'

251

Dingo whined again.

'Well, that's what I said, wasn't it?' Dragon Dog growled. 'Dingo insists on "evil disposition" rather than merely bad.'

'There's only one person it could be. Madame Delubovoska. My half brother's aunt.' Shaken out of her tenuous composure, lost in a seeming reality of danger, Marianne ran to the phone and punched long distance, jittering from foot to foot as she waited for an answer, telling herself she was not really calling, that it was only a dream call for which she would never receive a bill . . .

'Mama? How are you? How's Papa?

'Oh, yes, I miss everyone. And everything. Listen, are you all right? Is everyone there OK? No, nothing's wrong. I just got homesick, I guess.'

In the quiet apartment, the five momentary gods scratched, sniffed, groomed themselves, and nibbled at itchy places while Marianne concluded her conversation. 'Madame hasn't done anything to them,' she said at last. 'Not to Mama, or Papa. Last time — that other time, didn't she do something to them, first?'

'This is a new time,' said the Black Dog in his great, baying voice. 'This is a new time. And in this time, you may wish to put an end to the danger once and for all, Marianne. When you decide what you want to do . . . call on us.'

He turned and walked into the wallpaper. When she turned, the others were gone, Dingo's tail just disappearing into a kitchen cabinet.

When she decided what she wanted to do?

What could she do?

She raised her hand to her forehead, rubbing it, the pendant crystal that Makr Avehl had given her twinkling in the light from her west window. When she woke up, she would really call home.

She lay down on the couch, shutting her eyes. It was only a vision. Overwork. Homesickness. Stress. Reversion to an infantile fantasy life. She breathed deeply, willing herself to go into deep, unconscious sleep. She would wake, and it would be gone — all of it. Only a dreamed up nonsense put

252

together from fairy tales and recollections. The dogs were only her memory of the dogs that had attacked Harvey. The dark woman was only a remake of Disney's Snow White with its evil, hollow-cheeked queen. 'Mirror, mirror on the wall,' she chanted to herself defiantly.

Black Dog stuck his head out of the mirror and said in a stern voice, 'Mockery does not become you, Marianne.'

She turned over on the sofa pillow and wept herself truly asleep.

CHAPTER SIX

When she awoke in the morning, she tried to convince herself it had all been hallucination, brought about by stress, incited by the unpleasant gifts that someone had sent her. Staring at her own face in the mirror, she was unable to decide whether she really believed this or not. Before she went to work, she asked Pat Apple not to accept any more mail that had to be signed for. 'I don't care what it is, Pat. Letter, package, leaflet, registered mail − just don't sign for it. Let them leave me a notice and I'll pick it up. That box you signed for was a nasty joke, and it exploded when I opened it . . .'

'Exploded!' Pat screamed. 'My god, Marianne . . .'

'No damage done. It was all a joke. But it made a rotten smell, and I don't want any more. So, okay?'

'If I had friends who did things like that, they'd get a piece of my mind,' Pat grumbled. 'Honestly. Do I need to fumigate up there or anything? Deodorize?'

'It's all right now. Just don't accept anything else.'

She left feeling both prudent and dissatisfied, as though there were something else she should have done but could not remember. Some precaution in addition to the one she had just taken. What had this vague threat amounted to after all? Someone had played a couple of nasty jokes on her that had evoked her childhood fantasies, that's all. Nothing of any moment. Nothing she wasn't able to deal with — mostly by ignoring it.

And yet, perhaps there was something else she should have done. Something. On her wrist, the crystal bracelet sparkled in the morning light, unregarded. She was too preoccupied to notice it.

The day passed without incident. Friday followed, placid as a summer meadow. The weekend came and went. She did her laundry, went to a movie, told herself she had gotten over it, whatever it had been.

Monday, when she came home from work, there were chalk marks on the walk, looping swirls of yellow and red chalk, vertiginous spirals extending from the gate to the porch. Something inside her lurched, as though some essential organ had turned over, realigning itself into an unaccustomed position. Marianne gritted her teeth and crossed the lines, stepping from space to space in the design as though the marks had been barriers, surprised to find herself doing it without thought, more surprised to feel the wave of sheer terror that washed over her and was as unaccountably gone in the instant.

Pat was on the porch. 'Who's been messing up the sidewalk?' Marianne asked, looking back at the writhing lines, wondering what had just happened.

'Kids playing hopscotch, I suppose,' Pat said vaguely, fanning herself with a magazine. 'Doesn't really look like the hopscotch I remember, but things change. The marks were there about noon when I went out to get the mail. Funny. I did just what you did, walked in the spaces. A holdover from childhood, don't you suppose? It's been so hot today, I've been falling asleep all afternoon.'

Pat still looked half asleep, as though drugged, and her enervation seemed to be catching. It was like yawning, Marianne thought, opening her eyes wide and shaking her head. You see someone yawn, and it makes you yawn. She felt the same energy-draining lassitude Pat seemed to be feeling. It had not been this hot earlier; almost tropical. And

254

wet. The stairs were an endless climb, as though to some precipice.

There were more curiously twisted chalk marks on the upstairs hall floor and one on her apartment door. Some children must have come into the hallway and played around — Pat Apple often left the entry door unlocked. Marianne did not have the energy to rub the design out. Her key turned effortlessly.

The door opened.

Her eyes on the chalk marks, she went through . . .

In Alphenlicht, Makr Avehl sat up in bed, a shout trembling on his lips. There had been a flash, a very vivid flash. Someone knocked on his door.

'Come in, Ellat.'

'Something's happened to her, Makr Avehl.'

'I know. I felt it.'

'What are we going to do?'

'I don't know. I'm going to try to reach her . . .'

'She won't be there.'

'You think not?' He belted a robe around himself, rubbing his face with both hands.

'I know not. The crystal wouldn't have flashed if she were still there. She's been moved. Like last time.'

'Not quite. No. I don't think she consented verbally this time. It's some other variety of Madame's doing. Something more subtle. Oh, by the Gods and the Cave, I really didn't expect anything this soon . . .'

'Makr Avehl.'

'Yes, Ellat.'

'Maybe you shouldn't go after her. Maybe it's meant to end as it ended. She isn't the woman you loved. You admit that.'

He stared at his feet, wondering how he was to tell her, how he was to convince himself. 'Maybe she isn't the woman I loved, Ellat. But the woman I loved is still there.'

'Makr Avehl!'

'It's true. I'd stake my soul on it. She's there. Buried.

255

Unconscious. No. She's sleeping, Ellat. Sleeping and dreaming. Peering out at the world from time to time with wide, blinded, forsaken eyes.'

'You saw?'

'I saw what I thought was my *Marianne*. For an instant, only. Inside this other woman, somewhere.'

'Why? How?'

'I think she made a trade. Her life for Harvey's. She couldn't kill herself, so she just stopped . . . stopped being. No. Stopped expressing her being. She still *is*, but she doesn't give her existence any expression at all. She's just asleep.' He sighed deeply, feeling the familiar anguish that he had felt only weeks before when his *Marianne* had vanished, as suddenly, as cruelly.

'And even if that weren't true, even if Marianne is not the woman I loved at all, still she is in this difficulty at least partly because of what I did or didn't do. In a sense, this is my responsibility.'

'So you're going to go after her anyhow, aren't you?'

He didn't answer. The expression on his face was answer enough.

. . . through the door into her living room. It had a tidal smell to it, an abiding moisture, as though the sweats and steams from the laundry below had permeated the intervening walls and floor, making a swamp of these few rooms. Each evening when she climbed the narrow, dank stairs and opened the splintery door she expected to see crabs scurrying away behind the couch or a stand of cattails waving in the kitchen door. She would not have been amazed to find fish swimming in the kitchen sink or leaping in the tub. The greenish undersea colors of the worn carpet and the walls did nothing to refute this expectation. She was always surprised when she did not float into the place rather than plodding, as now, like an unwilling diver, across the sea floor of living room into a watery cave of kitchen to put the kettle on.

Most of her furniture had been collected from among things left in the laundry over the years. The bed had been found in the big indigo washer one evening after locking up. The green armchair had turned up in a dryer early one morning, though she thought she had checked the machine the night before as she had been told to do. Dishes and cushions appeared frequently, sometimes in the rose machine and sometimes in the green one. Once she had found a roaster and three live chickens in the ivory dryer. She had put the roaster on a high shelf in the kitchen; the three chickens still scratched a meagre living out of the weedy yard behind the laundry, nesting hopefully along the dilapidated board fence. One of them was, or believed itself to be, a rooster and greeted each day with a throaty chuckle that both it and Marianne supposed to be a crow. The cry had more of apologetics than of evangelism about it. On hearing it each morning, Marianne murmured 'pardon me,' as though she had been guilty of some egregious incongruity in harboring such an unsuitable chanticleer.

In addition to the more or less salvageable things found in the machines, there were great quantities of miscellany that she could find no use for. These she hauled out, as best she could, into the rear yard near the alley gate, and the trash men picked them up once each week or, for a sizeable tip, fetched the detritus from the laundry itself. She was always afraid that the tips, though accounted for on petty-cash slips and meticulously itemized, would not be considered accept-able expenses and would be deducted from her already tiny paycheck. Surely they could not expect her − or any one person − to carry the quantities of heavy things that the machines disgorged. Why, only two days ago there had been three sets of elephant harness as well as a crated harmonium and three pictures of the palace!

She had hung the pictures among the others in her office. Pictures of the palace or of the royal family almost covered the office walls, repetitive arrangements of the perpendicular: tall, thin members of the ruling family echoing tall, thin columns of the east portico, further paralleled by tall, thin trees on either side. Marianne could not remember seeing the palace personally, though the laundry must surely have been close to it at some time in the past. Still, she kept the pictures. It seemed less disrespectful than throwing them away. Disrespect was punishable, and she supposed she would start hanging them in the laundry itself when the walls of her office were filled.

The office was a mere cubicle in the rear corner of the laundry, a flimsy box of wallboard with one glass window set into it through which she could watch the customers at the machines and two doors, one leading to the back stairway and one into the laundry itself. That one she could shut when the noise became too overpowering, the sound of surf and whirlpool and tide and storm, a rush and surge and shush-shush of waters, a hum and whirl of air.

As one entered from the usually cobbled street one saw the seven huge machines down the left-hand wall, each labeled as to suggested contents, facing the seven matching dryers on the right-hand wall. Ivory washer opposite ivory dryer. Rose machine opposite rose machine. Great, indigo mechanism looming opposite another, equally monstrous. And on the back wall, the small, specialized machines, palest pink and baby blue and sea green, with their tiny soap dispensers tidily arrayed nearby.

In the center of the room was the spotting table and the table for folding clean laundry and half a dozen hard, molded chairs, reliably uncomfortable. The place was busy enough. No point in encouraging people to sit about by making it inviting.

She put the cash box on the kitchen table with a sense of relief, feeling more tired than usual tonight. It had been a sins day, with half the population of Badigor seeking redemption, and Marianne hadn't had time to sit down since seven this morning. The indigo washer had jammed along about noon, losing at least a dozen citizens in the process. They might show up again, or they might not. With Marianne's luck, she thought dismally, they'd show up in one of the dryers in the middle of the night and wake her up with their pounding and gargled cries for release.

The apartment looked strange to her, too, as it did sometimes.

As though she hadn't really seen it before, wasn't familiar with it, didn't belong in it. As though when she opened the door she should have been somewhere else. Somewhere drier, she thought, closing her eyes and visualizing it. A place where things didn't rust or mildew immediately. A place with a fireplace and light coming in through the windows instead of this constant, deadly fog. The thought of the fog made her think of being lost, and this brought her alert in a sudden panic.

She hadn't bought her map for tomorrow!

She stood up, mouth open in an expression of unconscious anxiety, hands twisting together. Usually she bought the map at noon, at a news vendor's kiosk. There was always a news vendor's kiosk somewhere within three or four blocks. Today she hadn't had time to go out to lunch, and she had forgotten it until this moment.

She fought panic by checking her watch, noting that she had at least fifteen minutes before the kiosk would close for the night. If she didn't get the map there, the nearest place would be the all-night restaurant at the corner of — there, she'd forgotten already. She'd need today's map in order to find either location.

She grabbed up the map and peered at it as she ran down the stairs, down the aisle between the monstrous, silent machines, their doors agape like snoring mouths, and out the door, stopping under the street light to find the nearest kiosk. There was one, just three blocks away!

She hurried, half running, paying little attention to her surroundings. At one time, she seemed to recall, she had spent hours just walking, entertaining herself with speculation about the strange houses and buildings and with the odd juxtapositions she discovered — infant nursery beside slaughterhouse; twin brothels flanking a church; doctors and apothecaries adjacent to mortuaries; a manufacturer of ear plugs next to a teacher of music. She seemed to remember that she had laughed at these arrangements once, with genuine amusement. No longer. She could not imagine what had made her think them laughable. Humor resulted from surprise, and

259

the combinations she had found were not novel, not even unusual. If she had found them funny, it meant there was something wrong with her, something different, something that didn't fit in. It was almost as though she had come from some other world in which such neighbors were unlikely. This idea had popped into her head unbidden, frightening her badly. The Map Police were known to seek out strangers, people who didn't fit in. She did not wish to be sought out, so she had stopped looking for weird combinations, stopped noticing the buildings she passed except for ones marking her progress toward her infrequent destinations. It was better just to stick to one's own obligatory business: a trip to a kiosk once a day to buy a map, a trip to take the laundry receipts to a bank and to shop at a grocery once every ten days, a trip to whatever temple or shrine was nearby on the infrequently declared holidays.

People who used the laundry sometimes talked of keeping in touch with friends or relatives. On holidays, they would meet in a previously agreed upon park. Or they would select a certain restaurant and gather there.

'I wanted to celebrate Mother's birthday,' one woman had said plaintively over her crocheting. 'But how would anyone know when it was?'

Marianne found herself wondering what a birthday was. Some kind of holiday she didn't know about. She, herself, had never known anyone well enough to meet them on a holiday. Whenever a holiday was announced, she would make her obligatory trip to the temple or shrine or church and then come back to the apartment over the laundry. She had no relatives. At least, she supposed she had none. Surely she would know if she had, she thought, hurrying along the empty street. It was the kind of thing a person ought to know.

The kiosk was in the middle of the block. The vendor had his back to her and was lowering the shutter as she approached. 'Tomorrow's map, please,' she called, her voice bouncing shrilly between buildings, a dwindling flutter of retreating sound. 'I'm sorry I'm so late.'

'So late is too late,' he grumbled, turning his lumpy face

toward her, the eroded skin circling a red, pendulous nose that swayed slightly as he turned. 'All sold out.'

'Oh, no!' she cried. 'You can't be.'

'Can't, can't I? Oh, yes I can. I say out, I mean I haven't got any. Except one for me. Now, if you'd like to share it?' He leaned toward her, one hand out as though to touch her, his face twisted into a suggestive leer. She turned away, keeping her face quiet, trying to be dignified about it. No doubt he meant what he said; he'd share if she'd come home with him, and it would be legal to do so. Cohabitors could share maps. Mothers and children. Married couples. Lovers. She shuddered in revulsion at the idea of sharing anything with the vendor who stood watching her, his nose twitching. Before he could say anything more, she moved away, fumbling with the map, which resisted being unfolded, almost as though it were a living thing with a natural resentment at being disturbed.

She had circled the laundry with red pencil, almost at the edge of the map, far from its important, stable center. From there she traced her way to the kiosk where she was now, then searched for the nearest location marked with a spoon and a large, red '24.' There were two twenty-four-hour restaurants within reasonable traveling distance. The street she was on ran directly toward one of them, then circled away at a narrow alley labeled 'Mock Street.' If she could catch a number twenty-seven bus — the number clearly marked on the map — and get off at Mock Street, it would be a walk of only a few blocks.

She went directly to the bus stop, ignoring whatever it was the vendor shouted after her, checking carefully to be sure the number twenty-seven stopped at this particular place. It was a favorite trick of the mappers to have busses halt at only every third or fourth stop, letting the people in between stand helplessly as the bus rumbled by, clattering over cobbles or sections of trolley track that led nowhere but seemed always to crop up in three or four block-long sections. This stop was scheduled for number twenty-seven busses at twenty-minute intervals.

What was scheduled had no connection with what actually happened. No bus arrived. She jittered, moving to and fro on the pavement. There was a vengeance booth on the corner, and the vendor leaned from behind her counter to solicit Marianne's business. 'Fine, fresh vengeance fish,' she called. 'Caught just this morning and spell cast before it was dead. Name it for your enemy and let him eat it. Stop his heart, stop his mind, stop his life, lady?'

'I don't have any enemies,' Marianne called softly. 'I don't need a fish, thank you.'

'No enemies? Think of that. Here in this city, and she says she has no enemies?' The woman cackled with laughter and closed the booth front. When Marianne looked up a moment later, she had gone, and Marianne sighed with relief. Sometimes the vendors were very persistent. Twice or three times, she had bought things that she didn't want, carried them home with her, and then had to put them out for the trash men. There had been a set of thumb screws, she remembered. And a whip braided out of human hair with little sharp bones set in it. Things that made her squirm with revulsion when she looked at them. She sighed, turning to stare down the street in the direction the bus should come from.

When forty-five minutes had passed, however, none had arrived. She counseled herself sternly not to start walking. As soon as she did, particularly if she were in between widely separated stops, the bus would come and pass her by. She checked her watch. Eight o'clock. Plenty of time. It was only a half-hour ride, and the streets would not shift until midnight. Eleven at the earliest. Or ten-thirty. Plenty of time.

She shifted from foot to foot, staring down the street, uttering silent invocations. 'Bus, good bus, come on, bus.'

At eight-thirty, she began to worry. If she started now, she could reach the all-night restaurant by walking. If she waited too long, it would be impossible to reach it at all. Good sense warred with her weariness. She didn't want to make the long walk.

'You have to,' she told herself. 'You have to.'

She turned and strode down the street, checking her progress against the map at every crossing. It would be a walk of some sixty blocks. About five miles. She could be there well before shift time.

A number twenty-seven bus passed her by and stopped two blocks down the street. She began to run, senselessly, knowing it wouldn't wait.

It pulled out just as she came close enough to touch the rear of it. A man who was passing shook his head and murmured, 'Tough luck. Why don't you just wait for the next one?'

She checked her watch. Nine o'clock. There wasn't time to wait. She lowered her head and kept walking. Another twenty-seven bus went by. She let it go. She had a hard, burning pain in her side and could not possibly run again. The pain in her side moved downward, slowly, first into her hip and then into her right knee and shin. The door of the orange dryer had fallen open and bruised her there. The half-healed muscle still hurt, more and more the farther she walked.

There were infrequent passersby. Sometimes people looked each other full in the face, as though searching for a face they knew. Other times, they ducked their heads and scurried past, as though afraid to encounter either an acquaintance or a stranger. Marianne, on her infrequent forays from the laundry, tried to take her cue from those she passed, but tonight she was too tired to care. She stared at her feet as people went by, praying they would not say anything to delay her.

By ten o'clock she had reached Mock Street. The all-night restaurant was now only a dozen blocks away, but the street she was on turned into a massive concrete overpass, soaring above the surrounding area. The next street over dived down, as though into a tunnel, and did not emerge again for blocks. There were half a dozen access ramps circling up and over, down and under, allowing access to every street except the one she needed. She puzzled at them, plotting her route. If she went down Mock Street one block then turned left she would come to an underpass that would take her under a highway and bring her within two blocks of the restaurant.

She trudged on. The street lights in this part of town threw puddles of dim, dun-yellow light onto the pavement and reflected a furtive glow into alleys and along the curbs, hiding as much as it disclosed. She stopped momentarily, thinking what might be hiding in those alleys. There were stories about bears living in alleys and crocodiles in the sewers under the street. And there were mapless gangs, not storied but real, ever-changing tribes of non-locus aberrants who preyed upon single pedestrians.

The underpass before her was not lighted at all except by a grayish shine at the far end, a perfect location for ambush. She dithered, trying to see if anything lurked against the distant glow, plunging into the semi-darkness at last in an almost fatalistic fit of panic. She got to the center of it, the deepest part, buffeted to the far edge of the sidewalk by gusts kicked up by passing trucks, when there was a shudder, a gelatinous shiver.

'No,' she said. 'No.' It had only been the vibration of the heavy trucks, she told herself. It couldn't have been the changeover. It was far too early.

The tunnel seemed endless. When she emerged, the street sign nearest her said 'Willis Boulevard.' She turned to her map, only to see it shrivel in her hands and fall to the side-walk in bits of ash, twisting in the light wind, disappearing around an anonymous corner. She stood at an intersection with featureless walls looming around her. A loudspeaker on the lamppost bellowed white noise at her, then muttered, 'Welcome to the City of Trallis.'

'Oh, God, no,' she moaned. 'God, please, no.'

The map she had used was obsolete. There was no more Badigor. She was too late. Now she could not buy a map that would tell her where anything was today. It was illegal — perhaps impossible — to sell anyone a map of today. Only tomorrow's maps would be available. It was illegal — or impossible — for anyone to share a map with her. She would be unable to find anything except by chance. And if she did not chance upon a map vendor, then the day after today would be even further lost.

She had had nightmares about this, as she imagined most of the people of the city did, though many would not admit doing so. She had considered what she would do if ever she found herself without a map. The one thing she had resolved upon was that she would kill herself before she would join the mapless ones with her name tattooed on her face and her hair dyed green.

'Search,' she told herself. 'I've got to search.'

'Sleep,' some interior voice demanded. 'You've got to sleep, first.'

She couldn't sleep on the street. She had money in her money belt, plus what was in her wallet. Only idiots went anywhere without money. She could find somewhere to sleep. Perhaps a hotel.

Something.

She began to walk. There were few signs on the buildings, and it would not have mattered if there were more or fewer. Juxtaposition meant nothing. The large blue building with the carved cornerstone — 'Wilkins Building, July 16, 1917' — might have stood next to the red stone building yesterday, as it did today, or it might have stood halfway across the district. Only the map and the directory could have told her. If one knew the name of the building, one could look it up in the directory, find the coordinates on the map, then find the building itself. If one didn't know the name of the building or have a map — then one was lost.

'Lost,' she whispered to herself. 'Lord, I'm lost.'

This block was lined with four- and five-story, narrow fronted apartment houses with ornate, Italianate cornices. From high above her the sound of a radio whined into darkness and a white curtain flapped from a dark window, a ghost making a futile attempt at escape. At the end of the block she turned one block left along a muddy path beside a dairy farm, then resumed her original direction. This was a warehouse area, lined with featureless walls and locked entries fronted with iron grates. Sometimes glassy doors showed a light from one back room filtering through to the street in a pallid, fungoid glow.

She moved left another block, a boardwalk past two gambling houses, then onto a tesselated pavement outside the townhouse of some grandee. At the corner, a neon sign identified a drugstore. She went in, searching fruitlessly for the symbol that would have identified the place as a map vendor. None. There was hot coffee, however, and a sweet, sticky doughnut, sustenance for the search. She went out again, noting in passing that she stood at the corner of Bruce and RP4. She walked down Bruce, crossing Eleanor and 5V and Shimstacks. Halfway down the block she entered a place that looked slightly like a hotel but turned out to be a brothel. Redfaced, she returned to the street.

'Quittin' early, sweetheart?' asked a constable, burly in his codpiece and high-laced sandals. He was loud enough to attract the attention of passersby.

'I thought it was a hotel,' she said without thinking.

'No map, eh? Move it, girly. No loitering.' He stood looking after her, slapping his riot gun into one beefy palm, a sneer on his face that she could feel through her light jacket. 'You should've applied for a job,' he yelled after her as she turned the corner. 'Then you'd know where you are!' Through the furious pounding of her blood in her ears, she could hear his laughter halfway down the next block, joined by that of the sycophants on the street corner.

Police persecuted non-locus people as legitimate prey. They harrassed people whose eyes were bad, as well, people who had trouble reading the maps. Or even foreigners who had trouble with the language. So far as the police were concerned, ignorance of the map was no excuse. She trudged on, leaving the dirty laughter behind.

She no longer tried to make an orderly search pattern. In order to avoid making circles, she turned alternately right and left, without any particular system. When she was so tired she could scarcely drag one foot in front of another, the street lights went off and she found herself in front of an all-night diner. She stared at the door for long, unconscious minutes before recognizing the red '24' painted on the glass. A map vendor.

She ordered coffee, went into the rest room and took enough money from her belt to pay for tomorrow's map, cursing in futile anger when she caught the crystal in her bracelet on the belt and could not get loose for long moments. 'Get rid of that bracelet,' she told herself in an unfamiliar voice. 'It's always catching on things.' As she was about to unclasp it and throw it away, however, someone came into the rest room and distracted her. Getting tomorrow's map was the important thing, she reminded herself. It would not help her today, but at the next shift, she would be able to find her way home.

'Gettin' it early, eh,' the counterman said as he handed her the map. 'Always smart to have your map early. Glad to see you, too. Didn't think I'd have any business today. Hate it when I end up surrounded by warehouses this way. At least, I guess they're warehouses. Just bad for business.'

'I suppose it would be better in the theatre district,' Marianne remarked. 'People staying out late.'

He nodded judiciously. 'That's a nice idea, a theatre district. Don't know I've ever seen a theatre district, if you mean a place where the theatres sort of cluster. Not much clustering any more. Lately it seems like every shift scatters things out more and more. I was surprised to see all these warehouses near each other this way when I came down to work this morning, to tell you the truth. Where I was yesterday, there was an aristocrat's mansion on one side of me and a junkyard on the other, and down the side streets was an amusement park and three office buildings. The noble had his screen up all day. Didn't blame him, either. That roller coaster practically ended up in my back booth.'

Marianne said something innocuous and noncommital.

'You on your way to work?'

She nodded, putting down coins to pay for the coffee, saying thank you, going out the door into the light of day with no idea where she was.

No one would be there to open the laundry. It might be all right. Business would be light on the day after sin day. Her legs felt like lead weights. She could not possibly lift them to walk another step. She had to find someplace she could sit, someplace she could stay until the next shift. A movie theatre. A park. No one would bother her in either place . . .

She walked slowly, pausing frequently to rest, leaning against fences, perching briefly on window sills while she pretended to take nonexistent stones out of her shoes. Shadows moved from one side of things to the other. She came to a botanical garden, which made her think of benches. After a moment's consideration, she paid the small fee to enter and moved among the scanty viewers along the sandy walks.

There was a grove of snatch trees set behind high fences with warning posters every few feet. Just past the snatch trees, a shallow lagoon was bordered with wide-mouthed maneaters, the ground littered with bones and the air thick with attractant scent. A weary-looking woman leaned pensively upon the protective wall, watching silently as the two oldest of her five screaming children teetered atop it. When they dropped safely to the ground beside her, she sighed, smiled apologetically at Marianne, and moved away toward the panther bushes where the barricades were in worse repair.

Beyond the homovores was a vegetable exhibition; beyond that a formal garden and reflecting pool; and beyond that an Oriental garden with a curved bridge over a chuckling stream and a miniature teahouse perched high upon a rock. People turned and moved curiously toward sounds of tragedy from the vicinity of the panther bushes. In moments Marianne was alone. The teahouse seemed to smile down at her from its perch. Without thought, she stepped across the bridge, climbed through the shrubbery and into the little structure, like a child into her own dollhouse. It was only six feet across. She lay down, stretched along one wall, hidden from any passerby. Immediately, she slept, curled like a cat, shivering, but oblivious to the outside world.

When she woke, it was almost dusk. She could not remember where she was. She should have been in her apartment. 'Pat,' she said. 'This room is ridiculously small for the rent I pay.' The words left no echo. They were forgotten as she spoke them. When she struggled out of the tiny house and across the bridge once more, the gates around the Oriental garden were closed and locked, six feet of close chain link with barbed wire at the top, both fence and wire red with rust but quite sound, for all that. She cried soundlessly as she walked back to the bridge, returning there because it would give her a sense of familiarity, however spurious. She sat for a time on the teahouse steps, watching the shadows grow thick among the carefully trimmed evergreens, listening to the lilt of water under the curved bridges. There was a boar scarer in the pool, a length of bamboo that filled with water, became overbalanced to spill the water out, then tipped back to let its momentarily empty length fall with an echoing blow onto a river-rounded stone. She had not noticed the sound in the afternoon among the chatter of sightseers and the cries of children. Now it seemed a drumbeat, slightly too slow to anticipate, coming each time as a surprise, like a hostile blow or shout.

She wept angrily. What good did it do to have tomorrow's map if one was locked up . . . though the gates would be unlocked fairly early in the morning. Perhaps. One couldn't be sure of that. Tomorrow might be declared a holiday, and nothing would be unlocked.

'Stop this,' she told herself. 'Don't just sit here. Find a way out!'

She began to wander, aimlessly, down across the high-backed bridges, toward the back of the garden where a fence of bamboo stood behind low evergreens and flowering shrubs. There was an unlocked gate. Behind it, she found a shed with loose boards making up the back wall of the gardens. She slipped through into a trash-filled yard only half a block from an evening world of restaurants and theatres.

She was sitting in one of the restaurants, finishing a third cup of coffee when the shift came. It was a soundless vibration, as though the world had been made of gelatine and was shaken, very slightly, making the outlines of everything quiver in semi-liquid confusion. All around her, silence fell, people looked at one another from the corners of their eyes, waiting for any sign that someone in the room might be non-locus. 'Welcome,' blared the loudspeakers, 'to the City of Bimbarnlegume.' Waiters began brushing up the scattered fragments of yesterday's maps; conversation resumed, people fished out their maps of today, plotting their way home or to whatever late evening diversion they had planned. The restaurant was called Chez Mazarin. She found it on the map. The Clean Machine was only one block away, much nearer the center of the map than yesterday — no, the day before.

Her lips trembled. It had been only one day, one change to be homeless, but it seemed much longer. If, indeed, she was not homeless still. Someone might have replaced her. Sometimes they did that. Fighting tears she stopped only briefly at the counter to pay her bill and to buy tomorrow's map before making her way home.

Inside the laundry, she opened all the machines, as she did every evening before going up the stairs. She would not have been surprised to find a note in her apartment telling her she was fired, or even to find someone else in her place, but all was as she had left it. She put the maps on the table by the door and fell into bed, grateful for the dank dampness of the sheets that told her she was in a place that she knew.

CHAPTER SEVEN

Her alarm went off as it always did, too early. The sheets were warm and dry from her body heat. Morning sleep was precious, and she had been dreaming of that other place, that other apartment. A strange dream that seemed to make that place more familiar than this one. She huddled in the bed, half sitting up, the blankets drawn about her neck. The alarm went off again, and she cursed, bitterly but briefly. The dream had left her. She could remember nothing about it. Staggering to the bathroom, she washed her face, surprised that it looked so familiar to her. It should have been another face, with darker hair, darker eyes, a different name.

A different name? She tried, very briefly, to remember her name. Marianne something, she thought. She had it written down somewhere. While she fixed her morning eggs, she tried to remember where, but could not bring it to mind. Sighing, she put the single dish and fork into the sink, running water over them but not taking time to wash them. She had to get the machines cleaned out before the first customers arrived.

At the bottom of the stairs she paused, listening. Sometimes there were living things in the machines, and in that case emptying them could be difficult. There were no rustling or thumping noises. Encouraged, she began at the end of the row, unlatching and opening the doors that she had unlatched and opened the night before.

The indigo machine was empty. So was the green one. When she moved toward the rose washer, she heard a peculiar sound, a high-pitched whining. When the door was opened, she saw a litter of puppies lying on a pile of miscellaneous laundry. Five of them, each a different color and shape, three males, two females, all of about the same age. They half crawled, half fell out of the machine to wobble about on infant legs, tugging at her trousers and whining to be fed. She brought a bottle of milk from her apartment as well as some bread and meat scraps that all five tore at with tiny teeth, growling as they tugged and fought for possession of the best pieces. They seemed to be housebroken already, barking in treble voices to be let out. She thought of taking them to the dog pound. Surely there was a dog pound? And if there were? It could mean a half block walk or an interminable journey.

She surprised herself by finding the nearest grocery, instead, and buying a large sack of puppy kibble, wondering why she was doing it, admitting to herself at last that she was lonely. She could not remember having had that thought before, and it astonished her with its obviousness. Of course she was lonely. Why hadn't she realized that in the past? Perhaps it had been yesterday's unpleasant adventure, wandering quite alone as she had. For whatever reason, she welcomed the pups and made them a bed of a violet chenille bedspread and a bright pink tablecloth in an old fruit crate near the back door. She propped the door ajar so they could get into the weedy backyard to do their business.

She named them for their colors. Rouge, Liquorice, and Delphinium − Delphy for short − were the red, black, and blue pups. Silver and Gold were the silver-gray and yellow ones. 'You can stay, at least temporarily,' she told them. 'And those names will do until something of your character becomes clear to me. Then I'll give you new names.' She did not know where this thought came from, either. The names she had given them were adequate. Why should they need or expect new ones? Why should she?

'You need friends,' something inside her spoke. 'You have no friends.'

She laughed. Who could have friends in this world of changing locations? Unless someone actually lived with you, in the same house, one day's neighbor could become another day's foreigner, adrift in some remote suburb.

When she closed the laundry to go for tomorrow's map, the puppies barked behind her, demandingly, then trailed at her heels in an untidy kite's tail of staggering doglets as she walked them three blocks to the kiosk and back.

'There's no excuse for not getting one's map,' she confided. 'There's always a kiosk within six blocks. It's arranged that way. If one doesn't get a map, it's because one is simply too scatterbrained.'

'Or ill,' her mind suggested with a discomforting and unusual percipience. 'Or busy, or unconscious, or held prisoner, or crippled, or old, or drunk, or not very bright.'

'Too scatterbrained,' she said firmly. 'We have ours, don't we?'

There was scattered agreement from five small throats. Already she was beginning to see differences among them. Liquorice was going to be smooth-haired and large − he had huge feet. Rouge was going to be fluffy. The tips of his ears barely showed above his puff of fur, and he had a tightly curled tail. The yellow female tended to be a slinker, a peerer from corners and under chairs, with curious and suspicious

272

brown eyes. The blue-gray one was afraid of nothing, and would have fur as sleek as lizard skin. The silver-gray one was quiet and thoughtful. She had this habit of looking wisely at Marianne, without blinking.

'I have no idea why they run things this way,' she told the puppy, sure she had asked a question about the city of Varnatur. 'It's always been this way.'

Though Marianne seemed to remember a place where things had stayed the same. Oh, the joyous recognition of a place like that. To see the same faces, the same places. To know them! Not always to be among strange places and people.

It was an aberrant thought. One she might be punished for, if anyone found out.

'The Map Police could find out,' she told the puppies. 'They really could. They know things about people. Sometimes they come into the laundry and arrest people. For the things they're trying to clean, you know?'

Silver looked at her with complete understanding, as though she knew all too well.

Usually in the evening, Marianne watched the television. There were always three music programs, two drama programs, and the obligatory palace broadcast, in no consistent order. There was also the half-hour lost-and-found program, which she always watched with complete attention. It wasn't the mappers' fault: every program started with a disclaimer by the map commission, but sometimes things got disconnected. Children from their parents. Husbands and wives. Parts of houses. Belongings.

First there was a fanfare. Then the disclaimer, read by the High Commissioner. Then the brief announcements, sometimes with pictures. 'Reward offered for the return of our beloved son, Roger Erickson, age three, lost during the last changeover.' Name of family, name of house. Marianne wrote it down. She always wrote the locations down. Who knew? She might find one of them. Picture of Roger. Fat. Dimpled. Not very bright looking.

'Not very bright looking,' said Marianne.

'Woof,' agreed Rouge.

273

'Reward offered for the location of our kitchen and servants' quarters, inadvertently misplaced during the last changeover.' Name of house. Floor plan of kitchen, as though that made any difference. 'If you found a kitchen attached to your house and it didn't belong there,' Marianne remarked, 'you'd call them, wouldn't you? Why show us the floor plan?'

Gold panted briefly, licked a paw, then returned her liquid brown gaze to Marianne's face.

'Reward offered for a set of five things taken from the palace,' the announcer intoned. 'Purposefully detached, not lost during changeover. All citizens are encouraged to keep their eyes open for five things that may have been stolen from the palace. Five similar things.'

Silver growled deep in her throat. Rouge laughed. Delphy tried to catch his tail. Gold and Liquorice were playing tag around the legs of a chair.

'No,' Marianne said, looking at them. 'Puppies aren't things. The announcement said five things.'

'Not many things come in fives,' her mind said.

'No,' she said again. 'Puppies aren't things. It couldn't be.'

CHAPTER EIGHT

Today's city was Brandton-Minor. Marianne checked the map over her morning coffee. The palace was at the center of the map, as it always was. Other things moved; the palace did not. Not the palace and not the Bureau of Maps. The Clean Machine had continued its slow approach and was now within six blocks of it. 'We'll probably never be this close again,' she told the pups. 'We can go see the palace this evening. After work. I'll get tomorrow's map at noon, and that'll leave plenty of time.' It seemed likely that palace viewing would need an hour or more. The television often showed endless

274

streams of pedestrians and bus passengers on their way to or from the palace.

When she set out, the puppies in a straggling tail at her heels, the streets were full of people headed in the same direction. Marianne followed along, part of the human procession, smiling, nodding, exchanging a few words. Today she was tempted to look for someone recognizable. Someone she might have seen before. Marianne played this game seldom and saw anyone she recognized less often yet, but she frequently met the same half-curious, half-searching glances she knew was on her own face.

The block nearest the palace fence was very crowded. The puppies whined. Marianne picked them up and put them in the large canvas bag she was carrying. Their heads poked above the top, peering curiously at the crowd.

People worked their way to the fence, stood there staring for a time, then departed. Those at the back of the crowd were gradually shifted forward. When Marianne's time at the fence came, she stared no less curiously than the rest. There was the sloping lawn, the two vast fountain basins to left and right, the slender pillars supporting the roof of the portico, the rows of flimsy trees. A line of black-clad guardsmen stood motionlessly upon the stairs. A gardener worked on his knees beside one of the fountains.

One of the puppies whined, briefly, and there was a small convulsion in the canvas bag. Marianne looked down to see the bag almost empty. Only Rouge and Liquorice stared up at her, their tongues out. The others had jumped out and run off. Somewhere.

'Cute pups,' someone said.

She looked through the fence into the eyes of a guardsman, his face immobile, as though carved from some dark stone. One hand held a leash from which a dog leaned toward the fence, straining, teeth exposed in an eager, hungry dog smile. 'I will bite you if I get a chance,' the smile said. 'They will reward me if I do it well.'

'How many of them do you have?' the guardsman asked in a significant voice.

She started to say, 'Five,' then choked the word off as Rouge barked a treble puppy bark and nipped at Liquorice's ear. 'This is Rouge,' Marianne said weakly. 'This is Liquorice.'

He nodded, moving off down the row of spectators. At the far, right-hand corner of the palace was a low tower, crowned with a row of arched and curtained windows. One of the curtains twitched as though someone had been standing behind it, watching.

Marianne turned away. She wanted to look for Gold and Silver and Delphy, but something told her it would be dangerously foolish to do so just now. The place felt like the streets did just before change, shivering with purpose. Something impended. She hurried away through the crowd, slowing as it thinned in order not to draw attention to herself.

There were only a few blocks to traverse, back to the laundry. As she turned the last corner, she noted half consciously that the street was empty, an unusual thing for this time of night. It was not until she had come halfway from the corner, however, that they stepped out of an alley and came toward her.

Their hair was stiffened into spikes and dyed in shades of bright green or purple or blue. Their faces were painted. She stopped where she was, thought of running, knew it would do no good. Her money belt was at home. They would take her wallet, but she could spare that. If that was all they took . . .

'Hey, mama,' the largest of them said. His voice was silky, insinuating, a rapist's voice. 'Hey, lady. Hey, you. Where you goin'?'

It would do no good to talk. Talking would only make it worse. If she could stay on the street, likely they would not kill her. The Map Police did not like people being killed on the street. She was silent, quiet, holding her bag across her chest like a shield.

His name was written on his forehead in blue ink. Ironballs. Fanning out behind him were Blueshit and Wrecker, their names tattooed above the brows in purple and red, and a huge, muscular woman with her name on both cheeks, Brasstits. Her gilded nipples thrust through holes in a leather vest.

Rouge whined, pawed at the edge of the sack, overbalanced and dropped to the sidewalk with an abrupt half-bark of surprise.

'Hey, she's got puppies,' said the woman in a narrow, nasal voice which was so surprised it was for the moment nonthreatening. 'Pups!'

'His name is Rouge,' Marianne found the voice to say. 'The other one is Liquorice.'

'Where'd you get 'em?' Ironballs asked in a mild tone.

'I guess they were abandoned,' she said, trying to keep her voice from trembling. 'I found them.'

'In a alley, huh?' he said, almost sympathetically. She did not correct him. She didn't want them to know where she lived, or worked. She merely nodded, not moving. Liquorice tried to climb out of the bag and she set him down beside Rouge.

'We could eat 'em,' offered Blueshit. 'I ate dog once.'

'You'd eat shit,' Brasstits offered mildly. 'You'd cut off your mother's tit and eat that. Trouble with you, Blue, is you got no discrimination.'

Rouge, moving with unpuppylike speed, darted toward the alley entrance from which the mapless ones had emerged. With a shout, half of amusement, half of challenge, Brasstits turned and pursued him, Blueshit and Wrecker close behind, whooping with glee. Ironballs stayed where he was, eyeing Marianne as though he planned to butcher her for the pot. 'What you got good, Mama? Got money? Love or money, which? Huh? Maybe both?' He raped her with his eyes, an anticipatory revel.

Liquorice barked briefly, lifted his infant leg and peed on the man's boots. Ironballs let out a yell of rage and snatched at the pup who darted just out of reach, toward the alley.

'Go home,' said a voice in Marianne's ear. 'Go home, fast.'

Ironballs was chasing Liquorice; the others of the gang were chasing Rouge. For the moment, none of them was watching her. Marianne got into the laundry and double-locked the door, then stood in the dark, watching the street through a crack in the shutter.

A sound drew her attention from the window. All five of the pups were sitting behind her in a line, watching her watching the street. Rouge and Liquorice had somehow rejoined the others.

Out in the street, the four mapless ones emerged from the alley once more to stare up and down the street, waving their arms and cursing one another loudly for the loss of their prey.

'Thank you,' said Marianne.

'You're welcome,' said the voice in her mind.

She looked into Gold's eyes, seeing something there of comprehension. 'You said that?' she challenged.

'Woof,' Gold replied in a puppyish treble, licking her front paw. 'Woof.'

The following morning, the Clean Machine was only a block from the palace. Marianne felt this was uncomfortably close. Too near the center of things. Early in the morning people started flowing toward the palace grounds; all day the crowds pushed to and fro, ripple-mobs of people ebbing and flowing. Her first customer of the day was a talkative old man with a cane. He had an ancient curve-topped trunk to be laundered.

'Got to frettin' me,' he said, counting out the coins that the chart gave as the correct charge for luggage − one piece, footlocker or larger. 'Don't know what might be in there. All kinds of memories, most likely. Things I don't want to rake up. Thought I'd launder it first.' He peered curiously about him, inspecting every corner of the place, taking a tottery step or two to look into Marianne's little office, committing it to memory. The eyes he turned on her were keen and youthful in the wrinkled face.

'We're very glad to take care of it for you,' Marianne murmured, maneuvering her loading cart through the door to the curb where the bus driver had dropped the trunk. 'We'll just put it here for the indigo washer as soon as this cycle's complete.'

'People in there?' he asked as she reentered with the trunk. 'Seem to hear them yellin' about somethin'.'

'No,' she answered absentmindedly. 'As a matter of fact, that's a mixed load. Two parrots from the pet store down the block and a set of encyclopedias. A mother brought the books in. Before she gives them to her children.'

'Ah,' he nodded wisely. 'Stuff she doesn't want the kiddy widdles to know, most likely. My ma was the same way. We knew all about it from the kids at school and watchin' the farm animals, but she'd have it we was innocent as daisies. Well. Mamas are like that.'

'Are they?' Matianne asked. It was one of those bits of conversation that annoyed her, often keeping her awake at night. Were mamas like that? How did he know? And if he knew, why didn't she?

'Most of 'em,' he confided, sitting down on one of the uncomfortable chairs and pulling a folded newspaper from his pocket. 'Says here there's going to be rain this summer.'

'Is there?'

'Yep. Says so here. Says the royal family's goin' on a tour. Foreign parts. The Queen and the Duke of Eyes.'

This was another thing that annoyed her. Foreign parts. Other places. Where? Why had she never thought of going? Why had she never met anyone who had gone? And who was the Duke of Eyes? His picture was not in any of the royal portraits she had hung in the office. Queen, King, the Jack of Japes, Lady Ten. No Duke at all.

The buzzer on the indigo washer went off with an ear-shattering shriek. Marianne shut it off hastily and opened the door. The two parrots emerged, damp and disheveled, to perch on the dryer door and complain to her. There seemed to be nothing left of the set of encyclopedias.

'Thought that'd happen,' the old man said, rising to help her get the trunk into the machine. 'That's the trouble with things in writin'. Sometimes you take one little word away and the whole thing falls apart. Ever notice that?'

Marianne thrust the trunk into the machine, set the dials, and turned purposefully toward the parrots. They, meantime, had flown up to one of the light fixtures and regarded her with disfavor from that lofty height.

'Quite dry enough, thank you,' one of them offered. 'As is my friend.'

'You're dripping all over the floor,' Marianne observed.

'As would you,' said the other parrot, regarding her warily, 'if you had been forcibly immersed in that monster. I want to say something but can't remember what.'

'That's what the laundering was for,' the first parrot reminded him. 'Language.'

'I'd forgotten,' said the second. 'Isn't that astonishing. 'Well, though I seem to be unable to remember the proper words, whatever vile and insulting language best suits the occasion, Miss, consider it said.' He began to preen himself with ostentatious fervor as Marianne and the old man watched, eyes wide.

'Thought I'd walk over and see the palace,' the old man observed, 'while that washes.'

'Feel free to do so,' she remarked absently. 'I'll put it in the dryer for you.' Silver had come into the room and appeared to be in silent conversation with the parrots, a colloquy of gesture, paw taps, wing shrugs, head twistings. As the old man left, the pet shop woman came to fetch her birds, a cage in either hand, and as she left a guardsman entered, his shiny little eyes peering into every corner of the room.

'Name?' he asked, flipping open a notebook.

'The Clean Machine,' she said, mouth open in astonishment. There had never been a guardsman in the laundry before.

'No, lovey, your name.'

'Marianne,' she replied. 'Just Marianne.'

'Well, Just Marianne, this is a routine procedure. Each day we investigate all premises within three blocks of the palace. Lookin' for anarchists and revolutionaries, so they tell us, not that we've ever found any. Found a nest of revisionists once, but nobody cared.'

'What were they revising?' she asked, truly curious.

'Don't know. Didn't ask 'em. Now. This is a cleaning establishment, right? You the proprietor?'

'No,' she admitted. 'I'm only the manager.'

'Live on the premises?'

'There's an apartment upstairs.'

'Married? Cohabiting? Children?'

'No.' She started to mention the dogs, but then was quite unaccountably silent.

'Where were you yesterday?'

'About six blocks away,' she admitted. 'I went to look at the palace after closing time.'

'Quite a sight, isn't it?'

No, she thought, even as her head nodded polite agreement. It wasn't much of a sight, really. There hadn't been that much to see. She didn't say it. He wrote busily in his book for a moment, starting as the buzzer on the indigo machine went off.

'What in hell!'

'It's just the machine,' she explained. 'Excuse me. I have to take the trunk out.' But when she opened the machine, she could not take the trunk out. It had vanished, in that unaccountable way in which things intended for cleaning sometimes did vanish, as though they were held together by dirt, by a kind of ephemeral filth that could be dismissed by water and soap. Of course, things sometimes reappeared, as well. Reconstituted, one might say. She stared into the washer, waiting for the trunk to emerge. In its place were five velvet cushions, sodden and steaming, a gemmed crown on each, glittering like malignant octopus eyes from a water cave.

'Aha,' said the guardsman. 'Got you.'

The cell in which they left her was not uncomfortable. There was a cot, a toilet, a basin, a glass for drinking water, even a screen so she could use the facilities without undue display to anyone peering in through the little grated window. The room was reasonably warm, and it was dry. On a table by the heavy door, barred with iron and studded with thick nails of gleaming bronze, the five crowns huddled like socialites in a drunk tank, making a fierce show of quality to cow whomever was responsible for the outrage.

Marianne was no longer looking at them. She had looked, for a time, trying to remember if she had indeed stolen any such thing, for this is what she was accused of. She had tried to explain to the guardsman that the crowns were not unlike the elephant harness or the double bed, having arrived in some similar and as unexplainable a fashion, but he had been unwilling to entertain any such possibility.

'You were at the palace, you admit it,' he said.

'Only out by the fence. Along with hundreds of other people.'

'But you were there. And five things disappeared, and now you have five things.'

What could she say to that? She did, indeed, have them. Even now she had them. 'The broadcast didn't say what things,' she pleaded. 'It didn't say what things at all!'

He sneered, pointing. Could anyone doubt that crowns like these belonged in a palace? Could anyone doubt they had no business in the indigo washer at the Clean Machine?

Marianne sank onto the cot. She wondered if the old man had ever come back for his trunk. She wondered if crying would help. She wondered if screaming would help and decided it would not; the sound of screaming had echoed through the prison almost since she had entered it, sometimes softly and plaintively, sometimes with an excess of agony that made it quite unbearable to hear.

'But I didn't take them,' she said again, aloud.

'You're not charged with taking them,' said a voice. 'You're charged with receiving them.'

There was someone at the grated window, peering in at her. She could see one glassy eye. 'I didn't receive them,' she said. 'The machine did. It does things like that.'

'You'll have a chance to explain that to the magistrates, tomorrow,' said the voice. 'I thought I'd warn you, in case you wanted to change your clothes and tidy up a bit.'

'I only have these clothes,' she shouted, suddenly angry. 'The ones I had on.'

'Closet,' said the voice. 'There's a closet.'

Of course there was a closet. It contained three pairs of overalls, a fireman's helmet, and a ball gown at least five sizes too large. 'I will appear before the magistrates as I am,' she said aloud, attempting to sound dignified. 'In my own clothes.' She was wearing a simple shirtwaist dress, now somewhat rumpled, and a wool sweater, both in mud shades.

The grating across the window in the cell door slammed shut, as though in frustration.

The five puppies came out from beneath her cot and gathered around her feet.

'This is ridiculous,' she said. 'How did I ever get into this mess? How did you get in here?'

CHAPTER NINE

The magistrates were informal in their treatment of those brought before them. There were seven chairs on the dais, and occasionally all seven of them were occupied, though usually only two or three of the magistrates were seated there at a time, often at least one of them asleep. The others wandered about the courtroom or left the room entirely and could occasionally be heard ordering someone around backstage, as it were. One magistrate played endless games of chess with himself. Another drew endless pictures of naked women without heads. Only the tall, dark woman at the left end of the row seemed to pay attention.

'Window dressing,' said the voice in Marianne's mind. 'She's the only real one. The others are merely window dressing.' The dark woman peered at her out of fiery eyes, hot, eager eyes, belying her casual demeanor.

'Just Marianne, charged with receiving stolen goods,' the

prosecutor intoned, tugging at the wig that seemed always about to slip off the back of his bald head. 'Material of national importance, stolen from the palace.'

'Trial by combat,' the dark woman drawled in a bored though somehow elated voice. 'Next case.'

CHAPTER TEN

'You have until the holiday to obtain a champion,' the voice said through the grate in the window. 'I told you you should have cleaned yourself up. The Queen thought your disheveled state was disrespectful.'

'The Queen?'

'You should feel honored. She heard your case personally.'

'Who did?'

'The Queen.'

'Not that I saw!'

'Oh, you must have seen her. A dark woman, very slender. With fiery eyes.'

'One of the magistrates was a dark woman.'

'First magistrate of the realm, the Queen is.'

'She didn't hear my case! She didn't hear anything but the charge! She didn't even give me a chance to plead guilty or not guilty.'

'Oh, she knew you were guilty. It's just a case of deciding punishment, don't you know.'

A tiny growl came from beneath the bunk. Marianne interpreted this as a warning and said nothing more about her innocence. 'Where am I supposed to get a champion! I don't know anyone.'

'Then you'll have to fight the Duke of Eyes yourself. Not, by the way, something I would choose to do on a holiday afternoon.'

'I don't even know who he is!'

'The Queen's champion, of course. Who else would he be?' The grating slammed closed. This anonymous informant always slammed the grating to end conversation, as though the very act of conversing led to unbearable frustration or annoyance. Marianne reviewed what she had said — certainly nothing to offend. The behavior of the grating voice had no logic to it. It told her things she did not ask to hear and seemed to expect some response she could not give. She lay down on the cot, hearing the scrabble of puppy feet beneath it. They had found some way to enter and leave the cell — some way she could not find though she had searched for hours — but they always hid when anyone was at the door. 'I don't know what's happening,' she whispered as a moist little tongue explored between her fingers. 'I'm terrified, and I don't know what's happening.'

CHAPTER ELEVEN

'I hope you know what you're doing,' Ellat said, picking up her teacup and pausing in the doorway as though wanting both to go and to stay. Behind her in the vaulted room, Makr Avehl frowned at her as he adjusted the sleeves of his ceremonial robe and sat down on the narrow bed.

'Of course I don't, Ellat. No more than I did last time. But I have at least as good a clue this time as I had then. She has the bracelet, and I can follow that. Also, this time there are momentary gods. They will certainly have trailed after her, and they will have left a track. Surely someone as skilled as I am reputed to be can sniff them out.' He shrugged in self deprecation, giving her a boyish smile.

'What makes you think . . .' she began in a maternal voice, then made a fretful motion and said, 'oh, never mind. It's just all so . . . uncertain.'

'You want to know what makes me think the woman

washing clothes is the operative symbol? A hunch, Ellat. And your favorite at the Cave, the one with the scary eyes.'

'Therat?'

'Yes. That one. She agrees that the symbol is very potent. So, for all intents and purposes, I'm looking for a laundress. I shall put myself into the proper frame of mind. I shall burn the right incense,' he gestured at the ceremonial brazier beside the bed, already wreathed in smoke. 'I shall recite the correct words and send my spirit self looking for a laundress. A laundress, mind you, with five dogs of five colors. I'll grant you there may be more than one set of beings meeting that description, but not many more than one.'

'You're not taking Aghrehond?'

'I would if he were here, Ellat, but he's either on his way home or still in New York. He may be here by morning. Perhaps he'll come after me as he did last time. I'll leave it to him. He certainly carried the brunt of the battle during our last foray against Madame. And he had all the best of it. He appeared more or less as himself while I — well, I was undoubtedly a monster.'

'Good-hearted, however,' Ellat interjected. 'You must have been good-hearted.'

'Some part of me may have been,' he agreed somberly. 'She gave me that role last time, an equivocal one, because she did not know how she felt about me. This time I will choose what role to take. I shall go this time as something every maiden dreams of.' He laughed, sardonically.

'What's that?'

'Why, Ellat. You were a maiden once. Can't you guess?'

'You don't mean . . .'

He waved to her, a small wave, dismissive as well as affectionate, as he lay down on the cot. 'I do mean, love. Wish me luck.'

CHAPTER TWELVE

In the dungeon, Marianne huddled on the hard cot, her eyes shut, trying to dream of that other place, trying desperately to pretend she was somewhere else.

'Hsss,' a low whisper at her ear. 'Hsss.'

She turned her head toward the wall, feeling the faintest breath against her cheek. Mortar had fallen from between two of the cyclopean stones of the dungeon wall, leaving a narrow slot through which the breath came, a fervent little wind, hot and smelling of grease and garlic.

'Hsss, can you hear me?'

She put her lips within an inch of the wall. 'Yes, I can hear you.'

'What are you in for?'

'Receiving stolen goods. Palace goods.'

'Ah. They'll probably hang you, then. Or feed you to the plants in the botanical garden. Queen Luby likes to do that. I'm in for sedition.'

'How long have you been here?'

'Haven't any idea. Don't even remember coming here. Just woke up here one day. Isn't it that way with everyone?'

A chill began just above Marianne's eyes, moving swiftly down her body to her toes, tingling along her arms. Within her mind something turned sluggishly, as though in drugged slumber, deeply somnolent and yet restless. The combination of cold and the vertiginous shifting within herself made her nauseated, and she gagged. What the voice said was true. She couldn't remember where she had been before. She couldn't remember coming to . . . to whatever town this was. Surely she couldn't always have worked for the laundry. 'What did you do before?' she begged of the wall, seeking a clue to her own past. Surely she had a past!

'Advertising,' it answered promptly, perhaps with a touch of pride. 'Something to do with advertising. Insurance, I think. Or perhaps toothpaste.'

'They don't seem similar.'

'Identical,' the voice hissed as though from some great distance. 'Actually, they're identical.'

She felt the source of the voice had withdrawn, though only temporarily, and this assumption was verified in a moment when it resumed. 'Had to check the corridor. They spy, you know. They sneak the gratings open and stand there, listening. Always check the grating before you say anything.'

'I don't have anything bad to say,' she objected.

'Oh, they don't care. Bad. Good. It doesn't matter. They'll use it against you anyhow. Where were we?'

'They say I have to have a trial by combat,' she blurted. 'With the Duke of Eyes. I don't know what it means.'

A long silence. A sound as of lips smacking, or it could be a tsking; malice or sympathy, impossible to tell which. 'Well, they won't hang you or feed you to the plants, then, which is too bad.'

'Bad? Not to be fed to the plants?' she demanded.

'Ever seen him?' the voice asked. 'The Duke?'

'No.'

'He's sort of a machine, you know. Only a tiny part human. Like his body doesn't . . . function. So he's in this machine. And they keep changing it. One time he'll have hooks for hands and the next time, kind of grabbers. Or clubs. And one time he'll have legs, but the next time tracks, like some kind of big earth mover. He doesn't talk. Just looks at you with his eyes. Wherever his eyes look, that's where the machine goes. Whatever his mind thinks, that's what the machine does. And it's big, you know. About twelve feet high.'

'What kind of a champion could fight that?' she asked, holding her terror at arm's length. 'How could I fight that?'

'Well, you can't, of course. Best thing to do is lie down, put your head on your arms and let him kill you. Not many people can do that, of course. He plays. Whips. Pincers. Things like that. It hurts, and it's hard not to run and leap and try to escape. That's what people come for, of course. To see the opponent try to escape.'

'In other words,' she whispered, 'a trial by combat with the Duke of Eyes is really just another way of saying someone is to be publicly tortured to death?'

'Well . . .' the voice faded away. There was a distant clanging, a sound of several voices raised, a long silence. Then the hissing once more, close, very close, 'That's what it amounts to, Marianne.'

She had not told the voice her name. She rolled away from the aperture, fighting her welling nausea, knowing it wasn't a prisoner who spoke to her through that rent in the masonry. Or, if a prisoner, then one who had been put up to it by someone else. By the nameless voice that spoke through the grating. By the dark woman on the magistrate's bench. By the Queen. By someone who wanted to be sure she knew what would happen. Someone who wanted to savor her terror.

A soft nose pushed into her palm. A moist tongue licked at it, a puppy voice whined.

'They're going to kill me,' she said, hopelessly. 'That's what this has all been about. They're going to kill me. And I don't even know why.'

CHAPTER THIRTEEN

In Alphenlicht, Makr Avehl lay silently on the narrow cot, eyes closed, his breathing so shallow he appeared hardly to breathe at all. Around him extended a gray vacancy that was brushed intermittently with hints of color, echoing occasionally with a distant sound, a melody, perhaps a voice. It smelled of mossy woods, then of cinnamon, then of something name-lessly disgusting. He had the sensation of walking, or swim-ming, or perhaps flying through this nameless void, reaching out with his senses toward a potent symbol. It was a familiar quest. He had floated here before, very recently. It was only a few weeks ago that he had followed the other *Marianne* into the false worlds that opened upon this nothingness, the dream worlds, the fantasy worlds that clustered within and beside and through the worlds of reality.

What would it be this time? One of Madame's worlds, certainly, and yet not wholly hers. Each time she drew a victim into one of her worlds, whether purposely or unwittingly, that victim would change the world, little or much. Marianne's presence would have modified the world in which she found herself, would have changed it and put a mark upon it that the follower might seek as a trailfinder seeks a cairn.

A woman washing clothes. The slap of sodden fabric. The slosh of water. The soggy enervation of steam. The fatty stink of soap. He turned his head on the pillow, evoking and following that fragrance. The smell of soap. He seemed to scent it, far off, coming closer. And a sound, as of some great tumble of waters. Thrashing. Gushing. A whirling sound.

He drifted. Drifted uncomfortably. Wet. Very wet. His whole body was soaked. He choked, drowning, forgetting, screaming at the dark thundering waters around him.

Someone opened the door of the indigo washer and he spilled onto the floor, wet as a flounder, his princely garb reeking of bleach.

'Gracious,' said the old man across the crook of his cane. 'It's Prince Charming! I thought you might be my trunk, coming back.'

'I've come to rescue the fair damsel,' The Prince gargled, gasping for air. 'Where is she?'

'If you're talking about Marianne,' the old man answered, 'She's imprisoned.' He nodded, his head tilting to and fro like a rocking chair sent into motion by some constant breeze, moving of itself, unable to stop. 'Sentenced to trial by combat. The whole town is talking of nothing else.'

The Prince rose with what dignity he could muster. His satin trousers leaked dye even as they shrank into sausage-skin tightness. Rust bloomed on the hilt of his sword all at

290

once, like a flower. His velvet cape was a rag, ripped into fragments by the waters. He cursed.

'You must be her champion,' the old man commented, gesturing as he did so at the great machine across the aisle. 'The indigo dryer,' he murmured, staring at Prince Charming's trousers. 'I'd recommend it.'

CHAPTER FOURTEEN

In the middle of the night, the voice returned, hissing once more between the impenetrable stones. 'Marianne. Marianne.' Insinuating as a serpent. 'Marianne? Your champion has arrived.'

It was impossible to ignore the voice, even though she told herself it was a ploy, a feint, an attempt to give her hope that would then be dashed. She tried to keep silent and could not. 'Who?' she begged. 'Who is it?'

'Prince Charming,' said the voice with a lewd giggle. 'All got up for the part.'

She turned away from the wall and put her arm across her eyes, willing herself not to cry, not to speak. The little grating opened and someone peered in. She kept her eyes shut, breathed slowly, pretended to be asleep.

'You'll meet him next holiday!' the voice exulted. 'At the colosseum. In the catacombs where the victims are prepared!'

Marianne didn't answer. She could not have answered. In this nightmare world, she could only endure for a time, then die. What was the point in argument or expostulation? What was the point of anything?

Slow tears crept down her face, hidden behind her arm. After a time, the grating slammed shut, as though in pique.

CHAPTER FIFTEEN

Prince Charming was hiding in an alley near the palace, hoping very strongly that the gang of mapless ones he had recently evaded would not find him again. He had had to fight off two such gangs already, and his rusty sword was proving to be of little help. He carried it in his hand, unsheathed, since if it was sheathed when he needed it, there was a strong likelihood it could not be pulled free at all. Once dry, he had assumed he would be able to obtain clothing, directions, perhaps a hot meal or a warm bed, all those things that civilized men take more or less for granted. His first disillusionment had come when he approached a store which purported, by the terms of its window displays and name, to sell clothing.

'Y'got a coupon?' the clerk had asked him curiously when Makr Avehl had asked to see something in a cloak and tights, size forty-two long.

'Coupon?'

'A coupon entitlin' you to go around in fancy dress like that there. I mean, I'm not goin' to say nothin' to the Map Police, they'll find you soon enough in that getup, Mack, but it'd be my job if I sold you somethin' like that without a coupon.'

Prince Charming sighed. He felt it would be unbecoming to succumb to local pressure in the matter of dress, but one could not go about the streets looking like a derelict. 'How about a regular sports coat and slacks, then. Shirt size sixteen-and-a-half, thirty-two.'

'Fine. Y'got the money?'

Prince Charming laid gems and gold upon the counter.

'I didn't ask did you have no joolry. I asked did you have money. Like coin of the realm, like moolah, like voskies,

292

double-voskies or maybe a ten vosky bill. I can't do nothing with those.'

Prince Charming asked the way to a pawn shop or exchange bank and encountered the realities of the city.

'Listen, Mack. You can't find nothin' without you got a map. First thing you got to do is lay your hands on tomorrow's map, got that? Then you can find yourself some pawn shop or whatever.'

A few incisive questions asked of passersby elicited the information that maps were available at kiosks or twenty-four-hour restaurants for one vosky the map.

Prince Charming repaired to the nearest restaurant he could find and asked for a job as dishwasher.

'It'd have to be that, wouldn't it,' said the manager, staring at him with obvious distaste. 'You sure couldn't wait tables in that getup. Yeah, I suppose you can wash dishes. One vosky an hour and your supper. Y'got your work permit?'

'Work permit?' asked Prince Charming.

A few incisive questions asked of the restaurant manager gave the Prince the information that work permits were issued at the palace, between the hours of eight a.m. and noon each day.

'Where will I find the palace?' the Prince asked, exiting the restaurant a few moments later to the sound of raucous laughter.

'It seems to me,' mused the Prince to himself, 'that there is something wickedly illogical at work here.'

He found a television store and watched the broadcast of the palace viewing. During the broadcast, the announcer used the phrase, 'Here at the center of the city.' Sighing, Prince Charming set out to find the center of the city, by trial and error.

By nightfall, he had worked his way within three blocks of the palace. Not wishing to draw himself to the attention of the guards, he took refuge in an alley, intending to apply for a work permit in the morning. When he awoke, he found himself in a different alley, with the palace nowhere in sight. He had not eaten in two days.

293

The Prince decided to beg a meal. He was promptly set upon by the Map Police and thrashed before being given a stern warning. Begging was not permitted in Bimbleton. The Prince decided to scavenge a meal. This brought him to the attention of the first of the mapless gangs.

'That trash can, in case you're interested, joker, is in our territory.' The speaker had green hair and his name tattooed on his forehead. Bonecracker.

'I'm sorry,' said the Prince. 'I didn't know trash cans were anybody's territory.'

'He didn't know,' Bonecracker advised his friends, Dangerous and Lethal. 'Ain't that a pity. He didn't know.'

The Prince tried his sword and found it locked in the sheath. He therefore leapt straight upward and caught the bottom rung of a fire escape which lowered itself under his weight into the waiting arms of the trio. The Prince gave an excellent accounting of himself with the sheathed sword, emerging with one black eye, a split lip, and assorted bruises around the ribs and belly. Dangerous had, as he recommended to Lethal and Bonecracker, split. The other two were stretched beside the disputed trash can, which, on examination, proved to be empty. Another can, further down the block, yielded half a sack of potato chips and an unopened flip-top can of Ruby Garcia's Bean Dip with extra jalapeños.

Later that day he found a public drinking fountain and stayed near it for some time, attempting to put out the fire in his stomach. By evening he had worked his way to the palace once more. Moving as casually as his strange garb, now further battle-worn, would allow, he found a place near the fence that was partially hidden by the overhanging limbs of a large tree. When the tremor of change came, he grasped the iron fence and held tight, emerging from the changeover still on the sidewalk adjacent to the palace.

Satisfied, he evaded a mapless gang set upon stealing his sword and found the nearby alley previously referred to in which to spend the rest of the night.

'Work permit, sure,' said the palace functionary the next

morning, polishing the brass buttons on his cuff. 'Y'got entry papers?'

'Entry papers?' said the Prince in a dignified voice with overtones of distress. 'Entry papers?'

'Apply for those at the Bureau of Maps. Be sure to have your vaccination documents, three letters of reference from local residents, and the quota number under which you entered the country.'

'Quota number,' said the Prince vaguely, beginning to get the idea.

When next violently approached by members of a mapless gang, Prince Charming asserted with a bare though rusty blade his intention of joining them. Brasstits believed it was because of her well displayed charms. Ironballs thought it was because of his obvious leadership capabilities. In reality, Prince Charming would have joined anyone he thought able to provide him with a decent meal and some idea of what was going on.

'Why don't we . . . ah . . . rip off a map vendor?' he asked. 'Then we'd know where we wanted to go tomorrow.'

Brasstits shook her head pityingly. She was drawn to this peculiar stranger, partly because he obviously needed mothering and partly because he was so — oh, polite. Most men — well, no need to go into that, but they didn't act like this one did. 'You poor jerk,' she said. 'That's not the way it works.'

Prince Charming smiled up at her from under his lashes. He was not above flirtation for a good purpose, though he had not used this particular technique since age ten. 'How does it work, Brassy? Tell me.'

'If you don't buy a map for one vosky, the map just falls apart. You can't steal one. You can't peek over anybody's shoulder, either, or the Map Police'll put your eyes out. You could find somebody's got a map and offer to cohabit, if you want to, but the people who're willing to do that are pretty repulsive, let me tell you.'

'So, if you can't buy a map, you don't know where you are. If you can't get a job, you can't buy a map. If you can't get a work permit, you can't get a job. If you don't have entry papers, you can't get a work permit. If you don't have local references, you can't get entry papers, and you can't get local references without having a map. Is that more or less it?'

'More or less,' she said admiringly. 'You catch on fast.'

'Which is why there are mapless ones, I guess. You've learned to do without.'

'Well, it's either that or the arena. I mean, you can volunteer to be a victim for the arena, to fight the Duke of Eyes, and they'll feed you and take care of you until the next game comes up.'

'Duke of Eyes?' asked the Prince with a shiver of foreboding. 'Duke of Eyes?'

Brasstits described the Duke with loving attention to the more formidable details. 'Like, he gets to fight the victims, you know. And he gets to fight the champions, too. Like there's this girl, Marianne, and she has a champion going to fight for her. I'd like to see that. He won't get anywhere with the Duke of Eyes, let me tell you.'

The Prince sighed, his worst fears fulfilled. 'Where will this take place, Brassy? And when?'

Once the Prince had the day-to-day details of survival under control — though he was unable to do anything about improving his clothing — he worked his way to the palace once more and announced himself as Marianne's champion. He asked to see the Fair Maiden and was greeted with a chorus of jeering laughter.

'Whadaya think this is, the Love Boat?' a functionary asked him. 'You get to fight for her, chum, not canoodle with her.'

'I didn't have canoodling in mind,' said the Prince in a very dignified voice. 'I simply thought I should meet her and assure her of my best efforts. She may not even know I've arrived.'

'Oh, she knows!' There was laughter again. 'You can see her at the arena, buddy. If you can find it.' There was more hooting laughter, and the Prince left the palace feeling quite downhearted.

'How would you find the arena, if you had to?' he asked Ironballs.

'Gosh, I dunno,' said Ironballs. 'It moves around, the arena does, just like everyplace else. Brasstits, how'd you find the arena if you had to?'

'Find somebody that was goin' there, I guess,' she said. 'Maybe you could do that.'

Two days later, Prince Charming awoke in front of a pawn shop.

He took the gems and gold he had hidden in his left boot heel and spread them upon the dirty counter.

'My, my, look at that,' the pawnshop owner gazed at the glittering hoard. 'Where'd you get all this, man?'

'It's mine,' said the Prince. 'Not stolen.'

'I didn't suppose it was. Just interested is all. What you want for 'em?'

'Clothing,' said the Prince. 'Voskies.'

The pawnshop owner shook his head. 'Sorry. Can't give you anything but coupons. Look through the coupon book if you like. If you see anything there you can use, let me know.'

The coupon book was dusty. Most of the coupons were handwritten. One offered a home-cooked meal, another to repair a saddle. One offered two nights' lodging with Mrs McAlister. One offered to tell his fortune.

'I'd like the meal and the lodging,' said the Prince. 'If that includes a bath.'

'Not unless it says so,' the pawnshop owner shook his head. 'I doubt Mrs McAlister would let you in, the way you look and smell. Tell you what. Why'n't you take the meal and the fortune. I'll sell you those two for this littlest jewel, right here.'

'I don't need my fortune told,' said the Prince. 'I already know how things are going.'

'Yeah, but I'm throwing it in. Won't cost you anything.'

The Prince took the coupon, was directed to the house where the meal was offered — corned beef and cabbage and pecan pie for dessert — and then to Madame Fifi's Emporium of Truth.

'Trouble with you is,' said Fifi, 'you got body odor.'

'So would you,' snarled Prince Charming, 'if you'd been sleeping in alleys and eating out of trash cans for the past week.'

'You know, that's a very good observation,' she remarked, rubbing her hands gently over the crystal ball. 'I probably would smell pretty bad. Of course this is your fortune we're doing here, so how I might smell under any circumstances at all is what you might tend to call kind of irrelevant.'

'That's so,' admitted the Prince.

'Let's see here. You gotta dangerous trial comin' up in the near future. You gotta rescue a Fair Maiden. Lord love a duck, it's been twenty years since I seen a rescue of a Fair Maiden in the crystal ball and that was a fireman. Well, what else. If you'll spend the night in the alley just across from this place, here, right after midnight the restaurant will throw out two T-bone steaks, medium-rare, not even touched. Man and his wife have an anniversary fight and storm outa the place without eatin'. What else. You expectin' a horse, maybe?'

Prince Charming said he was not expecting a horse.

' 'Fiuzyou, I'd expect a horse. *Also,* there's somethin' in here about a Holiday comin' up in about two days. Oh, boy, that means the Duke of Eyes'll be at it again. That machine goes through Fair Maidens like they was panty hose. That's it.'

'What's it?'

'That's yer fortune. Coupon please. Thank you very much.'

Prince Charming found himself back on the street. It was late enough to seek shelter for the night, and by paying strict attention to what the fortune-teller had told him, he was able to obtain two medium-rare steaks, two baked potatoes, one with butter one with sour cream, and a side of fried zucchini. As he sprawled in the rear doorway of the restaurant, licking his fingers, he thought how true it was that one's pleasures are measured by one's expectations. He could not remember having had a better or more satisfying meal.

Were it not for the plight of the Fair Maiden, he would have been almost content. He still had no idea how to find the colosseum when the terrible day came.

CHAPTER SIXTEEN

On the days that followed, Marianne would wake each morning to look out the high, barred window at a featureless sky, rather more gray than blue, without clouds, perhaps evenly painted with a high mist through which the sun let down a neutral, colorless light. She would rise wearily, use the toilet, splash tepid water on her face and chest at the stained basin, then retreat to the cot to await breakfast. It would always be the same: bread and tea, both tasteless. During the morning, the voice at the grating would offer intelligence of a kind. Lunch would follow: broth and bread, distinguishable from the previous meal only in that the liquid was served in a bowl rather than a cup. During the afternoon, the voice through the wall would hiss its messages of cheer, and in the evening there would be bread and a kind of mush that seemed to have a good deal of sawdust in it in addition to whatever nutrient it might have contained. Shortly after the evening meal, the light would go out as the shrieks began, and in the scream-wracked darkness she would lie awake, shaking and weeping silently while the puppies huddled around her, offering what comfort they could.

The voice through the wall told her foolproof ways of escaping the Duke of Eyes: running around him clockwise to make him dizzy; putting marbles under his wheels to make him skid; picking up a rock from the arena floor and using it to bash in his sensors. Hearing this merely increased Marianne's sense of hopelessness. Each tidbit was so obviously constructed to make her try desperate maneuvers in the arena, to increase her spectator value.

The voice from the hallway, however, gave her intelligence about her champion. How he tried to buy new clothing but could not pay for it in coin of the realm. How his sword had rusted into its sheath so it could not be drawn out. How he had attempted to eat with Marianne prior to the day of the trial only to have his request denied by the magistrates. About his piteous state of dishevelment and pathetic lack of armor. About his maplessness and homelessness and probable inability even to find the colosseum on the holiday. At each such recitation, the sluggish, nameless entity within Marianne stirred, each time more restively, as though about to awake. It was like being in a small boat, she thought, above the heaving of some great waterbeast that lifted and sagged the surface in dizzying waves so that her whole world tilted from the rising pressure of the monstrous thing beneath. Each time, Marianne retched, staggered, and then came to herself, unchanged yet newly terrified that the next time whatever it was would come up, breach the surface, and terrify her by letting her look into its face. When that happened . . . when that happened, she assured herself, she could not possibly survive it.

'It's six of one and half a dozen of the other,' she wept hysterically into the flat mattress. 'Whether I die of this heaving inside me or die at the hands or feet or whatever of the Duke of Eyes. Whichever comes first, I suppose.' Beneath the cot a moist nose and tongue touched her dangling hand, as though in comfort, and she dug her fingers into the loose skin of a pup. They were still there, still coming and going, present in twos and threes, always absent when anyone might be looking. If she could only find their route of entry. If she could only find one of her own.

So, each day. She lost count of them. There were ten or a dozen, all alike. Then the morning came on which the sky was a clear, empyrean blue, on which a fresh wind enlivened the cells with stomach-heaving smells of food and smoke, and on which some nearby loudspeaker broke the morning quiet with the blared announcement, 'The Queen is pleased to announce a HOLIDAY. All citizens are reminded of the obligation to visit a church or temple of your choice.'

Her cell door swung wide. A heavy-bellied guardsman told her to come along to church services, and she found herself in the company of some fifty or sixty other inmates, all with the same lost and shattered expression on their faces, being herded into a vaulted room crowded with images and symbols and hazed with rising veils of ceremonial smoke.

The service was conducted interminably in a language foreign to all those present. They bore it patiently as it wound its way through procession and recession, prophon and antiphon, prolapse and relapse, to its long delayed close. When they left the vault, blinking at the sudden access of light, they were given chunks of dried cake to eat and herded onto a waiting bus. Only when the bus approached the gates of the colosseum — which Marianne seemed to remember having seen before, whether personally or on TV she could not say — did she realize that this was the day of her trial. She tried to scream, but her mouth was full of dried cake, and she succeeded only in spraying gummy crumbs over an old woman sitting next to her and receiving an indignant glance and muttered curses in return.

She did not see where they took the others. They dragged her down a flight of worn stone stairs into the bowels of the place, into a kind of cell with two barred doors, one opening from the echoing corridor and the other into the arena itself. Through this grated opening she could hear and see the crowds streaming into the towering stands, could observe the velvet-draped grandeur of the royal box. This baroque edifice was garlanded with golden rope. Slender pillars reached from it to a gilded baldachin over the carved throne. Marianne clutched the bars and stared at it as though hypnotized, waiting for the moment when that dark woman would arrive.

The Duke of Eyes entered first.

From behind a mighty timbered door, a stupendous clatter overrode the crowd noises, a cacophonous thunder that shocked the muttering multitude into silence. As they watched, nudging one another, the vast door rose on creaking ropes and through it came the Duke himself.

Treads as high as Marianne's head moved inexorably with a metallic clanging. Between and above them towered a cylindrical housing with swinging tentacles on either side. Above that projected the top of a glass-fronted coffin with something barely discernible in it, a form that might have been human.

In one tentacle it carried a bludgeon; in another a flame thrower; in another a sword; in the last a lash made up of many little chains. The crowd roared. The Queen moved into the royal box and took her seat. Across from Marianne a barred door opened and a man was thrust out into the arena, half naked, bare-handed. He stared at the creature before him with horror and dismay.

Marianne watched as long as she could. For a time the man was agile enough to escape injury. After the Duke broke one of his legs with the bludgeon, however, the contest was less amusing and the crowd began to complain, querulously, like a hive of angry bees. The Queen watched all this with no change of expression. As Marianne turned away, her stomach heaving and the sound of the man's screams echoing in her ears, a voice spoke from behind her.

'Maiden? Marianne?'

He stood in the doorway. Someone had opened the grating to let him through. The tattered finery that hung upon him was caked with alley dirt and thrown ordure. His trousers were mere scraps, clinging to his thighs more out of habit than from any sensible continuity of fabric. His feet were wrapped in scraps of velvet rag, and his shirt was a filthy fiction. She stared, unable to believe him, even while knowing who it must be.

'I could not obtain a map,' he said with some dignity. 'So I merely followed the crowds. I'm sorry I'm so late.'

'You're my champion?' she asked, breaking into hysterical giggles. 'The man who will fight for me? Prince Charming?'

Something in his face stilled her helpless merriment. It was stern, hard, aching and yet determined. He crossed the room and stared through the window she had just left.

'So,' he said. 'That's what Madame has waiting for us.'

'You can't fight it,' she told him. 'No one can.'

Across the cell a yellow puppy slid between two stones to sit panting on the floor.

'If we can't fight it, we have to escape it,' he told her. 'You hear me, Fair Lady!'

The thing inside Marianne heaved. She retched with motion sickness as her interior landscape trembled.

'A nice trick that would be,' she said with a sick, feeble giggle, tears running down her face. 'Maybe it will kill us quickly.'

'Not on your life it won't,' he said. 'Maiden! Listen to me. We have to find a way out!'

'If we just lie down. Put our heads down. Don't move, no matter how much it hurts us . . .'

He came to her, the strength of him pouring before him like a palpable cloud. He took her in his arms as though it were a ritual and pressed his lips to hers. She could not move, could not breathe. She wanted to thrust him away but more than that to lose herself in that embrace and never come out of it. The thing inside her heaved again, and again, higher and higher, breaking upward through all the strata that had overlaid it, all the time, the endless time . . .

'My Prince!' cried *Marianne,* who had been sleeping for about ten years.

'Who are you?' cried Marianne at once and in the same voice. Something besides herself occupied her mind.

'Beloved,' Prince Charming cried, exultantly. 'Sleeping Beauty. My own!'

'Where?' *Marianne* asked, staring around herself at the stone walls, cocking her head at the screams of the crowd. 'Where are we?'

'We are ensorceled, enchanted, girded about with foul machination,' he said. 'In about five minutes, they'll kill us — you and me. There should be some way to escape. All ensorcelments have escape hatches . . .'

Behind them, a blue dog slipped into the cell, closely followed by a silver one.

'What's going on?' begged Marianne. 'What's happening?'

'Shh, shh,' said *Marianne*. 'Be still. Let me see what you know.' There was another of those seasick heavings, and Marianne felt her body move, without her volition, to the barred gate. 'Oh, Gods of Creation, what monster is that?'

'A very horrid one,' he answered. 'A crippled thing in both mind and body, given the wherewithal to accomplish its foul purposes despite its limitations.'

'We can't fight him.'

'Not conceivably.'

'We must find a way out.'

A black puppy slipped into the room, a red one close behind him, and with a rending shudder, the hoof and leg of a horse reached through just behind them.

'Oh, most elevated and supreme Prince, most lovely Lady, guidance!' whinnied a pathetic voice. 'I am lost among the stones, tracking these wee doglings, and cannot find my way.'

'Who is that?' The Prince turned toward the wall. 'Who calls my name?'

'Your faithful steed, left behind in the void, oh, Prince. Shout again, and I will follow the sound of your voice.'

The red dog disappeared into the stone, and the other front leg of the horse emerged, along with its nose. The black dog leapt up, seized the bridle, and tugged the horse forward. It nodded its head and neighed gratefully as the last of its tail came through the stone, then turned confidentially to Marianne. 'Lovely Lady, though I would walk through hell for the privilege of your company, I had not thought to make such a trip as that.' He turned his massive head as though to look at himself. He was a ponderous gray Shire horse, feather-footed and muscular, his back a veritable field on which a high saddle sat like a minaret, garlanded about with weapons.

'My steed?' asked the Prince, uncertainly. 'The fortune-teller did tell me to expect a horse.'

'Obviously,' said the horse. 'What good is a Prince Charming without his faithful horse?'

304

The five dogs sat down in a row and regarded Marianne with a mixture of skepticism and concern. They had grown considerably since she had seen them last.

'Are you really my doggies?' she asked at last, the words scarcely out of her mouth before someone else inside her used her mouth to ask quite another question.

'Haven't we met before?'

Black Dog panted, nodding. 'Elsewhere, *Marianne*. And in another time.'

Red Dog nodded assent. 'An evil place, this. We find ourselves very limited in what we can do to assist you.'

'Would your limitations extend to getting us out of here?' Prince Charming asked, his eyes fixed on the royal box where the Queen seemed about to make an announcement.

'There is an available nexus, yes,' said Black Dog. 'One. We know the momeg who holds a locus upon it, one Gojam, and he would be happy to let us through. His locus is, however, in an unfortunate juxtaposition relative to certain other material manifestations.'

'I don't understand.' The Prince wrinkled his brow and rubbed his forehead while Marianne engaged in an internal colloquy between herselves. 'You propose a way out? But say it is in an unfortunate place?'

'The spatial location to which we refer is out in the arena. Right in the middle. Under him,' said the momeg, pointing with one paw at the Duke of Eyes. 'Immediately under him. If you can get us all out there in the middle, Prince, I think we may be able to do something . . .'

In the arena the Duke of Eyes rumbled to and fro over the bloodstained patch of sand that had been his earlier opponent. Though he moved backward and forward and from side to side, he stayed generally in the center of the area in order to permit the audience the best possible unobstructed view. The Duke seemed to enjoy the sound of his treads, a rhythmic clumpety-wump-de-clangedy-wham which filled the blind-walled chasm with thundering echoes. This clattering stopped briefly as the Queen rose to her feet. Her voice filled the stadium, seeming to need no artificial amplification.

305

'Loyal Citizens,' she cried. 'For your delectation, we will now have a trial by combat. Just Marianne, guilty of receiving goods stolen from the palace — the evidence is there, before you,' she made two dramatic gestures, first toward a litter being carried around the arena on which the five gemmed crowns rested, then toward the barred gate. 'Represented by her champion, Prince Charming!'

The grating flew upward and two guardsmen entered to escort the Prince into the arena. He, however, had already leapt upon his horse and, heaving Marianne up behind him, he shouted a battle cry and thundered into the fray. The momegs, after only a moment's hesitation, pattered after him.

'What are we going to do?' the horse asked in an interested tone. 'Do you have anything specific in mind?'

'Get him over to one edge,' gritted the Prince. 'Away from the middle. Then get ourselves and the dogs into the middle.'

'An excellent plan, though somewhat easier said than done,' murmured the horse, sidestepping in a set of immaculately executed dressage steps to avoid a tentacle thrust forward by the Duke of Eyes. Momentarily, they were out of the Duke's vision and the crowd cheered.

'Seven to two on the Duke,' cried a hawker. 'Seven to two on the Duke.'

'Ooooh, Marianne,' squealed a clutch of colosseum groupies. 'Ooooh, Prince Charming.' They tossed circlets of flowers which fell around the Prince's head and over the horse's ears, blinding them both. 'Ooooh, Hooray for the Duke.'

One set of tracks thundered forward, the other back, as the Duke of Eyes rotated to keep them in view. From his central position, it was obvious that the tentacles could reach almost to the arena walls. 'Damn little maneuvering room, if you've noticed,' the horse whinnied, shaking a flower circlet into his mouth and mumbling around a crisp mouthful of carnations. 'Shouldn't you be doing something with that battle axe or that shield or something?'

'Oh, of course,' said the Prince, startled. He seized the battle axe and got the shield over one arm just in time to block a sword-bearing tentacle that the Duke lashed at them from behind his left shoulder. The Duke snarled, a metallic growl, twisting his flame-thrower-tentacle toward them. Before it could be brought to bear, both the Black and the Foo Dogs scampered wildly across the arena before the machine, leapt onto the right-hand tread and, running the great tread-mill madly on three legs, raised their left hind legs to pee industriously into the gears and linkages. Meantime, the faithful horse had raised himself on his hind legs into a wide, hopping turn that let him pound away in the opposite direction before the flame thrower could be readied for use.

'Got to get him out of the middle,' panted Prince Charming. 'Got to give him some bait!'

'Me,' breathed Marianne. 'Me?'

'Me, I'd rather thought,' he replied. 'I'll slide off. You get forward in the saddle here and hang on. When the thing comes after me, if it does, get behind him in the middle out there with the dogs. Got that?'

'But what about you?' *Marianne* wailed. 'What about you!'

'I'll have to run for it,' he said grimly, sliding off the wall side of the horse, shield at the ready and battle axe in hand.

Horse and Marianne circled counterclockwise. The Duke of Eyes stopped rotating and concentrated on Prince Charming, now huddled under his shield at the arena wall as though in a state of paralysis. The crowd was on its feet cheering, throwing popcorn, and releasing clouds of brightly colored balloons. The Queen was smiling widely, in very good temper, and now nodded magnanimously, signalling her champion to close in for the kill.

'Twelve to one on the Duke,' the hawker cried. 'Get yer bets down. Twelve to one on the Duke.'

Whatever victims the Duke had met in the past, he was not accustomed to meeting armed opponents. He lashed out clumsily with the flame thrower in an attempt to knock the shield to one side. The Prince jumped high, thrust down with the shield to catch the tentacle beneath it, then cut it through with a mighty swing of the axe while the crowd cheered.

The Queen frowned.

The cheering stopped as though cut off by a knife. The crowd murmured disapprobation. 'Foul,' several sycophantic voices called. 'Foul.'

'Five to one on the Duke,' the hawker cried again. 'Five to one on the Duke.'

The Prince retreated behind his shield once more and circled. The Duke's remaining weapons could not be used at a distance. The mighty treads began to revolve, shrieking as they did so. That same flowering rust that had bloomed on everything metal in the city now bloomed on the gears that moved the great treads. Swiveling and lurching, the Duke scrabbled toward the Prince crabwise, each movement accompanied by an ear-shattering shriek of corroding metal.

Behind the Duke, the horse and Marianne moved on tiptoe toward the center of the arena, dogs at either side.

Prince Charming stuck his head up from behind the shield to stick out his tongue at the Duke. 'The Queen is a coprophagist,' he cried in a stentorian voice. 'She's got steatopygia and her eyes are crossed!'

The Queen scowled. The crowd sat down, huddling in their thousands, making no sound.

'Nyaa, nyaa, nyaa,' cried the Prince. 'Old metal guts, afraid to fight.'

The Queen snarled and gestured: Forward!

The Duke of Eyes extended all remaining tentacles and lunged, only to find himself skidding wildly to the right because of the rust that had largely immobilized one tread.

From behind the mechanical monster, the Black Dog barked wildly. 'Now, Prince. Here, Prince, here, Prince, here!'

Prince Charming dropped shield and axe and ran for his life. Behind the Duke of Eyes the horse began to occult, winking in and out of existence, each time longer between reappearances. The momegs, too, began to wink. The crowd rose to its feet, screaming. The Queen made an imperious gesture, and the great machine lifted and turned, ponderously creaking and screaming, even as Prince Charming threw himself across the last few feet to the center of the arena and caught the momentarily visible horse around one rear leg.

Then they were gone.

With a scream of rage, the Queen turned and stormed out of the arena. With a clatter of treads, the Duke of Eyes wobbled through the great, timbered door. Later the people of whatever-city-it-was commented upon the strange lights that moved all night in the high, private wing of the palace.

CHAPTER SEVENTEEN

Slick as a frog's back, clay-gray, the flats stretched from under the wagon wheels in all directions to the veiled horizon. Water covered most of it, a mere sheen of moisture licking at mud edges, flattening the hollows, leaving only a narrowly wandering track above the waterline to glimmer like light on wet silk, an uncertain highway from somewhere to anywhere. Tracks came spinning endlessly off the wheels and meandered across the flats until they vanished into misty distance, the net result of all peregrinations yielding no particular direction. Four dogs, red and blue, gray and yellow, bent to the traces, following the black lead dog as he tracked the ridge to leave their paw, wheel and hoof prints in the firmly silted sand. It was forever from where they were to where the tracks vanished in mist. An equivalent featureless distance lay on every hand.

At times the drier ground split into two or three branches, making the lead dog whine with frustration until the momeg, Gojam, flicked the whip in one direction or another to indicate the chosen route. Nothing differentiated the choices. There was always as much water on one hand as on the other; there was always an equivalency of mud, a sufficiency of glimmer, shine, vapor, colorlessness, sourceless, shadowless light.

'A dull world,' said Gojam to no one in particular, 'yet one I have always favored.'

'These are tidal flats, aren't they?' asked Prince Charming.

'So I have always believed,' Gojam replied with a polite smile that showed his pointed teeth and crinkled several of his red little eyes.

'Then the tide ought to − come in, oughtn't it? At some time?'

'So I would suppose. Though I have never seen it do so.'

'You come here often?'

'When it seems appropriate.'

'May one ask,' whinnied the horse from his position at the rear of the wagon, 'what made it seem appropriate on this occasion?'

'Well,' Gojam mused for a moment, his dewlaps quivering and his long, pendant ears swaying to and fro with the power of his concentration. 'Firstly, it isn't inimical. I mean, you can all breathe here, and the temperature isn't unbearable. Secondly, it's a placid sort of place. Very little happens. At least, very little has happened when I've been here in the past. I thought that would give you all time to collect yourselves, as it were . . .'

'Very kind of you,' murmured Marianne, wondering if her tenant, *Marianne*, would interrupt her in mid-speech. 'I, for one, could stand a little collecting.'

'And, thirdly,' the momeg continued, 'I doubt that half a dozen momegs in the universe know about this place. Which means that though the dark woman, the Queen, Madame Delubovoska, will probably track you here eventually, it isn't likely to be a place she'll look for you right away.'

'Madame Delubovoska,' mused the Prince. 'That was the woman who was attempting to kill us, wasn't it?'

'I believe so,' offered Gojam. 'Switching nexi is a strain, and you may have forgotten. Let me take the liberty of reminding you. You were engaged in battle with a large, mechanical monster. Does that ring a bell? Ah, good. Your momeg friends approached me for a means of escape? Ah, you do recall.'

'I remember *that*,' said the Prince. 'I went there to rescue

310

a Fair Maiden — my own true love,' he cast Marianne a melting glance, 'but how I got there I really can't recollect.'

The lead dog stopped, abruptly, making the other four dogs pile up in the traces with muttered growls. 'Something,' the Black Dog said. 'Out there on the mud.'

They stared in the direction the dog's muzzle pointed, seeing nothing at first, then a tiny interruption in nothing, and finally, protruding above the water, two miniscule pimples that had attracted the dog's attention. The pimples blinked and disappeared, only to appear again, slightly to the right of their previous location.

'Eyes,' said Marianne. 'Something with eyes.'

The eyes regarded them balefully from the level of the water's surface before disappearing again. They might have been something quite small, close up, or something quite large, far away.

'I had no idea anything lived here,' Gojam remarked, scratching at a left ear with one pair of arms while twitching the reins with another. 'Of course, I haven't come here that frequently.'

'About the tide,' said the Prince, moodily attempting to pull two scraps of trouser together to cover an expanse of muscular thigh. 'Reason would indicate it must come in at some time or other.'

'I've always thought reason sadly overrated,' remarked Gojam. 'There are momegs who pay a lot of attention to it, just as there are some who disbelieve in it entirely. I tend to the middle view. Use it when it's helpful and ignore it when it isn't.'

'I merely meant, it would be unpleasant for us if the tide came in while we were out here.' The Prince sighed, turned to Marianne, gave her a long, burning look and touched her hand. *Marianne* stroked his in response, her eyes misty. The hand twitched and drew away as Marianne looked down and saw what it was doing.

'You say "out here" as though there were some "in there" which might be selected instead,' Gojam commented, uncrossing his third and fourth legs and stretching them

311

over the dashboard of the wagon. 'So far as I am aware, "out here" is all there is.'

'Wrong,' said the horse. 'It may be all you've seen, magnificent sir. All you have become aware of in your peregrinations. All you have intuited or assumed or inferred from the lack of structure around us. Not all, however, that there is. I suggest you gaze toward the horizon, slightly to the left of our present line of travel.'

'I see it,' said the Red Dog after a time. 'A tower.'

'Towers,' corrected Blue Dog. 'Misty, but still quite real.'

'I wouldn't have said real,' murmured Gojam. 'Evident, perhaps. Or perceivable. Not necessarily real.'

'A nice philosophical point,' commented the Prince, perking up a little. 'Could we direct our travel in the direction of those possibly spiritual and/or ephemeral structures?'

Gojam sighed, flicked the whip, and directed Black Dog slightly to the left at the next branch.

'Eyes,' said Marianne again, pointing toward the water. This time there were several pairs of lidded hemispheres blinking at them from the fluctuating surface.

'They seem interested in our progress but not hostile,' Gojam remarked. 'In keeping with the placidity I have always found here.'

'Wherever here is,' neighed the horse rudely, mostly to himself.

'How did you and the − the other momegs become acquainted?' Marianne asked hastily, giving the horse's nose an admonitory tap of her fingers.

'Become acquainted?' Gojam stared at her with one set of eyes, rapidly blinking the other to convey confusion. 'I am not aware that we are acquainted.'

'I only thought − you were kind enough to let them exit through your . . . your locus.'

'Through a nexus of which my locus was a part, most accurately. It's impossible to exit through a locus. A locus doesn't go anywhere. It merely is. Interminably and dully in most cases. Which is not responsive to your inquiry. Well, I would have done as much for any entity. Known or unknown. Recognizable or strange. Dynamic or static. Your friends approached me politely and I responded in kind. What kind of a universe would it be if we could not do small kindnesses for one another?'

'I see,' she murmured. 'What indeed.'

'Besides,' he confessed, compressing one set of lips while sneering with another, 'I do detest Madame Delubovoska. She has a nasty habit of summoning up momegs on the spur of the moment, without any concern for the inconvenience it may cause, and then splatting them back again whenever it suits her. If she returns them at all, which I have reason to doubt in some cases. A very *very* close friend of mine, virtually a contiguite, was used twice by Madame and actually burned both times as a dismissal. No lasting damage, of course. We're virtually indestructible, but we do have *feelings*.'

'How awful for him,' murmured Marianne, feeling faintly guilty without being able to remember why. 'How awful for you. How many — ah, contiguites do you have?'

'Oh, twelve. Depending upon the packing, don't you know. They do insist on shifting it about.'

'Twelve at my locus, too,' said the Black Dog. 'Of course, it's unstressed space in my neighborhood. Things can get packed a lot tighter than that around singularities, I understand.'

'Indeed,' said Gojam, playing idly with the whip. 'So I've been told by some momegs who've been there. And a lot looser around discontinuities, if it comes to that — which we all fervently hope it never does.' He shuddered delicately. 'No matter how dull the locus, it's better than no locus at all.' He sighed, moodily. 'Are we getting any closer to the whatevers?'

They were getting considerably closer. What had at first appeared to be towers now proved to be lumpish promontories culminating in tall, cylindrical structures that were either unfinished or in a state of ruinous decay.

'Eyes,' said Marianne again. This time there were a hundred pairs or more, moving gently along the surface of the water, observing their progress.

'A veritable metropolis, gentlemen and lady,' suggested the horse. 'An urban center. Who knows what delights and surprises may await us.'

'Whatever it is, it's made out of mud,' remarked the Red Dog. 'Wet mud.'

'Wettish,' corrected Black Dog. 'If it were really wet, it wouldn't hold shape.'

'Not necessarily true,' admonished Gojam. 'There you go, naughty, naughty, being reasonable again. You have to remember where we are.'

'Wherever that may be,' nickered the horse, very quietly, to himself.

'Wherever it is, we approach,' said the Black Dog, firmly.

As they drew closer, they could see that the structures were indeed made of mud, tiny dab on tiny dab built up in endless layers, like the nest of a cliff swallow or a mud dauber wasp, the accretion of protracted and focused effort, mud on mud on mud, higher and higher, a mighty mound with little jug-shaped dwellings covering it, the round jug necks peering in all directions. At the top of the great mound a slightly smaller mound began, and on top of that one, another still. Extending high above these three great clumps, like a mud-man with a tall hat, a long cylindrical chimney of mud dabs spiralled lumpishly upward into the mists.

'Wettish,' remarked the Black Dog with satisfaction. 'Damp.'

'Hail, great travelers,' called a small voice. 'Accept the hospitality of the Tower of Petition.'

It took them a little time to locate the speaker. It had crawled out of the water onto the track before them and lay there now, propped high on two front flippers with its eyes bulging toward them, the top of its head reaching approximately to Black Dog's knees.

'Hail,' said Gojam in a kindly voice. 'Very nice of you, I must say.'

The speaker flipped itself toward the mud hive, found an upward track among the dwellings and scuttled up this slick and obviously well-traveled incline until it was at their eye level. 'I would invite you in, but there seems to be some disparity in size.'

'Think nothing of it,' said the Prince. 'We may have been trespassing. If so, it was unintentional, and we apologize for any anxiety we may have caused.'

The speaker waved both flippers before its face as though to wave away such an idea. 'We are honored by your presence. Some of us have been following your progress with deep attention. Even now our philosophers are engaged in colloquy to determine which of the Great Questions should be put to you. Who knows? Your arrival may actually put an end to Construction!'

'Construction?' asked Marianne. 'This construction?' She gestured upward at the tower. 'It's very impressive. We wouldn't want to . . . interrupt anything.' Her eyes dropped to the water level where great numbers of the mud creatures were scuttling up into and upon the building. Many of the mud jugs were already occupied, and serious eyes peered at them from every direction.

'It would be a blessing,' the speaker said in a distracted tone. 'We've been building it with conscript labor for sixty generations, and everyone is tired to death of it. Is there anything I can do to increase your comfort? The water is potable. At least, we drink it. If you'd like some scum, I can have some gathered for you. No? We quite understand. Different creatures, different needs. Though until now we had only postulated the existence of different creatures. And now! To see — how many kinds of you are there? I count at least four, but perhaps there are subtleties of which I am unaware?'

'Three basic shapes,' said the Prince. 'Four if you distinguish on the basis of size as you seem to be doing. Two basic kinds. Nine entities, each different in some way from the others. I believe there are at least three sexes represented.'

'Oh, you,' said Gojam, twinkling.

'Remarkable,' twittered the mud creature. 'Oh, I am incredibly rude. I haven't given you my designation. I am philosopher's assistant Puy.'

'I am Prince Charming,' said the Prince. 'This is the Fair Maiden Marianne or Sleeping Beauty Marianne, I forget which. That is Gojam. That is a horse, nameless for the moment, though undoubtedly faithful. The dogs are all momentary gods, as is Gojam, designated by color.'

'Color?' asked Puy. 'I'm sorry, I don't recognize the concept.'

'Ah, a measure of the creature's ability to reflect certain wavelengths of light. Unimportant.'

'They are Rouge, Delphy, Liquorice, Gold, and Silver,' said Marianne, pointing to each in turn.

'Delighted,' said Puy, bowing on his flippers. 'Utterly delighted. Ah, I believe the council of philosophers is approaching.'

Having made this announcement, Puy peered upward from the edge of the slide. Following his gaze, they saw several rather bulbous mud creatures sliding down the mud track from the top of the structure, braking madly at the turns with their flippers, then thrusting themselves onward on the straightaways, much in the manner of skiers negotiating a challenging run. They had reached the bottom of the chimney shape and were now negotiating tortuous turns among the dwellings. They arrived, rather out of breath, bowed to Puy, who bowed in return, and then took their positions before the visitors, still panting.

'Honored guests,' their spokesman peeped. 'We, the council of philosophers, have determined which of the Great Questions shall be put to you.'

'Very flattering, I'm sure,' said Gojam. 'Is it your expectation we will answer this question or questions?'

The mud creatures stared at them, then at each other, murmuring rapidly.

'. . . always thought . . .'

'. . . never considered they might not . . .'

'. . . could always threaten them . . .'

'. . . try persuasion . . .'

'We will be happy to try to answer your questions,' said *Marianne* in a firm voice, frowning at Gojam.

'I was only asking,' said the momeg in a mild voice. 'Not all creatures really want their questions answered, you know.'

The rapid exchange among the mud peepers went on.

'Trying to answer just isn't good enough . . .'

'. . . anything that size ought to know . . .'

'. . . had to come from somewhere . . .'

'We have decided to threaten you,' the speaker went on at the conclusion of this conference. 'You must answer the questions.'

'Or?' asked Prince Charming, curiously.

'Or we'll summon the tide,' the creature answered.

'It will wash away your entire building,' the Prince remarked, with what Marianne regarded as commendable calm. 'Would you really want to do that?'

The conference resumed.

'. . . hadn't thought about . . .'

'. . . sixty generations by my count . . .'

'. . . all to do over again . . .'

'Maybe we'll just ask the questions,' the speaker said at last, eyes half shut and an expression of pain on its fishlike face.

'Ask away,' invited Gojam.

'We've been building this tower for over sixty generations,' the speaker peeped. 'Trying to get it high enough to see over the mist. You've probably noticed, you can't see very far.'

'We had noticed,' Marianne said.

'We were trying to answer several of the great questions for ourselves you see. It isn't that we're lazy, or lacking in endeavor. We've really worked very hard at this. It's difficult, you know. The mud won't dry thoroughly. It tends to slide. There've been some really bad accidents . . .'

'Your question?' asked Gojam.

'We need to know two things. Where are we, and is there anyone out there who can help us?'

Gojam frowned and began to speak, then frowned again. When he did speak, it was very gently. 'You're on a world

317

in the dream zone, which I identify as the Mud Flats.'

There was a long silence, broken at last by Puy. 'That . . . that isn't really helpful to us. I think what the philosophers want an answer to is the second question. Is there anyone out there who can help us?'

Gojam began to shake his head. Prince Charming very firmly took him by the neck and held him still.

'It would help us if you told us why you wanted to know.'

'Why . . . we *need* to know,' asserted Puy. 'There are certain problems we have been unable to solve. We have been unable even to agree on possible solutions. Basic philosophies differ. There is the question of the hatch rate, should it be encouraged or discouraged or should it be a matter of personal choice. There is the question of those among us who prefer not to provide their share of labor. Should they be conscripted against their will, and if not, are the rest of us under any obligation to feed them. There is the question of mechanicals. Some say they are diabolical and against the Will Of Him Who. Others maintain they are quite acceptable. We have come to bites and thrashings over these questions. Blood has been shed. Several of us have suffered quite severe lacerations. If there were someone neutral, someone from outside, who would arbitrate, perhaps give us another point of view . . .'

Gojam started to speak again, but the Prince held him firmly. 'You're saying there is considerable disagreement among you about how to solve your problems?'

The chief philosopher spoke up, nodding vigorously. 'Indeed. There is no agreement on how things should be handled. None at all. We need . . .'

'You need someone who will tell you what to do?'

'Well . . .' They scurried together for another hurried colloquy.

'. . . Not *tell*, precisely . . .'

'. . . still it wouldn't be a bad idea . . .'

'I can answer your question,' the Prince interrupted them. 'Yes, there are many worlds and creatures out there. Your next question will be, how do you reach them? Well, you cannot reach them until you have solved your own problems. And, no, we cannot help you with your problems. It is forbidden for us to do so. Each society must solve its own problems before it goes mixing about with other societies. That's the law. Isn't that right, Gojam?'

Gojam sulked only for a moment. 'Perfectly correct, Prince. Exactly what I was going to say.'

'In return for this information,' Prince Charming continued, inexorably, 'we'd like to ask a favor.'

'Anything,' breathed the philosophers sadly, banging their faces on their flippers, 'anything at all.'

'We have an enemy. A tall person shaped like one of us,' the Prince indicated Marianne and himself. 'A female person, if that concept is meaningful. She has a lot of very dark hair − this stuff. She is thinner than this person. She is as tall as I am. She has very fiery − ah, let me see − very intense-looking eyes. She may ask if you have seen us. She would not hesitate to destroy you if she did not get information to her liking.'

'Say no more,' breathed Puy. 'No more. At the first sight of such a one, we will summon the tide.'

'But your extraordinary building,' murmured Marianne.

'Thanks be to all the things that are or may be, we can quit building the damned thing,' Puy said. 'It's been very tiring. You have no idea. It's virtually destroyed our social system. Blessings on you for bringing us the law. Really.' He turned and kicked at a bit of mud with his right flipper, watching it with satisfaction as it tumbled into the water and dissolved. All over the structure, mud creatures were ripping off chunks of building material and dropping them to see the splash.

There seemed nothing further to discuss. Gojam flicked his whip. They moved off into the mist.

'Is what you said really the law?' *Marianne* asked.

'It is here,' murmured the Prince. 'It is now.'

When they had followed the wavering track until they could barely see the towers far behind them, Gojam muttered, 'Well, enough of this, all right? Where now? Someplace

Madame won't even consider looking for you. I have one or two ideas . . .'

'No,' said Prince Charming. 'Our encounter with these creatures has brought me to confront the true problem we face. We can run from her for a very long time, but it won't solve anything. Just as our mud friends have to solve their own problems, so do we.'

Marianne started to say something, then stopped, her tongue checked by that other person who seemed to be sharing her body. That person, in turn, stepped away, as though conscious she had been rude. In their common mind, Marianne could hear the half-humorous, half-hysterical laughter of that other person. 'After you, Marianne.'

'I was just going to say we have more problems than one.' Her voice was stiff and unforgiving, and she glared at the Prince as though it had been his fault, only to feel the glare turn into a wry smile as that other *Marianne* peered through her eyes.

'I know,' he said. 'I know. There are two of you in there, and I love at least one of you desperately. Since there were no provisions for that emotion in the world we fled from, it is obvious to me that the world from which we fled is not the world in which we belong. Gojam, can you take us through to our own real world?'

The momeg looked disappointed as he quirked his various eyebrows and twitched various parts of extremities. 'Of course. There's a likely nexus only a few steps from here. Though you have various real worlds. You, sir, have one. The woman has one. The other woman I sense to be present has another. The other momegs have their loci . . . well, you take my meaning.'

'I do,' Prince Charming mused, still attempting to draw the shreds of his clothing together, compulsively, as though he could find refuge behind or within some whole garment. 'Our basic problem seems to be Madame Delubovoska. Though I cannot at the moment remember why she is a difficulty for us. Still, it is evident we cannot accomplish anything without dealing with her. Presumably she has a place in the real world. We should, therefore, be returned as near that place as we can be without endangering ourselves. If we have allies anywhere near, then we would like to go to the place our allies dwell.'

'I will drop you,' Gojam said in his usual kindly voice, 'in the vicinity of Alphenlicht.'

CHAPTER EIGHTEEN

'But my dear, if you didn't tell the creature precisely where you wanted to be left off, you shouldn't be angry if he just dropped you nearby.' Ellat offered Marianne a towel. 'Perhaps dung doesn't mean to it what it does to us.'

Though Marianne did not remember Ellat, the woman's astonishing familiarity and friendliness did not permit Marianne to react as to a stranger. 'A dung pile is a dung pile,' Marianne objected. 'And I don't for one moment think Gojam didn't know it.'

'What was it you said it was? A momentary god? Makr Avehl mentioned momentary gods just before he went after you.'

'Gojam, the one with the peculiar sense of humor, went back, wherever they go. We have the other five with us, the dog ones.'

'Aghrehond said something about it. I suggested the kennels, but he . . . he didn't think that would do.'

'They're not really dogs, you know, Ellat. Not really.'

'As for that, Marianne, who are you, really?' The older woman turned Marianne around so she could look into her eyes. 'Are you the girl I knew?'

'Yes,' said *Marianne*.

'No,' said Marianne.

It came out as a gargle.

'You're not sure,' Ellat offered in a sympathetic tone. 'Or maybe you're both.'

321

'An uncomfortable both,' *Marianne* said, gritting her teeth. 'The thinking part works well, thank you. We each seem to have control of our own thoughts. But sometimes both of us try to use the body at once. I go left, she goes right. I say yes, she says no. We seem to gargle and stagger a lot. Well, you get the idea.'

'Not at all pleasant,' agreed Ellat. 'Couldn't you agree to take turns?'

'It may come to that,' Marianne agreed, closing her eyes wearily. 'Except that I'm still half convinced this whole thing is a dream. Did Makr Avehl tell you about the world he found me in?'

Ellat shook her head. Actually, he had said a few words, but only a few, and most of those had had to do with Madame Delubovoska.

'I was managing a laundry,' Marianne mused.

'The Cave of Light showed him a woman washing clothes,' Ellat offered. 'I imagine that's how he found you.'

'What I can't understand is why? Even in dream there should be some logic. Why a laundry?'

Ellat stirred, a little uncomfortably. 'You might discuss that with Therat . . .'

'Therat?'

'One of the Kavi. She is extremely interested in the power of symbols. I imagine she'll tell you that the laundry was symbolic of something in your life. Some need for cleanliness or being cleansed of something. Some unexpressed wish for redemption, perhaps. Madame summoned you into her world, but your own conscious or subconscious symbolic structure would largely have determined the specific role you would play in that environment. At least, that's my understanding of the way it works.'

'A laundry!' Marianne shook her head. 'And then there's this business of memory only working one way! When I'm there, I can't remember here. But when I'm here, I can remember there well enough. Not like a dream at all, which is upsetting, because if it's all a dream, which I believe it is, then I ought not to be able to remember it. Unless I'm

322

not awake yet.' She made a petulant gesture, aware of how ridiculous this sounded. 'Well, let it go. I think the important thing for me now is to find out about air schedules to get home. If it's a dream, I'll dream my flight back. I may have already lost my job, not showing up for so long.'

'How long do you think, my dear?'

'Days. Weeks. Maybe months. No — only weeks, I think.'

'Actually, less than one day.'

'You're joking?'

'Not at all. It was only last night that we awoke, Makr Avehl and I, knowing something had happened to you. It is only a few hours since Aghrehond went after Makr Avehl. Time does not move in the false worlds as it moves here. Madame can do a year's worth of damage in the false worlds in what passes for moments here in our world. In the dream worlds, one can live many lives in one lifetime or one can effectively experience an eternity of discomfort or horror.'

Both Mariannes took a moment to absorb this. 'Well, little time or a lot, I've still got to get back to work,' said the younger one. She rose with a bit of bustle, wanting to do something decisive, tired of being done to and with.

'Marianne,' said Makr Avehl from the doorway where, clad only in clean trousers, he stood vigorously toweling his head. 'Don't be silly. You can't.' His voice was fond, loving, concerned.

'I most certainly can,' she turned, eyes blazing, furious at his assumption of authority over her.

His lips clamped tight in disappointment and anger. 'Then you'll most certainly end up back in some laundry, or some library, or some dungeon once again! Madame is not going to give up. Can't you get that through your head?' He threw the towel on the floor and stamped on it with his bare feet as he left the room, shouting for someone to get him a shirt.

'He doesn't like me,' said Marianne, slightly discomfitted. 'He really doesn't.'

'It isn't that,' Ellat murmured. 'But you do rather stand between him and someone he loves very dearly.'

'Her,' snarled Marianne. 'I know.' She waited grimly for

Marianne to assert herself, but there was only a silent, somehow satisfied watchfulness inside.

'True, but it isn't only that. He feels responsible for you. You *both*, I should say. The situation must be resolved, and he's quite right. If you go back home, you'll only end up ensorceled once again.'

'If the damned woman wants to kill me, why doesn't she just do it and get it over with? Why all this folderol, this magic this and that. I really don't understand it. Don't believe it. Don't like it.'

'Well, my dear, none of us do. As to why she doesn't just hire some thug to murder you — well, the reason is fairly obvious I should think. She doesn't really want you dead. She wants you in a state of subservience. She needs something from you. You really should enquire about your parents' estate, Marianne. If Tabiti is seeking to enslave you, it must be because you have or will have some authority she wants.'

'Well, I already have inquired about the estate,' Marianne confessed, a little shamefacedly. 'When Makr Avehl visited our home, he said something about it which piqued my curiosity, so I asked Mama. Evidently my independence has impressed Papa sufficiently that he has named me as the executor, for everything. I had always assumed there would be a number of trustees — and there will be if anything happens to me — but if anything happens to Mama and Papa and I'm alive and well, I'll be the only one.'

'Well then, you have the explanation so don't be foolish,' said Makr Avehl from the door. He had managed to get himself almost fully dressed, and was now tucking in an unbuttoned shirt that displayed a generous extent of muscular and smooth-skinned chest. 'It's obvious what Tabiti wants — just what she's wanted all along: control of the Zahmani estates. She enslaves you, then does away with your parents, and she's what you Americans would call home free.'

Marianne withdrew her eyes from Makr Avehl's naked chest, surprised to find that simple action very difficult. 'Ah — um, I did think she was going to kill me, though, there in the arena.' The sight of his body was doing strange things to her breathing.

'I think not. The threat to you was a ploy designed to get me into the act,' Makr Avehl said, buttoning his shirt. 'Since I represent a challenge to her plans, naturally, she wants me out of the way entirely.'

'If she had killed you there, would you be . . . that is, would it have . . .'

'Would it have killed me here and now? Oh, very much so. Because everything that makes me me was there. All that was left here was a kind of anchor.'

'And yet when we're . . . there, we don't remember . . . here.'

'No, because if we did, we couldn't be fully involved in the dream world. Our memories of home would keep us from interacting with where we are and what we're doing. You couldn't really have been concerned about that laundry if you'd remembered home, could you? Could I have believed in myself as Prince Charming if I had remembered who I was?'

'Does Madame remember who she is when she's there?'

Makr Avehl looked puzzled. 'You know, I haven't the least idea. It wouldn't surprise me. In fact, that could be part of the secret of her power, an ability to take her memory intact into the false worlds. It would be quite a trick, wouldn't it, Ellat?'

'It would indeed,' she said with a harsh twist to her lips. 'Though I hate to think what she must have done to gain that ability. Not something I think we want to try for, Makr Avehl.'

'No fear, Sister.'

'May I enter, most exalted one?' Aghrehond stood at the door, his hair still wet from the thorough washing he had given it. Of them all, Aghrehond had been most completely buried in the dung pile. 'May I greet our guest in my own inimitable person? May I say hello and how-de-do and welcome to Alphenlicht?'

Ellat beckoned him. 'Don't be an ass, Hondi. Come in.'

'But I am an ass, Lady. Or was. First cousin to one. Did I make an excellent horse, Marianne? Was I splendid?'

'Perfectly splendid, Aghrehond,' she choked, fighting her internal twin for possession of her voice.

'I liked you better as the grassy dog,' said *Marianne*, taking over. 'I liked you as Cani Grassi, Aghrehond. Fighting the Manticore.'

Makr Avehl stepped forward to embrace her, holding her very tightly only for a moment, then stepping back as she started to writhe away from him.

'I wish you wouldn't do that,' said Marianne, not entirely convincingly. She found herself panting.

'It was the other one I embraced,' he whispered. 'Don't take it personally.'

She, however, was taking it very personally, since every inch of her body yearned toward him. Her limbs felt loosened, somehow separated from her, as though they were floating. Hot, sweet liquid was running through her veins, and there was a tingle in her breasts. She breathed as though she had been running. She sat down abruptly, sending a confused, hostile thought toward her tenant.

'Damn it, do you have to melt like that?'

'I love him, silly girl. What do you want me to do? Simply ignore how I feel?'

'I want you to go back where you came from.'

'I am where I came from. Precisely.'

'Then go wherever you went when I was twelve.'

'Not on your life. I tried that, and all it did was almost get us both killed.'

'What brought you back, anyhow?'

'You know very well!' Marianne felt the internal blush.

'Oh, the Sleeping Princess was awakened by Prince Charming's kiss? Isn't that a dreadful cliché?'

'Marianne!' Ellat was shaking her. 'Stop that. Your eyes are crossed and you're making disgusting noises. If you have to argue with yourself, go out in the garden and do it out loud.' She pushed the embarrassed girl out the door and made a gesture at the two men who had been watching, openmouthed. 'And as for you two, go away. Makr Avehl, I'm ashamed of you. You're not helping, not at all.'

'What do you want me to do, Ellat?' he echoed *Marianne*'s silent question. 'Pretend she isn't here?'

'You could try that. For a time. While we try or she tries or they try to sort it out.'

He gave her a surly look, but did not argue with that particular point. 'I've reached a decision, Ellat.'

'I thought you might have,' she replied mildly, folding the towel he had dropped on the floor. 'Since you wouldn't have come back to Alphenlicht, otherwise.'

'We're going to have to confront Madame.'

'I assumed that, also.'

'Sometimes I despair, Ellat. Will I ever be able to surprise you?'

'Yes. If you'd listen to me, ever, it would surprise me enormously. I told you years ago we would have to deal with Tabiti, forthrightly and personally. You, on the other hand, preferred diplomatic maneuver and, more recently, this dream-world pursuit.'

'Not my choice!'

'True. However, in my opinion, the best time to have struck at Tabiti would have been immediately on your return from — what shall I say? — episode one. Before you went searching for *Marianne* again. While Tabiti was still confused.'

'You overlook one thing,' he replied in a dry voice. 'If she was confused, which I'm not at all certain of, I was even more so.'

'Yes. Well. That's as may be, and nothing was done at the time, so it's fruitless to speak of it. What do you plan now?'

'I plan a visit to the Cave of Light, Ellat. With Marianne. Tabiti gets her power from somewhere . . .'

'I thought her power had always been attributed to shaman-istic influences.'

'That's only a label. Yes, I have no doubt she was taught whatever she knows by the black shamans, but what did they teach her? Where does she draw her force from?'

'And if you find out?'

'We must find a way to cut it off. Marianne will never be safe until we do — the world may not be safe until we do.'

'You're aware that there is a great deal of risk in such an endeavor.'

'So far as I can see, there's more risk in doing nothing. It's a case of being damned if we do and damned if we don't.'

Ellat said nothing to this, choosing instead to cling tightly to a serenity of spirit that had cost her a good deal to achieve. He would do it. She could not in good conscience advise otherwise. She would do what she had done so often in the past.

Wait and hope.

CHAPTER NINETEEN

Therat recommended an afternoon reading from the Cave of Light, then spent the morning hours with Marianne, telling her of the history of the Cave. 'I can't expect you to believe in it totally,' she smiled, her lips belying her eyes which burned into Marianne's own with a fervid glow. 'We do expect that you not come into the Cave as a skeptic. Just be open to whatever happens.'

'Do I need to do anything? Learn any chants or responses or anything?'

'Nothing at all. We'll do the reciting. You will need to stand in darkness for a few moments, which makes some people rather dizzy. I'll be next to you and you can hold on to me if you like.'

'Do I get to see the — symbols or whatever they are?'

'Certainly. All those present are requested to verify whatever message the Cave seems to be offering.'

'What do I wear?'

'Whatever you like. Ellat will give you a robe to cover

whatever you're wearing, but that's tradition, not ritual. I've recommended about two o'clock, if that's all right with you.'

'I don't know why not,' said Marianne. She had been waiting all morning for *Marianne* to interrupt her or supersede her in some action, but nothing of the kind had happened. Still, the sense of being occupied was very strong. *Marianne* had not gone away.

When they arrived at the Cave that afternoon — Ellat, Aghrehond, Makr Avehl and Marianne — Therat, along with Nalavi and Cyram, met them at the entrance cavern and escorted them down the winding, sandy-floored tunnel by the light of flaring lanterns. Every wall, every pillar, every square inch of exposed stone was decorated with symbols: words, phrases, or numbers; some superimposed upon others; some ancient, some newly chiseled or painted on the stone.

They placed their lanterns upon the central altar. Words were chanted that Marianne did not recognize. She knew what they meant, however. In the ancient language of the Magi, the question that the Cave was to answer had been asked. What was the source of Madame's power?

She felt Therat take her arm as the lanterns were turned off. They stood in darkness. Above them the great, perforated bulk of the mountain rested, spongy with micalined worm holes, through which the light from the outer world was reflected in and down, faint glimmerings, no more than the smallest candle glow, falling through all that weight of rock and earth into the cavern below. Light, reflected from leaf or stream or animal or stone. Never twice the same.

'I see light,' whispered Marianne.

'The light rests on an hourglass,' said Therat.

'A sundial,' said Nalavi.

'A clock,' said Cyram, all three of them at once, looking in three different directions. Then they were in darkness once more, unrelieved and absolute. After a moment, Therat sighed and struck a light. 'Well, Makr Avehl?'

'Time,' he said. 'The source of her power is time.'

'What's the matter, Makr Avehl?' asked *Marianne*. 'You don't sound hopeful.'

'Time?' he replied. 'How does one get at it? What does one do with it? How has she gained access to it?'

'The momentary gods,' *Marianne* replied. 'They'd know. They give time its reality, or so they say. No, that's not quite it. They give space its reality, and that gives time its reality.'

Therat stared at her in the glare of the lantern light. 'You have spoken with momentary gods?' Therat asked.

'There are five of them with us,' Marianne began.

'I summoned them,' said *Marianne*. 'It's something I learned to do from . . . from Madame, I think. I was in this place, a library, I seem to remember, and she did this thing. Summoned something terrible. All the world was full of snakes, I remember that. And she had this Manticore. She summoned it up, too, from time to time. And she used . . . used the momentary gods to transport people into her worlds, I remember that. She would reach up and twist the tail of a momentary god, and it would establish a nexus and let someone through. Oh, I do remember that.'

'And you learned to do this by merely observing her?'

Marianne shook her head, confused. 'I'm not sure that's exactly it. Let's say I absorbed enough to do it once, once only, without knowing what I was really doing and without any idea how to undo it.'

'Shamanism,' said Therat in a flat, dismissive tone. 'Trifling with the structure of the universe. Foolish! Dangerous!'

'Dangerous, yes, but we'll have to deal with it somehow,' mused Makr Avehl.

'I still think we ought to talk to the momentary gods,' advised *Marianne*, turning toward the entrance of the Cave. 'They may tell us something of value.'

Therat came with them to the Residence, where *Marianne* called the momegs. Black Dog came in answer to her call, but he was most unwilling to talk. He arrived. He listened briefly, then vanished. Marianne called him again, he returned to lie on the floor, head on paws, scowling at them all.

'Come on,' *Marianne* said. 'You know something. You told me the momegs give time its reality, or something like that.'

'It's true,' he mumbled. 'Each of us holds a chunk. Our birthright, so to speak.'

'How big a chunk?' asked Makr Avehl.

'You don't understand. It's not like that. Not bigness or longness.'

'Well tell me, what is it then?'

'What it is, is duration. Or very rarely beginningness.'

Makr Avehl was relentless. 'Explain that.'

Black Dog whined, pawed his nose, gnawed at some imaginary itch on his hind leg, then said, 'Something happens. Then after that, something else happens. Let's say, a light wave comes to my locus. It has duration there, a chunk of it, the only size there is, then it has to go somewhere, so it goes to my contiguite. Anyhow, my contiguite has a chunk of duration, too. *After* something happens somewhere else, something happens with him. Usually it's light. Sometimes it's quarks. We do a lot of durations and aftering with quarks.'

'What about beforeness?' asked Marianne, puzzled. 'Don't any of you have that?'

'There's no such thing,' Black Dog barked, almost howling, putting his front paws over his ears. 'That's heresy. We give time its reality by duration and afterness. Everything happens after something else. Nothing happens before something else. It can't! That's just a human heresy, that's all.'

'Why are you so upset?' asked Makr Avehl. 'You're saying time is quantized, aren't you? I don't see why it shouldn't be. Does this have anything to do with where Madame gets her power?'

'She twists things,' sulked the Black Dog.

'She's evil,' said the Foo Dog, erupting into the room from behind a chair. 'She'll end up destroying the universe, or at least this piece of it.'

'Because?'

'Because she keeps beforing things. She takes momegs and bends them double, so that things don't go on to after, they twist around and go back before. That's how *she*,' the momeg indicated Marianne, 'went back in her own time that way. She learned it from Madame and she borrowed Madame's power to do it. Not that we blame her. She didn't know what she was doing . . .'

'I really didn't,' said *Marianne*, aghast. 'Do you mean when I did that, I actually destroyed something?'

'A momeg is all. One of us. Not one any of us liked very much. He was from a locus way out at the edge of things. Madame keeps a stock of rural momegs around. She thinks as long as she just nibbles away at the edges of things, it won't really affect anything. She's wrong, of course. Everyone with any sense knows that the edges of things are really the middle. There have already been disruptions.' The Foo Dog brooded. 'I suppose we should have told you this be . . . uh, at some prior eventuality.'

'It would have been helpful,' said Makr Avehl. 'I'm not sure I understand it yet. Let's see if I do. The black shamans taught Madame how to evoke momegs. They taught her how to twist momegs in half — is that right? — so that things go backwards or make loops in time instead of going forward?'

'Taught her how, or gave her some device to do it with, I'm not sure which. Anyhow, she does it, and that makes holes in time where she can stick her false worlds,' the Foo Dog nodded. 'And it allows her to fool around with people in very unpleasant ways. And it's all wrong, of course. Nobody ought to do it, ever. Up until recently, it was only the black shamans who talked about it, but more recently there was some respected human person who taught that time doesn't always seem to come afterward, even though we know it does.'

'Are you talking about relativity?' asked Makr Avehl. 'Really?'

'That's what he called it,' said Wolf Dog, melting through a wall. 'That's not what we call it. We call it messing about with things that ought to be left alone. Though of course so long as people just talk about it, no harm is done. It's when people start actually messing about with it that things start to go wrong.'

'Then Gojam was right,' said *Marianne*.

Makr Avehl stared at her in perplexity. It was Aghrehond who snapped his fingers in sudden memory. 'He said something about Madame taking momegs and — what? Not sending them back at all?'

'To quote him exactly,' said *Marianne*, 'Gojam said, "She has a nasty habit of summoning up momegs on the spur of the moment, without any concern for the inconvenience it may cause, and then splatting them back again whenever it suits her. If she returns them at all, which I have reason to doubt in some cases." '

Makr Avehl ran his fingers through his hair, then smoothed it, then rolled it again. 'She's using them up. Burning them up, as we would burn gasoline. Through some — some mechanism, some spell, something. We need to find how she does it. If the mechanism can be destroyed — assuming she can't build another one — that will do. If the source can be eliminated, that will do.'

'If Madame can be done away with,' said Marianne, 'that will do as well.'

The others in the group looked at one another uncomfortably.

'No?' she asked, surprised.

'Not except as a last resort,' Ellat said. 'People like Madame — often trade off vital parts of themselves in return for power. That, too, is a shamanistic tendency. Black shaman, I should say. Those vital parts are often — well, potentiated, I suppose one might say, when the person dies.'

'You're talking ghosts, here?' Marianne challenged.

'Something like that.'

'So? What harm can a ghost do?'

'I'm talking real ghosts, not comic-book creatures,' Ellat said patiently. 'Concatenations of evil intention. Which, after sufficient aggregation, become what we would call demons. As to what harm, a very great deal. To you. To Makr Avehl. To nameless third parties we don't even know of.'

'Take her word for it,' said Therat, who had listened silently to the entire conversation with the momegs and who now spoke for the first time. 'It would be better to render Madame helpless than to kill her. Truly. If you can figure out a way to do that, you will have done all that needs doing.'

'And how do we do that?'

'We go to Lubovosk,' said Makr Avehl. 'We go to Lubovosk and talk to the same people Madame talked to when she learned all this. We start with the black shamans.'

CHAPTER TWENTY

Three bodies and four people went. Two Mariannes, one Makr Avehl, one Aghrehond. Makr Avehl's beard and hair were dyed white, he led the packhorse and walked with a cane. Marianne wore the typical peasant dress of the region; her hair was braided; her face was dirty. Dressed in leather trousers and a full-sleeved shirt under a filthy sheepskin jacket, Aghrehond drove a small flock of sheep with the help of a couple of the momegs who showed up from time to time to nip at a lagging heel or bark at a straying woolface. They climbed over a mountain by a secret trail maintained by the Alphenlicht border guards; they appeared in Lubovosk some miles inside the border with all the requisite papers tucked in one pocket or another.

Before they left, certain processes had been set in motion in Alphenlicht, behind them. Functionaries at the Residence started the day by announcing that the Prime Minister would shortly be married, that even now his intended bride, an American girl of impecccable Kavi descent, was visiting the family. All attention was drawn south, to the Prime Minister's Residence in Alphenlicht. Such had been Makr Avehl's intention.

When advised of this ruse, Marianne was furious. 'I never said I'd marry you.'

'Since I didn't propose to you, that doesn't surprise me.'

'You can't marry *her* unless I consent to it. It's my body, damn it.'

334

Makr Avehl considered this for a long time, looking her up and down, walking around her as though she had been a filly for auction. 'I think I could, don't you know. We'd simply divide up the time. Monday, Wednesdays, Fridays, and alternate Sundays would be yours. The other time would be ours. That would work out well, wouldn't it? You'd have lots of time to yourself. *Marianne* and I would have time to ourselves. You could learn to sleep through our times, just as Marianne did during yours.'

'I'm going back to Colorado.'

'That would make what I propose very difficult.'

'You're impossible.'

'Not impossible, no. Merely very unlikely. Face it, Marianne. We are all unlikely. You, me, Ellat, Aghrehond. The world is unlikely. But not impossible.'

She had stormed at him then and did so now, clomping along the trail in her felt boots, unable to set aside her anger even for the moment.

Aghrehond caught her by the hand. 'Oh, beauteous lady, most glorious master, please. For the sake of my poor, outraged heart. Here are we all, in the very belly of the beast, here on the slippery slopes of Lubovosk, here in the necromantic north, in the wicked woods, in the very gut of this dreadful country, and you argue over such trifles as who shall love whom. Truly, it may be none of us will love again, and then you will be sorry to have wasted your time in this fashion.' Aghrehond sounded much aggrieved, taking out his temper on the sheep as he boomed at them to move in the direction he wished and no other. He had a tired lamb draped around his neck, which somewhat mitigated his attempts at fierceness.

Marianne subsided, though only a little. 'What are we going to do when we get there? And where is there, come to that?'

Makr Avehl answered her. 'We're going to the place Tabiti lives. Not a palace, or residence, I've been told, but something more like a villa or chateau, outside the capital city — or what passes for one in Lubovosk. Somewhere nearby, there should be an encampment where we'll find the shamans. My spies tell me that she consults them or uses them almost daily, so they'll have to be close by. On the other hand, she wouldn't want their presence obvious to visitors, so I think they will not actually be part of her establishment.'

The sun marked their progress, from morning until noon, into the late afternoon. Along about dusk they heard the city before they saw it, a dull hum, like a hive of dispirited bees. From the crest of a hill they stared down at it, squatting like a toad in a desolate valley, surrounded by an ancient and anciently ruined wall. Here and there around the perimeter of the city were gun emplacements, and fully half the persons moving about on the streets seemed to be in uniform.

'Madame's friends,' growled Makr Avehl. 'Invited in to help her keep order.'

'I should think she would keep order by — by her own methods,' *Marianne* remarked.

'It would take too much of her time. Easier to do it by brute force and a little official terrorism, I should think. No, Madame's ambition extends far beyond this pathetic excuse for a country, believe me.'

'Where's her place?'

'I see half a dozen largish houses on the surrounding hills. I think that one must be it.' He pointed to the left, where a fully walled villa crowned a forested hill. 'It makes some pretense at looking civilized.'

'And what do we do?'

'We look around. We start by driving the sheep down that road past the place, into the woods, looking around in the woods, seeing what we see, and then pitching a tent.'

'Do we have a tent?'

Aghrehond burbled, 'Oh, indeed, lovely lady, we have a tent. Would we come into this despicable wilderness without some amenities for so admirable a person? What of your privacy? Your dignity? Would we come without a tent?'

'Probably,' said Marianne. 'Where is it?'

'On the packhorse,' said Makr Avehl.

'I hope there's something for supper there as well.'

'That was the idea, yes.'

They passed under the walls of the chateau, studiously ignoring the impersonal insults shouted down at them by lounging guards, and went toward the forest on a narrow track.

'Smoke coming from up ahead,' said Makr Avehl softly. 'Could be anything, including what we're looking for.' They went on, Wolf Dog and Dingo trotting behind, an ill-assorted pair of shepherds. 'The shamans have a style about them. They go in for feathers and hair quite a bit. Beads, too. Also they try not to bathe very often. Not more than once every two or three years, I'd say. We may smell the camp before we see it. Or we may hear it. Shamans go in for drums, too . . .'

Under the eaves of the forest, monstrous firs shut out the light to leave a gray-green gloom beneath their branches. From beyond a brush-covered rise, they could hear the sounds of people moving about, a muffled shout, the crack of an axe — and a drum. Makr Avehl disappeared into the brush, returning after a time brushing twigs and leaves from his jacket.

'Here, I should think,' he said, nodding significantly toward the noise. While Marianne sat on a fallen log, watching them, the two men set up a camp, two small tents, a cookfire with a kettle suspended above it, and a line of ropes strung around several trees to make a pen for the sheep. When all was settled, Aghrehond and Makr Avehl began a loud and, so far as Marianne could see, pointless argument, with much shouting.

The drum which had been tum-te-tumming away behind the brush fell silent. So did the voices.

'You've forgotten it, dunderhead,' growled Makr Avehl in an old man's voice. 'Forgotten it completely. How can I fry sausages without my pan?'

'It was there,' grumbled Aghrehond loudly and angrily. 'I put it there myself.'

'Greetings,' said a strange voice from under the trees. 'Is something wrong?'

He was tall and very dark, with feathers and beads woven into his hair. In his hand he held a staff decorated with more feathers and bones and long hanks of hair attached to chunks of skin which looked suspiciously scalplike. His mouth was bent into an obviously unaccustomed smile that displayed a few discolored teeth and did not succeed in making him look less threatening.

It was almost as though he had been expecting them, thought *Marianne*.

'This dunderhead lost my frying pan,' snarled Makr Avehl.

'It's right here,' said Aghrehond, triumphantly, waving it. 'I told you I put it in.'

'My name is Chevooskak,' the dark man said with a toothy grin. The remaining teeth, though yellow, were very sharp. 'Who are you?'

'Shepherds,' mumbled Makr Avehl. 'Trying to get these fool sheep home. Name's Dommle. He's my son. Hondi Dommle. She's his wife, Dummy Dommle. She's mute. Can't talk, thanks be. There's too much talk, anyway, in my opinion.'

'Ah,' murmured Chevooskak, showing his teeth once more. 'Would you be interested in selling a sheep? Our camp needs meat. You could join us, if you liked. Just through the brush there. It's closer to the water than you are here.'

Makr Avehl and Aghrehond discussed this while Marianne attempted to look bored and slightly half-witted. At length, Makr Avehl agreed both to sell one sheep and to move nearer to the larger camp where, on arrival, they found a dozen hide yurts arranged around a sizeable clearing with a sturdy pole coral at one side.

'You can put the sheep in there,' Chevooskak said. 'We won't be using it for a day or two. The horses are all out on pasture.'

The language was almost the same as that spoken in Alphenlicht, though the accent was harsher. Marianne understood much of what he said, and every word made her cringe, though she could not say why.

'It's obvious why,' said *Marianne*, silently. 'Because he's lying to you. He intends to kill at least two of you and take the sheep.'

'Which two?' she asked, then flushed. It was obvious which two. 'How do you know that?'

'I just know. Ask Makr Avehl if I'm not right.'

When she whispered her suspicions to Makr Avehl, he merely nodded. 'We figured on it, Marianne. Just go on as you are. Remember, you can't talk.'

She was not tempted to talk aloud. Even one or two words in her unmistakably American accent would have given them away. 'What are we going to do?' she whispered.

'Wait until dark. Then do a little worm turning if the momegs will help.'

'I can't see that we have any choice,' said the Wolf Dog, leering at a recalcitrant sheep. 'Not ethically.'

Dingo merely whined and thrust her head into Marianne's lap, tongue licking delicately between Marianne's fingers.

'Why don't you ever talk?' Marianne murmured. 'So silent, Dingo Dog.'

'She's telepathic,' said the Wolf Dog, returning the recalcitrant sheep to the corral, from which she promptly tried to escape once more. 'These sheep have no brains.'

'Shh,' muttered Makr Avehl to the momegs. 'You're going to make them suspicious with all this chatter.'

Chevooskak stood at the side of the pole corral, commenting upon the edibility of various of the animals. Aghrehond argued with him vehemently. Sheep after sheep was proposed, argued over, and discarded in favor of another. When the entire flock had been considered, agreement was reached, and the stubborn wool-head who had evaded Wolf Dog was led away to the slaughter.

'Serves her right,' muttered the dog.

'Quiet,' urged Makr Avehl. 'Sheep-dogs do not discuss their charges with the shepherd.'

Fires were built. Within the hour, roasting meat smells began to drift across the clearing. Marianne found herself salivating profusely, and the dried sheet of bread which Aghrehond offered her did little to alleviate her hunger. She raised her head, sniffing, as Chevooskak brought them a fat, dripping leg, redolent of garlic and herbs.

'Welcome,' he breathed at them with his toothy smile. 'Welcome to our home. Eat. Enjoy.'

Makr Avehl bowed, Aghrehond bowed, both cut bite-sized chunks from the meat and pretended to eat while surreptitiously tossing the chunks into the fire. Aghrehond offered a dripping slice to Marianne, gesturing pointedly at the burning fat. She took it hungrily, but managed to follow their example. Between pretend mouthfuls of the savory smelling meat, she took real bites of the dry bread along with sips of sour yoghurt.

'I think we're due to get very sleepy along about now,' muttered Makr Avehl. 'Tent time.' He yawned ostentatiously and crept into one tent. After a moment, Aghrehond followed his example by crawling into the other one. 'Get in here, wife,' he bellowed. 'Don't sit there dreaming by the fire.'

Marianne, who had forgotten her role as Hondi Dommle's wife, started in surprise, then recovered herself and crawled into the tent where Aghrehond promptly thrust her into a corner and sat down beside the entrance, a wicked-looking knife in his hand.

'Can you call them?' he asked. 'All five of them.'

'That would be unnecessary,' Black Dog mumbled from the pile of blankets. 'We are here.'

'You understand what to do?'

'A little menacing. Perhaps a bit of human chewing and tearing. A touch of mild laceration. We've done it before.'

They had no opportunity to do it again for a long time. It was almost midnight before Chevooskak lurked across the clearing, a shadow among darker shadows. He paused for endless moments outside the tent, listening. Aghrehond breathed slowly, rhythmically, loudly. At last the shaman went down on all fours and crept within.

Marianne restrained herself with difficulty. The man's eyes glowed, like a cat's eyes, reflecting light.

They glowed only for a moment. Then there was a rush of bodies, a thrashing, then silence.

'Light the lantern,' said Makr Avehl.

Marianne complied, feeling for the matches in the darkness. In the dim light she saw Chevooskak lying prone, one of the momegs grasping each extremity, the wolf at his throat. Aghrehond sat on the shaman's back, testing with his thumb the knife the shaman had carried.

'A simple thing,' Makr Avehl said conversationally, entering the tent through a slit in the back and crouching next to Marianne. 'A simple thing, Chevooskak. A request for information. These are momentary gods at your throat, at your limbs. They will not hesitate to tear you apart. You cannot control them by guile or lore, for they were not summoned by you. You see, I know some few things about this matter.'

'What do you want?' the shaman gargled, staring sideways into the red glare of the Foo Dog's eyes. *Marianne* did not think he was as frightened as he pretended to be.

'How does Madame control the momentary gods? What device does she use? What words or incantation? How does she do it? Tell me.'

The shaman shook his head. 'She would kill me.'

'Come now. It was you who taught her in the first place.'

'Not me. No. My father taught her.'

'Well, are you not privy to your father's secrets?'

'He did not tell me everything.'

'He told you of this, though, didn't he?'

The man started to shake his head, but the dog at his throat growled softly, so he changed his mind and whispered instead. 'He said — he said he gave her the time bender.'

'What is it, this time bender?'

'I don't know. I never saw it. She has it.'

'How big a thing, then? Small, or large?'

'I don't know. Truly. I don't know!'

'Come, come.' The momegs growled, closing their teeth upon the shaman's arms and legs. The Wolf leaned forward to get a better grip on the man's throat.

'Where did your father get it?' whispered *Marianne*. 'Did he tell you that?' Something was not right about this, but she

341

couldn't tell what it was. The man's reluctance seemed real, and yet it did not. He was too easily persuaded.

'It fell. Out of the sky.'

'Let him up,' said *Marianne*. 'I believe he will talk with us.' And that fact disturbed her. He would talk with them. He would tell them the truth. She knew it. Why did it upset her?

Makr Avehl tied the man's hands behind him, and Aghrehond saw that two of the momegs were at either side of him before he was allowed to sit up against the canvas, glaring at them in the light of the lantern. 'Who are you?' he hissed. 'Who?' This at least seemed an honest question. He really didn't know.

'Never mind,' said *Marianne*. 'You don't really want to know. Now, tell us what your father told you.'

The man's eyes glazed. He mumbled a moment, 'Fell from the sky, he said. Dreaming, all night, under the stars . . . stars like a great river, running away across the sky, and near morning a red star, burning, like a forge, hot over his head, east to west, falling. He went where it fell . . . all the trees bent down around it. A great hole, hot. And when it cooled, this thing was in it. So he picked it up and put it in his ghost bag and went away from there.'

'So, then, we know how large it is,' *Marianne* murmured. 'Small enough to be carried away in his ghost bag. How big was his bag, Chevooskak? You saw it many times, how big was it?'

'So,' he motioned with his hands, a small square, perhaps a foot on a side.

'With many things in it, no? Bones, perhaps?'

He nodded, unwillingly. 'Many things.'

'What did your father do with this time bender?'

'He could make time stop. He could make people stop moving. He could make animals stop moving. He was very powerful. Very great. Until she came.'

'She,' crooned *Marianne*. 'Did he love her, Chevooskak?' Perhaps this was what bothered her.

The man glared, spat, honestly angry. 'Like a dog after a

342

bitch. Everything he knew, he told her. Everything he had, he gave her.'

'Instead of to you, his son?'

The shaman growled, deep in his throat. 'When she had it all, she killed him.'

Marianne looked at Makr Avehl and shrugged. This last was real, very real. Chevooskak felt that. The other? She was not comfortable with what little they had learned, but she knew of no way to get at the source of her discomfort. Makr Avehl leaned forward to press his hands on the shaman's neck. The shaman fell forward, unconscious, and the momegs stepped fastidiously away from him.

'He smells terrible,' said the Blue Dragon Dog. 'I don't think he ever bathes.'

'I would have hated to bite him,' admitted Wolf Dog, 'though honor would have constrained me to do so.'

'It wasn't necessary,' commented Makr Avehl. '*Marianne* seems to have found out what we needed to know. Let's dose him with that potion Ellat gave me, Hondi, then haul him back to his yurt. The potion should guarantee he remembers none of this.' He turned to Marianne with a puzzled look, a look he retained when he returned to the tent. 'Don't you think that was too easy?' he murmured.

'Perhaps not,' Aghrehond argued, without real conviction. 'He is not the man his father was. That is clear. Perhaps the power which would have passed from father to son passed instead to her — Madame?'

'Possible,' Makr Avehl acknowledged, 'but I still think it was much too easy.' The expression of concern stayed on his face and was still there early in the morning, before most of the camp was astir, when they left with their flock. Chevooskak came out of his yurt to stare bleary-eyed after them, a look of confusion on his face.

'Too easy,' said Makr Avehl again.

'I wish you wouldn't keep saying that,' said Marianne. 'It doesn't seem easy to me. You may know more or less what you're looking for, but you still have no idea where she keeps it or what it really looks like.'

'We know a few things about it,' said Makr Avehl. 'She uses it to move people into her false worlds. She used it on *Marianne* — my Marianne — at the top of a flight of stairs in Marianne's own house. She had it with her. Was she carrying anything at that time?'

Marianne answered. 'Nothing but a clipboard with a piece of paper on it. Nothing in her hands.'

'And what was she wearing?'

'A cap, like a uniform cap, and dark shirt and trousers, I think. Yes, I'm sure. I thought she was a delivery person until she raised her head.'

'Shirt and trousers. Nothing voluminous. Something, then, that would fit in a pocket or, more likely, on a chain around the neck.'

'She never wears low-cut clothes,' *Marianne* said. 'I have been trying to remember every time I've seen her. She always wore a high-necked dress or shirt.'

'So, we assume when she leaves her home, she wears the thing around her neck. When she's at home, however, she could put it almost anywhere.'

'So,' Aghrehond continued, 'we have a better chance if we get her to come out than if we go in after her.'

Marianne snorted. 'How do you expect to do that?'

'Very simple,' said Makr Avehl. 'We invite her to the wedding.'

CHAPTER TWENTY-ONE

Marianne was furious. 'I know why he's doing it. I know it's a good plan. I know Madame will probably come like a shot, if just to have a chance at me! But this kind of haste — well, it's unseemly, that's what it is. People will think I'm pregnant.'

Ellat said reasonably, 'Well, what's that matter in this day and age? What's that matter in any day and age, come to that?

344

Even here in Alphenlicht, it's not that unusual.'

'Papa will split a gusset,' Marianne snarled, quoting Cloud-haired mama, who always asserted that Papa would split a gusset. Marianne herself had no very clear idea of what a gusset might be. 'He'll name a new executor. He'll . . . Besides, I don't want to get married.'

'My brother won't be marrying you, dear.'

'You tell me how he's going to marry *her* without marrying *me*. We just happen to be sharing a body. There are certain − intimacies that go with marriage you know.' She stopped, flushing. When it came right down to it, she could not be repelled by the idea of those intimacies, though she tried. 'It's like rape,' she told herself vehemently, not believing a word of it. Her body − *their* body − refused to consider it rape.

'My dear, be calm. Please. Be calm. Makr Avehl will do nothing to offend your sensibilities, you have my word. Take a nap. You look tired.'

'I do nothing these days but take naps. I slept half of yesterday. Don't try to put me off, Ellat. It's international news. Papa will hear of it.'

'Leave that to the Prime Minister, my dear. He will handle everything.'

Marianne subsided, wondering as she did so where the other *Marianne* had taken herself. Though her presence could still be felt, she had not recently interrupted or taken over. She yawned. It was true that she seemed to do nothing but sleep, lately. And she was becoming forgetful. This morning when she woke from a quick nap, she was not wearing the same blouse she remembered having on when she lay down. This morning, she remembered putting her slippers on one side of the bed and woke to find them on the other. Why did Marianne have this feeling that something was going on, that *Marianne* and Makr Avehl were plotting something, when they could not possibly plot anything without her knowing. Was there some way that *Marianne* could remain active while Marianne was asleep? 'Lying low, are you?' she snarled at the mirror. 'If I could get my hands on you.'

All Alphenlicht had been delighted to learn that the wedding would take place only a few weeks hence. A couturier had been summoned from Paris to create a wedding gown, and the tiny state newspaper had run pictures of previous gowns created by this master. The menu for the nuptial banquet was published, occasioning much comment, particularly on the matter of wines. The Residence servants brought in their cousins and sisters and started an orgy of cleaning out and refurbishing. Various members of the Kavi were said to be rehearsing the rituals that would be used. Plate and porcelain were unpacked and polished. It would be a small wedding. Only three hundred guests were invited, virtually all of them from Alphenlicht.

Marianne did not recall being interviewed, but various international publications ran stories about her, quoting her view on the Alphenlicht-Lubovosk controversy, on feminism, on agricultural management. One writer commented on the soundness of her opinions concerning sheep. Her image smiled brightly from the pages of *Time* and *Newsweek*, Makr Avehl's striking darkness looming protectively in the background.

Cloud-haired mama called. Papa called. Somehow neither of them was as upset as Marianne had supposed they might be. Somehow she was unable to tell either of them that she was being kidnapped, shanghaied, invaded by an alternate self and married off without her consent. Even during her phone conversations with them, she yawned, sleepily, wondering what was going on.

A week in advance of the ceremony, there was to be a small 'family' dinner, to which certain aunts and uncles and cousins were invited, along with some of the Kavi and Marianne's parents. A special messenger was sent to deliver an invitation for Tabiti Delubovoska to attend this event.

'I worded it very carefully,' said Ellat. 'Along the lines of "let bygones be bygones, join us in celebration, all one heritage after all." I have no idea if she'll believe any of it, or even if she thinks I believe it, but it should do the job.'

'I wouldn't believe it,' said Marianne, flatly. 'I don't think she will either. She won't think it's natural.'

'It all seems very natural,' objected Makr Avehl. 'Our getting married.'

'To you, perhaps,' Marianne jeered. 'It feels anything but natural to me. Besides, that's not what I meant. I meant after everything we've been through with her, she won't think the invitation is natural. As to this putative wedding, I still haven't agreed to go through with it!'

'Well, perhaps it won't be necessary to go through with it.'

'And what do you mean by that?' Her heart had stopped, and she was trying to cope with an emotional flood. Surely she didn't want to marry the man! Then why this terror at the thought she might not?

'We believe Madame will make her move at the family dinner,' said Ellat. 'And, if she does, and if we are successful, then one of the major reasons for the wedding will have vanished . . .'

'The family dinner! Mama and Papa will be here. She might do something to them!'

'No, they won't be here. They'll be delayed, in Paris. I've arranged for that. They'll have to charter a plane to get here, and I've arranged for that, too. They won't get here until after — well, after.'

'So — it's just me and you, and Ellat, and Aghrehond.'

'And a few aunts and uncles, and Therat, and Cyram, and Nalavi. A dozen or two people. Nothing threatening at all.'

Marianne wasn't at all sure of that. She could not get it out of her head that something was going on that she didn't know about.

'You know, this dress looks familiar to me, and yet I know I've never had one like it.' Marianne looked at herself in the mirror, glittering and swaying in her silver sequined sheath. 'It was kind of you to order it for me, Ellat.'

'Well, that silly man was making such a fuss over one wedding dress, I decided he needed something to occupy his mind. I've had him do half a dozen things for me, as well. I even talked Therat into having a few gowns made. She's such a dear woman — though Makr Avehl claims to find her

347

scary, she's really very sensible — but she's never paid any attention to clothes at all. Before you came along, my dear, I often hoped that she and Makr Avehl would get to know one another better.' Ellat smiled sweetly at her, and Marianne felt something clutch her stomach at the thought of Makr Avehl and Therat.

'Still, the gown does look familiar,' she faltered, needing to say something.

'Well, you know, the other *Marianne* may have one like it.' Did have, Ellat told herself. Definitely did have. Fought Madame off in it, she did, for a whole evening. She pressed a hand flat on her own stomach, quieting the slightly sick feeling of apprehension that kept coming and going, remembering a recent conversation with Makr Avehl.

'My dear, it is so risky my heart stops, thinking of it!'

'Of course it's risky, Ellat. Life is risky. However, you yourself said we had to confront her. So, we're going to confront her.'

'She'll twist. She'll fight. She'll bite you like a serpent, brother.'

'She will that. She'll come in all smiles, but she'll plan to leave with me dead and Marianne in her pocket.'

'You've been to the Cave?'

'You know I have, dear Ellat. The Cave says fishes. whole walls full of fishes. Therat thinks she has it figured out.'

'And yet she's letting you go ahead?'

He shook his head at her, sadly. *'Let, Ellat? Let? It has to be done, and that's all there is to it.'*

Now she took Marianne's hand to descend the curving main stair of the Residence, smiling bravely and wondering if she were going to be able to eat anything at all.

The guests arrived. There was much sparkle and laughter, many congratulations for Makr Avehl, many good wishes for Marianne. Tabiti arrived in a long, black limousine, escorted by a much bemedaled officer of uncertain rank. She twinkled and glittered, congratulating Makr Avehl, exclaiming over Marianne's dress, falling fulsomely upon Ellat's neck, her eyes and mouth in ceaseless motion.

The guests drank champagne, ate hors d'oeuvres, chatted. Dinner was announced. The guests were seated. Tabiti was down the table from Makr Avehl and Marianne, separated from Ellat by only one guest. Marianne could not take her eyes from Madame's dramatically high-necked gown. At the throat was a spider done in jet-black beads, and the web extended across the bosom of the dress and down the long sleeves. Butterflies in bright sequins lay upon this web, seeming to struggle as Madame moved and laughed and turned to throw long, significant glances up the table.

'What is she going to do?' Marianne demanded.

'Shhh, my love,' said Makr Avehl. 'Smile. Finish your consommé.'

A whole fish on a vast silver tray was carried to the buffet to be carved and served with many flourishes while the footmen poured wine.

The guests tasted, approved, ate hungrily.

'What kind of fish is this?' Marianne asked Makr Avehl. 'I don't think I've seen the kind before.'

He shook his head at her. 'Something the cook found,' he said rather loudly. 'She's a marvel, that woman. I ought to give her a raise.'

For all his admiration, he didn't seem to be eating much of it. Then the fish was gone. The plates and one set of wine glasses were cleared away . . .

And the world slowed down.

Voices fell lower and lower, like a record played at slow speed, lower until they stopped.

Faces moved less and less until they did not move at all.

Hands with glasses in them remained halfway to lips, which remained half parted.

'You should have paid more attention to where your cook got her fish, Prime Minister,' said Madame, the words ringing down the long table like a struck anvil, hard and metallic. 'A vengeance fish, that one, from a certain world of mine, a world perhaps you remember? I named that fish with the names of everyone at this table. Cold, that fish, and now cold all of those here. Unmoving, that fish, and now unmoving all those here. Except myself and my escort, of course. And now, if you and Marianne don't mind coming with me?' She stood, smiling. Marianne found herself getting up and walking, though she was not conscious of any volition to do so. She was beside Makr Avehl. They were walking out of the Residence, getting into Madame's car. 'At the border,' Madame instructed, 'you will tell your people you are going to Lubovosk with me for a nightcap. It's only fifteen miles. Tell them you'll be back by midnight. And you will be back. You and your little love, here. Both of you will be back.'

'He said it was too easy,' thought Marianne. 'We weren't waiting for her. She was waiting for us.' Then she couldn't think any more for it took too much effort.

The car drove away. Marianne wondered, vaguely, what the servants at the Residence would think when they came to clear for the next course and found all the guests sitting there, frozen. Perhaps the servants wouldn't come in at all. Perhaps Madame had named a fish for them, as well.

'Do you know, dear girl, I have had dreams about you,' said Madame in the car as it sped through the darkness toward the high, guarded border. 'I dreamed once that your dear brother, my nephew, Haurvatat — named for your father by my dear dead sister who was his first wife — I dreamed that Harvey had not had his unfortunate accident and that he and I were able to entertain you as we had once planned. I dreamed once that your dear parents had succumbed to some misfortune and died. Then I woke, and it was all a dream. Was it a dream, little Marianne?'

Marianne felt a compulsion to answer, to tell the entire story of what had happened to Harvey and her own part in it. Her lips opened, her tongue vibrated . . .

And *Marianne* said calmly, 'It must have been a dream. Poor Harvey had an accident.'

'How did I do that?' Marianne asked from deep within herself. 'How?'

'She forgot to name the fish for me,' said *Marianne*, silently. 'She named it for only one of us, and that one was you.'

350

Madame looked dissatisfied, as though the answer she had received was not the one she had expected. 'Only a dream, Marianne? Are you quite sure?'

'Harvey had an accident,' said *Marianne* in a child's voice. 'It was very sad. Papa cried.'

'That's too bad,' said Madame, petulantly. 'When I dream, I remember it otherwise.'

The car stopped at the border. In an emotionless voice, Makr Avehl gave the message he had been directed to give. The car sped on.

'In my dream,' Madame went on, 'Harvey inherited a great deal of wealth. I let him enjoy parts of it, though most came to me. With it, I was able to subvert some of the Prime Minister's key supporters. With it, I planned to gain control of the Cave of Light.'

'Yes,' said *Marianne* in an uninflected voice, like a sigh. 'That is what you planned to do.'

'We had only to remove you, little Marianne, when we had made what use of you we could. It was all planned, how we would do it. In my dream. There would be dogs, and a horse, and an accident. In my dream. But it was Harvey who had the accident.'

'Papa cried,' said *Marianne* again.

Madame was sulkily silent for some miles. When she spoke again, the car was on the high ridge above the city.

'We are going to my villa. Not that it's really necessary to do so. I could have concluded my business with you anywhere, but I wanted to do it there. So I could remember it, later . . .

'I have a room there, in my villa, in the tower at the back of the garden. There are windows all around it. I take my tower to all my worlds, did you know that? Wherever I go, there is a tower there. On the embassy. On the palace. On the library. In the center of town. Somewhere, there is always a tower . . .'

'Always a tower,' agreed *Marianne*.

'That's where I'm taking you and your lover. When you are my servants, you and the Prime Minister, I will sit in my high, lovely tower and remember how it came about. Won't that be amusing?'

Again Marianne felt a terrible compulsion to tell the truth, to say, 'No, it will be horrible.'

But *Marianne* answered for her in a low, emotionless voice, 'Amusing.'

Madame pouted. She had wanted more sport than this. In the seat across from her, Makr Avehl sat motionless, his eyes fixed before him as though he saw something there from which he could not move his gaze. Silence as the car rushed on. The city fled away to their right. They began to climb the hill on which the villa stood. Before them, gates swung open onto a dark courtyard. As they went through the gates, the headlights disclosed several figures outside the wall, tall, with feathers in their hair and high, scalp-decked staffs.

'Dear Chevooskak,' murmured Madame. 'Come to see if you've arrived safely.'

'It was too easy,' thought Marianne.

'Shhh,' said *Marianne*. 'We thought so, too.'

'And here we are.' Madame alighted from the car, summoning men who came to take each of Makr Avehl's arms, each of Marianne's. 'I thought you might like a tour of the villa. You've never been here, Makr Avehl.' She laughed, a tiny frozen glitter of sound. 'You know, in my dream, I once thought we would be married, you and I. Oh, I know I'm somewhat older than you, but still — it would have reunified our countries. You would have enjoyed it, Makr Avehl.'

'I would rather have died,' said Makr Avehl, like an automaton.

'That, too, can be arranged,' said Madame.

They went into the villa, through a wide hall and into a long gallery. 'I call this my gallery of worlds,' Madame said as she turned on the lights. 'It will amuse you both. See, here is a favorite world of mine.'

Marianne stared at the picture, a long avenue ending at the Gates of Darius. There was scaffolding against the Gates, and dwarfs huddled upon it, pecking at the stones with tiny hammers. Far down the Avenue shone the pale stones of the embassy, and it seemed to Marianne that she might see herself drifting aimlessly down that Avenue toward that building . . .

'Or this one,' said Madame. 'Not one of mine, originally, but I rather like it.'

A peculiar city under a lowering sky, with tattered posters covering almost every wall. Marianne shuddered, without knowing she had done so. Somewhere in that city, something violent and horrible was abroad, hunting. She knew it.

'Or this,' said Madame.

A stretch of lawn before the tall, slender pillars of the palace. Twin fountain basins at either side. And at the back of the building, a tower, at one of the windows of which a curtain twitched as though someone were watching.

'But this is one I want you to pay particular attention to, Prime Minister. Marianne. Look.'

The world was covered with water. In one place, the remains of a mud tower protruded above the surface, crumbling even as they watched. A long avenue of stakes had been driven into the shallow water, and chained to those were a variety of creatures, one of which had multiple eyes and legs and arms and an expression of patient terror.

'Gojam,' said *Marianne*. 'She caught him.'

'The silly creatures who live there called in the tide,' yawned Madame. 'Now I use it to keep things in. Things — and people.' She sighed. 'Enough. It's time we went up to my tower, Marianne, to my lovely room, Makr Avehl. The little elevator is just over here. You may release my guests now, gentlemen. They will be quite safe with me . . .'

The guards went away. They were in a tiny box which purred its way upward, quite alone except for Madame. She let them out into a high room surrounded by arched windows. Curtains closed these arches against the dark sky, but Madame made a slow circuit of the room, opening them to let the stars look in.

'We need only a little light to do what we will do. Starlight is enough, don't you think?'

They did not answer.

She fished in the neck of her gown and drew out a little sack.

353

From the sack she took something, a small something, the size of a walnut, and set it upon a table at the center of the room.

It shone, a twisting of light. It glimmered with lines and points of shining white. As their eyes fastened upon it, it grew. Where there had been only a few points of light, there were now many. Where there had been only two or three spiraling lines, now there were hundreds . . .

'The time bender,' gloated Madame. 'What people do you suppose created it, Prime Minister? What starship do you suppose it was on? What unimaginable accident caused it to crash on our world? And what luck, for me, that old Chevooskak Anuk found it. And what luck, for me, that he found me irresistible.' She laughed, a quiver of sound so cold that even in her ice-bound lethargy, Marianne shivered.

'You shouldn't have sought out his son, Prime Minister. I listen in on all Chevooskak's thoughts, all his conversations. He does what I tell him. When he told you about the time bender, I heard it all. He did only what I told him to do, said only what I told him to say. Even his fury at me, I told him to let you see that. It's true enough. He hates me, but he obeys me. Old Chevooskak Anuk might have been able to protect himself against me — though he never would have — but his son, no.'

She began to dance around the twist of light, a slow, bending waltz, humming to herself as she did so. 'What shall we do with it tonight? Eh? I had thought to send you and Makr Avehl away for a time, to that wet world you traveled before. You would not escape from it now. I would leave you there, chained to a stake, for a time. Only a hundred years or so. And then bring you back when only an hour had passed. Would you love one another then, I wonder? After a hundred years up to your hips in water, with only the mud creatures to talk to? You are their law giver, Prime Minister. I have no doubt they would feed you the very best of their scum . . .

'Or shall we simply set the chains upon you both now and forget the amusement?' She whirled, her skirts swirling around her, her arms raised, a dervish of evil intent. 'Yes. I think we will set the chains of servitude upon you. Bind you in time. Forever.'

'Now,' called *Marianne* in her mind. 'Now, Dingo Dog. Now, momegs! Do it now, do it now!'

From somewhere beneath Madame's feet, a howling broke loose, a hideous caterwauling so clamorous that Madame clapped her hands to her ears, eyes slitted. 'What?' she grated. 'What?'

Marianne and Makr Avehl were unmoving, seeming not to hear. The sound renewed itself, even louder. There were screams and shouts of people mixed in with a kind of barking yodel, the sound of a pack on the hunt.

Madame twitched, snarled. 'Do wait for me, children,' she instructed, pointing her long, bony fingers at each of them. 'Don't run away.' Then she was back in the little elevator, the door closing behind her.

As soon as they were alone, *Marianne* walked calmly to the table where the time bender stood and took it into her hand. 'She didn't name me at all, did she? Just as you thought, Makr Avehl, she didn't know I was there.' *Marianne* leaned forward and snapped her fingers beneath his nose, seeing him twitch into sudden life. 'Come on, love. We're going away from here just as we planned. But first, there are a few things I need to do.'

CHAPTER TWENTY-TWO

There were no words in her mind at all. None of the tools of thinking were there, not yet. Nonetheless, she saw faces peering down at her, saw smiles on lips, heard chortling words and knew them. They were people. The words of recognition came swimming through her mind like familiar fish. Mama. Papa. Great-aunt Dagma.

She was three days old.

'Third time is the charm,' said *Marianne*.

CHAPTER TWENTY-THREE

'The wedding was very, very beautiful,' said Cloud-haired mama. 'I was so afraid we'd miss it. When we got held up in Paris that way, I thought for sure you'd have to get married without us!'

'Even I thought it was lovely,' Marianne laughed, 'once you and Papa got here. Though I was afraid you'd think it was terribly sudden.'

'No more sudden than the way Haurvatat married me. He met me on the third of June and by the tenth we were married. They have this way with them, the men of Alphenlicht. And he's as happy for you as I am, Mist Princess. Though how you got here and married when the last thing we knew you were in Denver, working for the feds — that's what Papa says — "the feds" . . .'

'Well, as you said, the men of Alphenlicht have a way with them. Makr Avehl just wouldn't rest until I came here, and I'd no sooner arrived than he announced the wedding.'

'I do hope he proposed properly in between.'

'You know, I really can't remember. He must have, don't you think? Surely I wouldn't have consented to a wedding if he hadn't proposed?'

'Of course not, darling. Look, there's Papa beckoning to me. He has someone he wants me to meet.' And Cloud-haired mama drifted away across the room looking almost as young and lovely as Marianne herself.

'Happy?' asked Makr Avehl from behind her. 'Would you like more champagne?'

She turned and kissed him, feeling her whole body come alive as she pressed against him, catching her breath in a shaky laugh as she said, 'Very happy. But I haven't had any champagne at all, yet. You've been hogging it all for yourself.'

'Lovely wedding,' murmured Ellat, offering her a glass and a curious look, both at once. 'I was thinking during the ceremony how little you've changed, Marianne. When you first arrived here in Alphenlicht, you were a bit of a stranger, but now you're so much the girl I knew — before.'

'Oh, I finally got myself together,' laughed Marianne, looking up at Makr Avehl with a twinkle. 'Or we did. I think personalities tend to integrate as we get a little older, don't you, Ellat? Most of us are rather schizy when we're young.'

'There's certainly nothing the matter with your integration,' Ellat admitted with a continuing searching look into Marianne's face. There was a lot of courage there, and determination. A lot of intelligence, too, as well as an almost violent alacrity, given to sudden decisions. Ellat was looking for a kind of untried girlishness that she thought she remembered seeing recently, but it wasn't there. She tipped her glass in salute and smiled again as she moved away. It had been a beautiful wedding.

'Isn't it time we were running off somewhere?' Marianne whispered to Makr Avehl. 'Isn't it time you were taking me to bed, love?'

'Forward wench.' He grinned at her, eating her with his eyes. 'Just a few more minutes and we'll escape. I hadn't told you, but we're going up to the hunting lodge for a proper honeymoon. We can leave in just a bit, but I think there are just one or two guests who may put in an appearance . . .'

There was a momentary hush from across the room as one of the belated guests arrived — a very old woman, leaning on the arms of two attendants. Her hair was white and her expression was mildly vacant.

'Oh, look,' said Marianne in a voice that anyone who did not know her very well would have thought to be sympathetic. 'Isn't that Tabiti Delubovoska? One of Papa's relatives by his first marriage. I met her once when I was only a child. She's aged terribly. Heavens, she must be ninety-five if she's a day.' She smiled up at Makr Avehl again, seeing his eyes riveted on the old woman.

'Over a hundred,' he offered. 'So I've been told. Though

357

she looked remarkably young for her age until just — well, recently.'

'Pity,' said Marianne, drinking her champagne. 'I don't think she'll last much longer. Well, we women can only hold time at bay for so long. It gets all of us in the end.'

'Does it indeed?' asked Makr Avehl. 'Does it, Marianne?'

They stood looking at one another for a long moment, each still holding a celebratory glass in hand. Makr Avehl's expression was loving, watchful, a little wary, as though something had happened of which he was only partially aware. 'Does time get all of us in the end?'

'Of course,' said Marianne, touching her breast where something hung on a chain beneath her high-necked dress. Across the room, a black dog with Gojam on its back poked its head through a door and winked at her.

Marianne looked up at her lover and smiled.

'Of course it does, darling,' she said.

MARIANNE,
THE
MATCHBOX,
AND THE
MALACHITE
MOUSE

Dagma's Parchment

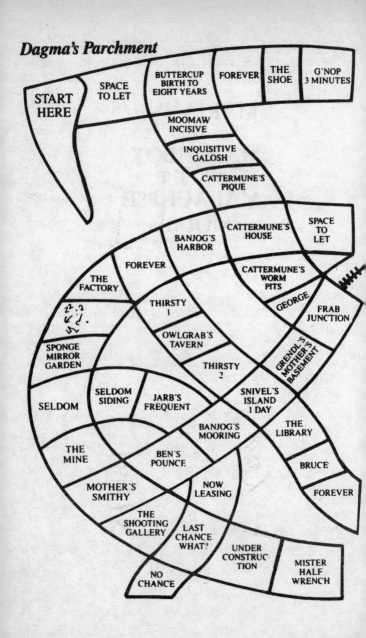

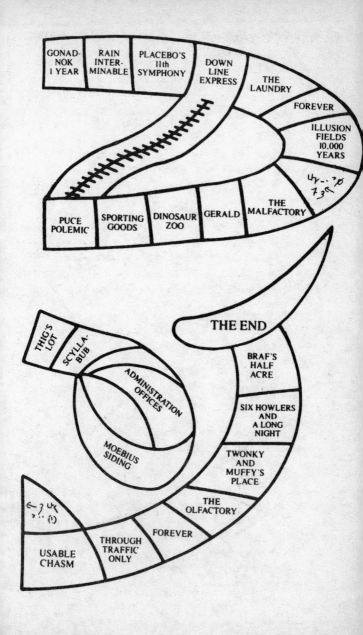

CHAPTER ONE

Marianne, well ensconced in the Prime Minister's Residence in Alphenlicht, half a world away from the state of Virginia, had no idea that her Great-aunt Dagma was dying until she received a letter from her saying so. 'Not long to go,' it said. 'Possibly two or three months, and don't upset yourself about it, my dear, because I'm not in any pain at all . . .'

Marianne's first reaction was not to believe it. Aunt Dagma was immortal! She had been living with Marianne's parents for as long as Marianne could remember, as long as her father could remember − small, slender, dark-haired, with eyes that snapped. In recent years the hair had not been as black as formerly, true. And the eyes were possibly, though only slightly, less hawklike. But Dagma dying? Surely not!

'I need your help, my dear,' Dagma's letter went on. 'A little matter that I think should be taken care of and one that neither of your dear parents would have adequate skills to cope with. It is a matter requiring someone with your rather − shall we say − *individual* abilities.'

Which was as close as Aunt Dagma would care to come to guessing at Marianne's abilities, though there were other words which might have described them better. Peculiar? Odd? Weird? Supernatural? Uncanny? Eldtrich? Or perhaps merely bizarre?

'Makr Avehl,' Marianne said to her husband, the Prime Minister of Alphenlicht, 'I've had this sad, strange letter from Great-aunt Dagma.'

Makr Avehl, who was trying to eat his breakfast egg while going through a pile of documents, merely grunted at her.

'Prime Minister,' Marianne tried again. 'I have this matter of state . . .'

He looked up at her, focusing vaguely. 'Ah. Sorry, love. What was it you said?'

She handed him the letter and watched him read it while the egg was eaten, while the coffee was drained, while the last bite of toast was munched. Though Makr Avehl was Alphenlichtian to his fingernails, he did prefer an American-style breakfast to broiled lamb, flat bread, and yoghurt of the peculiarly sour variety which suited most Alphenlichtians. 'I'm fond of Dagma,' he said at last. 'There are other people I would be less sorry to hear this news from.'

Marianne got up and went around the table to give him a hug, a difficult matter to manage as her melon-shaped self kept getting in the way. 'I'll be very glad when this child is born,' she said. 'She keeps coming between us. What do you think, Makr Avehl? Should I go?'

'I don't see why not. If you want to. The daughter and heir isn't due for almost two months. Virginia is lovely this time of year. It would give you a chance to visit with your parents.'

'But . . . what if the baby decides to be born while I'm in the States? Would that upset you?'

He shook her gently. 'You were born there, Marianne. If our first girlchild gets born there, too, I'm sure all Alphenlicht will be able to accept that fact.'

Marianne, who had spent the last year getting to know the country and people of Alphenlicht, wasn't that sure. She walked to the wall of French doors which opened from the small breakfast room onto the area of the Residence known as the 'summer terrace.' The other, larger, breakfast room opened onto the knot garden; the various dining rooms, of assorted sizes and degrees of formality, opened onto the rose garden, the water garden, and the sculpture terrace. This, the summer terrace, was much the nicest of the lot, she thought, with its own small fountain and reflecting pool, surrounded by shade-loving flowers and sheltered from the summer sun by the branches of an enormous oak.

A low balustrade separated the terrace from the sloping grounds of the Residence. The orchard bloomed at the bottom

364

of the slope, where the road ran off through fields and woods to what passed, in Alphenlicht, for a city. It was there that the House of Delegates met, there that Makr Avehl served as Hereditary Prime Minister for the Council of Kavi, made up of largely hereditary religious dignitaries. Makr Avehl called the form of government a democratic parliamentary theocracy. Or a theocratic parliamentary democracy, or, sometimes, 'that stubborn bunch of reactionaries,' depending upon how he was feeling about it at the time.

'I'm not sure I want to leave right now,' Marianne said.

He came up behind her and put his arms around her. 'You'll get no argument from me, love. The only real question is whether you want to write to your great-aunt and tell her that.'

'No,' she sighed. 'I really can't do that.'

'I didn't think you could.'

'She wants me to do something weird, you know. Otherwise she'd ask Father.'

'I rather guessed that from the letter.'

'Perhaps it will be something I'd rather not do while I'm pregnant.'

'Then you'll do it later, when you're not pregnant. The point is that Great-aunt Dagma won't be around later to tell you whatever it is she wants done. She has to do that now, while she has time.'

'You're so sensible,' she told him, burrowing into his chest. 'Such a sensible, practical man.'

He, remembering certain wildly impractical and totally unsensible things from their separate and collective pasts, chose to say nothing at all about that. 'Remember,' he whispered. 'If there's anything troublesome, you're to let me know at once. And there's always the Cave of Light.'

There was indeed the Cave of Light, the heartstone of the Alphenlicht theocratic system, a kind of national soothsaying machine, a natural source of augury. 'Do you think I should go there before I make the trip?' she asked. 'Would it be a good idea?'

'It's always a good idea. Call up whats-her-name . . .'

'You know perfectly well what her name is. Her name is Therat. Why don't you ever call her by her name, Makr Avehl?'

'The name doesn't suit her.'

'It's a little wildflower, isn't it? A therat?'

'There's nothing flowery about her. The woman galls me. She's never surprised at anything. Just once I'd like to take her totally unaware.'

'You should be glad she foresees things.'

'I suppose I should. Well, call Therat. Ask her to arrange a reading for you.'

'I'll do that if someone in your office will make plane reservations for me. Through Turkey, I suppose.' Alphenlicht lay in a hidden twist of mountains at a place where the border of Turkey, Iran, and the USSR approached one another to the point of virtual overlap.

'Not through Iran,' he said. 'It's regimes like that that give theocracy a bad name.' He rose, stretching, putting his papers together. It was difficult at the best of times for a small country — no, a *tiny* country — to maintain its neutrality or even its existence when surrounded by larger and far less sensible nations. However, Alphenlicht had been doing it for something over 1700 years, and Makr Avehl swore that with the help of the Cave, they would do it for 1700 more. Luckily, the mountainous little nation did not lie on any direct invasion route from any one of its neighbors to any other one. Isolated and serene — more or less — it continued in its own timeless fashion while turmoil boiled around it.

'I'll have one of the choppers readied. You'll want Aghrehond as pilot, won't you?'

'Amazing,' she murmured. 'I didn't think he'd really ever learn to fly those things.'

'Took to it like a bird,' he murmured. 'He can fly you down to the airport at Van whenever you're ready. And I want him to go with you, Marianne. No! Not a word. I can't go just now, as you well know, but I'd rather you weren't alone. Aghrehond will go, and that's that. Besides, he'd be hurt if you didn't ask him.

366

'Now! I really must get myself to work . . .'

'What are you working on?'

'Well, the thing this morning is a meeting concerning disappearances!'

'Disappearances? Who?'

'People,' he said vaguely. 'They do, you know. Disappear. All the time. Young people run away from home, and older people get disgusted with life and go off to start over. It's a well-known phenomenon, and no one in authority gets overly concerned about it.'

'So?'

'So this: lately a great many people seem to have been disappearing in ways no one can seem to explain! Threes and fours of them at a time. The disappearance rate has almost doubled.'

'Here? In Alphenlicht?'

'No. Not here. Not that I know of, at least. But in quite a lot of places. In the eastern part of the United States, particularly. And in England. And, funnily enough, in Japan. Some other places, too. None of the underdeveloped countries, however, which is rather interesting. At any rate, it's become worrying enough that the United Nations is attempting to gather some data. I have a great, complicated questionnaire which a group of the Kavi are going to fill out this morning, and afternoon, from the look of the thing. Then, when that's finished, we have a religious holiday to plan for.'

'You always have at least one of those.'

'Quite right. Every good theocracy should have at least one religious holiday looming on every horizon, and I'd better get to it or I'll find myself supplanted by someone else . . .'

He kissed her and bustled out, and a moment later Marianne saw the long, silver car slide effortlessly down the drive and away behind the apple trees of the distant orchard.

'Would you care for anything else, ma'am?' The serving maid was standing politely by the buffet, her hand on the silver coffeepot.

'Thank you, Bella, no. You can clear. And would you find Aghrehond for me. And my secretary.'

367

'My secretary.' The words sounded slightly pretentious. It would have been better to say, 'Janice,' or 'Thomas,' or some other name. Except that she didn't know what her secretary's name was today. It would be one of the Kavi, one of the ruling class of Alphenlicht, probably a young one, though, on occasion, it had been someone old enough to be her grandparent. It was their way of getting to know her; their way of influencing her, giving her Alphenlichtian values.

'You asked for me?' said Therat, her slender young form poised gracefully in the doorway.

'Therat! Don't tell me you're playing amanuensis!'

'Um, well, I had a premonition.'

'I wasn't counting on a premonition.' Marianne smiled warily at her, feeling more than slightly uncomfortable. Even though she had teased Makr Avehl about his attitude toward Therat, Marianne knew just how he felt. Therat might well have had a premonition; she was that kind of person. 'But since you had one, what did it say?'

'That you'd be taking a trip, that you'd want to visit the Cave first, and that you'd be somewhat troubled about it.'

Wordlessly Marianne picked Great-aunt Dagma's letter from the table and held it out. Therat took it, turning her piercing eyes upon it and letting Marianne off the hook of scrutiny she had felt herself hanging on ever since Therat came into the room. No, Therat was not surprised. Makr Avehl was quite right: Therat was never surprised at anything. Just once, Marianne would like to surprise her. Somehow Marianne could not imagine Therat being astonished. She couldn't imagine Therat in love, or Therat pregnant, or Therat shaving her legs, or Therat taking a bath. She had tried, without success, to imagine Therat doing anything personal and intimate. One only saw the eyes, felt the mind, and was vaguely aware of the body that carried these around, like a kind of vehicle.

'Do you care greatly for her?' Therat asked. It was typical of her that her voice contained no sympathetic tones whatsoever.

'Yes. I do.'

'Then I grieve for you.' And it was equally typical that one knew she did, in her own way. 'You're going? When? Tomorrow?'

'Whenever my "secretary" can call the Prime Minister's office and check on the travel arrangements.' Marianne smiled.

'I'll take care of it. However — Marianne . . .'

'Yes, Therat.'

'This tone in your great-aunt's letter. Is she possibly involving you in something that . . . in your present condition . . .'

'Makr Avehl says to find out what she needs. I can always take care of it later, after I'm not in my present condition.'

'Ah.' Therat didn't sound convinced. 'Well, we'll see what the Cave has to say.'

'Will you ask someone to send a message, please, telling my great-aunt that I am coming.'

And after that she took the time to speak to her maid Renee about packing. She did not want to make a major production of it. It was not to be a very social visit, after all. She would need something flowing and pretty for dinners. She would need several practical things — equally flowing, considering her shape — for daytime. Despite Renee's expostulations, Marianne insisted that she keep the luggage to a minimum: one case and a makeup kit.

In midafternoon, Marianne went with Therat to the Cave, driven by Aghrehond the first part of the way, walking up the last bit of winding path to the tunnel mouth. As she always did when she came here, Marianne stood for a moment on the doorstep of the mountain, looking up and around her at the prominence beneath which the Cave lay. A hill, large and pleasantly wooded, full of little valleys and gullies, decked with clearings and copses, wandered over by deer and goats and occasional hunters. Beneath the hill, far beneath, was a cavern, and winding down to that cavern were hundreds of twisting worm holes lined with mica which reflected the surface light deep into the cave that lay at the center of the mountain. Holes that reflected light, here and there. Now and then. On this spot and on that.

369

And there, far underground, every square inch of the cavern was carved and painted with symbols and pictures and words and numbers, so that the light fell, inevitably, on some sign or omen. Never twice the same, so said the canon of the Kavi.

And certainly Marianne had never seen it twice the same. She shook her head at the sunlit foliage and followed Therat into the lamplit tunnel and down it into the lantern-spotted darkness.

'Ah, pretty lady,' said Aghrehond, 'it makes a spookiness, does it not, a kind of ghosty feeling to come into this darkness.'

'Reverence,' said Therat in a no-nonsense-now kind of voice. 'That would be a more proper emotion.'

'Perhaps proper, for members of the priesthood, for those worshipful ones who guide and protect us, but for me, a driver of vehicles, a mere carrier from place to place, for me it makes a genuine shiver, Therat.' His large form quivered beside Marianne and he grinned at her as he put one great hand beneath her elbow, guiding her. To hear Aghrehond, he was the worst coward in the country. To recall what he actually did — that was another matter.

A simple stone altar stood at the center of the cave. They set their lanterns upon it and turned them off. Marianne, with only partial success, tried to assume the vacant, waiting frame of mind which the Kavi asserted was appropriate for visits to the Cave. Aghrehond, beside her, seemed under no such stricture. He was humming, very softly, under his breath. From Therat, not a sound. The darkness was full of darting spots of light, false impressions of light left when the lantern was turned off. Gradually the darkness took their place.

Marianne breathed deeply, folded her hands, and went through the formula silently. 'I seek guidance. I seek knowledge. I seek that which will avoid harm to living things. I seek not for selfish purposes but for the good of all . . .'

'A roadway,' said Therat in her emotionless voice. Marianne searched through the darkness, finding the beam of light at last where it swam with dust motes. The cave wall where it made a tiny, irregular circle was carved with something. Marianne would have said it was a snake, but Therat knew every symbol. If she said it was a road, it was a road!

Marianne breathed deeply again. A usual reading was considered to be three or four signs.

'A leopard,' said Therat, sounding puzzled. 'No, a demon, no, a leopard.' There was something in her voice that made Marianne think Therat would have used an obscenity if they were somewhere else. Then she said, 'I don't understand this one at all . . .'

There was silence for a moment. 'And finally a rope,' said Therat finally, leaning forward to turn on the lantern once more.

'Was it a cat thing or a demon thing, Highmost Kavi,' asked Aghrehond in his bantering tone. 'You seemed unable to make up your mind.'

'Look for yourself,' said Therat. 'Here,' she pointed to a place on the wall where a carved leopard — one assumed it was a leopard, as it had a spotted coat — was surrounded on three sides by devil faces. 'The light overlapped. First on the cat, then on the face, then back again, wavering. Most unusual. Not the most unusual thing about this particular reading, however. Look over here. The light lit this place.' She pointed.

'There's nothing there,' said Marianne in surprise.

'Exactly. There's nothing there. There was something there until last week. There was a carving of a flowerpot there. But the man who came in to clean the floors knocked over his little cart, and it bumped just there, knocking the carving to bits. So! Does this reading mean that the flowerpot was supposed to be there? Or that nothing was supposed to be there? And if nothing, then what does that mean?' Therat sounded excessively annoyed.

'A road and a rope, a cat demon, and a vacancy?' asked Marianne, trying not to sound amused.

'The meaning may be something quite different,' Therat answered her stiffly. 'As you know, Your Excellency.'

'Oh, Therat, don't Excellency me. I've told you I hate it.

The signs meant nothing to me, I'm sorry. I will rely on you to figure it out and let me know.'

'The journey should be postponed until I have accomplished that,' said Therat.

'The journey can't be postponed,' Marianne answered. 'You read the letter. You know. I know enough about the Cave to know there were no omens of destruction, Therat. I've at least skimmed through the great lectionary, so I do know that. And from what I've gathered from the lectionary, spotted cats and roads and ropes do not constitute serious warnings.'

'Perhaps,' the Kavi assented grudgingly. 'I'll study the implications. If I come up with anything, I'll let you know.'

Marianne barely had time to get back to the Residence and dress for dinner before the arrival of four visiting dignitaries from neighboring countries. She spent the evening being a polite and accomplished hostess, and then, at last, was able to retire to the quiet of the master suite.

'So you're leaving tomorrow morning?' Makr Avehl said, holding her close. 'What did the Cave say?'

'Something about roads and ropes and a spotted cat. Not even a black cat. Even I could have interpreted that.'

'Call me if you need me,' he said. 'You know.'

She did know. She could call Makr Avehl without using any technological assistance. This was one of the *individual* abilities Great-aunt had been referring to in her letter. Marianne had several of them, and Makr Avehl had others.

'Are you taking the . . . you know?' He was referring to the timetwister, a device which Marianne had obtained on a former quite dangerous and mystical adventure.

From her pillow, she shook her head. No. No mystical devices. She might be tempted to use it if she had it, and using such things could be dangerous. She yawned.

He nodded his satisfaction with that. 'Just find out what's needed, love. Don't get yourself involved in anything right now, but assure Dagma we'll take care of it at the earliest opportunity.'

'Mmmm,' she assured him, drowsily.

372

He, hearing her sleepy breathing, did not insist that she promise him. Later, of course, he was very much to wish that he had. Though it might not have made any difference at all.

At Heathrow Airport, Marianne and Aghrehond had over an hour to spend between flights, and they wandered about, stretching their legs, shopping for magazines and Marianne's favorite type of fruit gumdrop, which she couldn't find.

'Damn,' she fussed. 'You'd think any country with a confectionary industry could make nice, soft, fruit-flavored gumdrops instead of these rubbery awful things.'

'Ah, pretty lady,' sighed Aghrehond. 'I know a place in Boston they may be had.'

'I know that place, too. They import them from England! So why aren't there any here?'

'Possibly because the confectionary has been supplanted by that,' he said, waving his hand at a brightly festooned store, obviously newly opened.

'Cattermune's,' she read. 'Now what in heaven's name is that.'

'We shall go see,' he said ponderously, tucking her hand beneath his arm.

She started off obediently enough, but then the annunciator began its thunderous chatter, among which she heard the flight number and airline name she had half been listening for.

'Our plane,' she said definitely, turning about with Aghrehond tugged behind. 'Come on, my friend, or we'll miss it and be stuck in England overnight.'

Staring over his shoulder, Aghrehond complied. Cattermune's. A very bright, festive store which seemed given over to games and amusements. Pity they didn't have time to see it. Perhaps they could take time on the way back.

CHAPTER TWO

Arti and Haurvatat Zahmani, Marianne's mother and father, met the plane and talked Marianne's ear off most of the way back to the estate while Aghrehond sat placidly beaming. Marianne peered out at the green countryside and asked questions about all her friends and neighbors and her horse.

'Rustam is getting terribly fat,' her father said. 'You're in no shape to ride, Marianne, but you should arrange to ship Rustam to Alphenlicht as soon as the baby comes. I hired a stable boy, but he . . . well, Rustam just isn't getting enough exercise.'

'I didn't write to tell you,' her mother said, 'but there've been a rash of disappearances, Marianne. The boy your father hired was one of them.'

'Disappearances, Mama? Here? Do you know, almost the last thing Makr Avehl was talking to me about was disappearances.'

'Don't trouble your head about it, Mist Princess,' her father said heavily with a disapproving glance at her mother. Haurvatat Zahmani was of that school which believed that no woman should be bothered with troublesome or unpleasant facts, particularly not when pregnant, as their fragile minds could easily be overstressed by any burden at that time. How he equated this with his usual demanding attitude toward all the female servants at the estate or his female employees, Marianne had never asked. She didn't really need to. He would say that Arti and Marianne were different. They were family. Therefore fragile, and lovely, and to be treasured. Never mind that it didn't make any sense, Haurvatat Zahmani would believe it anyhow. Who should know that better than Marianne, who had had to fight over and over again for the right to be something other than an unwilling bird in a luxuriously gilded cage.

Now she indicated that independence of spirit which he deplored. 'I certainly will pay attention, Daddy. Who has disappeared, Mother?'

'People. Just people. The postman, for one. A very happily married man with a new baby he absolutely doted on. And the butcher's wife. You remember her, Marianne. The big, jolly woman with the laugh that sounded like it started down around her knees somewhere. People do vanish, of course. Children run away. Husbands get fed up and leave home. And so do wives. Old people decide to see the world. It's just there've been so many disappearances lately, and most of them such very unlikely people.'

'Police think they've found an anomaly,' snorted Haurvatat.

'A statistical anomaly,' explained Arti. 'Evidently there have been more people disappearing in our part of the United States than the statistical average.'

'How long has this been going on?' Marianne asked in wonder.

'Well, one man at the capital says the anomaly started at least fifty years ago,' her mother offered. 'Of course, the governor says the man is mistaken.'

'Governor says he's a stupid ass,' muttered Haurvatat. 'I think the man has a glitch in his software somewhere.'

'It does seem odd that if something has been going on for fifty years, it should only be noticed now,' Marianne commented.

'Oh, no, pretty lady,' Aghrehond interjected cheerfully. 'Many things go on for centuries occasioning no remark whatsoever, then, suddenly, someone will notice they are quite remarkable. Planets, you know. They did what they did for many centuries and no one thought much of it until someone said they did not do what people imagined at all. Then, of course, everyone paid attention to them. And genetics. Pink blossoms and white ones and no one having any idea what caused the one or the other. I, for example, had never noticed this place called Cattermune's, but we have seen now four of them since leaving Alphenlicht.'

'Four, Aghrehond?'

'The one in England, pretty lady, and one at the airport here, and two more since, in shopping centers we have driven by.'

'It's a chain operation,' said Haurvatat. 'Games, I think, and hobby supplies, and toys for children.'

'Ah,' said Aghrehond. 'I had not seen them before.'

'I don't think it's a new company,' Marianne's father mused. 'Seems to me there was one in New York City ten or twelve years ago. They must have just recently expanded.'

'Another thing I have just noticed,' Aghrehond went on irrepressibly, 'is how like your mother you look, Marianne, though I have seen you both many times, but now I see it and remark upon it. Very much alike, are they not, Mr Zahmani, sir.'

'Entirely too much,' Haurvatat blustered. 'Both as stubborn as mules. Still, I'm rather fond of them.'

'And we of you, dear,' murmured Arti with a wink at Marianne. 'We'll stop talking about disappearances if you think we should, if it upsets you.'

'Doesn't upset me,' he mumbled, flushing a little. 'Don't want it upsetting you.'

'Nonetheless, it is upsetting, isn't it,' said Marianne. 'All very mysterious.'

'Let's get back to the subject of that horse of yours,' said her father with ponderous cheer.

CHAPTER THREE

Great-aunt Dagma, who had always seemed to fill any room she happened to be in, was shrunken to the capacity of one narrow bed. When she opened her eyes, however, they were almost as snappingly black as ever, with the old 'I will have 'no nonsense' expression which Marianne remembered and treasured.

'Great-aunt,' she said, leaning forward to kiss her aged relative. 'You were asleep when I got here.'

'Marianne,' Dagma said in return, her voice quite calm though not as strong as Marianne would have liked. 'Thank you for coming. I've left this matter foolishly late. To tell you the truth, I'd totally forgotten about it. If it hadn't been for that man, coming to ask about Father . . . Well, I am so thankful that you were within reach, that you responded, that you are here − though, even now, I'm not certain I should have bothered you with . . .'

'I'm here, Aunt Dagma. You knew I'd come, for heaven's sake.'

'Oh, I knew you'd want to, child. Of course. I didn't know if that husband of yours would want you to, not so close to the time for the baby, you know.'

'Well, he did. Now why don't you tell me what all this is about.'

The old woman didn't respond at once. Instead, she shifted her eyes from Marianne's face to the window across the room, looking out onto the green meadows and billowing trees of the Virginia countryside. The window stretched from the floor almost to the ceiling. Before it, muslin curtains blew gently into the room across polished walnut floors. There was the smell of lemon oil and pot pourri, and Marianne breathed it deeply, relishing it, the smell of home, ignoring the other smell that lay under it, the scent of mortality, age, and dissolution.

'My father,' Dagma said at last, 'whom you never knew, my dear, was a very foolish man.'

Not knowing what else to do, Marianne merely looked sympathetic, cocking her head to acknowledge that there must be more to it than that. 'You said a man came to ask about him?'

'Just last week. So strange. If my father were still alive, he would be one hundred thirty years old, and he certainly wouldn't be *here*, living with your dear papa, and yet this very strange person came to ask for him. "Does anyone here know of Staurbat Zahmani?" He had a very furry, portentous voice, quite loud. Even from my room here, I heard him myself, down in the front hall.'

'That is strange,' murmured Marianne. 'Maybe he was thinking of someone else.'

'No. He said Staurbat Zahmani, and then he said, "He had a daughter, Dagma." Well, then I heard your father say something about his uncle having been dead for fifty years and his daughter being very ill, "Not expected to get better, I'm afraid," is what your dear papa said. Haurvatat has always been quite diplomatic. He could just as well have told the man I'm dying.'

'What happened then, Great-aunt?'

'The man went away. Haurvatat came up to tell me about it. It made no sense to either of us, but it did start me thinking about my father. When he was young he was foolish, Marianne, and he matured into a very silly man. When he was well along in years, younger than I am now but still what one would think of as having attained the age of wisdom, he got himself into a good deal of difficulty with a . . . well, with the supernatural.'

Without meaning to, Marianne exclaimed a non-word of shock and dismay.

'Oh, I know. You've had your troubles with such things, too. Witches, and warlocks, and shamans, I have no doubt. I've put two and two together, my dear. I'm not entirely unschooled in some of the things you've — well, what shall we say — "happened upon." I spent my youth in Alphenlicht. I learned of, well . . . the things one does learn about in Alphenlicht. Everyone there takes the supernatural very seriously. Your dear parents don't know anything about *those* things, of course. They love to talk about their Alphenlichtian heritage, but they're fully acculturated here. They certainly have no idea about what you really are — or what your half brother really was before he died. I was speaking of you the other day to your dear mother, and I called you "Marianne Three," and your mother gave me this very odd look. You are the third Marianne, though, aren't you?'

Marianne did not answer. She merely gave her great-aunt a slightly questioning look as though to say, 'Dear one, what *are* you talking about.'

'Never mind. If you are what I think you are, you have lived your life over *at least* three times and have learned things that other people could not even imagine. However, I wouldn't expect you to tell me about it. If you aren't what I think you are, you possibly can't help me at all. So, I'm going to assume that you are . . .' She cocked her head at Marianne, but Marianne made no response. Her silence came partly from surprise and partly from shock — she had thought no one but Makr Avehl and Aghrehond and Makr Avehl's sister Ellat and certain of the Kavi could possibly have known about . . . well, about all that. Though if any member of her family could have understood about it all, it would probably have been Great-aunt Dagma.

The old woman went on. 'Be that as it may. That's your business and I won't try to intrude on it, certainly not at this late date. Getting back to my problem . . .

'My foolish father was an inveterate gambler. In these days we know it can be a kind of illness, like alcoholism, but in his day he was regarded by his family and friends merely as having a defective moral nature. He would gamble on anything, with anyone. And he did so, more than once, at times and in places which were not at all appropriate to say nothing of being sensible! Or safe! On one such occasion my father made a bet with, well, with a supernatural being, and my father lost.' She paused, as though uncertain how to go on.

'He couldn't pay?' prompted Marianne.

The old woman shook her head. 'Well he *could*, of course, but he very much wished to avoid it. He had bet his life and his soul, Marianne. He had been what we would say in this country, "set up." The bet had not been a fair one, but nonetheless, his life and his soul had been lost. By "soul" was meant, I believe, whatever essential nature it is that we

379

humans persist in believing exists. His life was merely his life, but his soul was his "selfhood." To give him credit, he was a good deal more worried about that than he was about his life. Father took ridiculous risks with his life from time to time, and it never seemed to concern him at all. Now, I don't know whether souls really exist. When I was younger, I shrugged the question off, but at my age, of course, one wonders. If they do exist, there are certain conditions under which it would be quite terrible for one to be lost . . .'

'I should imagine so,' Marianne interjected, appalled.

'. . . such as losing one's identity to some malignant being for all eternity.'

'What being?' Marianne asked, having had some experience with malignant beings in the past.

'My father never said. I had the impression it was . . . well. Do you believe in demons, Marianne?'

'Makr Avehl tells me there are . . . such things.'

'I think so, too. Well, when my father had lost his bet and became fully aware of the implications of what he had done, he was in sheer desperation and he went to someone for help. An expatriate Lubovoskan living here in the United States, a shaman named Grutch. Not his real name, of course, which is or was unpronounceable, but Father called him Grutch.'

This was bad news for Marianne. Lubovosk was infamous for its shamans, and she, herself, had reason to know how well deserved that reputation was. 'Your father felt this Grutch was very powerful?' suggested Marianne.

'There would have been little point in going to someone who wasn't,' Dagma snapped. 'And, believe me, whatever you are thinking at this moment concerning my father's sanity, I thought at the time and said, at some length, to Father. I expatiated on foolishness and irresponsibility and so forth, so we needn't go over all that again . . .' Dagma panted a little, raising herself in the bed. Marianne helped her, then smoothed down the pillow and coverlet.

'Now, my dear, this is all very muddled because though my father did tell me about it, he told me a slightly different story each time — trying to make himself appear in a more flattering light, I should think. Putting two and two together, I pieced out what had happened. This shaman, Grutch, obtained for my father a very powerful talisman that belonged to a creature named Cattermune. Grutch told my father that this talisman was from some Other Place.'

'Cattermune! Other Place?'

'Well, when one hears that phrase, one thinks of hell, doesn't one? But it was not hell, my dear. I really don't think so. No, just an Other Place. At any rate, Grutch told my father how he could use this talisman — and I have no idea myself how it was done — and when the supernatural being came to collect my father's life and soul, the talisman protected my father and the being went away in a fury.'

'Had this Cattermune set a price for this talisman?'

'My father said not, and each time he told the story he was consistent in this particular detail, which made me believe it was more or less true. Grutch told my father that this being, Cattermune, simply liked helping people. That though Cattermune — let me see, what were Papa's exact words — "That though Cattermune expected any grateful person would return the talisman by the indicated date, he was happy to lend it out of the goodness of his heart." Cattermune's heart, that is.'

'What was this talisman that your father borrowed?'

'It was . . . is . . . appears to be a matchbox.'

'A matchbox,' Marianne repeated expressionlessly.

'It's over there, on the table by the window. A gold matchbox. There may have been matches in it at one time. Perhaps they were ensorcelled matches. Or if not matches, something else.'

'I see.'

Great-aunt Dagma turned restlessly upon the pillow and gave Marianne a grumpy look. 'Well, you know that you don't "see," and neither do I, because the entire matter made very little sense. However, I do remember very distinctly that the matchbox was supposed to be returned. My father said, in this infuriatingly casual way he had when he was skating along the very edge of disaster, "He wants it back, of course." And I said, "Who does, Father?" and he replied, "This fellow Cattermune, from the Other Place, of course. He wants it back by his birthday." And then Father laughed and told me when the birthday was. "If I don't get it back to him by then, I'll be overdue," he said.'

'Did you ask him what "overdue" meant?'

'I did. He didn't seem greatly concerned. And the date it was to be returned was so very far in the future that, quite frankly, I didn't take it seriously.'

'Umm. Perhaps your father thought it would be like an overdue book at the library.'

'Well, that's about what *I* thought originally. Nothing serious. Something rather casual. Twenty cents a day fine. Something like that. But I'm afraid it was really rather more than that.' Dagma pushed herself up on her pillows, an angry flush making her cheeks red and hectic-looking. 'Father talked to me a lot. He told me stories about himself even when I wished very much he would not, because he seldom told them completely or with any accuracy and I found his tales confusing. In addition to which they deprived me of something every daughter should be allowed to have: respect for her father! It was as though by telling me of his failings, even though he minimized everything when he did so, he had somehow exculpated himself from any responsibility for them. In this case, he actually did free himself of any responsibility . . .' Her voice faded away and her eyes closed.

Marianne waited for a moment and then prompted gently, 'Dagma, what happened?'

The aged woman opened her eyes, shook her head from side to side, very gently, as though she were afraid it might come off at the neck, then said, 'At the time of the initial incident, Father spoke to me about the matchbox half a dozen times, over a period of three or four months. Then, after that, he didn't mention it for years. I quite forgot about it. Much later — I think it must have been at least ten or eleven years later — Father made a trip to Alphenlicht. I'm quite sure he made a visit to the Cave of Light. Father was entirely capable of going to the Cave of Light for a tip on a horse race.'

'Not very respectful,' murmured Marianne, wondering how Therat would have reacted to a petitioner taking advantage of Alphenlicht's national religious shrine to get a gambling tip.

'Father was not a respectful kind of person. Well, in any event, he returned from Alphenlicht very gray in the face. I recall it well. I had a dinner engagement the night he returned, a man I loved very much, a man I believed would have asked me to marry him on that evening. I was tired of being a spinster. I was, quite frankly, middle-aged. Father asked me to break the date. He said he had something he had to tell me, and then when I had done what he asked — which offended my friend greatly, by the way. Though we saw one another after that, he never did . . . well, that night was the end of all my hopes — when I sat down with father, he trembled and rambled and contradicted himself and it was very difficult to make any sense whatsoever of it. The gist of the matter was that the matchbox, which he had always treated as a kind of joke, had to be returned. He had to return it! He had forgotten about it, he told me, he had not thought it was important, but it *had to be* returned.'

'Well then,' Marianne said impatiently, 'why didn't he?'

'I'm telling you, child. By the time he got to the point it was rather late in the evening. He said, "In the morning. First thing in the morning. You'll find the things in my second desk drawer on the left, Dagma. Bring them up when you bring my tea." I always used to take him tea in the morning. He treasured my doing so, and it was little enough in the way of filial duty. Mind you, he said all this in a very serious voice, quite a frightened voice, a tone which transfixed me because it was so unlike him. Father always treated disaster as though it were some kind of minor inconvenience, and to hear him actually frightened . . .'

'Yes?' Marianne prompted once more.

'Well, when I took up his tea along with the paper and other things from his desk drawer, I found he had died in his sleep, smiling quite peacefully. He had died very conveniently. I'm afraid I have always felt that he knew the heart

383

attack was coming, that he had passed on his responsibilities purposely, merely to avoid cleaning up the messy details of his life. They were many, and some of them were quite unpleasant. His relationships with women after my poor mother died were convoluted in the extreme. He had made certain representations to at least six ladies, representations which he had no way at all of making good even if he had lived for some time longer.'

'I'm sorry,' said Marianne inadequately.

'So was I, and so, needless to say, were they. Ah, well, it's long ago. I was very angry and hurt at the time, but it is far in the past. I did get everything take care of, bit by bit, except for this matter . . .'

'I should have thought you would have seen to this at once, especially since he had mentioned it just before he died.'

'When Papa died, Marianne, there were things that seemed of more immediate concern, believe me. The date he had mentioned as the deadline for the return of the matchbox was ludicrously far in the future. Fifty *years* in the future. Even though he had said he intended to take care of it immediately, there were more urgent things that had to be done right then. I did not really forget about it, Marianne. From time to time I would remind myself . . .'

'Dagma.'

'Yes, child.'

'If your father was dead, surely the responsibility to return the thing died with him.'

'Well, of course it did, if we were speaking only of responsibility and not of *consequences*. When I went through Father's things, I found a letter which he had written on the plane on his way back from Alphenlicht. He had written it to me, perhaps intending to post it and then disappear, leaving it to me to take care of. That would have been a bit much, however, even for Father, and he hadn't sent it.'

'And it said?'

'That if the matchbox was not returned, there would be terrible consequences. His exact words were, "To me, and to my nearest and dearest and to theirs . . ." How could

384

one interpret this? I judged it to mean there were dreadful consequences to him, and if not to him, to his nearest kin.'

'You?'

'Me. And failing me, my nearest kin, my nephew — your dear papa. And failing him, his nearest kin, which would be you, Marianne. Or your baby.'

'Oh, my God,' Marianne said feelingly.

'Precisely. Well, finding the letter was more or less the last straw. My love had abandoned me. Father had died. There was all his mess and confusion. I had what in those days was called a "nervous breakdown" and spent several months in hospital. When I came out, I fully intended to take care of it but didn't. I should have taken care of it years ago. I didn't. Funk, probably. Not knowing how to go about it.' The dark eyes fixed on the garden shifted around the room. 'And anger at him, of course, for leaving me with all his unfinished business. And then, he had told me that it didn't need to be done until fifty years in the future! It's so *unlikely*. Perhaps I thought I would die and someone else would have to . . . No. I hope I was not that craven! I simply postponed the matter. Over and over again, postponed it. Half the time I didn't even believe it.'

'And the other half . . .'

'I did, and it frightened me. So I didn't think about it. I must have inherited that ability from Father, the ability to conveniently forget . . .'

'When does it have to be returned by, Aunt Dagma.'

'Next Thursday, dear. Six days from now . . .'

Marianne felt a tumbling wave of panic. She had assumed it would be something she could take care of after the baby came. This had to be done at once.

'Perhaps Makr Avehl . . .' she began.

'Father's letter said the matchbox had to be returned by a blood member of the family,' Great-aunt Dagma concluded. 'So you see, it's no good our asking Makr Avehl to help.'

'How, where . . .' she stuttered.

'Well, that's really the problem, how and where. If I had known how and where, I would likely have taken care of the

385

matter long ago. The whole thing is rather mysterious. I still have the original paper and things that I took from his desk drawer the morning I found him dead,' said Dagma, pulling out the drawer in the nightstand beside her bed and removing a folded sheet of parchment. Her fingers trembled as she unfolded it and went on trembling as Marianne leaned closer. 'I did look at them at the time. I can't say they made sense to me.' She whispered this last, leaning over the parchment.

Marianne turned the sheet, examining it closely. Printed or drawn on it was a twining line of squares, with various offshoots from the main line. Some of the squares were printed with meaningless words, others were squiggles. It reminded Marianne of something, but for a time she could not think what it was. Then it came to her.

'It's like a board game, isn't it?' Marianne cried. 'Snakes and ladders. I used to play that with my English cousins. What's this? It says, "Start Here," then there's a square reading "Space to let," then the next one reads, "Buttercup, Birth to Eight Years." '

Dagma pulled herself into a half sitting position. 'After that one comes a square reading "Forever," then one that says "The Shoe," then one that reads, "G'nop, 3 Minutes." '

'A game? Some kind of game.' Marianne stared at it, trying to force it to make sense. 'Dagma, do you have any idea what the consequences are if we don't get the matchbox back to its owner?'

'I have no idea, except that Father described them as horrible.'

'Loss of one's . . . um . . . soul?'

'I suppose that's possible.'

'You? And then my father? And then me, and the baby?'

Dagma nodded slowly, her eyes suddenly ancient and no longer bright. 'I would play the game myself, right now, if I only knew how . . .'

Marianne went to the table by the window where the matchbox lay and took it into her hand. A simple thing, but heavy, clearly made of gold, with a slide-out drawer to hold matches or whatever it had held or did hold. Around the outside were lines of deeply engraved characters, not in any written language Marianne had ever seen before, and on the top and bottom of the matchbox was the deeply etched design of an anchor attached to a chain. The chain curled up, over the edge of the box, and disappeared into the crack where the drawer went. The carved inscription was probably a spell, she thought, source of the power of the box. She shook it. Something inside rattled harshly. Not matches. Something harder than that. She tried to open the box, unsuccessfully.

'I don't think you can open it except when you have to,' Dagma said.

'I find it very strange. That is, the name of the creature who lent this to your father.'

'Is that any stranger than any other part of it? Someone named Cattermune? From some Other Place? Here, on this parchment, there are several references to Cattermune. One square is labeled "Cattermune's House," and another is "Cattermune's Pique." An odd name, yes, and yet there is a shop of that name in the city. I saw an advertisement in the paper only last week, just after the man had been here. I took it as another reminder . . .'

'That name has popped up half a dozen times in the last few days,' Marianne replied. 'If it is a reminder, it seems to be reminding the whole world! Aghrehond and I saw a shop with that name in London. And at the airport here. And twice more, in shopping centers . . .'

'It could be only coincidence,' Dagma murmured. 'Couldn't it?'

'You said your father left the original paper "and things." What "things," Dagma?' Marianne returned to the bed, absentmindedly dropping the matchbox into her pocket.

Dagma reached into the drawer beside her once more, bringing out a thick envelope which she spilled onto the bedcover — a pair of dice and several inch-long figures which appeared to have been carved from semi-precious jewels. Marianne picked them up and examined them one by one. A turquoise tortoise. A rhodolite rhinoceros. An amethyst ape. A malachite mouse. Marianne stared at them, childhood memories stirring. 'Game pieces,' she said. 'That's what they are. And, that tells us how to play, Dagma.' She spread the parchment on the bedside table and placed the malachite mouse on the square lettered 'Start Here.'

'Now,' she said without thinking about it, utterly unaware of what she was saying. 'I think we can assume it would be played this way. The first thing to do would be roll the dice . . .'

She threw them out upon the game and they came to rest, one, and one.

'Snake eyes,' said Marianne, just before she vanished.

CHAPTER FOUR

Buttercup saw nothing. Mouse saw everything. To Buttercup, sounds were only sensations, some pleasurable, some not. To Mouse they were voices and tocsins and occasions for fear or reassurance. To Buttercup, the world went by in a haze of milky unconsciousness, but to Mouse, it germinated, grew, assumed proportions of threat and vengeance — and opportunity.

The worst part of it was, from Mouse's point of view, that she could do nothing about anything except perceive it. In the beginning, she could not even stop Buttercup's aimless arm-waving and thumb-sucking. Later on, when it would have been possible for her to stop the thumb-sucking or the howling or anything else she pleased, Mouse had settled down into her observer's role and was, if not content, at least reconciled to letting time pass.

There was the physical anomaly, of course. Certain parts of Buttercup's anatomy were not what Mouse was accustomed to, particularly certain parts of the face and feet. For a time this half-familiar, half-strange feeling made her feel panicky, almost hysterical, but then some recollection of other, similar, occurrences soothed her. Time, she told herself. Time would work things out. She settled herself into the mostly milky nothingness to wait it out. There was plenty of time.

And with every passing day, it became easier, she had to admit that. As Buttercup acquired understanding and volition and even a limited ability to communicate, it became easier for Mouse to bear. Sheer tedium gave way to matters of at least transitory interest.

Time passed. The milky unconsciousness turned into perception, into sounds and smells and sights, into the feel of hands on her skin. Single things, at first, and then sequences. And, finally, a full perception of something actually happening: the arrival with her wet nurse at the house of Mr Thrumm.

It was her first clear memory. Before that she might have heard people in some other and previous location speculating as to whether it was yet safe for her to travel, and she did recall a thin and insinuating voice saying something about her safety — 'The Van Hoost rogue's safety!' — being of no possible concern to anyone. She remembered very little of the journey. Perhaps it had been brief. Perhaps she had slept through it. Perhaps, and it was not impossible, she had been drugged. Much later, recollecting Nursey's predeliction for saving trouble by any and every means at hand, she thought it not unlikely that Nursey had simply given her something to keep her quiet until they arrived. By that time, she had stopped distinguishing between herself, Mouse, and her other self, Buttercup. It was futile. One could only watch and listen and wait for the time when things would straighten themselves out again.

Arrival at Mr Thrumm's house, however, she perceived in all its details.

'Here you are,' burbled Mr Thrumm, peering at her through his thick glasses. 'From the Palace of the Old Queen, as promised, one article. A sweet one, Nurse, yes she is. But I do see what they meant, indeed I do. She has the Van Hoost chin, doesn't she?'

'So they say, sir,' boomed Nurse. 'Though I can't think

why. It seems a very babylike chin to me. Not unlike most babies. And if it is a bit Van Hoosty, what of it?'

'Well,' he replied, opening the door and beckoning them in (part of her remembered the wheels of a carriage leaving just then, the grating sound of gravel underlying his voice). 'Well, now, what of it? My dear Nurse, during the reign of one of the aunts of the current Queen — was it during Grislda's time or Hermione's? Or could it have been Euthasia? I can never recall — it was determined that the fall in the fortunes of the Royal House had come about because of the admixture of the tainted Van Hoost blood.'

'Van Hoost was only a young rooster, for heaven's sake,' said Nursey. 'And it was all of a long time ago.'

'Be that as it may, Nurse. This charge of yours is only the latest in a long line of Van Hoost chins, elbows, and heels — the Van Hoost heel is unmistakable even at an early age — to be sent into banishment — that is, into the care of the Thrumms.'

The three of them, Thrumm, Nursey, and infant went in, taking Mouse along perforce, unseen, unregarded, unsuspected. Buttercup, the infant, had no means of knowing that it was impossible for a child of her tender age to understand, much less remember this occasion. She, the infant, Buttercup, had no means of knowing that such perception was beyond one of her extreme youth and that she must, therefore, be possessed in some very strange way. The urgency and uniqueness of that arrival faded into memory as time went by. There had been only the one arrival, and Buttercup — or Mouse — remembered that distinctly, but subsequently there were many days and seasons of living in Thrumm House, all much alike. They tended to fade together into one endless montage, though the infant still retained very clear and detailed memories of her early months, phrasing these memories to herself in language. The infant had not, as yet, any understanding of language. She did not recognize language, much less speak it, but Mouse did, and Mouse remembered it for her.

Thrumm House was remarkable neither for its size nor

for its rather undistinguished exterior architecture, a style referred to in some quarters as Nuvo Obfuscian. It was a dwelling of some fifteen or twenty major rooms, interesting mainly in the extent of its internal drawering. The number and variety of drawers was uncommon, if not unique. They covered every wall from floor to ceiling: the bathing chambers, the stairways, the kitchens — even the little porch where Nursey sat on rainy days singing nursery songs and rubbing thube shrinking salve into her charge's Van Hoost chin — all the rooms were lined with drawers. There were large ones, including those in which the inhabitants slept, medium-sized and smallish ones for the storage of a multitude of necessary things, and then hundreds of very tiny ones along the floor or up beneath the coving of the stained and cracked ceilings. Some had heavy, ornamental castings as handles. Others had simple knobs of porcelain or simulacre or gold.

In the child's own room there were one thousand six hundred and forty-three drawers. She *learned* this as soon as she was able to count though she had *known* it before. She learned at the same time that most of the drawers were quite empty. Only one of them had anything in it that she had previously put there. As soon as she could walk, she had taken the jar of thube salve which Nursey was wont to rub into her chin and emptied it into one of the tiniest drawers, refilling the jar with tallow from the kitchen. What moved her to this effort, Buttercup the infant could not have said. Mouse would have said that the thube salve smelled abominably and, more to the point, it itched. The kitchen grease did not smell quite the same, but Nursey, who had very little sense of smell, never noticed the difference and went on tallowing her charge's chin every afternoon for years.

A tribe of small waltzing mice lived in several of the medium-sized drawers, drawers which Mouse, though not Buttercup, thought were probably connected to the kitchen because of the smell of toasted cheese which emanated each time she opened them. The mice were companions, not useful for conversation but infinitely amusing in the long, dusky holiday hours when the shutters were closed and there was nothing to do. Some of the drawers in the orangery had lizards living in them, and there were bright, glistening snakes in the drawers of the small porch. All in all, she preferred the mice for the bedroom.

When Buttercup was still quite young, after she had learned to walk and count but before she was weaned or could talk with clarity, Mr Thrumm began to object to the name 'Buttercup.'

'Not a name which will do,' opined Mr Thrumm. 'Not one which will be acceptable on the occasion.'

'Well, for heaven's sake, I've got to call her something!' Nursey objected with that stubborn intransigence which was natural to all Nurseys. 'I can't go on saying "her" all the time.'

Mr Thrumm grumbled, but did not insist. Acceptable or not, it was the name by which the infant became known to those around her. As herself, she accepted the name, thinking nothing of it. The mouse part thought to itself that it was a ridiculous name for anyone, but most especially a ridiculous name for this — this being that she was inhabiting.

Mr Thrumm, in whose house they dwelt, was not the only Mr Thrumm. Buttercup was to meet three Mr Thrumms, virtually identical in appearance though somewhat varied in habit. Each of them, seemingly, had been awarded the care and custody of Van Hoost rogues since the time, approximately, of Hermione. Buttercup's own Mr Thrumm was named Raphael. The others, who visited from time to time, were Jonas and Cadmon. Buttercup came to understand that there had always been three Mr Thrumms, always so named. Whether these were the original or successor ones, she was never able to establish, and in fact she — including her separate inhabitant self — grew to feel that it did not really matter.

Mr Thrumm, whether the current Mr Thrumm or a predecessor, had to have collected everything stored away in the drawers of Thrumm House. The current Mr Thrumm, however, passed his time looking for things he or his predecessors had hidden. In the evenings he would sit in a half-open drawer staring into the fire while he made lists of things he hoped to find on the following day. Then, on the morrow, he would look for these things, always finding others which were not on his list. Exclamations of interest and amusement followed these discoveries, though he never actually laughed, and the fact that he seldom if ever found what he sought did not dissuade him from making another interminable list on the following evening. He was not in the least disheartened. He would say to Buttercup, 'Well, lass, try again, what? Got to be there somewhere, that's what I say. Those memorabilia of the Great Grisl-Threepian War, for example. Couldn't have been thrown away, could they? Keep looking, and eventually they'll turn up.'

Perhaps it was the constant repetition of these words, or perhaps it was that Mouse finally managed to get through to her, that caused Buttercup to hear a reverberation of his words in her own mind, an almost echo instructing her in a firm and not unfamiliar voice, 'There's something in this house that I need. Something I had with me when I left. It isn't in here, where I am, so it must be out there, in the house. You'll have to find it for me. Don't forget it, now. It's important.'

Buttercup could not imagine what this something might be, but the reminder irritated her, causing her to lose sleep, making her lie awake in the closely shuttered dark wondering what might possibly be in any of the drawers that was important to her. Mouse saw this restlessness with satisfaction. She knew she had had the matchbox with her when she left . . . left wherever she had been. Where had she been? Sometimes it was almost on the tip of her tongue. She had been in . . . She had been on . . . Never mind. Wherever it had been, she knew it had not simply been 'lost in transit.' The matchbox could not be lost in that way. Intrinsic to its nature or structure was an inviolability of direction. If she, Mouse, had come here, then it, matchbox, had come here as well. It was nearby, and it was up to Buttercup to find it.

In the course of time, Buttercup was weaned, toilet-trained, and taught proper speech and elementary deportment. She achieved her third birthday. It was time for Nursey to depart and for the tutor to arrive. Buttercup did not weep when Nursey went. There was a feeling almost of relief to smell the last of that thube-reeking, deep-uddered being. When night came, however, grief came with it bringing shuddering sobs which Buttercup could in no wise understand. It was as though the very foundation of her life had been torn away without her realizing it. That night she experienced a strong, almost imperative dream in which the unknown voice reminded her to search for something — something very important to her. She wakened from it half terrified.

She sought no comfort from Mr Thrumm. Even in the midst of her grief, she was cognizant that Mr Thrumm would offer her no consolation, even if he had known how.

The tutor was a tall, pale individual who wore tight trousers and short, many-pocketed jackets worked with scenes of forests and glades in tapestry stitch. He carried a slender cane with which he switched the heads off of grasses and wildflowers while on walks. His name was John Henry Sneeth. He confessed in an embarrassed whisper that he did not like the names John and Henry and would prefer to be called simply 'Sneeth.' Buttercup had had no intercourse with the outer world and therefore did not at the time think this a ridiculous request, though Mr Thrumm rolled his eyes and pinched his mouth as though to keep back laughter and Mouse rolled about in amusement, figuratively speaking, since Mouse, being disembodied, had no ability to roll about in actuality.

Ribble the cook also quivered with merriment for days after first meeting Sneeth. There were, in addition to Thrumm and Sneeth, two other older persons in Thrumm House, the Ribble couple: cadaverous Ribble who tended the gardens and fat Ribble who cooked. Cook Ribble made up for all the laughter no one else used. Cook was always aquiver: chins, belly, bosom, tiny jiggly bits and pieces around the elbows and knees moving in a constant delirium of motion. Cook's laughter was as without end as without cause. Cook simply moved in it, like a fish in water, unconscious of its being a medium of transport.

Cadaverous Gardener Ribble was as dry and brittle as a burnt bird's bone. Gardener Ribble seldom spoke and was never amused.

Sneeth took up the Buttercup's tutelage with something approaching enthusiasm, at least he did so at first. Simple reading, writing, arithmetic, basic history — though Buttercup had the feeling that he left things out of history, either through carelessness or ignorance, or from some other motive she could not discern — and, of course, deportment. Mr Thrumm recurrently suggested the importance of deportment. Why it should be important for someone virtually expunged from the memory of the Royal Family to be instructed in the minutia of aristocratic customs and behavior made no sense at all. According to Mr Thrumm, it was important. Sneeth always complied with Mr Thrumm's suggestions, however gently they might be phrased, and deportment became important to Sneeth.

It was Sneeth's inclination, however, no less than Buttercup's own, to ignore the curriculum laid down *as much as possible*, that is, at any point at which the basics were well in hand. Once the subject matter was reasonably well understood, Sneeth found no reason to continue with the dull texts prescribed by custom (or Thrumm) when there were other, more interesting — even though forbidden — books available.

And there were. The drawers in the library were packed with volumes. Others filled the lower stairway drawers and those in the back pantry. In the root cellar, where no one would expect to find books at all, Buttercup found a collection of what were possibly the most interesting volumes on the property. These included books of wonder stories, some purely fanciful and others based in fact, concerning other worlds and peoples. There was also a collection of the Palace Newspapers, a rich trove of mystery and intrigue beside which mere history (however truncated to eliminate boring detail) paled to nothing. From them, and without Sneeth's knowledge, Buttercup learned many things she was not supposed to know. She learned, for example, what had happened to the Van Hoost consorts. She learned the ritual of Royal Challenge, during which the Heiress Presumptive, challenged by at least one other Grisl of Royal Blood, must prove herself able to emerge victorious from combat. She read with interest accounts of current and bygone fads and fashions at the Palace, who and what was in and who and what was out, and why. Though all these matters were but dimly understood, scarcely more relevant than if they had recounted the customs of savage Earthians or Jambanders, they had a certain fascination and served to fill up the vacant corners of an eager young mind.

It was in one of these same drawers that she found a small gold box, greeting this discovery with a wash of grateful emotion so ecstatic that it left her limp. Under Mouse's direction, Buttercup took the box to her room and secreted it in one of the tiny drawers, where she, guided by Mouse, could take it out and fondle it from time to time, though she had no idea why. 'Never mind why,' Mouse said within her mind. 'It's important, that's all.'

Sneeth and Buttercup were largely unsupervised, so long as the examiners, who arrived once each year, were satisfied with the progress of Mr Thrumm's protégée. A Van Hoost chin, taken alone, was not sufficient to warrant actual execution, but such a chin coupled with intransigent ignorance of deportment and protocol might well be. Mr Thrumm was at some pains to point this out. As a result of this threat, the latter part of each winter was spent in a feverish attempt to master all the information which had been largely ignored since the previous spring. Buttercup rather liked these intellectual sprints. She quite enjoyed the haunted expression which Sneeth came to wear on these occasions, realizing full well that his own destiny was tied to hers. If Buttercup failed, so did Sneeth. For Buttercup, contemplation of this fact lent piquancy to what might have been an otherwise tedious span of years.

In the spring the examiners came. In company with one or two who changed from visit to visit there was always one named Fribberle who came again and again. He had a dour and reproving countenance. He sat with the others at one end of the table in the formal dining room while Buttercup stood at the other end of the table, hands folded in front of her, face composed. This was elementary deportment. One did not twitch. And, despite Cook's example, one did not laugh. And one did not show interest beyond mere politeness. One answered briefly, accurately, demonstrating if requested. The bow direct. The bow deferential. The bow obsequious. The challenge Royal. The challenge covert. The nod of dismissal. The nod of repudiation. She learned them all and practiced them in front of her mirror. There was never any trouble with the examinations. Buttercup always passed.

And each time the examiners left, Sneeth and Buttercup were left to their own devices once more. There were weeks and months during which they could amuse themselves, weeks and months in which Buttercup experienced virtual contentment — except for the internal voice of Mouse which sometimes wakened her in the night trying to give her unwanted advice.

Thrumm House was situated on a pleasant prominence overlooking the Welling Valley and the village of Lesser Wellingford. Greater Wellingford had been widely distributed by flood some years before and was no longer sufficiently aggregate to merit attention. Lesser Wellingford offered plentiful amusements, however. Sneeth and Buttercup could shop in the main street, or visit the parrot market or buy hot seed pies from the piemonger, and do all these things without offending against what Sneeth was pleased to call Buttercup's 'dignity.' Certain other pleasures, such as watching a grisling show, were forbidden lest they result in this offense.

'I don't know what you mean by "dignity," Sneeth,' she complained when he refused for the third time to allow her to see the grisling show. The two of them were standing on the midway of a traveling circus that came frequently to the Welling Valley during the summer, and Buttercup was staring up at the banners that advertised this event. 'I am a rogue daughter of the ruling house. I've been banished. I don't know what dignity I've got.'

'More than me,' he mumbled.

'Well, yes,' she admitted, 'but then I am female. That means I have more dignity that you or Thrumm or Cook and more than all the villagers, too, because you and they are all males, but that doesn't signify much. I don't know what it has to do with watching a grisling show.'

'Mr Thrumm would have a fit if he found out.'

'How in the world would he find out! He doesn't come down to the village. None of these oafs are going to go up to Thrumm House and tell him.'

'You won't tell him?'

'Of course I won't tell him. Don't be silly. I don't want to get into trouble.'

Sneeth bought tickets, insisting that they enter the show through the rear tent flap and set themselves well toward the back, where they would not make themselves a part of the spectacle.

The stage was small. Grislings themselves were small. Buttercup watched, entranced, as the little females decked themselves in their finery — they had been trained to do this, of course, it was no part of the wild behavior — and then went through the classic motions of challenge and attack. A cage of males was surreptitiously placed near the platform to provoke this behavior. The little females looked almost Grisllike, almost human with their cocky little heads and delicate arms. Their ivory spurs had been replaced with false, flexible ones so they could not hurt one another, and the growth of their paralyzing fangs had been suppressed with thube. They had been cleaned and groomed until they were very pretty, and Buttercup thought that she preferred them even to the waltzing mice. They looked so very human. Almost as though they might speak at any moment, demanding access to the cage of males which had been hastily taken away as soon as battle was joined.

'That's not fair,' Buttercup protested. 'Taking the males away from the little pink one. She won the fight.'

'Well — but,' Sneeth stuttered, turning quite red. 'That's not a nice thing to say! If they had left the males there, she would have . . . well, it's not something we could watch. Not good deportment, at all. Not civilized!'

She subsided, still thinking it had been quite unfair, but distracting herself with the thought of hot seed pie. She and Sneeth usually bought pies for themselves plus two to carry back, one for Gardener Ribble and one for the gardener's boy. Ribble always had a boy, someone from the village or the surrounding area who was willing to work for three meals a day, a drawer to sleep in, and a seed pie now and again.

They wandered munchingly along the valley, licking syrup from their chins, climbing over a stile to ascend the hill toward Thrumm House, then stopping as they heard a sound in the underbrush nearby, a kind of stifled snigger.

Sneeth dithered, turning toward and then away from the noise.

'Come on,' instructed Buttercup. 'I want to see what that is.' She streaked away through the grasses, Sneeth tiptoeing guiltily behind, and threw herself at the top of an embankment to peer between two shrubs.

Below her in a tiny clearing was the latest gardener's boy, and on the earth before him were two wild grislings engaged in battle. They were in no wise as lovely as the groomed ones Buttercup had seen so recently upon the stage but no less human-looking for that. Buttercup drew in her breath, letting it out in one long shriek of fury. The boy, the filthy *boy*, had cut the spurs from one of the grislings leaving her helpless before the paralyzing attack of the other. She had already been cut to ribbons while the boy sat there sniggering and playing with himself.

Buttercup was about to launch herself at him, with no clear idea of what she might accomplish — he outweighed her by half — when Sneeth came down the embankment, lashing away with his cane, catching the boy full across his face and sending him screaming away across the fields, blood streaming down his neck.

Buttercup cradled the maimed grisling, but it was far too late. As she held the little creature it sighed and expired in her arms.

She turned, hiding tears with difficulty. Only her long study of deportment let her continue the journey home without showing her feelings on her face. When they arrived there, she went up the stairs, intending to shut herself into her room, but was stopped halfway down the hall by the sound of conversation in the foyer below.

'. . . whipped him and he ran off, but she had already seen it. *Never* should have been done where she could see it!'

Where she could see it? What had Sneeth meant by that? The rigged battle had been something *no* one should ever have to see. A fair fight in nature is one thing, she told herself. Nature is bloody and violent, as many of the books she had read had made quite clear. A battle during which one opponent is rendered helpless, however, was simply not to be thought of without disgust, even a battle between creatures as tiny as wild grislings. *Where she could see it*, indeed. Buttercup was angry all over again, and it took a long evening alone with the mice — feeding them the seed pie which had been destined for the gardener's boy — before she could show herself with an unperturbed face.

That night she had particularly violent dreams in which a previously indulgent voice directed her with some hostility to quit fooling around and pay attention to what was going on. The dream, like most dreams, bothered her on first awaking and was forgotten by breakfast time. Inside Buttercup, Mouse was in a state.

Since it was a holiday, breakfast was served in the gloomy kitchen. On holidays the shutters were left closed all day. Those civilized beings so foolish as to leave secure shelter on holidays were said to deserve whatever happened to them, as those were the days when the tribes of wild Grisls moved down out of the mountains seeking — well — seeking whatever they sought. What they sought was never specified in Buttercup's presence, and she had imagined several things which they might be after, some of which brought shivers of revulsion.

When Nursey had been present, she had insisted upon spending all of every holiday in the kitchen, as it had the fewest windows. Sneeth, however, considered it appropriate to sit in the schoolroom and do whatever work was needed, and he repaired there with Buttercup as soon as Cook cleared the table. Sneeth, unaccountably sleepy-looking, as though he had spent a wakeful night, managed to maintain an instructive manner for only about an hour, after which repeated yawns turned into a breathy snore and he laid his head upon his desk and slept.

Buttercup, at a loss for anything interesting to do, went to a shutter which was tightly closed across one of the classroom windows and found a knot at which she had been working for some time. A bit more prying and the knot popped into her hand, leaving behind a large, slanted knothole through which she could examine the hidden outer world of holiday-time.

And how strange an outer world it proved to be! Thrumm House had been invaded by wild Grisls. At least three camps of them huddled beneath the trees at the edge of the meadow. On the meadow itself, half a dozen robed females engaged in a stately dance. Observing them from the shelter of the trees were a number of males including a number whom Buttercup recognized from the village.

The tempo of the dance increased. Buttercup cast a quick glance at Sneeth, but he was quite unconscious of her misbehavior. She applied her eye to the knothole once more.

One by one the Grisls removed their robes until all six of them were standing quite naked except for their rather tawdry veils and gems. They began to display, rumps flushing crimson, eyes flashing, venom tooth gleaming, spurs positively glittering in the sun. Oh, the lovely length of those spurs, as white and unsullied as peeled wood, gently curved, sharp as needles. Here was no pretense! No flexible spurs to save wounding!

The females paired off and began to battle. Out of the shade of the woods the males crept, hypnotized by the scent of combat, fascinated by the sight of it, until a ring of them surrounded the combatants. Two battles were swiftly concluded, and while the losers lay bleeding and paralyzed upon the sward, the winners engaged one another. The males crept closer, showing obvious signs of arousal.

The third couple concluded its fight, a winner emerged from the second battle, and the two successful fighters now poised before one another, heads back, crowing, casting flirtatious glances at the circle of males . . .

And then the Grisls decided, simultaneously, that they need not fight one another, that there were plenty of males to go around. They turned, instead, to prance before the circle of wide-eyed, hypnotized males, selecting this one and that one to receive a love bite from their dripping fangs until each had three or four laid out on the meadow grasses.

As the rejected males slunk away, those accepted were used repeatedly by the successful females while Buttercup watched, entranced. When the females had finished, which took some time, they packed up their wagons and tents and went off down the valley, leaving the paralyzed males lying on the meadow.

Sneeth sighed dreamily.

Buttercup slipped the knot back into the hole and turned back to her books.

'. . . reign of Euthasia,' said Sneeth, completing a thought he had begun some hours before.

'I'm tired,' said Buttercup, much aroused. 'I think I'll go to my room and take a nap.'

'Oh, very well,' said Sneeth. 'It probably wouldn't hurt either of us.'

Buttercup left, only to return to the vacant schoolroom and put her eye to the knothole once more. Men from the village had come to the dusky meadow to pile the paralyzed lovers in barrows and carts, preparatory to hauling them back to the village, Buttercup supposed.

'So that's what it all meant,' she murmured to herself, thinking on all the references to sex she had seen in this book and that. 'That's how it's done.' There were still things that were quite unclear to her, but she would not ask either Sneeth or Mr Thrumm. It was not something one wanted to discuss with a male. Not for the first time, Buttercup wished

402

for Nursey. If she wanted to know something about sex and had no member of her own sex to ask, the next best thing would be to have a Nursey to inquire from.

Not, she reminded herself, that she would necessarily get a truthful answer.

It was shortly after the knothole experience that Buttercup began to experience certain bodily manifestations. The hard, callused lumps on her heels began to itch, and it was not long before two ivory spikes showed there, glistening against the pinkness of her skin. A similar itchiness attacked her chin, and another ivory spike emerged from its tip to grow both upward toward her upper lip and downward into a hollow point. These protuberances grew very rapidly, and soon Buttercup herself could see her spurs and venom tooth emerging from the chrysalis of her childhood. When she looked in the mirror, it was with a sense of recurrent wonder, as though she expected to see someone else reflected there, someone without a venom tooth, someone without spurs on her heels. Someone with round ears. Someone green. And behind that someone, still another someone, a vaguely bipedal form which came and vanished like a windblown ghost.

Someone, Sneeth or Mr Thrumm or even one of the Ribbles, first commented on the change in her. Cook began giggling about it, making sly remarks. Mr Thrumm announced his intention of 'sending word to the Palace.' Sneeth merely looked more uncomfortable than usual, which, since the incident of the gardener's boy, had been quite uncomfortable indeed.

Buttercup had naively supposed that the Van Hoostness which had caused her banishment had also disqualified her for consideration by the Palace. In this, she was quite mistaken. The punctilious arrival of the examiners should have informed her otherwise. Of course the Palace considered her. Why else would the examiners have bothered?

This insight came to her with some force when a personage arrived from the Palace in response to Mr Thrumm's report. It was Fribberle, the perennial examiner, now arrived to take up residence at Thrumm House. Not to give lessons. Not to visit with Mr Thrumm. Merely to occupy a room from which he emerged at intervals to stare at Buttercup and make some remark apropos of nothing. On one occasion he said, 'You need not think you will become a femme fatale just because you are growing up.' Though Buttercup kept an imperturbable face, the remark disturbed her. She had never thought of becoming any such thing. She had never known there was any such thing. None of the books had mentioned such a creature, not even the ones in the root cellar.

Breaking one of her own rules, she asked Sneeth to define a 'femme fatale.' Sneeth flushed, stuttered, and fled. Obviously, she had entered upon a subject which was taboo. This irritated her. She was already irritated at the dream voice which was becoming a nightly presence, abjuring her to pay attention because something inimical was going on. Her conscious mind and that strange, inhabiting mind were washing at her like the flow of the Welling River, telling her again and again that she, Buttercup, was in danger and that there were things she must do about it. Even the composure resulting from seven years study of deportment could not hold back such a flow, and Buttercup acceded to it at last. She accepted that neither Mr Thrumm nor Sneeth nor Fribberle had been forthcoming in telling her what was going on. Somewhere there had to be information she needed, information which had been withheld from her, information she assumed could be found in Thrumm House, somewhere, which meant it had to be in one of the thousands of drawers.

Her search began with a systematic mental review of the contents of every drawer she had seen opened in Thrumm House. Her own room could be ignored. She had been through all of her own drawers repeatedly, even the ones near the ceiling, borrowing Gardener Ribble's ladder for the process. She felt that some walls of drawers could probably be ignored as she had closely observed Mr Thrumm rummaging through them. These included virtually all those in the library, the salon, the dining room, and the three major suites, not including Mr Thrumm's own room. Therefore, her search would concentrate on other areas than these. Every night,

when the house was quiet, she would rise from her bed, take
a lantern and begin her quest, retiring only at dawn. Since
Sneeth, with the advent of Fribberle, had virtually abdicated
his responsibility to educate her, there was no impediment
to her napping in the daytime.

At length, only the upper drawers in the great hall remained
unsearched. The ladder was too short to reach more than
halfway up the wall. Making a stairway out of half opened
drawers proved impossible as many of them were stuck. She
resorted, finally, to a knotted rope let down from the balcony
which let her reach a drawer she could open enough to stand
upon. From this vantage place, other drawers could be
opened, some of the drawers containing things evidently
unseen since the time of Hermione.

She searched one drawer, then another, and another. And
another still . . .

In which she found, wrapped in tissue paper, some white
as though recently cut, others yellow with age, a dozen pairs
of ivory spurs.

Grisl spurs.

They were not prostheses. Their bases bore the clear marks
of the saw. They had been cut from the heels of Grisls —
probably living Grisls. They had probably been cut here, in
Thrumm House.

The sight of the amputated spurs brought back memories
of the gardener's boy and the wild grislings, and she heard
Sneeth's voice saying, '. . . never should have been done
where she could see it!'

He had meant that she should not have seen a rigged battle
between grislings, where one of them had had her spurs
amputated. She remembered Sneeth's discomfort with the
grisling show. She should not really have been allowed to
see the grisling show either, and only Sneeth's desire for
amusement had moved him to permit it. There had been
something in both those spectacles she was supposed to be
unaware of.

Buttercup had asked Mr Thrumm at one time why there
were no other Grisls in residence. He had replied with his

405

usual, vague insouciance, 'There aren't many needed, lass. Only a few. They come and they go.'

Inside her, Mouse's voice spoke clearly. 'Smarten up, dumdum. You've got all the pieces. Put them together.'

And in response to that voice, she saw what they had been hiding from her. It was evident to her at last and all at once that the Grisls who came into Thrumm House did indeed go — go as the pathetic wild grisling had gone before the gardener's boy — to a prearranged and ugly defeat, despurred, and with their fangs undoubtedly suppressed with thube salve. Defenseless. Offenseless. Unable to do battle.

But why? Why? Why had this been done in the past? Was it being planned again? Why had an employee from the Palace been sent to . . . to observe.

'Nitwit,' said the voice from inside her somewhere. 'Are you not a Grisl of Royal Blood? And do not Heiresses Presumptive have to emerge victorious from open combat with at least one heiress of Royal Blood?' The voice had more than a hint of annoyance in it, as of an elder chastising a child guilty of an ignorance almost insolent in its totality.

Nonetheless, the voice was right. It all came back to her now. Those forbidden books in the root cellar. The system of Royal Challenge. And everyone knew, even Buttercup — for it was talked about constantly, by everyone — that the Old Queen was coming very close to the end of her reign, the end of her very long life.

So, Buttercup hissed to herself, feeling a coldness on one foot, raising it to find it wet with something . . . wet with venom dripping from the slender, hollow fang growing on her Van Hoost chin. So, they intended her to be a victim, did they. They intended to cut off her spurs. They thought the thube salve had suppressed the venom sacks in her chin. They thought she would be helpless. Incapable. They intended her to challenge the Heiress Presumptive, and they intended for the heiress to kill her.

She could imagine how they planned to do it. They would transport her to the Palace, fit her out with a pair of flexible false spurs, drug her into some kind of hypnotized trance, and then let the heiress make away with her.

Buttercup shut the various drawers she had opened, unknotted the rope from the balcony, and went back to her bed. No matter when they planned, they would do nothing until the Old Queen died or was very close to death. She was sure of it. When the time came for the Heiress Presumptive to confront a challenger, they would want the challenger to look as normal as possible. This could only be achieved if they let the challenger alone until the last possible moment.

Well then, they had taught her deportment and imperturbability. Now was certainly the time to use it.

Some months passed. Occasionally, Buttercup would take the matchbox from the small drawer and look at it, wondering why it was important. Several times she tried to open it, but found it proof against her curiosity. Occasionally she would query that intrusive inner voice to learn whether some other intelligence knew something that would help her. The voice was stubbornly silent.

And then, in the middle of the night, in springtime, as the year was wakening from chill, everyone in Thrumm House was roused by the tolling of the village bell. From a distance, across a fold of hills, another bell gave answer, and from other valleys far and near, more bells rang out. There could be only one reason for such a clamor. The Old Queen was dead.

Buttercup had barely time to get out of bed and hide herself behind the door. Fribberle entered with the sound of the final knell, Mr Thrumm close behind him. Fribberle carried a saw in one hand and a hypodermic syringe in the other. Buttercup did not bother to ask him what it contained. That he carried a saw was evidence enough of his evil intent.

She had been practicing the leap and jab she had seen the Grisls using when she watched through the knothole. Fribberle, who was the larger of the two males, caught the first dose, impeccably delivered at the juncture of neck and shoulder. Her fang slid into and out of his flesh like a skewer into and out of a succulent roast. Thrumm saw it, but he did

407

not react swiftly enough to save himself. Though she missed the exact location with her second bite, it did well enough. By the time she had caught her breath, both of them were quite paralyzed, staring at the wall, awaiting her instructions. She appreciated that. She had not wanted anything messy. She had given them little more than a love bite, as she wanted them ambulatory and cooperative.

There was a small, virtually unused sun porch on the second floor. She took them there and sat them comfortably in chairs where they could look out onto the Welling Valley. There were things she wanted to know which she inquired of Fribberle. He gave the information freely, and she sighed with relief. In the room he had used, there was a device to communicate with the Palace. It was simple to operate, one simply picked up the speaking disk and announced one's message. She felt that Fribberle's voice would not be difficult to counterfeit.

As a precaution, once they were seated, she nipped them again. Grisl venom could be reversed by antidote or, if given in small enough doses, it did wear off in time. Larger doses, of course, could be fatal. Buttercup assured herself that neither Mr Thrumm nor Fribberle was dead. She had not decided yet whether she wanted them dead.

Sneeth was next, then Ribble the Cook and Gardener Ribble. Unfortunately, there was a new gardener's boy, and he had to be included. After which Buttercup took herself to the communication device and, speaking in an approximation of Fribberle's haughty voice, asked when the Van Hoost Grisl would be wanted at the Palace. How much of this was her own idea and how much had come from Mouse's prompting it never occurred to her to inquire.

A barely intelligible quacking and gargling ensued. Translated into the closest approximation of recognizable words, the sense of it seemed to be that nothing needed to be done for a few weeks. Obsequies were underway. There would be a state funeral. Only then would the heiress need her properly prepared opponent.

Buttercup went to her room, stripped, and examined herself

with care. Her spurs were longer than some she had seen through the knothole. Her fang was well developed, thanks no doubt to those years of careful rubbing with tallow. While she was unpracticed in actual combat, she was young and better fed than most of the wild Grisls she had seen.

'Risk not, gain not,' the internal voice advised. 'I hate to be involved, kid, but I think you'd better get some practice.' Buttercup could not but agree. It would certainly not do to meet the Heiress Presumptive without any practical experience at all.

Since she could not very well simply go out into the countryside looking for experience, she felt it would be well to take advantage of the opportunity brought to her gate, as it were. On the next holiday, when the wild Grisls assembled in the meadow, Buttercup emerged from the house to take part in the combat. She was, quite frankly, frightened half to death. The inner voice which had plagued her for years was mercifully silent, as though holding its tongue, but she was afraid she might not be able to concentrate.

The preliminaries to challenge took care of that. As she told herself later, one needed only to get to a certain point by determination. After that, the hormones took over.

When the bout had concluded, Buttercup selected one of the young males who had been aroused to erotic suppliance by the battle and took him back to the house with her. Not to have done so would have caused antagonism and violence, even though she had previously decided that she could not, *must* not risk actual dalliance. The conclusion was inescapable that untrammeled eroticism led inevitably to egg-maturation. A Grisl's chances of winning a challenge would undoubtedly be lessened if one was swollen and lethargic with egg. Therefore, once the young male had been given the love bite, she ensconced him in a chair next to the gardener's boy. That much was easy. The harder part was to leave him there. He was remarkably attractive.

On successive holidays she engaged in battle, emerging victorious each time. The number of young males in the sun porch swelled to seven, and Buttercup had to fetch more chairs. She felt actual pity as she realized that unless someone carrying the antidote arrived at the house — one of the other Mr Thrumms, perhaps — or unless the house fell down around them, they would sit there for years while the seasons passed and Thrumm House was given over to mice and lizards.

Came a morning when the communication device quacked and gargled once more. The Van Hoost rogue was to be brought to the Palace in ten days time. Mimicking Fribberle's voice, Buttercup assented.

Fribberle would undoubtedly have procured a conveyance. Buttercup did not wish to have a conveyance. She wished to explore the world and see something of its ways. She spent the last evening in Thrumm House in nostalgic reminiscences of her peaceful and unsuspecting childhood and in searching the only drawers she had been unable to search before, those in Mr Thrumm's own room. Aside from stacks of pictures which intrigued her inasmuch as she had not known that males did that with one another, she found nothing of interest.

On the following morning, just before she left, she paused before the portraits of the recent Queens — Hermiones I, II and III; Euthasias I through IV; Grislda, surnamed 'the only.' None of them had the Van Hoost chin, but she resolved that the next Queen would have that attribute, Heiress Presumptive or no Heiress Presumptive. When the time came, she would rule under her own name, or under some new name, something original, perhaps something she would pick for herself. Grisls were not given formal names, as a general rule, until they had challenged and won at least once. What would be the point, after all? 'Short, anonymous lives,' the poet had said of early losers. 'Short, anonymous lives.' Nurseys, being uniformly sentimental, often attached some baby name to their Grisl charges just as they did their male ones. The males kept their baby names, but Grisls did not.

Therefore it must be as Buttercup that she emerged into the

410

world. It was, she thought, quite fitting. As Buttercup she had come. As Buttercup she would go.

'Quite right, too,' said Mouse. Buttercup, of course, did not know it was Mouse. She accepted the reinforcement as though it had come from some alter ego of her own.

CHAPTER FIVE

In order to avoid challenges, which would have slowed the trip to an interminable crawl, Buttercup wore the so-called 'quiet garb,' a light though opaque garment, a head to spur dust-gown with a flap to cover the lower face and fang. She had not gone over five miles before she realized that if it had not been for the garment, she would not have been able to keep her resolution about the males. Every group that passed seemed to have half a dozen of them, burgeoning with health and juices, tippy-toeing along with their cute little behinds twitching, not at all like the placid villagers she had been used to seeing. Not for the first, or last, time, she regretted the seven sitting there on the sun porch, nipped into impotent insensibility.

Except for this, there seemed to be no impediment to a swift and pleasant journey. Buttercup found the weather delightful, warm and yet airy, with light breezes from the fragrant forests, cooled from the heat of the day with gentle showers, dry by evening so that one could sleep in comfort. She was glad not to be confined in a conveyance. Those that passed on the road looked hot and uncomfortable, like ovens on wheels. This was not quite her own thought, but it was not so unfamiliar as to seem disturbing. As she walked, she rehearsed what she would do and say at the Palace, how she would get by the guard Nurseys to emerge into the arena at the proper time. She spent some time considering whether the Heiress Presumptive would have been well trained in combat, deciding probably not. All this conjecture was so compelling that she failed to keep her attention on the road. As the sun dropped behind the trees she looked up in sudden confusion, realizing that for some time she had not seen another person and that the trail she was on had, at some point behind her, departed from the route she should have been following.

'Oh, fine,' snarled Mouse. Buttercup ignored this interpolation since it was very close to her own feelings.

There was nothing around her but forest and the path which meandered through it, seemingly without destination, certainly without observable direction.

She was not frightened. That is, at that time, she did not identify her feelings as fright. She was distinctly uncomfortable, disliking the idea of being quite so surrounded by woods with the night coming on and annoyed with herself for having allowed the predicament to occur. It was while she was working through this feeling of annoyance that she heard the sound. Someone or something was blundering about in the underbrush at no great distance from the path and making a noise which was, perhaps, a whuffling. Or a hruff. Perhaps both, she thought, in sequence. An ungrislish sound.

At a greater distance a person was shouting, words which made no sense at all to her though she was pleased that someone else was abroad in the falling dark. 'Hiya, wurfle, wurfle, heah, heah,' the voice called unintelligibly. 'Heah, heah.'

The underbrush quaked, shivered, rattled with leaves and twigs as a monstrous form erupted onto the path to turn toward Buttercup with an expression of brutish ferocity. Without knowing how she got there, Buttercup found herself with her back against a tree and her robe hiked high so that her spurs could be brought into play. The creature crouched, ready to spring, then began a series of stiff-legged hops in her direction, all the while making wuffling and hruffing noises. An inner voice was saying, 'Just a minute, here. I seem to remember that animal,' to which Buttercup was paying no attention whatsoever.

Just as she was about to leap, fang fully extended, a person moved out of the trees behind the creature and called plaintively, 'Damn it, Whurfle, down I say, let the Grisl alone.' The person, a young male of a slight build and pallid aspect, came toward her, saying in an apologetic tone, 'Damn dog! Please accept my apologies, Grisl. This animal of mine keeps running off and making a nuisance of itself. It really only wants to be friends, and I'm sorry if it frightened you.'

Buttercup adjusted her clothing in a mood of frosty hauteur, remarking that she had not been in the least frightened. The 'dog,' meantime, continued its stiff-legged gambol, obviously overjoyed to be the center of attention. Buttercup thought briefly of nipping him, only slightly, to teach him a lesson, but decided that this would undoubtedly offend the young male who was, after all, the only person she had seen for hours and likely her only guide back to the road. Besides, now that she was calmer, she recalled reading of dogs, a rare animal imported from the planet of the barbarian Earthians with whom the creature was said to have a symbiotic or perhaps parasitic relationship. She had not seen a dog before, however, and could not, quite frankly, find any charm in the one before her.

The young male, who introduced himself as Honsl, a printer from the nearby village of Rivvelford, continued his apologetic expostulations, ending with, 'And now I seem to be lost. Can you direct me?'

Sternly quelling a response to this question which would have directed him to depart in an unmentionable direction, Buttercup replied that she, too, was lost, having misplaced the road in her abstraction. He, in a manner which Buttercup considered to be very considerate, offered to accompany her back down the path in the hope they would come upon some more commodious and better traveled way. She found him a pleasant-looking young person, interesting in that he seemed unconscious of her as a Grisl. He quietly accepted her as a thinking being, or so it seemed, without any of that coy shyness which so many males used on all occasions of converse with Grisls of any age or condition. He was

413

relaxing, somewhat as she had often found Sneeth to be.

They returned along the path, stopping in bewilderment at a fork in the way. Buttercup had not noticed it on the way, and she had no idea which of the two paths before them had been her original one. They chose the left-hand path, which seemed a bit less overgrown, only to confront still another fork before they had wound their way another five hundred paces. Again choosing the left-hand way − for Buttercup seemed to remember that the forest had been on her left as she came up the river and therefore the road should lie to the left if she was faced in the opposite direction − they went on until darkness made it impossible to go farther. It was obvious to both of them that they would have to wait until morning when the sun would give them direction.

Honsl settled himself against a tree with his animal and spoke in a desultory way about the weather, happenings at the Palace, the funeral observances conducted in the village for the Old Queen, and other such trivial conversation. He spoke of the state of agriculture in the province (it had been a wet spring) and of how he had acquired the dog. It had been part of the stock in trade of an importer who had gone bankrupt, owing Honsl a large printing bill. Honsl had taken the dog, so he said, 'for company,' in settlement of the debt. He had no knowledge of where the creature originated or what system it may have been native to, and Buttercup told him what she had read of dogs, also mentioning that she found the example before her in every way inferior to the native fauna. It had no grace. It made no attractive noises. It smelled.

Honsl admitted that it did smell but said that one grew attached to the noises the thing made and to its affectionate nature. Buttercup reflected that males were notoriously whimsical in their desires; that many of them made collections of useless and trivial things − witness Mr Thrumm! − and that it was no part of her duty to educate this village printer in matters esthetic. She congratulated him on his acquisition and settled herself to rest.

It was at this moment that the dog, who had been quiet for some time, hruffed. He was standing, muzzle pointed at a spark of light which flickered among the windblown branches. Honsl saw it as well, and Buttercup suggested that they walk toward it, slowly, in order not to fall into any holes or ditches. As they grew closer, the light was seen to come from a cottage window. The dog went ahead, uttering a brusque 'harf, harf, harf' sound. Considering the unpleasantness of the sound, Buttercup was not surprised when the occupant of the cottage, an aged and unattractive Grisl of forbidding aspect, came out to see who was approaching, light streaming from the doorway behind her to fill the dooryard with shadows.

The dwelling was small, done up in a style popular during the reign of Hermione, called variously 'Marple Cookie' or 'Marple Bread,' after the spicy and highly ornamented cakes which it much resembled. Buttercup was hungry enough that the idea made her mouth water. The Grisl beckoned them forward, identifying herself as Mother Marple, at which Buttercup could not suppress a giggle. It was exactly like something out of a children's story. What followed was precisely as might have been foretold. Mother Marple offered them marple bread. At that, Buttercup did laugh, though the old Grisl patted her head very kindly, searching her face, or that of it which could be seen, with serious concentration. Buttercup chose not to take offense. There would be time for that in daylight.

The old Grisl pointed the direction and told them they could find the road easily in the morning, then offered them two pallets before the fire on which to sleep. The dog had, for some reason known best to dogs, either decided not to come in or had not been invited, which was more likely. Feeling particularly drowsy, Buttercup did not worry over the animal. Seemingly, neither did Honsl, for in a moment, lulled by the heat of the fire and the warmth in their bellies of the freshly baked marple cake, they were both asleep.

Buttercup had very odd dreams. The nagging voice which had not lately bothered her had returned to tease at her with nebulous commands and comments. 'I hope to hell you can get out of this' was one, as well as, 'You never learn, do

415

you?' When she woke it was with an ominous sense of something very wrong. When she came fully awake, she found herself in a stout cage behind the marple-bread cottage. Honsl was sitting disconsolately beside a tree, his ankle chained to a nearby post. The dog was nowhere to be seen, but Buttercup could hear his atrocious harf, harf, harf off somewhere in the woods. Though she was somewhat disoriented, she pulled herself together enough to address the pale young male before her.

'Honsl! What has happened?'

'The old witch caught us, is what.'

'Not a nice way to refer to an elderly Grisl, Honsl.'

'Don't care,' he sulked. 'She is.'

'Why in the world are we confined in this way?'

'Got the _____ for us,' he mumbled, the mid-part of the information lost in mid-mutter. Nor would he repeat what he had said.

Buttercup was at first inclined to think it was some kind of joke. Perhaps the old Grisl had taken offense at the dog. Perhaps she was merely a bit scattered, as the very old sometimes become. As the day wore on, however, she began to believe that it was the old Grisl's intention to starve her to death.

During the day Honsl received several plates of cakes with tea. Buttercup was given only water. All attempts to communicate with the aged Grisl met with a sly smile and complete silence. By evening, Buttercup was beginning to feel slightly dizzy from hunger, and it was at that time that the dog, crawling on its belly through the tall grasses, brought to the cage the bodies of several small, juicy examples of the local fauna.

Buttercup had been schooled to avoid raw meat. As she was about to turn from the still warm bodies in disgust, however, her interior voice said so loudly and so very clearly that it should have been audible across the clearing, 'For the sake of good sense, Buttercup, eat the damn things. You must. If you can't see the plot outline emerging here, I can!'

Buttercup had no idea what was meant by this, but as things

stood, she was both ravenous and had little choice of menu. Calling softly to Honsl, she offered to share the meat and was met with a shudder of rejection. An obscure impulse (Mouse, who wished to guarantee a continued source of sustenance) moved her to say, 'Good dog,' and she watched with interest as it wagged its posterior appendage to and fro in response to each utterance of this phrase. 'Good dog.'

When Buttercup had finished her meal, she tossed the bones away into the shrubbery, licked her bloody fingers clean, and lay down to sleep, aware of Honsl's reproachful eyes upon her. She would like to have cheered him, but since he would not share the provender furnished by his own dog, there was little she could do. Now that she had eaten the raw and bloody meat, she felt much better — well enough, in fact, that she wondered why she had been taught not to eat it.

Some days went by. The aged Grisl offered her nothing but water, but the dog brought dead animals at evening and at dawn. On the fifth day, the old Grisl began to approach the cage frequently, peering at Buttercup with wicked old eyes, totally ignoring all attempts at conversation. She was looking for something. Toward evening, when dog brought the catch of the day, Buttercup realized what the old Grisl was looking for. Mother Marple expected Buttercup to show signs of weakness! Five days of starvation would normally be enough to reduce even a well-conditioned Grisl to semi-consciousness.

Buttercup (encouraged by Mouse) resolved that, when morning came, she would play the part just to see what happened. During the night she was disturbed, as on the previous two nights, by erotic dreams. Such dreaming, she had been told, was a well-known consequence of eating raw meat, especially in the quantities Buttercup had recently been consuming. She had not been told, however, how amusing such dreams were. When morning came, she found herself looking at Honsl in a frankly lubricious way which should, in most circumstances, have stirred some signs of appreciation. Honsl, however, merely went on looking depressed and rather constipated.

Buttercup preened. He paid no attention. Irritated, she

417

began a full display, only to catch a glimmer of motion at the corner of the house. Hastily she pulled her robe together and, as she had rehearsed in her mind the previous evening, dropped to the ground in feigned weakness, tongue lolling unattractively. The aged Grisl approached the cage, peered at her captive for long moments before beginning to jig about in an obscene way, grinning widely. Then, to Buttercup's complete amazement, the witch dropped her garments and began a pre-challenge display as she jogged her unlovely self around the clearing. The scent of her had its inevitable effect upon Buttercup. Her spurs twitched. Seeing this, Mother Marple unlocked the cage.

Honsl's head came up sharply, eyes wide with surprise. He was no more surprised than Buttercup herself. Grisls of the age of Mother Marple and in that stage of decrepitude were commonly supposed to be neither interested in sex nor capable of instigating it, since no one in such a state of decay would be able to withstand combat.

Unless — Mouse shrieked at her — unless such an old hen had starved an opponent into terminal weakness, as this one had planned to do.

If that had been the plan, it went sadly awry for Mother Marple. Buttercup dropped her robe and emerged from the cage in one giant leap, in full possession of her faculties, of gleaming spurs, of a dripping fang, and of hands still red from breakfast.

The old witch, as Honsl called her, might have been a worthy opponent at one time. The old movements were all there, though weakly and unsatisfactorily executed. At one point, she so far forgot herself as to screech, though Buttercup, intent upon the battle, hardly heard it. All that raw meat had had its effect. Though she admitted to herself that it was unmaidenly to do so, Buttercup was drawing out the battle in order to maximize its erotic effect upon Honsl. Egg-maturation or not, she felt she had been celibate long enough! As she fought, she thought of Honsl, of his arousal, of the expression on his pretty face when she turned to him at last, triumphant, spurs dripping, fang flirtatiously extended.

He would greet her with welcoming, tremulous expectation, she thought as she finally tired of the play and pierced Mother Marple's throat with a nicely judged side slash.

She turned to the chained male, flushed with anticipation.

Staring at her across the carcass of Mother Marple with his usual constipated expression, Honsl held the ankle chain out toward Buttercup. He showed no signs of arousal whatsoever. He showed no signs of interest.

There was a lengthy and uncomfortable silence, broken when he said, finally, in a rather self-conscious whine, 'She would have been most awfully disappointed, wouldn't she?'

She would have been? thought Buttercup.

'I don't know why it is,' he went on plaintively, 'that Grisls always assume males *like* being — well, you know — wanted in that way. Sought after. Lots of them don't. I never have. It's just not all that amusing.' He held out the ankle chain once more, obviously expecting her to find the key and let him loose.

She could not stop herself. Later, she could not recall that she had even tried. She nipped him firmly, rather more than a love bite, and glared at him as she snarled, 'Not all that amusing, indeed!'

The faithful dog came out of the underbrush to sniff at Honsl a time or two, raising his hind leg at the paralyzed figure in a gesture unfamiliar to Buttercup. She wondered what it signified as the creature left his erstwhile master and came bounding toward her. He smelled no better than he had at first, rather worse, in fact, but she saw the animal through clearer eyes. Clever, clever boy. Nice dog. Large enough to be useful in many ways — to carry baggage, or even to ride upon if one chose.

With the sun moving toward noon, it would be easy for her to find her way back to the road. She left Honsl where he was, striking off through the forest in the direction Mother Marple had indicated on the night they had arrived, Whurfle in close pursuit. She thought that in future she would pay more attention to where she was going. She thought she would find a way to show gratitude to the dog. She thought that when she grew weary, she might ride upon him. She hoped she would reach the nearest village well before dark.

'Whurfle is a clever animal, true,' said a voice in her head. 'But you wouldn't really want to spend the night out on a dog like this.'

CHAPTER SIX

By sundown, Buttercup reached the village of Rivvelford. She thought that perhaps it should be called a town, inasmuch as it was the seat of government for the surrounding area and had not one but two excellent inns. Whatever one might choose to call it, she was glad to reach it. Though she had not suffered malnutrition under Mother Marple's care, she had suffered emotional exhaustion and wanted nothing more than a quiet room, a warm bath, cooked food, and escape, however temporarily, from dog. She stabled him appropriately though he howled dismally after her as she left him to the tender care of the stable boy and the enjoyment of a large dish of bones and table scraps. She drew the line at sharing quarters with anything that smelled quite so much like wet winter-wear. The stable boys seemed to find Whurfle irresistible, which was congruent with thoughts she had already expressed about the essential triviality of the male mind.

She had brought with her from Thrumm House a quantity of coin, sufficient, she had estimated, for a journey much longer than the one contemplated, so there was no problem in obtaining a pleasant dinner of baked moor-hen, fresh vegetables, and a wine of the area which, while young, had a certain foolhardy insouciance which she found intriguing. Mr Thrumm had been quite a connoisseur of wines, and some of his snobbish delight seemed to have rubbed off on her. Well, she thought (Mouse thought) after all, if one must travel, one might as well travel with enjoyments appropriate to one's station. One was, after all, a daughter of the Royal House, Van Hoost or not. Not that she intended to say anything about that.

The inn specialized in elaborate confections, but she had smelled enough marple bread recently to make anything sweet seem abhorrent. She contented herself with the wine, sitting late in the dining room as she watched the fire flicker low and the moon peer through the mullioned window over the branches of the sorbish grove. It was while she was so pleasantly occupied that she overheard the conversation of a group of males at a nearby table who, warmed overmuch by spiritous indulgence, had so far forgotten themselves as to become loud.

One was exhorting to another to attend a 'revival' which was to be held in the village square on the following evening at which time the populace would be addressed by a traveling preacher. Though it was unclear what was to be revived, Buttercup had never heard a preacher and was curious enough to spend an additional day in Rivvelford. She was, at this point, only two days journey from the Palace and did not want to arrive too early.

'Early to bed and early to rise,' said a hectoring voice from inside. 'Get a head start to make you wise. Better early than never!' Buttercup, as was her habit, ignored it. The days spent at Mother Marple's had already delayed her. Surely one or two days more would not matter.

On the following evening, Buttercup, soberly clad in her quiet robe, joined a crowd made up almost entirely of males with only three of four constabulary Nurseys standing about looking bored. Besides herself, there were not half a dozen robed Grisls in the square. Of unrobed Grisls there were none, as the presence of such a one would have been provocative, inappropriate, and uncivil. In good time the preacher was introduced: Sensalee, a young, slim, serious-looking male, not unlike Sneeth in general appearance and demeanor though far, far better looking. He was well spoken and made an excellent impression upon the crowd.

That impression, so far as the Grisls were concerned, was quickly dissipated when they began to understand what he had to say. He was speaking for a cause he called 'Male Rights,' by which they understood him to mean that he wished males to be allowed Grisl privileges or, conversely, that he wished Grisl privileges in connection with males to be curtailed. Most of his remarks were concerned with his disapproval of the Grisl habit of what he called 'casual sex.'

Casual indeed, scowled Buttercup beneath her robe. It seemed ridiculous that a matter so urgent could be called 'casual' by anyone!

The preacher, however, called it casual again and again, spoke of the male being a mere 'plaything,' and went on at painful length about the pathetic fortunes of males 'casually used' by Grisls and then 'casually' disposed of. By which he meant, if Buttercup understood what he was attempting to say, that males should not be left precisely as she had left Honsl. Or, as she had also left Fribberle and Thrumm, Sneeth, two Ribbles, a gardener's boy, and seven suitors. That is, in some remote or infrequented place to be found or not, as chance dictated.

Buttercup felt that she had never heard quite such un-mitigated rubbish. Even Sneeth had never uttered such blather. If males were casually disposed of, it is because they were not pleasing to the Grisl involved. This taught them and others to be more pleasing in future, and in doing so they achieved the epitome of masculine virtue and charm. No male worth displaying for would want anything more than to be regarded with that indulgent delight of which the romantic ardor of a satisfied Grisl is capable. Males were most delightful when they knew their place and did not attempt to leave it. So the books in the root cellar had said, and so Buttercup thought as well.

'You shouldn't be here,' said the internal voice. 'Really, Buttercup. You're getting involved!'

Buttercup didn't listen. The preacher, unconscious of the effect his words were having upon her, went on to say that males ought to be allowed careers in the constabulary,

422

opportunities as administrators, even, heaven help the Queen-dom, consideration as rulers. Buttercup noted that she was not the only Grisl fighting down laughter. Poor little males. So silly and misguided. She was torn from her amusement, however, when she looked at the face and stance of the preacher once more. He was lean, sweet in an unprepossessing way. Almost delicate. Virginal. Was it really his fault he had been led into the pernicious philosophy he avowed? Perhaps no one had taken the time or trouble to talk with him. It was likely that no Grisl had taken the time or trouble to tell him why his reasoning was so far astray from reality and natural law. She felt almost ashamed for her sex. Well, though it had not been done before, certainly it could be done now.

Several Grisls were murmuring dangerously. Others approached the constabulary Nurseys. There was a confabulatory mutter and the Nurseys strode throughout the crowd, loudly demanding that the meeting be brought to an end before arrests for sedition and disloyalty to the crown were brought against those in the assembly. The preacher stood with bowed head, shaking it again and again in pitiful dismay. Buttercup almost wept for him.

'Please . . .' begged the internal voice.

'Shut up,' Buttercup told herself.

When he left, she followed him to the quiet district where he was evidently lodged. He entered an inn and sat down in the common room. She approached him and asked, as gently as possible, if she might speak with him. He responded modestly, with a pretty air of confusion, and the two of them chatted in a general way about the town and his audience for the evening. He explained that he went from place to place speaking for his 'cause,' living on donations. He also confessed, in a slightly elevated manner, that he had been hatched at the Palace and was of the Royal line — as though that were of any consideration where males were concerned. She did not chide him for this little conceit. He seemed to set so much store by his 'Royal' pretentions that it would have seemed discourteous to attack them.

They talked thus for over an hour, Buttercup listening as

he conveyed his winsome dreams and desires, his simple opinions about the world and the nature of things. She was moved to murmur sympathetically from time to time, reaching to stroke his hand where it lay on the table. At this, he blushed, casting his eyes downward to peer at her through the fringing lashes. She found this adorable.

'I shouldn't say this,' he murmured. 'But I must. If all Grisls were like you, we wouldn't feel as we do about being males. You are so sympathetic, so strong. You understand so much of what I'm trying to say.'

Buttercup dropped the hood of her robe and preened, only so much as was acceptable in a public place. If she had learned nothing else in the custody of Mr Thrumm, she had learned what acceptable behavior was. Under the table she touched his leg with the side of her spur, sliding it sensuously along his calf. He blushed again, murmuring, 'I wonder if I might have a little wine.'

Might he have a little wine! The sweet creature, obviously inexperienced, obviously attracted to Buttercup, not quite knowing how to handle the experience. Display and challenge were not the only way of sex among Grisls. There were tenderer styles of wooing. If the truth were known, Buttercup was almost as inexperienced as he, but her wide reading in the root cellar had prepared her for moments such as this — or so she fondly assumed. Her blood warmed to think of it. This was no pasty Honsl with chilled and torpid blood. This was a male she could respect, one whose every word showed him to be of impeccable judgment and discrimination.

'You even look different from most of them,' he said with acute perception. 'Your face is more refined, somehow. You don't pant at one and insist on pawing all the time.'

Buttercup removed her hand from his in order to summon the waiter. Examining the wine card with care, she ordered a light Themsafel, delicate and unobtrusive, but lingering on the palate like the aftertaste of love. Or so Mr Thrumm's dictionary of wine had said. Buttercup explained this to Sensalee in a manner which was, unfortunately, rather pedantic. Occasionally, she felt, one had to sacrifice the affectionate tone in order to maintain an authoritative position. They drank, savoring the vintage, which seemed to Buttercup to have an odd, almost acrid taste beneath its unequaled fragrance.

Sensalee sighed.

'What is it?' Buttercup asked.

'It's just that — oh, I don't know how to say it . . .'

She encouraged him.

'You're so . . . perceptive. You make me feel so *protected*. All that . . . you know, the male-rights thing, it seems so *unnecessary* when I'm with you.'

Gently Buttercup suggested that perhaps he would like to remain with her for some indeterminate time. She saw a suspicious glint in the corners of his eyes as he hastily excused himself to go to the little males' room. She leaned back in her chair, feeling expansive and pleased. The room was warm, comfortable. Her little companion was proving more than amenable to her suggestions and hopes. The room was warm, comfortable, and the ceiling swam above her. The room was warm . . .

When she awoke, she was under the table. A nagging voice somewhere was saying, '. . . tried to tell you, but no, you had to go chasing after . . . after whatever you call it. Honestly, Buttercup, young or not, you have absolutely no sense . . .'

The common room was quite empty and there was no sign of Sensalee. Her clothing was somewhat disarranged, and when she felt for her purse, which contained almost all her coin, she found that it was gone. Back at her own inn she would find a modest sum which she had left with her spare clothing. She tried to clear her head of the wavering vapors in which it swam. Only a few scattered embers gleamed on the hearth. Obviously time had passed. How much? It was difficult to say. Probably several watches of the night.

Nothing was to be gained by sitting stupidly on the floor. She staggered to her feet, realizing for the first time that she had been drugged. In the wine, undoubtedly. By Sensalee, undoubtedly.

She was enraged.

As she staggered from the room, something she had read of the habits and abilities of dogs entered her mind. Propping the inn door ajar, she made her way to her own inn and to the stable where the dog slept, twitching and panting in some dreamed escapade. Returning with him to the inn of misadventure, she directed the animal's attention to the chair where Sensalee had sat and to the floor. With one of those atrocious 'harfs,' the animal sniffed his way out of the inn and down one of the twisting streets of Rivvelford, out of the city, into the wooded lands, and down a well-worn trail to the edge of an encampment centered upon an open area where great steaming cookpots hung above the fire. There, on the lap of an enormous wild Grisl, basking in the warmth of her embrace, was Sensalee.

'You're a dear marvel you are,' the huge Grisl said. 'A veritable marvel, Sensy my sweet. It never fails, do it? A little preachering, and some silly Grisl or other must see to your enlightenment. Well, this one that came after you this time was better gilded than most, I'll say that.' She clinked coin, *Buttercup's* coin, with one hand while stroking Sensalee with the other. He quivered, actually quivered with delight.

'Ooh, Grendy, you're so mistressful,' he cooed. 'Your hands just send shivers all up and down me, I swear they do.'

Behind the screening bushes, Buttercup seethed with nauseated fury. The male didn't even sound like Sensalee. He oozed with sycophantic smarm. Buttercup prepared herself for challenge.

'She'll kill you,' said her internal voice calmly. 'She'll kill you quite easily. You'll never get to the capital. You'll never fight in the arena. One more Van Hoost idiot down the drain!'

The voice was even more infuriating than Sensalee's presence.

'I wonder,' the huge Grisl went on, 'whether there is any more gilt where this came from? You might go back, tomorrow say, and tell her you were set on by thieves? Make up some other tale? Ah, well, it would stretch luck a bit.'

426

'It would,' agreed Sensalee as he patted the pendulous cheek of the Grisl. 'It really would, Grendy. It was touch and go as it was. The innkeeper wanted half, you know. I had to hide how much there really was and give him only a little.'

Everything in Buttercup screamed 'Challenge!' except for a nagging voice which went on and on and on . . .

'She outweighs you three to one. She outreaches you by your arm's length. Remember what Sneeth used to say. "Outweighed may be outplayed, but outreached is unbreeched." She's huge, Buttercup, absolutely huge. Which means, of course, that you will do whatever is most stupid and childish. You've forgotten the Palace. You've forgotten the Old Queen!'

'Smiss,' whispered Buttercup. It was the dirtiest word she knew, naming an act she could not even conceive of committing, but she said it several more times. 'Smiss, smiss, smiss.' Reason should have told her this could happen, but reason had never described a Grisl like this to her. Huge. Implacable. Probably almost impossible to defeat. What if the Heiress Presumptive at the Palace was like this . . .

'Not at all,' the inner voice suggested. 'At the Palace they care for grace, elegance, beauty, charm. Would they be content to be ruled by a hulk like this?'

It was true. The Palace would not be ruled by a slovenly, obese monster, no matter how forceful. Still, it was something to think on before Buttercup went plummeting into Royal society.

Slowly, reluctantly, she tugged dog back onto the trail and led him away, not without one or two muffled and longing 'whurfs' from him. He wanted to attack, but Buttercup pulled him firmly along. The voice, whatever it was, had some truth in it. Her concern had to be for other things at the moment, such things as repairing her fortune. Sensalee had taken the greater part of her funds. There was not enough left to get to the Palace in even moderate comfort, much less to keep herself in the town while awaiting time for the challenge.

Her need was answered when she arrived at the inn, as

427

though by some benevolent spirit. Posted on the wall of the courtyard was a flyer issued by the Male Protective League offering a reward, no questions asked, for the whereabouts of several listed males. Among them was Honsl, printer of the village of Rivvelford, missing seven days, last seen . . . and so on and so on. Buttercup sent a message by a sulky stable boy, giving Honsl's location. The promised reward arrived by noon. While it was not exorbitant, Buttercup felt it was a good deal more than Honsl was worth.

She went up to her room, recounting to herself that she had learned a valuable lesson. She had learned that duplicity and treachery could be hidden behind a pretty face. She had learned that what had been read in books was not adequate preparation for reality. Most valuable, though most horrifying, she had learned that some males felt Grisls to be fair game though she could not comprehend why this should be so.

'The Palace,' whispered her internal voice impatiently.

'What are you?' snarled Grisl. 'Who asked you?'

'The Palace,' the voice said again imperturbably. 'Never mind who I am. I will leave you at the Palace and you won't be bothered with me anymore.'

Buttercup left the room in a mood of seething frustration. It had all been almost enough to make her doubt the fundamental rationality of natural law which assigns each sex to its place in the vast scheme of things. She felt . . . she felt as she had felt when she was only three and Nursey had told her there was not, in fact, a Fang Fairy.

Disillusionment is hard for the young, she told herself. Very hard for the young.

'No harder than for anyone else,' the voice snorted. 'The trouble with you, Buttercup, is that you take yourself entirely too seriously.'

CHAPTER SEVEN

Buttercup arrived at the Palace — or, more precisely, in the vicinity of the Palace — on the day before the Heiress Presumptive was to accept challenge in the Royal arena. Placards were posted throughout the town announcing the event, though only ticket holders would be allowed to attend and only Grisls of the aristocracy and certain males of the bureaucracy had been furnished with tickets. Certain pre-selected males would, of course, be in the arena itself. To the victor would go the spoils. Public consummation was part of the ritual, after all.

The sound of a familiar voice drew Buttercup's attention to a small group of males on a street corner, and she was surprised to see the Misters Jonas and Cadmon Thrumm talking with a male who looked, dressed, and acted very much like Fribberle. Had the other two Thrumms also brought Van Hoost challengers to the city? Had they, too, prepared young Grisls to die in the arena, helpless before the assault of the Heiress Presumptive? Or were they merely there for the festivities?

Buttercup, thankful that she had left the dog at her place of lodging, drew her quiet garment about her and approached closely enough to hear what they were saying.

'I simply can't imagine what's keeping him,' muttered Jonas Thrumm. 'He said he'd meet us here yesterday, with the candidate — the only candidate! A policy which I continue to maintain is shortsighted and parsimonious — and no one has seen him.'

'It's unlike Raphael to be late,' said Cadmon Thrumm. 'Of the set of us, he is the most punctilious.'

'The same with Fribberle,' said the man who looked like Fribberle, sounding quite put out and distressed. 'Where was Raphael to meet you?'

429

'We have rooms at the Insensitive Galosh,' said Cadmon. 'A suite. Raphael was to have joined us there yesterday.'

Buttercup moved away from them into the crowd. Well and well. Perhaps something could be done with this.

'Be careful,' said the voice inside her. 'Your birthday isn't until tomorrow.'

'My birthday?' Buttercup said aloud, drawing curious glances from passersby. 'My birthday?'

'You will be eight tomorrow.'

'How do you know? Who are you?' Buttercup demanded, half angrily. 'What are you doing sneaking about in my mind?'

'Not sneaking,' the voice replied. 'Merely hitchhiking. Just wanted to warn you to be especially careful . . .'

Buttercup chose to ignore the voice, birthday or no birthday. She inquired as to the location of the Insensitive Galosh and went there, walking up the stairs hidden in her all-concealing robe and finding the suite with no difficulty at all. It was not even locked.

There was notepaper in the desk. She wrote, scratched out, wrote again, then took time to copy it all over in the clear, anonymous script which Mr Thrumm had advocated for cultivated personal use.

'My dear Cadmon and Jonas,' she had written. 'I have run into a slight contretemps which will keep me occupied with the candidate until challenge time tomorrow. Would you be kind enough to advise the officials of our arrival. Tell them please that one of us will bring the candidate to the arena only slightly before challenge time. As ever, Raphael.'

Buttercup, in her searching through the drawers of Thrumm House had had occasion to read various pieces of Thrumm correspondence. She felt she had Raphael's style, or lack of it, very clearly in mind and had reproduced it fairly.

She left the suite only moments before the Thrumms returned to it.

'Now what?' asked the voice in her head.

'Supper,' replied Buttercup. 'Rare roast, lots of it, and no wine.'

'Very sensible of you,' said the voice in her head.

Buttercup spent some time wondering about the voice, particularly inasmuch as it had become more and more obtrusive during the past several days, advising her for and against various courses of action with increasing fervor. Undoubtedly it was the same voice which had been with her since childhood. Certainly it had never harmed her. On occasion, as in the case of Sensalee, it had probably helped her to some extent. Perhaps it was an aberration of some kind. Perhaps it was a guardian spirit.

At the moment, it didn't matter which or whether. Buttercup returned to her lodgings, ordered a plentiful supper, and consumed it with good appetite. Various of the placards about the town had carried pictures of the Heiress Presumptive. She was portrayed as being quite young. Very slender. Almost, one might say, unformed. Buttercup was more sanguine about her chances of success than at any time since seeing Sensalee in the lap of the giant wild Grisl.

She slept the sleep of the just.

On the morrow, slightly before challenge time, she presented herself at the Insensitive Galosh and asked for Mr Cadmon Thrumm. When he appeared, she greeted him in a dreamy manner, her eyes wide, her voice monotonous, her gait slightly staggering.

'Mr Thrumm has sent me, Mr Thrumm. He has been unavoidably delayed. He says you must take me to the . . . to the arena. We are to watch the battle. Won't that be exciting?'

Mr Thrumm regarded her with deep suspicion. 'Where is Raphael?'

'With . . . with his . . . with a male,' she murmured. 'I will tell you his name if I can whisper it.'

Mr Thrumm turned quite pink. 'At it again, is he! Tell me,' and leaned forward to receive the tip of her fang just below his ear.

'Take me to the Palace,' said Buttercup. 'I believe they are expecting us.'

The whole town was expecting them! There were banners

431

across the streets, balloons clustered on lampposts, drifts of confetti, and small wandering bands making frenzied music. There were platoons of uniformed Nurseys marching to and fro with a rat-a-tat of drums. There were booths selling roast fleeb nuts and seed pies and ice cream. There were vendors of illustrated books of the adventures of Great Grisl among the savage Earthians. There were salesmen of mugs with a picture of the Heiress Presumptive upon them and pillows with a picture of the Heiress Presumptive upon them and toilet seats which played the national anthem when one sat down. Indeed, the Heiress Presumptive stared at the merrymakers from every conceivable surface, including some which were in questionable taste.

Cadmon Thrumm led Buttercup among crowds which grew ever thicker as they approached the arena walls. On the higher roofs surrounding the arena were crowds of males and Nurseys who had paid dearly for the privilege of watching the challenge ceremony through telescopes from these lofty vantage points.

Once at the arena itself, they found their way to a small side door guarded by two monstrous Nurseys. 'Cadmon Thrumm,' her putative escort announced. 'Bringing the candidate as arranged.'

'Supposed to be Raphael this time, Thrumm,' opined one of the Nurseys, giving him a keen glance. 'Where is he?'

'Indisposed,' said Cadmon. 'A digestive upset of some kind. Jonas and I decided I should bring her on ahead. We were afraid Raphael might not recover soon enough.'

'The candidate all prepared, is she?'

Cadmon nodded. 'She's been at Thrumm House almost since birth.'

'Fribberle get there in good time, did he?'

Cadmon nodded again. One of the Nurseys reached out and lifted Buttercup's veil away from her face, remarking, 'That's the Van Hoost chin, all right. Can't mistake it. Did his usual good job with the spurs, did he?'

Buttercup remained passive with enormous effort. When this was over, she was going to bite whole battalions of Nurseys!

'Well, go on in. Third room to the right. The garb's all laid out.'

They went through the gate. The third room on the right had a grated window which looked out on the arena itself, a sand-floored circular space surrounded by a head-high wall. Above the wall were rows on rows of seats, filled for the most part with robed Grisls and soberly dressed functionaries.

Buttercup disposed of Cadmon in a closet, instructing him not to move until she told him to and resolving never to tell him to move in a million years. This room probably wouldn't be used until the next challenge, and he could sit there and rot until then, reward or no reward.

The caparison she was to wear was, indeed, laid out. Delicate, silken veils for head and shoulders. Glittering jewels for neck, wrists, and ankles. Even in this they had played false. The necklace was so tight that it would cut off her breathing if she wore it. The bracelets were loose and jangling and would prove to be a distraction. The gemmed footlets would have fouled her spurs in moments. With her face set, Buttercup removed the robe, laid it on the bed, and then dressed herself in the abbreviated veils, leaving the ornaments where they were.

Through the window she could hear the band. A roar from the crowd as the Heiress Presumptive arrived in the Royal box, then again as she left the box to descend to the arena floor. Buttercup peeked out. The heiress was there, seated at the far end of the arena, bowing, left, right, lifting her hands to wave, left, right. Fanfare.

Fanfare.

The entry of the challenger. Her entry.

Buttercup turned to the mirror to check her appearance one last time, feeling as she did so a shiver as though something had torn loose within her, as though something had ripped away, as though half her being was being amputated from her.

Suddenly beside her in the mirror was a small green creature with whiskers and round ears. Buttercup whirled.

433

'You look very nice,' said the familiar voice as the green creature looked up at her, wrinkling its nose. 'Happy Birthday, and go give 'em hell. But I need my matchbox first.'

Another, irritated-sounding, fanfare.

'Who are you!' Buttercup demanded.

'You don't have time to find out,' the green creature whispered between its two huge front teeth. It cocked its round ears toward the window. 'That's your entry, Buttercup. Let me have the box, quickly, then you'd better get cracking!'

Hypnotized, Buttercup fished the box from the pocket of her robe where she had carried it. The green creature opened the gold box, took two cubes out of it, then knelt and rattled the cubes in its paw — cubes with dots on them . . .

Fanfare once more. An impatient roar from the crowd.

Buttercup opened the arena door. On a low dais across the arena the Heiress Presumptive sat waiting, rising now to a roar of acclamation and excitement. She was about Buttercup's size. Maybe even a little larger. She had an excellent set of spurs. And her fang was even longer than Buttercup's fang.

With a stagger which was not altogether feigned, Buttercup went forth . . .

Behind her the dice tumbled and came up two and one.

'Three,' said Marianne, the malachite mouse.

'You will forgive me, won't you?' pled Great-aunt Dagma from her bed. 'I wasn't thinking. I never intended it to happen that way.'

'I will forgive you, of course,' said Aghrehond. 'Though what my forgiveness might mean to you, madam, or what currency it might have in the world at large, I am at some difficulty to identify. And as for my master, Makr Avehl, whether he will forgive you is another matter yet. Still, from what you tell me, she didn't mean to do it . . .'

'She didn't. I know she didn't. She was simply going to demonstrate how the game should be played. It was a matter of here one moment, gone the next, and she didn't plan it, I'm sure.'

'There is a young Kavi who attends upon the Cave of Light,

in my home in Alphenlicht, you understand? Ah, I was sure you did. Her name is Therat, this Kavi, an innocuously floral name for someone so omniscient, and she has eyes like a hawk, all seeing, far seeing, only sometimes they do not see what one wants them to look at. So, before I left with my master's wife, it was Therat who told me something awkward would probably happen. She spent all night consulting the lectionaries, and when she could not find what she sought — well, she was surprised and then upset. Still, what was there to do about it? We could not say, Therat or I, that Marianne should stay in Alphenlicht and let her loved relative die! Who could say such a thing. So, one comes and one hopes, only to have one's hopes dashed and the danger comes anyway. Alas.' Aghrehond rubbed his large head, shaking it to and fro. 'I should have come up here with her to visit you instead of staying below in the kitchens.'

'I doubt you would have moved fast enough even if you'd been standing right beside her,' whispered Dagma from her bed. She was desperately tired and worried, and her voice was feeble. 'She just did it, suddenly, all at once.'

'Tell me, Madame Zahmani, how long has Marianne been gone?'

'Only about fifteen minutes, Aghrehond. I haven't said anything to Arti, that is Marianne's mother, yet. She would be sure to have hysterics. She would think Marianne had fallen victim to the local epidemic of vanishment.'

'An epidemic? Ah, so it is happening here, as well? I had not known that. It is possible Marianne is a victim of it.'

'Well, don't tell Arti. She would not be able to hold herself together.'

'I have told no one yet except Makr Avehl himself, and for him I have had to leave a message because he is not near a phone. Now we must decide what to do, Madame Zahmani.'

'Please don't call me "Madame Zahmani," Aghrehond, or I shall have to call you "Mr Aghrehond," which is too formal for the occasion. "Madame" is a courtesy title, in any case. I was never married.'

'Very well, Great-aunt. Tell me about this epidemic.'

Dagma did so, as much as she knew. 'According to the statistician, it's been going on for decades. According to the governor's office, the whole thing is a computational error!'

'For decades, ah?' Aghrehond sighed. 'And when Marianne threw the dice, how did they come up?'

'I heard her say "snake eyes," and I blinked. When I opened my eyes she was gone. And so was the malachite mouse. And the matchbox, of course.'

'Of course,' Aghrehond brooded over the game diagram. 'It could only be that, could it not? Everything that happens has purpose, or so I have always felt, and when one is caught in a net such as this, things happen as they must. Ah, well. It would do no good at all to play in behind her. We must try to get ahead of her, then wait for her. But, she could leapfrog right over us. What was on the second square?'

'Before Marianne threw the dice, it said, "Buttercup, Birth to Eight Years." Now it says, "Queen Buttercup, the first month of her reign."'

'So it does,' said Aghrehond. 'Which means Marianne must have done something in that square to change things there. She has that quality, does she not? Always busy, upsetting apple carts, turning over kettles. I have seen her — well, of no matter. That was in another time and place. She will have gone past the Buttercup point by now, so there is no point in discussing it. And that raises the point of how she got past that point. The dice are still here.'

'There was something rattly in the matchbox,' Dagma offered.

'Rattly. Well, of course. Game makers must provide for those who play. Dice available here to start the game. And if there are none in there to continue playing with — then perhaps one is trapped? Who knows. Let us suppose she had two dice with her. Using two dice, she could not throw a one, which is fortunate. The square after the Buttercup square is labeled "Forever."'

'What does that mean?'

'It probably means exactly what it says. If she had thrown

a three, she would have landed in Forever and no matter all
our machinations, Great-aunt, there is no doubt we would not
have seen our Marianne again, weep though we might and
wait at the horrors of fate.'

'I . . . I didn't have any idea . . .'

'No. Well. She would have thought of it if she hadn't been
overtaken by events. Now, by my great, wobbly belly, if one
wanted to get to the end of the game quickly, how could it
be done? What do the rules say?'

'Rules?'

'I make the assumption that verbiage printed at the bottom
of the game must be the rules of play. It has that aspect,
has it not? That solidity imparted by black ink on a lighter
surface which says, "I am official. Pay attention." ' He
turned the printed parchment toward him and read, ' "Players
may pass through previously occupied spaces but may not
occupy any space twice in the same game." If one has been
to Buttercup once, one may not go back to Buttercup again.'

'But it's not the same Buttercup,' objected Dagma. 'It says
something else now.'

'Leaving that aside for the moment, which we must do since
we have no one to interpret the rules for us, and returning
to my question: How would one get to the end of the game
most quickly?' He mused, ticking off the squares with his
fingertip. 'One would throw a nine, which would take one to
the Down Line Express. From there, presumably though not
surely, one would reach Frab Junction without another throw.
At that point, if one could achieve any combination of throws
resulting in fourteen − except for one totaling five or nine
if we wished to avoid these other Forevers − one would reach
the point labeled "The End." Of course, it's unlikely one
could throw exactly the right number. One might end up at
The Library or Usable Chasm.' He mused for some time
longer. 'Or even at Seldom Siding, which has a certain feeling
of non-quotidian misadventure about it. Since there is no way
to know where she *is* in the game, we must hope that she
reaches the end of it and attempt to meet her there. What is
the end of the game, after all?' he asked. 'Here, in the last

square — though it isn't precisely a square, is it? — where it says, "The End." So, if we can't intercept her, then we need to play to get there? Don't we?'

'Do we?' faltered Dagma.

'Yes, because if she doesn't show up, we might be able to go backward, or come out and start over. We do. We must. Time wastes and we dally.'

'We?' she faltered again.

'We,' said Aghrehond with a glance of forbearance which was almost cruel in its charity. 'Accepting that it was really your father's responsibility, still, when he died without fulfilling it, it became your task, Great-aunt. Even if you had only a week, or a day, or even an hour, you should have tried to complete it to spare our Marianne. Ah, but then, you know that already.'

'I knew that,' she wept. 'There seemed to be so little time left.'

'Time enough to try,' he said. 'Who will you be? The rhodolite rhinoceros? The amethyst ape?'

'The turquoise tortoise,' she said in a slightly firmer voice. 'I've been so slow about it.'

'Of course. Stupid of me not to have thought of that. In case there are no dice in the game, we'll need dice to carry with us. Are there any in the house?'

'Over in the drawer by the window. I used to sit at that table with my nephew — Marianne's father — and beat him at backgammon.'

He fetched them, putting one pair in his pocket, another pair in the pocket of her bed jacket. 'You first then.'

'Shouldn't I change into clothing a little more suitable for travel?'

'The tortoise won't know the difference,' he told her.

In the face of his quiet stare she could delay no longer. She rolled the dice. Nine. Perhaps she said something, perhaps not. She was gone, the tortoise was gone.

'All or nothing,' said Aghrehond, putting the amethyst ape on the space that said, 'Start Here.'

And rolled nine again.

CHAPTER EIGHT

The Malachite Mouse clung to a root, a root which bulged
like an enormous bulwark against the unimaginable hulk of
the trunk looming upward through a layer of gray and oozing
clouds.

'G'nop,' said something. It was a combination of inquiry
and swallow, as though a very large being had asked for
sustenance and had been given it all in one instant, satisfaction
following hunger instantaneously, only to be immediately
succeeded by hunger once more. 'G'nop.'

The source of the sound moved among the roots with a
monstrous squelching, a flatulent bubbling, like mud dropped
into mud, the one only slightly more solid than the other so
that the two surfaces sucked at one another, stopping only
one degree short of mingling.

'G'nop.'

A long thing darted across the root above the malachite
mouse, being at one moment not there and at the next there,
then gone once more as though it had solidified out of nothing
only long enough to be perceived before vanishing, a kind of
solid and rubbery-looking horizontal lightning. And yet there
had been time to identify the thing as 'darting,' that is coming
from somewhere.

'G'nop,' the thing went again. The mouse saw it this time,
from right to left, then back to the right again, a mighty hawser
of viscous stuff with a sticky sheen to it and something fluttery
at the end of it. Something fluttery when it withdrew, though
not, so far as Mouse could tell, when it had emerged.

If one could say emerged.

'G'nop.' The squelching repeated itself, a sodden movement,
as of a wet sponge being manipulated in a pot of hot oatmeal.

Mouse turned her head very quietly, very slowly, peering

along the side of the great buttress of root to the place it edged into the shadow filling the spaces between roots. There was nothing here but shadow and wet, blotches of filthy duns and ochres, deep feculent smells of bog. The wall edge of the root made a long diagonal line running upward from right to left. Mouse clung flat against it, all claws extended to bite into tiny fissures in the bark. Below was the glug of water; above, layers of discolored light in a viridescent collage, deepening toward the trunk.

Mouse began to move, very slowly, toward a hole in the root, a fissure deeper than most, almost a cave.

'G'nop.'

Above the edge of the root an orb began to emerge.

Mouse did not wait for it but leapt, all at once, into the fissure to cower there, panting silently, nose turned outward, and all whiskers atremble. It had been an eye, she told herself, an eye as large as a dome, a glowing dirigible of eye rising over the root wall like a pallid and hungry moon.

'Zup,' went the hawser, returning with something screaming at the end of it, then 'Zup' again, returning empty.

'Roawrrr,' howled the swamp in fury. 'Roawrrr.'

The mouse shook the dice out of the matchbox and threw them, very carefully, on the tiny level patch at the bottom of the fissure.

'Eleven,' it sighed, grabbing up the dice and disappearing from the fissure just as the great tongue entered it.

CHAPTER NINE

At the home of Marianne's parents, in Virginia, where Dagma lived, where Marianne and Aghrehond were supposed to be visiting, the phone rang.

A maid answered it and then went in search of Aghrehond. Not finding him, she reported with some discomfiture to Marianne's father that the visiting gentleman seemed to have gone out.

'Out, Briggs?'

'Yes, sir.'

'But he was with Dagma and Marianne.'

'Your daughter and the old ma'am's gone out, too, sir.'

'Don't be silly, Briggs. Dagma is far too ill to have gone out.'

'Well, sir, she's gone. I don't know out or where, but she's not there. Not in her bathroom or her bedroom or the little sitting room, neither.'

'Either, Briggs,' Marianne's father corrected as he gave this matter some thought. 'Is my wife still napping?' Arti had not been sleeping well, and she had announced her intention of taking a pill and a long nap.

'Yes, sir. I peeked in on her just a little while ago.'

'Who is it calling for Aghrehond?'

'Overseas phone, sir.'

'I'll speak to them.'

Which he did. 'Makr Avehl? How nice to hear your voice again. It seems an enormous time since the wedding.'

'_____.'

'What was that about the Cave of Light?'

'_____!'

'I'm to tell Aghrehond that Makr Avehl is on his way?'

'_____?'

'He seems to have stepped out, Makr Avehl. Dagma and Marianne as well. They can't have gone far. Dagma was far too unwell . . . Yes, I understand. If I see Aghrehond, I'm to tell him to wait for you.' The connection broke, and Haurvatat was left holding the buzzing instrument, a feeling of sick vacancy deep inside him. Until this moment he had not taken seriously the fact that Briggs had been unable to find Marianne or Dagma or Aghrehond. Until this moment he had not believed there was, really, an epidemic of vanishment. Until this moment — but when one of the Kavi called to warn his daughter about a reading from the Cave of Light . . .

Shaking, Haurvatat went upstairs, first to search Dagma's room, then to sit by his wife's bed and keep an eye on her. He was determined not to leave her until she woke.

441

CHAPTER TEN

'To the departure area for the Down Line Express,' the amethyst ape directed the cabdriver, grasping the shell of the turquoise tortoise more tightly under his arm to prevent its falling into the street.

'Right-ee-oh,' the cabman assented, hardly waiting until the ape was seated before flicking his whip over the backs of the matched pair of umble-geese which set off at once with a loud clacking complaint. 'Where's yer destination, guvner?' he asked. 'You goin' far?'

'Ah,' the ape considered, 'Frab Junction? There should be a good deal going on in Frab Junction, shouldn't there?'

'Depends,' the cabman said, unfolding an atrophied wing and scratching beneath it with every evidence of enjoyment. 'On whatcher mean by goin' on. There's things doin' here, too, y'know. People comin' and goin' orf again. Stuff comin' through all the time on its way to Cattermune's 'Ouse.'

'I'm very curious about Cattermune's House,' said the ape. 'What can you tell me about it?'

'Well, not much, and that's the truth,' the driver replied, snapping his whip at an intrusive squozzle lizard drawing a heavy dray in the opposing lane. 'Everybody's been there, don't you know, but nobody talks much about it. Oh, they'll say this and that 'appened to 'em, or this or that occurred, if you take my meanin', but they'll not say where, and then you ask 'em and they'll whisper it at you without seemin' real sure of it, like as if they didn't remember it much. "Cattermune's 'Ouse," they'll say. "I think it was Cattermune's 'Ouse." '

'Who or what is Cattermune?' asked the tortoise in a leisurely tone. The tortoise was incapable of any tone except a leisurely one or of any locomotory speed except slow forward.

'It's a *he*,' the cabdriver asserted darkly, 'and that says 'alf of what I know about 'im.'

'What's the other half?' asked the ape.

'You wouldn't want to end up in 'is Worm Pits is the other half,' the driver retorted. 'That's a 'undred years is Worm Pits. That's a long time stay. Illusion Fields is ten thousand years, and that's a long time, too, but you don't feel it so much, if you take my meanin'. Worm Pits you'd feel every second, and a 'undred years'd seem like a few thousand, so they say.'

'I'll try to stay away from the Worm Pits,' the ape agreed.

'Throw a three at Frab Junction and likely you'll meet Cattermune. Can't go back three on the Down Line. Three left takes you to the Administrative Offices, which leads right into the Moebius Siding. Nobody in 'is right mind wants to go there. Three forward takes you to Banjog's Mooring. Give me a choice like that, prob'ly I'd go on to Cattermune's 'Ouse, Worm Pits or no Worm Pits.'

'Besides,' opined the tortoise, 'you wouldn't get to the Worm Pits from Cattermune's House. There's no way to throw a one.'

'That's as may be,' the driver agreed. 'But there's ways and there's ways. Here's the terminal. Mind your step.'

'How much?' asked the ape.

' 'Ow much what?' the driver asked in return. 'No charge, guvner. We're all in the game together, ain't we.' He flicked the whip over the backs of the umble-geese and went clacking back into the surge of wagons and cabs which filled the streets of Down Line Express.

The terminal was typical of railway buildings of the period, a spider's web of steel clad with high, dirty windows through which a dusty effulgence fell sadly into an echoing cavern, making puddles of melancholy light on the enormous paved floor. Creatures moved into and out of the light to the accompaniment of a continuous barrage of sound, the rattle of wheels, the roar of great locomotives in tunnels, the unintelligible quack and babble of someone announcing departures and arrivals.

At a central kiosk labeled 'Information,' the ape asked, 'When does the next Down Line Express leave?'

'As soon as it's full.' The Information creature smiled vaguely, looking up from its crossword puzzle with one pair of eyes. 'Be a while, I should think. One left yesterday.'

'Where are all the other trains going?'

'Other trains?' Another vague smile.

'The ones we hear coming in and going out?'

'Oh,' the creature pointed at a shelf near its feet where a tape player hummed. 'That's all just for atmosphere, don't you know. Actually, the Down Line is a gravity train. Very quiet.'

'We could use a little quiet in here,' the tortoise said. 'This racket is giving me a headache.'

'Would you like it turned off?' The creature reached down and switched the player off and silence fell into the enormous room like snow into a bucket. Only a few reverberating hoof-falls broke the peace. High above, in the web of steel, a flock of winged creatures argued melodically over a scrap of food. Somewhere someone asked, 'Can I arrange a throw for Usable Chasm from there?' the voice falling away into hush.

'I rather like that,' said the Information creature. 'It makes a nice change. Perhaps we'll just leave it like that until the train fills up.'

'You said it might take a while?'

'Several days, perhaps.'

'But it's supposed to be an express!'

'Oh, it is. Expressly for Frab Junction. And very fast. When it leaves.'

'Which is when it's full.'

'Exactly.'

'Is there somewhere we can get food? Perhaps a bed for the night?'

'Food booths are all along that wall,' the creature pointed. 'Medium of exchange is information about the game. New-

444

comers are allowed to use imaginative assumptions and valid extrapolations from known data against future redemption.'

The ape thought this one over. 'Like IOUs?'

'Hmm, rather. There's a dormitory up on the balcony. Better sleep in relays. They don't announce departure, you know, and if you're not there when it leaves, you may miss it.'

'Thank you,' said the tortoise weakly. 'You've been very helpful.'

- They wandered off toward the food wall, selecting a booth which provided sandwiches and beverages as well as fresh fruit of both familiar and exotic types.

'So, what have you got to tell?' the tentacled vendor asked them.

'I have an imaginative assumption,' said the ape.

'First-timer, humph. The assumptions never come to anything, you now. Still, I'm required to accept them, so you might as well spit it out.'

'I assume,' said the ape, 'that this game is played in many worlds, and that the creatures inhabiting the game are those who are currently playing it and haven't yet found their way out.'

The creature barked with laughter, waving three tentacles and jittering on the remaining four. 'That's what I call an assumption. Now I'll tell you one. If that's true, what you just said, how come this place is getting more and more crowded all the time. You tell me that?'

'Hmmm,' mused the ape as he read the menu posted on the wall above the counter. 'Do I need to answer in order to get two butterfilk sandwiches and a couple of pints of bitter?'

'Not at all,' the vendor replied, filling their order with alacrity. 'I thought it might amuse you, that's all. He who laughs last.'

'Well, it does. If the place is getting more and more populated all the time, it would mean A) that more and more people are playing the game or B) that more and more people are unable to complete the game or C) that more and more people have no desire to complete the game. If the former is true, there are so many implications it would be

445

difficult to list them all. If the latter is true, it could be because A) they enjoy the ambience of this particular place more than wherever they are from or B) the act of completing the game is, for some reason, unacceptable to them.'

The vendor twinkled in their direction as it provided woe cones in various flavors to an ill-assorted group of travelers. 'Unacceptable is mild, stranger, mild, but clever of you, nonetheless. Easy come isn't always easy go. For that little exercise in extrapolation there, I can offer you dessert. Cheese cake? Hot mud sundae? A nice piece of ripe squap?'

'Melon,' said the ape.

'Perhaps an apple,' said the tortoise, her head in the bottom of the bitter glass where she was attempting to sup up the last few drops.

'Don't you want your sandwich?' asked the ape.

'Not really,' sighed the tortoise. 'What I'd really like is a bowl of earthworms and some lettuce.'

The vendor removed the sandwich and supplied the requested articles, from which the ape averted his eyes. Only when he heard the first crunch of the apple did he look back again. The worm bowl was empty and the vendor was staring at the tortoise with contemplative eyes.

'One man's meat,' he murmured to himself or to them. 'You'd love Cattermune's Worm Pits. You really would.'

The ape shuddered, delicately, as the tortoise nodded. 'We're together,' she said. 'Though I might relish a visit to the pits, I'm afraid the ape wouldn't like it.'

'Strange bedfellows,' sighed the vendor, wrapping each of their empty glasses in a tentacle and dousing them in a bucket of soapy water.

'Speaking of bed,' said the ape. 'I'm suffering from jet lag.'

'And what might that be?'

'I can't remember,' said the ape, 'except that I've got it.' He turned and climbed the stairs to the balcony, carrying the tortoise under one arm, where he found two adjacent cots. 'Half an hour's nap,' the ape said. 'Then we'll go wait on the platform.'

They slept longer than half an hour, but the train was still there when they gained the platform. Thereafter, it was not as long a wait as they had feared. The train, consisting of a number of open cars like those on a roller coaster, stood at the platform untended, gradually filling up as this one and that one sat down and strapped itself in with every indication of staying until the device moved. Behind each seat was hinged a clear bubble, obviously designed to protect the bodies of the passengers from the lash of air or from something falling from above. The train was held back by a barricade of heavy wooden planks. When the last seat had been filled, the barricade pivoted outward and up, and the train slowly began to roll beneath it. When the last car had passed, the barricade rotated into place once more with a sonorous clang. The Down Line Express was under way.

It was not unlike a roller-coaster ride, except that there were long stretches of virtually level track and the few major inclines were brief. There was an initial drop to pick up speed, and from that point on, the cars rolled silently forward into what appeared to be limitless space. Ahead and behind the tracks ran into infinity, slender lines extending into forever, crosshatched by ties which were tied, thought the ape, to nothing at all.

Far away to the left was a tumbled glory of clouds and precipices, interspersed with rays of many colored lights. The aspect of this area changed from moment to moment, at one instant lending itself to interpretation as a landscape and at the next seeming to be an enormous garden of moving flowers.

'The Illusion Fields,' cried the scaled being behind them, reaching forward to point with a lengthy talon. 'I was there once.'

'Only once, though, isn't that right?' asked the ape. 'You can't go back again?'

'True,' said the being sadly. 'The time for the Illusion Fields is ten thousand years. It was a very long time, but not bad. Better than ending the game, that's for sure.'

'What is this business about ending the game,' drawled the tortoise. 'I don't like it at all, Ape.'

447

'It does give one pause,' replied the ape. 'As I recall, it was our intention to get to the end of the game and await our friend there. We may have to change that intention.'

'Our friend,' mused Tortoise. 'That would have been Mouse, would it not?'

'It would indeed. Mouse. Malachite mouse. Who is now either behind us or ahead of us. Who could be anywhere at all. Who could be in the Illusion Fields, where she would stay for ten thousand years.' The ape chewed a knuckle gloomily. 'I have the feeling that all is not what it seems to be in this place.'

Some time passed. Ahead of them and still to the left they made out a mass, extending from illimitable space below to endless space above, vaguely man-shaped, the feet dwindling away into a bottomless chasm, the head lost in mist. 'Gerald,' commented their co-traveler. 'I've never been there.'

'Never been to Gerald?'

'On Gerald. Or perhaps in. I've never been to George, either, but I suppose I'll have to go sometime soon. I've been almost everywhere else. As we go past Gerald, take a good look off to the left, slightly up, and you'll catch a glimpse of the Dinosaur Zoo. Sometimes the express stops for a while on a siding so the passengers can enjoy the view.'

'A whole zoo of dinosaurs,' marveled the tortoise.

'For dinosaurs,' corrected their guide.

The tortoise started to say something, then thought better of it.

Gerald grew larger and larger on their left until he filled the entire sky, the top button of his striped trousers even with the tracks on which they ran. Far below, dwarfed to baby bootees by the distance, were Gerald's shoes, which even from this height could be seen to need polishing. As the train ran on, Gerald grew smaller once more behind them.

Another structure evidenced itself before them, also to the left, a clutter, a ragtag of color and movement, a confettilike swirl, suspended as though it were cloud, except that its edges were definite and unchanging. It came closer, growing larger in their view. The train slowed and ran off on a

448

platformed siding on which were mounted a number of coin-operated telescopes. A conductor with a change dispenser moved along the cars, passing out coins in various denominations. 'The company apologizes for a brief delay,' it intoned in a funereal voice. 'The company offers free viewing of the Dinosaur Zoo while you are waiting.' It dropped coins into the ape's hand and moved on. 'The company apologizes . . .'

'Would you like to see the zoo?' Ape asked the tortoise.

'Go ahead,' said the tortoise faintly. 'I'll wait here.'

The ape put a coin in one of the telescopes and stared through it at the distant zoo, surprised at how close and immediate it appeared. It was a rather old-fashioned zoo, with rows of cages rather than 'habitats,' and strolling viewers dressed mostly in striped jackets and straw hats or shawls and bonnets, depending, he supposed, upon sex. They were all of the upright type of dinosaur with heavy hind legs and kangaroolike tails which served as props when groups of them stopped, as they frequently did, to chat together or share refreshments.

After gaping at the dinosaurs for a moment, the ape turned his attention to the inhabitants of the few cages he could see clearly. One was occupied by a large furry pig and its family; another by a very large bird with legs like an elephant; two more by several dozen serpents of various colors and diameters; and finally a malachite mouse in a cage by itself.

The ape left the platform hastily, returning in moments with the tortoise. 'Is that her?' he asked. 'I never saw the mouse. It looks like a malachite mouse, but there might be more than one. Or perhaps not . . .'

'It does look like her,' replied the tortoise somewhat doubtfully. 'If she has the matchbox, we'd be sure.'

The mouse took a golden matchbox from her pocket, removed something from it, and made the unmistakable motion of throwing dice. The mouse had only time to seize the dice before she vanished.

'That was her,' said the tortoise slowly. 'That was her.'

'I don't suppose you could see how the dice fell,' asked the ape plaintively.

'I'm sorry, I couldn't,' answered the tortoise.

'This is madness,' responded the ape in a fretful tone. 'A kind of madness which has no equal in any world I have yet contemplated. Complete madness. It's like trying to go up on a down escalator.'

'Wouldn't that be a descalator?' Tortoise asked. 'From the word "descend." '

'All on board,' cried the conductor. 'Close the noiseproof hoods over your seats, please. We will be passing under the Puce Polemic. All on board!'

They hastily strapped themselves back in, lowered the clear, noiseproof hoods over their heads, watched as the conductor gave the train a small push to get it started, then reconciled themselves to the dubious pleasure of the Puce Polemic and what could not but be an interesting arrival in Frab Junction.

CHAPTER ELEVEN

When Mouse arrived at the Dinosaur Zoo, she was relieved to find herself behind bars. An onlooker peered at her with a large and saurian eye, one which inevitably reminded her of that vast, moonlike orb which had been about to spy her as she so precipitously left G'nop, and she cowered timorously for a moment until she realized both that the bars were stout and that the creature staring at her was a civilized being. The first observer turned away to be replaced by two bonneted saurians, and when they noticed her discomfort, they politely averted their gaze and moved on. The dinosaurs were certainly courteous. A sign just inside her own cage made it clear that the zoo cages were occupied by transients. The sign read, 'Time of transit, Dinosaur Zoo, from three to twenty-two hours.' Next to this notice was a map of the game with a red arrow marked, 'You are here,' pointing to the zoo and a number of cards which Marianne did not bother to examine.

A large, furry pig in the next cage asked, rather breathlessly, 'Where from, dearie?'

'G'nop, most recently,' replied the mouse.

'Oh, by my own blessed piglets,' the pig cried. 'I spent the worst three minutes of my entire existence at G'nop. Lost three out of the litter and would have been gone, myself, if the time hadn't run out.'

'Do you know the game well?' Marianne asked politely.

'As well as anyone. They change it from time to time, but I've been around three times, including all the sidings except Moebius, thank the Alltime Boar, and take my word for it, avoid Banjog's Mooring if you *possibly* can.'

Mouse nodded thoughtfully. 'Let's suppose I hadn't thrown the dice, there at G'nop. What would have happened?'

'Why, you'd have had another three minutes, dearie. I thought everyone knew that.'

'And, if I were in the Illusion Fields, and ten thousand years passed, and I didn't throw?'

'You'd be in for another ten millennia. You want to watch your step there. Along about nine thousand and eight hundred years, you want to start paying very close attention to the passage of time! If you want out, that is.'

'And if you throw a square where you've already been?'

'Automatic skip over to the next square where you haven't. Unless it's a junction, of course. It's all very simple, really.'

'What if that square's a Forever?'

'If you land on a Forever, we all say ta-ta. Ta-ta, dearie, and it's been nice to play with you. Forever's pretty well gone and lost forever, dreadful sorry, pal of mine.'

'It sounds to me as though the safest bet is just to stay in the Illusion Fields time after time,' the mouse remarked in a depressed voice.

'Oh, but so dull! I hate to say it about my own kind, but piggishly dull, dearie. Somnolent, slovenly, sluggardly, lie-about, do-nothing, dreadfully dull. One gets so sick of special effects! Along about the seven thousandth year, one gets absolutely fed up!'

451

The mouse sighed. 'I didn't intend to play this game just now. You see, I'm pregnant.'

'Well so was I, dearie, when I began. And here you see me with what's left of the litter, still getting along. Don't fret. Everything will happen in its own time.'

'Which is what?'

The pig shrugged, a most expressive gesture when done with furry shoulders, furry hips, furry ears and snout. 'You mean time inside versus time outside? But, dearie, who knows? Who knows?'

'Some think they know,' said a ponderous voice from the cage on the other side. Mouse turned to meet the scrutiny of round, golden eyes in a vast, owllike head that was perched on a dumpy feathered body supported by elephantine legs. 'Some think they know how long in-here is how long out-there, but then the question arises, doesn't it, which out-there one is speaking of and which in-here one is speaking of also.'

'There would be that,' agreed the mouse.

'Feeding time here at the zoo is in about an hour,' the bird advised. 'You still have time to fill out your menu selection and put it on the outside of the door.'

'Thank you very much,' breathed the mouse, suddenly aware of hunger. 'I don't think I've eaten in a very long time.'

'Exactly,' said the bird. 'That's how some people think they know.' He or she then turned its back on the mouse and settled into a squat, as though sleeping.

'That's the aepyowl. Been here for simply ages,' the pig whispered. 'Refuses to throw the dice. Says it likes the food. And the food is very good, dearie. Do what it said. Fill out your menu card.'

Mouse settled on a seafood bisque, a green salad, and hot buttered rolls, with coffee to follow. The meal was delivered by a short, liveried staurikosaurus who wheeled in a low, rolling table, chatted about the weather, 'Unusually fine for this part of the game,' and poured the coffee before leaving. When the mouse had eaten, she felt much better. As she sipped the last of the coffee, she saw something far off in the sky, rather like a contrail. 'What's that?' she asked, attracting the pig's attention and pointing upward.

'Hmmm?' The pig ambled over to get a better look. 'Down Line Express, dearie. It goes right by here on its way to Frab Junction. Everybody in the game gets to Frab Junction sooner or later. You'll find if you try, you can throw any number you really want to. Also, you need to have the direction you're going in mind before you throw. Try real hard to throw a seven from here and concentrate on a left turn at Cattermune's House. You'll end up at the junction, sure as sure. Interesting places, junctions.'

'What makes them interesting?'

'There are nine junction squares — not counting the Forever one — and they aren't like anyplace else in the game. You can go there twice or three times or a dozen. You can meet people you've met before. Catch up on what's happening in all the squares. Find out who the current Grisl Queen is, and who G'nop's swallowed recently. Hear the latest on Gerald and George. Find out what's going on at Cattermune's House.' The pig shuddered delicately. 'It's just interesting.'

The mouse patted its whiskers on the napkin which had been provided with dinner and watched the Down Line Express come nearer. It seemed to be running on a dim tracery, like the faintest cobweb stretched across the sky. When it was at its closest point it stopped. Various creatures, dwarfed by distance, got off the train and stared toward the zoo. There was something about one or two of them that tickled at Mouse, worrying her. Where had she seen those shapes before? She stared and stared, almost but not quite recognizing them.

With an exclamation of impatience, Mouse got the dice out of her matchbox. Surely at least three hours had passed since she first entered the zoo! Remembering the advice of pig, she concentrated on what she was doing and threw a seven.

CHAPTER TWELVE

'I can't understand how you got here so quickly,' exclaimed
the tortoise. 'We passed you, way back there, behind the
Polemic.' Tortoise still had shreds of Polemic caught on her
back claws, and she shuffled them on the pavement. The stuff
was like chewing gum!

'I know you did,' answered the mouse, who had remembered them the minute she had seen them up close.

'Mouse threw the dice when she saw us go by,' said the
amethyst ape, thoughtfully, stroking the malachite mouse
with both hands. 'Oh, lovely Mouse, are you well, are you
coherent, are you in one piece, are you all right?'

'Perfectly all right,' the mouse said with a tiny catch in
the voice, like the smallest possible sob. 'I spent eight
interminable years in Buttercup. I was almost eaten in G'nop.
I did, however, have an excellent supper in the Dinosaur
Zoo, and I am here, so, yes, I'm all right.'

They were sitting on a bench just outside the terminus of
the Down Line Express, among a fuming welter of passersby,
hawkers, mongers, and kiosk-holders, all greeting one another
or calling out their wares in loud and uninhibited voices.
Beyond this hubbub were streets full of wanderers and
windows full of watchers. A streetcar clanged busily up a
hill, striking sparks from the wires strung above the street,
its bell ringing frantically. Food carts offered roast nuts,
ethnic dishes, and brightly colored galoshes for those traveling
to the Puce Polemic, the Worm Pits, or the Six Howlers. A
newsmonger was doing a brisk business and the ape went to
fetch one of the red lettered tabloids. 'NEW GRISL QUEEN
REIGNS AS BUTTERCUP I,' headlined the front page, subheaded
by 'DOGS ARE LATEST ROYAL FAD,' and 'DOG IMPORTERS
DO BRISK BUSINESS.' Other front page headlines included,

'SELDOM SIDING TRANSIENTS IN RIOT. DEMAND MORE FRE-QUENT SERVICE,' and 'PUCE POLEMIC SEEN AS HEALTH HAZARD.'

On page two was a lengthy list of names headed, 'G'NOP VICTIMS INCREASE IN RECENT,' followed by an even longer list headed, 'VACATIONERS RETURNING TO GAME FROM ILLUSION FIELDS.' Ape read these lists almost compulsively, wondering if he would recognize anyone, realizing that he could not recognize anyone under the guise of carnelian cocks or emerald emus. On page three was a brief interview in which George confided that he hadn't really meant what he said about Gerald, and another putatively conducted in the Dinosaur Zoo with a short-time visitor, a malachite mouse, in which the mouse was quoted as saying, 'I didn't plan to make this trip just now as I'm pregnant.'

'That pig,' breathed Mouse.

'Never mind,' said the ape. 'It would seem the item to which our attention must inevitably be drawn is this one, here.' He pointed to a feature article on the back page, 'CATTERMUNE'S HOUSE HOSTS CELEBRITIES FOR BIRTHDAY FETE.' 'It is the only mention of a birthday I can find, and didn't someone say that something had to be done by someone's birthday?'

'I wonder if it's the same Cattermune?' asked Mouse.

'Surely there wouldn't be more than one,' commented Tortoise.

'What Cattermune is that?' asked the ape. 'The name does sound familiar. Do you know this Cattermune?'

'The Cattermune who lent a certain matchbox to the father of a certain person,' said Mouse. 'If you know who I mean.'

The tortoise sighed. 'You don't need to try to spare my feelings. It was my father who borrowed the matchbox from Cattermune. Presumably, if we are to avoid disaster, it must be returned to Cattermune, at Cattermune's House, in time for Cattermune's birthday.'

'You didn't mention the name Cattermune,' said the ape. 'When we discussed doing . . . coming . . . proceeding after Mouse, you didn't so much as hint at Cattermune. We could have gone right past Cattermune's and missed Mouse completely.'

'You don't need to be testy,' said Tortoise. 'It had slipped my mind, that's all. In all this flurry and haste, the reason for the whole matter had simply slipped my mind.'

'The matchbox,' Mouse told Ape vehemently. 'That's what it's all about. The return of the matchbox to Cattermune!'

'A matchbox?' the ape asked. 'Do you have it?'

In answer the mouse took the box from her pocket and rattled it. 'It was in one of the drawers at Buttercup's house, that is, at Thrumm House. I was inhabiting Buttercup herself . . .'

'Which is what the game square said,' the tortoise interrupted. 'It said Buttercup.'

'Well, I was in Buttercup, and there was no room in there for anything but me and her, but at least the matchbox didn't end up far away.'

'Thank heaven you didn't mislay it,' said the tortoise fervently.

'I had some trouble getting Buttercup to find it, but I certainly wouldn't have mislaid it,' replied the mouse. 'That's what I came for. Or what I would have come for if I had intended to come at all.'

'Oh, most sweet and excellent companions, I am correct in thinking that a birthday was mentioned, am I not?' Ape received two solemn nods in confirmation of this. 'And since this paper indicates that a birthday is imminent, and since we have no idea how much time goes by within the game as compared to our customary world, hadn't we better get ourselves to Cattermune's House at once?'

'If we're in a hurry, we will need to throw a three,' said Mouse plaintively.

'But what if we don't. Or one of us doesn't?' Tortoise asked.

The ape laid his hands on Tortoise's shell, patting her gently. 'Come, come, now. Let us not give way to hysteria or melancholy. I seem to have noticed that when we really concentrate, we can throw any number we really desire to throw.'

'It did seem that was what's been going on, but it makes no sense. If one can throw any number one wishes, then . . .'

'Oh, most excellent Tortoise, then there are a finite number of choices,' said the ape. 'And that number gets smaller and smaller the longer one stays in the game.'

'Until, at last, there is nothing left but junctions, Forevers, and The End,' said Mouse, examining the huge game map mounted on the wall behind them. 'Players can gyrate back and forth between junctions for a long, long time. From Buttercup to Cattermune to Frab, from there to Snivel's Island — and Mother's Smithy. Over to Seldom and Last Chance What? and Usable Chasm. And then you'd throw two elevens and be back at the Down Line again. It could go on and on and on and on . . .' Her voice dwindled away.

'Shh,' comforted the ape. 'We must not allow ourselves to be disheartened. Someone I once knew well always told me that a stout heart is the only true requisite in the game of life. I am not at all sure what he meant, but it sounds exemplary, doesn't it? Let's not get ahead of ourselves. The most important thing right now is to return the matchbox, don't you agree?'

'It's certainly a place to start,' the mouse assented. 'If Tortoise thinks so.'

'I think so,' said Tortoise slowly. 'I really do think so.'

'I'd been looking forward to sight-seeing here for a while,' Mouse sighed. She looked tired. The malachite around her eyes had faded to a limey green and her whiskers were limp.

'Every moment we spend here might be the last moment for return,' remarked the tortoise.

'Of course.' Mouse sighed again, getting out her dice as she saw the other two doing so. 'Three, from here, didn't you say?' Listlessly she rolled the dice. 'To Cattermune's House.'

CHAPTER THIRTEEN

The man turned around and saw her, putting out his hands to hold hers, very tightly. As for the young woman, she cried, her tears running down her face to make a salty wetness.

'So here we are,' he said.

'I didn't, didn't,' she gulped.

'Oh, but my dear young woman, you didn't mean to, I know.'

'I told him you didn't,' the old woman said, peering down at her nightgown. 'Didn't whatever it was, though I seem to have forgotten what you didn't do. I knew I should have changed my clothes! I told someone so!' She pulled her shawl more firmly around herself, thankful for the thickness of the flannel gown and the solid support of the slippers on her feet.

'Where are we?' the large man asked, swiveling his belly before him as he examined their surroundings.

'Who are we?' asked the young woman.

'Why are we here?' concluded the old woman. 'And how did we get here?'

They stood very closely together, looking first at themselves in the high mirrors before them, then at each other, and finally around themselves at the room they were in, an enormous, rectangular ballroom, one not used recently, for the floor was thick with dust and the crystal chandeliers above them hung like dirty icicles from a vast, vaulted ceiling painted with gloomy scenes of the hunt — a chase through immemorial forests and across vast, edgeless moors in the gloom of an autumn dusk for an illusive and dangerous prey whose painted eyes and gleaming teeth menaced them fiercely from behind painted bracken.

To one side opened a row of tall arched windows draped

with begrimed dark velvet and curtained with webs of torn fabric. Opposite the windows an equal number of high, round topped doors stood, enigmatically closed except for the farthest one which moved silently to and fro as if blown by opposing breezes. The curved tops of the windows and doors were like the arches of great trunked trees; the tattered fabric of the curtains hung in the windows like dangling moss. Gilt chairs with broken legs huddled in corners and staggered along the shorter walls like visitors from a more civilized world, abandoned to die in this darkling glen. On a dais, rusty music stands huddled like skeletal victims of some long-ago hunt above a litter of musical scores, yellowed by time into a forest floor deep piled with autumn's leaves.

On both short walls were gold-framed portraits, larger than life-size, veiled in cobwebs. Brass plates labeled these as Cattermunes, fathers and daughters, mothers and sons, then sons and daughters again, for generations. All of them shared the same heavy eyelids, like the lids on a marble statue, lips slightly parted to reveal sharpened teeth; neat, small ears which lay oddly horizontal on their heads as though tilted backward; nostrils, widely distended, seeming to scent game even through the paint which bound them to their canvases.

Hypnotized by the painted stares of those dozen pairs of eyes, the three travelers drew near enough to read the labels attached to the frames. Amerie Cattermune. Grendla Cattermune. Ostrey Cattermune the Elder. Ostrey Cattermune the Younger and his mate, Sulina. Ostrey Cattermune the Third. And more.

Without exception, the Cattermunes had been painted with weapon in hand or upon shoulder or carried in some other fashion, and with one foot poised upon something dead. Even Sulina smiled around the poniard she carried between her teeth as she glanced with satisfaction at the stripe-hided hulk beneath her tiny boot.

From somewhere a breath of icy air stirred the chandeliers into shrill, tinkling complaint.

'The door,' breathed the man, leading the way toward the single door which stood open, swinging soundlessly in and

459

out. They slipped through into a corridor as the breeze caught the door behind them, slamming it, caroming an assault of echoes down the length of the hallway behind and before them with the sound of a shouted word.

'Hush,' said the man, holding up one hand, but the word was lost in echoes. He had not needed to hush them. Neither of them had dared say anything at all.

One side of the hallway was taken up with the high arched doors into the long room they had just left. The other side was lined with niches in which lamps burned over great bronze busts, each statue festooned with cobwebs, veloured in dust, labeled in bronze. Evenyl Cattermune the Elder. Evenyl Cattermune the Younger. Starwold Cattermune. Ogfire Cattermune and his mate, Mordinor.

'One would not doubt,' said the old woman, 'that this is the Cattermune's House.'

'But what are we doing here?' asked the young woman. 'It is not a place I would want to visit. Why are we here?'

The large-bellied man led them on down the corridor, stopping only briefly at each niche to confirm that yet another Cattermune was immortalized there. At the end of the corridor a passageway led to their left, slightly narrower but noticeably cleaner. They turned and followed it. The marble floor gave way to threadbare carpet and this in turn gave way to carpet in a reasonable state of repair. The corridor turned once more, this time to the right.

'Good, merciful Moomaw,' a voice said from a suddenly opened door. 'What are you people doing wandering around back here? You're half a mile from where you're supposed to be, and late at that!'

They turned to confront an emaciated old person with flyaway white hair and shoulders so high they appeared to be roughly at ear level. 'Come along, now. Lost, I suppose? How else end up in the west wing! No one's used the west wing since the time of Alphia Cattermune. Nothing back there but dust, spiders, and broken furniture. You, Green, are supposed to be down in the butler's pantry helping polish the silver for the Cattermune's birthday fete next week, when the new Grisl Queen comes calling. Take the next right, down two flights, then two sharp lefts, got that. You women come along with me . . .'

The women, young one and old one, trailed after him, turning to catch a last glimpse of the man called Green, now departing down a cross corridor. The old being went on, 'You, young woman, you're the wet nurse, right? Mary Ann? Two flights up at this next stairway, then through the green baize door on your right and you'll find the nurseries. Nanny hasn't arrived yet, but the nurserymaid is up there. Fanetta, her name is. Poor thing. Yours is the room next to the night nursery.' He turned to the old woman and gave her a piercing glance. 'You must be the layette seamstress, Mrs Smani? Your room is right next to the wet nurse's room. You'll find everything you need laid out there, including several uniforms. If I may say so, it was hardly sensible of you to come to work in your night clothes.'

'. . . very suddenly,' said the old woman he had named Mrs Smani. 'Didn't have time to . . .'

'Yes, well, that's understandable. Blessed event, and all that. New Cattermune heir or heiress? Ah? Lord Cattermune's young mate fooled us all, she did. Here she is, almost ready to kindle — just as you are, my dear — and no one knew until just now. And aren't the older children fit to be tied! AND the other wives!'

'Excuse me, sir,' said the young woman, Mary Ann, 'but could we ask your name?'

'Me? Oh, I'm Groff. Old Groff. Or Groff the Pensioner. I was butler here once, long ago. Now I just make myself useful. Finding servants who show up in the wrong place. Replacing those who leave at awkward times. Giving information and advice. Speaking of which . . .' He folded his hands and gave them a stern look.

'Staff dining room is down the way I sent Green. Nursery staff won't have their meals delivered until after the blessed event, or until your baby comes, young woman, but after that you'll have meals in the nursery dining room. Staff meal times are six, eleven, and five, with tea and snacks laid on

461

after the Cattermunes have finished dinner in the evenings. You must wear uniforms at all times in the house. Nursery staff shouldn't be wandering about. When you aren't in the staff dining room or out taking exercise in the servants' yard, you should be in the nurseries or on your way there. When a Cattermune comes by, or a guest, you stand back at the wall with your hands at your sides and your eyes respectfully down. Other than that, do your work well and no one will bother you . . .' He gestured grandly at the staircase beside them and repeated himself, 'Two flights up, through the green baize door, and you're in nurseryland.'

Mary Ann started up the stairs, the old woman trailing behind. 'Seamstress,' the old woman muttered. 'Layette seamstress. Somehow that comes as a surprise.'

'Wet nurse,' mused Mary Ann. 'Not too surprising, considering everything. Green is my brother, isn't he?'

'Why do you think so?'

'He looks like me. Come to think of it, we both look like you. Are you our mother?'

'I don't think so,' said Mrs Smani. 'I don't feel like your mother. I certainly don't feel like that man's mother.'

'An aunt, perhaps?' asked Mary Ann. 'Then he might be my cousin. It would be nice to have a cousin.'

'He seemed quite fond of you,' Mrs Smani opined. 'Perhaps he's your husband. I suppose you do have a husband.'

Mary Ann stroked her rounded belly and nodded. 'It would be appropriate, wouldn't it? I wonder when the Cattermune blessed event is expected.'

'Sometime after yours, I should think, if you're to be wet nurse. Sometime after the layette is sewn. From the looks of you, they've left it rather late.'

'This must be the door.' Mary Ann pushed her way through the green baize door and found herself in a murky hallway with a strip of blood-red carpet down the center and dark-paneled walls on either side. Iron brackets in the shapes of bats bore red lanterns. Daggers and javelins hung in groups between the doors, which stood open upon the right side. The first door opened into a flagstoned room with toy shelves ranked beneath the windows, the second into a long, low room with cribs lined against one wall, the third into a small bedroom with a rocking chair in one corner, the fourth into a sewing room with a cot. On the other side of the hall the doors were closed, but as they went by, one of them popped open an inch and a pale face peeked at them through the crack.

Mary Ann said in a gentle voice, 'Fanetta? I'm the . . . I'm the wet nurse. And this is the seamstress.'

'Oh, thank Moomaw,' squeaked the nursery maid. 'I've been up here all alone! I didn't want the nanny to come, you know what nannies are! Especially Cattermune nannies.'

Mary Ann didn't know, but she thought it unwise to say so. Mrs Smani was as tight-lipped as she went into the sewing room and lay down on the cot, breathing a deep, weary sigh. 'My bones feel as though they'd been pinched,' she said. 'As though I'd been walking around all bent over.'

The room was lined in shelves piled with folded lengths of fabric in one mud color or another. A sewing machine sat beneath the one narrow window, the cabinet beside it stacked with spools of thread, scissors, binding tape, and buttons of various sizes.

'Can you sew?' Mary Ann asked.

'I suppose so,' replied the old woman. 'Sometimes when you get to be my age, you forget what you've done. It will come back to me.'

'I'll help you,' the younger woman said. 'There's a list here on the sewing machine. It says, "Seven sets of crib linens, including changes of linen, or as needed." Why seven sets? I wonder.' She went to the window, drew aside the heavy drapes, and looked outside. Beyond the walls was a dreary and unpleasant landscape of stone and contorted thorn; inside the walls another wing of Cattermune's House loomed across a plaza where a fountain played, so lit by red lanterns that it appeared to be a fountain of blood.

Mary Ann went through the connecting door into her own room. An armoire of black wood with uniforms in a trying shade of earthy plum hung in a sparse array next to a narrow

463

bed with a single pillow. Against one wall stood a crib like a cage, with a top which could be shut and locked. The batwinged key in the lock had a loop of thong tied through it so that it could be hung up — or put around one's neck. Shuddering, Mary Ann left it where it was and went through the connecting door. In the night nursery was nothing at all but one straight-backed chair and the cribs, seven of them. These cradles, like the one in her own room, had tops that locked. Next door was the day nursery, with a floor as hard as iron and one small, soft rug before the great deep fireplace. The toys on the surrounding shelves were strange to her. Dolls, of course, and small, soft animals, but also model racks and guillotines and whips and lances and gibbets. From one of these, a teddy bear hung with its head awry, and Mary Ann shuddered again.

She returned to her room, closing the door behind her. She had not liked the looks of the nurseries.

Each room had a clock with a swinging pendulum; each room had its own rhythm of tic and toc, toc-toc, tac-tac, each loud enough that when the connecting doors were open the clocks spoke to one another in a tiny, percussive rustle, as though the rooms were alive with beetles. From every window, the same view presented itself: the bloody fountain and the landscape beyond. They had evidently come at evening, for the light grew dimmer, and Mary Ann turned to look for lamps.

There were no lights of any kind in her room except a candle beside her bed, and an ornate iron tinderbox in the drawer of the table. She rapped at the door to the old woman's room and went in. Here there was a lamp beside the sewing machine where the treadle clattered and the needle replied as lengths of dirty-colored fabric moved from the old woman's lap through the machine.

'Seven sets,' Mrs Smani hummed. 'Seven sets.'

'What time did that old person say dinner was?'

'Five.'

'The clocks say nine.'

'Then we came after dinner.'

464

'I'm hungry.'

'Snacks after the Cattermunes have eaten. I wonder what time that is?'

'Let's find out.' She went back into her own room and changed into one of the plum-colored dresses, a garment with buttons down the front from neck to ankle and a dark blue apron and cap. Mrs Smani's garb was the same, except that hers buttoned in the back and had a cap with cerise ribbons on one side.

'So they'll know who we are,' Mrs Smani murmured. 'The uniform tells them. Dark blue apron and cap, that's the wet nurse. Cap with ribbons, that's the layette seamstress.' They had just emerged into the hallway and turned toward the green baize door when the door opposite Mary Ann's popped open again and Fanetta's head appeared. She was wearing a cap very much like Mrs Smani's except that the ribbons were deep blue.

'Where are you going!' she demanded.

'Down to see if we can get something to eat,' Mary Ann replied.

'Oh, my, no, no. You'd be finished off in a minute. Don't dare go that way. There'll be Cattermunes and their cousins all over out there. See!' She stood back, gesturing them to come through and look out her window. From here they could see another court of Cattermune's House, far below them, with carriages arriving and departing and a great clutter of figures walking among the formal gardens of clipped yew and black cypresses and peonies as dark as clotted gore.

'Then they haven't eaten yet?'

'Oh, my, no. No, not until ten or eleven, or even midnight. They're night people, are the Cattermunes. If you want to wander about, the time to do it is very early in the morning, about dawn, and for a few hours after that. Then the Cattermunes are all asleep.'

'But I am hungry,' said Mary Ann plaintively. 'I really am.'

'So am I,' confided Fanetta. 'We can go down. Just not the way you were going.'

She went down the hallway away from the green baize

door, leading them around a turn and into a dismal cul-de-sac hung with tapestries. Behind one of these she found a knob, twisted it to reveal a black space, which she entered, calling, 'Follow me!'

'What about a light?' objected Mary Ann.

'I've got one,' came the answer as a gleam of matchlight showed from the black pit. 'I keep candles and matches down here on a kind of ledge thing. The housekeeper gives me candles to replace the ones burned in the nursery, and I always bring the stub ends down here . . .' The voice drifted away. Mary Ann and Mrs Smani hurried to follow it, the hidden door swinging shut behind them.

There was a seemingly endless flight of stairs, with odd little corridors which corkscrewed away from it through the walls of the place. 'You can get to almost every room in the Cattermune's House through the walls,' murmured Fanetta. 'Or, at the very least, you can look and listen through spy holes. They've forgotten about these ways. Nobody uses them anymore except us.'

'Us?'

'Us mouslings. Us little people. If you're smart, you'll learn your way around. Sometimes a Cattermune takes after one of us for no reason. If we're lucky, we can get into the walls before we get caught.'

'And then?'

'Then sometimes I get out of Cattermune's House for a while, you know. Even though I know I'll probably just come back later. I go to Frab Junction or Mother's Smithy for a time . . .'

Mary Ann frowned. Frab Junction. Surely she remembered something about that. And Mother's Smithy. She rubbed her head, as though the memory only needed stimulation to emerge, fully fledged. She lost it as Fanetta went on.

'Chances are, the Cattermunes'll have forgotten about it by the time I get back . . .' Her voice faded away and the light flickered on before them, down and down, and around, and down once more. Here and there were spy holes extending through the mighty walls into rooms which were evidently in use for light came through, and the sounds of voices. 'Kitchens are next level down,' said Fanetta. 'Remember that. From the end of the nursery hall, it's straight down the stairway to the kitchens. Do you know anyone there?'

'Green,' replied Mrs Smani. 'A kind of under-butler, perhaps?'

'Footman,' suggested Fanetta. 'Well, when we go in, stay out of the way of the cooks, that's all. Most of them have been here a long, long time, and they don't take to new-comers. They don't take to anybody much, and that's the truth.'

She found a knob similar to the one at the top of the stairs and twisted it counterclockwise, making a loud click. The hidden door swung open into a short corridor off an enormous, stone-floored kitchen filled with scurrying people in white coats and flat white caps, others in slightly taller headgear, and a few in towering hats topped with fabric puffs like billows of cream. The room reeked of roasted meats and baking breads, steam from kettles seethed over the monstrous iron stoves, heat beat like a desert wind from the doors of opened ovens where brobdingnagian pies sweltered, their tops bubbling with juices. Everywhere was the scurry and chop of cooklets fleeting like sheep before the advance of the mighty cooks.

'First course,' cried a stentorian voice from the doorway. 'The guests are seated.'

'Send up the seethed snivel,' shouted a tall cook, waving an enormous ladle. 'Go!' Five cooklets staggered out the doorway under an enormous laden platter, headed toward a barely visible immensity of stairs.

At the foot of the stairs the cooks were surrounded by a crowd of footmen and harried on their way with sharp cries of 'Mind the step,' 'Sharp left here,' and 'Hold up your end, you fool.'

'Quick now,' bellowed a cook, 'dabble fish into the poacher. Cravvle and Journ! Start chopping twelve cups of parsley.'

'I think we can sneak around here to the staff dining room,' whispered Fanetta. 'Don't, for Moomaw's sake, get in their way.'

The three women, staying as close to the wall as possible, slipped a quarter way round the huge kitchen and through a narrow door into a shabby, low-ceilinged room furnished only with long, scarred tables and dilapidated straight chairs. At one of the tables a group leaned confidentially toward one another in quiet talk. At another, a liveried servant slept, face hidden in pillowing arms. 'Those're the staff cooks,' Fanetta whispered, pointing at the group. 'They're the ones that feed us. There'll be something over there on the buffet. There's always bread and cheese and something to drink.' They scurried to the buffet and found not only the promised bread and cheese but also half an enormous meat pie and a bowl of slightly wilted salad.

'Not that they eat salad,' Fanetta murmured. 'The Cattermunes, I mean. But some of their guests fancy it, so there's usually some about.'

'Do all these people know about the passages in the walls?' Mary Ann asked.

'Oh, no. Well, they know there *are* passages in the walls, but not *where* they are. There's only a few of us know where all of the passages are. Groff. And me. And some of the housemaids. We're the only ones that've been around long enough.'

'Why have you been here so long?'

'Because . . . I've been everywhere in the game, at least once, and there's nothing left for me but junctions. Except The End, of course, but I'm not ready for that yet.' She jutted her chin at them and glared, a mouse glare. 'That's the rules, and even the Cattermune has to obey the rules! Even the Cattermune can't go anywhere he's been before except junctions!'

Mary Ann and Mrs Smani shared glances. When Fanetta spoke of junctions, they suddenly remembered something about junctions though they had not thought of them until that moment. 'Which is the best junction?'

'Well, for me, this one is. I know my way about. I'm so

unimportant, it isn't likely any of the Cattermunes will get offended at me. Sometimes there isn't anyone in the nursery but me, the young ones grow up so fast. Even when there aren't any young ones there, someone has to keep the place clean. I've got a fairly comfortable room, and the food isn't bad. Sometimes it's kind of interesting, too, what you can see and hear through the walls.'

'Dear and valuable young woman, tell us about the other junctions,' said a male voice. They looked up to see that Green, who had been asleep at another table, had joined them, still rubbing his eyes. 'Now that you speak of junctions, I seem to remember such places. Tell us about Seldom.'

'There's not much to tell. There's a corral for horses and a well for water and a cave with some supplies of food and firewood. There's a haystack. And a privy. And once in a while a stagecoach comes through. There's a desert all around, nothing but lizards and cactus.'

'How about Snivel's Island?'

'Oh, the snivels are worse than G'nop. They've got such teeth, and they're everywhere. You can't lie down without one of them trying to chew on you. You can climb a tree and stay away from the big ones, like the one they had for dinner tonight, but the little ones can climb anything. Oh, no, no, you wouldn't want to go to Snivel's Island.'

'How about Last Chance What?' asked Mary Ann.

'It's in the bottom of a well full of spiders,' she replied. 'And Mother's Smithy is so hot, and such hard work all the time, and no sleep with that hammer going night and day. Then there's the Forever junction! Be very careful leaving here if you're going on the main gameline. Don't throw a two, whatever you do!'

'Isn't there any way out of a Forever?'

'No. Land on a Forever, and you're gone and that's it! But, it's easy enough to stay out of them. Just concentrate on which way you're going and don't throw a wrong number!'

'What about Usable Chasm?' Mrs Smani asked.

'If you've got wings, that's just the place. For the rest of us, it's cling to the side and pray. It's got no top, at least

469

no top anybody knows about, and I've never been to the bottom. Last time I had to chew out a place flat enough to roll the dice!'

'And Moebius Siding?' Green asked in a bemused voice. 'What about that?'

'Like a roller coaster. Around and around and around, with no end and no beginning to it, every office you go to they send you someplace else, and just when you think you've got somewhere, they send you back right where you started. And no place to sit down and nothing to eat, and the drinking fountains don't work and there's a line a mile long waiting to get into the rest rooms . . . if they aren't out of order.'

'That reminds me of someplace I've been before,' mused Mary Ann. 'I wonder if I've been to Moebius?'

'You'd remember if you had.'

A clamor in the corridor made them look up to see the under-cooks struggling back to the kitchen under the weight of the great platter, empty now except for a litter of bones and a broad, toothy skull, its jaws propped open with another skull, one that looked very human.

'Well, it looks like they've finished with the seethed snivel,' Fanetta remarked. 'They've even eaten the meat off the binker's head in its jaws.'

'Binker's head?' Mrs Smani faltered.

'Game. Prey. You know, what the Cattermunes hunt, out there, in the wilds. That's what they hunt, binkers.'

'That thing is a *human* skull.'

'Shhh!' hissed Fanetta. 'Never say that. Never for a minute say that. That was a binker, that was. Never mind what it might have been before. It was a binker, and that's all there is to it.' Her face was very white, and she was trembling uncontrollably. 'Don't, don't say that other thing. Don't ever.'

'Shhh,' said Mary Ann. 'I won't say it. Calm down.' She cast a quick glance at Green's face, seeing there a quiet, calculating look more frightening in its rigorous calm than was Fanetta's hysteria.

'Ahh,' he said softly, 'if the Cattermunes are . . . ah . . .

470

displeased, I presume those they are displeased with are or
. . . shall we say become . . . binkers?'

Fanetta did not reply, but neither did she contradict him.
She merely shivered, glancing the way the cooks had gone.
'They only eat binkers when it's just family and cousins,'
she said. 'When there are guests, like the Grisl Queen, they
don't. At least not whole. In pies, mostly.'

'You mean . . .' Green's eyes strayed to the leftover pie
on the buffet. 'You mean . . .'

'Most likely.' She shivered again. 'You don't see anybody
down here eating it, do you?'

'I did,' he remarked faintly. 'I did.'

The others watched his retreating back. 'I suppose he'll be
sick,' said Mrs Smani. 'I would be in his place.'

'Stick with the bread and cheese,' recommended Fanetta.
'It's safest.'

They waited for Green's return which happened coinciden-
tally with the conclusion of dessert. Under-cooks, bearing
trays of pastries and fruit, stopped off in the staff dining
room to offer leftovers to those present. Gratefully, Mary
Ann and Mrs Smani stocked up on apples and pears and
bunches of red grapes, borrowing a basket from the kitchen
to carry the harvest in.

'Lovely companions, I have a feeling, wrenched up from
Moomaw knows what depth of former existence,' said Green
from his huddle at the end of the table, 'that there is something we should be attending to here at Cattermune's House.'

'That's strange,' said Mary Ann. 'So have I.'

'Well of course,' remarked Fanetta. 'You'll both have
plenty to attend to, just getting your jobs done, and I don't
envy either one of you, let me tell you.'

'More than that,' the man said, sighing. 'More than that.
Not something I'm supposed to do as part of being *here*.
Something I was supposed to do when I *came* here.'

'I've had that feeling,' said Fanetta. 'It usually goes away
if I have a hot bath and some sleep.'

'Hot bath,' breathed Mary Ann.

'Sleep,' whispered Mrs Smani. 'Oh, yes, please.'

471

'Something we should be doing,' mused Green. 'Maybe it will come to me tomorrow.'

The three women made their way back through the kitchen to the hidden door in the paneling, then up the endless stairs to the door behind the tapestry, with Mary Ann carrying Mrs Smani the last few flights. In the nursery hallway, the lanterns were alight. Mary Ann left the hall door ajar as she put the little old woman on her bed, covering her with a blanket, then closed it behind her and opened the door into her own room. The dress she had taken off was lying across the bed. As she went to hang it up, something in the pocket knocked on the door of the armoire. She fished it out. A gold matchbox.

A gold matchbox. Belonging to someone. Now whose matchbox was it?

'Is this yours?' she asked Fanetta, who had come to her door.

'Not mine,' the maid said. 'I just came to tell you the bathroom's across the hall from the night nursery. There's hot water this time of night or very early in the morning. I put the fruit in my window. It's cool there.' She turned to leave. 'If you don't want that matchbox, I'll take it.'

'No,' mused Mary Ann. 'I think I'm supposed to give it to someone.' She put the matchbox in the pocket of her uniform and lit the candle by her bed, surprised to find that the warm, yellow light made her want to weep with pleasure. There was too much red light in Cattermune's House, and this warm glow made her remember the yellow sun of some other world.

'Give the matchbox to Cattermune, for his birthday.' Fanetta laughed. 'That'd be a kick.'

'Why? Why would it be?'

'Oh, I don't know. Cattermune gets big things for his birthday. Maybe he'd like something little for a change.' She drifted away, humming to herself. 'Just don't put your name on it. That way, if he doesn't like it, he won't know who gave it to him.'

Mary Ann, obscurely moved by this suggestion, set it aside for the time. There was a long flannel nightgown among the clothing in the armoire. She put it on and crawled into her bed, forgetting Cattermunes and matchboxes and everything connected with them in a long timeless, lightless slide into sleep.

CHAPTER FOURTEEN

Green was roused early, dragged from his bed in the footmen's dormitory and chivvied into a line waiting to take care of sanitary and grooming matters. Half an hour later, a long file of identically dressed figures submitted to inspection by a haughty individual identified as Cribbs, an under-butler, who took pleasure in advising Green that he was not an important figure in the affairs of Cattermune's House. There were, Cribbs said, a steward, two butlers, four under-butlers, two wine stewards, twenty footmen, a housekeeper, two under-housekeepers, forty housemaids, a kitchen staff of thirty, plus the nursery staff and personal servants and a staff for the stables and gardens comprising several dozen individuals. In addition there were tutors, seamstresses, costume makers, musicians, artists, dancing masters, game keepers, librarians, decorators, carpenters, assorted grooms, and several masters of the hunt. All of these in service to the thirty or forty Cattermunes currently present at Cattermune's House.

'Though there'll be more, for the fete,' sniffed Cribbs. 'There'll be sixty or seventy of the family here by then.'

'Where are they now?' asked Green daringly. His words fell into a ghastly silence.

'About,' said Cribbs. 'Where is none of your business.' He began to read off assignments for the day. During the morning, Green was to station himself in the gaming rooms, where he was to attend to the needs of any family member who might go in that direction.

The gaming rooms were on a lower floor, underground, without a window or a breath of air. Dice tables and card tables were scattered about, cluttered with the accoutrements of gaming — decks of cards, dice in their cups, chips printed with strange symbols.

Morning wore away to noon. Green was replaced by another footman and went to have his lunch. After lunch, he was assigned to man the small library, and he headed in that direction, fighting sleep.

The small library was in the direction of the abandoned wing in which Green had first found himself. It looked out upon a quiet stretch of sward surrounded by bleak cypresses and centered upon a reflecting pool in which pallid lilies bloomed, ghostlike in the still light. Green stationed himself in a corner, almost hidden behind a bookcase and the fall of drapery from the nearby window.

'How do you stay awake?' he had asked another footman at lunch. 'There's nothing going on!'

'Pinch yourself,' said the other as he left. 'Or play with yourself. Or imagine what the Cattermunes would do to you if they caught you asleep.'

Green had some difficulty with this, inasmuch as he had not yet even seen or heard a Cattermune — a deficiency which was almost immediately remedied.

A noise in the hallway brought Green's head up. Someone or something massive entered the room, saying in a heavy, furry voice. 'Ah, no one here. Come in, Cornutes, come in.' There was the sound of someone else coming in, the noise of two people moving about, a chair scraping on the floor, then another, before the voice spoke again. 'I don't want to miss the gaming, so you must not keep me long. Now, what was it?'

'Just wanted to reassure you. So far so good, Cattermune,' said another voice, a lighter voice, though one similar in its furry quality. 'I checked the placement of the thing, as you suggested. You did brilliantly. The daughter of the man you gave it to is old and dying, and any knowledge of the thing will die with her. Meantime, the supply of immigrants is more than adequate and seems to be increasing. You didn't need to have been concerned. Nothing's going to go wrong.'

'Of course nothing will go wrong,' said the heavy, furry voice with enormous self-satisfaction. 'I was never concerned, though I suppose it never hurts to check. I told the family they could trust me in this matter. The sacrifices were heavy, but within hours our waiting will be over. Finality will occur. Cattermune's House will be immortal!' There was a gelatinous chuckle in the furry voice.

'Clever of you! Though there were some . . .'

'Ah, well, it was a dreadful risk at the time. And it took the sacrifice of fifty of our family to create the thing. I told them what the benefits would be, but they weren't what one might call willing. I suggested a lottery, but they'd have none of that, so I ended up picking them out myself. I'm sorry that your mother had to be among them, Cornutes, but she would go on nagging at me. And several of your littermates, too. She'd got to them. And then before we were through, it took the blood of another fifty to break through to the world. And then, finally, it took fifty years to implant, fifty years to become permanent. A long, hard process, but there was no shorter way.' The heavy voice sighed, again with satisfaction, as a man might who had completed a hard task to his own total satisfaction.

'What would you have done if it had come back somehow? If the man you gave it to had returned it?'

'Oh, if it had been returned, I would simply have placed it in the world again. It would have taken another fifty lives, another fifty years, but still, whatever the cost, it would have been well worth it. However, there was little chance of that. The man I gave it to — he wouldn't have returned it. I read the man well. A fool. An irresponsible fool. The risk was that his daughter would return it, but even there — she delayed.'

'Yes. She delayed.'

'And now you say she has grown old and is dying. When

475

she dies, all knowledge of the thing dies. When she is gone, someone will take the anchor and put it away, or sell it, or, better yet, melt it down to make something else, perhaps a dozen other things. That's why it was made of gold, so that it will be kept, somehow, in some form. There's no way it can get back here. It will be divided up and scattered about in the world, no one will ever put it together and bring it back! The House of Cattermune will be tied directly into a source of supply and the future of the House will be assured!'

'Players,' said the lighter voice. Green could hear the sound of hands being rubbed briskly together, a swish, swish, swish of flesh on flesh, celebrating.

'Players, yes,' purred the heavy voice.

'Binkers,' said the other, with a kind of bubbling snigger. 'Binkers unlimited.'

'That, too,' replied the other voice with a deeply gelatinous and shivering laugh. 'Come now, you've kept me from the gaming long enough. You uncle Cadermon bilked me at dice last night. Tonight I will have my revenge.' And he laughed again.

Green, in his hidden corner, for no reason that he could identify, shivered with an uncontrollable aversion at the sound of that voice.

CHAPTER FIFTEEN

Arti Zahmani answered the door herself, unsurprised to find Makr Avehl on the doorstep since he had called from the airport to say he was on his way. His face under the porch light was drawn and tired-looking. She scarcely noticed.

'Where are they?' she blurted. 'Where is my daughter? Where is Dagma? She was too weak to get out of bed without help. Haurvatat is having an absolute fit. The doctor knocked

476

me out for simply hours. I suppose you know Aghrehond is gone as well! Where are they, Makr Avehl?' The tears she had been fighting began to run down her cheeks and she made an ugly, gulping noise.

He put his arms around her and patted her back, trying to calm her. 'At the moment, we don't know where they are, Arti, and if you distress yourself in this fashion, you can't help me find them. Try to calm down.' Even as he said it, he knew how futile and silly he sounded. How could she calm down?

'You must know something? You were already on the way when I called Alphenlicht!'

'Aghrehond called me, Arti. He left one of his usual enigmatic messages. And Therat had a feeling. She'd been musing over a strange reading from the Cave of Light, and suddenly it came to her that what was usually interpreted as a harmless set of symbols was in fact rather threatening. She and Ellat insisted that all three of us get here as quickly as possible. Until I talked to you from the airport, we had no idea that Marianne and the others had disappeared, but I am sure that it is somehow connected with whatever it is that your aunt Dagma asked Marianne to do.' He reached out to take Arti Zahmani by the shoulders, shaking her gently. 'We can't do any good by going to pieces, now settle down.'

'This whole thing is ridiculous,' Arti cried, barely controlling her hysteria. 'Dagma was asleep when Marianne got here. Marianne had luncheon with us. We talked about all the plans for the baby. Then Dagma woke up, her nurse came down to tell Marianne, and she went up. After about half an hour, Dagma's bell rang, and she asked for Aghrehond! Aghrehond! Why? Then you called, and we looked for him, and they were gone. All of them.' She shivered and began weeping. 'I don't understand it! Haurvatat is ready to kill someone, probably me.'

'Nonsense, Arti. Just because it's mysterious is no reason to believe it's necessarily dangerous. Marianne and the others may be perfectly all right. Have you touched anything in Dagma's room?'

'You said not to, so we didn't. Not after we talked to you.'

'Then let's start there. Will you show me the way?'

'Oh,' she started, coming to herself, the well practiced routines of the hostess for the moment derailing her anxiety. 'Of course, Makr Avehl. I'm sorry. Up here.' She turned to lead the way up the curving stairs and down the wide corridor to the door of Dagma's room.

The room bore evidence of a hasty and cursory search. The covers of the bed were thrown back. The closet doors stood open and hangers were disarrayed, as though someone had looked behind the clothing hanging there. A sheet of thick, creased parchment lay half under the coverlet. On the floor at Makr Avehl's feet was a tiny carved gem and a pair of dice. He picked them up, inspected the dice, grunted and pocketed them while closely examining the tiny animal he had found: a rhinoceros cut from gleaming rose-colored stone. Rhodolite, he told himself, recognizing the color. A rhodolite rhinoceros. 'Ah,' he murmured to himself. 'Interesting. Alliterative. Accidentally, or as part of something very complex? Therat may know. And very fine work to be trodden underfoot. Now why is that?'

He sat heavily upon the bed and turned over the folded sheet, seeing that it was parchment, believing that it was hand drawn. 'Personally drawn,' he corrected himself. 'Who knows if the one who drew it had hands or not.' When he had mused over it for some time while Arti stood at the window — alternately staring at him and staring out, as though the missing ones might materialize upon the lawn or at the end of the drive — he folded the parchment and secreted it in his inside jacket pocket, dropping the carved animal in after it before taking Arti by the hand and leading her downstairs.

'Will you stay to dinner?' Arti asked him. 'I was afraid you were going to disappear, right in front of me.'

'No, no, Arti. Not me. Where's Haurvatat? In the city? Even as upset as he must be?'

'*Because* he's so upset, Makr Avehl. He was sitting around here driving me mad. I told him to go consult someone, anyone, for heaven's sake. Marianne and Dagma and Aghre-hond have been gone for two days now. Well, one day and part of another one. And you know as well as I do that they aren't the only ones. This business of mysterious disappearance is gaining epidemic proportions. My neighbor down the road vanished a week ago Wednesday! And her son and daughter at the same time, only teenagers. A man who serves on a charity board with me disappeared last Sunday! I'm beginning to read about it every day in the newspapers! And it's all around here! Not New York or Chicago or London. No, here, in Virginia! Hundreds of people gone, disappeared, no one knows where.'

'Shh, Arti. Hold it together, dear. We can't do any good by falling apart. Do you have a maid who usually cleans Dagma's room?'

'Yes, of course. Her name is Briggs.'

'May I see her, please?'

The maid, when summoned, proved to be stocky and plain-featured, with an open countenance and a confiding smile. Makr Avehl laid the parchment out on the desk in the library and invited her to look at it. 'Have you seen this before?'

She studied it for the briefest moment. 'It looks like the game my brother's got. I think it's the same. His has little animals to play with. He showed it to me, but I haven't had a chance to play it with him yet . . .'

Makr Avehl showed her the rhinoceros, and she nodded. 'Well, his were that size, but his was a kangaroo, I think, and a bird of some kind and some other things I'd never seen before.'

'How many game pieces?'

'Four, I think.' She furrowed her brow. 'Yes, four.'

'Where did he get the game, do you know?'

'There's a shop that sells them. In the mall. All the kids hang out at the mall. It's a store where they sell records and tapes and posters and games, and there are video games there for them to play, you know.'

'And the name of this place?'

She furrowed her forehead in concentration. 'I've never

479

been in there, but I've passed it. On the upper level, beside the shoe store . . . Cat something. Catfields?'

'Cattermune's,' suggested Makr Avehl, who had noticed the name blazoned on several shopping centers on his way from the airport.

'That's it,' said Briggs, leaning forward to inspect the parchment. 'You know, the one my brother has is on a board, not just paper like this.'

'A more recent issue, likely,' agreed Makr Avehl. 'This may have been the original. I should not be surprised to learn that old Madame Dagma has had it for many years.'

'Oh, she has,' Briggs confirmed. 'I've been here eleven years, and all that time she's kept her handkerchiefs in the top drawer of her bedside table, and whenever she asked me to give her a hanky, I've seen this folded paper under it. It's kind of splotchy, you know. Not exactly all white.'

'That's because it isn't paper.' Makr Avehl smiled at her, thanking her for her observation. 'It's parchment. Skin.'

'Sheepskin, maybe?' asked the maid.

'Something like that,' he agreed, thinking that it was probably something quite unlike that. 'Did you by any chance see the game pieces that went with this?'

The maid shook her head. 'I never did. She had an envelope in that drawer, but I never looked inside it.'

'Well, it's still confirmation of a kind. Thank you, Briggs. You've been very helpful.' He smiled, and the maid went out, shaking her head over it all. 'Now, Arti, forgive me for refusing your kind invitation, but I must tell Ellat and Therat what has happened and then go here and there for the next several hours.'

After a few more tears and protestations, he was allowed to go.

CHAPTER SIXTEEN

At the hotel where Makr Avehl had decided they should stay — believing they would have more freedom of action there than at the Zahmanis — he cleared the phone, a lamp, and assorted cardboard advertisements from the top of the table and spread the parchment game upon it. Ellat sat in one chair with Therat across from her, each of them leaning forward, chin in hand, to examine the twisting lines and labeled squares. Makr Avehl placed the dice upon the parchment and the rhinoceros beside it.

'Notice the dice,' he said.

Ellat stared at them. 'I notice them, Makr Avehl, but I don't know what it is I'm noticing.'

He rolled them over with a finger. 'Dice are usually made so that opposite sides add to seven. The one dot is opposite the six. The five is opposite the two, and the three opposite the four.'

Therat picked them up. 'These add to three, seven, and eleven.'

'Does it mean anything to you?'

'They are numbers used in conjury. Here, let me hold them.' She picked them up, closed her fist, her face knotted in concentration. Suddenly she exclaimed, dropped them shaking her hand. 'By Zurban, Makr Avehl! These are evil things!'

'And the animal?'

She touched the little rhinoceros with a tentative forefinger, shivering at the touch. 'This, too. It is not that the things themselves are evil, rather that the intent for which they were made is evil.'

'They lend themselves?'

'I would say, yes. It would be hard to bend them to a good purpose.'

'Let me tell you what I think happened,' said Makr Avehl. 'Dagma asked Marianne to do something which involved this game. I believe there were originally four game pieces. Animals, probably, or birds. Living things, at any rate. My guess is that they were alliterative, the substance and the shape starting with the same sound . . .'

'To lend force to the enchantment.'

'Yes. I think Marianne, probably without any sense of what would happen, placed a game piece on the parchment and then threw the dice. She vanished.'

'How do you know that?' Ellat asked.

'Because Dagma rang and asked for Aghrehond. If Marianne had wanted him, she would have asked for him herself. If she had been present, she would have asked for him. She didn't. Dagma did. So — what would Aghrehond do?'

'He would enter the game, going after Marianne,' said Ellat definitely. 'You couldn't have stopped him with a large piece of machinery.'

'And Dagma?' asked Therat.

'I think he took her along. For reasons of his own, which, probably, were very good ones. I wish I knew what the three missing game pieces had looked like, but I don't.'

'But you wouldn't want to . . .' mused Ellat.

'I would not want to use Cattermune's game pieces. I don't think.'

'Cattermune?'

'Look, there on the parchment. Cattermune's House. Cattermune's Pique. Cattermune's Worm Pits. Then think. How many "Cattermune's" did we see on our way here.'

'The London airport,' said Ellat.

'The Washington airport,' said Therat. 'And there were those two shopping centers we passed.' The three of them stared at one another, puzzled. 'A connection, Makr Avehl?'

'Have you ever heard the name before this week?'

'No.'

'And now, everywhere?'

'It does seem unlikely.'

'It seems unlikely by accident, yes. It is not at all unlikely as part of a plan. Besides which, the maid, Briggs, says her little brother purchased a similar game at Cattermune's. I would say a plan. A conspiracy.'

'A plan to what?'

'To disappear a great many people. And don't ask me for what reason, Ellat. I don't know.'

'What are you going to do?'

'I'm going to do what Aghrehond did, go in after them.'

'I don't think you can,' said Therat, running her fingers over the parchment. 'I don't think anyone can.'

'What do you mean?' Makr Avehl put his own hands on the parchment, trying to feel whatever it was she was feeling. There was nothing.

'It feels dead,' she said. 'Turned off. Not like the dice or the little animal.'

'Turned off?' asked Ellat. 'Therat, what are you talking about.'

Therat flushed. 'I can feel − connections. I've always been able to. If I put my hand on a woman's shoulder and she is in love with someone, I can feel a kind of current running out of her toward the person she loves. Like a pulse. A vibration. If you hand me a letter someone has written, even though it's in a sealed envelope, if that person is anywhere near, I can feel the connection. It feels like a circuit, like something flowing. If the person who wrote the letter is dead, the letter feels dead.'

'And this parchment feels dead?'

'It feels like its connections have been turned off.'

'Hmph,' growled Makr Avehl. 'Since when? Therat, will you call the papers and the police and ask if anyone has disappeared in this strange fashion since − what is today?'

'Wednesday.'

'Since . . . since Monday afternoon.'

'When Marianne disappeared?'

'When Marianne and Dagma and Aghrehond disappeared.'

He got up and stalked about the room, scowling, eyes squinted

483

almost shut. 'Connections. Maybe that was what it was about. What did the Cave of Light say again, Therat? Roads? Ropes? Something like that?'

'Exactly like that.'

'Something had established a connection. And something that Marianne did broke it.'

'Not at once,' said Therat. 'Not if your theory about what happened is true, because Dagma and Aghrehond still went.'

'Maybe what Marianne did to break it didn't happen all at once,' he said. 'Maybe it happened after she disappeared. Maybe it happened when she moved to a certain . . . to a certain place in the game.' He turned, stared at the parchment, and put his right forefinger on the square marked 'Cattermune's House.' 'When she got there,' he said. 'I can feel it.'

'Which means?'

'Which means I'll have to get in there on my own. Using my own dice. And my own game piece, too. Which is fortunate. I really didn't fancy being a rhinoceros.'

'They're quite short-sighted, aren't they?' asked Ellat in an annoyingly meaningful voice.

'Quite,' he snarled, 'Not that I've been exactly clairvoyant about this whole thing.'

'Don't blame yourself, Makr Avehl,' said Therat. 'If anyone's to blame, it's I. I should have . . .'

'We all should have. But we didn't. So let's remedy the situation now. Ellat, will you go get a taxi and go to that Cattermune's place we passed on the way here. Buy one of these games and bring it back. I think we already know what we will find, but it won't hurt to double check. Meantime — I need to find a jeweler.'

Makr Avehl needed go no farther than the lobby of the hotel to find a most prestigious shop, a name he recognized as being identified anywhere in the world with fabulous objects of great value.

The jeweler peered at the tiny rhinoceros through his loupe, making admiring noises. 'Beautifully done. The detail! Almost miscroscopic.'

484

'Is there anyone you know who can . . .'

'Duplicate this?' He put down the loupe and thought, pulling on one earlobe to assist the process of thought. 'One man, possibly. Actually, he does most of his carving in jade, and the pieces I've seen are a good deal larger than this. Some of the details he does on the large carvings — blossoms, or insects on a branch — are no larger than this, though, and they're equally well done.'

'Is he local?'

'Well, yes, in a way. He's Chinese, but he's lived here for a decade or more. Won Sin is his name. He has a shop in the fourteen hundred block of Cleveland Street.' When Makr Avehl left, rather hurriedly, the merchant was still exclaiming about the little rhinoceros.

Makr Avehl found the Precious Stone Tree, a tiny shop in a quiet neighborhood of no particular distinction. He found the owner, the owner's wife, and the owner's eleven half-grown and fully grown children occupied in various craftish endeavors concerned with carving stone and gems and what looked suspiciously like illegal ivory but was said, by Mrs Won, to be an artificial substance.

Makr Avehl put the rhinoceros on the counter. Thirteen pairs of eyes fastened upon it.

'Quite remarkable,' said Won Sin, with no accent at all.

'I need . . .' began Makr Avehl, then stopped, for the moment uncertain.

'Yes,' prompted the carver.

'I need a carving, of about this size, of the fiercest animal in the universe.'

'Oh, my,' said Mrs Won. 'A tiger, do you think?'

'Is that the fiercest?'

'Mythological animals are acceptable?' asked Won Sin. 'If so, what about a chimera.'

'Not, I think, a chimera,' said Makr Avehl with a reminiscent smile. 'No. Not nearly fierce enough. Too given to committee decisions and involuntary introspection.'

'Ah.' The carver smiled a secret smile. 'So, you have had experiences with chimerae.'

'One, at least. A manticore won't do, either.' He frowned, remembering a manticore.

'Griffin? Wyvern? Rok?'

'A dragon,' said one of the younger children. 'A Chinese dragon.'

'Not fierce enough,' commented another. 'You would need a Western dragon, one with wings, who spouts fire out of his nose.'

'A dragon might do,' said Makr Avehl in sudden thought. 'I happen to have something with me that might make a dragon a good choice. A particularly fierce dragon. I like the idea of fire coming out of the nose, too. How long would it take you to make one?'

'Out of what?'

'Out of something I have in my pocket that starts with a D. I have here a rhodolite rhinoceros. I imagine elsewhere in these games there are emerald emus and sapphire serpents. I am assuming alliteracy, on the basis of . . . well, magical requirements.'

'Diamond is too hard,' offered Won Sin.

'I have the stone,' said Makr Avehl. He reached deep into one pocket and pulled it out, a roughly oval black stone, gleaming as with an internal light.

'What is it?' the carver asked. 'It looks like obsidian. Except that the light in it is red instead of gold.'

'It is a demon's gall stone,' said Makr Avehl. 'Demons are frequently afflicted with a surfeit of gall, more often with that complaint than with any other. It is why, in many cases, they are so demonic.'

'How did you get it?' asked one of the little ones.

'I had need of a demon, then I had need to send him away. When the demon went, this was left,' said Makr Avehl. 'And since I need something starting with a D, a demon's gall stone will do well enough. How long will it take?'

'A day,' said the carver. 'Using my power tools. If I do nothing else.'

'Please,' said Makr Avehl, piling money on the counter. 'I would be deeply grateful if you would do nothing else.'

CHAPTER SEVENTEEN

'I wish we were doing something,' Ellat fumed. 'Marianne is gone, heaven knows what is happening to her, and here we sit, dillying.'

'I am not dillying,' said Makr Avehl in as patient a voice as he could manage. 'Listen, Ellat, there is a villain out there. A most horribly noxious but subtle villain. His name, for lack of a better and because it has become ubiquitous, is Cattermune. I think it is no coincidence that this chain of game stores springs up and at the same time people begin to disappear. It is no coincidence that we find this game in a place where Marianne and Dagma and the faithful Aghrehond have just vanished from. You've been to a Cattermune store. You brought back a game, the same game, and Therat says it, too, is dead. The dice that came with it are those strange dice. The game pieces are all alliterative little animals. Ruby rats and chalcedony chickens. Bloodstone bats and garnet geese. Little animals which disappear when their players do. So, and so, Ellat, I, too, will disappear . . .'

'Makr Avehl,' she wailed. 'I wish you didn't have to do it, not again.'

'What can I do when my beloved has gone off in this mysterious way? Can I leave her there, wherever she may be? At the mercy of this Cattermune. Can I leave this Cattermune in peace, to continue his depredations? No, of course not. I must go. But I will not use this game piece which was made by Cattermune. No. I will use another, made of something violent and strange which belongs to me. I will go in a guise that suits myself. Besides, you were right about rhinoceri being very shortsighted with disablingly bad tempers. I will need to be far more subtle than that.'

'And I will help you,' said Therat. 'I am ashamed of myself.

I should have caught the strangeness of the reading in the Cave of Light. The vacancy. It meant nothing to me then. Now, well . . .'

'You've blamed yourself quite enough,' said Makr Avehl. 'Who knows what higher purpose may be achieved through your failure.'

'I don't like it,' said Therat through gritted teeth. 'Failure! I don't like it at all.'

'Bear up, Therat,' rumbled Makr Avehl. 'Bear up and turn your considerable talents to making our dragon invincible.'

'How would you suggest?' asked Ellat.

'I would suggest a few spells and invocations,' Makr Avehl responded. 'I would suggest asking a few of Marianne's friends from among the momentary gods for assistance. I would suggest a guidance reading from the Cave of Light, conducted by you, Therat, by long-distance phone. See whether it tells us the same thing now that it told you before. I would suggest some protection spells done by you, Ellat. Does this give you any ideas?'

Both of the women flushed, admitting that it did.

'Then get with it,' Makr Avehl suggested. 'While I do some thinking of my own.'

Thereafter, Makr Avehl meditated. Ellat burned incense and spoke persuasively to the powers and confusions. Therat called her fellow Kavi in Alphenlicht and asked for a reading. Some hours went by. Evening came. They ate and slept and began doing the same things again.

'Have the Kavi any help to offer?' Makr Avehl asked of Therat as he unwrapped the tiny package which had just been delivered.

'There have been confirming readings twice in succession. An anchor, a rope, a road on the first session. A bridge, a chain, a gateway on the second. There can be only one interpretation.'

'A way to travel between two points,' said Ellat promptly.

'A tie between two points,' said Makr Avehl. 'The anchor, the chains, the bridge, the line. Things that fasten two places together.'

'Things that permit passage between two places,' amended

488

Therat. 'During the last reading the gateway was marked with a death's head; the road went by a cemetery.'

'Oof,' said Makr Avehl. 'Passage between two places, this place and some other not-so-nice place? What kind of creature will this Cattermune be?'

'I'd like to know what Marianne's great-aunt Dagma could have done that got her involved with this Cattermune.'

'Involved she was, whether purposely or by accident. And not happy about it, I should think. That was what Dagma wanted. She wanted Marianne to do something about this linkage, whatever it is,' Ellat sighed.

'Which Marianne either tried to do or not. If not, she was simply caught and vanished, as hundreds of others seem to have been caught and vanished. Which changes nothing, so far as I can see. I still have to go, and here is my game piece.'

He unfolded the last piece of tissue paper and disclosed what had been wrapped in it. A dragon, neck curved and front claw raised, tail stretched behind into a sinuous line, wings half unfurled. The red glow within the stone made it appear to be on fire, and Makr Avehl nodded his head.

A note had been enclosed with the dragon. 'My family has taken the liberty of invoking some help for you,' it said. It was signed by Won Sin in a splash of ideographs which looked very much like dragon tracks. Makr Avehl read it, half smiling, then put it away with a sigh.

'There's no point in delay is there? Do you have the dice, Therat?'

'Two to use here, and eight identical-looking ones to take with you, Makr Avehl. All ten of them loaded as you asked. You can throw any number you need to.'

He took them from her, threw each one to see how it rolled, then carefully separated two from the eight others, which he pocketed, remarking as he did so, 'I will go to Cattermune's House. I will see if I can find Marianne. If I cannot, I will find out anything I can about Marianne, then go elsewhere as needs must.' He spread the parchment out on the table in front of him and placed the dragon in the space marked 'Start Here.' 'Is there anything else you can think of?'

'Watch out for Cattermune,' said Therat.

Makr Avehl sighed. 'I had intended to do so.'

'What do we tell Marianne's parents?' asked Ellat.

'As little as possible,' Therat answered. 'He'll either have her back very soon or . . .'

She didn't finish the statement but all three of them knew what she meant. Makr Avehl would either have the vanished ones back fairly soon, or he wouldn't bring them — or himself — back at all. Makr Avehl nodded once and swallowed rather hard, then muttering the opening enchantment which he hoped would get him into the game and concentrating very hard on Cattermune's House, he threw a six.

CHAPTER EIGHTEEN

And found himself rolling into a vast, funereal courtyard in a capacious gilded coach which swayed and thumped with every turn of its wheels. Out one side window he could see red-lit fountains, out of the other, black cypresses and hedges of dark yew and tree peonies laden with darkly scarlet bloom. The pavement beneath the carriage wheels was black, polished to a leaden glimmer, over which the wind chased red petals as though toying with drops of blood.

'Cattermune's,' said the driver, climbing down from his high perch to open the door. 'You here for his birthday fete tonight or for the celebratory hunt tomorrow?'

'Both,' said Mondragon, wiping traces of road dust from his lips and returning his handkerchief to his cuff. 'I have an invitation somewhere . . .'

'No matter. Here come the footmen now, so it looks as though you're expected.'

Indeed, a flurry of footmen had come out of the door and

490

were scurrying across the pavement to gather Mondragon's luggage, of which he seemed to have an exorbitant quantity.

'Careful, oaf!' he demanded, as one of the pallid footmen allowed the stacked cases to totter. 'Cattermune's birthday gift is in there. He won't thank you if it's broken!'

The footman turned, if anything, slightly paler.

'What's your name, my man?' said Mondragon in a more friendly tone.

'Green, sir.'

'Green, eh. Something familiar about you, Green. Do you remember seeing me before?'

'You have a very distinctive face, sir. It does seem familiar, but I couldn't say where we might have encountered one another.'

'I know we have, Green. Would you by any chance have a friend named Marianne?'

'Mary Ann? The wet nurse? Funny you should mention her, sir. Why, I saw her just today.'

'And Dagma?'

'I'm afraid I don't know any Dagma, sir.'

'Hmm. Mrs Zahmani?'

'Mrs Smani? The layette seamstress. Now how would you have known about her?'

Mondragon intercepted an angry and suspicious look from a liveried supervisor who was hovering in the background. 'She was in service with my family. They both were. Come, now. Gather up my bags. Can't stand here all night.' Folding the great, winglike panels of his cape around him, Mondragon followed the footman into the great hall. So, Aghrehond didn't know him. Which meant that Marianne wouldn't know him either. Difficult to make contact under those circumstances, he thought. He thought so even more after several members of the Cattermune family had introduced themselves to him, taking his long, agile hand in their own short, fat ones, tickling his palm with their curved fingernails, smiling with sharp teeth at his polite greetings, their whiskers twitching, only slightly. The women couldn't really be said to have whiskers. Only the tiniest hint of whiskers. Freckles at the corners of their mouths from which the finest gossamer protruded, visible only in certain lights. But they all had the Cattermune teeth. Mondragon smiled and nodded, bowed and murmured, before escaping to follow the footman up the wide sweep of stairs to an upper hall.

'Your room is just down here, sir,' said Green. He and another footman had carried up the baggage. Now the other footman bowed himself away as Green opened the door and began carrying the cases inside to dispose them about the room. 'Will you be wanting me to unpack for you, sir?'

'Just those two,' Mondragon said, indicating two cases. 'The others are for . . .' What in heaven's name was all this luggage for? 'For later journeys and eventualities.' He went to the window and looked out across the courtyard, letting his eyes drift up the façade which confronted him. Story after story, window after window. A movement at one of the third-floor windows caught his eye. Pale faces there. He turned and fumbled in one of the open cases, returning to the window with a pair of binoculars.

'Green,' he said. 'Tell me who that is.'

Green came to stand beside him at the window. Mondragon passed him the glasses, pointing.

'Oh, that's Mary Ann, sir. The wet nurse for the Cattermune infants.'

'She had a child of her own, then?' Mondragon growled in his throat, thinking of the threat to the child, of not being there when the child was born.

'Oh, not yet, sir. No. Soon, probably. We are all assured the Cattermune's young wife will be having her own very soon. The woman with Mary Ann is Mrs Smani, the layette seamstress.'

'There are three women there.'

Green put the glasses back to his eyes. 'The other one is the nursery maid, sir. Fanetta. They would be in the nursery maid's room. When we had . . . when we had supper together last night, she mentioned having a room which faced the courtyard.'

'She is pregnant,' said Mondragon.

'The Cattermune's young wife? She is indeed, sir, to the consternation of some members of the family, I'm told.'

'I don't mean Cattermune's anybody. I mean that girl, Mary Ann.'

'Oh, yes, sir. Unmistakably. Quite, ah, rotund.'

'I would like to meet her,' whispered Mondragon.

'Oh, sir. Quite improper.' Green's words were belied by his expression, which was full of unconscious surmise.

'I know that. Therefore, we won't do anything precipitant, will we, Green. No. I know I can trust you. Meet me here, tonight, after the birthday dinner. We'll talk about it then.'

CHAPTER NINETEEN

From the high window in Fanetta's room, Mary Ann continued to stare down at the window in which she had just seen a face. Not only a face, but a face looking at her — a face which had used glasses to look at her more closely.

She was interrupted in this pastime by sounds from the nursery hallway, thumpings and loud expostulations issued in a hard, baritone voice with unmistakably metallic tones in it. Fanetta opened her door, peeked out, then shut it, leaned against it, and said in a terrified voice, 'It's the nanny. The Cattermune nanny has arrived.'

The door vibrated to a thunderous knocking and the sound of the metallic voice. 'Fanetta! Fanetta, I know you're in there, so don't play silly games. Come out here at once and bring the others with you.'

Gulping, smoothing her apron, wiping away tears which had appeared at the corners of her eyes, Fanetta complied. Waiting for them in the hall was an enormous woman of uncertain age clad in the ritual garb of nannies: a dark suit, impeccably brushed, with a watch-pin upon the lapel; a snowy white shirtwaist; sensible dark shoes and stockings; and a flat straw hat set squarely upon her head. She carried an umbrella with which she now poked the terrified nursery maid, making her squeak in fear.

'So, Fanetta! What have you been up to, eh? Sedition and sneakery, no doubt. Crawling about through the walls?'

'Only down to kitchen and back, Nanny.'

'Well, there'll be no more of that! You,' she fixed Mary Ann with a cruel, hard stare. 'When is your baby coming?'

'I'm not exactly sure,' whispered Mary Ann, as terrified as Fanetta obviously was. 'Soon.'

'It had better be soon. Cattermune's young wife is due to kindle anytime now. Could be tomorrow.'

'I don't think that soon,' Mary Ann cried in panic. 'Not nearly that soon.'

'You,' the nanny said, poking Mrs Smani in her turn. 'How many layettes are finished?'

'All the crib sheets, Nanny. I did them yesterday. I'm working on the nightgowns now.'

'You are not,' said the nanny. 'You are lolly-gagging about in Fanetta's room, doing nothing. Watching your betters, no doubt. Wishing you were Cattermunes so you could ride about in carriages, going to birthday parties.'

'Yes, ma'am,' 'No, ma'am,' said Mary Ann and Mrs Smani simultaneously.

'I suggest you get on with your work. You' − she poked Mary Ann once more − 'since you have nothing to do at the moment, could assist Fanetta in cleaning the nursery. She slacks. I know she slacks.' The enormous woman turned and stalked away, entering a room down the hall, as Fanetta whimpered slightly.

Mary Ann, musing, was reminded of someone else. 'Nurseys,' she whispered to herself. 'Constabulary Nurseys.'

'What did you say?' begged Fanetta. 'What about Nurseys?'

'I don't quite know,' remarked Mary Ann. 'Except that the nanny reminds me of them. I must have encountered them somewhere. Before. Before I came here. It's hard to remember.'

'I know,' sobbed Fanetta. 'It's always hard to remember

in Cattermune's House. Lots of people can't, or don't. I remember because I've been back and forth so many times, you see, and I wrote it all down on the bottom of my bureau drawers, so all I have to think of when I come to Cattermune's is to read the bottom of my bureau drawers, and I have that written on my knee. Once you remember, everything is much clearer.'

'What did you write? Where?' begged Mary Ann.

'All about the game, and the game squares, and where everything is, and where the junctions are from here.'

'But how did you remember that first time?' asked Mrs Smani eagerly. 'We're here for the first time, and we don't remember. How did you remember?'

'Groff has a rememberer. Every now and then they use it on somebody, to find out who they really are, you know? Every now and then the Cattermune will tell Groff to use it on somebody. All I did was, I was cleaning his room — there weren't any babies in the nursery that time, so they had me working upstairs — so I used it on myself.'

'And who are you?' asked Mrs Smani.

'Fanny Farroway of Seattle, Washington,' said Fanetta with a faraway look. 'Caught into the game on the fifth of April, 1982. I was a dental technician. It's all written down on the bottom of my underwear drawers. And on my knee, in indelible ink, I've written, "Read the bottom of your drawers." I have to keep renewing that, of course, because it wears off.'

'I wonder who I am,' murmured Mary Ann. 'I wonder who you are, Mrs Smani, and who Green is and who that man is who looked at me in such a strange way.'

'He's probably a Cattermune,' said Fanetta. 'If he's a guest, he's probably a Cattermune.'

'Buttercup is going to be a guest, and she's not a Cattermune, is she?'

'Next thing to it,' murmured Fanetta.

'You there!' came the imperious voice. 'I told you to get busy.' The nanny stood in her doorway, glaring through rimless spectacles and threatening them with her umbrella.

The three of them fled, Mrs Smani to her sewing machine and Mary Ann with Fanetta to the nursery, where they began to dust and sweep the already spotless furniture and floors.

'Why do these cribs have tops on them?' whispered Mary Ann.

'To keep the Cattermune children from eating one another,' whispered Fanetta in return.

'Why does the crib in my room have a top on it?' cried Mary Ann, with a half-suppressed shriek.

'To keep them from eating your baby,' Fanetta replied. 'Which they will do, if they get the chance. Last time I was here, the wet nurse had twins, and the Cattermunes ate them both. The wet nurse dried up from grief and they made a binker of her.'

'Oh, by blessed Moomaw,' said Mary Ann, holding her bulging stomach. 'What dreadful place have I got myself into.'

'Cattermune's House, is all,' said Fanetta. 'And if you think that's bad, you ought to see some of the other places I've been.'

CHAPTER TWENTY

A manservant, not Green, arrived to help Mondragon dress for dinner. Cocktails, he said, would be served at the first bell. The second bell would be struck ten minutes before dinner was served, just time to get down to the drawing rooms. If Mondragon had brought a gift, it could be put with the others in the library.

'Green asked me to tell you, sir. It would be wise to avoid the meat pie.'

'Thank Green for me. I always avoid meat pie. So anonymous, don't you think? Meat pie and mince meat and paté. So subject to abuse.'

'Exactly Green's thought, my lord.'

'Not "my lord," ' said Mondragon abstractedly. 'I may be addressed as "Your Excellency." '

The manservant, a lean and pallid creature given to sudden twitches and starts, bowed. 'Green also said, Your Excellency, that he would see to that small matter of yours following dinner.' The speaker did not look precisely human, Mondragon thought. Not precisely. Something about the face was odd. Also, there was something repellently obsequious in his tone.

Still, he replied politely. 'Thank Green again.'

'May I say, Your Excellency, that if Green is ever unavailable to take care of Your Excellency's needs, you have only to ask for me. I would be happy to . . .'

'And what is your name?'

'Sneeth, sir. John Henry Sneeth. I was at one time in service to Her Majesty, Queen Buttercup the First.' A strange expression, half terror, half pride, flitted across the creature's face. 'The Guest of Honor at Cattermune's fete. She arrived just moments ago.'

'So we are to see Her Majesty at this celebration?'

The expression again, this time with terror predominating. 'She came down the highway through the Moomaw Incisive and the Inquisitive Galosh, crossing Cattermune's Pique on the causeway, which he had fenced off for the occasion.'

'Cattermune's Pique?'

'Where the hunt takes place, sir. Where they . . . where they always release the binkers. For the hunt. The Queen will take part in the hunt. Of course. Tomorrow.'

Mondragon started to ask, 'Binkers?' then changed his mind. Something in Sneeth's voice indicated that it might be better not to ask. Still, he tucked the word away, waiting to hear it again in a context which might explain it.

Mondragon's partner for dinner was a Cattermune cousin, Eulalienne Cattermune, she told him, of the highland Cattermunes. She was inquisitive and predacious, but Mondragon managed to keep her talking about herself rather than inquiring about him, though her curiosity was evident. Looking about,

Mondragon could understand why. He was one of very few non-Cattermunes, and none of the others looked precisely human. They, like the creature Sneeth, seemed to have something wrong with them.

'So this is the big banquet,' he smiled. 'Cattermune's birthday.'

'At last,' she grinned, pointed teeth showing at the corner of her mouth. 'No more worries about supplies. Plenty of good hunting from now on.'

'Binkers,' he smiled.

She gave him a glance of startled attention.

'One hears things,' he shook his head.

'You're no Cattermune, so I wouldn't talk of binkers,' she purred, pointed teeth showing at the corners of her mouth.

'Inappropriate of me,' he said.

'Rather. Yes.'

'But still, such a very elegant affair. And Queen Buttercup is here!'

'Grisls,' she sneered. 'I claim we're not related at all, though the Cattermune says we are a kind of cousin to that line. Still, she's seated down there on the Cattermune's right. The man on Cattermune's left is the surviving son and heir − not counting what the wife will produce. Rather throws a rock into the machinery, that.'

'Um,' nodded Mondragon, around a mouthful of something safely vegetable. There was a good deal of cheerful laughter at the table, resulting at least partly from much drinking of wine. 'Will we have an opportunity to meet her?'

'After dinner. Or tomorrow, at the hunt.' Eulalienne seemed to have lost interest in him, turning to her neighbor on the other side with some laughing remark.

Mondragon became inconspicuous, taking every opportunity to examine the features of Queen Buttercup and those of the Cattermune.

The Grisl Queen had a triangular face, mouth and chin coming to a point in front from which a long, ivory fang depended. The fang moved with the jaw. She looked much less human than Sneeth, and yet not precisely inhuman.

No less than the Cattermunes, who also looked rather human. Bipedal, bimanual, eyes, ears, noses, and mouths in the right places, facial expressions quite readable. The Queen was delighted to be here. One could see it in every gesture.

The brooding hulk which was the Cattermune was not so obviously pleased. Furry brows curled over dark eyes which seemed to see everyone, everything. As though aware of Mondragon's scrutiny, the Cattermune darted a glance down the table and Mondragon dropped his eyes to his plate, pretending to say something to his neighbor. The Cattermune's glance went by him like a laser, visibly hot.

A chinkling of glassware brought his attention back to the head of the table where the Cattermune's eldest son stood up and grinned voraciously at the other guests. 'Honored guests!' he cried. 'Friends! Family! A toast to my father – *our Cattermune!*'

'Hear, hear,' thundered the Cattermunes.

'Tonight at midnight, he will have successfully concluded a coup which has been a generation in the making.'

'Hooray,' yowled the Cattermunes, striking their wine glasses with their spoons.

'It was a generation ago that our Cattermune, braving dangers which we cannot even conceive of, traveled to the World Outside and established there – The Connection!'

'Hooraw for The Connection,' the diners cried, echoed by their guests and the servants lined along the walls.

'The only Connection,' continued the toastmaster. 'The One Connection. Purchased at a terrible price and totally irreplaceable.'

The large figure at the head of the table smiled grimly, nodding in agreement.

'And since that time, how many hundreds – nay – thousands of participants have traveled The Connection and become part of Cattermune's Game!'

'Binkers,' cried a drunken young Cattermune male, possibly a feckless nephew. 'Binkers and the hunt!'

The toastmaster lifted his glass in acknowledgement. 'And

binkers, of course. Now, you all know what great occasions tonight and tomorrow are.'

' 'Ray! Wonderful night. Whoopee,' cried the diners.

'Tonight, The Connection becomes *permanent*!'

Wild cheers and outcries. Mondragon, paying close attention, waved his hands with the rest as he adopted an expression of feigned delight.

'Thereafter, it may not be dislodged. The location of The Connection has been checked by yours truly. I went there a week ago. The anchor is in place. Nothing threatens it. I invite you all to rise and drink to — the Cattermune!'

Chairs scraped. Some fell over backward, propelled by the enthusiasm of those who rose, waving their wine glasses, caterwauling, 'The Cattermune.' 'Long live the Cattermune,' and other such sentiments. Out of the corner of his right eye, Mondragon saw that Eulalienne Cattermune was watching him closely over the rim of her glass. He gave her a drunkenly lecherous grin and appeared to gulp deeply from his own glass. She returned his lecherous expression with one of her own. Well, no help for it. He counterfeited drunkenness, then increasing physical distress, and between the next two courses he excused himself hastily and slipped away as inconspicuously as possible while Eulalienne stared sullenly after him.

As he went through the reception hall, he saw a gray-haired Cattermune arguing hotly with one of the butlers.

'I must see him now! It's an emergency.'

'You must be quite mad. They're in the middle of the birthday dinner!'

'I must see him. I'm the immigration master. It's my responsibility. The Cattermune must be told what's happened.'

'After dessert,' sniffed the butler. 'I'll tell him you're here.'

Mondragon didn't linger. Green would be waiting for him. Probably. If Green had not attracted some suspicion. If Green could get away.

And Green had somehow managed it.

'The under-butler kept watching me,' he murmured from

his place behind Mondragon's door, taken, so he said, so that he could hide in a moment if necessary. 'There's a sneak down there in the servant's quarters. A sneak named Sneeth, I'll warrant. A slimy sort.'

'Not human,' suggested Mondragon.

'Why, no,' Green agreed with surprise. 'Come to think of it, I don't believe he is.'

'And no more are the Cattermunes,' Mondragon suggested again. 'Are they?'

'I'd never thought of it,' said the large-bellied man, shaking his head in amazement. 'Isn't that strange. I remember arriving here among them, with Mary Ann and Mrs Smani, but until this moment, I never considered where here was or what they were. How very strange.'

'Your real name is Aghrehond,' said Mondragon. 'My real name is Makr Avehl. Mary Ann's name is, indeed, Marianne, and Mrs Smani is Dagma Zahmani, Marianne's great-aunt. Does any of that mean anything at all to you?'

Green-Aghrehond's face wrinkled in concentration. 'I have no sense of disbelief,' he said at last. 'Though nothing going on in my head at this moment confirms that what you say is true.'

'Damn,' said Mondragon-Makr Avehl. 'And I suppose Marianne will know no more than you?'

'I consider it unlikely, sir.'

'Please, don't sir me. Simply be quiet for a moment and let me think.' Which Mondragon did, furiously, considering alternatives of action. Suspicion had already been aroused. He could not wait any longer to act. 'Can you take me to Marianne? Or, better yet, can you bring her and Mrs Smani here?'

Green shook his head worriedly. 'They're in the nursery. It's another wing of the house altogether. There are ways through the walls, but I don't know how to get there from here and there's no one I could ask. Fanetta knows the way, of course. She may be in the kitchen this time of night, and I do know the way to the kitchen. Come to think of it, I've seen the entrance from the kitchen that they use when they return to the nursery. Perhaps I could find my way from there.'

'There would be no reason for a guest to go to the kitchens, would there?'

'You could be a footman. A new footman. They come and go all the time. With most of the Cattermunes still at dinner, we might make it if we hurry.'

'We would need the livery.'

'That Sneeth is about your size.'

'True. And did offer his services.'

Mondragon turned to the bellpull, and when a maid tapped at his door a moment later, he asked her to find Sneeth. Green was, meantime, busy tearing up pillow cases.

Sneeth arrived with suspicious promptness. He was indeed about Mondragon's size, though less robust. Still, in a pinch, the clothing would do. Green sat upon him while Mondragon gagged him, stripped him of his livery, tied him securely, and deposited him in the wardrobe. When Mondragon put the clothing on, Sneeth's inhumanness became even more apparent. The proportions of the trousers and coat were subtly wrong, and Mondragon found himself walking in a high-crotched spidery sidle that was totally unlike his usual stride.

They went down a back staircase and through a network of hallways, standing aside, politely heads down, whenever any of the upper servants came by. There was another staircase, narrower halls, then a doorway opening into a shabby, low-ceilinged room with long tables and battered chairs. 'The staff dining room,' said Green, eyes darting from side to side. Except for a huge woman who was loudly slurping soup at one of the tables, the room was empty.

'She's not here?' murmured Mondragon. The woman at the table could not be the Fanetta he had seen through his glasses. 'Who's that?'

'I don't know,' mumbled Green in return. 'I've never seen her before. As I said, they come and go. Sometimes one doesn't see the same faces twice!'

'Where's the door you mentioned?'

'Out along the kitchen wall, in a little side corridor.'

'We'd be noticed if we went now.' It was true. The kitchen was having a momentary hiatus. The next course stood upon a side table, ready to go up. Washers were scrubbing pans in desultory fashion. Chief cooks sat on high stools, chatting together. 'Wait until the next course leaves the kitchen, and we'll try it then.'

Mondragon sat down, leaning casually on the table while Green fetched two cups of tea from the buffet. The large woman fixed them with an incredulous stare and sniffed audibly before saying, 'You are on your legitimate break time, I presume.'

Mondragon gave her a haughty look. 'Who are you, madam?'

'I am the Cattermune nanny. And you?'

'Green, ma'am. And Sneeth. Yes, ma'am. On our break. We'll be only a few moments.'

As they sipped the tepid tea, a burst of noise came from the kitchen, cries of disbelief, the crash of broken crockery. The nanny darted to the door with Mondragon and Green close behind. 'It's true,' an under-butler was exclaiming. 'I was in the dining room when the immigration manager came to tell the Cattermune! There've been no immigrants for some time.'

'What does it mean?' cried a cook, his high, puffy hat flopping to and fro as he twisted his head about, seeking information. 'That there have been no immigrants?'

'There's talk the anchor has come loose,' the under-butler mumbled, casting a hasty look behind him as though afraid to be heard uttering this heresy. 'That The Connection is broken.'

'Surely not?'

'It couldn't be!'

'The Cattermune put it there personally.'

'I thought it was permanently in place.'

'Not until midnight tonight. Midnight it would have been permanent. If it had still been there.'

'The Cattermune will be furious.'

'They'll be binkering everyone . . .'

'Now,' whispered Mondragon. 'In all the confusion.' He followed Green along the wall of the kitchen and into the side corridor. A little door opened upon darkness and they slipped within, though not before Mondragon cast a look behind him to find the Cattermune nanny staring after them, her mouth half open.

'Hurry,' cried Mondragon. 'The nanny saw us.'

'I am hurrying, sir, but it's pitch-dark in here.'

'I had thought it might be,' said Mondragon, taking a flashlight from his pocket. 'I seem to have come very well prepared. Ellat's doing, no doubt. Or Therat's. I have no doubt that if we needed an inflatable boat or a pair of trained yaks, we would find them in the luggage. Which way?'

'I haven't the slightest notion,' said Green, peering at the stairs that split into three before him.

'Hello?' came a tentative hail from above. 'Who's down there?'

'Fanetta?' cried Green. 'Is that you?'

'Green? Who's with you?'

'Somebody who wants to see Mary Ann.'

'She's here, with me. So's Mrs Smani.'

'Thank whatever,' said Mondragon, climbing steadily toward the voice. He found the three women huddled on a narrow landing.

'Have you heard?' begged Fanetta. 'One of the maids came to tell me. The Cattermune will be furious. He'll be making binkers right and left. I told Mary Ann we had to get out of the nursery and hide.'

'The nanny saw us come in here,' said Mondragon.

'Oh, by the Galosh's pet plaice! We'll have to get off these stairs or she'll find us sure. Come along after me,' and Fanetta dashed off down a winding mouse tunnel, so narrow and low that Mondragon had to stoop and Green grunted as he squeezed himself around and through the corners and turns. They climbed, descended, then made several turns to arrive at last in a small roomlike space with a bench along one wall.

'Be very quiet,' murmured Fanetta. 'We're just outside the dining room.'

'Is there a hole?' whispered Mondragon. 'We need to know what's going on.'

Laying her fingers across her lips, Fanetta held her candle to the wall to disclose two eyeholes with a shutter latch to one side. 'Slide that and they'll open,' she whispered. 'You'll be looking right out of the eyes of the portrait of Gormdab Cattermune.'

He slid the latch to one side. Dim light came through the two holes before he pressed his eyes to them and peered down into the dining room he had left less than an hour before. No one seemed to be present except Cattermunes. Some stood on chairs, yowling. Others scratched the walls in a fury, leaving long claw marks in the silk brocade.

'How!' howled the Cattermune. 'I ask you, how?'

The person of whom this question was asked was the gray-haired Cattermune that Mondragon had seen in the entry hall. He had a long, lugubrious face and a large, bumpy head which he shook slowly from side to side. 'I don't know and it isn't my doing and not my fault. I've said and I've said. Nobody came through for a long time, and I thought it was just — oh, maybe a war or something happening there to keep them from playing the game, you know. Not that it would stop them for long. But then, time went on and nobody came, so I ran a test on The Connection. Closed. Shut tight. No way through. They couldn't get into the game if they tried.'

'With the anchor in the World Outside, it couldn't happen!' screamed the Cattermune.

'Then the anchor isn't there anymore, and that's all there is to it,' said the lugubrious one.

Mondragon slid the shutter closed and turned to Marianne. 'Marianne, my dearest, did you bring anything with you when you came?'

'Dearest?' she faltered. 'Have we met?'

'Damn,' he said, not for the first time. 'I am Mondr — I am Makr Avehl, your husband. You are Marianne, my wife. This lady is Dagma Zahmani, your great-aunt. And we desperately need to know if you brought anything with you when you came.'

'She wouldn't remember,' said Fanetta. 'None of us do. I don't know how you do, but none of us do. Except for me, of course, but that was just once.'

'Ah.' Mondragon ground his teeth together. 'Tell me about the once, dear girl. How did you manage it?'

'Old Groff has a rememberer,' she said. 'I sneaked it once and used it on me.'

'And where is Old Groff now?'

'In the butler's pantry. Listening to what's going on in the dining room.'

'And his rememberer is where?'

'In his room.'

'And, lovely maiden, can you get us there?'

She stared at him, mouth open, then nodded slowly. 'You're something else, aren't you? Something different from these other ones.'

'I do hope so, maiden, since the situation desperately calls for something of the kind. Lead the way.'

As they went, they heard a consternation of sound off in the wallways, a bellowing and cursing, a sound of hammering. 'They're looking for us,' whispered Fanetta. 'They'll never find us. Not in a million years.'

'We don't have a million years,' suggested Mondragon. 'Quickly, girl. Find this thing you mentioned.'

She found Groff's room with only a few false trails. The room did not yield the thing she called the rememberer, however.

'What did it look like?' begged Green.

'Was it bigger than a breadbox?' asked Mrs Smani.

'Could he have put it elsewhere?' asked Mondragon.

'It looks like a hat. It isn't bigger than a breadbox. He could have put it anywhere, but why would he?'

'Look for a hat,' said Mondragon. 'Spread out.'

The closet was stripped, the wardrobe laid bare. Every drawer was pulled out and emptied. At last, to the accompaniment of furious noise in the corridor outside, Mary Ann looked up at the chandelier and cried out, 'There!'

It was hanging on an iron branch, obviously tossed there

506

in a moment of carelessness. Green lifted Mondragon, and he fished the thing down. It did look like a very curious hat. 'Now' — he thrust them back toward the open panel through which they had entered the room — 'Get back into hiding!'

They were no sooner behind the wall than they heard the door to the room they had left banged open and a huge voice shouting. 'Groff! Groff! Where is that fool?'

'How does it work?' asked Mondragon, retreating down the hidden corridor.

'Just put it on. You'll remember.'

'Not me, her,' he said, fitting the hat onto Marianne's head. 'Darling? Sweetheart? Did you bring anything in here with you?'

'Makr Avehl,' she cried, breaking into tears. 'Oh, thank God you're here.'

There was a rustle of patting and hugging and tear drying while the others tried to look elsewhere. 'Dear one, please. Concentrate. Did you bring anything in here with you?'

'I . . .' she said. 'We . . . Let me think. I did. Yes. Of course I did. I brought — ah, what was it. The matchbox. I brought the matchbox!' She fished in the pocket of her uniform and brought it out for them all to see. 'This matchbox!'

'Ah!' He took it, turned it in his hands, shut his eyes and felt of it. 'Yes. Well. So that's why no one can come into the game anymore. Clever girl. You've broken his Connection. Not that he can't restore it, if he gets his hands on this, though I imagine it would take another generation to make it permanent. Well. We must make sure he doesn't. We really must think of a way to get out of here! Nothing obvious.'

Fanetta burbled, 'They'll never find us. We can stay right here until the whole thing blows over. I've done it. Sometimes for weeks at a time. Late at night we can steal food from the kitchen. It's easy. I've done it.'

'My dear young woman,' said Makr Avehl. 'Believe me. If we stay anywhere within reach, they will find us. If they have to tear Cattermune's House down stone by stone, they will find us. I know that as surely as I know my own

507

name.' He kissed Marianne again, removing the rememberer from her head and setting it firmly upon Green-Aghrehond's. 'The only chance we have is to take this thing somewhere else — somewhere where the Cattermune quite simply will not think to look!'

'But the Cattermune goes everywhere,' Fanetta said. 'That is, everywhere he can. To all the junctions. And he has spies everywhere else. Where could you go where he wouldn't suspect you'd be?'

'To Cattermune's Pique,' said Mondragon. 'All of us.'

'To the Pique?' she screamed. 'But that's where . . .'

'Exactly. That is where,' asserted Mondragon. 'Precisely why he won't look for us there.'

'You can't throw a one,' Fanetta objected. 'You just can't.'

'They're my dice,' said Mondragon, fishing a particular die from his pocket. 'I can throw anything I please. Hold on to me, please. We're about to go elsewhere.'

CHAPTER TWENTY-ONE

The dragon soared above the forests and moors of Cattermune's Pique holding a turquoise tortoise firmly in his left foretalon. On his shoulders sat an amethyst ape wearing a peculiar hat and holding a malachite mouse firmly on his lap. From the dragon's rear talons dangled a gneissic gnu which had not ceased bleating since they had begun the flight.

'Where are we going?' asked the mouse plaintively. 'Where are we from?'

'Down,' cried the ape to the dragon. 'She doesn't remember where we are.'

'In a moment,' bellowed the dragon. 'I've spotted a likely lair.' They slanted through the darkling air toward a many forked peak with a cloud of bats circling it. 'Bats mean caves.'

'So they do,' said the ape. He stared at the mouse for a

moment, then removed his peculiar hat and placed the mouse in it.

'How are you managing, Marianne?' he asked.

'Aghrehond?' the mouse said plaintively. 'Is that you?'

'I believe so,' he said.

'Where's Dagma?'

'Dangling, at the moment. As is Fanetta. I believe Makr Avehl has found us a lair.'

'These changes of shape are unsettling,' she complained. 'I feel very peculiar.'

The dragon's wings cupped the air and he settled toward a stony step beside a dark cavity in the mountain. Laden as he was, the landing was not smooth, and the ape clutched the mouse in the hat to keep her from being thrown into the chasm beside them.

'A likely place,' said the dragon. 'Feels like home.'

'Not to me,' said the tortoise.

'Nor me,' bleated the gnu. 'A nice veldt. A bit of grass. A few hundred thousand close friends. Now that would be home.'

'Put the hat on them both,' said the mouse. 'They're silly.'

The ape complied, applying Groff's rememberer first to the gnu and then to the tortoise. Both made noises of astonishment and then settled into a meditative mood, staring down on the stretching moors from their high roost.

'What's going to happen now?' asked the tortoise.

'It will depend,' said the dragon. 'It will depend on how clever the Cattermune is. On how well he can put two and two together. On whether the immigration manager noticed who came into the game last.'

The mouse nodded. 'You mean, it' all depends on who they're looking for.'

'Exactly. It won't take them long to figure out that one of the last players to enter the game brought the anchor — that is, the matchbox — back to Cattermune's House. The arrival of the matchbox at Cattermune's House is what shut down the entry port. Now, if Marianne and Dagma and you, Aghrehond, have attracted no notice whatsoever . . .'

'I'm afraid she has,' said the tortoise. 'She was in the paper. At Frab Junction. A pig interviewed her in the Dinosaur Zoo. A lot of stuff about being pregnant. It was obvious from what she said that she hadn't been in the game long . . .'

'And there was Buttercup,' said the mouse in a rueful voice. 'She saw me when I left Buttercup for G'nop. Buttercup is still very early in her reign, so she'd know that it wasn't long ago. Though by that time I had been in Buttercup for eight years.'

'Game time,' mused the dragon. 'Game time hardly counts. Eight years,' he snapped his talons. 'No time at all. Now, the Illusion Fields, that might be a bit of time.'

'Ten thousand years,' said the mouse. 'But that's no time, either. The pig I met at the zoo had been there for a whole ten thousand, but this game has only been going for fifty!'

'But a Forever . . .' mused the gnu. 'A Forever is a Forever, no matter what. Everyone says so. A Forever really is.'

'That's what the pig said, too. Ta-ta, she said. Good-bye and gone forever.' The mouse sighed, scratching behind an ear with one hind foot. 'Gone forever.'

'Right,' said the dragon. 'I think you may safely say that a Forever is a Forever. Though at the moment I'm not sure that's relevant to anything. Ape, do you see something over there on the causeway?'

The lands of Cattermune's Pique were bisected by a dike, mounted high above the surrounding moors and copses, topped by a wide road. At the far end of this road, almost at the limit of their vision, there seemed to be something going on.

'All I can see is movement,' said the ape. 'Your eyes should be better than mine.'

'I would have thought so,' said the dragon. 'And yet, I can't make it out with any clarity.'

'You don't need to make it out,' whined the gnu. 'You know what it is. It's the hunt. Cattermunes out of their clothes, running naked on all fours, their teeth showing.

510

Cattermunes and their "guests." Queen Buttercup — she'll be right in with the rest of them, though they'll have to give her a wagon to ride in.'

'What are they hunting?' asked the dragon, sucking a fang. 'I thought it was binkers.'

'We're binkers, stupid,' cried the gnu. 'Out here we're whatever we are, good sport, good hunting, but when they take our carcasses back to Cattermune's House, we're binkers. Meat for the table and guts for the Worm Pits, that's what we are.' She began sobbing. 'I should have just stayed in the walls where I was.'

'Do you think they'll see us up here? If we go in the cave?'

'Cattermunes? Don't be silly! They can smell an ant from a mile away, see a flea at the bottom of a chasm. They've already seen you, Dragon. And me, most likely.'

'But they can't know that we . . .'

'Doesn't matter do they know, don't they know. They're hunting. Everything that moves. Anything that lives.'

'It does matter,' said the mouse firmly. 'We've got the matchbox, and we've got to keep them from getting it. Even if they get us, they mustn't get the matchbox.'

'True,' the ape remarked. 'The Cattermune would simply put it in place again, even though it would take fifty years and the blood of fifty Cattermunes to do it.'

'Ah,' mused the dragon. 'I'd wondered about that.'

'What will we do?' cried the gnu.

'Hide, for starters,' said the dragon, eyes firmly fixed on the distant causeway. He could see them now, Cattermunes in their striped hided hundreds, packs of them running along the roadway on their padded feet, teeth gleaming like diamonds. Behind them rolled a light carriage with Buttercup driving a team of four matched Cattermunes, young ones, yowling as they raced after their unburdened elders.

'No weapons,' remarked the dragon.

'Claws. Fangs. Speed. Strength. Endurance,' murmured the gnu. 'Who needs more than that.'

'In their portraits, they all had weapons,' said the ape. 'I remember it distinctly.'

'Convention,' said the tortoise. 'Mere convention. In order to appear civilized.'

'All aboard,' said the dragon. 'Let's get out of sight.' He waited until the ape was seated, grasped the other two in the nearest available talons, and launched himself off the mountain peak, down into the canyon, dropping below the level of the treetops as he sailed downward.

'It won't do any good,' muttered the gnu. 'They'll smell you.'

'A delaying action,' murmured the dragon through his teeth. 'While I'm thinking.'

'What are you thinking?' begged the mouse.

'Where to hide that matchbox so that Cattermune will never find it.'

'In a Forever, obviously,' grunted the gnu.

'And who's going to take it there,' snorted the tortoise. 'Did I hear you volunteering?'

The gnu was silent.

The dragon landed among some towering trees at one side of the canyon. 'Explain it to me,' he demanded of the gnu. 'How do you get from one square to another?'

'Concentrate on where you intend to go, then throw the right number,' said the gnu.

'Let's say you intended to go to — oh — Mother's Smithy,' the dragon mused. 'And you needed a six but somehow threw a four. What would happen?'

'You'd go toward Mother's Smithy,' said the gnu, 'but you'd stop two squares short. Except if you'd been on that square before, you'd skip to the next one. Unless it was a junction, of course. If it was a junction, you'd stop there.'

'Ah,' said the dragon.

'Ah,' said the mouse.

'Um,' said the ape.

'I've caused you all a great deal of trouble,' said the tortoise sadly. 'We may never get out of here.'

'True,' said the dragon. 'Perfectly true. Though — there may be a way.'

The sound of yowling brought their heads up. Somewhere

512

on the slopes behind them were Cattermunes, coming closer.

'Tell me,' the dragon said to the ape in a conversational tone of voice while examining the talons of his left forefoot, 'do the Cattermunes gamble?'

'There are gaming rooms,' the ape said in an uncertain voice. 'I've seen the rooms, but never with anyone in them.'

'Of course they gamble,' said the gnu. 'There's no bad habit the Cattermunes don't have. Can we get out of here. They're coming very close.'

'Does *the* Cattermune himself play dice . . .?'

'He plays dice with his brothers, after dinner usually.' The gnu shifted restlessly. 'Those hunting Cattermunes are really coming quite close.'

'Is *the* Cattermune hunting with the ones who are after us?'

'He never leaves Cattermune's House. I heard him say once that leaving Cattermune's House was just an invitation to sedition. He likes to keep an eye on things. Ah. Oh. I just saw four Cattermunes coming over the ridge.' The gnu sounded rather hopeless, as though she believed they were done for.

'Just leaving,' said the dragon, picking her up and bearing down on both wings, throwing dust in the approaching Cattermunes' eyes.

He darted away down the canyon like a swallow, slipping behind standing pillars of stone and through tall-trunked trees, bearing toward the causeway entrance to Cattermune's Pique. 'I'm going to drop you all close to the border,' he said softly, barely audible over the sound of his own wings. 'Ape, I want you to hide Mouse, Tortoise, and yourself and stay hidden. Mouse, I will need the matchbox. Gnu, you're coming back with me, back to Cattermune's House.'

'Thank Moomaw,' bleated the gnu. 'If I have to die, I'd rather die as Fanetta in the walls than out here like some poor beast.'

The dragon dropped to the ground and relieved himself of his passengers. 'Quickly,' he steamed. 'A hiding place.'

'Nothing much except a hollow tree here,' suggested the ape. 'We'd fit nicely, except that the hollow is quite visible.'

'Give me the matchbox,' the dragon demanded. He took it, tucking it into a corner of his mouth, behind the dagger-shaped teeth. 'Now get yourselves in,' and he thrust them toward the tree hollow with buffets of great wings. 'There will be some flame out here, deodorizing, so to speak, so they don't smell you. Then I'm going to lead them away. *You are to stay put.* I don't care what you hear, stay where you are.'

They crawled into the tree hollow, a tall cylinder of punky brown wood with beetles crawling up and down the cracks and light slanting down on them from places where branches had rotted out. Fine dust sifted in the beams of light. Mouse sneezed. Ape sat down, putting Tortoise beside him and Mouse on his shoulder. Through a small hole she could see the dragon picking up stones and placing them in front of the hole through which they had crawled. The hollow grew dim. There was a vast roaring, as of some great furnace. Wisps of smoke crept into the hollow. Mouse sneezed again, her eyes watering. When she looked out once more the dragon was aloft and the clearing behind him was blackened by flame and veiled with smoke.

'I can't smell anything but burning,' sniffed the tortoise.

'I think that was the idea,' said the ape. 'He'll let them see him and the gnu. He'll lead them away. And then what?'

'I haven't the slightest idea,' said Mouse sadly. 'I don't know anything with any certainty except that I'm almost sure I just had a labor pain.'

'We'd better be silent,' said the tortoise. 'Cattermunes will probably come to investigate the smoke.'

Which they did only moments later, in howling groups, sniffing and yowling, standing on their hind legs to claw at the trees around the hollow, jumping high to catch a glimpse of the fleeing dragon, then leaping away in the direction the dragon had gone.

'Somehow, when they have their clothes on, they don't look exactly like that,' said the mouse.

'Sweet Marianne,' said the ape. 'They look feral in any guise. How could I have accepted service in such a beastly hole as that?'

'Because you didn't remember anything,' said the tortoise plaintively. 'One can accept almost anything if one doesn't remember anything. Do you suppose one remembers anything in a Forever? Or is it just day on day, with everything new.'

'Madame Dagma, I have no idea,' returned the ape with a sudden access of dignity. 'How would anyone know?'

The tortoise was quiet for a time, then she said, 'Do you have the dice, Aghrehond? May I see them for a moment?' When Aghrehond had given them to her, she stared at them, her clawed, webbed front feet moving over them again and again, as though to cast some enchantment upon them.

'What are you doing?' asked the mouse.

'Thinking,' said the tortoise. 'Just thinking.'

Meantime, the dragon had skimmed along the canyon, making great, furious roars, crisping a tree from time to time or making an acre of ash among lower growing things, attracting the attention of the Cattermunes and causing the gnu though she was firmly gripped in the front talons, to bleat pitifully now and again at the speed, the height, the risk.

'Oh, do be quiet,' muttered the dragon impatiently. 'Everything I'm doing is absolutely necessary. We have to decoy the Cattermunes away from the others.'

'I know,' grunted the gnu. 'It's just that I can't help myself. I've always been afraid of heights.'

'Try to forget that,' urged the dragon.

'Now that I've remembered, it would be quite impossible to forget,' the gnu replied with some dignity. 'Quite impossible.'

'I'm going to commit some carnage,' said the dragon. 'I'll have to leave you alone for a time. Try not to attract attention.' He dropped into another narrow arroyo, flew down it with dizzying speed, hastily dropped the gnu into a small copse at the mouth of the canyon, then ascended into clear view as he darted toward a prowl of Cattermunes with his ears back and flame belching from his nose.

Concealed in the copse, the cowering gnu heard the screeches of scalded cats.

'We'll get you.' 'You have to come down sometime.' 'You

515

can't fly forever.' 'Thief!' 'Assassin!' 'Cheat!' Those Cattermunes remaining — though there were several of whom talons, fangs, and flame had made broiled mince — yowled themselves away after the dragon.

The dragon darted here and there over the moor, disappearing from the gnu's sight. Sometime later she heard his voice from behind her. 'I lost them up a canyon and then walked,' he said. 'It's getting dark. I wondered if it would get dark at all here in Cattermune's Pique, but evidently the place has day and night.'

'To let the Cattermunes know when it's dinnertime,' she replied. 'They do love to eat, the Cattermunes.'

'Lucky for us,' said the dragon. 'Come back into this canyon with me. As soon as it's a bit darker, we're going to go back to Cattermune's House.'

In the hollow tree, time wore on. Mouse's labor pains came and then went, leaving only an empty ache behind. 'I'm hungry,' she said.

'So sorry, pretty lady,' said ape-Aghrehond. 'If there were anything edible about, I would fetch it for you. Truly I would.'

'There are raspberries growing at the edge of the clearing,' said the mouse. 'I can smell them.'

'Surely not over that charred smell. Surely not at this time of year,' said the tortoise.

'What time of year?' asked the mouse in an annoyed tone. 'Dagma, it could be anytime of year at all. Spring. Fall. High summer. Maybe some season we don't even have a name for. It could be Clunch, for all we know, and Clunch may be raspberry season here in the Pique. All I know is that I'm tired and I ache and I'm hungry and I'm worried about us and about Makr Avehl and I smell raspberries.'

'I suppose it wouldn't hurt anything to pick a few raspberries,' said the ape doubtfully. 'The Cattermunes have gone far away by now.'

'I recommend against it,' said the tortoise in a remote voice. 'Not a good idea.'

'Please,' urged the mouse, feeling naughty but unable to control herself. She really did smell raspberries. She really was terribly hungry.

Ape pushed the stones away and crawled out of the tree, the mouse close behind him. He picked his way gingerly across the clearing, trying to avoid places where tiny wisps of smoke were still rising. At the edge of the clearing there were indeed raspberry canes, short ones, laden with berries.

Mouse began to nibble. Ape reached out with both hands.

'Aha,' said a voice.

They turned in panic to confront the figure which stood half hidden among the trees at the edge of the clearing. 'I thought this much fire would hardly have been lit for no reason at all,' said the voice.

'Buttercup!' said Mouse in a shocked voice. 'Queen Buttercup.'

'Fool Cattermunes,' said the Queen in a delighted voice. 'I made a bet with the Cattermune himself that I'd be the one to kill. A little silence, I told him. A little tracking and sneaking instead of all this yowling and chasing. He laughed. Well, we'll see who laughs when I bring you two back. Binkers! Aha.'

Ape shivered at the tone which was lusty, predatory, and quite merciless.

'That would be very dishonorable,' said the mouse firmly. 'You would be forever dishonored as a Queen.'

The Grisl regarded her with a sneer. 'What do you mean?'

'You were living with Mr Thrumm,' said the mouse. 'They meant to kill you. They meant to cut off your spurs and put you into the arena helpless, didn't they?'

'Aragh,' growled the Grisl.

'A voice told you to find out what they were up to. A little voice. A mouse voice!'

'You?' Buttercup was incredulous.

'Who else would know what you did. I know. You found the spurs. You bit Thrumm and Fribberle. And Sneeth, too, though I suppose he got away later.'

'Sneeth,' the Grisl sneered. 'When I became Queen, I felt

517

sorry for him so I sent someone to give him the antidote. I should have let him die.'

'He was very useful to us,' said the ape in a conciliatory tone. 'Really very useful.'

'At any rate,' continued Mouse. 'Since I saved your life, it would be quite dishonorable for you to kill me. It would cast a pall over your reign.'

The Grisl snarled again. 'So. So. Well then, I'll leave you and kill it!' She bared her fang in the direction of the ape. 'He'll be binker enough.'

'No,' said the mouse firmly. 'He belongs to me, and that would be stealing. That would also be dishonorable. As bad as being sent into the arena without spurs.'

The Grisl seemed to be thinking it over. Twice she bared her fang. Twice she nodded thoughtfully. 'It's like dog,' she said at last. 'Faithful dog. Though I am not fond of him, he does me nothing but good, therefore I owe him consideration. It took me some time to ascertain this, but I feel it is a truth. This would be the same thing.' She sounded slightly aggrieved.

'Exactly the same thing,' said Mouse. 'I did you nothing but good. A certain amount of goodwill is appropriate among – ah – well-intentioned beings.'

'Unusual,' said the Grisl. 'In my square, everybody is always doing everybody else. It's only you – you outside creatures, like you and dog, who do this other thing.'

Mouse nodded, still firmly. 'It's part of our religion.'

Queen Buttercup shrugged. 'So, I'll lose my bet with the Cattermune. It wasn't a very big bet anyhow. He bet me a free trip on the Down Line Express against some of my males for binkers, and I've got lots of them.' Sighing, she turned away. 'Oh, Mouse!'

'Yes?'

'It was, well, it was interesting to see you again. Or see you, I should say, since I never really . . . We shared certain . . . experiences . . .' The Grisl gave Mouse a strange look, one might almost have said a pleading look. 'There really isn't anyone who knows me.'

Mouse gulped. It was true. 'Yes, Your Majesty. You were not allowed to have . . . well, friends.'

'Were you . . . that is . . . would you call yourself my friend?'

Mouse gulped again. 'Ah, yes. I think I would say that I am the closest thing you have to a friend, Queen Buttercup.'

'It wasn't exactly easy,' whined the Queen.

'They were distressing times,' said Mouse bravely. 'I was most sympathetic with Your Majesty's distress.'

'I wish you could stop at my square again, but I know that's not possible. I'd like it very much if you would have dinner with me at Frab Junction. We'll go to the Marveling Galosh. They have the most wonderful . . . Oh, say that you will!'

'I'd be most pleased,' said the mouse, bowing.

'Promise!'

'I promise,' said Mouse, feeling as though she had just signed away her soul.

'Do send word with any player who is coming my way,' the Queen said. She shook her head, as though astonished at herself and then went up and over the hill, continuing to shake her head as she thoughtfully twonged the end of her fang with one finger.

Mouse sighed and went limp.

Ape made a wordless noise and went behind a bush. The encounter had been a stressful one.

After a time they returned to the hollow tree to get Tortoise. There was nothing in the hollow except the pair of dice. Tortoise had thrown a nine.

CHAPTER TWENTY-TWO

Mondragon, who had managed to get both to his own room and to the gaming rooms with Fanetta's assistance in guiding him through the walls, stood with Eulalienne Cattermune near the dicing table, one hand in his pocket, the other resting casually on the edge of the table where the Cattermune and his brothers were gambling.

'Any word, Cattermune?' an elderly member of the family asked, offering a cigar to the head of the family. 'Any word at all?'

'It got dark in the Pique,' the Cattermune rumbled. 'So they've called it off until morning. They'll catch them, though. Immigration manager says the last three through were a mouse, an ape, and a tortoise kind of thing. Somebody on the Down Line Express saw the mouse thing with the matchbox. They've got to be the ones. Have to. Never fear. We'll get The Connection back and we'll start over, that's all.'

'That's the spirit! Never say die!'

Several nearby Cattermunes, remembering the blood price which would be needed to *start over*, blanched at these words, but the Cattermune did not seem to notice. 'Never too late to start over,' he growled to himself. 'Never too late.'

Mondragon sighed deeply and inwardly. It was his intention to keep the Cattermune from starting anything over. The time to act was now, at once, before any suspicion could attach to him, and yet the whole matter was so dangerous, so fraught with dreadful consequence. The nanny had seen him in company with Green. Of course, the nanny thought his name was Sneeth. Perhaps the nanny had seen only the livery. 'Bear up,' he told himself. 'Now or never.'

Moving smoothly, quietly, his expression one of unruffled calm, Mondragon moved toward a waiter who held a tray of champagne glasses. His route took him immediately behind the Cattermune, and he delayed, timing his nearest approach to the moment when Cattermune threw the dice.

At which moment he was leaning forward, across the table, his jacket open with the pocket exposed.

Mondragon slipped the matchbox into the Cattermune's pocket and continued toward the waiter, returning in a moment with two glasses, one of which he handed to Eulalienne. She took it, purring. He returned her smile, squeezed her paw-like hand, and turned back to the table. Now he stood at the

520

center of the table, nearest the place where the dice usually rebounded.

'What is it they're looking for?' murmured Mondragon sotto voce to the nearest gambler, another elderly Cattermune. Evidently all the younger members of the family had been taking part in the hunt and had not yet rejoined the party. 'What is it that the Cattermune says they will find?'

'The Connection,' murmured his neighbor in return. 'The anchor. Everyone knows that.'

'Well of course,' agreed Mondragon. 'But what is it? An actual anchor? Not that it matters, of course, merely my curiosity plaguing me.'

'Now that's interesting,' replied the elderly Cattermune. 'You know, I've never asked.' He moved toward the Cattermune, elbowing his way among the gamblers. 'I say, Cattermune, what did the thing look like? The Anchor. The Connection. What was it actually?'

The Cattermune looked up with a snarl.

Timing, thought Mondragon. Now it had to be entirely a matter of timing.

'It was a matchbox,' the Cattermune growled. 'A golden matchbox. Valuable enough not to destroy! Small enough to be easily hidden.' He threw the dice. They rebounded far down the table, out of Mondragon's reach, and the Cattermune grunted in satisfaction. He had made his point. Someone handed him the dice and he gathered them into the leather dice cup again.

'You know,' said Mondragon in a clear carrying voice just as the dice were being thrown. 'I saw a golden matchbox just the other day. Now where was that?'

The Cattermune looked up from the dice, letting them lie as he searched for the person who had spoken. His golden eyes came to rest upon Mondragon. 'You saw what?' His voice was a deep and phlegmy growl.

Mondragon reached down onto the table, gathered up the dice, half holding them toward the Cattermune. 'A golden matchbox. It was about so big. It had an anchor on it. And some writing.'

'Where?' howled the Cattermune. 'Where did you see it?'

Mondragon held out the dice, dropped them into the Cattermune's cup. 'Why — at Mother's Smithy! That's where I saw it. On a shelf beside the door . . .'

'Mother's Smithy!' yowled the Cattermune. 'They're going to melt it down! Not if I get there first!' And he threw the dice, crying, 'Eight squares to Mother's Smithy . . .'

The dice rolled, rebounded, bounced and jounced and came to rest on the table. Everyone around the table was looking at the place the Cattermune had been. Only Mondragon's eyes were on the dice, his dice, Makr Avehl's loaded dice. He picked them up, dropped them in his pocket and waited, holding his breath.

A moment went by.

The Cattermune next to him became misty, indistinct, shadowed. The table turned into smoke, into mist, then vanished. Someone said, 'So I told the Cattermune . . .' the voice fading away into a reverberating silence. The outlines of the room began to quiver and shake, like a mirage. Darkness approached, enveloped everything, and was gone in its turn. He felt himself falling, endlessly, through absolute nothingness.

'Marianne,' he cried, wondering for a hopeless moment if he had miscalculated.

'Makr Avehl,' said Ellat in a sharp, imperative tone. 'Answer me!'

He opened his eyes. The hotel room swam before him.

'What's wrong?' she cried again. 'When are you going to go?'

He took the dice which the Cattermune had used from his pocket and threw them onto the table, watching with satisfaction as they turned up one, and one. Snake eyes.

'I've been,' he said.

'Where's Marianne!' asked Therat. 'Where is she?'

'Call the Zahmanis,' he yawned. 'Unless I'm very much mistaken, Marianne will be in Dagma's room. Dagma and Aghrehond are probably there as well.' He threw the dice again, smiling when they came up snake eyes again.

'What are you playing with those dice for?' Ellat asked in exasperation as she dialed the phone.

'Admiring them,' he said. 'Admiring a one-way ticket to a Forever.'

CHAPTER TWENTY-THREE

'I would have thought,' Haurvatat Zahmani said with an expression of acute annoyance, 'that your great-aunt would have come back with you.'

'She . . .' Marianne hesitated, wondering just how to say it. 'I think she felt that if Makr Avehl managed to get us back at all, she had very little to come back for. She said pretty much that to me before I . . . well, before I left. Evidently while Aghrehond and I were busy with Buttercup, Dagma simply concentrated on where she wanted to go and threw a nine.'

'At the time,' said Aghrehond gloomily, 'I could not recall precisely where a nine might take her. Now, of course, it is obvious that she went to the Illusion Fields . . .'

'Or to Mother's Smithy. Or some other place,' said Marianne. 'We really don't know.'

'And you think she's there still?' Arti wiped a tear from the corner of her eye, whether from joy over Marianne's return or from sorrow over Dagma, she herself could not have said.

'I doubt it,' said Makr Avehl. 'Haven't vanished people been showing up in droves? I know Fanetta did, because I called Seattle to find out. Your postman, Arti? I'll wager he's back. Your butcher's wife. The man who sits on that charity board with you? Your neighbor and her children. I imagine all of them are back unless they happened to get into a Forever.'

'Or,' said Aghrehond ominously. 'Or . . .'

'Well, yes. Or the ones who were hunted down in Cattermune's Pique.'

'Dagma wasn't hunted down. But she hasn't come back, either,' said Arti.

Marianne sighed. 'Mother, there was one Forever nine squares from Cattermune's Pique. Not an obvious one, to be sure, but then Dagma seldom did the obvious . . .'

'Dagma is not the only one in this family of whom that can be said,' grumped Haurvatat. 'And here you are within weeks, within days, of having a baby. What if it had been born there?'

Marianne shuddered delicately. 'I'd rather not think about that.'

'I should hope not. Think of something else. Something cheerful. Such as, what are you going to name the baby?' He looked at her triumphantly, sure, from what he was pleased to think of as his intimate knowledge of feminine psychology, that this subject would drive all others from her mind.

'Ah,' sighed Marianne. 'Well, Daddy, it's going to be a girl, you know. Makr Avehl and I have considered many names. Family names. Historic names. Old Alphenlichtian names. Kavi names, even. Considering everything — and I do mean everything — I really think there's only one thing I can call her. It will be my way, at least in part, of making up for a broken promise.' Her tone was rather stiff as she said this, and she avoided meeting Makr Avehl's eyes.

He shook his head in dismay. Her bearing, her tone, everything told him he was not going to like what she would say next. He swore silently to himself that he would not say one thing, not one thing.

'But I've never known you to break a promise, Marianne,' said her mother. 'Never once.'

'You taught me not to, Mama. But this is one I'm going to have to break. There is no way that I can go to Frab Junction, to the Marveling Galosh, and have lunch with the Queen. That's why I'm going to name the baby Buttercup.'

'Buttercup!' roared Haurvatat. 'Of all the . . .'

'Shhh,' said Makr Avehl, shaking his head at Marianne with a fondly rueful expression. 'Father-in-law, don't upset the mother-to-be. In English it does sound rather silly. We could do it in Latin, of course. Ranunculus.'

'I won't have a granddaughter named Ranunculus!'

'No. I couldn't take that seriously myself. There is one — a buttercup — that grows in our mountains, however. Ranunculus asiaticus. A rather charming flower, actually. It has a common name, of course. An Alphenlichtian name.'

'What is it in Alphenlichtian?' asked Haurvatat suspiciously.

'*Therat,*' said Marianne. 'This time I think she really will be surprised.'

THE END

THE AWAKENERS
by Sheri S. Tepper

'Tepper creates a true refuge, one of those rare worlds into which the reader can escape completely'
Locus

In the savage and magical world of the River, the pace of life is dictated by the ebb and flow of the great tides – and by the power of a fearsome religion. Yet dangerous currents gather force beneath the placid surface.

Together, Pamra Don and Thrasne the Boatman seek to uncover the terrible truth about the river and its awesome strength. But in the world of the Awakeners, the truth can kill . . .

'Sheri S. Tepper has a remarkable talent, and with each new book she outdoes herself. I don't know which I like more, the worlds she creates or the ways she writes about them'
Stephen R. Donaldson

'The plot is rich . . . the characters come alive. The whole is imbued with a marvellous sense of dream . . . Don't miss'
Analog

'Tepper is something special'
Orson Scott Card

0 552 13295 0

THE TRUE GAME
by Sheri S. Tepper

In the lands of the True Game, your lifelong identity will emerge as you play. Prince or Sorcerer, Armiger or Tragamor, Demon or Doyen . . .

Which will it be?

The neophyte necromancer Peter embarks on a long and hazardous quest, to uncover the truth behind the disappearance of the prominent Gamesmen from the lands of the True Game. As the Wizard's Eleven sleep, trapped by their dreams, a giant stalks the mountains, the Shadowpeople gather by the light of the moon, and the Bonedancers raise up armies of the dead.

The truth unfolds, revealing that magic is science and science is magic, and Peter, son of Mavin Manyshaped, must realize his true identity, and become the wild card that threatens the True Game itself.

Players, take your places. The Game begins . . .

'Very good! It moves with all the precision of a chess game with fate'
Roger Zelazny

0 552 12620 9

SHERI S. TEPPER TITLES
AVAILABLE FROM CORGI BOOKS

☐	01559 2	THE AWAKENERS (Trade paperback)	£6.95
☐	13295 0	THE AWAKENERS	£3.99
☐	12620 9	THE TRUE GAME	£3.99
☐	12834 1	THE CHRONICLES OF MAVIN MANYSHAPED	£3.99
☐	13373 6	THE ENIGMA SCORE	£3.50
☐	01604 1	THE GATE TO WOMEN'S COUNTRY (Trade paperback)	£6.95
☐	01784 6	GRASS (Trade paperback)	£6.95
☐	13189 X	JINIAN FOOTSEER	£2.50
☐	13190 3	DERVISH DAUGHTER	£2.75
☐	13191 1	JINIAN STAR-EYE	£2.99
☐	13466 X	STILL LIFE	£2.99